By C. S. Lewis

The Abolition of Man

Mere Christianity

The Great Divorce

The Problem of Pain

The Weight of Glory and Other Addresses

The Screwtape Letters (with "Screwtape Proposes a Toast")

Miracles

The Case for Christianity

The Lion, the Witch and the Wardrobe

Prince Caspian

The Voyage of the Dawn Treader

The Silver Chair

The Magician's Nephew

The Horse and His Boy

The Last Battle

Perelandra

That Hideous Strength

Out of the Silent Planet

The Joyful Christian

George Macdonald: An Anthology

C. S. Lewis: Letters to Children

C. S. Lewis

THE SPACE TRILOGY

OUT OF THE SILENT PLANET
PERELANDRA
THAT HIDEOUS STRENGTH

SCRIBNER

NEW YORK LONDON TORONTO SYDNEY NEW DELHI

SCRIBNER
A Division of Simon & Schuster, Inc.
1230 Avenue of the Americas
New York, NY 10020

First Scribner trade paperback edition September 2011

SCRIBNER and design are registered trademarks of
The Gale Group, Inc., used under license by Simon & Schuster, Inc.,
the publisher of this work.

For information about special discounts for bulk purchases,
please contact Simon & Schuster Special Sales at 1-866-506-1949
or business@simonandschuster.com.

The Simon & Schuster Speakers Bureau can bring authors to your live event.
For more information or to book an event contact the Simon & Schuster Speakers Bureau
at 1-866-248-3049 or visit our website at www.simonspeakers.com.

Designed by Brooke Koven
Set in Sabon

Manufactured in the United States of America

11 13 15 17 19 20 18 16 14 12

ISBN 978-1-4516-6482-9

These titles have been previously published individually.

C. S. Lewis

OUT OF THE SILENT PLANET

A NOVEL

SCRIBNER
NEW YORK LONDON TORONTO SYDNEY NEW DELHI

To my brother W. H. L.
a life-long critic of the space-and-time story

NOTE: Certain slighting references to earlier stories of this type which will be found in the following pages have been put there for purely dramatic purposes. The author would be sorry if any reader supposed he was too stupid to have enjoyed Mr. H. G. Wells's fantasies or too ungrateful to acknowledge his debt to them.

C. S. L.

I

The last drops of the thundershower had hardly ceased falling when the Pedestrian stuffed his map into his pocket, settled his pack more comfortably on his tired shoulders, and stepped out from the shelter of a large chestnut-tree into the middle of the road. A violent yellow sunset was pouring through a rift in the clouds to westward, but straight ahead over the hills the sky was the colour of dark slate. Every tree and blade of grass was dripping, and the road shone like a river. The Pedestrian wasted no time on the landscape but set out at once with the determined stride of a good walker who has lately realised that he will have to walk farther than he intended. That, indeed, was his situation. If he had chosen to look back, which he did not, he could have seen the spire of Much Nadderby, and, seeing it, might have uttered a malediction on the inhospitable little hotel which, though obviously empty, had refused him a bed. The place had changed hands since he last went for a walking-tour in these parts. The kindly old landlord on whom he had reckoned had been replaced by someone whom the barmaid referred to as "the lady," and the lady was apparently a British innkeeper of that orthodox school who regard guests as a nuisance. His only chance now was Sterk, on the far side of the hills, and a good six miles away. The map marked an inn at Sterk. The Pedestrian was too experienced to build any very sanguine hopes on this, but there seemed nothing else within range.

He walked fairly fast, and doggedly, without looking much about him, like a man trying to shorten the way with some interesting train of thought. He was tall, but a little round-shouldered, about thirty-five to forty years of age, and dressed with that particular kind of shabbiness which marks a member of the intelligentsia on a holiday. He might easily have been mistaken for a doctor or a schoolmaster at first sight, though he had not the man-of-the-world air of the one or the indefinable breeziness of the other. In fact, he was a philologist, and fellow of a Cambridge college. His name was Ransom.

He had hoped when he left Nadderby that he might find a night's lodging at some friendly farm before he had walked as far as Sterk. But the land this side of the hills seemed almost uninhabited. It was a desolate, featureless sort of country mainly devoted to cabbage and turnip, with poor hedges and few trees. It attracted no visitors like the richer country south of Nadderby and it was protected by the hills from the industrial areas beyond Sterk. As the evening drew in and the noise of the birds came to an end it grew more silent than an English landscape usually is. The noise of his own feet on the metalled road became irritating.

He had walked thus for a matter of two miles when he became aware of a light ahead. He was close under the hills by now and it was nearly dark, so that he still cherished hopes of a substantial farmhouse until he was quite close to the real origin of the light, which proved to be a very small cottage of ugly nineteenth-century brick. A woman darted out of the open doorway as he approached it and almost collided with him.

"I beg your pardon, sir," she said. "I thought it was my Harry."

Ransom asked her if there was any place nearer than Sterk where he might possibly get a bed.

"No, sir," said the woman. "Not nearer than Sterk. I dare say as they might fix you up at Nadderby."

She spoke in a humbly fretful voice as if her mind were intent on something else. Ransom explained that he had already tried Nadderby.

"Then I don't know, I'm sure, sir," she replied. "There isn't hardly any house before Sterk, not what you want. There's only The Rise, where my Harry works, and I thought you was coming from that way, sir, and that's why I come out when I heard you, thinking it might be him. He ought to be home this long time."

"The Rise," said Ransom. "What's that? A farm? Would they put me up?"

"Oh no, sir. You see there's no one there now except the Professor and the gentleman from London, not since Miss Alice died. They wouldn't do anything like that, sir. They don't even keep any servants, except my Harry for doing the furnace like, and he's not in the house."

"What's this professor's name?" asked Ransom, with a faint hope.

"I don't know, I'm sure, sir," said the woman. "The other gentleman's Mr. Devine, he is, and Harry says the *other* gentleman is a professor. He don't know much about it, you see, sir, being a little simple, and that's why I don't like him coming home so late, and they said they'd always send him home at six o'clock. It isn't as if he didn't do a good day's work either."

The monotonous voice and the limited range of the woman's vocabulary did not express much emotion, but Ransom was standing sufficiently near to perceive that she was trembling and nearly crying. It occurred to him that he ought to call on the mysterious professor and ask for the boy to be sent home: and it occurred to him just a fraction of a second later that once he were inside the house—among men of his own profession—he might very reasonably accept the offer of a night's hospitality. Whatever the process of thought may have been, he found that the mental picture of himself calling at The Rise had assumed all the solidity of a thing determined upon. He told the woman what he intended to do.

"Thank you very much, sir, I'm sure," she said. "And if you would be so kind as to see him out of the gate and on the road before you leave, if you see what I mean, sir. He's that frightened of the Professor and he wouldn't come away once your back was turned, sir, not if they hadn't sent him home themselves like."

Ransom reassured the woman as well as he could and bade her good-bye, after ascertaining that he would find The Rise on his left in about five minutes. Stiffness had grown upon him while he was standing still, and he proceeded slowly and painfully on his way.

There was no sign of any lights on the left of the road—nothing but the flat fields and a mass of darkness which he took to be a copse. It seemed more than five minutes before he reached it and found that he had been mistaken. It was divided from the road by a good hedge and in the hedge was a white gate: and the trees which rose above him as he examined the gate were not the first line of a copse but only a belt, and the sky showed through them. He felt quite sure now that this must be the gate of The Rise and that these trees surrounded a house and garden. He tried the gate and found it locked. He stood for a moment undecided, discouraged by the silence and the growing darkness. His first inclination, tired as he felt, was to continue his journey to Sterk: but he had committed himself to a troublesome duty on behalf of the old woman. He knew that it would be possible, if one really wanted, to force a way through the hedge. He did not want to. A nice fool he would look, blundering in upon some retired eccentric—the sort of a man who kept his gates locked in the country—with this silly story of a hysterical mother in tears because her idiot boy had been kept half an hour late at his work! Yet it was perfectly clear that he would have to get in, and since one cannot crawl through a hedge with a pack on, he slipped his pack off and flung it over the gate. The moment he had done so, it seemed to him that he had not till now fully made up his mind—now that he must break into the garden if only in order to recover the pack. He became very angry with the woman, and with himself, but he got down on his hands and knees and began to worm his way into the hedge.

The operation proved more difficult than he had expected and it was several minutes before he stood up in the wet darkness on the inner side of the hedge smarting from his contact with thorns and nettles. He groped his way to the gate, picked up his pack, and then for the first time turned to take stock of his surroundings. It was lighter on the drive than it had been under the trees and he had no difficulty in making out a large stone house divided from him by a width of untidy neglected lawn. The drive branched into two a little way ahead of him—the righthand path leading in a gentle sweep to the front door, while the left ran straight ahead, doubtless to the back premises of the house. He noticed that this path was churned up into deep ruts—now full of water—as if it were used to carrying a traffic of heavy lorries. The other, on which he now began to approach the house, was overgrown with moss. The house itself showed no light: some of the windows were shuttered, some gaped blank without shutter or curtain, but all were lifeless and inhospitable. The only sign of occupation was a column of smoke that rose from behind the house with a density which suggested the chimney of a factory, or at least of a laundry, rather than that of a kitchen. The Rise was clearly the last place in the world where a stranger was likely to be asked to stay the night, and Ransom, who had already wasted some time in exploring it, would certainly have turned away if he had not been bound by his unfortunate promise to the old woman.

He mounted the three steps which led into the deep porch, rang the bell, and waited. After a time he rang the bell again and sat down on a wooden bench which ran along one side of the porch. He sat so long that though the night was warm and starlit the sweat began to dry on his face and a faint chilliness crept over his shoulders. He was very tired by now, and it was perhaps this which prevented him from rising and ringing a third time: this, and the soothing stillness of the garden, the beauty of the summer sky, and the occasional hooting of an owl somewhere in the neighbourhood which seemed only to emphasize the underlying tranquillity of his surroundings. Something like drowsiness had already descended upon him when he found himself startled into vigilance. A peculiar noise was going on—a scuffing, irregular noise, vaguely reminiscent of a football scrum. He stood up. The noise was unmistakable by now. People in boots were fighting or wrestling or playing some game. They were shouting too. He could not make out the words but he heard the monosyllabic barking ejaculations of men who are angry and out of breath. The last thing Ransom wanted was an adventure, but a conviction that he ought to investigate the matter was already growing upon him when a much louder cry rang out in which he could distinguish the words, "Let me go. Let me go," and then, a second later, "I'm not going in there. Let me go home."

Throwing off his pack, Ransom sprang down the steps of the porch, and ran round to the back of the house as quickly as his stiff and footsore condition allowed him. The ruts and pools of the muddy path led him to what seemed to be a yard, but a yard surrounded with an unusual number of outhouses. He had a momentary vision of a tall chimney, a low door filled with red firelight, and a huge round shape that rose black against the stars, which he took for the dome of a small observatory: then all this was blotted out of his mind by the figures of three men who were struggling together so close to him that he almost cannoned into them. From the very first Ransom felt no doubt that the central figure, whom the two others seemed to be detaining in spite of his struggles, was the old woman's Harry. He would like to have thundered out, "What are you doing to that boy?" but the words that actually came—in rather an unimpressive voice—were, "Here! I say! . . ."

The three combatants fell suddenly apart, the boy blubbering. "May I ask," said the thicker and taller of the two men, "who the devil you may be and what you are doing here?" His voice had all the qualities which Ransom's had so regrettably lacked.

"I'm on a walking-tour," said Ransom, "and I promised a poor woman——"

"Poor woman be damned," said the other. "How did you get in?"

"Through the hedge," said Ransom, who felt a little ill-temper coming to his assistance. "I don't know what you're doing to that boy, but——"

"We ought to have a dog in this place," said the thick man to his companion, ignoring Ransom.

"You mean we should have a dog if you hadn't insisted on using Tartar for an experiment," said the man who had not yet spoken. He was nearly as tall as the other, but slender, and apparently the younger of the two, and his voice sounded vaguely familiar to Ransom.

The latter made a fresh beginning. "Look here," he said. "I don't know what you are doing to that boy, but it's long after hours and it is high time you sent him home. I haven't the least wish to interfere in your private affairs, but——"

"Who are you?" bawled the thick man.

"My name is Ransom, if that is what you mean. And——"

"By Jove," said the slender man, "not Ransom who used to be at Wedenshaw?"

"I was at school at Wedenshaw," said Ransom.

"I thought I knew you as soon as you spoke," said the slender man. "I'm Devine. Don't you remember me?"

"Of course. I should think I do!" said Ransom as the two men shook hands with the rather laboured cordiality which is traditional in such meetings. In actual fact Ransom had disliked Devine at school as much as anyone he could remember.

"Touching, isn't it?" said Devine. "The far-flung line even in the wilds of Sterk and Nadderby. This is where we get a lump in our throats and remember Sunday-evening Chapel in the D.O.P. You don't know

Weston, perhaps?" Devine indicated his massive and loud-voiced companion. "*The* Weston," he added. "You know. The great physicist. Has Einstein on toast and drinks a pint of Schrödinger's blood for breakfast. Weston, allow me to introduce my old schoolfellow, Ransom. Dr. Elwin Ransom. *The* Ransom, you know. The great philologist. Has Jespersen on toast and drinks a pint——"

"I know nothing about it," said Weston, who was still holding the unfortunate Harry by the collar. "And if you expect me to say that I am pleased to see this person who has just broken into my garden, you will be disappointed. I don't care two-pence what school he was at nor on what unscientific foolery he is at present wasting money that ought to go to research. I want to know what he's doing here: and after that I want to see the last of him."

"Don't be an ass, Weston," said Devine in a more serious voice. "His dropping in is delightfully apropos. You mustn't mind Weston's little way, Ransom. Conceals a generous heart beneath a grim exterior, you know. You'll come in and have a drink and something to eat of course?"

"That's very kind of you," said Ransom. "But about the boy——"

Devine drew Ransom aside. "Balmy," he said in a low voice. "Works like a beaver as a rule but gets these fits. We are only trying to get him into the wash-house and keep him quiet for an hour or so till he's normal again. Can't let him go home in his present state. All done by kindness. You can take him home yourself presently if you like—and come back and sleep here."

Ransom was very much perplexed. There was something about the whole scene suspicious enough and disagreeable enough to convince him the he had blundered on something criminal, while on the other hand he had all the deep, irrational conviction of his age and class that such things could never cross the path of an ordinary person except in fiction and could least of all be associated with professors and old schoolfellows. Even if they had been ill-treating the boy, Ransom did not see much chance of getting him from them by force.

While these thoughts were passing through his head, Devine had been speaking to Weston, in a low voice, but no lower than was to be expected of a man discussing hospitable arrangements in the presence of a guest. It ended with a grunt of assent from Weston. Ransom, to whose other difficulties a merely social embarrassment was now being added, turned with the idea of making some remark. But Weston was now speaking to the boy.

"You have given enough trouble for one night, Harry," he said. "And in a properly governed country I'd know how to deal with you. Hold your tongue and stop snivelling. You needn't go into the wash-house if you don't want——"

"It weren't the wash-house," sobbed the half-wit, "you know it weren't. I don't want to go in *that* thing again."

"He means the laboratory," interrupted Devine. "He got in there and was shut in by accident for a few hours once. It put the wind up him for some reason. Lo, the poor Indian, you know." He turned to the boy. "Listen, Harry," he said. "That kind gentleman is going to take you home as soon as he's had a rest. If you'll come in and sit down quietly in the hall I'll give you something you like." He imitated the noise of a cork being drawn from a bottle—Ransom remembered it had been one of Devine's tricks at school—and a guffaw of infantile knowingness broke from Harry's lips.

"Bring him in," said Weston as he turned away and disappeared into the house. Ransom hesitated to follow, but Devine assured him that Weston would be very glad to see him. The lie was barefaced, but Ransom's desire for a rest and a drink were rapidly overcoming his social scruples. Preceded by Devine and Harry, he entered the house and found himself a moment later seated in an arm-chair and awaiting the return of Devine, who had gone to fetch refreshments.

2

The room into which he had been shown revealed a strange mixture of luxury and squalor. The windows were shuttered and curtainless, the floor was uncarpeted and strewn with packing-cases, shavings, newspapers and boots, and the wallpaper showed the stains left by the pictures and furniture of the previous occupants. On the other hand, the only two armchairs were of the costliest type, and in the litter which covered the tables, cigars, oyster-shells and empty champagne-bottles jostled with tins of condensed milk and opened sardine-tins, with cheap crockery, broken bread, and teacups a quarter full of tea and cigarette-ends.

His hosts seemed to be a long time away, and Ransom fell to thinking of Devine. He felt for him that sort of distaste we feel for someone whom we have admired in boyhood for a very brief period and then outgrown. Devine had learned just half a term earlier than anyone else that kind of humour which consists in a perpetual parody of the sentimental or idealistic clichés of one's elders. For a few weeks his references to the Dear Old Place and to Playing the Game, to the White Man's Burden and a Straight Bat, had swept everyone, Ransom included, off their feet. But before he left Wedenshaw Ransom had already begun to find Devine a bore, and at Cambridge he had avoided him, wondering from afar how anyone so flashy and, as it were, ready-made, could be so successful. Then had come the mystery of Devine's election to the Leicester fellowship, and the further mystery of his increasing wealth. He had long since abandoned Cambridge for London, and was presumably something "in the city." One heard of him occasionally and one's informant usually ended either by saying, "A damn clever chap, Devine, in his own way," or else by observing plaintively, "It's a mystery to me how that man has got where he is." As far as Ransom could gather from their brief conversation in the yard, his old schoolfellow had altered very little.

He was interrupted by the opening of the door. Devine entered alone, carrying a bottle of whiskey on a tray with glasses, and a syphon.

"Weston is looking out something to eat," he said as he placed the tray on the floor beside Ransom's chair, and addressed himself to opening the bottle. Ransom, who was very thirsty indeed by now, observed that his host was one of those irritating people who forget to use their hands when they begin talking. Devine started to prise up the silver paper which covered the cork with the point of a corkscrew, and then stopped to ask:

"How do you come to be in this benighted part of the country?"

"I'm on a walking-tour," said Ransom; "slept at Stoke Underwood last night and had hoped to end at Nadderby to-night. They wouldn't put me up, so I was going on to Sterk."

"God!" exclaimed Devine, his corkscrew still idle. "Do you do it for money, or is it sheer masochism?"

"Pleasure, of course," said Ransom, keeping his eye immovably on the still unopened bottle.

"Can the attraction of it be explained to the uninitiate?" asked Devine, remembering himself sufficiently to rip up a small portion of the silver paper.

"I hardly know. To begin with, I like the actual walking——"

"God! You must have enjoyed the army. Jogging along to Thingummy, eh?"

"No, no. It's just the opposite of the army. The whole point about the army is that you are never alone for a moment and can never choose where you're going or even what part of the road you're walking on. On a walking-tour you are absolutely detached. You stop where you like and go on when you like. As long as it lasts you need consider no one and consult no one but yourself."

"Until one night you find a wire waiting at your hotel saying, 'Come back at once,' " replied Devine, at last removing the silver paper.

"Only if you were fool enough to leave a list of addresses and go to them! The worst that could happen to me would be that man on the wireless saying, 'Will Dr. Elwin Ransom, believed to be walking somewhere in the Midlands——' "

"I begin to see the idea," said Devine, pausing in the very act of drawing the cork. "It wouldn't do if you were in business. You are a lucky devil! But can even you just disappear like that? No wife, no young, no aged but honest parent or anything of that sort?"

"Only a married sister in India. And then, you see, I'm a don. And a don in the middle of long vacation is almost a non-existent creature, as you ought to remember. College neither knows nor cares where he is, and certainly no one else does."

The cork at last came out of the bottle with a heart-cheering noise.

"Say when," said Devine, as Ransom held out his glass. "But I feel sure there's a catch somewhere. Do you really mean to say that no one knows where you are or when you ought to get back, and no one can get hold of you?"

Ransom was nodding in reply when Devine, who had picked up the syphon, suddenly swore. "I'm afraid this is empty," he said. "Do you mind having water? I'll have to get some from the scullery. How much do you like?"

"Fill it up please," said Ransom.

A few minutes later Devine returned and handed Ransom his long-delayed drink. The latter remarked, as he put down the half-emptied tumbler with a sigh of satisfaction, that Devine's choice of residence was at least as odd as his own choice of a holiday.

"Quite," said Devine. "But if you knew Weston you'd realise that it's much less trouble to go where he wants than to argue the matter. What you call a strong colleague."

"Colleague?" said Ransom inquiringly.

"In a sense." Devine glanced at the door, drew his chair closer to Ransom's, and continued in a more confidential tone. "He's the goods all right, though. Between ourselves, I am putting a little money into some experiments he has on hand. It's all straight stuff—the march of progress and the good of humanity and all that, but it has an industrial side."

While Devine was speaking something odd began to happen to Ransom. At first it merely seemed to him that Devine's words were no longer making sense. He appeared to be saying that he was industrial all down both sides but could never get an experiment to fit him in London. Then he realised that Devine was not so much unintelligible as inaudible, which was not surprising, since he was now so far away—about a mile away, though perfectly clear like something seen through the wrong end of a telescope. From that bright distance where he sat in his tiny chair he was gazing at Ransom with a new expression on his face. The gaze became disconcerting. Ransom tried to move in his chair but found that he had lost all power over his own body. He felt quite comfortable, but it was as if his legs and arms had been bandaged to the chair and his head gripped in a vice; a beautifully padded, but quite immovable vice. He did not feel afraid, though he knew that he ought to be afraid and soon would be. Then, very gradually, the room faded from his sight.

Ransom could never be sure whether what followed had any bearing on the events recorded in this book or whether it was merely an irresponsible dream. It seemed to him that he and Weston and Devine were all standing in a little garden surrounded by a wall. The garden was bright and sunlit, but over the top of the wall you could see nothing but darkness. They were trying to climb over the wall and Weston asked them to give him a hoist up. Ransom kept on telling him not to go over the wall because it was so dark on the other side, but Weston insisted, and all three of them set about doing so. Ransom was the last. He got astride on the top of the wall, sitting on his coat because of the broken bottles. The other two had already dropped down on the outside into the darkness, but before he followed them a door in the wall—which none of them had noticed—was opened from without and the queerest people he had ever seen came into the garden bringing Weston and Devine back with them. They left them in the garden and retired into the darkness themselves, locking the door behind them. Ransom found it impossible to get down from the wall. He remained sitting there, not frightened but rather uncomfortable because his right leg, which was on the outside, felt so dark and his left leg felt so light. "My leg will drop off if it gets much darker," he said. Then he looked down into the darkness and asked, "Who are you?" and the Queer People must still have been there for they all replied, "Hoo—Hoo—Hoo?" just like owls.

He began to realise that his leg was not so much dark as cold and stiff, because he had been resting the other on it for so long: and also that he was in an arm-chair in a lighted room. A conversation was going on near him and had, he now realised, been going on for some time. His head was comparatively clear. He realised that he had been drugged or hypnotized, or both, and he felt that some control over his own body was returning to him though he was still very weak. He listened intently without trying to move.

"I'm getting a little tired of this, Weston," Devine was saying, "and specially as it's my money that is being risked. I tell you he'll do quite as well as the boy, and in some ways better. Only, he'll be coming round very soon now and we must get him on board at once. We ought to have done it an hour ago."

"The boy was ideal," said Weston sulkily. "Incapable of serving humanity and only too likely to propagate idiocy. He was the sort of boy who in a civilized community would be automatically handed over to a state laboratory for experimental purposes."

"I dare say. But in England he is the sort of boy in whom Scotland Yard might conceivably feel an interest. This busybody, on the other hand, will not be missed for months, and even then no one will know where he was when he disappeared. He came alone. He left no address. He has no family. And finally he has poked his nose into the whole affair of his own accord."

"Well, I confess I don't like it. He is, after all, human. The boy was really almost a—a preparation. Still, he's only an individual, and probably a quite useless one. We're risking our own lives too. In a great cause——"

"For the Lord's sake don't start all that stuff now. We haven't time."

"I dare say," replied Weston, "he would consent if he could be made to understand."

"Take his feet and I'll take his head," said Devine.

"If you really think he's coming round," said Weston, "you'd better give him another dose. We can't start till we get the sunlight. It wouldn't be pleasant to have him struggling in there for three hours or so. It would be better if he didn't wake up till we were under weigh."

"True enough. Just keep an eye on him while I run upstairs and get another."

Devine left the room. Ransom saw through his half-closed eyes that Weston was standing over him. He had no means of foretelling how his own body would respond, if it responded at all, to a sudden attempt of movement, but he saw at once that he must take his chance. Almost before Devine had closed the door he flung himself with all his force at Weston's feet. The scientist fell forward across the chair, and Ransom, flinging him off with an agonizing effort, rose and dashed out into the hall. He was very weak and fell as he entered it: but terror was behind him and in a couple of seconds he had found the hall door and was working desperately to master the bolts. Darkness and his trembling hands were against him. Before he had drawn one bolt, booted feet were clattering over the carpetless floor behind him. He was gripped by the shoulders and the knees. Kicking, writhing, dripping with sweat, and bellowing as loud as he could in the faint hope of rescue, he prolonged the struggle with a violence of which he would have believed himself incapable. For one glorious moment the door was open, the fresh night air was in his face, he saw the reassuring stars and even his own pack lying in the porch. Then a heavy blow fell on his head. Consciousness faded, and the last thing of which he was aware was the grip of strong hands pulling him back into the dark passage, and the sound of a closing door.

3

When Ransom came to his senses he seemed to be in bed in a dark room. He had a pretty severe headache, and this, combined with a general lassitude, discouraged him at first from attempting to rise or to take stock of his surroundings. He noticed, drawing his hand across his forehead, that he was sweating freely, and this directed his attention to the fact that the room (if it was a room) was remarkably warm. Moving his arms to fling off the bedclothes, he touched a wall at the right side of the bed: it was not only warm, but hot. He moved his left hand to and fro in the emptiness on the other side and noticed that there the air was cooler—apparently the heat was coming from the wall. He felt his face and found a bruise over the left eye. This recalled to his mind the struggle with Weston and Devine, and he instantly concluded that they had put him in an outhouse behind their furnace. At the same time he looked up and recognised the source of the dim light in which, without noticing it, he had all along been able to see the movements of his own hands. There was some kind of skylight immediately over his head—a square of night sky filled with stars. It seemed to Ransom that he had never looked out on such a frosty night. Pulsing with brightness as with some unbearable pain or pleasure, clustered in pathless and countless multitudes, dreamlike in clarity, blazing in perfect blackness, the stars seized all his attention, troubled him, excited him, and drew him up to a sitting position. At the same time they quickened the throb of his headache, and this reminded him that he had been drugged. He was just formulating to himself the theory that the stuff they had given him might have some effect on the pupil and that this would explain the unnatural splendour and fullness of the sky, when a disturbance of silver light, almost a pale and miniature sunrise, at one corner of the skylight, drew his eyes upward again. Some minutes later the orb of the full moon was pushing its way into the field of vision. Ransom sat still and watched. He had never seen such a moon—so white, so blinding and so large. "Like a great football just outside the glass," he thought, and then, a moment later, "No—it's bigger than that." By this time he was quite certain that something was seriously wrong with his eyes: no moon could possibly be the size of the thing he was seeing.

The light of the huge moon—if it was a moon—had by now illuminated his surroundings almost as clearly as if it were day. It was a very strange room. The floor was so small that the bed and a table beside it occupied the whole width of it: the ceiling seemed to be nearly twice as wide and the walls sloped outwards as they rose, so that Ransom had the impression of lying at the bottom of a deep and narrow wheelbarrow. This confirmed his belief that his sight was either temporarily or permanently injured. In other respects, however, he was recovering rapidly and even beginning to feel an unnatural lightness of heart and a not disagreeable excitement. The heat was still oppressive, and he stripped off everything but his shirt and trousers before rising to explore. His rising was disastrous and raised graver apprehensions in his mind about the effects of being drugged. Although he had been conscious of no unusual muscular effort, he found himself leaping from the bed with an energy which brought his head into sharp contact with the skylight and flung him down again in a heap on the floor. He found himself on the other side against the wall—the wall that ought to have sloped outwards like the side of a wheelbarrow, according to his previous reconnaissance. But it didn't. He felt it and looked at it: it was unmistakably at right angles to the floor. More cautiously this time, he rose again to his feet. He felt an extraordinary lightness of body: it was with difficulty that he kept his feet on the floor. For the first time a suspicion that he might be dead and already in the ghost-life crossed his mind. He was trembling, but a hundred mental habits forbade him to consider this possibility. Instead, he explored his prison. The result was beyond doubt: all the walls looked as if they sloped outwards so as to make the room wider at the ceiling than it was at the floor, but each wall as you stood beside it turned out to be perfectly perpendicular—not only to sight but to touch also if one stooped down and examined with one's fingers the angle between it and the floor. The same examination revealed two other curious facts. The room was walled and floored with metal, and was in a state of continuous faint vibration—a silent vibration with a strangely life-like and unmechanical quality about it. But if the vibration was silent, there was plenty of noise going on—a series of musical raps or percussions at quite irregular intervals which seemed to come from the ceiling. It was as if the metal chamber in which he found himself was being bombarded with small, tinkling missiles. Ransom was by now thoroughly frightened—not with the prosaic fright that a man suffers in a war, but with a heady, bounding kind of fear that was hardly distinguishable from his general excitement: he was poised on a sort of emotional watershed from which, he felt, he might at any moment pass into delirious terror or into an ecstasy of joy. He knew now that he was not in a house, but in some moving vessel. It was clearly not a submarine: and the infinitesimal quivering of the metal did not suggest the motion of any wheeled vehicle. A ship then, he supposed, or some kind of airship . . . but there was an oddity in all his sensations for which neither supposition accounted. Puzzled, he sat down again on the bed, and stared at the portentous moon.

An airship, some kind of flying-machine . . . but why did the moon look so big? It was larger than he had thought at first. No moon could really be that size; and he realised now that he had known this from the first but had repressed the knowledge through terror. At the same moment a thought came into his head which stopped his breath—there could be no full moon at all that night. He remembered distinctly that he had walked from Nadderby in a moonless night. Even if the thin crescent of a new moon had escaped his notice, it could not have grown to this in a few hours. It could not have grown to this at all—this megalomaniac disk, far larger than the football he had at first compared it to, larger than a child's hoop, filling almost half the sky. And where was the old "man in the moon"—the familiar face that had looked down on all the generations of men? The thing wasn't the Moon at all; and he felt his hair move on his scalp.

At that moment the sound of an opening door made him turn his head. An oblong of dazzling light appeared behind him and instantly vanished as the door closed again, having admitted the bulky form of a naked man whom Ransom recognised as Weston. No reproach, no demand for an explanation, rose to Ransom's lips or even to his mind; not with that monstrous orb above them. The mere presence of a human being, with its offer of at least some companionship, broke down the tension in which his nerves had long been resisting a bottomless dismay. He found, when he spoke, that he was sobbing.

"Weston! Weston!" he gasped. "What is it? It's not the moon, not that size. It can't be, can it?"

"No," replied Weston, "it's the Earth."

4

Ransom's legs failed him, and he must have sunk back upon the bed, but he only became aware of this many minutes later. At the moment he was unconscious of everything except his fear. He did not even know what he was afraid of: the fear itself possessed his whole mind, a formless, infinite misgiving. He did not lose consciousness, though he greatly wished that he might do so. Any change—death or sleep, or, best of all, a waking which should show all this for a dream—would have been inexpressibly welcome. None came. Instead, the lifelong self-control of social man, the virtues which are half hypocrisy or the hypocrisy which is half a virtue, came back to him and soon he found himself answering Weston in a voice not shamefully tremulous.

"Do you mean that?" he asked.

"Certainly."

"Then where are we?"

"Standing out from Earth about eighty-five thousand miles."

"You mean we're—in space." Ransom uttered the word with difficulty as a frightened child speaks of ghosts or a frightened man of cancer.

Weston nodded.

"What for?" said Ransom. "And what on earth have you kidnapped me for? And how have you done it?"

For a moment Weston seemed disposed to give no answer; then, as if on a second thought, he sat down on the bed beside Ransom and spoke as follows:

"I suppose it will save trouble if I deal with these questions at once, instead of leaving you to pester us with them every hour for the next month. As to how we do it—I suppose you mean how the space-ship works—there's no good your asking that. Unless you were one of the four or five real physicists now living you couldn't understand: and if there were any chance of your understanding you certainly wouldn't be told. If it makes you happy to repeat words that don't mean anything— which is, in fact, what unscientific people want when they ask for an explanation—you may say we work by exploiting the less observed properties of solar radiation. As to why we are here, we are on our way to Malacandra. . . ."

"Do you mean a star called Malacandra?"

"Even you can hardly suppose we are going out of the solar system. Malacandra is much nearer than that: we shall make it in about twenty-eight days."

"There isn't a planet called Malacandra," objected Ransom.

"I am giving it its real name, not the name invented by terrestrial astronomers," said Weston.

"But surely this is nonsense," said Ransom. "How the deuce did you find out its real name, as you call it?"

"From the inhabitants."

It took Ransom some time to digest this statement. "Do you mean to tell me you claim to have been to this star before, or this planet, or whatever it is?"

"Yes."

"You can't really ask me to believe that," said Ransom. "Damn it all, it's not an everyday affair. Why has no one heard of it? Why has it not been in all the papers?"

"Because we are not perfect idiots," said Weston gruffly.

After a few moments' silence Ransom began again. "Which planet is it in our terminology?" he asked.

"Once and for all," said Weston, "I am not going to tell you. If you know how to find out when we get there, you are welcome to do so: I don't think we have much to fear from your scientific attainments. In the meantime, there is no reason for you to know."

"And you say this place is inhabited?" said Ransom.

Weston gave him a peculiar look and then nodded. The uneasiness which this produced in Ransom rapidly merged in an anger which he had almost lost sight of amidst the conflicting emotions that beset him.

"And what has all this to do with me?" he broke out. "You have assaulted me, drugged me, and are apparently carrying me off as a prisoner in this infernal thing. What have I done to you? What do you say for yourself?"

"I might reply by asking you why you crept into my backyard like a thief. If you had minded your own business you would not be here. As it is, I admit that we have had to infringe your rights. My only defence is that small claims must give way to great. As far as we know, we are doing what has never been done in the history of man, perhaps never in the history of the universe. We have learned how to jump off the speck of matter on which our species began; infinity, and therefore perhaps eternity, is being put into the hands of the human race. You cannot be so small-minded as to think that the rights or the life of an individual or of a million individuals are of the slightest importance in comparison with this."

"I happen to disagree," said Ransom, "and I always have disagreed, even about vivisection. But you haven't answered my question. What do you want me for? What good am I to do you on this—on Malacandra."

"That I don't know," said Weston. "It was no idea of ours. We are only obeying orders."

"Whose?"

There was another pause. "Come," said Weston at last, "there is really no use in continuing this cross-examination. You keep on asking me questions I can't answer: in some cases because I don't know the answers, in others because you wouldn't understand them. It will make things very much pleasanter during the voyage if you can only resign your mind to your fate and stop bothering yourself and us. It would be easier if your philosophy of life were not so insufferably narrow and individualistic. I had thought no one could fail to be inspired by the role you are being asked to play: that even a worm, if it could understand, would rise to the sacrifice. I mean, of course, the sacrifice of time and liberty, and some little risk. Don't misunderstand me."

"Well," said Ransom, "you hold all the cards, and I must make the best of it. I consider *your* philosophy of life raving lunacy. I suppose all that stuff about infinity and eternity means that you think you are justified in doing anything—absolutely anything—here and now, on the off chance that some creatures or other descended from man as we know him may crawl about a few centuries longer in some part of the universe."

"Yes—anything whatever," returned the scientist sternly, "and all educated opinion—for I do not call classics and history and such trash education—is entirely on my side. I am glad you raised the point, and I advise you to remember my answer. In the meantime, if you will follow me into the next room, we will have breakfast. Be careful how you get up: your weight here is hardly appreciable compared with your weight on Earth."

Ransom rose and his captor opened the door. Instantly the room was flooded with a dazzling golden light which completely eclipsed the pale earthlight behind him.

"I will give you darkened glasses in a moment," said Weston as he preceded him into the chamber whence the radiance was pouring. It seemed to Ransom that Weston went up a hill towards the doorway and disappeared suddenly downwards when he had passed it. When he followed—which he did with caution—he had the curious impression that he was walking up to the edge of a precipice: the new room beyond the doorway seemed to be built on its side so that its farther wall lay almost in the same plane as the floor of the room he was leaving. When, however, he ventured to put forward his foot, he found that the floor continued flush and as he entered the second room the walls suddenly righted themselves and the rounded ceiling was over his head. Looking back, he perceived that the bedroom in its turn was now heeling over—its roof a wall and one of its walls a roof.

"You will soon get used to it," said Weston, following his gaze. "The ship is roughly spherical, and now we are outside the gravitational field of the Earth 'down' means—and feels—towards the centre of our own little metal world. This, of course, was foreseen and we built her accordingly. The core of the ship is a hollow globe—we keep our stores inside it—and the surface of that globe is the floor we are walking on. The cabins are arranged all round this, their walls supporting an outer globe which from our point of view is the roof. As the centre is always "down," the piece of floor you are standing on always feels flat or horizontal and the wall you are standing against always seems vertical. On the other hand, the globe of floor is so small that you can always see over the edge of it— over what would be the horizon if you were a flea—and then you see the floors and wall of the next cabin in a different plane. It is just the same on Earth, of course, only we are not big enough to see it."

After this explanation he made arrangements in his precise, ungracious way for the comfort of his guest or prisoner. Ransom, at his advice, removed all his clothes and substituted a little metal girdle hung with enormous weights to reduce, as far as possible, the unmanageable lightness of his body. He also assumed tinted glasses, and soon found himself seated opposite Weston at a small table laid for breakfast. He was both hungry and thirsty and eagerly attacked the meal which consisted of tinned meat, biscuit, butter and coffee.

But all these actions he had performed mechanically. Stripping, eating and drinking passed almost unnoticed, and all he ever remembered of his first meal in the space-ship was the tyranny of heat and light. Both were present in a degree which would have been intolerable on Earth, but each had a new quality. The light was paler than any light of comparable intensity that he had ever seen; it was not pure white but the palest of all imaginable golds, and it cast shadows as sharp as a floodlight. The heat, utterly free from moisture, seemed to knead and stroke the skin like a gigantic masseur: it produced no tendency to drowsiness: rather, intense alacrity. His headache was gone: he felt vigilant, courageous and magnanimous as he had seldom felt on Earth. Gradually he dared to raise his eyes to the skylight. Steel shutters were drawn across all but a chink of the glass, and that chink was covered with blinds of some heavy and dark material; but still it was too bright to look at.

"I always thought space was dark and cold," he remarked vaguely.

"Forgotten the sun?" said Weston contemptuously.

Ransom went on eating for some time. Then he began, "If it's like this in the early morning," and stopped, warned by the expression on Weston's face. Awe fell upon him: there were no mornings here, no evenings, and no night—nothing but the changeless noon which had filled for centuries beyond history so many millions of cubic miles. He glanced at Weston again, but the latter held up his hand.

"Don't talk," he said. "We have discussed all that is necessary. The ship does not carry oxygen enough for any unnecessary exertion; not even for talking."

Shortly afterwards he rose, without inviting the other to follow him, and left the room by one of the many doors which Ransom had not yet seen opened.

5

The period spent in the space-ship ought to have been one of terror and anxiety for Ransom. He was separated by an astronomical distance from every member of the human race except two whom he had excellent reasons for distrusting. He was heading for an unknown destination, and was being brought thither for a purpose which his captors steadily refused to disclose. Devine and Weston relieved each other regularly in a room which Ransom was never allowed to enter and where he supposed the controls of their machine must be. Weston, during his watches off, was almost entirely silent. Devine was more loquacious and would often talk and guffaw with the prisoner until Weston rapped on the wall of the control-room and warned them not to waste air. But Devine was secretive after a certain point. He was quite ready to laugh at Weston's solemn scientific idealism. He didn't give a damn, he said, for the future of the species or the meeting of two worlds.

"There's more to Malacandra than that," he would add with a wink. But when Ransom asked him what more, he would lapse into satire and make ironical remarks about the white man's burden and the blessings of civilization.

"It *is* inhabited, then?" Ransom would press.

"Ah—there's always a native question in these things," Devine would answer. For the most part his conversation ran on the things he would do when he got back to Earth: ocean-going yachts, the most expensive women and a big place on the Riviera figured largely in his plans. "I'm not running all these risks for fun."

Direct questions about Ransom's own role were usually met with silence. Only once, in reply to such a question, Devine, who was then in Ransom's opinion very far from sober, admitted that they were rather "handing him the baby."

"But I'm sure," he added, "you'll live up to the old school tie."

All this, as I have said, was sufficiently disquieting. The odd thing was that it did not very greatly disquiet him. It is hard for a man to brood on the future when he is feeling so extremely well as Ransom now felt. There was an endless night on one side of the ship and an endless day on the other: each was marvellous and he moved from the one to the other at his will, delighted. In the nights, which he could create by turning the handle of a door, he lay for hours in contemplation of the skylight. The Earth's disk was nowhere to be seen; the stars, thick as daisies on an uncut lawn, reigned perpetually with no cloud, no moon, no sunrise to dispute their sway. There were planets of unbelievable majesty, and constellations undreamed of: there were celestial sapphires, rubies, emeralds and pin-pricks of burning gold; far out on the left of the picture hung a comet, tiny and remote: and between all and behind all, far more emphatic and pal-pable than it showed on Earth, the undimensioned, enigmatic blackness. The lights trembled: they seemed to grow brighter as he looked. Stretched naked on his bed, a second Danaë, he found it night by night more difficult to disbelieve in old astrology: almost he felt, wholly he imag-ined, "sweet influence" pouring or even stabbing into his surrendered body. All was silence but for the irregular tinkling noises. He knew now that these were made by meteorites, small, drifting particles of the world-stuff that smote continually on their hollow drum of steel; and he guessed that at any moment they might meet something large enough to make meteorites of ship and all. But he could not fear. He now felt that Weston had justly called him little-minded in the moment of his first panic. The adventure was too high, its circumstance too solemn, for any emo-tion save a severe delight. But the days—that is, the hours' spent in the sun-ward hemisphere of their microcosm—were the best of all. Often he rose after only a few hours' sleep to return, drawn by an irresistible attraction, to the regions of light; he could not cease to wonder at the noon which always awaited you however early you went to seek it. There, totally immersed in a bath of pure ethereal colour and of unrelenting though unwounding brightness, stretched his full length and with eyes half closed in the strange chariot that bore them, faintly quivering, through depth after depth of tranquillity far above the reach of night, he felt his body and mind daily rubbed and scoured and filled with new vitality. Weston, in one of his brief, reluctant answers, admitted a scientific basis for these sensations: they were receiving, he said, many rays that never penetrated the terrestrial atmosphere.

But Ransom, as time wore on, became aware of another and more spiritual cause for his progressive lightening and exultation of heart. A nightmare, long engendered in the modern mind by the mythology that follows in the wake of science, was falling off him. He had read of "Space': at the back of his thinking for years had lurked the dismal fancy of the black, cold vacuity, the utter deadness, which was supposed to separate the worlds. He had not known how much it affected him till now—now that the very name "Space" seemed a blasphemous libel for this empyrean ocean of radiance in which they swam. He could not call it "dead'; he felt life pouring into him from it every moment. How indeed should it be otherwise, since out of this ocean the worlds and all their life had come? He had thought it barren: he saw now that it was the womb of worlds, whose blazing and innumerable offspring looked down nightly even upon the earth with so many eyes—and here, with how many more! No: space was the wrong name. Older thinkers had been wiser when they named it simply the heavens—the heavens which declared the glory—the

> "*happy climes that ly*
> *Where day never shuts his eye*
> *Up in the broad fields of the sky.*"

He quoted Milton's words to himself lovingly, at this time and often.

He did not, of course, spend all his time in basking. He explored the ship (so far as he was allowed), passing from room to room with those slow movements which Weston enjoined upon them lest exertion should overtax their supply of air. From the necessity of its shape, the space-ship contained a good many more chambers than were in regular use: but

Ransom was also inclined to think that its owners—or at least Devine—intended these to be filled with cargo of some kind on the return voyage. He also became, by an insensible process, the steward and cook of the company; partly because he felt it natural to share the only labours he could share—he was never allowed into the control-room—and partly in order to anticipate a tendency which Weston showed to make him a servant whether he would or no. He preferred to work as a volunteer rather than in admitted slavery: and he liked his own cooking a good deal more than that of his companions.

It was these duties that made him at first the unwilling, and then the alarmed, hearer of a conversation which occurred about a fortnight (he judged) after the beginning of their voyage. He had washed up the remains of their evening meal, basked in the sunlight, chatted with Devine—better company than Weston, though in Ransom's opinion much the more odious of the two—and retired to bed at his usual time. He was a little restless, and after an hour or so it occurred to him that he had forgotten one or two small arrangements in the galley which would facilitate his work in the morning. The galley opened off the saloon or day-room, and its door was close to that of the control-room. He rose and went there at once. His feet, like the rest of him, were bare.

The galley skylight was on the dark side of the ship, but Ransom did not turn on the light. To leave the door ajar was sufficient, as this admitted a stream of brilliant sunlight. As everyone who has "kept house" will understand, he found that his preparations for the morning had been even more incomplete than he supposed. He did his work well, from practice, and therefore quietly. He had just finished and was drying his hands on the roller-towel behind the galley door when he heard the door of the control-room open and saw the silhouette of a man outside the galley—Devine's, he gathered. Devine did not come forward into the saloon, but remained standing and talking—apparently into the control-room. It thus came about that while Ransom could hear distinctly what Devine said he could not make out Weston's answers.

"I think it would be dam' silly," said Devine. "If you could be sure of meeting the brutes where we alight there might be something in it. But suppose we have to trek? All we'd gain by your plan would be having to carry a drugged man and his pack instead of letting a live man walk with us and do his share of the work."

Weston apparently replied.

"But he *can't* find out," returned Devine. "Unless someone is fool enough to tell him. Anyway, even if he suspects, do you think a man like that would have the guts to run away on a strange planet? Without food? Without weapons? You'll find he'll eat out of your hand at the first sight of a *sorn*."

Again Ransom heard the indistinct noise of Weston's voice.

"How should I know?" said Devine. "It may be some sort of chief: much more likely a mumbo-jumbo."

This time came a very short utterance from the control-room: apparently a question. Devine answered at once.

"It would explain why he was wanted."

Weston asked him something more.

"Human sacrifice, I suppose. At least it wouldn't be human from *their* point of view; you know what I mean."

Weston had a good deal to say this time, and it elicited Devine's characteristic chuckle.

"Quite, quite," he said. "It is understood that you are doing it all from the highest motives. So long as they lead to the same actions as *my* motives, you are quite welcome to them."

Weston continued; and this time Devine seemed to interrupt him.

"You're not losing your own nerve, are you?" he said. He was then silent for some time, as if listening. Finally, he replied:

"If you're so fond of the brutes as that you'd better stay and inter-breed—if they have sexes, which we don't yet know. Don't you worry. When the time comes for cleaning the place up we'll save one or two for you, and you can keep them as pets or vivisect them or sleep with them or all three—whichever way it takes you. . . . Yes, I know. Perfectly loathsome. I was only joking. Good night."

A moment later Devine closed the door of the control-room, crossed the saloon and entered his own cabin. Ransom heard him bolt the door of it according to his invariable, though puzzling, custom. The tension with which he had been listening relaxed. He found that he had been holding his breath, and breathed deeply again. Then cautiously he stepped out into the saloon.

Though he knew that it would be prudent to return to his bed as quickly as possible, he found himself standing still in the now familiar glory of the light and viewing it with a new and poignant emotion. Out of this heaven, these happy climes, they were presently to descend—into *what? Sorns,* human sacrifice, loathsome sexless monsters. What was a *sorn?* His own role in the affair was now clear enough. Somebody or something had sent for him. It could hardly be for him personally. The somebody wanted a victim—any victim—from Earth. He had been picked because Devine had done the picking; he realised for the first time—in all circumstances a late and startling discovery—that Devine had hated him all these years as heartily as he hated Devine. But what was a *sorn?* "When he saw them he would eat out of Devine's hands." His mind, like so many minds of his generation, was richly furnished with bogies. He had read his H. G. Wells and others. His universe was peopled with horrors such as ancient and mediæval mythology could hardly rival. No insect-like, vermiculate or crustacean Abominable, no twitching feelers, rasping wings, slimy coils, curling tentacles, no monstrous union of superhuman intelligence and insatiable cruelty seemed to him anything but likely on an alien world. The *sorns* would be . . . would be . . . he dared not think what the *sorns* would be. And he was to be given to them. Somehow this seemed more horrible than being caught by them. Given, handed over, offered. He saw in imagination various incompatible monstrosities—bulbous eyes, grinning jaws, horns, stings, mandibles. Loathing of insects, loathing of snakes, loathing of things that squashed and squelched, all played their horrible symphonies over his nerves. But the reality would be worse: it would be an extra-terrestrial Otherness—something one had never thought of, never could have thought of. In that moment Ransom made a decision. He could face death, but not the *sorns.* He must escape when they got to Malacandra, if there were any possibility. Starvation, or even to be chased by *sorns,* would be better than being handed over. If escape were impossible, then it must be suicide. Ransom was a pious man. He hoped he would be forgiven. It was no more in his power, he thought, to decide otherwise than to grow a new limb. Without hesitation he stole back into the galley and secured the sharpest knife: henceforward he determined never to be parted from it.

Such was the exhaustion produced by terror that when he regained his bed he fell instantly into stupefied and dreamless sleep.

6

He woke much refreshed, and even a little ashamed of his terror on the previous night. His situation was, no doubt, very serious: indeed the possibility of returning alive to Earth must be almost discounted. But death could be faced, and rational fear of death could be mastered. It was only the irrational, the biological, horror of monsters that was the real difficulty: and this he faced and came to terms with as well as he could while he lay in the sunlight after breakfast. He had the feeling that one sailing in the heavens, as he was doing, should not suffer abject dismay before any earthbound creature. He even reflected that the knife could pierce other flesh as well as his own. The bellicose mood was a very rare one with Ransom. Like many men of his own age, he rather underestimated than overestimated his own courage; the gap between boyhood's dreams and his actual experience of the War had been startling, and his subsequent view of his own unheroic qualities had perhaps swung too far in the opposite direction. He had some anxiety lest the firmness of his present mood should prove a short-lived illusion; but he must make the best of it.

As hour followed hour and waking followed sleep in their eternal day, he became aware of a gradual change. The temperature was slowly falling. They resumed clothes. Later, they added warm underclothes. Later still, an electric heater was turned on in the centre of the ship. And it became certain, too—though the phenomenon was hard to seize—that the light was less overwhelming than it had been at the beginning of the voyage. It became certain to the comparing intellect, but it was difficult to *feel* what was happening as a diminution of light and impossible to think of it as "darkening" because, while the radiance changed in degree, its unearthly quality had remained exactly the same since the moment he first beheld it. It was not, like fading light upon the Earth, mixed with the increasing moisture and phantom colours of the air. You might halve its intensity, Ransom perceived, and the remaining half would still be what the whole had been—merely less, not other. Halve it again, and the residue would still be the same. As long as it was at all, it would be itself—out even to that unimagined distance where its last force was spent. He tried to explain what he meant to Devine.

"Like thingummy's soap!" grinned Devine. "Pure soap to the last bubble, eh?"

Shortly after this the even tenor of their life in the space-ship began to be disturbed. Weston explained that they would soon begin to feel the gravitational pull of Malacandra.

"That means," he said, "that it will no longer be 'down' to the centre of the ship. It will be "down" towards Malacandra—which from our point of view will be under the control-room. As a consequence, the floors of most of the chambers will become wall or roof, and one of the walls a floor. You won't like it."

The result of this announcement, so far as Ransom was concerned, was hours of heavy labour in which he worked shoulder to shoulder now with Devine and now with Weston as their alternating watches liberated them from the control-room. Water-tins, oxygen-cylinders, guns, ammunition and foodstuffs had all to be piled on the floors alongside the appropriate walls and lying on their sides so as to be upright when the new "downwards" came into play. Long before the work was finished disturbing sensations began. At first Ransom supposed that it was the toil itself which so weighted his limbs: but rest did not alleviate the symptom, and it was explained to him that their bodies, in response to the planet that had caught them in its field, were actually gaining weight every minute and doubling in weight with every twenty-four hours. They had the experiences of a pregnant woman, but magnified almost beyond endurance.

At the same time their sense of direction—never very confident on the space-ship—became continuously confused. From any room on board, the next room's floor had always looked downhill and felt level: now it looked downhill and felt a little, a very little, downhill as well. One found oneself running as one entered it. A cushion flung aside on the floor of the saloon would be found hours later to have moved an inch or so towards the wall. All of them were afflicted with vomiting, headache and palpitations of the heart. The conditions grew worse hour by hour. Soon one could only grope and crawl from cabin to cabin. All sense of direction disappeared in a sickening confusion. Parts of the ship were definitely below in the sense that their floors were upside down and only a fly could walk on them: but no part seemed to Ransom to be indisputably the right way up. Sensations of intolerable height and of falling—utterly absent in the heavens—recurred constantly. Cooking, of course, had long since been abandoned. Food was snatched as best they could, and drinking presented great difficulties: you could never be sure that you were really holding your mouth below, rather than beside, the bottle. Weston grew grimmer and more silent than ever. Devine, a flask of spirits ever in his hand, flung out strange blasphemies and coprologies and cursed Weston for bringing them. Ransom ached, licked his dry lips, nursed his bruised limbs and prayed for the end.

A time came when one side of the sphere was unmistakably down. Clamped beds and tables hung useless and ridiculous on what was now wall or roof. What had been doors became trapdoors, opened with difficulty. Their bodies seemed made of lead. There was no more work to be done when Devine had set out the clothes—their Malacandrian clothes—from their bundles and squatted down on the end of the saloon (now its floor) to watch the thermometer. The clothes, Ransom noticed, included heavy woollen underwear, sheepskin jerkins, fur gloves and eared caps. Devine made no reply to his questions. He was engaged in studying the thermometer and in shouting down to Weston in the control-room.

"Slower, slower," he kept shouting. "Slower, you damned fool. You'll be in air in a minute or two." Then sharply and angrily, "Here! Let me get at it."

Weston made no replies. It was unlike Devine to waste his advice: Ransom concluded that the man was almost out of his senses, whether with fear or excitement.

Suddenly the lights of the Universe seemed to be turned down. As if some demon had rubbed the heaven's face with a dirty sponge, the splendour in which they had lived for so long blenched to a pallid, cheerless and pitiable grey. It was impossible from where they sat to open the shutters or roll back the heavy blind. What had been a chariot gliding in the fields of heaven became a dark steel box dimly lighted by a slit of window, and falling. They were falling out of the heaven, into a world. Nothing in all his adventures bit so deeply into Ransom's mind as this. He wondered how he could ever have thought of planets, even of the Earth, as islands of life and reality floating in a deadly void. Now, with a certainty which never after deserted him, he saw the planets—the "earths" he called them in his thought—as mere holes or gaps in the living heaven—excluded and rejected wastes of heavy matter and murky air, formed not by addition to, but by subtraction from, the surrounding brightness. And yet, he thought, beyond the solar system the brightness ends. Is that the real void, the real death? Unless . . . he groped for the idea . . . unless visible light is also a hole or gap, a mere diminution of something else. Something that is to bright unchanging heaven as heaven is to the dark, heavy earths. . . .

Things do not always happen as a man would expect. The moment of his arrival in an unknown world found Ransom wholly absorbed in a philosophical speculation.

7

aving a doze?" said Devine. "A bit blasé about new planets by now?"

"Can you see anything?" interrupted Weston.

"I can't manage the shutters, damn them," returned Devine. "We may as well get to the manhole."

Ransom awoke from his brown study. The two partners were working together close beside him in the semi-darkness. He was cold and his body, though in fact much lighter than on Earth, still felt intolerably heavy. But a vivid sense of his situation returned to him; some fear, but more curiosity. It might mean death, but what a scaffold! Already cold air was coming in from without, and light. He moved his head impatiently to catch some glimpse between the labouring shoulders of the two men. A moment later the last nut was unscrewed. He was looking out through the manhole.

Naturally enough all he saw was the ground—a circle of pale pink, almost of white: whether very close and short vegetation or very wrinkled and granulated rock or soil he could not say. Instantly the dark shape of Devine filled the aperture, and Ransom had time to notice that he had a revolver in his hand—"For me or for *sorns* or for both?" he wondered.

"You next," said Weston curtly.

Ransom took a deep breath and his hand went to the knife beneath his belt. Then he got his head and shoulders through the manhole, his two hands on the soil of Malacandra. The pink stuff was soft and faintly resilient, like india-rubber; clearly vegetation. Instantly Ransom looked up. He saw a pale blue sky—a fine winter-morning sky it would have been on Earth—a great billowy cumular mass of rose-colour lower down which he took for a cloud, and then—

"Get out," said Weston from behind him.

He scrambled through and rose to his feet. The air was cold but not bitterly so, and it seemed a little rough at the back of his throat. He gazed about him, and the very intensity of his desire to take in the new world at a glance defeated itself. He saw nothing but colours—colours that refused to form themselves into things. Moreover, he knew nothing yet well enough to see it: you cannot see things till you know roughly what they are. His first impression was of a bright, pale world—a water-colour world out of a child's paint-box; a moment later he recognised the flat belt of light blue as a sheet of water, or of something like water, which came nearly to his feet. They were on the shore of a lake or river.

"Now then," said Weston, brushing past him. He turned and saw to his surprise a quite recognizable object in the immediate foreground—a hut of unmistakably terrestrial pattern though built of strange materials.

"They're human," he gasped. "They build houses?"

"*We* do," said Devine. "Guess again," and, producing a key from his pocket, proceeded to unlock a very ordinary padlock on the door of the hut. With a not very clearly defined feeling of disappointment or relief Ransom realised that his captors were merely returning to their own camp. They behaved as one might have expected. They walked into the hut, let down the slats which served for windows, sniffed the close air, expressed surprise that they had left it so dirty, and presently re-emerged.

"We'd better see about the stores," said Weston.

Ransom soon realised that he was to have little leisure for observation and no opportunity of escape. The monotonous work of transferring food, clothes, weapons and many unidentifiable packages from the ship to the hut kept him vigorously occupied for the next hour or so, and in the closest contact with his kidnappers. But something he learned. Before anything else he learned that Malacandra was beautiful; and he even reflected how odd it was that this possibility had never entered into his speculations about it. The same peculiar twist of imagination which led him to people the universe with monsters had somehow taught him to expect nothing on a strange planet except rocky desolation or else a network of nightmare machines. He could not say why, now that he came to think of it. He also discovered that the blue water surrounded them on at least three sides: his view in the fourth direction was blotted out by the vast steel football in which they had come. The hut, in fact, was built either on the point of a peninsula or on the end of an island. He also came little by little to the conclusion that the water was not merely blue in certain lights like terrestrial water but "really" blue. There was something about its behaviour under the very gentle breeze which puzzled him—something wrong or unnatural about the waves. For one thing, they were too big for such a wind, but that was not the whole secret. They reminded him somehow of the water that he had seen shooting up under the impact of shells in pictures of naval battles. Then suddenly realization came to him: they were the wrong shape, out of drawing, far too high for their length, too narrow at the base, too steep in the sides. He was reminded of something he had read in one of those modern poets about a sea rising in "turreted walls."

"Catch!" shouted Devine. Ransom caught and hurled the parcel on to Weston at the hut door.

On one side the water extended a long way—about a quarter of a mile, he thought, but perspective was still difficult in the strange world. On the other side it was much narrower, not wider than fifteen feet per-haps, and seemed to be flowing over a shallow—broken and swirling water that made a softer and more hissing sound than water on Earth; and where it washed the hither bank—the pinkish-white vegetation went down to the very brink—there was a bubbling and sparkling which suggested effervescence. He tried hard, in such stolen glances as the work allowed him, to make out something of the farther shore. A mass of something purple, so huge that he took it for a heather-covered moun-tain, was his first impression: on the other side, beyond the larger water, there was something of the same kind. But there, he could see over the top of it. Beyond were strange upright shapes of whitish green: too jagged and irregular for buildings, too thin and steep for mountains. Beyond and above these again was the rose-coloured cloud-like mass. It might really be a cloud, but it was very solid-looking and did not seem to have moved since he first set eyes on it from the manhole. It looked like the top of a gigantic red cauliflower—or like a huge bowl of red soapsuds—and it was exquisitely beautiful in tint and shape.

Baffled by this, he turned his attention to the nearer shore beyond the shallows. The purple mass looked for a moment like a clump of organ-pipes, then like a stack of rolls of cloth set up on end, then like a forest of gigantic umbrellas blown inside out. It was in faint motion. Suddenly his eyes mastered the object. The purple stuff was vegetation: more precisely it was vegetables, vegetables about twice the height of English elms, but apparently soft and flimsy. The stalks—one could hardly call them trunks—rose smooth and round, and surprisingly thin, for about forty feet: above that, the huge plants opened into a sheaf-like development, not of branches but of leaves, leaves large as lifeboats but nearly transparent. The whole thing corresponded roughly to his idea of a submarine forest: the plants, at once so large and so frail, seemed to need water to support them, and he wondered that they could hang in the air. Lower down, between the stems, he saw the vivid purple twilight, mottled with paler sunshine, which made up the internal scenery of the wood.

"Time for lunch," said Devine suddenly. Ransom straightened his back: in spite of the thinness and coldness of the air, his forehead was moist. They had been working hard and he was short of breath. Weston appeared from the door of the hut and muttered something about "finishing first." Devine, however, overruled him. A tin of beef and some biscuits were produced, and the men sat down on the various boxes which were still plentifully littered between the space-ship and the hut. Some whiskey—again at Devine's suggestion and against Weston's advice—was poured into the tin cups and mixed with water; the latter, Ransom noticed, was drawn from their own water-tins and not from the blue lakes.

As often happens, the cessation of bodily activity drew Ransom's attention to the excitement under which he had been labouring ever since their landing. Eating seemed almost out of the question. Mindful, however, of a possible dash for liberty, he forced himself to eat very much more than usual, and appetite returned as he ate. He devoured all that he could lay hands on either of food or drink: and the taste of that first meal was ever after associated in his mind with the first unearthly strangeness (never fully recaptured) of the bright, still, sparkling, unintelligible landscape—with needling shapes of pale green, thousands of feet high, with sheets of dazzling blue soda-water, and acres of rose-red soapsuds. He was a little afraid that his companions might notice, and suspect, his new achievements as a trencherman; but their attention was otherwise engaged. Their eyes never ceased roving the landscape; they spoke abstractedly and often changed position, and were ever looking over their shoulders. Ransom was just finishing his protracted meal when he saw Devine stiffen like a dog, and lay his hand in silence on Weston's shoulder. Both nodded. They rose. Ransom, gulping down the last of his whiskey, rose too. He found himself between his two captors. Both revolvers were out. They were edging him to the shore of the narrow water, and they were looking and pointing across it.

At first he could not see clearly what they were pointing at. There seemed to be some paler and slenderer plants than he had noticed before amongst the purple ones: he hardly attended to them, for his eyes were busy searching the ground—so obsessed was he with the reptile fears and insect fears of modern imagining. It was the reflections of the new white objects in the water that sent his eyes back to them: long, streaky, white reflections motionless in the running water—four or five, no, to be precise, six of them. He looked up. Six white things *were* standing there. Spindly and flimsy things, twice or three times the height of a man. His first idea was that they were images of men, the work of savage artists; he had seen things like them in books of archæology. But what could they be made of, and how could they stand?—so crazily thin and elongated in the leg, so top-heavily pouted in the chest, such stalky, flexible-looking distortions of earthly bipeds . . . like something seen in one of those comic mirrors. They were certainly not made of stone or metal, for now they seemed to sway a little as he watched; now with a shock that chased the blood from his cheeks he saw that they were alive, that they were moving, that they were coming at him. He had a momentary, scared glimpse of their faces, thin and unnaturally long, with long, drooping noses and drooping mouths of half-spectral, half-idiotic solemnity. Then he turned wildly to fly and found himself gripped by Devine.

"Let me go," he cried.

"Don't be a fool," hissed Devine, offering the muzzle of his pistol.

Then, as they struggled, one of the things sent its voice across the water to them: an enormous horn-like voice far above their heads.

"They want us to go across," said Weston.

Both the men were forcing him to the water's edge. He planted his feet, bent his back and resisted donkey-fashion. Now the other two were both in the water, pulling him, and he was still on the land. He found that he was screaming. Suddenly a second, much louder and less articulate noise broke from the creatures on the far bank. Weston shouted too, relaxed his grip on Ransom and suddenly fired his revolver not across the water but up it. Ransom saw why at the same moment.

A line of foam like the track of a torpedo was speeding towards them, and in the midst of it some large, shining beast. Devine shrieked a curse, slipped and collapsed into the water. Ransom saw a snapping jaw between them, and heard the deafening noise of Weston's revolver again and again beside him and, almost as loud, the clamour of the monsters on the far bank, who seemed to be taking to the water too. He had had no need to make a decision. The moment he was free he had found himself automatically darting behind his captors, then behind the space-ship and on as fast as his legs could carry him into the utterly unknown beyond it. As he rounded the metal sphere a wild confusion of blue, purple and red met his eyes. He did not slacken his pace for a moment's inspection. He found himself splashing through water and crying out not with pain but with surprise because the water was warm. In less than a minute he was climbing out onto dry land again. He was running up a steep incline. And now he was running through purple shadow between the stems of another forest of the huge plants.

8

A month of inactivity, a heavy meal and an unknown world do not help a man to run. Half an hour later, Ransom was walking, not running, through the forest, with a hand pressed to his aching side and his ears strained for any noise of pursuit. The clamour of revolver-shots and voices behind him (not all human voices) had been succeeded first by rifle-shots and calls at long intervals and then by utter silence. As far as eye could reach he saw nothing but the stems of the great plants about him receding in the violet shade, and far overhead the multiple transparency of huge leaves filtering the sunshine to the solemn splendour of twilight in which he walked. Whenever he felt able he ran again; the ground continued soft and springy, covered with the same resilient weed which was the first thing his hands had touched in Malacandra. Once or twice a small red creature scuttled across his path, but otherwise there seemed to be no life stirring in the wood; nothing to fear—except the fact of wandering unprovisioned and alone in a forest of unknown vegetation thousands or millions of miles beyond the reach or knowledge of man.

But Ransom was thinking of *sorns*—for doubtless those were the *sorns,* those creatures they had tried to give him to. They were quite unlike the horrors his imagination had conjured up, and for that reason had taken him off his guard. They appealed away from the Wellsian fan-

tasies to an earlier, almost an infantile, complex of fears. Giants—
ogres—ghosts—skeletons: those were its key words. Spooks on stilts, he
said to himself; surrealistic bogy-men with their long faces. At the same
time, the disabling panic of the first moments was ebbing away from
him. The idea of suicide was now far from his mind; instead, he was
determined to back his luck to the end. He prayed, and he felt his knife.
He felt a strange emotion of confidence and affection towards himself—
he checked himself on the point of saying, "We'll stick to one another."

The ground became worse and interrupted his meditation. He had
been going gently upwards for some hours with steeper ground on his
right, apparently half scaling, half skirting a hill. His path now began to
cross a number of ridges, spurs doubtless of the higher ground on the
right. He did not know why he should cross them, but for some reason
he did; possibly a vague memory of earthly geography suggested that the
lower ground would open out to bare places between wood and water
where *sorns* would be more likely to catch him. As he continued crossing ridges and gullies he was struck with their extreme steepness; but
somehow they were not very difficult to cross. He noticed, too, that even
the smallest hummocks of earth were of an unearthly shape—too narrow, too pointed at the top and too small at the base. He remembered
that the waves on the blue lakes had displayed a similar oddity. And
glancing up at the purple leaves he saw the same theme of perpendicu-
larity—the same rush to the sky—repeated there. They did not tip over
at the ends; vast as they were, air was sufficient to support them so that
the long aisles of the forest all rose to a kind of fan tracery. And the
sorns, likewise—he shuddered as he thought it—they too were madly
elongated.

He had sufficient science to guess that he must be on a world lighter
than the Earth, where less strength was needed and nature was set free
to follow her skyward impulse on a superterrestrial scale. This set him
wondering where he was. He could not remember whether Venus was
larger or smaller than Earth, and he had an idea that she would be hotter than this. Perhaps he was on Mars; perhaps even on the Moon. The
latter he at first rejected on the ground that, if it were so, he ought to
have seen the Earth in the sky when they landed; but later he remembered having been told that one face of the Moon was always turned
away from the Earth. For all he knew he was wandering on the Moon's

outer side; and, irrationally enough, this idea brought about him a bleaker sense of desolation than he had yet felt.

Many of the gullies which he crossed now carried streams, blue hissing streams, all hastening to the lower ground on his left. Like the lake they were warm, and the air was warm above them, so that as he climbed down and up the sides of the gullies he was continually changing temperatures. It was the contrast, as he crested the farther bank of one such small ravine, which first drew his attention to the growing chilliness of the forest; and as he looked about him he became certain that the light was failing too. He had not taken night into his calculations. He had no means of guessing what night might be on Malacandra. As he stood gazing into the deepening gloom a sigh of cold wind crept through the purple stems and set them all swaying, revealing once again the startling contrast between their size and their apparent flexibility and lightness. Hunger and weariness, long kept at bay by the mingled fear and wonder of his situation, smote him suddenly. He shivered and forced himself to proceed. The wind increased. The mighty leaves danced and dipped above his head, admitting glimpses of a pale and then a paler sky; and then, discomfortingly, of a sky with one or two stars in it. The wood was no longer silent. His eyes darted hither and thither in search of an approaching enemy and discovered only how quickly the darkness grew upon him. He welcomed the streams now for their warmth.

It was this that first suggested to him a possible protection against the increasing cold. There was really no use in going farther; for all he knew he might as well be walking towards danger as away from it. All was danger; he was no safer travelling than resting. Beside some stream it might be warm enough to lie. He shuffled on to find another gully, and went so far that he began to think he had got out of the region of them. He had almost determined to turn back when the ground began falling steeply; he slipped, recovered and found himself on the bank of a torrent. The trees—for as "trees" he could not help regarding them—did not quite meet overhead, and the water itself seemed to have some faintly phosphorescent quality, so that it was lighter here. The fall from right to left was steep. Guided by some vague picnicker's hankering for a "better" place, he went a few yards upstream. The valley grew steeper, and he came to a little cataract. He noticed dully that the water seemed to be descending a little too slowly for the incline, but he was too tired to speculate about it. The water was apparently hotter than that of the lake—perhaps nearer its subterranean source of heat. What he really wanted to know was whether he dared drink it. He was very thirsty by now; but it looked very poisonous, very unwatery. He would try not to drink it; perhaps he was so tired that thirst would let him sleep. He sank on his knees and bathed his hands in the warm torrent; then he rolled over in a hollow close beside the fall, and yawned.

The sound of his own voice yawning—the old sound heard in night-nurseries, school dormitories and in so many bedrooms—liberated a flood of self-pity. He drew his knees up and hugged himself; he felt a sort of physical, almost a filial, love for his own body. He put his wrist-watch to his ear and found that it had stopped. He wound it. Muttering, half whimpering to himself, he thought of men going to bed on the far-distant planet Earth—men in clubs, and liners, and hotels, married men, and small children who slept with nurses in the room, and warm, tobacco-smelling men tumbled together in forecastles and dug-outs. The tendency to talk to himself was irresistible . . . "We'll look after you, Ransom . . . we'll stick together, old man." It occurred to him that one of those creatures with snapping jaws might live in the stream. "You're quite right, Ransom," he answered mumblingly. "It's not a safe place to spend the night. We'll just rest a bit till you feel better, then we'll go on again. Not now. Presently."

9

It was thirst that woke him. He had slept warm, though his clothes were damp, and found himself lying in sunlight, the blue waterfall at his side dancing and coruscating with every transparent shade in the whole gamut of blue and flinging strange lights far up to the underside of the forest leaves. The realization of his position, as it rolled heavily back upon consciousness, was unbearable. If only he hadn't lost his nerve the *sorns* would have killed him by now. Then he remembered with inexpressible relief that there was a man wandering in the wood—poor devil—he'd be glad to see him. He would come up to him and say, "Hullo, Ransom,"—he stopped, puzzled. No, it was only himself: it *was* Ransom. Or was he? Who was the man whom he had led to a hot stream and tucked up in bed, telling him not to drink the strange water? Obviously some new-comer who didn't know the place as well as he. But whatever Ransom had told him, he was going to drink now. He lay down on the bank and plunged his face in the warm rushing liquid. It was good to drink. It had a strong mineral flavour, but it was very good. He drank again and found himself greatly refreshed and steadied. All that about the other Ransom was nonsense. He was quite aware of the danger of madness, and applied himself vigorously to his devotions and his toilet. Not that madness mattered much. Perhaps he was mad already, and not really on Malacandra but safe in bed in an English asylum. If only it might be so! He would ask Ransom—curse it! there his mind went playing the same trick again. He rose and began walking briskly away.

The delusions recurred every few minutes as long as this stage of his journey lasted. He learned to stand still mentally, as it were, and let them roll over his mind. It was no good bothering about them. When they were gone you could resume sanity again. Far more important was the problem of food. He tried one of the "trees" with his knife. As he expected, it was toughly soft like a vegetable, not hard like wood. He cut a little piece out of it, and under this operation the whole gigantic organism vibrated to its top—it was like being able to shake the mast of a full-rigged ship with one hand. When he put it in his mouth he found it almost tasteless but by no means disagreeable, and for some minutes he munched away contentedly. But he made no progress. The stuff was quite unswallowable and could only be used as a chewing-gum. As such he used it, and after it many other pieces; not without some comfort.

It was impossible to continue yesterday's flight as a flight— inevitably it degenerated into an endless ramble, vaguely motivated by the search for food. The search was necessarily vague, since he did not know whether Malacandra held food for him nor how to recognise it if it did. He had one bad fright in the course of the morning, when, passing through a somewhat more open glade, he became aware first of a huge, yellow object, then of two, and then of an indefinite multitude coming towards him. Before he could fly he found himself in the midst of a herd of enormous pale furry creatures more like giraffes than anything else he could think of, except that they could and did raise themselves on their hind legs and even progress several paces in that position. They were slenderer, and very much higher, than giraffes, and were eating the leaves off the tops of the purple plants. They saw him and stared at him with their big liquid eyes, snorting in *basso profondissimo,* but had apparently no hostile intentions. Their appetite was voracious. In five minutes they had mutilated the tops of a few hundred "trees" and admitted a new flood of sunlight into the forest. Then they passed on.

This episode had an infinitely comforting effect on Ransom. The planet was not, as he had begun to fear, lifeless except for *sorns.* Here was a very presentable sort of animal, an animal which man could probably tame, and whose food man could possibly share. If only it were possible to climb the "trees"! He was staring about him with some idea of attempting this feat, when he noticed that the devastation wrought by the leaf-eating animals had opened a vista overhead beyond the plant-tops to a collection of the same greenish-white objects which he had seen across the lake at their first landing.

This time they were much closer. They were enormously high, so that he had to throw back his head to see the top of them. They were something like pylons in shape, but solid; irregular in height and grouped in an apparently haphazard and disorderly fashion. Some ended in points that looked from where he stood as sharp as needles, while others, after narrowing towards the summit, expanded again into knobs or platforms that seemed to his terrestrial eyes ready to fall at any moment. He noticed that the sides were rougher and more seamed with fissures than he had realised at first, and between two of them he saw a motionless line of twisting blue brightness—obviously a distant fall of water. It was this which finally convinced him that the things, in spite of their improbable shape, were mountains; and with that discovery the mere oddity of the prospect was swallowed up in the fantastic sublime. Here, he understood, was the full statement of that *perpendicular* theme which beast and plant and earth all played on Malacandra—here in this riot of rock, leaping and surging skyward like solid jets from some rock-fountain, and hanging by their own lightness in the air, so shaped, so elongated, that all terrestrial mountains must ever after seem to him to be mountains lying on their sides. He felt a lift and lightening at the heart.

But the next moment his heart stood still. Against the pallid background of the mountains and quite close to him—for the mountains themselves seemed but a quarter of a mile away—a moving shape appeared. He recognised it instantly as it moved slowly (and, he thought, stealthily) between two of the denuded plant-tops—the giant stature, the cadaverous leanness, the long, drooping, wizard-like profile of a *sorn*. The head appeared to be narrow and conical; the hands or paws with which it parted the stems before it as it moved were thin, mobile, spidery and almost transparent. He felt an immediate certainty that it was looking for him. All this he took in in an infinitesimal time. The ineffaceable image was hardly stamped on his brain before he was running as hard as he could into the thickest of the forest.

He had no plan save to put as many miles as he could between himself and the *sorn*. He prayed fervently that there might be only one; perhaps the wood was full of them—perhaps they had the intelligence to make a circle round him. No matter—there was nothing for it now but sheer running, running knife in hand. The fear had all gone into action; emotionally he was cool and alert, and ready—as ready as he ever would be—for the last trial. His flight led him downhill at an ever-increasing speed; soon the incline was so steep that if his body had had terrestrial gravity he would have been compelled to take to his hands and knees and clamber down. Then he saw something gleaming ahead of him. A minute later he had emerged from the wood altogether; he was standing, blinking in the light of sun and water, on the shore of a broad river, and looking out on a flat landscape of intermingled river, lake, island and promontory—the same sort of country on which his eyes had first rested in Malacandra.

There was no sound of pursuit. Ransom dropped down on his stomach and drank, cursing a world where *cold* water appeared to be unobtainable. Then he lay still to listen and to recover his breath. His eyes were upon the blue water. It was agitated. Circles shuddered and bubbles danced ten yards away from his face. Suddenly the water heaved and a round, shining, black thing like a cannon-ball came into sight. Then he saw eyes and mouth—a puffing mouth bearded with bubbles. More of the thing came up out of the water. It was gleaming black. Finally it splashed and wallowed to the shore and rose, steaming, on its hind legs—six or seven feet high and too thin for its height, like everything in Malacandra. It had a coat of thick black hair, lucid as seal-skin, very short legs with webbed feet, a broad beaver-like or fish-like tail, strong forelimbs with webbed claws or fingers, and some complication half-way up the belly which Ransom took to be its genitals. It was something like a penguin, something like an otter, something like a seal; the slenderness and flexibility of the body suggested a giant stoat. The great round head, heavily whiskered, was mainly responsible for the suggestion of seal; but it was higher in the forehead than a seal's and the mouth was smaller.

There comes a point at which the actions of fear and precaution are purely conventional, no longer felt as terror or hope by the fugitive. Ransom lay perfectly still, pressing his body as well down into the weed as he could, in obedience to a wholly theoretical idea that he might thus pass unobserved. He felt little emotion. He noted in a dry, objective way that this was apparently to be the end of his story—caught between a *sorn* from the land and a big, black animal from the water. He had, it is true, a vague notion that the jaws and mouth of the beast were not those of a carnivore; but he knew that he was too ignorant of zoology to do more than guess.

Then something happened which completely altered his state of mind. The creature, which was still steaming and shaking itself on the back and had obviously not seen him, opened its mouth and began to make noises. This in itself was not remarkable; but a lifetime of linguistic study assured Ransom almost at once that these were articulate noises. The creature was *talking*. It had a language. If you are not yourself a philologist, I am afraid you must take on trust the prodigious emotional consequences of this realization in Ransom's mind. A new world he had already seen—but a new, an extra-terrestrial, a non-human language was a different matter. Somehow he had not thought of this in connection with the *sorns;* now, it flashed upon him like a revelation. The love of knowledge is a kind of madness. In the fraction of a second which it took Ransom to decide that the creature was really talking, and while he still knew that he might be facing instant death, his imagination had leaped over every fear and hope and probability of his situation to follow the dazzling project of making a Malacandrian grammar. *An Introduction to the Malacandrian language—The Lunar verb—A Concise Martian-English Dictionary* . . . the titles flitted through his mind. And what might one not discover from the speech of a non-human race? The very form of language itself, the principle behind all possible languages, might fall into his hands. Unconsciously he raised himself on his elbow and stared at the black beast. It became silent. The huge bullet head swung round and lustrous amber eyes fixed him. There was no wind on the lake or in the wood. Minute after minute in utter silence the representatives of two so far-divided species stared each into the other's face.

Ransom rose to his knees. The creature leaped back, watching him intently, and then became motionless again. Then it came a pace nearer, and Ransom jumped up and retreated, but not far; curiosity held him. He summoned up his courage and advanced, holding out his hand; the beast misunderstood the gesture. It backed into the shallows of the lake and he could see the muscles tightened under its sleek pelt, ready for sudden movement. But there it stopped; it, too, was in the grip of curiosity. Neither dared let the other approach, yet each repeatedly felt the impulse to do so himself, and yielded to it. It was foolish, frightening, ecstatic and unbearable all in one moment. It was more than curiosity. It was like a courtship—like the meeting of the first man and the first woman in the world; it was like something beyond that; so natural is the contact of sexes, so limited the strangeness, so shallow the reticence, so mild the repugnance to be overcome, compared with the first tingling intercourse of two different, but rational, species.

The creature suddenly turned and began walking away. A disappointment like despair smote Ransom.

"Come back," he shouted in English. The thing turned, spread out its arms and spoke again in its unintelligible language; then it resumed its progress. It had not gone more than twenty yards away when Ransom saw it stoop down and pick something up. It returned. In its hand (he was already thinking of its webbed forepaw as a hand) it was carrying what appeared to be a shell—the shell of some oyster-like creature, but rounder and more deeply domed. It dipped the shell in the lake and raised it full of water. Then it held the shell to its own middle and seemed to be pouring something into the water. Ransom thought with disgust that it was urinating in the shell. Then he realised that the protuberances on the creature's belly were not genital organs nor organs at all; it was wearing a kind of girdle hung with various pouch-like objects, and it was adding a few drops of liquid from one of these to the water in the shell. This done it raised the shell to its black lips and drank—not throwing back its head like a man but bowing it and sucking like a horse. When it had finished it refilled the shell and once again added a few drops from the receptacle—it seemed to be some kind of skin bottle—at its waist. Supporting the shell in its two arms, it extended them towards Ransom. The intention was unmistakable. Hesitantly, almost shyly, he advanced and took the cup. His finger-tips touched the webbed membrane of the creature's paws and an indescribable thrill of mingled attraction and repulsion ran through him; then he drank. Whatever had been added to the water was plainly alcoholic; he had never enjoyed a drink so much.

"Thank you," he said in English. "Thank you very much."

The creature struck itself on the chest and made a noise. Ransom did not at first realise what it meant. Then he saw that it was trying to teach him its name—presumably the name of the species.

"*Hross*," it said, "*Hross*," and flapped itself.

"*Hross*," repeated Ransom, and pointed at it; then "Man," and struck his own chest.

"*Hmā—hmā—hmān*," imitated the *hross*. It picked up a handful of earth, where earth appeared between weed and water at the bank of the lake.

"*Handra*," it said. Ransom repeated the word. Then an idea occurred to him.

"*Malacandra?*" he said in an inquiring voice. The *hross* rolled its eyes and waved its arms, obviously in an effort to indicate the whole landscape. Ransom was getting on well. *Handra* was earth the element; *Malacandra* the "earth" or planet as a whole. Soon he would find out what *Malac* meant. In the meantime "H disappears after C" he noted, and made his first step in Malacandrian phonetics. The *hross* was now trying to teach him the meaning of *handramit*. He recognised the root *handra-* again (and noted "They have suffixes as well as prefixes'), but this time he could make nothing of the *hross's* gestures, and remained ignorant what a *handramit* might be. He took the initiative by opening his mouth, pointing to it and going through the pantomime of eating. The Malacandrian word for *food* or *eat* which he got in return proved to contain consonants unreproducible by a human mouth, and Ransom, continuing the pantomime, tried to explain that his interest was practical as well as philological. The *hross* understood him, though he took some time to understand from its gestures that it was inviting him to follow it. In the end, he did so.

It took him only as far as where it had got the shell, and here, to his not very reasonable astonishment, Ransom found that a kind of boat was moored. Man-like, when he saw the artifact he felt more certain of the *hross's* rationality. He even valued the creature the more because the boat, allowing for the usual Malacandrian height and flimsiness, was really very like an earthly boat; only later did he set himself the question, "What else could a boat be like?" The *hross* produced an oval platter of some tough but slightly flexible material, covered it with strips of spongy, orange-coloured substance and gave it to Ransom. He cut a convenient length off with his knife and began to eat; doubtfully at first and then ravenously. It had a bean-like taste but sweeter; good enough for a starving man. Then, as his hunger ebbed, the sense of his situation returned with dismaying force. The huge, seal-like creature seated beside him became unbearably ominous. It seemed friendly; but it was very big, very black, and he knew nothing at all about it. What were its relations to the *sorns*? And was it really as rational as it appeared?

It was only many days later that Ransom discovered how to deal with these sudden losses of confidence. They arose when the rationality of the *hross* tempted you to think of it as a man. Then it became abominable—a man seven feet high, with a snaky body, covered, face and all, with thick black animal hair, and whiskered like a cat. But starting from the other end you had an animal with everything an animal ought to have—glossy coat, liquid eye, sweet breath and whitest teeth—and added to all these, as though Paradise had never been lost and earliest dreams were true, the charm of speech and reason. Nothing could be more disgusting than the one impression; nothing more delightful than the other. It all depended on the point of view.

10

When Ransom had finished his meal and drunk again of the strong waters of Malacandra, his host rose and entered the boat. He did this head-first like an animal, his sinuous body allowing him to rest his hands on the bottom of the boat while his feet were still planted on the land. He completed the operation by flinging rump, tail and hind legs all together about five feet into the air and then whisking them neatly on board with an agility which would have been quite impossible to an animal of his bulk on Earth.

Having got into the boat, he proceeded to get out again and then pointed to it. Ransom understood that he was being invited to follow his example. The question which he wanted to ask above all others could not, of course, be put. Were the *hrossa* (he discovered later that this was the plural of *hross*) the dominant species on Malacandra, and the *sorns,* despite their more man-like shape, merely a semi-intelligent kind of cattle? Fervently he hoped that it might be so. On the other hand, the *hrossa* might be the domestic animals of the *sorns,* in which case the latter would be superintelligent. His whole imaginative training somehow encouraged him to associate superhuman intelligence with monstrosity of form and ruthlessness of will. To step on board the *hross's* boat might mean surrendering himself to *sorns* at the other end of the journey. On the other hand, the *hross's* invitation might be a golden opportunity of leaving the *sorn*-haunted forests for ever. And by this time the *hross* itself was becoming puzzled at his apparent inability to understand it. The urgency of its signs finally determined him. The thought of parting from the *hross* could not be seriously entertained; its animality shocked him in a dozen ways, but his longing to learn its language, and, deeper still, the shy, ineluctable fascination of unlike for unlike, the sense that the key to prodigious adventure was being put in his hands—all this had really attached him to it by bonds stronger than he knew. He stepped into the boat.

The boat was without seats. It had a very high prow, an enormous expanse of free-board, and what seemed to Ransom an impossibly shallow draught. Indeed, very little of it even rested on the water; he was reminded of a modern European speed-boat. It was moored by something that looked at first like rope; but the *hross* cast off not by untying but by simply pulling the apparent rope in two as one might pull in two a piece of soft toffee or a roll of plasticine. It then squatted down on its rump in the stern-sheets and took up a paddle—a paddle of such enormous blade that Ransom wondered how the creature could wield it, till he again remembered how light a planet they were on. The length of the *hross's* body enabled him to work freely in the squatting position despite the high gunwale. It paddled quickly.

For the first few minutes they passed between banks wooded with the purple trees, upon a waterway not more than a hundred yards in width. Then they doubled a promontory, and Ransom saw that they were emerging on to a much larger sheet of water—a great lake, almost a sea. The *hross*, now taking great care and often changing direction and looking about it, paddled well out from the shore. The dazzling blue expanse grew moment by moment wider around them; Ransom could not look steadily at it. The warmth from the water was oppressive; he removed his cap and jerkin, and by so doing surprised the *hross* very much.

He rose cautiously to a standing position and surveyed the Malacandrian prospect which had opened on every side. Before and behind them lay the glittering lake, here studded with islands, and there smiling uninterruptedly at the pale blue sky; the sun, he noticed, was almost immediately overhead—they were in the Malacandrian tropics. At each end the lake vanished into more complicated groupings of land and water, softly, featherily embossed in the purple giant weed. But this marshy land or chain of archipelagoes, as he now beheld it, was bordered on each side with jagged walls of the pale green mountains, which he could still hardly call mountains, so tall they were, so gaunt, sharp, narrow and seemingly unbalanced. On the starboard they were not more than a mile away and seemed divided from the water only by a narrow strip of forest; to the left they were far more distant, though still impressive—perhaps seven miles from the boat. They ran on each side of the watered country as far as he could see, both onwards and behind them; he was sailing, in fact, on the flooded floor of a majestic canyon nearly ten miles wide and of unknown length. Behind and sometimes above the mountain peaks he could make out in many places great billowy piles of the rose-red substance which he had yesterday mistaken for cloud. The mountains, in fact, seemed to have no fall of ground behind them; they were rather the serrated bastion of immeasurable tablelands, higher in many places than themselves, which made the Malacandrian horizon left and right as far as eye could reach. Only straight ahead and straight astern was the planet cut with the vast gorge, which now appeared to him only as a rut or crack in the tableland.

He wondered what the cloud-like red masses were and endeavoured to ask by signs. The question was, however, too particular for sign-language. The *hross,* with a wealth of gesticulation—its arms or forelimbs were more flexible than his and in quick motion almost whip-like—made it clear that it supposed him to be asking about the high ground in general. It named this *harandra.* The low, watered country, the gorge or canyon, appeared to be *handramit.* Ransom grasped the implications, *handra* earth, *harandra* high earth, mountain, *handramit* low earth, valley. Highland and lowland, in fact. The peculiar importance of the distinction in Malacandrian geography he learned later.

By this time the *hross* had attained the end of its careful navigation. They were a couple of miles from land when it suddenly ceased paddling and sat tense with its paddle poised in the air; at the same moment the boat quivered and shot forward as if from a catapult. They had apparently availed themselves of some current. In a few seconds they were racing forward at some fifteen miles an hour and rising and falling on the strange, sharp, perpendicular waves of Malacandra with a jerky motion quite unlike that of the choppiest sea that Ransom had ever met on

Earth. It reminded him of disastrous experiences on a trotting horse in the army; and it was intensely disagreeable. He gripped the gunwale with his left hand and mopped his brow with his right—the damp warmth from the water had become very troublesome. He wondered if the Malacandrian food, and still more the Malacandrian drink, were really digestible by a human stomach. Thank heaven he was a good sailor! At least a fairly good sailor. At least——

Hastily he leaned over the side. Heat from blue water smote up to his face; in the depth he thought he saw eels playing: long, silver eels. The worst happened not once but many times. In his misery he remembered vividly the shame of being sick at a children's party . . . long ago in the star where he was born. He felt a similar shame now. It was not thus that the first representative of humanity would choose to appear before a new species. Did *hrossa* vomit too? Would it know what he was doing? Shaking and groaning, he turned back into the boat. The creature was keeping an eye on him, but its face seemed to him expressionless; it was only long after that he learned to read the Malacandrian face.

The current meanwhile seemed to be gathering speed. In a huge curve they swung across the lake to within a furlong of the farther shore, then back again, and once more onward, in giddy spirals and figures of eight, while purple wood and jagged mountain raced backwards and Ransom loathingly associated their sinuous course with the nauseous curling of the silver eels. He was rapidly losing all interest in Malacandra: the distinction between Earth and other planets seemed of no importance compared with the awful distinction of earth and water. He wondered despairingly whether the *hross* habitually lived on water. Perhaps they were going to spend the night in this detestable boat. . . .

His sufferings did not, in fact, last long. There came a blessed cessation of the choppy movement and a slackening of speed, and he saw that the *hross* was backing water rapidly. They were still afloat, with shores close on each side; between them a narrow channel in which the water hissed furiously—apparently a shallow. The *hross* jumped overboard, splashing abundance of warm water into the ship; Ransom, more cautiously and shakily, clambered after it. He was about up to his knees. To his astonishment, the *hross*, without any appearance of effort, lifted the boat bodily on to the top of its head, steadied it with one forepaw, and proceeded, erect as a Grecian caryatid, to the land. They walked forward—if the swinging movement of the *hross*'s short legs from its flexible hips could be called walking—beside the channel. In a few minutes Ransom saw a new landscape.

The channel was not only a shallow but a rapid—the first, indeed, of a series of rapids by which the water descended steeply for the next half-mile. The ground fell away before them and the canyon—or *handramit*—continued at a very much lower level. Its walls, however, did not sink with it, and from his present position Ransom got a clearer notion of the lie of the land. Far more of the highlands to left and right were visible, sometimes covered with the cloud-like red swellings, but more often level, pale and barren to where the smooth line of their horizon marched with the sky. The mountain peaks now appeared only as the fringe or border of the true highland, surrounding it as the lower teeth surround the tongue. He was struck by the vivid contrast between *harandra* and *handramit*. Like a rope of jewels the gorge spread beneath him, purple, sapphire blue, yellow and pinkish white, a rich and variegated inlay of wooded land and disappearing, reappearing, ubiquitous water. Malacandra was less like earth than he had been beginning to suppose. The *handramit* was no true valley rising and falling with the mountain chain it belonged to. Indeed, it did not belong to a mountain chain. It was only an enormous crack or ditch, of varying depth, running through the high and level *harandra;* the latter, he now began to suspect, was the true "surface" of the planet—certainly would appear as surface to a terrestrial astronomer. To the *handramit* itself there seemed no end; uninterrupted and very nearly straight, it ran before him, a narrowing line of colour, to where it clove the horizon with a V-shaped indenture. There must be a hundred miles of it in view, he thought; and he reckoned that he had put some thirty or forty miles of it behind him since yesterday.

All this time they were descending beside the rapids to where the water was level again and the *hross* could relaunch its skiff. During this walk Ransom learned the words for boat, rapid, water, sun and carry; the latter, as his first verb, interested him particularly. The *hross* was also at some pains to impress upon him an association or relation which it tried to convey by repeating the contrasted pairs of words *hrossa-handramit* and *séroni-harandra*. Ransom understood him to mean the *hrossa* lived down in the *handramit* and the *séroni* up on the *harandra*.

What the deuce were *séroni*, he wondered. The open reaches of the *harandra* did not look as if anything lived up there. Perhaps the *hrossa* had a mythology—he took it for granted they were on a low cultural level—and the *séroni* were gods or demons.

The journey continued, with frequent, though decreasing, recurrences of nausea for Ransom. Hours later he realised that *séroni* might very well be the plural of *sorn*.

The sun declined, on their right. It dropped quicker than on Earth, or at least on those parts of Earth that Ransom knew, and in the cloudless sky it had little sunset pomp about it. In some other queer way which he could not specify it differed from the sun he knew; but even while he speculated the needle-like mountain-tops stood out black against it and the *handramit* grew dark, though eastward (to their left) the high country of the *harandra* still shone pale rose, remote and smooth and tranquil, like another and more spiritual world.

Soon he became aware that they were landing again, that they were treading solid ground, were making for the depth of the purple forest. The motion of the boat still worked in his fantasy and the earth seemed to sway beneath him; this, with weariness and twilight, made the rest of the journey dream-like. Light began to glare in his eyes. A fire was burning. It illuminated the huge leaves overhead, and he saw stars beyond them. Dozens of *hrossa* seemed to have surrounded him; more animal, less human, in their multitude and their close neighborhood to him, than his solitary guide had seemed. He felt some fear, but more a ghastly inappropriateness. He wanted men—any men, even Weston and Devine. He was too tired to do anything about these meaningless bullet heads and furry faces—could make no response at all. And then, lower down, closer to him, more mobile, came in throngs the whelps, the puppies, the cubs, whatever you called them. Suddenly his mood changed. They were jolly little things. He laid his hand on one black head and smiled; the creature scurried away.

He never could remember much of that evening. There was more eating and drinking, there was continual coming and going of black forms, there were strange eyes luminous in the firelight; finally, there was sleep in some dark, apparently covered place.

II

Ever since he awoke on the space-ship Ransom had been thinking about the amazing adventure of going to another planet, and about his chances of returning from it. What he had not thought about was *being* on it. It was with a kind of stupefaction each morning that he found himself neither arriving in, nor escaping from, but simply living on, Malacandra; waking, sleeping, eating, swimming and even, as the days passed, talking. The wonder of it smote him most strongly when he found himself, about three weeks after his arrival, actually going for a walk. A few weeks later he had his favourite walks, and his favourite foods; he was beginning to develop habits. He knew a male from a female *hross* at sight, and even individual differences were becoming plain. Hyoi who had first found him—miles away to the north—was a very different person from the grey-muzzled, venerable Hnohra who was daily teaching him the language; and the young of the species were different again. They were delightful. You could forget all about the rationality of *hrossa* in dealing with them. Too young to trouble him with the baffling enigma of reason in an inhuman form, they solaced his loneliness, as if he had been allowed to bring a few dogs with him from the Earth. The cubs, on their part, felt the liveliest interest in the hairless goblin which appeared among them. With them, and therefore indirectly with their dams, he was a brilliant success.

Of the community in general his earlier impressions were all gradually being corrected. His first diagnosis of their culture was what he called "old stone age." The few cutting instruments they possessed were made of stone. They seemed to have no pottery but a few clumsy vessels used for boiling, and boiling was the only cookery they attempted. Their common drink vessel, dish and ladle all in one, was the oyster-like shell in which he had first tasted *hross* hospitality; the fish which it contained was their only animal food. Vegetable fare they had in great plenty and variety, some of it delicious. Even the pinkish-white weed which covered the whole *handramit* was edible at a pinch, so that if he had starved before Hyoi found him he would have starved amidst abundance. No *hross*, however, ate the weed (*honodraskrud*) for choice, though it might be used *faute de mieux* on a journey. Their dwellings were beehive-shaped huts of stiff leaf and the villages—there were several in the neighbourhood—were always built beside rivers for warmth and well upstream towards the walls of the *handramit* where the water was hottest. They slept on the ground. They seemed to have no arts except a kind of poetry and music which was practised almost every evening by a team or troupe of four *hrossa*. One recited half chanting at great length while the other three, sometimes singly and sometimes antiphonally, interrupted him from time to time with song. Ransom could not find out whether these interruptions were simply lyrical interludes or dramatic dialogue arising out of the leader's narrative. He could make nothing of the music. The voices were not disagreeable and the scale seemed adapted to human ears, but the time-pattern was meaningless to his sense of rhythm. The occupations of the tribe or family were at first mysterious. People were always disappearing for a few days and reappearing again. There was a little fishing and much journeying in boats of which he never discovered the object. Then one day he saw a kind of caravan of *hrossa* setting out by land each with a load of vegetable food on its head. Apparently there was some kind of trade in Malacandra.

He discovered their agriculture in the first week. About a mile down the *handramit* one came to broad lands free of forest and clothed for many miles together in low pulpy vegetation in which yellow, orange and blue predominated. Later on, there were lettuce-like plants about the height of a terrestrial birch-tree. Where one of these overhung the warmth of water you could step into one of the lower leaves and lie deliciously as in a gently moving, fragrant hammock. Elsewhere it was not warm enough to sit still for long out of doors; the general temperature of the *handramit* was that of a fine winter's morning on Earth. These food-producing areas were worked communally by the surrounding villages, and division of labour had been carried to a higher point than he expected. Cutting, drying, storing, transport and something like manuring were all carried on, and he suspected that some at least of the water channels were artificial.

But the real revolution in his understanding of the *hrossa* began when he had learned enough of their language to attempt some satisfaction of their curiosity about himself. In answer to their questions he began by saying that he had come out of the sky. Hnohra immediately asked from which planet or earth (*handra*). Ransom, who had deliberately given a childish version of the truth in order to adapt it to the supposed ignorance of his audience, was a little annoyed to find Hnohra painfully explaining to him that he could not live in the sky because there was no air in it; he might have come through the sky but he must have come from a *handra*. He was quite unable to point Earth out to them in the night sky. They seemed surprised at his inability, and repeatedly pointed out to him a bright planet low on the western horizon—a little south of where the sun had gone down. He was surprised that they selected a planet instead of a mere star and stuck to their choice; could it be possible that they understood astronomy? Unfortunately he still knew too little of the language to explore their knowledge. He turned the conversation by asking them the name of the bright southern planet, and was told that it was Thulcandra—the silent world or planet.

"Why do you call it *Thulc?*" he asked. "Why silent?" No one knew.

"The *séroni* know," said Hnohra. "That is the sort of thing they know."

Then he was asked how he had come, and made a very poor attempt at describing the space-ship—but again:

"The *séroni* would know."

Had he come alone? No, he had come with two others of his kind—bad men ('bent" men was the nearest *hrossian* equivalent) who tried to kill him, but he had run away from them. The *hrossa* found this very difficult, but all finally agreed that he ought to go to Oyarsa. Oyarsa would protect him. Ransom asked who Oyarsa was. Slowly, and with many misunderstandings, he hammered out the information that Oyarsa (1) lived at Meldilorn; (2) knew everything and ruled everyone; (3) had always been there; and (4) was not a *hross,* nor one of the *séroni.* Then Ransom, following his own idea, asked if Oyarsa had made the world. The *hrossa* almost barked in the fervour of their denial. Did people in Thulcandra not know that Maleldil the Young had made and still ruled the world? Even a child knew that. Where did Maleldil live, Ransom asked.

"With the Old One."

And who was the Old One? Ransom did not understand the answer. He tried again.

"Where was the Old One?"

"He is not that sort," said Hnohra, "that he has to live anywhere," and proceeded to a good deal which Ransom did not follow. But he followed enough to feel once more a certain irritation. Ever since he had discovered the rationality of the *hrossa* he had been haunted by a conscientious scruple as to whether it might not be his duty to undertake their religious instruction; now, as a result of his tentative efforts, he found himself being treated as if *he* were the savage and being given a first sketch of civilized religion—a sort of *hrossian* equivalent of the shorter catechism. It became plain that Maleldil was a spirit without body, parts or passions.

"He is not *hnau,*" said the *hrossa.*

"What is *hnau?*" asked Ransom.

"You are *hnau.* I am *hnau.* The *séroni* are *hnau.* The *pfifltriggi* are *hnau.*"

"*Pfifltriggi?*" said Ransom.

"More than ten days' journey to the west," said Hnohra. "The *harandra* sinks down not into a *handramit* but into a broad place, an open place, spreading every way. Five days' journey from the north to the south of it; ten days' journey from the east to the west. The forests are of other colours there than here, they are blue and green. It is very deep there, it goes to the roots of the world. The best things that can be dug out of the earth are there. The *pfifltriggi* live there. They delight in digging. What they dig they soften with fire and make things of it. They are little people, smaller than you, long in the snout, pale, busy. They have long limbs in front. No *hnau* can match them in making and shaping things as none can match us in singing. But let *Hmān* see."

He turned and spoke to one of the younger *hrossa* and presently, passed from hand to hand, there came to him a little bowl. He held it close to the firelight and examined it. It was certainly of gold, and Ransom realised the meaning of Devine's interest in Malacandra.

"Is there much of this thing?" he asked.

Yes, he was told, it was washed down in most of the rivers; but the best and most was among the *pfifltriggi,* and it was they who were skilled in it. *Arbol hru,* they called it—Sun's blood. He looked at the bowl again. It was covered with fine etching. He saw pictures of *hrossa* and of smaller, almost frog-like animals; and then, of *sorns.* He pointed to the latter inquiringly.

"*Séroni,*" said the *hrossa,* confirming his suspicions. "They live up almost on the *harandra.* In the big caves."

The frog-like animals—or tapir-headed, frog-bodied animals—were *pfifltriggi.* Ransom turned it over in his mind. On Malacandra, apparently, three distinct species had reached rationality, and none of them had yet exterminated the other two. It concerned him intensely to find out which was the real master.

"Which of the *hnau* rule?" he asked.

"Oyarsa rules," was the reply.

"Is he *hnau?*"

This puzzled them a little. The *séroni,* they thought, would be better at that kind of question. Perhaps Oyarsa was *hnau,* but a very different *hnau.* He had no death and no young.

"These *séroni* know more than the *hrossa?*" asked Ransom.

This produced more a debate than an answer. What emerged finally was the *séroni* or *sorns* were perfectly helpless in a boat, and could not fish to save their lives, could hardly swim, could make no poetry, and even when *hrossa* had made it for them could understand only the inferior sorts; but they were admittedly good at finding out things about the stars and understanding the darker utterances of Oyarsa and telling what happened in Malacandra long ago—longer ago than anyone could remember.

"Ah—the intelligentsia," thought Ransom. "They must be the real rulers, however it is disguised."

He tried to ask what would happen if the *sorns* used their wisdom to make the *hrossa* do things—this was as far as he could get in his halting

Malacandrian. The question did not sound nearly so urgent in this form as it would have done if he had been able to say "used their scientific resources for the exploitation of their uncivilized neighbours." But he might have spared his pains. The mention of the *sorns*" inadequate appreciation of poetry had diverted the whole conversation into literary channels. Of the heated, and apparently technical, discussion which followed he understood not a syllable.

Naturally his conversations with the *hrossa* did not all turn on Malacandra. He had to repay them with information about Earth. He was hampered in this both by the humiliating discoveries which he was constantly making of his own ignorance about his native planet, and partly by his determination to conceal some of the truth. He did not want to tell them too much of our human wars and industrialisms. He remembered how H. G. Wells's Cavor had met his end on the Moon; also he felt shy. A sensation akin to that of physical nakedness came over him whenever they questioned him too closely about men—the *hmāna* as they called them. Moreover, he was determined not to let them know that he had been brought there to be given to the *sorns;* for he was becoming daily more certain that these were the dominant species. What he did tell them fired the imagination of the *hrossa:* they all began making poems about the strange *handra* where the plants were hard like stone and the earth-weed green like rock and the waters cold and salt, and *hmāna* lived out on top, on the *harandra.*

They were even more interested in what he had to tell them of the aquatic animal with snapping jaws which he had fled from in their own world and even in their own *handramit.* It was a *hnakra,* they all agreed. They were intensely excited. There had not been a *hnakra* in the valley for many years. The youth of the *hrossa* got out their weapons—primitive harpoons with points of bone—and the very cubs began playing at *hnakra*-hunting in the shallows. Some of the mothers showed signs of anxiety and wanted the cubs to be kept out of the water, but in general the news of the *hnakra* seemed to be immensely popular. Hyoi set off at once to do something to his boat, and Ransom accompanied him. He wished to make himself useful, and was already beginning to have some vague capacity with the primitive *hrossian* tools. They walked together to Hyoi's creek, a stone's throw through the forest.

On the way, where the path was single and Ransom was following

Hyoi, they passed a little she-*hross*, not much more than a cub. She spoke as they passed, but not to them: her eyes were on a spot about five yards away.

"Who do you speak to, Hrikki?" said Ransom.

"To the *eldil*."

"Where?"

"Did you not see him?"

"I saw nothing."

"There! There!" she cried suddenly. "Ah! He is gone. Did you not see him?"

"I saw no one."

"Hyoi!" said the cub. "the *hmān* cannot see the *eldil*."

But Hyoi, continuing steadily on his way, was already out of earshot, and had apparently noticed nothing. Ransom concluded that Hrikki was "pretending" like the young of his own species. In a few moments he rejoined his companion.

12

They worked hard at Hyoi's boat till noon and then spread themselves on the weed close to the warmth of the creek, and began their midday meal. The war-like nature of their preparations suggested many questions to Ransom. He knew no word for war, but he managed to make Hyoi understand what he wanted to know. Did *séroni* and *hrossa* and *pfifltriggi* ever go out like this, with weapons, against each other?

"What for?" asked Hyoi.

It was difficult to explain. "If both wanted one thing and neither would give it," said Ransom, "would the other at last come with force? Would they say, give it or we kill you?"

"What sort of thing?"

"Well—food, perhaps."

"If the other *hnau* wanted food, why should we not give it to them? We often do."

"But how if we had not enough for ourselves?"

"But Maleldil will not stop the plants growing."

"Hyoi, if you had more and more young, would Maleldil broaden the *handramit* and make enough plants for them all?"

"The *séroni* know that sort of thing. But why should we have more young?"

Ransom found this difficult. At last he said:

"Is the begetting of young not a pleasure among the *hrossa?*"

"A very great one, *Hmān*. This is what we call love."

"If a thing is a pleasure, a *hmān* wants it again. He might want the pleasure more often than the number of young that could be fed."

It took Hyoi a long time to get the point.

"You mean," he said slowly, "that he might do it not only in one or two years of his life but again?"

"Yes."

"But why? Would he want his dinner all day or want to sleep after he had slept? I do not understand."

"But a dinner comes every day. This love, you say, comes only once while the *hross* lives?"

"But it takes his whole life. When he is young he has to look for his mate; and then he has to court her; then he begets young; then he rears them; then he remembers all this, and boils it inside him and makes it into poems and wisdom."

"But the pleasure he must be content only to remember?"

"That is like saying "My food I must be content to eat." "

"I do not understand."

"A pleasure is full grown only when it is remembered. You are speaking, *Hmān,* as if the pleasure were one thing and the memory another. It is all one thing. The *séroni* could say it better than I say it now. Not better than I could say it in a poem. What you call remembering is the last part of the pleasure, as the *crah* is the last part of a poem. When you and I met, the meeting was over very shortly, it was nothing. Now it is growing something as we remember it. But still we know very little about it. What it will be when I remember it as I lie down to die, what it makes in me all my days till then—that is the real meeting. The other is only the beginning of it. You say you have poets in your world. Do they not teach you this?"

"Perhaps some of them do," said Ransom. "But even in a poem does a *hross* never long to hear one splendid line over again?"

Hyoi's reply unfortunately turned on one of those points in their language which Ransom had not mastered. There were two verbs which both, as far as he could see, meant to *long* or *yearn;* but the *hrossa* drew a sharp distinction, even an opposition, between them. Hyoi seemed to him merely to be saying that every one would long for it (*wondelone*) but no one in his senses could long for it (*hluntheline*).

"And indeed," he continued, "the poem is a good example. For the most splendid line becomes fully splendid only by means of all the lines after it; if you went back to it you would find it less splendid than you thought. You would kill it. I mean in a good poem."

"But in a bent poem, Hyoi?"

"A bent poem is not listened to, *Hmān*."

"And how of love in a bent life?"

"How could the life of a *hnau* be bent?"

"Do you say, Hyoi, that there are no bent *hrossa*?"

Hyoi reflected. "I have heard," he said at last, "of something like what you mean. It is said that sometimes here and there a cub of certain age gets strange twists in him. I have heard of one that wanted to eat earth; there might, perhaps, be somewhere a *hross* likewise that wanted to have the years of love prolonged. I have not heard of it, but it might be. I have heard of something stranger. There is a poem about a *hross* who lived long ago, in another *handramit*, who saw things all made two—two suns in the sky, two heads on a neck; and last of all they say that he fell into such a frenzy that he desired two mates. I do not ask you to believe it, but that is the story: that he loved two *hressni*."

Ransom pondered this. Here, unless Hyoi was deceiving him, was a species naturally continent, naturally monogamous. And yet, was it so strange? Some animals, he knew, had regular breeding seasons; and if nature could perform the miracle of turning the sexual impulse outward at all, why could she not go further and fix it, not morally but instinctively, to a single object? He even remembered dimly having heard that some terrestrial animals, some of the "lower" animals, were naturally monogamous. Among the *hrossa*, anyway, it was obvious that unlimited breeding and promiscuity were as rare as the rarest perversions. At last it dawned upon him that it was not they, but his own species, that were the puzzle. That the *hrossa* should have such instincts was mildly surprising; but how came it that the instincts of the *hrossa* so closely resembled the unattained ideals of that far-divided species Man whose instincts were so deplorably different? What was the history of Man? But Hyoi was speaking again.

"Undoubtedly," he said. "Maleldil made us so. How could there ever be enough to eat if everyone had twenty young? And how could we endure to live and let time pass if we were always crying for one day or one year to come back—if we did not know that every day in a life fills the whole life with expectation and memory and that these *are* that day?"

"All the same," said Ransom, unconsciously nettled on behalf of his own world, "Maleldil has let in the *hnakra.*"

"Oh, but that is so different. I long to kill this *hnakra* as he also longs to kill me. I hope that my ship will be the first and I first in my ship with my straight spear when the black jaws snap. And if he kills me, my people will mourn and my brothers will desire still more to kill him. But they will not wish that there were no *hnéraki;* nor do I. How can I make you understand, when you do not understand the poets? The *hnakra* is our enemy, but he is also our beloved. We feel in our hearts his joy as he looks down from the mountain of water in the north where he was born; we leap with him when he jumps the falls; and when winter comes, and the lake smokes higher than our heads, it is with his eyes that we see it and know that his roaming time is come. We hang images of him in our houses, and the sign of all the *hrossa* is a *hnakra.* In him the spirit of the valley lives; and our young play at being *hnéraki* as soon as they can splash in the shallows."

"And then he kills them?"

"Not often them. The *hrossa* would be bent *hrossa* if they let him get so near. Long before he had come down so far we should have sought him out. No, *Hmān,* it is not a few deaths roving the world around him that make a *hnau* miserable. It is a bent *hnau* that would blacken the world. And I say also this. I do not think the forest would be so bright, nor the water so warm, nor love so sweet, if there were no danger in the lakes. I will tell you a day in my life that has shaped me; such a day as comes only once, like love, or serving Oyarsa in Meldilorn. Then I was young, not much more than a cub, when I went far, far up the *handramit* to the land where stars shine at midday and even water is cold. A great waterfall I climbed. I stood on the shore of Balki the pool, which is the place of most awe in all worlds. The walls of it go up for ever and ever and huge and holy images are cut in them, the work of old times. There is the fall called the Mountain of Water. Because I have stood there alone, Maleldil and I, for even Oyarsa sent me no word, my heart has been higher, my song deeper, all my days. But do you think it would have been so unless I had known that in Balki *hnéraki* dwelled? There I drank life because death was in the pool. That was the best of drinks save one."

"What one?" asked Ransom.

"Death itself in the day I drink it and go to Maleldil."

Shortly after that they rose and resumed their work. The sun was declining as they came back through the wood. It occurred to Ransom to ask Hyoi a question.

"Hyoi," he said, "it comes into my head that when I first saw you, and before you saw me, you were already speaking. That was how I knew that you were *hnau*, for otherwise I should have thought you a beast, and run away. But who were you speaking to?"

"To an *eldil*."

"What is that? I saw no one."

"Are there no *eldila* in your world, *Hmān?* That must be strange."

"But what are they?"

"They come from Oyarsa—they are, I suppose, a kind of *hnau*."

"As we came out to-day I passed a child who said she was talking to an *eldil*, but I could see nothing."

"One can see by looking at your eyes, *Hmān*, that they are different from ours. But *eldila* are hard to see. They are not like us. Light goes through them. You must be looking in the right place and the right time; and that is not likely to come about unless the *eldil* wishes to be seen. Sometimes you can mistake them for a sunbeam or even a moving of the leaves; but when you look again you see that it was an *eldil* and that it is gone. But whether your eyes can ever see them I do not know. The *séroni* would know that."

13

The whole village was astir next morning before the sunlight—already visible on the *harandra*—had penetrated the forest. By the light of the cooking-fires Ransom saw an incessant activity of *hrossa*. The females were pouring out steaming food from clumsy pots; Hnohra was directing the transportation of piles of spears to the boats; Hyoi, in the midst of a group of the most experienced hunters, was talking too rapidly and too technically for Ransom to follow; parties were arriving from the neighbouring villages; and the cubs, squealing with excitement, were running hither and thither among their elders.

He found that his own share in the hunt had been taken for granted. He was to be in Hyoi's boat, with Hyoi and Whin. The two *hrossa* would take it in turns to paddle, while Ransom and the disengaged *hross* would be in the bows. He understood the *hrossa* well enough now to know that they were making him the noblest offer in their power, and the Hyoi and Whin were each tormented by the fear lest he should be paddling when the *hnakra* appeared. A short time ago, in England, nothing would have seemed more impossible to Ransom than to accept the post of honour and danger in an attack upon an unknown but certainly deadly aquatic monster. Even more recently, when he had first fled from the *sorns,* or when he had lain pitying himself in the forest by night, it would hardly have been in his power to do what he was intending to do to-day. For his intention was clear. Whatever happened, he must show that the human species also were *hnau*. He was only too well aware that such resolutions might look very different when the moment came, but he felt an unwonted assurance that somehow or other he would be able to go through with it. It was necessary, and the necessary was always possible. Perhaps, too, there was something in the air he now breathed, or in the society of the *hrossa,* which had begun to work a change in him.

The lake was just giving back the first rays of the sun when he found himself kneeling side by side with Whin, as he had been told to, in the bows of Hyoi's ship, with a little pile of throwing-spears between his knees and one in his right hand, stiffening his body against the motion as Hyoi paddled them out into their place. At least a hundred boats were taking part in the hunt. They were in three parties. The central, and far the smallest, was to work its way up the current by which Hyoi and Ransom had descended after their first meeting. Longer ships than he had yet seen, eight-paddled ships, were used for this. The habit of the *hnakra* was to float down the current whenever he could; meeting the ships, he would presumably dart out of it into the still water to left or right. Hence while the central party slowly beat up the current, the light ships, paddling far faster, would cruise at will up and down either side of it to receive the quarry as soon as he broke what might be called his "cover." In this game numbers and intelligence were on the side of the *hrossa;* the *hnakra* had speed on his side, and also invisibility, for he could swim under water. He was nearly invulnerable except through his open mouth. If the two hunters in the bows of the boat he made for muffed their shots, this was usually the last of them and of their boat.

In the light skirmishing parties there were two things a brave hunter could aim at. He could keep well back and close to the long-ships where the *hnakra* was most likely to break out, or he could get as far forward as possible in the hope of meeting the *hnakra* going at its full speed and yet untroubled by the hunt, and of inducing it, by a well-aimed spear, to leave the current then and there. One could thus anticipate the beaters and kill the beast—if that was how the matter ended—on one's own. This was the desire of Hyoi and Whin; and almost—so strongly they infected him—of Ransom. Hence, hardly had the heavy craft of the beaters begun their slow progress up-current amid a wall of foam when he found his own ship speeding northward as fast as Hyoi could drive her, already passing boat after boat and making for the freest water. The speed was exhilarating. In the cold morning the warmth of the blue expanse they were clearing was not unpleasant. Behind them arose, re-echoed from the remote rock pinnacles on either side of the valley, the bell-like, deep-mouthed voices of more than two hundred *hrossa,* more musical than a cry of hounds but closely akin to it in quality as in pur-port. Something long sleeping in the blood awoke in Ransom. It did not seem impossible at this moment that even he might be the *hnakra*-slayer; that the fame of *Hmān hnakrapunt* might be handed down to posterity in this world that knew no other man. But he had had such dreams before, and knew how they ended. Imposing humility on the newly risen riot of his feelings, he turned his eyes to the troubled water of the current which they were skirting, without entering, and watched intently.

For a long time nothing happened. He became conscious of the stiff-ness of his attitude and deliberately relaxed his muscles. Presently Whin reluctantly went aft to paddle, and Hyoi came forward to take his place. Almost as soon as the change had been effected, Hyoi spoke softly to him and said, without taking his eyes off the current:

"There is an *eldil* coming to us over the water."

Ransom could see nothing—or nothing that he could distinguish from imagination and the dance of sunlight on the lake. A moment later Hyoi spoke again, but not to him.

"What is it, sky-born?"

What happened next was the most uncanny experience Ransom had yet had on Malacandra. He heard the voice. It seemed to come out of the air, about a yard above his head, and it was almost an octave higher than the *hross's*—higher even than his own. He realised that a very little dif-ference in his ear would have made the *eldil* as inaudible to him as it was invisible.

"It is the Man with you, Hyoi," said the voice. "He ought not to be there. He ought to be going to Oyarsa. Bent *hnau* of his own kind from Thulcandra are following him; he should go to Oyarsa. If they find him anywhere else there will be evil."

"He hears you, sky-born," said Hyoi. "And have you no message for my wife? You know what she wishes to be told."

"I have a message for Hleri," said the *eldil.* "But you will not be able to take it. I go to her now myself. All that is well. Only—let the Man go to Oyarsa."

There was a moment's silence.

"He is gone," said Whin. "And we have lost our share in the hunt."

"Yes," said Hyoi with a sigh. "We must put *Hmān* ashore and teach him the way to Meldilorn."

Ransom was not so sure of his courage but that one part of him felt an instant relief at the idea of any diversion from their present business. But the other part of him urged him to hold on to his new-found manhood; now or never—with such companions or with none—he must leave a deed on his memory instead of one more broken dream. It was in obedience to something like conscience that he exclaimed:

"No, no. There is time for that after the hunt. We must kill the *hnakra* first."

"Once an *eldil* has spoken," began Hyoi, when suddenly Whin gave a great cry (a "bark" Ransom would have called it three weeks ago) and pointed. There, not a furlong away, was the torpedo-like track of foam; and now, visible through a wall of foam, they caught the metallic glint of the monster's sides. Whin was paddling furiously. Hyoi threw and missed. As his first spear smote the water his second was already in the air. This time it must have touched the *hnakra*. He wheeled right out of the current. Ransom saw the great black pit of his mouth twice open and twice shut with its snap of shark-like teeth. He himself had thrown now—hurriedly, excitedly, with unpractised hand.

"Back," shouted Hyoi to Whin who was already backing water with every pound of his vast strength. Then all became confused. He heard Whin shout "Shore!" There came a shock that flung him forward almost into the *hnakra*'s jaws and he found himself at the same moment up to his waist in water. It was at him the teeth were snapping. Then as he flung shaft after shaft into the great cavern of the gaping brute he saw Hyoi perched incredibly on its back—on its nose—bending forward and hurling from there. Almost at once the *hross* was dislodged and fell with a wide splash nearly ten yards away. But the *hnakra* was killed. It was wallowing on its side, bubbling out its black life. The water around him was dark and stank.

When he recollected himself they were all on shore, wet, steaming, trembling with exertion and embracing one another. It did not now seem strange to him to be clasped to a breast of wet fur. The breath of the *hrossa* which, though sweet, was not human breath, did not offend him. He was one with them. That difficulty which they, accustomed to more than one rational species, had perhaps never felt, was now overcome. They were all *hnau*. They had stood shoulder to shoulder in the face of an enemy, and the shapes of their heads no longer mattered. And he, even Ransom, had come through it and not been disgraced. He had grown up.

They were on a little promontory free of forest, on which they had run aground in the confusion of the fight. The wreckage of the boat and the corpse of the monster lay confused together in the water beside them. No sound from the rest of the hunting party was audible; they had been almost a mile ahead when they met the *hnakra*. All three sat down to recover their breath.

"So," said Hyoi, "we are *hnakrapunti*. This is what I have wanted all my life."

At that moment Ransom was deafened by a loud sound—a perfectly familiar sound which was the last thing he expected to hear. It was a terrestrial, human and civilized sound; it was even European. It was the crack of an English rifle; and Hyoi, at his feet, was struggling to rise and gasping. There was blood on the white weed where he struggled. Ransom dropped on his knees beside him. The huge body of the *hross* was too heavy for him to turn round. Whin helped him.

"Hyoi, can you hear me?" said Ransom with his face close to the round seal-like head. "Hyoi, it is through me that this has happened. It is the other *hmāna* who have hit you, the bent two that brought me to Malacandra. They can throw death at a distance with a thing they have made. I should have told you. We are all a bent race. We have come here to bring evil on Malacandra. We are only half *hnau*—Hyoi . . ." His speech died away into the inarticulate. He did not know the words for "forgive," or "shame," or "fault," hardly the word for "sorry." He could only stare into Hyoi's distorted face in speechless guilt. But the *hross* seemed to understand. It was trying to say something, and Ransom laid his ear close to the working mouth. Hyoi's dulling eyes were fixed on his own, but the expression of a *hross* was not even now perfectly intelligible to him.

"*Hnā—hmā*," it muttered and then, at last, *Hmān, hnakrapunt.*" Then there came a contortion of the whole body, a gush of blood and saliva from the mouth; his arms gave way under the sudden dead weight of the sagging head, and Hyoi's face became as alien and animal as it had seemed at their first meeting. The glazed eyes and the slowly stiffening, bedraggled fur were like those of any dead beast found in an earthly wood.

Ransom resisted an infantile impulse to break out into imprecations on Weston and Devine. Instead he raised his eyes to meet those of Whin who was crouching—*hrossa* do not kneel—on the other side of the corpse.

"I am in the hands of your people, Whin," he said. "They must do as they will. But if they are wise they will kill me and certainly they will kill the other two."

"One does not kill *hnau*," said Whin. "Only Oyarsa does that. But these others, where are they?"

Ransom glanced around. It was open on the promontory but thick wood came down to where it joined the mainland, perhaps two hundred yards away.

"Somewhere in the wood," he said. "Lie down, Whin, here where the ground is lowest. They may throw from their thing again."

He had some difficulty in making Whin do as he suggested. When both were lying in dead ground, their feet almost in the water, the *hross* spoke again.

"Why did they kill him?" he asked.

"They would not know he was *hnau*," said Ransom. "I have told you that there is only one kind of *hnau* in our world. They would think he was a beast. If they thought that, they would kill him for pleasure, or in fear, or" (he hesitated) "because they were hungry. But I must tell you the truth, Whin. They would kill even a *hnau*, knowing it to be *hnau*, if they thought its death would serve them."

There was a short silence.

"I am wondering," said Ransom, "if they saw me. It is for me they are looking. Perhaps if I went to them they would be content and come no farther into your land. But why do they not come out of the wood to see what they have killed?"

"Our people are coming," said Whin, turning his head. Ransom looked back and saw the lake black with boats. The main body of the hunt would be with them in a few minutes.

"They are afraid of the *hrossa*," said Ransom. "That is why they do not come out of the wood. I will go to them, Whin."

"No," said Whin. "I have been thinking. All this has come from not obeying the *eldil*. He said you were to go to Oyarsa. You ought to have been already on the road. You must go now."

"But that will leave the bent *hmāna* here. They may do more harm."

"They will not set on the *hrossa*. You have said they are afraid. It is more likely that we will come upon them. Never fear—they will not see us or hear us. We will take them to Oyarsa. But you must go now, as the *eldil* said."

"Your people will think I have run away because I am afraid to look in their faces after Hyoi's death."

"It is not a question of thinking but of what an *eldil* says. This is cubs" talk. Now listen, and I will teach you the way."

The *hross* explained to him that five days" journey to the south the *handramit* joined another *handramit;* and three days" up this other *handramit* to west and north was Meldilorn and the seat of Oyarsa. But there was a shorter way, a mountain road, across the corner of the *harandra* between the two canyons, which would bring him down to Meldilorn on the second day. He must go into the wood before them and through it till he came to the mountain wall of the *handramit;* and he must work south along the roots of the mountains till he came to a road cut up between them. Up this he must go, and somewhere beyond the tops of the mountains he would come to the tower of Augray. Augray would help him. He could cut weed for his food before he left the forest and came into the rock country. Whin realised that Ransom might meet the other two *hmāna* as soon as he entered the wood.

"If they catch you," he said, "then it will be as you say, they will come no farther into our land. But it is better to be taken on your way to Oyarsa than to stay here. And once you are on the way to him, I do not think he will let the bent ones stop you."

Ransom was by no means convinced that this was the best plan either for himself or for the *hrossa*. But the stupor of humiliation in which he had lain ever since Hyoi fell forbade him to criticize. He was anxious only to do whatever they wanted him to do, to trouble them as little as was now possible, and above all to get away. It was impossible to find out how Whin felt; and Ransom sternly repressed an insistent, whining impulse to renewed protestations and regrets, self-accusations that might elicit some word of pardon. Hyoi with his last breath had called him *hnakra*-slayer; that was forgiveness generous enough and with that he must be content. As soon as he had mastered the details of his route he bade farewell to Whin and advanced alone towards the forest.

14

Until he reached the wood Ransom found it difficult to think of anything except the possibility of another rifle bullet from Weston or
Devine. He thought that they probably still wanted him alive rather than
dead, and this, combined with the knowledge that a *hross* was watching
him, enabled him to proceed with at least external composure. Even
when he had entered the forest he felt himself in considerable danger.
The long branchless stems made "cover" only if you were very far away
from the enemy; and the enemy in this case might be very close. He
became aware of a strong impulse to shout out to Weston and Devine
and give himself up; it rationalized itself in the form that this would
remove them from the district, as they would probably take him off to
the *sorns* and leave the *hrossa* unmolested. But Ransom knew a little
psychology and had heard of the hunted man's irrational instinct to give
himself up—indeed, he had felt it himself in dreams. It was some such
trick, he thought, that his nerves were now playing on him. In any case
he was determined henceforward to obey the *hrossa* or *eldila*. His efforts
to rely on his own judgment in Malacandra had so far ended tragically
enough. He made a strong resolution, defying in advance all changes of
mood, that he would faithfully carry out the journey to Meldilorn if it
could be done.

This resolution seemed to him all the more certainly right because he had the deepest misgivings about that journey. He understood that the *harandra,* which he had to cross, was the home of the *sorns.* In fact he was walking of his own free will into the very trap that he had been trying to avoid ever since his arrival on Malacandra. (Here the first change of mood tried to raise its head. He thrust it down.) And even if he got through the *sorns* and reached Meldilorn, who or what might Oyarsa be? Oyarsa, Whin had ominously observed, did not share the *hrossa*'s objection to shedding the blood of a *hnau.* And again, Oyarsa ruled *sorns* as well as *hrossa* and *pfifltriggi.* Perhaps he was simply the arch-*sorn.* And now came the second change of mood. Those old terrestrial fears of some alien, cold intelligence, super-human in power, sub-human in cruelty, which had utterly faded from his mind among the *hrossa,* rose clamoring for readmission. But he strode on. He was going to Meldilorn. It was not possible, he told himself, that the *hrossa* should obey any evil or monstrous creature; and they had told him—or had they? he was not quite sure—that Oyarsa was not a *sorn.* Was Oyarsa a god?—perhaps that very idol to whom the *sorns* wanted to sacrifice him. But the *hrossa,* though they said strange things about him, clearly denied that he was a god. There was one God, according to them, Maleldil the Young; nor was it possible to imagine Hyoi or Hnohra worshipping a bloodstained idol. Unless, of course, the *hrossa* were after all under the thumb of the *sorns,* superior to their masters in all the qualities that human beings value, but intellectually inferior to them and dependent on them. It would be a strange but not an inconceivable world; heroism and poetry at the bottom, cold scientific intellect above it, and overtopping all some dark superstition which scientific intellect, helpless against the revenge of the emotional depths it had ignored, had neither will nor power to remove. A mumbo-jumbo . . . but Ransom pulled himself up. He knew too much now to talk that way. He and all his class would have called the *eldila* a superstition if they had been merely described to them, but now he had heard the voice himself. No, Oyarsa was a real person if he was a person at all.

He had now been walking for about an hour, and it was nearly midday. No difficulty about his direction had yet occurred; he had merely to keep going uphill and he was certain of coming out of the forest to the mountain wall sooner or later. Meanwhile he felt remarkably well, though greatly chastened in mind. The silent, purple half-light of the woods spread all around him as it had spread on the first day he spent in Malacandra, but everything else was changed. He looked back on that time as on a nightmare, on his own mood at that time as a sort of sickness. Then all had been whimpering, unanalysed, self-nourishing, self-consuming dismay. Now, in the clear light of an accepted duty, he felt fear indeed, but with it a sober sense of confidence in himself and in the world, and even an element of pleasure. It was the difference between a landsman in a sinking ship and a horseman on a bolting horse: either may be killed, but the horseman is an agent as well as a patient.

About an hour after noon he suddenly came out of the wood into bright sunshine. He was only twenty yards from the almost perpendicular bases of the mountain spires, too close to them to see their tops. A sort of valley ran up in the re-entrant between two of them at the place where he had emerged: an unclimbable valley consisting of a single concave sweep of stone, which in its lower parts ascended steeply as the roof of a house and farther up seemed almost vertical. At the top it even looked as if it hung over a bit, like a tidal wave of stone at the very moment of breaking; but this, he thought, might be an illusion. He wondered what the *hrossa*'s idea of a road might be.

He began to work his way southward along the narrow, broken ground between wood and mountain. Great spurs of the mountains had to be crossed every few moments, and even in that light-weight world it was intensely tiring. After about half an hour he came to a stream. Here he went a few paces into the forest, cut himself an ample supply of the ground-weed, and sat down beside the water's edge for lunch. When he had finished he filled his pockets with what he had not eaten and proceeded.

He began soon to be anxious about his road, for if he could make the top at all he could do it only by daylight, and the middle of the afternoon was approaching. But his fears were unnecessary. When it came it was unmistakable. An open way through the wood appeared on the left—he must be somewhere behind the *hross* village now—and on the right he saw the road, a single ledge or, in places, a trench, cut sidewise and upwards across the sweep of such a valley as he had seen before. It took his breath away—the insanely steep, hideously narrow staircase without steps, leading up and up from where he stood to where it was an almost invisible thread on the pale green surface of the rock. But there was no time to stand and look at it. He was a poor judge of heights, but he had no doubt that the top of the road was removed from him by a more than Alpine distance. It would take him at least till sundown to reach it. Instantly he began the ascent.

Such a journey would have been impossible on earth; the first quarter of an hour would have reduced a man of Ransom's build and age to exhaustion. Here he was at first delighted with the ease of his movement, and then staggered by the gradient and length of the climb which, even under Malacandrian conditions, soon bowed his back and gave him an aching chest and trembling knees. But this was not the worst. He heard already a singing in his ears, and noticed that despite his labour there was no sweat on his forehead. The cold, increasing at every step, seemed to sap his vitality worse than any heat could have done. Already his lips were cracked; his breath, as he panted, showed like a cloud; his fingers were numb. He was cutting his way up into a silent arctic world, and had already passed from an English to a Lapland winter. It frightened him, and he decided that he must rest here or not at all; a hundred paces more and if he sat down he would sit for ever. He squatted on the road for a few minutes, slapping his body with his arms. The landscape was terrifying. Already the *handramit* which had made his world for so many weeks was only a thin purple cleft sunk amidst the boundless level desolation of the *harandra* which now, on the farther side, showed clearly between and above the mountain peaks. But long before he was rested he knew that he must go on or die.

The world grew stranger. Among the *hrossa* he had almost lost the feeling of being on a strange planet; here it returned upon him with desolating force. It was no longer "the world," scarcely even "a world': it was a planet, a star, a waste place in the universe, millions of miles from the world of men. It was impossible to recall what he had felt about Hyoi, or Whin, or the *eldila,* or Oyarsa. It seemed fantastic to have thought he had duties to such hobgoblins—if they were not hallucinations—met in the wilds of space. He had nothing to do with them: he was a man. Why had Weston and Devine left him alone like this?

But all the time the old resolution, taken when he could still think, was driving him up the road. Often he forgot where he was going, and why. The movement became a mechanical rhythm—from weariness to stillness, from stillness to unbearable cold, from cold to motion again.

He noticed that the *handramit*—now an insignificant part of the land-scape—was full of a sort of haze. He had never seen a fog while he was living there. Perhaps that was what the air of the *handramit* looked like from above; certainly it was different air from this. There was something more wrong with his lungs and heart than even the cold and the exertion accounted for. And though there was no snow, there was an extraordinary brightness. The light was increasing, sharpening and growing whiter; and the sky was a much darker blue than he had ever seen on Malacandra. Indeed, it was darker than blue; it was almost black, and the jagged spires of rock standing against it were like his mental picture of a lunar landscape. Some stars were visible.

Suddenly he realised the meaning of these phenomena. There was very little air above him: he was near the end of it. The Malacandrian atmosphere lay chiefly in the *handramits;* the real surface of the planet was naked or thinly clad. The stabbing sunlight and the black sky above him were that "heaven" out of which he had dropped into the Mala-candrian world, already showing through the last thin veil of air. If the top were more than a hundred feet away, it would be where no man could breathe at all. He wondered whether the *hrossa* had different lungs and had sent him by a road that meant death for man. But even while he thought of this he took note that those jagged peaks blazing in sunlight against an almost black sky were level with him. He was no longer ascending. The road ran on before him in a kind of shallow ravine bounded on his left by the tops of the highest rock pinnacles and on his right by a smooth ascending swell of stone that ran up to the true *harandra.* And where he was he could still breathe, though gasping, dizzy and in pain. The blaze in his eyes was worse. The sun was setting. The *hrossa* must have foreseen this; they could not live, any more than he, on the *harandra* by night. Still staggering forward, he looked about him for any sign of Augray's tower, whatever Augray might be.

Doubtless he exaggerated the time during which he thus wandered and watched the shadows from the rocks lengthening towards him. It cannot really have been long before he saw a light ahead—a light which showed how dark the surrounding landscape had become. He tried to run but his body would not respond. Stumbling in haste and weakness, he made for the light; thought he had reached it and found that it was far farther off than he had supposed; almost despaired; staggered on again, and came at last to what seemed a cavern mouth. The light within was an unsteady one and a delicious wave of warmth smote on his face. It was firelight. He came into the mouth of the cave and then, unsteadily, round the fire and into the interior, and stood still blinking in the light. When at last he could see, he discerned a smooth chamber of green rock, very lofty. There were two things in it. One of them, dancing on the wall and roof, was the huge, angular shadow of a *sorn;* the other, crouched beneath it, was the *sorn* himself.

15

"Come in, Small One," boomed the *sorn*. "Come in and let me look at you."

Now that he stood face to face with the spectre that had haunted him ever since he set foot on Malacandra, Ransom felt a surprising indifference. He had no idea what might be coming next, but he was determined to carry out his programme; and in the meantime the warmth and more breathable air were a heaven in themselves. He came in, well in past the fire, and answered the *sorn*. His own voice sounded to him a shrill treble.

"The *hrossa* have sent me to look for Oyarsa," he said.

The *sorn* peered at him. "You are not from this world," it said suddenly.

"No," replied Ransom, and sat down. He was too tired to explain.

"I think you are from Thulcandra, Small One," said the *sorn*.

"Why?" said Ransom.

"You are small and thick and that is how the animals ought to be made in a heavier world. You cannot come from Glundandra, for it is so heavy that if any animals could live there they would be flat like plates—even you, Small One, would break if you stood up on that world. I do not think you are from Parelandra, for it must be very hot; if any came from there they would not live when they arrived here. So I conclude you are from Thulcandra."

"The world I came from is called Earth by those who live there," said Ransom. "And it is much warmer than this. Before I came into your cave I was nearly dead with cold and thin air."

The *sorn* made a sudden movement with one of its long forelimbs. Ransom stiffened (though he did not allow himself to retreat), for the creature might be going to grab him. In fact, its intentions were kindly. Stretching back into the cave, it took from the wall what looked like a cup. Then Ransom saw that it was attached to a length of flexible tube. The *sorn* put it into his hands.

"Smell on this," it said. "The *hrossa* also need it when they pass this way."

Ransom inhaled and was instantly refreshed. His painful shortness of breath was eased and the tension of chest and temples was relaxed. The *sorn* and the lighted cavern, hitherto vague and dream-like to his eyes, took on a new reality.

"Oxygen?" he asked; but naturally the English word meant nothing to the *sorn*.

"Are you called Augray?" he asked.

"Yes," said the *sorn*. "What are you called?"

"The animal I am is called Man, and therefore the *hrossa* call me *Hmān*. But my own name is Ransom."

"Man—Ren-soom," said the *sorn*. He noticed that it spoke differently from the *hrossa*, without any suggestion of their persistent initial H.

It was sitting on its long, wedge-shaped buttocks with its feet drawn close up to it. A man in the same posture would have rested his chin on his knees, but the *sorn*'s legs were too long for that. Its knees rose high above its shoulders on each side of its head—grotesquely suggestive of huge ears—and the head, down between them, rested its chin on the protruding breast. The creature seemed to have either a double chin or a beard; Ransom could not make out which in the firelight. It was mainly white or cream in colour and seemed to be clothed down to the ankles in some soft substance that reflected the light. On the long fragile shanks, where the creature was closest to him, he saw that this was some natural kind of coat. It was not like fur but more like feathers. In fact it was almost exactly like feathers. The whole animal, seen at close quarters, was less terrifying than he had expected, and even a little smaller. The face, it was true, took a good deal of getting used to—it was too long, too solemn and too colourless, and it was much more unpleasantly like a human face than any inhuman creature's face ought to be. Its eyes, like those of all very large creatures, seemed too small for it. But it was more grotesque than horrible. A new conception of the *sorns* began to arise in his mind: the ideas of "giant" and "ghost" receded behind those of "goblin" and "gawk."

"Perhaps you are hungry, Small One," it said.

Ransom was. The *sorn* rose with strange spidery movements and began going to and fro about the cave, attended by its thin goblin shadow. It brought him the usual vegetable foods of Malacandra, and strong drink, with the very welcome addition of a smooth brown substance which revealed itself to nose, eye and palate, in defiance of all probability, as cheese. Ransom asked what it was.

The *sorn* began to explain painfully how the female of some animals secreted a fluid for the nourishment of its young, and would have gone on to describe the whole process of milking and cheesemaking, if Ransom had not interrupted it.

"Yes, yes," he said. "We do the same on Earth. What is the beast you use?"

"It is a yellow beast with a long neck. It feeds on the forests that grow in the *handramit*. The young ones of our people who are not yet fit for much else drive the beasts down there in the mornings and follow them while they feed; then before night they drive them back and put them in the caves."

For a moment Ransom found something reassuring in the thought that the *sorns* were shepherds. Then he remembered that the Cyclops in Homer plied the same trade.

"I think I have seen one of your people at this very work," he said. "But the *hrossa*—they let you tear up their forests?"

"Why should they not?"

"Do you rule the *hrossa*?"

"Oyarsa rules them."

"And who rules you?"

"Oyarsa."

"But you know more than the *hrossa*?"

"The *hrossa* know nothing except about poems and fish and making things grow out of the ground."

"And Oyarsa—is he a *sorn?*"

"No, no, Small One. I have told you he rules all *nau*" (so he pronounced *hnau*), "and everything in Malacandra."

"I do not understand this Oyarsa," said Ransom. "Tell me more."

"Oyarsa does not die," said the *sorn*. "And he does not breed. He is the one of his kind who was put into Malacandra to rule it when Malacandra was made. His body is not like ours, nor yours; it is hard to see and the light goes through it."

"Like an *eldil?*"

"Yes, he is the greatest of *eldila* who ever come to a *handra*."

"What are these *eldila?*"

"Do you tell me, Small One, that there are no *eldila* in your world?"

"Not that I know of. But what are *eldila,* and why can I not see them? Have they no bodies?"

"Of course they have bodies. There are a great many bodies you cannot see. Every animal's eyes see some things but not others. Do you know of many kinds of body in Thulcandra?"

Ransom tried to give the *sorn* some idea of the terrestrial terminology of solids, liquids and gases. It listened with great attention.

"That is not the way to say it," it replied. "Body is movement. If it is at one speed, you smell something; if at another, you hear a sound; if at another you see a sight; if at another, you neither see nor hear nor smell, nor know the body in any way. But mark this, Small One, that the two ends meet."

"How do you mean?"

"If movement is faster, then that which moves is more nearly in two places at once."

"That is true."

"But if the movement were faster still—it is difficult, for you do not know many words—you see that if you made it faster and faster, in the end the moving thing would be in all places at once, Small One."

"I think I see that."

"Well, then, that is the thing at the top of all bodies—so fast that it is at rest, so truly body that it has ceased being body at all. But we will not talk of that. Start from where we are, Small One. The swiftest thing that touches our senses is light. We do not truly see light, we only see slower things lit by it, so that for us light is on the edge—the last thing we know before things become too swift for us. But the body of an *eldil* is a movement swift as light; you may say its body is made of light, but not of that which is light for the *eldil*. His "light" is a swifter movement which for us is nothing at all; and what we call light is for him a thing like water, a visible thing, a thing he can touch and bathe in—even a dark thing when not illumined by the swifter. And what we call firm things—flesh and earth—seem to him thinner, and harder to see, than our light, and more like clouds, and nearly nothing. To us the *eldil* is a thin, half-real body that can go through walls and rocks: to himself he goes through them because he is solid and firm and they are like cloud. And what is true light to him and fills the heaven, so that he will plunge into the rays of the sun to refresh himself from it, is to us the black nothing in the sky at night. These things are not strange, Small One, though they are beyond our senses. But it is strange that the *eldila* never visit Thulcandra."

"Of that I am not certain," said Ransom. It had dawned on him that the recurrent human tradition of bright, elusive people sometimes appearing on the Earth—*albs, devas* and the like—might after all have another explanation than the anthropologists had yet given. True, it would turn the universe rather oddly inside out; but his experiences in the space-ship had prepared him for some such operation.

"Why does Oyarsa send for me?" he asked.

"Oyarsa has not told me," said the *sorn*. "But doubtless he would want to see any stranger from another *handra*."

"We have no Oyarsa in my world," said Ransom.

"That is another proof," said the *sorn*, "that you come from Thulcandra, the silent planet."

"What has that to do with it?"

The *sorn* seemed surprised. "It is not very likely if you had an Oyarsa that he would never speak to ours."

"Speak to yours? But how could he—it is millions of miles away."

"Oyarsa would not think of it like that."

"Do you mean that he ordinarily receives messages from other planets?"

"Once again, he would not say it that way. Oyarsa would not say that he lives on Malacandra and that another Oyarsa lives on another earth. For him Malacandra is only a place in the heavens; it is in the heavens that he and the others live. Of course they talk together. . . ."

Ransom's mind shied away from the problem; he was getting sleepy and thought he must be misunderstanding the *sorn*.

"I think I must sleep, Augray," he said. "And I do not know what you are saying. Perhaps, too, I do not come from what you call Thulcandra."

"We will both sleep presently," said the *sorn*. "But first I will show you Thulcandra."

It rose and Ransom followed it into the back of the cave. Here he found a little recess and running up within it a winding stair. The steps, hewn for *sorns,* were too high for a man to climb with any comfort, but using hands and knees he managed to hobble up. The *sorn* preceded him. Ransom did not understand the light, which seemed to come from some small round object which the creature held in its hand. They went up a long way, almost as if they were climbing up the inside of a hollow mountain. At last, breathless, he found himself in a dark but warm chamber of rock, and heard the *sorn* saying:

"She is still well above the southern horizon." It directed his attention to something like a small window. Whatever it was, it did not appear to work like an earthly telescope, Ransom thought; though an attempt, made next day, to explain the principles of the telescope to the *sorn* threw grave doubts on his own ability to discern the difference. He leaned forward with his elbows on the sill of the aperture and looked. He saw perfect blackness and, floating in the centre of it, seemingly an arm's length away, a bright disk about the size of a half-crown. Most of its surface was featureless, shining silver; towards the bottom markings appeared, and below them a white cap, just as he had seen the polar caps in astronomical photographs of Mars. He wondered for a moment if it was Mars he was looking at; then, as his eyes took in the markings better, he recognised what they were—Northern Europe and a piece of North America. They were upside down with the North Pole at the bottom of the picture and this somehow shocked him. But it was Earth he was seeing—even, perhaps, England, though the picture shook a little and his eyes were quickly getting tired, and he could not be certain that he was not imagining it. It was all there in that little disk—London, Athens, Jerusalem, Shakespeare. There everyone had lived and everything had happened; and there, presumably, his pack was still lying in the porch of an empty house near Sterk.

"Yes," he said dully to the *sorn*. "That is my world." It was the bleakest moment in all his travels.

16

Ransom awoke next morning with the vague feeling that a great weight had been taken off his mind. Then he remembered that he was the guest of a *sorn* and that the creature he had been avoiding ever since he landed had turned out to be as amicable as the *hrossa*, though he was far from feeling the same affection for it. Nothing then remained to be afraid of in Malacandra except Oyarsa . . . "The last fence," thought Ransom.

Augray gave him food and drink.

"And now," said Ransom, "how shall I find my way to Oyarsa?"

"I will carry you," said the *sorn*. "You are too small a one to make the journey yourself and I will gladly go to Meldilorn. The *hrossa* should not have sent you this way. They do not seem to know from looking at an animal what sort of lungs it has and what it can do. It is just like a *hross*. If you died on the *harandra* they would have made a poem about the gallant *hmān* and how the sky grew black and the cold stars shone and he journeyed on and journeyed on; and they would have put in a fine speech for you to say as you were dying . . . and all this would seem to them just as good as if they had used a little forethought and saved your life by sending you the easier way round."

"I like the *hrossa*," said Ransom a little stiffly. "And I think the way they talk about death is the right way."

"They are right not to fear it, Ren-soom, but they do not seem to look at it reasonably as part of the very nature of our bodies—and therefore often avoidable at times when they would never see how to avoid it. For example, this has saved the life of many a *hross*, but a *hross* would not have thought of it."

He showed Ransom a flask with a tube attached to it, and at the end of the tube a cup, obviously an apparatus for administering oxygen to oneself.

"Smell on it as you have need, Small One," said the *sorn*. "And close it up when you do not."

Augray fastened the thing on his back and gave the tube over his shoulder into his hand. Ransom could not restrain a shudder at the touch of the *sorn*'s hands upon his body; they were fan-shaped, seven-fingered, mere skin over bone like a bird's leg, and quite cold. To divert his mind from such reactions he asked where the apparatus was made, for he had as yet seen nothing remotely like a factory or a laboratory.

"We thought it," said the *sorn*, "and the *pfifltriggi* made it."

"Why do they make them?" said Ransom. He was trying once more, with his insufficient vocabulary, to find out the political and economic framework of Malacandrian life.

"They like making things," said Augray. "It is true they like best the making of things that are only good to look at and of no use. But sometimes when they are tired of that they will make things for us, things we have thought, provided they are difficult enough. They have not the patience to make easy things however useful they would be. But let us begin our journey. You shall sit on my shoulder."

The proposal was unexpected and alarming, but seeing that the *sorn* had already crouched down, Ransom felt obliged to climb on to the plume-like surface of its shoulder, to seat himself beside the long, pale face, casting his right arm as far as it would go round the huge neck, and to compose himself as well as he could for this precarious mode of travel. The giant rose cautiously to a standing position and he found himself looking down on the landscape from a height of about eighteen feet.

"Is all well, Small One?" it asked.

"Very well," Ransom answered, and the journey began.

Its gait was perhaps the least human thing about it. It lifted its feet very high and set them down very gently. Ransom was reminded alternately of a cat stalking, a strutting barn-door fowl, and a high-stepping carriage horse; but the movement was not really like that of any terrestrial animal. For the passenger it was surprisingly comfortable. In a few minutes he had lost all sense of what was dizzying or unnatural in his position. Instead, ludicrous and even tender associations came crowding into his mind. It was like riding an elephant at the zoo in boyhood—like riding on his father's back at a still earlier age. It was fun. They seemed to be doing between six and seven miles an hour. The cold, though severe, was endurable; and thanks to the oxygen he had little difficulty with his breathing.

The landscape which he saw from his high, swaying post of observation was a solemn one. The *handramit* was nowhere to be seen. On each side of the shallow gully in which they were walking, a world of naked, faintly greenish rock, interrupted with wide patches of red, extended to the horizon. The heaven, darkest blue where the rock met it, was almost black at the zenith, and looking in any direction where sunlight did not blind him, he could see the stars. He learned from the *sorn* that he was right in thinking they were near the limits of the breathable. Already on the mountain fringe that borders the *harandra* and walls the *handramit*, or in the narrow depression along which their road led them, the air is of Himalayan rarity, ill breathing for a *hross,* and a few hundred feet higher, on the *harandra* proper, the true surface of the planet, it admits no life. Hence the brightness through which they walked was almost that of heaven—celestial light hardly at all tempered with an atmospheric veil.

The shadow of the *sorn,* with Ransom's shadow on its shoulder, moved over the uneven rock unnaturally distinct like the shadow of a tree before the headlights of a car; and the rock beyond the shadow hurt his eyes. The remote horizon seemed but an arm's length away. The fissures and moulding of distant slopes were clear as the background of a primitive picture made before men learned perspective. He was on the very frontier of that heaven he had known in the space-ship, and rays that the air-enveloped worlds cannot taste were once more at work upon his body. He felt the old lift of the heart, the soaring solemnity, the sense, at once sober and ecstatic, of life and power offered in unasked and unmeasured abundance. If there had been air enough in his lungs he would have laughed aloud. And now, even in the immediate landscape, beauty was drawing near. Over the edge of the valley, as it had frothed down from the true *harandra*, came great curves of the rose-tinted, cumular stuff which he had seen so often from a distance. Now on a nearer view they appeared hard as stone in substance, but puffed above and stalked beneath like vegetation. His original simile of giant cauliflower turned out to be surprisingly correct—stone cauliflowers the size of cathedrals and the colour of pale rose. He asked the *sorn* what it was.

"It is the old forests of Malacandra," said Augray. "Once there was air on the *harandra* and it was warm. To this day, if you could get up there and live, you would see it all covered with the bones of ancient creatures; it was once full of life and noise. It was then these forests grew, and in and out among their stalks went a people that have vanished from the world these many thousand years. They were covered not with fur but with a coat like mine. They did not go in the water swimming or on the ground walking; they glided in the air on broad flat limbs which kept them up. It is said they were great singers, and in those days the red forests echoed with their music. Now the forests have become stone and only *eldila* can go among them."

"We still have such creatures in our world," said Ransom. "We call them birds. Where was Oyarsa when all this happened to the *harandra?*"

"Where he is now."

"And he could not prevent it?"

"I do not know. But a world is not made to last for ever, much less a race; that is not Maleldil's way."

As they proceeded the petrified forests grew more numerous, and often for half an hour at a time the whole horizon of the lifeless, almost airless, waste blushed like an English garden in summer. They passed many caves where, as Augray told him, *sorns* lived; sometimes a high cliff would be perforated with countless holes to the very top and unidentifiable noises came hollowly from within. "Work" was in progress, said the *sorn*, but of what kind it could not make him understand. Its vocabulary was very different from that of the *hrossa*. Nowhere did he see anything like a village or city of *sorns*, who were apparently solitary not social creatures. Once or twice a long pallid face would show from a cavern mouth and exchange a horn-like greeting with the travellers, but for the most part the long valley, the rock-street of the silent people, was still and empty as the *harandra* itself.

Only towards afternoon, as they were about to descend into a dip of the road, they met three *sorns* together coming towards them down the opposite slope. They seemed to Ransom to be rather skating than walking. The lightness of their world and the perfect poise of their bodies allowed them to lean forward at right angles to the slope, and they came swiftly down like full-rigged ships before a fair wind. The grace of their movement, their lofty stature, and the softened glancing of the sunlight on their feathery sides, effected a final transformation in Ransom's feelings towards their race. "Ogres" he had called them when they first met his eyes as he struggled in the grip of Weston and Devine; "Titans" or "Angels" he now thought would have been a better word. Even the faces, it seemed to him, he had not then seen aright. He had thought them spectral when they were only august, and his human reaction to their lengthened severity of line and profound stillness of expression now appeared to him not so much cowardly as vulgar. So might Parmenides or Confucius look to the eyes of a Cockney schoolboy! The great white creatures sailed towards Ransom and Augray and dipped like trees and passed.

In spite of the cold—which made him often dismount and take a spell on foot—he did not wish for the end of the journey; but Augray had his own plans and halted for the night long before sundown at the home of an older *sorn*. Ransom saw well enough that he was brought there to be shown to a great scientist. The cave, or, to speak more correctly, the system of excavations, was large and many-chambered, and contained a multitude of things that he did not understand. He was specially interested in a collection of rolls, seemingly of skin, covered with characters, which were clearly books; but he gathered that books were few in Malacandra.

"It is better to remember," said the *sorns*.

When Ransom asked if valuable secrets might not thus be lost, they replied that Oyarsa always remembered them and would bring them to light if he thought fit.

"The *hrossa* used to have many books of poetry," they added. "But now they have fewer. They say that the writing of books destroys poetry."

Their host in these caverns was attended by a number of other *sorns* who seemed to be in some way subordinate to him; Ransom thought at first that they were servants but decided later that they were pupils or assistants.

The evening's conversation was not such as would interest a terrestrial reader, for the *sorns* had determined that Ransom should not ask, but answer, questions. Their questioning was very different from the rambling inquiries of the *hrossa*. They worked systematically from the geology of Earth to its present geography, and thence in turn to flora, fauna, human history, languages, politics and arts. When they found that Ransom could tell them no more on a given subject—and this happened pretty soon in most of their inquiries—they dropped it at once and went on to the next. Often they drew out of him indirectly much more knowledge than he consciously possessed, apparently working from a wide background of general science. A casual remark about trees when Ransom was trying to explain the manufacture of paper would fill up for them a gap in his sketchy answers to their botanical questions; his account of terrestrial navigation might illuminate mineralogy; and his description of the steam-engine gave them a better knowledge of terrestrial air and water than Ransom had ever had. He had decided from the outset that he would be quite frank, for he now felt that it would be not *hnau*, and also that it would be unavailing, to do otherwise. They were astonished at what he had to tell them of human history—of war, slavery and prostitution.

"It is because they have no Oyarsa," said one of the pupils.

"It is because every one of them wants to be a little Oyarsa himself," said Augray.

"They cannot help it," said the old *sorn*. "There must be rule, yet how can creatures rule themselves? Beasts must be ruled by *hnau* and *hnau* by *eldila* and *eldila* by Maleldil. These creatures have no *eldila*. They are like one trying to lift himself by his own hair—or one trying to see over a whole country when he is on a level with it—like a female trying to beget young on herself."

Two things about our world particularly stuck in their minds. One was the extraordinary degree to which problems of lifting and carrying things absorbed our energy. The other was the fact that we had only one kind of *hnau*: they thought this must have far-reaching effects in the narrowing of sympathies and even of thought.

"Your thought must be at the mercy of your blood," said the old *sorn.* "For you cannot compare it with thought that floats on a different blood."

It was a tiring and very disagreeable conversation for Ransom. But when at last he lay down to sleep it was not of the human nakedness nor of his own ignorance that he was thinking. He thought only of the old forests of Malacandra and of what it might mean to grow up seeing always so few miles away a land of colour that could never be reached and had once been inhabited.

17

Early next day Ransom again took his seat on Augray's shoulder. For more than an hour they travelled through the same bright wilderness. Far to the north the sky was luminous with a cloud-like mass of dull red or ochre; it was very large and drove furiously westward about ten miles above the waste. Ransom, who had yet seen no cloud in the Malacandrian sky, asked what it was. The *sorn* told him it was sand caught up from the great northern deserts by the winds of that terrible country. It was often thus carried, sometimes at a height of seventeen miles, to fall again, perhaps in a *handramit,* as a choking and blinding dust-storm. The sight of it moving with menace in the naked sky served to remind Ransom that they were indeed on the *outside* of Malacandra—no longer dwelling in a world but crawling the surface of a strange planet. At last the cloud seemed to drop and burst far on the western horizon, where a glow, not unlike that of a conflagration, remained visible until a turn of the valley hid all that region from his view.

The same turn opened a new prospect to his eyes. What lay before him looked at first strangely like an earthly landscape—a landscape of grey downland ridges rising and falling like waves of the sea. Far beyond, cliffs and spires of the familiar green rock rose against the dark blue sky. A moment later he saw that what he had taken for downlands was but the ridged and furrowed surface of a blue-grey valley mist—a mist which would not appear a mist at all when they descended into the *handramit*. And already, as their road began descending, it was less visible and the many-coloured pattern of the low country showed vaguely through it. The descent grew quickly steeper; like the jagged teeth of a giant—a giant with very bad teeth—the topmost peaks of the mountain wall down which they must pass loomed up over the edge of their gully. The look of the sky and the quality of the light were infinitesimally changed. A moment later they stood on the edge of such a slope as by earthly standards would rather be called a precipice; down and down this face, to where it vanished in a purple blush of vegetation, ran their road. Ransom refused absolutely to make the descent on Augray's shoulder. The *sorn,* though it did not fully understand his objection, stooped for him to dismount, and proceeded, with that same skating and forward-sloping motion, to go down before him. Ransom followed, using gladly but stiffly his numb legs.

The beauty of this new *handramit* as it opened before him took his breath away. It was wider than that in which he had hitherto lived and right below him lay an almost circular lake—a sapphire twelve miles in diameter set in a border of purple forest. Amidst the lake there rose like a low and gently sloping pyramid, or like a woman's breast, an island of pale red, smooth to the summit, and on the summit a grove of such trees as man had never seen. Their smooth columns had the gentle swell of the noblest beech-trees: but these were taller than a cathedral spire on earth, and at their tops, they broke rather into flower than foliage; into golden flower bright as tulip, still as rock, and huge as summer cloud. Flowers indeed they were, not trees, and far down among their roots he caught a pale hint of slab-like architecture. He knew before his guide told him that this was Meldilorn. He did not know what he had expected. The old dreams which he had brought from Earth of some more than American complexity of offices or some engineers" paradise of vast machines had indeed been long laid aside. But he had not looked for anything quite so classic, so virginal, as this bright grove—lying so still, so secret, in its coloured valley, soaring with inimitable grace so many hundred feet into the wintry sunlight. At every step of his descent the comparative warmth of the valley came up to him more deliciously. He looked above—the sky was turning to a paler blue. He looked below—and sweet and faint the thin fragrance of the giant blooms came up to him.

Distant crags were growing less sharp in outline, and surfaces less bright. Depth, dimness, softness and perspective were returning to the landscape. The lip or edge of rock from which they had started their descent was already far overhead; it seemed unlikely that they had really come from there. He was breathing freely. His toes, so long benumbed, could move delightfully inside his boots. He lifted the ear-flaps of his cap and found his ears instantly filled with the sound of falling water. And now he was treading on soft ground-weed over level earth and the forest roof was above his head. They had conquered the *harandra* and were on the threshold of Meldilorn.

A short walk brought them into a kind of forest "ride"—a broad avenue running straight as an arrow through the purple stems to where the vivid blue of the lake danced at the end of it. There they found a gong and hammer hung on a pillar of stone. These objects were all richly decorated, and the gong and hammer were of a greenish blue metal which Ransom did not recognize. Augray struck the gong. An excitement was rising in Ransom's mind which almost prevented him from examining as coolly as he wished the ornamentation of the stone. It was partly pictorial, partly pure decoration. What chiefly struck him was a certain balance of packed and empty surfaces. Pure line drawings, as bare as the prehistoric pictures of reindeer on Earth, alternated with patches of design as close and intricate as Norse or Celtic jewellery; and then, as you looked at it, these empty and crowded areas turned out to be themselves arranged in larger designs. He was struck by the fact that the pictorial work was not confined to the emptier spaces; quite often large arabesques included as a subordinate detail intricate pictures. Elsewhere the opposite plan had been followed—and this alternation, too, had a rhythmical or patterned element in it. He was just beginning to find out that the pictures, though stylized, were obviously intended to tell a story, when Augray interrupted him. A ship had put out from the island shore of Meldilorn.

As it came towards them Ransom's heart warmed to see that it was paddled by a *hross*. The creature brought its boat up to the shore where they were waiting, stared at Ransom and then looked inquiringly at Augray.

"You may well wonder at this *hnau*, Hrinha," said the *sorn*, "for you have never seen anything like it. It is called Ren-soom and has come through heaven from Thulcandra."

"It is welcome, Augray," said the *hross* politely. "Is it coming to Oyarsa?"

"He has sent for it."

"And for you also, Augray?"

"Oyarsa has not called me. If you will take Ren-soom over the water, I will go back to my tower."

The *hross* indicated that Ransom should enter the boat. He attempted to express his thanks to the *sorn* and after a moment's consideration unstrapped his wrist-watch and offered it to him; it was the only thing he had which seemed a suitable present for a *sorn*. He had no difficulty in making Augray understand its purpose; but after examining it the giant gave it back to him, a little reluctantly, and said:

"This gift ought to be given to a *pfifltrigg*. It rejoices my heart, but they would make more of it. You are likely to meet some of the busy people in Meldilorn: give it to them. As for its use, do your people not know except by looking at this thing how much of the day has worn?"

"I believe there are beasts that have a sort of knowledge of that," said Ransom, "but our *hnau* have lost it."

After this, his farewells to the *sorn* were made and he embarked. To be once more in a boat and with a *hross,* to feel the warmth of water on his face and to see a blue sky above him, was almost like coming home. He took off his cap and leaned back luxuriously in the bows, plying his escort with questions. He learned that the *hrossa* were not specially concerned with the service of Oyarsa, as he had surmised from finding a *hross* in charge of the ferry: all three species of *hnau* served him in their various capacities, and the ferry was naturally entrusted to those who understood boats. He learned that his own procedure on arriving in Meldilorn must be to go where he liked and do what he pleased until Oyarsa called for him. It might be an hour or several days before this happened. He would find huts near the landing-place where he could sleep if necessary and where food would be given him. In return he related as much as he could make intelligible of his own world and his journey from it; and he warned the *hross* of the dangerous bent men who had brought him and who were still at large on Malacandra. As he did so, it occurred to him that he had not made this sufficiently clear to Augray; but he consoled himself with the reflection that Weston and Devine seemed to have already some liaison with the *sorns* and that they would not be likely to molest things so large and so comparatively man-like. At any rate, not yet. About Devine's ultimate designs he had no illusions; all he could do was to make a clean breast of them to Oyarsa. And now the ship touched land.

Ransom rose, while the *hross* was making fast, and looked about him. Close to the little harbour which they had entered, and to the left, were low buildings of stone—the first he had seen in Malacandra—and fires were burning. There, the *hross* told him, he could find food and shelter. For the rest the island seemed desolate, and its smooth slopes empty up to the grove that crowned them, where, again, he saw stonework. But this appeared to be neither temple nor house in the human sense, but a broad avenue of monoliths—a much larger Stonehenge, stately, empty and vanishing over the crest of the hill into the pale shadow of the flower-trunks. All was solitude; but as he gazed upon it he seemed to hear, against the background of morning silence, a faint, continual agitation of silvery sound—hardly a sound at all, if you attended to it, and yet impossible to ignore.

"The island is all full of *eldila*," said the *hross* in a hushed voice.

He went ashore. As though half expecting some obstacle, he took a few hesitant paces forward and stopped, and then went on again in the same fashion.

Though the ground-weed was unusually soft and rich and his feet made no noise upon it, he felt an impulse to walk on tiptoes. All his movements became gentle and sedate. The width of water about this island made the air warmer than any he had yet breathed in Malacandra; the climate was almost that of a warm earthly day in late September—a day that is warm but with a hint of frost to come. The sense of awe which was increasing upon him deterred him from approaching the crown of the hill, the grove and the avenue of standing stones.

He ceased ascending about half-way up the hill and began walking to his right, keeping a constant distance from the shore. He said to himself that he was having a look at the island, but his feeling was rather that the island was having a look at him. This was greatly increased by a discovery he made after he had been walking for about an hour, and which he ever afterwards found great difficulty in describing. In the most abstract terms it might be summed up by saying that the surface of the island was subject to tiny variations of light and shade which no change in the sky accounted for. If the air had not been calm and the ground-weed too short and firm to move in the wind, he would have said that a faint breeze was playing with it, and working such slight alterations in the shading as it does in a corn-field on the Earth. Like the silvery noises in the air, these footsteps of light were shy of observation. Where he looked hardest they were least to be seen: on the edges of his field of vision they came crowding as though a complex arrangement of them were there in progress. To attend to any one of them was to make it invisible, and the minute brightness seemed often to have just left the spot where his eyes fell. He had no doubt that he was "seeing"—as much as he ever would see—the *eldila*. The sensation it produced in him was curious. It was not exactly uncanny, not as if he were surrounded by ghosts. It was not even as if he were being spied upon; he had rather the sense of being looked at by things that had a right to look. His feeling was less than fear; it had in it something of embarrassment, something of shyness, something of submission, and it was profoundly uneasy.

He felt tired and thought that in this favoured land it would be warm enough to rest out of doors. He sat down. The softness of the weed, the warmth and the sweet smell which pervaded the whole island, reminded him of Earth and gardens in summer. He closed his eyes for a moment; then he opened them again and noticed buildings below him, and over the lake he saw a boat approaching. Recognition suddenly came to him. That was the ferry, and these buildings were the guest-house beside the harbour; he had walked all round the island. A certain disappointment succeeded this discovery. He was beginning to feel hungry. Perhaps it would be a good plan to go down and ask for some food; at any rate it would pass the time.

But he did not do so. When he rose and looked more closely at the guest-house he saw a considerable stir of creatures about it, and while he watched he saw that a full load of passengers was landing from the ferry-boat. In the lake he saw some moving objects which he did not at first identify but which turned out to be *sorns* up to their middles in the water and obviously wading to Meldilorn from the mainland. There were about ten of them. For some reason or other the island was receiving an influx of visitors. He no longer supposed that any harm would be done to him if he went down and mixed in the crowd, but he felt a reluctance to do so. The situation brought vividly back to his mind his experience as a new boy at school—new boys came a day early—hanging about and watching the arrival of the old hands. In the end he decided not to go down. He cut and ate some of the ground-weed and dozed for a little.

In the afternoon, when it grew colder, he resumed his walking. Other *hnau* were roaming about the island by this time. He saw *sorns* chiefly, but this was because their height made them conspicuous. There was hardly any noise. His reluctance to meet these fellow-wanderers, who seemed to confine themselves to the coast of the island, drove him half consciously upwards and inwards. He found himself at last on the fringes of the grove and looking straight up the monolithic avenue. He had intended, for no very clearly defined reason, not to enter it, but he fell to studying the stone nearest to him, which was richly sculptured on all its four sides, and after that curiosity led him on from stone to stone.

The pictures were very puzzling. Side by side with representations of *sorns* and *hrossa* and what he supposed to be *pfifltriggi* there occurred again and again an upright wavy figure with only the suggestion of a face, and with wings. The wings were perfectly recognizable, and this puzzled him very much. Could it be that the traditions of Malacandrian art went back to that earlier geological and biological era when, as Augray had told him, there was life, including bird-life, on the *harandra?* The answer of the stones seemed to be Yes. He saw pictures of the old red forests with unmistakable birds flying among them, and many other creatures that he did not know. On another stone many of these were represented lying dead, and a fantastic *hnakra*-like figure, presumably symbolizing the cold, was depicted in the sky above them shooting at them with darts. Creatures still alive were crowding round the winged, wavy figure, which he took to be Oyarsa, pictured as a winged flame. On the next stone Oyarsa appeared, followed by many creatures, and apparently making a furrow with some pointed instrument. Another picture showed the furrow being enlarged by *pfifltriggi* with digging tools. *Sorns* were piling the earth up in pinnacles on each side, and *hrossa* seemed to be making water channels. Ransom wondered whether this were a mythical account of the making of *handramits* or whether they were conceivably artificial in fact.

Many of the pictures he could make nothing of. One that particularly puzzled him showed at the bottom a segment of a circle, behind and above which rose three-quarters of a disk divided into concentric rings. He thought it was a picture of the sun rising behind a hill; certainly the segment at the bottom was full of Malacandrian scenes—Oyarsa in Meldilorn, *sorns* on the mountain edge of the *harandra,* and many other things both familiar to him and strange. He turned from it to examine the disk which rose behind it. It was not the sun. The sun was there, unmistakably, at the centre of the disk: round this the concentric circles revolved. In the first and smallest of these was pictured a little ball, on which rode a winged figure something like Oyarsa, but holding what appeared to be a trumpet. In the next, a similar ball carried another of the flaming figures. This one, instead of even the suggested face, had two bulges which after long inspection he decided were meant to be the udders or breasts of a female mammal. By this time he was quite sure that he was looking at a picture of the solar-system. The first ball was Mercury, the second Venus—"And what an extraordinary coincidence," thought Ransom, "that their mythology, like ours, associates some idea of the female with Venus." The problem would have occupied him longer if a natural curiosity had not drawn his eyes on to the next ball which must represent the Earth. When he saw it, his whole mind stood still for a moment. The ball was there, but where the flame-like figure should have been, a deep depression of irregular shape had been cut as if to erase it. Once, then—but his speculations faltered and became silent before a series of unknowns. He looked at the next circle. Here there was no ball. Instead, the bottom of this circle touched the top of the big segment filled with Malacandrian scenes, so that Malacandra at this point touched the solar system and came out of it in perspective towards the spectator. Now that his mind had grasped the design, he was astonished at the vividness of it all. He stood back and drew a deep breath preparatory to tackling some of the mysteries in which he was engulfed. Malacandra, then, was Mars. The Earth—but at this point a sound of tapping or hammering, which had been going on for some time without gaining admission to his consciousness, became too insistent to be ignored. Some creature, and certainly not an *eldil,* was at work, close to him. A little startled—for he had been deep in thought—he turned round. There was nothing to be seen. He shouted out, idiotically, in English:

"Who's there?"

The tapping instantly stopped and a remarkable face appeared from behind a neighbouring monolith.

It was hairless like a man's or a *sorn's*. It was long and pointed like a shrew's, yellow and shabby-looking, and so low in the forehead that but for the heavy development of the head at the back and behind the ears (like a bag-wig) it could not have been that of an intelligent creature. A moment later the whole of the thing came into view with a startling jump. Ransom guessed that it was a *pfifltrigg*—and was glad that he had not met one of this third race on his first arrival in Malacandra. It was much more insect-like or reptilian than anything he had yet seen. Its build was distinctly that of a frog, and at first Ransom thought it was resting, frog-like, on its "hands." Then he noticed that that part of its fore-limbs on which it was supported was really, in human terms, rather an elbow than a hand. It was broad and padded and clearly made to be walked on; but upwards from it, at an angle of about forty-five degrees, went the true fore-arms—thin, strong fore-arms, ending in enormous, sensitive, many-fingered hands. He realized that for all manual work from mining to cutting cameos this creature had the advantage of being able to work with its full strength from a supported elbow. The insect-like effect was due to the speed and jerkiness of its movements and to the fact that it could swivel its head almost all the way round like a mantis; and it was increased by a kind of dry, rasping, jingling quality in the noise of its moving. It was rather like a grasshopper, rather like one of Arthur Rackham's dwarfs, rather like a frog, and rather like a little, old taxidermist whom Ransom knew in London.

"I come from another world," began Ransom.

"I know, I know," said the creature in a quick, twittering, rather impatient voice. "Come here, behind the stone. This way, this way. Oyarsa's orders. Very busy. Must begin at once. Stand there."

Ransom found himself on the other side of the monolith, staring at a picture which was still in process of completion. The ground was liberally strewn with chips and the air was full of dust.

"There," said the creature. "Stand still. Don't look at me. Look over there."

For a moment Ransom did not quite understand what was expected of him; then, as he saw the *pfifltrigg* glancing to and fro at him and at the stone with the unmistakable glance of artist from model to work which is the same in all worlds, he realized and almost laughed. He was standing for his portrait! From his position he could see that the creature was cutting the stone as if it were cheese and the swiftness of its movements almost baffled his eyes, but he could get no impression of the work done, though he could study the *pfifltrigg*. He saw that the jingling and metallic noise was due to the number of small instruments which it carried about its body. Sometimes, with an exclamation of annoyance, it would throw down the tool it was working with and select one of these; but the majority of those in immediate use it kept in its mouth. He realized also that this was an animal artificially clothed like himself, in some bright scaly substance which appeared richly decorated though coated in dust. It had folds of furry clothing about its throat like a comforter, and its eyes were protected by dark bulging goggles. Rings and chains of a bright metal—not gold, he thought—adorned its limbs and neck. All the time it was working it kept up a sort of hissing whisper to itself; and when it was excited—which it usually was—the end of its nose wrinkled like a rabbit's. At last it gave another startling leap, landed ten yards away from its work, and said:

"Yes, yes. Not so good as I hoped. Do better another time. Leave it now. Come and see yourself."

Ransom obeyed. He saw a picture of the planets, not now arranged to make a map of the solar system, but advancing in a single procession towards the spectator, and all, save one, bearing its fiery charioteer. Below lay Malacandra and there, to his surprise, was a very tolerable picture of the space-ship. Beside it stood three figures for all of which Ransom had apparently been the model. He recoiled from them in disgust. Even allowing for the strangeness of the subject from a Malacandrian point of view and for the stylization of their art, still, he thought, the creature might have made a better attempt at the human form than these stocklike dummies, almost as thick as they were tall, and sprouting about the head and neck into something that looked like fungus.

He hedged. "I expect it is like me as I look to your people," he said. "It is not how they would draw me in my own world."

"No," said the *pfifltrigg*. "I do not mean it to be too like. Too like, and they will not believe it—those who are born after." He added a good deal more which was difficult to understand; but while he was speaking it dawned upon Ransom that the odious figures were intended as an *idealization* of humanity. Conversation languished for a little. To change the subject Ransom asked a question which had been in his mind for some time.

"I cannot understand," he said, "how you and the *sorns* and the *hrossa* all come to speak the same speech. For your tongues and teeth and throats must be very different."

"You are right," said the creature. "Once we all had different speeches and we still have at home. But everyone has learned the speech of the *hrossa*."

"Why is that?" said Ransom, still thinking in terms of terrestrial history. "Did the *hrossa* once rule the others?"

"I do not understand. They are our great speakers and singers. They have more words and better. No one learns the speech of my people, for what we have to say is said in stone and suns" blood and stars" milk and all can see them. No one learns the *sorns*" speech, for you can change their knowledge into any words and it is still the same. You cannot do that with the songs of the *hrossa*. Their tongue goes all over Malacandra. I speak it to you because you are a stranger. I would speak it to a *sorn*. But we have our old tongues at home. You can see it in the names. The *sorns* have big-sounding names like Augray and Arkal and Belmo and Falmay. The *hrossa* have furry names like Hnoh and Hnihi and Hyoi and Hlithnahi."

"The best poetry, then, comes in the roughest speech?"

"Perhaps," said the *pfifltrigg*. "As the best pictures are made in the hardest stone. But my people have names like Kalakaperi and Parakataru and Tafalakeruf. I am called Kanakaberaka."

Ransom told it his name.

"In our country," said Kanakaberaka, "it is not like this. We are not pinched in a narrow *handramit*. There are the true forests, the green shadows, the deep mines. It is warm. It does not blaze with light like this, and it is not silent like this. I could put you in a place there in the forests where you could see a hundred fires at once and hear a hundred hammers. I wish you had come to our country. We do not live in holes like the *sorns* nor in bundles of weed like the *hrossa*. I could show you houses with a hundred pillars, one suns" blood and the next of stars" milk, all the way . . . and all the world painted on the walls."

"How do you rule yourselves?" asked Ransom. "Those who are digging in the mines—do they like it as much as those who paint the walls?"

"All keep the mines open; it is a work to be shared. But each digs for himself the thing he wants for his work. What else would he do?"

"It is not so with us."

"Then you must make very bent work. How would a maker understand working in suns" blood unless he went into the home of suns" blood himself and knew one kind from another and lived with it for days out of the light of the sky till it was in his blood and his heart, as if he thought it and ate it and spat it?"

"With us it lies very deep and hard to get and those who dig it must spend their whole lives on the skill."

"And they love it?"

"I think not . . . I do not know. They are kept at it because they are given no food if they stop."

Kanakaberaka wrinkled his nose. "Then there is not food in plenty on your world?"

"I do not know," said Ransom. "I have often wished to know the answer to that question but no one can tell me. Does no one keep your people at their work, Kanakaberaka?"

"Our females," said the *pfifltrigg* with a piping noise which was apparently his equivalent for a laugh.

"Are your females of more account among you than those of the other *hnau* among them?"

"Very greatly. The *sorns* make least account of females and we make most."

18

That night Ransom slept in the guest-house, which was a real house built by *pfifltriggi* and richly decorated. His pleasure at finding himself, in this respect, under more human conditions was qualified by the discomfort which, despite his reason, he could not help feeling in the presence, at close quarters, of so many Malacandrian creatures. All three species were represented. They seemed to have no uneasy feelings towards each other, though there were some differences of the kind that occur in a railway carriage on Earth—the *sorns* finding the house too hot and the *pfifltriggi* finding it too cold. He learned more of Malacandrian humour and of the noises that expressed it in this one night than he had learned during the whole of his life on the strange planet hitherto. Indeed, nearly all Malacandrian conversations in which he had yet taken part had been grave. Apparently the comic spirit arose chiefly from the meeting of the different kinds of *hnau*. The jokes of all three were equally incomprehensible to him. He thought he could see differences in kind—as that the *sorns* seldom got beyond irony, while the *hrossa* were extravagant and fantastic, and the *pfifltriggi* were sharp and excelled in abuse—but even when he understood all the words he could not see the points. He went early to bed.

It was at the time of early morning, when men on Earth go out to milk the cows, that Ransom was awakened. At first he did not know what had roused him. The chamber in which he lay was silent, empty and nearly dark. He was preparing himself to sleep again when a high-pitched voice close beside him said, "Oyarsa sends for you." He sat up, staring about him. There was no one there, and the voice repeated, "Oyarsa sends for you." The confusion of sleep was now clearing in his head, and he recognized that there was an *eldil* in the room. He felt no conscious fear, but while he rose obediently and put on such of his clothes as he had laid aside he found that his heart was beating rather fast. He was thinking less of the invisible creature in the room than of the interview that lay before him. His old terrors of meeting some monster or idol had quite left him: he felt nervous as he remembered feeling on the morning of an examination when he was an undergraduate. More than anything in the world he would have liked a cup of good tea.

The guest-house was empty. He went out. The bluish smoke was rising from the lake and the sky was bright behind the jagged eastern wall of the canyon; it was a few minutes before sunrise. The air was still very cold, the ground-weed drenched with dew, and there was something puzzling about the whole scene which he presently identified with the silence. The *eldil* voices in the air had ceased and so had the shifting network of small lights and shades. Without being told, he knew that it was his business to go up to the crown of the island and the grove. As he approached them he saw with a certain sinking of heart that the monolithic avenue was full of Malacandrian creatures, and all silent. They were in two lines, one on each side, and all squatting or sitting in the various fashions suitable to their anatomies. He walked on slowly and doubtfully, not daring to stop, and ran the gauntlet of all those inhuman and unblinking eyes. When he had come to the very summit, at the middle of the avenue where the biggest of the stones rose, he stopped—he never could remember afterwards whether an *eldil* voice had told him to do so or whether it was an intuition of his own. He did not sit down, for the earth was too cold and wet and he was not sure if it would be decorous. He simply stood—motionless like a man on parade. All the creatures were looking at him and there was no noise anywhere.

He perceived, gradually, that the place was full of *eldila*. The lights, or suggestions of light, which yesterday had been scattered over the island, were now all congregated in this one spot, and were all stationary or very faintly moving. The sun had risen by now, and still no one spoke. As he looked up to see the first, pale sunlight upon the monoliths, he became conscious that the air above him was full of a far greater complexity of light than the sunrise could explain, and light of a different kind, *eldil*-light. The sky, no less than the earth, was full of them; the visible Malacandrians were but the smallest part of the silent consistory which surrounded him. He might, when the time came, be pleading his cause before thousands or before millions: rank behind rank about him, and rank above rank over his head, the creatures that had never yet seen man, and whom man could not see, were waiting for his trial to begin. He licked his lips, which were quite dry, and wondered if he would be able to speak when speech was demanded of him. Then it occurred to him that perhaps this—this waiting and being looked at—was the trial; perhaps even now he was unconsciously telling them all they wished to know. But afterwards—a long time afterwards—there was a noise of movement. Every visible creature in the grove had risen to its feet and was standing, more hushed than ever, with its head bowed; and Ransom saw (if it could be called seeing) that Oyarsa was coming up between the long lines of sculptured stones. Partly he knew it from the faces of the Malacandrians as their lord passed them; partly he saw—he could not deny that he saw—Oyarsa himself. He never could say what it was like. The merest whisper of light—no, less than that, the smallest diminution of shadow—was travelling along the uneven surface of the ground-weed; or rather some difference in the look of the ground, too slight to be named in the language of the five senses, moved slowly towards him. Like a silence spreading over a room full of people, like an infinitesimal coolness on a sultry day, like a passing memory of some long-forgotten sound or scent, like all that is stillest and smallest and most hard to seize in nature, Oyarsa passed between his subjects and drew near and came to rest, not ten yards away from Ransom in the centre of Meldilorn. Ransom felt a tingling of his blood and a pricking on his fingers as if lightning were near him; and his heart and body seemed to him to be made of water.

Oyarsa spoke—a more unhuman voice than Ransom had yet heard, sweet and seemingly remote; an unshaken voice; a voice, as one of the *hrossa* afterwards said to Ransom, "with no blood in it. Light is instead of blood for them." The words were not alarming.

"What are you so afraid of, Ransom of Thulcandra?" it said.

"Of you, Oyarsa, because you are unlike me and I cannot see you."

"Those are not great reasons," said the voice. "You are also unlike me, and, though I see you, I see you very faintly. But do not think we are utterly unlike. We are both copies of Maleldil. These are not the real reasons."

Ransom said nothing.

"You began to be afraid of me before you set foot in my world. And you have spent all your time then in flying from me. My servants saw your fear when you were in your ship in heaven. They saw that your own kind treated you ill, though they could not understand their speech. Then to deliver you out of the hands of those two I stirred up a *hnakra* to try if you would come to me of your own will. But you hid among the *hrossa,* and though they told you to come to me, you would not. After that I sent my *eldil* to fetch you, but still you would not come. And in the end your own kind have chased you to me, and *hnau*'s blood has been shed."

"I do not understand, Oyarsa. Do you mean that it was you who sent for me from Thulcandra?"

"Yes. Did not the other two tell you this? And why did you come with them unless you meant to obey my call? My servants could not understand their talk to you when your ship was in heaven."

"Your servants . . . I cannot understand," said Ransom.

"Ask freely," said the voice.

"Have you servants out in the heavens?"

"Where else? There is nowhere else."

"But you, Oyarsa, are here on Malacandra, as I am."

"But Malacandra, like all worlds, floats in heaven. And I am not 'here' altogether as you are, Ransom of Thulcandra. Creatures of your kind must drop out of heaven into a world; for us the worlds are places in heaven. But do not try to understand this now. It is enough to know that I and my servants are even now in heaven; they were around you in the sky-ship no less than they are around you here."

"Then you knew of our journey before we left Thulcandra?"

"No. Thulcandra is the world we do not know. It alone is outside the heaven, and no message comes from it."

Ransom was silent, but Oyarsa answered his unspoken questions.

"It was not always so. Once we knew the Oyarsa of your world—he was brighter and greater than I—and then we did not call it Thulcandra. It is the longest of all stories and the bitterest. He became bent. That was before any life came on your world. Those were the Bent Years of which we still speak in the heavens, when he was not yet bound to Thulcandra but free like us. It was in his mind to spoil other worlds besides his own. He smote your moon with his left hand and with his right he brought the cold death on my *harandra* before its time; if by my arm Maleldil had not opened the *handramits* and let out the hot springs, my world would have been unpeopled. We did not leave him so at large for long. There was great war, and we drove him back out of the heavens and bound him in the air of his own world as Maleldil taught us. There doubtless he lies to this hour, and we know no more of that planet: it is silent. We think that Maleldil would not give it up utterly to the Bent One, and there are stories among us that He has taken strange counsel and dared terrible things, wrestling with the Bent One in Thulcandra. But of this we know less than you; it is a thing we desire to look into."

It was some time before Ransom spoke again and Oyarsa respected his silence. When he had collected himself he said:

"After this story, Oyarsa, I may tell you that our world is very bent. The two who brought me knew nothing of you, but only that the *sorns* had asked for me. They thought you were a false *eldila,* I think. There are false *eldila* in the wild parts of our world; men kill other men before them—they think the *eldil* drinks blood. They thought the *sorns* wanted me for this or for some other evil. They brought me by force. I was in terrible fear. The tellers of tales in our world make us think that if there is any life beyond our own air it is evil."

"I understand," said the voice. "And this explains things that I have wondered at. As soon as your journey had passed your own air and entered heaven, my servants told me that you seemed to be coming unwillingly and that the others had secrets from you. I did not think any creature could be so bent as to bring another of its own kind here by force."

"They did not know what you wanted me for, Oyarsa. Nor do I know yet."

"I will tell you. Two years ago—and that is about four of your years—this ship entered the heavens from your world. We followed its journey all the way hither and *eldila* were with it as it sailed over the *harandra,* and when at last it came to rest in the *handramit* more than half my servants were standing round it to see the strangers come out. All beasts we kept back from the place, and no *hnau* yet knew of it. When the strangers had walked to and fro on Malacandra and made themselves a hut and their fear of a new world ought to have worn off, I sent certain *sorns* to show themselves and to teach the strangers our language. I chose *sorns* because they are most like your people in form. The Thulcandrians feared the *sorns* and were very unteachable. The *sorns* went to them many times and taught them a little. They reported to me that the Thulcandrians were taking suns" blood wherever they could find it in the streams. When I could make nothing of them by report, I told the *sorns* to bring them to me, not by force but courteously. They would not come. I asked for one of them, but not even one of them would come. It would have been easy to take them; but though we saw they were stupid we did not know yet how bent they were, and I did not wish to stretch my authority beyond the creatures of my own world. I told the *sorns* to treat them like cubs, to tell them that they would be allowed to pick up no more of the suns" blood until one of their race came to me. When they were told this they stuffed as much as they could into the sky-ship and went back to their own world. We wondered at this, but now it is plain. They thought I wanted one of your race to eat and went to fetch one. If they had come a few miles to see me I would have received them honourably; now they have twice gone a voyage of millions of miles for nothing and will appear before me none the less. And you also, Ransom of Thulcandra, you have taken many vain troubles to avoid standing where you stand now."

"That is true, Oyarsa. Bent creatures are full of fears. But I am here now and ready to know your will with me."

"Two things I wanted to ask of your race. First I must know why you come here—so much is my duty to my world. And secondly I wish to hear of Thulcandra and of Maleldil's strange wars there with the Bent One; for that, as I have said, is a thing we desire to look into."

"For the first question, Oyarsa, I have come here because I was brought. Of the others, one cares for nothing but the suns" blood, because in our world he can exchange it for many pleasures and powers. But the other means evil to you. I think he would destroy all your people to make room for our people; and then he would do the same with other worlds again. He wants our race to last for always, I think, and he hopes they will leap from world to world . . . always going to a new sun when an old one dies . . . or something like that."

"Is he wounded in his brain?"

"I do not know. Perhaps I do not describe his thoughts right. He is more learned than I."

"Does he think he could go to the great worlds? Does he think Maleldil wants a race to live for ever?"

"He does not know there is any Maleldil. But what is certain, Oyarsa, is that he means evil to your world. Our kind must not be allowed to come here again. If you can prevent it only by killing all three of us, I am content."

"If you were my own people I would kill them now, Ransom, and you soon; for they are bent beyond hope, and you, when you have grown a little braver, will be ready to go to Maleldil. But my authority is over my own world. It is a terrible thing to kill someone else's *hnau*. It will not be necessary."

"They are strong Oyarsa, and they can throw death many miles and can blow killing airs at their enemies."

"The least of my servants could touch their ship before it reached Malacandra, while it was in the heaven, and make it a body of different movements—for you, no body at all. Be sure that no one of your race will come into my world again unless I call him. But enough of this. Now tell me of Thulcandra. Tell me all. We know nothing since the day when the Bent One sank out of heaven into the air of your world, wounded in the very light of his light. But why have you become afraid again?"

"I am afraid of the lengths of time, Oyarsa . . . or perhaps I do not understand. Did you not say this happened before there was life on Thulcandra?"

"Yes."

"And you, Oyarsa? You have lived . . . and that picture on the stone where the cold is killing them on the *harandra*? Is that a picture of something that was before my world began?"

"I see you are *hnau* after all," said the voice. "Doubtless no stone that faced the air then would be a stone now. The picture has begun to crumble away and been copied again more times than there are *eldila* in the air above us. But it was copied right. In that way you are seeing a picture that was finished when your world was still half-made. But do not think of these things. My people have a law never to speak much of sizes or numbers to you others, not even to *sorns*. You do not understand, and it makes you do reverence to nothings and pass by what is really great. Rather tell me what Maleldil has done in Thulcandra."

"According to our traditions———" Ransom was beginning, when an unexpected disturbance broke in upon the solemn stillness of the assembly. A large party, almost a procession, was approaching the grove from the direction of the ferry. It consisted entirely, as far as he could see, of *hrossa,* and they appeared to be carrying something.

19

As the procession drew nearer Ransom saw that the foremost *hrossa* were supporting three long and narrow burdens. They carried them on their heads, four *hrossa* to each. After these came a number of others armed with harpoons and apparently guarding two creatures which he did not recognize. The light was behind them as they entered between the two farthest monoliths. They were much shorter than any animal he had yet seen on Malacandra, and he gathered that they were bipeds, though the lower limbs were so thick and sausage-like that he hesitated to call them legs. The bodies were a little narrower at the top than at the bottom so as to be very slightly pear-shaped, and the heads were neither round like those of *hrossa* nor long like those of *sorns,* but almost square. They stumped along on narrow, heavy-looking feet which they seemed to press into the ground with unnecessary violence. And now their faces were becoming visible as masses of lumped and puckered flesh of variegated colour fringed in some bristly, dark substance. . . . Suddenly, with an indescribable change of feeling, he realized that he was looking at men. The two prisoners were Weston and Devine and he, for one privileged moment, had seen the human form with almost Malacandrian eyes.

The leaders of the procession had now advanced to within a few yards of Oyarsa and laid down their burdens. These, he now saw, were three dead *hrossa* laid on biers of some unknown metal; they were on their backs and their eyes, not closed as we close the eyes of human dead, stared disconcertingly up at the far-off golden canopy of the grove. One of them he took to be Hyoi, and it was certainly Hyoi's brother, Hyahi, who now came forward, and after an obeisance to Oyarsa began to speak.

Ransom at first did not hear what he was saying, for his attention was concentrated on Weston and Devine. They were weaponless and vigilantly guarded by the armed *hrossa* about them. Both of them, like Ransom himself, had let their beards grow ever since they landed on Malacandra, and both were pale and travel-stained. Weston was standing with folded arms, and his face wore a fixed, even an elaborate, expression of desperation. Devine, with his hands in his pockets, seemed to be in a state of furious sulks. Both clearly thought that they had good reason to fear, though neither was by any means lacking in courage. Surrounded by their guards as they were, and intent on the scene before them, they had not noticed Ransom.

He became aware of what Hyoi's brother was saying.

"For the death of these two, Oyarsa, I do not so much complain, for when we fell upon the *hmāna* by night they were in terror. You may say it was as a hunt and these two were killed as they might have been by a *hnakra*. But Hyoi they hit from afar with a coward's weapon when he had done nothing to frighten them. And now he lies there (and I do not say it because he was my brother, but all the *handramit* knows it) and he was a *hnakrapunt* and a great poet and the loss of him is heavy."

The voice of Oyarsa spoke for the first time to the two men.

"Why have you killed my *hnau*?" it said.

Weston and Devine looked anxiously about them to identify the speaker.

"God!" exclaimed Devine in English. "Don't tell me they've got a loud-speaker."

"Ventriloquism," replied Weston in a husky whisper. "Quite common among savages. The witch-doctor or medicine-man pretends to go into a trance and he does it. The thing to do is to identify the medicine-man and address your remarks to *him* wherever the voice seems to come from; it shatters his nerve and shows you've seen through him. Do you see any of the brutes in a trance? By jove—I've spotted him."

Due credit must be given to Weston for his powers of observation: he had picked out the only creature in the assembly which was not standing in an attitude of reverence and attention. This was an elderly *hross* close beside him. It was squatting; and its eyes were shut. Taking a step towards it, he struck a defiant attitude and exclaimed in a loud voice (his knowledge of the language was elementary):

"Why you take our puff-bangs away? We very angry with you. We not afraid."

On Weston's hypothesis his action ought to have been impressive. Unfortunately for him, no one else shared his theory of the elderly *hross*'s behavior. The *hross*—who was well known to all of them, including Ransom—had not come with the funeral procession. It had been in its place since dawn. Doubtless it intended no disrespect to Oyarsa; but it must be confessed that it had yielded, at a much earlier stage of the proceedings, to an infirmity which attacks elderly *hnau* of all species, and was by this time enjoying a profound and refreshing slumber. One of its whiskers twitched a little as Weston shouted in its face, but its eyes remained shut.

The voice of Oyarsa spoke again. "Why do you speak to him?" it said. "It is I who ask you. Why have you killed my *hnau*?"

"You let us go, then we talkee-talkee," bellowed Weston at the sleeping *hross*. "You think we no power, think you do all you like. You no can. Great big head-man in sky he send us. You no do what I say, he come, blow you all up—Pouff! Bang!"

"I do not know what *bang* means," said the voice. "But why have you killed my *hnau*?"

"Say it was an accident," muttered Devine to Weston in English.

"I've told you before," replied Weston in the same language. "You don't understand how to deal with natives. One sign of yielding and they'll be at our throats. The only thing is to intimidate them."

"All right! Do your stuff, then," growled Devine. He was obviously losing faith in his partner.

Weston cleared his throat and again rounded on the elderly *hross*.

"We kill him," he shouted. "Show what we can do. Every one who no do all we say—pouff! bang!—kill him same as that one. You do all we say and we give you much pretty things. See! See!" To Ransom's intense discomfort, Weston at this point whipped out of his pocket a brightly coloured necklace of beads, the undoubted work of Mr. Woolworth, and began dangling it in front of the faces of his guards, turning slowly round and round and repeating, "Pretty, pretty! See! See!"

The result of this manœuvre was more striking than Weston himself had anticipated. Such a roar of sounds as human ears had never heard before—baying of *hrossa,* piping of *pfifltriggi,* booming of *sorns*—burst out and rent the silence of that august place, waking echoes from the distant mountain walls. Even in the air above them there was a faint ringing of the *eldil* voices. It is greatly to Weston's credit that though he paled at this he did not lose his nerve.

"You no roar at me," he thundered. "No try make me afraid. Me no afraid of you."

"You must forgive my people," said the voice of Oyarsa—and even it was subtly changed—"but they are not roaring at you. They are only laughing."

But Weston did not know the Malacandrian word for *laugh:* indeed, it was not a word he understood very well in any language. He looked about him with a puzzled expression. Ransom, biting his lips with mortification, almost prayed that one experiment with the beads would satisfy the scientist; but that was because he did not know Weston. The latter saw that the clamour had subsided. He knew that he was following the most orthodox rules for frightening and then conciliating primitive races; and he was not the man to be deterred by one or two failures. The roar that went up from the throats of all spectators as he again began revolving like a slow-motion picture of a humming-top, occasionally mopping his brow with his left hand and conscientiously jerking the necklace up and down with his right, completely drowned anything he might be attempting to say; but Ransom saw his lips moving and had little doubt that he was working away at "Pretty, pretty!" Then suddenly the sound of laughter almost redoubled its volume. The stars in their courses were fighting against Weston. Some hazy memory of efforts made long since to entertain an infant niece had begun to penetrate his highly trained mind. He was bobbing up and down from the knees and holding his head on one side; he was almost dancing; and he was by now very hot indeed. For all Ransom knew he was saying "Diddle, diddle, diddle."

It was sheer exhaustion which ended the great physicist's performance—the most successful of its kind ever given on Malacandra—and with it the sonorous raptures of his audience. As silence returned Ransom heard Devine's voice in English:

"For God's sake stop making a buffoon of yourself, Weston," it said. "Can't you see it won't work?"

"It *doesn't* seem to be working," admitted Weston, "and I'm inclined to think they have even less intelligence than we supposed. Do you think, perhaps, if I tried it just once again—or would you like to try this time?"

"Oh, Hell!" said Devine, and, turning his back on his partner, sat down abruptly on the ground, produced his cigarette-case and began to smoke.

"I'll give it to the witch-doctor," said Weston during the moment of silence which Devine's action had produced among the mystified spectators; and before anyone could stop him he took a step forward and attempted to drop the string of beads round the elderly *hross*'s neck. The *hross*'s head was, however, too large for this operation and the necklace merely settled on its forehead like a crown, slightly over one eye. It shifted its head a little, like a dog worried with flies, snorted gently, and resumed its sleep.

Oyarsa's voice now addressed Ransom. "Are your fellow-creatures hurt in their brains, Ransom of Thulcandra?" it said. "Or are they too much afraid to answer my questions?"

"I think, Oyarsa," said Ransom, "that they do not believe you are there. And they believe that all these *hnau* are—are like very young cubs. The thicker *hmān* is trying to frighten them and then to please them with gifts."

At the sound of Ransom's voice the two prisoners turned sharply around. Weston was about to speak when Ransom interrupted him hastily in English:

"Listen, Weston. It is not a trick. There really is a creature there in the middle—there where you can see a kind of light, or a kind of something, if you look hard. And it is at least as intelligent as a man—they seem to live an enormous time. Stop treating it like a child and answer its questions. And if you take my advice, you'll speak the truth and not bluster."

"The brutes seem to have intelligence enough to take you in, anyway," growled Weston; but it was in a somewhat modified voice that he turned once more to the sleeping *hross*—the desire to wake up the supposed witch-doctor was becoming an obsession—and addressed it.

"We sorry we kill him," he said, pointing to Hyoi. "No go to kill him. *Sorns* tell us bring man, give him your big head. We go away back into sky. *He* come (here he indicated Ransom) with us. He very bent man, run away, no do what *sorns* say like us. We run after him, get him back for *sorns*, want to do what we say and *sorns* tell us, see? He not let us. Run away, run, run. We run after. See big black one, think he kill us, we kill him—pouff! bang! All for bent man. He no run away, he be good, we no run after, no kill big black one, see? You have bent man—bent man make all trouble—you plenty keep him, let us go. He afraid of you, we no afraid. Listen——"

At this moment Weston's continual bellowing in the face of the *hross* at last produced the effect he had striven for so long. The creature opened its eyes and stared mildly at him in some perplexity. Then, gradually realizing the impropriety of which it had been guilty, it rose slowly to its standing position, bowed respectfully to Oyarsa, and finally waddled out of the assembly still carrying the necklace draped over its right ear and eye. Weston, his mouth still open, followed the retreating figure with his gaze till it vanished among the stems of the grove.

It was Oyarsa who broke the silence. "We have had mirth enough," he said, "and it is time to hear true answers to our questions. Something is wrong in your head, *hnau* from Thulcandra. There is too much blood in it. Is Firikitekila here?"

"Here, Oyarsa," said a *pfifltrigg*.

"Have you in your cisterns water that has been made cold?"

"Yes, Oyarsa."

"Then let this thick *hnau* be taken to the guest-house and let them bathe his head in cold water. Much water and many times. Then bring him again. Meanwhile I will provide for my killed *hrossa*."

Weston did not clearly understand what the voice said—indeed, he was still too busy trying to find out where it came from—but terror smote him as he found himself wrapped in the strong arms of the surrounding *hrossa* and forced away from his place. Ransom would gladly have shouted out some reassurance, but Weston himself was shouting too loud to hear him. He was mixing English and Malacandrian now, and the last that was heard was a rising scream of "Pay for this—pouff! bang!—Ransom, for God's sake—Ransom! Ransom!"

"And now," said Oyarsa, when silence was restored, "let us honour my dead *hnau*."

At his words ten of the *hrossa* grouped themselves about the biers. Lifting their heads, and with no signal given as far as Ransom could see, they began to sing.

To every man, in his acquaintance with a new art, there comes a moment when that which before was meaningless first lifts, as it were, one corner of the curtain that hides its mystery, and reveals, in a burst of delight which later and fuller understanding can hardly ever equal, one glimpse of the indefinite possibilities within. For Ransom, this moment had now come in his understanding of Malacandrian song. Now first he saw that its rhythms were based on a different blood from ours, on a heart that beat more quickly, and a fiercer internal heat. Through his knowledge of the creatures and his love for them he began, ever so little, to hear it with their ears. A sense of great masses moving at visionary speeds, of giants dancing, of eternal sorrows eternally consoled, of he knew not what and yet what he had always known, awoke in him with the very first bars of the deep-mouthed dirge, and bowed down his spirit as if the gate of heaven had opened before him.

"Let it go hence," they sang. "Let it go hence, dissolve and be no body. Drop it, release it, drop it gently, as a stone is loosed from the fingers drooping over a still pool. Let it go down, sink, fall away. Once below the surface there are no divisions, no layers in the water yielding all the way down; all one and all unwounded is that element. Send it voyaging where it will not come again. Let it go down; the *hnau* rises from it. This is the second life, the other beginning. Open, oh coloured world, without weight, without shore. You are second and better; this was first and feeble. Once the worlds were hot within and brought forth life, but only the pale plants, the dark plants. We see their children when they grow to-day, out of the sun's light in the sad places. After, the heaven made grow another kind on worlds: the high climbers, the bright-haired forests, cheeks of flowers. First were the darker, then the brighter. First was the worlds" blood, then the suns" blood."

This was as much of it as he contrived later to remember and could translate. As the song ended Oyarsa said:

"Let us scatter the movements which were their bodies. So will Maleldil scatter all worlds when the first and feeble is worn."

He made a sign to one of the *pfifltriggi,* who instantly arose and approached the corpses. The *hrossa,* now singing again but very softly, drew back at least ten paces. The *pfifltrigg* touched each of the three dead in turn with some small object that appeared to be made of glass or crystal—and then jumped away with one of his frog-like leaps. Ransom closed his eyes to protect them from a blinding light and felt something like a very strong wind blowing in his face, for a fraction of a second. Then all was calm again, and the three biers were empty.

"God! That would be a trick worth knowing on earth," said Devine to Ransom. "Solves the murderers" problem about the disposal of the body, eh?"

But Ransom, who was thinking of Hyoi, did not answer him; and before he spoke again everyone's attention was diverted by the return of the unhappy Weston among his guards.

20

The *hross* who headed this procession was a conscientious creature and began at once explaining itself in a rather troubled voice.

"I hope we have done right, Oyarsa," it said. "But we do not know. We dipped his head in the cold water seven times, but the seventh time something fell off it. We had thought it was the top of his head, but now we saw it was a covering made of the skin of some other creature. Then some said we had done your will with the seven dips, and others said not. In the end we dipped it seven times more. We hope that was right. The creature talked a lot between the dips, and most between the second seven, but we could not understand it."

"You have done very well, Hnoo," said Oyarsa. "Stand away that I may see it, for now I will speak to it."

The guards fell away on each side. Weston's usually pale face, under the bracing influence of the cold water, had assumed the colour of a ripe tomato, and his hair, which had naturally not been cut since he reached Malacandra, was plastered in straight, lank masses across his forehead. A good deal of water was still dripping over his nose and ears. His expression—unfortunately wasted on an audience ignorant of terrestrial physiognomy—was that of a brave man suffering in a great cause, and rather eager than reluctant to face the worst or even to provoke it. In explanation of his conduct it is only fair to remember that he had already that morning endured all the terrors of an expected martyrdom and all the anticlimax of fourteen compulsory cold douches. Devine, who knew his man, shouted out to Weston in English:

"Steady, Weston. These devils can split the atom or something pretty like it. Be careful what you say to them and don't let's have any of your bloody nonsense."

"Huh!" said Weston. "So you've gone native too?"

"Be silent," said the voice of Oyarsa. "You, thick one, have told me nothing of yourself, so I will tell it to you. In your own world you have attained great wisdom concerning bodies and by this you have been able to make a ship that can cross the heaven; but in all other things you have the mind of an animal. When first you came here, I sent for you, meaning you nothing but honour. The darkness in your own mind filled you with fear. Because you thought I meant evil to you, you went as a beast goes against a beast of some other kind, and snared this Ransom. You would give him up to the evil you feared. To-day, seeing him here, to save your own life, you would have given him to me a second time, still thinking I meant him hurt. These are your dealings with your own kind. And what you intend to my people, I know. Already you have killed some. And you have come here to kill them all. To you it is nothing whether a creature is *hnau* or not. At first I thought this was because you cared only whether a creature had a body like your own; but Ransom has that and you would kill him as lightly as any of my *hnau*. I did not know that the Bent One had done so much in your world and still I do not understand it. If you were mine, I would unbody you even now. Do not think follies; by my hand Maleldil does greater things than this, and I can unmake you even on the borders of your own world's air. But I do not yet resolve to do this. It is for you to speak. Let me see if there is anything in your mind besides fear and death and desire."

Weston turned to Ransom. "I see," he said, "that you have chosen the most momentous crisis in the history of the human race to betray it." Then he turned in the direction of the voice.

"I know you kill us," he said. "Me not afraid. Others come, make it our world——"

But Devine had jumped to his feet, and interrupted him.

"No, no Oyarsa," he shouted. "You no listen him. He very foolish man, he have dreams. We little people, only want pretty sun-bloods. You give us plenty sun-bloods, we go back into sky, you never see us no more. All done, see?"

"Silence," said Oyarsa. There was an almost imperceptible change in the light, if it could be called light, out of which the voice came, and Devine crumpled up and fell back on the ground. When he resumed his sitting position he was white and panting.

"Speak on," said Oyarsa to Weston.

"Me no . . . no," began Weston in Malacandrian and then broke off. "I can't say what I want in their accursed language," he said in English.

"Speak to Ransom and he shall turn it into our speech," said Oyarsa.

Weston accepted the arrangement at once. He believed that the hour of his death was come and he was determined to utter the thing—almost the only thing outside his own science—which he had to say. He cleared his throat, almost he struck a gesture, and began:

"To you I may seem a vulgar robber, but I bear on my shoulders the destiny of the human race. Your tribal life with its stone-age weapons and bee-hive huts, its primitive coracles and elementary social structure, has nothing to compare with our civilization—with our science, medicine and law, our armies, our architecture, our commerce, and our transport system which is rapidly annihilating space and time. Our right to supersede you is the right of the higher over the lower. Life——"

"Half a moment," said Ransom in English. "That's about as much as I can manage at one go." Then, turning to Oyarsa, he began translating as well as he could. The process was difficult and the result—which he felt to be rather unsatisfactory—was something like this:

"Among us, Oyarsa, there is a kind of *hnau* who will take other *hnau*'s food and—and things, when they are not looking. He says he is not an ordinary one of that kind. He says what he does now will make very different things happen to those of our people who are not yet born. He says that, among you, *hnau* of one kindred all live together and the *hrossa* have spears like those we used a very long time ago and your huts are small and round and your boats small and light and like our old ones, and you have only one ruler. He says it is different with us. He says we know much. There is a thing happens in our world when the body of a living creature feels pains and becomes weak, and he says we sometimes know how to stop it. He says we have many bent people and we kill them or shut them in huts and that we have people for settling quarrels between the bent *hnau* about their huts and mates and things. He says we have many ways for the *hnau* of one land to kill those of another and some are trained to do it. He says we build very big and strong huts of stones and other things—like the *pfifltriggi*. And he says we exchange many things among ourselves and can carry heavy weights very quickly a long way. Because of all this, he says it would not be the act of a bent *hnau* if our people killed all your people."

As soon as Ransom finished, Weston continued.

"Life is greater than any system of morality; her claims are absolute. It is not by tribal taboos and copy-book maxims that she has pursued her relentless march from the amoeba to man and from man to civilization."

"He says," began Ransom, "that living creatures are stronger than the question whether an act is bent or good—no, that cannot be right—he says it is better to be alive and bent than to be dead—no—he says, he says—I cannot say what he says, Oyarsa, in your language. But he goes on to say that the only good thing is that there should be very many creatures alive. He says there were many other animals before the first men and the later ones were better than the earlier ones; but he says the animals were not born because of what is said to the young about bent and good action by their elders. And he says these animals did not feel any pity."

"She——" began Weston.

"I'm sorry," interrupted Ransom, "but I've forgotten who She is."

"Life, of course," snapped Weston. "She has ruthlessly broken down all obstacles and liquidated all failures and to-day in her highest form—civilized man—and in me as his representative, she presses forward to that interplanetary leap which will, perhaps, place her for ever beyond the reach of death."

"He says," resumed Ransom, "that these animals learned to do many difficult things, except those who could not; and those ones died and the other animals did not pity them. And he says the best animal now is the kind of man who makes the big huts and carries the heavy weights and does all the other things I told you about; and he is one of these and he says that if the others all knew what he was doing they would be pleased. He says that if he could kill you all and bring our people to live in Malacandra, then they might be able to go on living here after something had gone wrong with our world. And then if something went wrong with Malacandra they might go and kill all the *hnau* in another world. And then another—and so they would never die out."

"It is in her right," said Weston, "the right, or, if you will, the might of Life herself, that I am prepared without flinching to plant the flag of man on the soil of Malacandra: to march on, step by step, superseding, where necessary, the lower forms of life that we find, claiming planet after planet, system after system, till our posterity—whatever strange form and yet unguessed mentality they have assumed—dwell in the universe wherever the universe is habitable."

"He says," translated Ransom, "that because of this it would *not* be a bent action—or else, he says, it *would* be a possible action—for him to kill you all and bring us here. He says he would feel no pity. He is saying again that perhaps they would be able to keep moving from one world to another and wherever they came they would kill everyone. I think he is now talking about worlds that go round other suns. He wants the creatures born from us to be in as many places as they can. He says he does not know what kind of creatures they will be."

"I may fall," said Weston. "But while I live I will not, with such a key in my hand, consent to close the gates of the future on my race. What lies in that future, beyond our present ken, passes imagination to conceive: it is enough for me that there is a Beyond."

"He is saying," Ransom translated, "that he will not stop trying to do all this unless you kill him. And he says that though he doesn't know what will happen to the creatures sprung from us, he wants it to happen very much."

Weston, who had now finished his statement, looked round instinctively for a chair to sink into. On Earth he usually sank into a chair as the applause began. Finding none—he was not the kind of man to sit on the ground like Devine—he folded his arm and stared with a certain dignity about him.

"It is well that I have heard you," said Oyarsa. "For though your mind is feebler, your will is less bent than I thought. It is not for yourself that you would do all this."

"No," said Weston proudly in Malacandrian. "Me die. Man live."

"Yet you know that these creatures would have to be made quite unlike you before they lived on other worlds."

"Yes, yes. All new. No one know yet. Strange! Big!"

"Then it is not the shape of body that you love?"

"No. Me no care how they shaped."

"One would think, then, that it is for the mind you care. But that cannot be, or you would love *hnau* wherever you met it."

"No care for *hnau*. Care for man."

"But if it is neither man's mind, which is as the mind of all other *hnau*—is not Maleldil maker of them all?—nor his body, which will change—if you care for neither of these, what do you mean by man?"

This had to be translated to Weston. When he understood it, he replied:

"Me care for man—care for our race—what man begets—" He had to ask Ransom the words for *race* and *beget*.

"Strange!" said Oyarsa. "You do not love any one of your race—you would have let me kill Ransom. You do not love the mind of your race, nor the body. Any kind of creature will please you if only it is begotten by your kind as they now are. It seems to me, Thick One, that what you really love is no completed creature but the very seed itself: for that is all that is left."

"Tell him," said Weston when he had been made to understand this, "that I don't pretend to be a metaphysician. I have not come here to chop logic. If he cannot understand—as apparently you can't either—anything so fundamental as a man's loyalty to humanity, I can't make him understand it."

But Ransom was unable to translate this and the voice of Oyarsa continued:

"I see now how the lord of the silent world has bent you. There are laws that all *hnau* know, of pity and straight dealing and shame and the like, and one of these is the love of kindred. He has taught you to break all of them except this one, which is not one of the greatest laws; this one he has bent till it becomes folly and has set it up, thus bent, to be a little, blind Oyarsa in your brain. And now you can do nothing but obey it, though if we ask you why it is a law you give no other reason for it than for all the other and greater laws which it drives you to disobey. Do you know why he has done this?"

"Me think no such person—me wise, new man—no believe all that old talk."

"I will tell you. He has left you this one because a bent *hnau* can do more evil than a broken one. He has only bent you; but this Thin One who sits on the ground he has broken, for he has left him nothing but greed. He is now only a talking animal and in my world he could do no more evil than an animal. If he were mine I would unmake his body for the *hnau* in it is already dead. But if you were mine I would try to cure you. Tell me, Thick One, why did you come here?"

"Me tell you. Make man live all the time."

"But are your wise men so ignorant as not to know that Malacandra is older than your own world and nearer its death? Most of it is dead already. My people live only in the *handramits;* the heat and the water have been more and will be less. Soon now, very soon, I will end my world and give back my people to Maleldil."

"Me know all that plenty. This only first try. Soon they go on another world."

"But do you not know that all worlds will die?"

"Men go jump off each before it deads—on and on, see?"

"And when all are dead?"

Weston was silent. After a time Oyarsa spoke again.

"Do you not ask why my people, whose world is old, have not rather come to yours and taken it long ago?"

"Ho! Ho!" said Weston. "You not know how."

"You are wrong," said Oyarsa. "Many thousands of thousand years before this, when nothing yet lived on your world, the cold death was coming on my *harandra*. Then I was in deep trouble, not chiefly for the death of my *hnau*—Maleldil does not make them long-livers—but for the things which the lord of your world, who was not yet bound, put into their minds. He would have made them as your people are now— wise enough to see the death of their kind approaching but not wise enough to endure it. Bent counsels would soon have risen among them. They were well able to have made sky-ships. By me Maleldil stopped them. Some I cured, some I unbodied——"

"And see what come!" interrupted Weston. "You now very few— shut up in *handramits*—soon all die."

"Yes," said Oyarsa, "but one thing we left behind us on the *harandra*: fear. And with fear, murder and rebellion. The weakest of my people do not fear death. It is the Bent One, the lord of your world, who wastes your lives and befouls them with flying from what you know will overtake you in the end. If you were subjects of Maleldil you would have peace."

Weston writhed in the exasperation born of his desire to speak and his ignorance of the language.

"Trash! Defeatist trash!" he shouted at Oyarsa in English; then, drawing himself up to his full height, he added in Malacandrian, "You say your Maleldil let all go dead. Other one, Bent One, he fight, jump, live—not all talkee-talkee. Me no care Maleldil. Like Bent One better: me on his side."

"But do you not see that he never will nor can," began Oyarsa, and then broke off, as if recollecting himself. "But I must learn more of your world from Ransom, and for that I need till night. I will not kill you, not even the Thin One, for you are out of my world. To-morrow you shall go hence again in your ship."

Devine's face suddenly fell. He began talking rapidly in English.

"For God's sake, Weston, make him understand. We've been here for months—the Earth is not in opposition now. Tell him it can't be done. He might as well kill us at once."

"How long will your journey be to Thulcandra?" asked Oyarsa.

Weston, using Ransom as his interpreter, explained that the journey, in the present position of the two planets, was almost impossible. The distance had increased by millions of miles. The angle of their course to the solar rays would be totally different from that which he had counted upon. Even if by a hundredth chance they could hit the Earth, it was almost certain that their supply of oxygen would be exhausted long before they arrived.

"Tell him to kill us now," he added.

"All this I know," said Oyarsa. "And if you stay in my world I must kill you: no such creature will I suffer in Malacandra. I know there is small chance of your reaching your world; but small is not the same as none. Between now and the next moon choose which you will take. In the meantime, tell me this. If you reach it at all, what is the most time you will need?"

After a prolonged calculation, Weston, in a shaken voice, replied that if they had not made it in ninety days they would never make it, and they would, moreover, be dead of suffocation.

"Ninety days you shall have," said Oyarsa. "My *sorns* and *pfifltriggi* will give you air (we also have that art) and food for ninety days. But they will do something else to your ship. I am not minded that it should return into the heaven if once it reaches Thulcandra. You, Thick One, were not here when I unmade my dead *hrossa* whom you killed: the Thin One will tell you. This I can do, as Maleldil has taught me, over a gap of time or a gap of place. Before your sky-ship rises, my *sorns* will have so dealt with it that on the ninetieth day it will unbody, it will become what you call nothing. If that day finds it in heaven your death will be no bitterer because of this; but do not tarry in your ship if once you touch Thulcandra. Now lead these two away, and do you, my children, go where you will. But I must talk with Ransom."

21

All that afternoon Ransom remained alone answering Oyarsa's questions. I am not allowed to record this conversation, beyond saying that the voice concluded it with the words:

"You have shown me more wonders than are known in the whole of heaven."

After that they discussed Ransom's own future. He was given full liberty to remain in Malacandra or to attempt the desperate voyage to Earth. The problem was agonizing to him. In the end he decided to throw in his lot with Weston and Devine.

"Love of our own kind," he said, "is not the greatest of laws, but you, Oyarsa, have said it is a law. If I cannot live in Thulcandra, it is better for me not to live at all."

"You have chosen rightly," said Oyarsa. "And I will tell you two things. My people will take all the strange weapons out of the ship, but they will give one to you. And the *eldila* of deep heaven will be about your ship till it reaches the air of Thulcandra, and often in it. They will not let the other two kill you."

It had not occurred to Ransom before that his own murder might be one of the first expedients for economizing food and oxygen which would occur to Weston and Devine. He was now astonished at his obtuseness, and thanked Oyarsa for his protective measures. Then the great *eldil* dismissed him with these words:

"You are guilty of no evil, Ransom of Thulcandra, except a little fear-fulness. For that, the journey you go on is your pain, and perhaps your cure: for you must be either mad or brave before it is ended. But I lay also a command on you; you must watch this Weston and this Devine in Thulcandra if ever you arrive there. They may yet do much evil in, and beyond, your world. From what you have told me, I begin to see that there are *eldila* who go down into your air, into the very stronghold of the Bent One; your world is not so fast shut as was thought in these parts of heaven. Watch those two bent ones. Be courageous. Fight them. And when you have need, some of our people will help. Maleldil will show them to you. It may even be that you and I shall meet again while you are still in the body; for it is not without the wisdom of Maleldil that we have met now and I have learned so much of your world. It seems to me that this is the beginning of more comings and goings between the heavens and the worlds and between one world and another—though not such as the Thick One hoped. I am allowed to tell you this. The year we are now in—but heavenly years are not as yours—has long been prophesied as a year of stirrings and high changes and the siege of Thulcandra may be near its end. Great things are on foot. If Maleldil does not forbid me, I will not hold aloof from them. And now, farewell."

It was through vast crowds of all the Malacandrian species that the three human beings embarked next day on their terrible journey. Weston was pale and haggard from a night of calculations intricate enough to tax any mathematician even if his life did not hang on them. Devine was noisy, reckless and a little hysterical. His whole view of Malacandra had been altered overnight by the discovery that the "natives" had an alcoholic drink, and he had even been trying to teach them to smoke. Only the *pfifltriggi* had made much of it. He was now consoling himself for an acute headache and the prospect of a lingering death by tormenting Weston. Neither partner was pleased to find that all weapons had been removed from the space-ship, but in other respects everything was as they wished it. At about an hour after noon Ransom took a last, long look at the blue waters, purple forest and remote green walls of the familiar *handramit* and followed the other two through the manhole. Before it was closed Weston warned them that they must economize air by absolute stillness. No unnecessary movement must be made during their voyage; even talking must be prohibited.

"I shall speak only in an emergency," he said.

"Thank God for that, anyway," was Devine's last shot. Then they screwed themselves in.

Ransom went at once to the lower side of the sphere, into the chamber which was now most completely upside down, and stretched himself on what would later become its skylight. He was surprised to find that they were already thousands of feet up. The *handramit* was only a straight purple line across the rose-red surface of the *harandra*. They were above the junction of two *handramits*. One of them was doubtless that in which he had lived, the other that which contained Meldilorn. The gully by which he had cut off the corner between the two, on Augray's shoulders, was quite invisible.

Each minute more *handramits* came into view—long straight lines, some parallel, some intersecting, some building triangles. The landscape became increasingly geometrical. The waste between the purple lines appeared perfectly flat. The rosy colour of the petrified forests accounted for its tint immediately below him; but to the north and east the great sand deserts of which the *sorns* had told him were now appearing as illimitable stretches of yellow and ochre. To the west a huge discoloration began to show. It was an irregular patch of greenish blue that looked as if it were sunk below the level of the surrounding *harandra*. He concluded it was the forest lowland of the *pfifltriggi*—or rather one of their forest lowlands, for now similar patches were appearing in all directions, some of them mere blobs at the intersection of *handramits*, some of vast extent. He became vividly conscious that his knowledge of Malacandra was minute, local, parochial. It was as if a *sorn* had journeyed forty million miles to the Earth and spent his stay there between Worthing and Brighton. He reflected that he would have very little to show for his amazing voyage if he survived it: a smattering of the language, a few landscapes, some half-understood physics—but where were the statistics, the history, the broad survey of extra-terrestrial conditions, which such a traveller ought to bring back? Those *handramits*, for example. Seen from the height which the space-ship had now attained, in all their unmistakable geometry, they put to shame his original impression that they were natural valleys. They were gigantic feats of engineering, about which he had learned nothing; feats accomplished, if all were true, before human history began . . . before animal history began. Or was that only mythology? He knew it would seem like mythology when he got back to Earth (if he ever got back), but the presence of Oyarsa was still too fresh a memory to allow him any real doubts. It even occurred to him that the distinction between history and mythology might be itself meaningless outside the Earth.

The thought baffled him, and he turned again to the landscape below—the landscape which became every moment less of a landscape and more of a diagram. By this time, to the east, a much larger and darker patch of discoloration than he had yet seen was pushing its way into the reddish ochre of the Malacandrian world—a curiously shaped patch with long arms or horns extended on each side and a sort of bay between them, like the concave side of a crescent. It grew and grew. The wide dark arms seemed to be spread out to engulf the whole planet. Suddenly he saw a bright point of light in the middle of this dark patch and realized that it was not a patch on the surface of the planet at all, but the black sky showing behind her. The smooth curve was the edge of her disk. At this, for the first time since their embarkation, fear took hold of him. Slowly, yet not too slowly for him to see, the dark arms spread farther and even farther round the lighted surface till at last they met. The whole disk, framed in blackness, was before him. The faint percussions of the meteorites had long been audible; the window through which he was gazing was no longer definitely beneath him. His limbs, though already very light, were almost too stiff to move, and he was very hungry. He looked at his watch. He had been at his post, spell-bound, for nearly eight hours.

He made his way with difficulty to the sunward side of the ship and reeled back almost blinded with the glory of the light. Groping, he found his darkened glasses in his old cabin and got himself food and water: Weston had rationed them strictly in both. He opened the door of the control-room and looked in. Both the partners, their faces drawn with anxiety, were seated before a kind of metal table; it was covered with delicate, gently vibrating instruments in which crystal and fine wire were the predominant materials. Both ignored his presence. For the rest of the silent journey he was free of the whole ship.

When he returned to the dark side, the world they were leaving hung in the star-strewn sky not much bigger than our earthly moon. Its colours were still visible—a reddish-yellow disk blotched with greenish-blue and capped with white at the poles. He saw the two tiny Malacandrian moons—their movement quite perceptible—and reflected that they were among the thousand things he had not noticed during his sojourn there. He slept, and woke, and saw the disk still hanging in the sky. It was smaller than the Moon now. Its colours were gone except for a faint, uniform tinge of redness in its light; even the light was not now incomparably stronger than that of the countless stars which surrounded it. It had ceased to be Malacandra; it was only Mars.

He soon fell back into his old routine of sleeping and basking, punctuated with the making of some scribbled notes for his Malacandrian dictionary. He knew that there was very little chance of his being able to communicate his new knowledge to man, that unrecorded death in the depth of space would almost certainly be the end of their adventure. But already it had become impossible to think of it as "space." Some moments of cold fear he had; but each time they were shorter and more quickly swallowed up in a sense of awe which made his personal fate seem wholly insignificant. He could not feel that they were an island of life journeying through an abyss of death. He felt almost the opposite— that life was waiting outside the little iron egg-shell in which they rode, ready at any moment to break in, and that, if it killed them, it would kill them by excess of its vitality. He hoped passionately that if they were to perish they would perish by the "unbodying" of the space-ship and not by suffocation within it. To be let out, to be free, to dissolve into the ocean of eternal noon, seemed to him at certain moments a consummation even more desirable than their return to Earth. And if he had felt some such lift of the heart when first he passed through heaven on their outward journey, he felt it now tenfold, for now he was convinced that the abyss was full of life in the most literal sense, full of living creatures.

His confidence in Oyarsa's words about the *eldila* increased rather than diminished as they went on. He saw none of them; the intensity of light in which the ship swam allowed none of the fugitive variations which would have betrayed their presence. But he heard, or thought he heard, all kinds of delicate sound, or vibrations akin to sound, mixed with the tinkling rain of meteorites, and often the sense of unseen presences even within the space-ship became irresistible. It was this, more than anything else, that made his own chances of life seem so unimportant. He and all his race showed small and ephemeral against a background of such immeasurable fullness. His brain reeled at the thought of the true population of the universe, the three-dimensional infinitude of their territory, and the unchronicled æons of their past; but his heart became steadier than it had ever been.

It was well for him that he had reached this frame of mind before the real hardships of their journey began. Ever since their departure from Malacandra, the thermometer had steadily risen; now it was higher than it had stood at any time on their outward journey. And it still rose. The light also increased. Under his glasses he kept his eyes habitually tight shut, opening them only for the shortest time for necessary movements. He knew that if he reached Earth it would be with permanently damaged sight. But all this was nothing to the torment of heat. All three of them were awake for twenty-four hours out of the twenty-four, enduring with dilated eyeballs, blackened lips and froth-flecked cheeks the agony of thirst. It would be madness to increase their scanty rations of water: madness even to consume air in discussing the question.

He saw well enough what was happening. In his last bid for life Weston was venturing inside the Earth's orbit, leading them nearer the Sun than man, perhaps than life, had ever been. Presumably this was unavoidable; one could not follow a retreating Earth round the rim of its own wheeling course. They must be trying to meet it—to cut across . . . it was madness! But the question did not much occupy his mind; it was not possible for long to think of anything but thirst. One thought of water; then one thought of thirst; then one thought of thinking of thirst; then of water again. And still the thermometer rose. The walls of the ship were too hot to touch. It was obvious that a crisis was approaching. In the next few hours it must kill them or get less.

It got less. There came a time when they lay exhausted and shivering in what seemed the cold, though it was still hotter than any terrestrial climate. Weston had so far succeeded; he had risked the highest temperature at which human life could theoretically survive, and they had lived through it. But they were not the same men. Hitherto Weston had slept very little even in his watches off; always, after an hour or so of uneasy rest, he had returned to his charts and to his endless, almost despairing, calculations. You could see him fighting the despair—pinning his terrified brain down, and again down, to the figures. Now he never looked at them. He even seemed careless in the control-room. Devine moved and looked like a somnambulist. Ransom lived increasingly on the dark side and for long hours he thought of nothing. Although the first great danger was past, none of them, at this time, had any serious hope of a successful issue to their journey. They had now been fifty days, without speech, in their steel shell, and the air was already very bad.

Weston was so unlike his old self that he even allowed Ransom to take his share in the navigation. Mainly by signs, but with the help of a few whispered words, he taught him all that was necessary at this stage of the journey. Apparently they were racing home—but with little chance of reaching it in time—before some sort of cosmic "trade-wind." A few rules of thumb enabled Ransom to keep the star which Weston pointed out to him in its position at the centre of the skylight, but always with his left hand on the bell to Weston's cabin.

This star was not the Earth. The days—the purely theoretical "days" which bore such a desperately practical meaning for the travellers— mounted to fifty-eight before Weston changed course, and a different luminary was in the centre. Sixty days, and it was visibly a planet. Sixty- six, and it was like a planet seen through field-glasses. Seventy and it was like nothing that Ransom had ever seen—a little dazzling disk too large for a planet and far too small for the Moon. Now that he was navigat- ing, his celestial mood was shattered. Wild, animal thirst for life, mixed with homesick longing for the free airs and the sights and smells of earth—for grass and meat and beer and tea and the human voice— awoke in him. At first his chief difficulty on watch had been to resist drowsiness; now, though the air was worse, feverish excitement kept him vigilant. Often when he came off duty he found his right arm stiff and sore; for hours he had been pressing it unconsciously against the control-board as if his puny thrust could spur the space-ship to yet greater speed.

Now they had twenty days to go. Nineteen—eighteen—and on the white terrestrial disk, now a little larger than a sixpence, he thought he could make out Australia and the southeast corner of Asia. Hour after hour, though the markings moved slowly across the disk with the Earth's diurnal revolution, the disk itself refused to grow larger. "Get on! Get on!" Ransom muttered to the ship. Now ten days were left and it was like the Moon and so bright that they could not look steadily at it. The air in their little sphere was ominously bad, but Ransom and Devine risked a whisper as they changed watches.

"We'll do it," they said. "We'll do it yet."

On the eighty-seventh day, when Ransom relieved Devine, he thought there was something wrong with the Earth. Before his watch was done, he was sure. It was no longer a true circle, but bulging a little on one side; it was almost pear-shaped. When Weston came on duty he gave one glance at the skylight, rang furiously on the bell for Devine, thrust Ransom aside, and took the navigating seat. His face was the colour of putty. He seemed to be about to do something to the controls, but as Devine entered the room he looked up and shrugged his shoulders with a gesture of despair. Then he buried his face in his hands and laid his head down on the control-board.

Ransom and Devine exchanged glances. They bundled Weston out of the seat—he was crying like a child—and Devine took his place. And now at last Ransom understood the mystery of the bulging Earth. What had appeared as a bulge on one side of her disk was becoming increasingly distinct as a second disk, a disk almost as large in appearance as her own. It was covering more than half of the Earth. It was the Moon—between them and the Earth, and two hundred and forty thousand miles nearer. Ransom did not know what fate this might mean for the space-ship. Devine obviously did, and never had he appeared so admirable. His face was as pale as Weston's, but his eyes were clear and preternaturally bright; he sat crouched over the controls like an animal about to spring and he was whistling very softly between his teeth.

Hours later Ransom understood what was happening. The Moon's disk was now larger than the Earth's and very gradually it became apparent to him that both disks were diminishing in size. The space-ship was no longer approaching either the Earth or the Moon; it was farther away from them than it had been half an hour ago, and that was the meaning of Devine's feverish activity with the controls. It was not merely that the Moon was crossing their path and cutting them off from the Earth; apparently for some reason—probably gravitational—it was dangerous to get too close to the Moon, and Devine was standing off into space. In sight of harbour they were being forced to turn back to the open sea. He glanced up at the chronometer. It was the morning of the eighty-eighth day. Two days to make the Earth, and they were moving away from her.

"I suppose this finishes us?" he whispered.

"Expect so," whispered Devine, without looking round.

Weston presently recovered sufficiently to come back and stand beside Devine. There was nothing for Ransom to do. He was sure now, that they were soon to die. With this realization, the agony of his suspense suddenly disappeared. Death, whether it came now or some thirty years later on Earth, rose up and claimed his attention. There were preparations a man likes to make. He left the control-room and returned into one of the sunward chambers, into the indifference of the moveless light, the warmth, the silence and the sharp-cut shadows. Nothing was farther from his mind than sleep. It must have been the exhausted atmosphere which made him drowsy. He slept.

He awoke in almost complete darkness in the midst of a loud continuous noise, which he could not at first identify. It reminded him of something—something he seemed to have heard in a previous existence. It was a prolonged drumming noise close above his head. Suddenly his heart gave a great leap.

"Oh God," he sobbed. "Oh God! It's *rain*."

He was on Earth. The air was heavy and stale about him, but the choking sensations he had been suffering were gone. He realized that he was still in the space-ship. The others, in fear of its threatened "unbodying," had characteristically abandoned it the moment it touched Earth and left him to his fate. It was difficult in the dark, and under the crushing weight of terrestrial gravity, to find his way out. But he managed it. He found the manhole and slithered, drinking great draughts of air, down the outside of the sphere; slipped in mud, blessed the smell of it, and at last raised the unaccustomed weight of his body to its feet. He stood in pitch-black night under torrential rain. With every pore of his body he drank it in; with every desire of his heart he embraced the smell of the field about him—a patch of his native planet where grass grew, where cows moved, where presently he would come to hedges and a gate.

He had walked about half an hour when a vivid light behind him and a strong, momentary wind informed him that the space-ship was no more. He felt very little interest. He had seen dim lights, the lights of men, ahead. He contrived to get into a lane, then into a road, then into a village street. A lighted door was open. There were voices from within and they were speaking English. There was a familiar smell. He pushed his way in, regardless of the surprise he was creating, and walked to the bar.

"A pint of bitter, please," said Ransom.

22

At this point, if I were guided by purely literary considerations, my story would end, but it is time to remove the mask and to acquaint the reader with the real and practical purpose for which this book has been written. At the same time he will learn how the writing of it became possible at all.

Dr. Ransom—and at this stage it will become obvious that that is not his real name—soon abandoned the idea of his Malacandrian dictionary and indeed all idea of communicating his story to the world. He was ill for several months, and when he recovered be found himself in considerable doubt as to whether what he remembered had really occured. It looked very like a delusion produced by his illness, and most of his apparent adventures could, he saw, be explained psychoanalytically. He did not lean very heavily on this fact himself, for he had long since observed that a good many "real" things in the fauna and flora of our own world could be accounted for in the same way if you started with the assumption that they were illusions. But he felt that if he himself half doubted his own story the rest of the world would disbelieve it completely. He decided to hold his tongue, and there the matter would have rested but for a very curious coincidence.

This is where I come into the story. I had known Dr. Ransom slightly for several years and corresponded with him on literary and philological subjects, though we very seldom met. It was, therefore, quite in the usual order of things that I should write him a letter some months ago, of which I will quote the relevant paragraph. It ran like this:

"I am now working at the Platonists of the twelfth century and incidentally discovering that they wrote damnably difficult Latin. In one of them, Bernardus Silvestris, there is a word I should particularly like your views on—the word *Oyarses*. It occurs in the description of a voyage through the heavens, and an *Oyarses* seems to be the 'intelligence" or tutelary spirit of a heavenly sphere, i. e. in our language, of a planet. I asked C. J. about it and he says it ought to be *Ousiarches*. That, of course, would make sense, but I do not feel quite satisfied. Have you by any chance ever come across a word like *Oyarses,* or can you hazard any guess as to what language it may be?"

The immediate result of this letter was an invitation to spend a week-end with Dr. Ransom. He told me his whole story, and since then he and I have been almost continuously at work on the mystery. A good many facts, which I have no intention of publishing at present, have fallen into our hands; facts about planets in general and about Mars in particular, facts about mediæval Platonists, and (not least in importance) facts about the Professor to whom I am giving the fictitious name of Weston. A systematic report of these facts might, of course, be given to the civilized world: but that would almost certainly result in universal incredulity and in a libel action from "Weston." At the same time, we both feel that we cannot be silent. We are being daily confirmed in our belief that the *oyarses* of Mars was right when it said that the present "celestial year" was to be a revolutionary one, that the long isolation of our own planet is nearing its end, and that great doings are on foot. We have found reason to believe that the mediæval Platonists were living in the same celestial year as ourselves—in fact, that it began in the twelfth century of our era—and that the occurrence of the name Oyarsa (Latinized as *oyarses*) in Bernardus Silvestris is not an accident. And we have also evidence—increasing almost daily—that "Weston," or the force or forces behind "Weston," will play a very important part in the events of the next few centuries, and, unless we prevent them, a very disastrous one. We do not mean that they are likely to invade Mars—our cry is not merely "Hands off Malacandra."

The dangers to be feared are not planetary but cosmic, or at least solar, and they are not temporal but eternal. More than this it would be unwise to say.

It was Dr. Ransom who first saw that our only chance was to publish in the form of *fiction* what would certainly not be listened to as fact. He even thought—greatly overrating my literary powers—that this might have the incidental advantage of reaching a wider public, and that, certainly, it would reach a great many people sooner than "Weston." To my objection that if accepted as fiction it would for that very reason be regarded as false, he replied that there would be indications enough in the narrative for the few readers—the very few—who at *present* were prepared to go further into the matter.

"And they," he said, "will easily find out you, or me, and will easily identify Weston. Anyway," he continued, "what we need for the moment is not so much a body of belief as a body of people familiarized with certain ideas. If we could even effect in one per cent of our readers a change-over from the conception of Space to the conception of Heaven, we should have made a beginning."

What neither of us foresaw was the rapid march of events which was to render the book out of date before it was published. These events have already made it rather a prologue to our story than the story itself. But we must let it go as it stands. For the later stages of the adventure—well, it was Aristotle, long before Kipling, who taught us the formula, "That is another story."

POSTSCRIPT

*(Being extracts from a letter written by the original
"Dr. Ransom" to the author.)*

. . . I think you are right, and after the two or three corrections (marked in red) the MS. will have to stand. I won't deny that I am disappointed, but then any attempt to tell such a story is bound to disappoint the man who has really been there. I am not now referring to the ruthless way in which you have cut down all the philological part, though, as it stands, we are giving our readers a mere caricature of the Malacandrian language. I mean something more difficult—something which I couldn't possibly express. How can one "get across" the Malacandrian *smells?* Nothing comes back to me more vividly in my dreams . . . especially the early morning smell in those purple woods, where the very mention of "early morning" and "woods" is misleading because it must set you thinking of earth and moss and cobwebs and the smell of our planet, but I'm thinking of something totally different. More "aromatic" . . . yes, but then it is not hot or luxurious or exotic as that word suggests. Something aromatic, spicy, yet very cold, very thin, tingling at the back of the nose—something that did to the sense of smell what high, sharp violin notes do to the ear. And mixed with that I always hear the sound of the singing—great hollow hound-like music from enormous throats, deeper than Chaliapin, a "warm, dark noise." I am homesick for my old Mala-candrian valley when I think of it; yet God knows when I heard it there I was homesick enough for the Earth.

Of course you are right; if we are to treat it as a story you *must* tele-scope the time I spent in the village during which "nothing happened." But I grudge it. Those quiet weeks, the mere living among the *hrossa*, are to me the main thing that happened. I *know* them, Lewis; that's what you can't get into a mere story. For instance, because I always take a thermometer with me on a holiday (it has saved many a one from being spoiled) I know that the normal temperature of a *hross* is 103°. I know—though I can't remember learning it—that they live about 80 Martian years, or 160 earth years; that they marry at about 20 (=40); that their droppings, like those of the horse, are not offensive to them-selves, or to me, and are used for agriculture; that they don't shed tears, or blink; that they do get (as you would say) "elevated" but not drunk on a gaudy night—of which they have many. But what can one do with these scraps of information? I merely analyse them out of a whole living memory that can never be put into words, and no one in this world will be able to build up from such scraps quite the right picture. For exam-ple, can I make even you understand how I know, beyond all question, why it is that the Malacandrians don't keep pets and, in general, don't feel about their "lower animals" as we do about ours? Naturally it is the sort of thing they themselves could never have told me. One just sees why when one sees the three species together. Each of them is to the oth-ers *both* what a man is to us *and* what an animal is to us. They can talk to each other, they can cooperate, they have the same ethics; to that extent a *sorn* and a *hross* meet like two men. But then each finds the other different, funny, attractive as an animal is attractive. Some instinct starved in us, which we try to soothe by treating irrational creatures almost as if they were rational, is really satisfied in Malacandra. They don't need pets.

By the way, while we are on the subject of species, I am rather sorry that the exigencies of the story have been allowed to simplify the biology so much. Did I give you the impression that each of the three species was perfectly homogeneous? If so, I misled you. Take the *hrossa;* my friends were black *hrossa,* but there are also silver *hrossa,* and in some of the western *handramits* one finds the great crested *hross*—ten feet high, a dancer rather than a singer, and the noblest animal, after man, that I have ever seen. Only the males have the crest. I also saw a pure white *hross* at Meldilorn, but like a fool I never found out whether he represented a sub-species or was a mere freak like our terrestrial *albino*. There is at least one other kind of *sorn* besides the kind I saw—the *soroborn* or red *sorn* of the desert, who lives in the sandy north. He's a corker by all accounts.

I agree, it is a pity I never saw the *pfifltriggi* at home. I know nearly enough about them to "fake" a visit to them as an episode in the story, but I don't think we ought to introduce any mere fiction. "True in substance" sounds all very well on earth, but I can't imagine myself explaining it to Oyarsa, and I have a shrewd suspicion (see my last letter) that I have not heard the end of *him*. Anyway, why should our "readers" (you seem to know the devil of a lot about them!), who are so determined to hear nothing about the language, be so anxious to know more of the *pfifltriggi*? But if you can work it in, there is, of course, no harm in explaining that they are oviparous and matriarchal, and short-lived compared with the other species. It is pretty plain that the great depressions which they inhabit are the old ocean-beds of Malacandra. *Hrossa,* who had visited them, described themselves as going down into deep forests over sand, "the bone-stones (fossils) of ancient wave-borers about them." No doubt these are the dark patches seen on the Martian disk from Earth. And that reminds me—the "maps" of Mars which I have consulted since I got back are so inconsistent with one another that I have given up the attempt to identify my own *handramit*. If you want to try your hand, the desideratum is "a roughly north-east and south-west 'canal" cutting a north and south 'canal" not more than twenty miles from the equator." But astronomers differ very much as to what they can see.

Now as to your most annoying question: "Did Augray, in describing the *eldila*, confuse the ideas of a subtler body and a superior being?" No. The confusion is entirely your own. He said two things: that the *eldila* had bodies different from those of planetary animals, and that they were superior in intelligence. Neither he nor anyone else in Malacandra ever confused the one statement with the other or deduced the one from the other. In fact, I have reasons for thinking that there are also irrational animals with the *eldil* type of body (you remember Chaucer's "airish beasts"?).

I wonder are you wise to say nothing about the problem of *eldil* speech? I agree that it would spoil the narrative to raise the question during the trial-scene at Meldilorn, but surely many readers will have enough sense to ask how the *eldila,* who obviously don't breathe, can talk. It is true that we should have to admit we don't know, but oughtn't the readers to be told that? I suggested to J.—the only scientist here who is in my confidence—your theory that they might have instruments, or even organs, for manipulating the air around them and thus producing sounds indirectly, but he didn't seem to think much of it. He thought it probable that they directly manipulated the ears of those they were "speaking" to. That sounds pretty difficult . . . of course one must remember that we have really no knowledge of the shape or size of an *eldil,* or even of its relations to space (*our* space) in general. In fact, one wants to keep on insisting that we really know next to nothing about them. Like you, I can't help trying to fix their relation to the things that appear in terrestrial tradition—gods, angels, fairies. But we haven't the data. When I attempted to give Oyarsa some idea of our own Christian angelology, he certainly seemed to regard our "angels" as different in some way from himself. But whether he meant that they were a different species, or only that they were some special military caste (since our poor old earth turns out to be a kind of Ypres Salient in the universe), I don't know.

Why must you leave out my account of how the shutter jammed just before our landing on Malacandra? Without this, your description of our sufferings from excessive light on the return journey raises the very obvious question, "Why didn't they close their shutters?" I don't believe your theory that "readers never notice that sort of thing." I'm sure I should.

There are two scenes that I wish you could have worked into the book; no matter—they are worked into me. One or other of them is always before me when I close my eyes.

In one of them I see the Malacandrian sky at morning; pale blue, so pale that now, when I have grown once more accustomed to terrestrial skies, I think of it as almost white. Against it the nearer tops of the giant weeds—the "trees" as you call them—show black, but far away, across miles of that blinding blue water, the remoter woods are water-colour purple. The shadows all around me on the pale forest floor are like shadows on snow. There are figures walking before me; slender yet gigantic forms, black and sleek as animated tall hats; their huge round heads, poised on their sinuous stalk-like bodies, give them the appearance of black tulips. They go down, singing, to the edge of the lake. The music fills the wood with its vibration, though it is so soft that I can hardly hear it: it is like dim organ music. Some of them embark, but most remain. It is done slowly; this is no ordinary embarkation, but some ceremony. It is, in fact, a *hross* funeral. Those three with the grey muzzles whom they have helped into the boat are going to Meldilorn to die. For in that world, except for some few whom the *hnakra* gets, no one dies before his time. All live out the full span allotted to their kind, and a death with them is as predictable as a birth with us. The whole village has known that those three will die this year, this month; it was an easy guess that they would die even this week. And now they are off, to receive the last counsel of Oyarsa, to die, and to be by him "unbodied." The corpses, as corpses, will exist only for a few minutes: there are no coffins in Malacandra, no sextons, churchyards, or undertakers. The valley is solemn at their departure, but I see no signs of passionate grief. They do not doubt their immortality, and friends of the same generation are not torn apart. You leave the world, as you entered it, with the "men of your own year." Death is not preceded by dread nor followed by corruption.

The other scene is a nocturne. I see myself bathing with Hyoi in the warm lake. He laughs at my clumsy swimming; accustomed to a heavier world, I can hardly get enough of me under the water to make any headway. And then I see the night sky. The greater part of it is very like ours, though the depths are blacker and the stars brighter; but something that no terrestrial analogy will enable you fully to picture is happening in the west. Imagine the Milky Way magnified—the Milky Way seen through our largest telescope on the clearest night. And then imagine this, not painted across the zenith, but rising like a constellation behind the mountain-tops—a dazzling necklace of lights brilliant as planets, slowly heaving itself up till it fills a fifth of the sky and now leaves a belt of blackness between itself and the horizon. It is too bright to look at for long, but it is only a preparation. Something else is coming. There is a glow like moonrise on the *harandra*. *Ahihra!* cries Hyoi, and other baying voices answer him from the darkness all about us. And now the true king of night is set up, and now he is threading his way through that strange western galaxy and making its lights dim by comparison with his own. I turn my eyes away, for the little disk is far brighter than the Moon in her greatest splendour. The whole *handramit* is bathed in colourless light; I could count the stems of the forest on the far side of the lake; I see that my fingernails are broken and dirty. And now I guess what it is that I have seen—Jupiter rising beyond the Asteroids and forty million miles nearer than he has ever been to earthly eyes. But the Malacandrians would say "within the Asteroids," for they have an odd habit, sometimes, of turning the solar system inside out. They call the Asteroids the "dancers before the threshold of the Great Worlds." The Great Worlds are the planets, as we should say, "beyond" or "outside" the Asteroids. Glundandra (Jupiter) is the greatest of these and has some importance in Malacandrian thought which I cannot fathom. He is "the centre," "great Meldilorn," "throne" and "feast." They are, of course, well aware that he is uninhabitable, at least by animals of the planetary type; and they certainly have no pagan idea of giving a local habitation to Maleldil. But somebody or something of great importance is connected with Jupiter; as usual "The *séroni* would know." But they never told me. Perhaps the best comment is in the author whom I mentioned to you: "For as it was well said of the great Africanus that he was never less alone than when alone, so, in our philosophy, no parts of this universal frame are less to be called solitarie than those which the vulgar esteem most solitarie, since the withdrawing of men and beasts signifieth but the greater frequency of more excellent creatures."

More of this when you come. I am trying to read every old book on the subject that I can hear of. Now that "Weston" has shut the door, the way to the planets lies through the past; if there is to be any more space-travelling, it will have to be time-travelling as well . . . !

By C. S. Lewis

The Abolition of Man

Mere Christianity

The Great Divorce

The Problem of Pain

The Weight of Glory and Other Addresses

The Screwtape Letters (with "Screwtape Proposes a Toast")

Miracles

The Case for Christianity

The Lion, the Witch and the Wardrobe

Prince Caspian

The Voyage of the Dawn Treader

The Silver Chair

The Magician's Nephew

The Horse and His Boy

The Last Battle

Perelandra

That Hideous Strength

Out of the Silent Planet

The Joyful Christian

George Macdonald: An Anthology

C. S. Lewis: Letters to Children

C. S. Lewis

—

PERELANDRA

A Novel

SCRIBNER

NEW YORK   LONDON   TORONTO   SYDNEY   NEW DELHI

SCRIBNER
1230 Avenue of the Americas
New York, NY 10020

First Scribner trade paperback edition 2003
SCRIBNER and design are trademarks
of Macmillan Library reference USA, Inc., used under license
by Simon & Schuster, the publisher of this work.

For information about special discounts for bulk purchases,
please contact Simon & Schuster Special Sales:
1-800-456-6798 or business@simonandschuster.com

Designed by Brooke Koven
Set in Sabon

Manufactured in the United States of America

15 17 19 20 18 16

Library of Congress Cataloging-in-Publication Data is available.

ISBN-13: 978-0-684-83365-1
ISBN-10:   0-684-83365-4
ISBN-13: 978-0-7432-3491-7 (Pbk)
ISBN-10:   0-7432-3491-X (Pbk)

To Some Ladies *at* Wantage

PREFACE

This story can be read by itself but is also a sequel to *Out of the Silent Planet* in which some account was given of Ransom's adventures in Mars—or, as its inhabitants call it, *Malacandra*. All the human characters in this book are purely fictitious and none of them is allegorical.

C.S.L.

I

As I left the railway station at Worcester and set out on the three-mile walk to Ransom's cottage, I reflected that no one on that platform could possibly guess the truth about the man I was going to visit. The flat heath which spread out before me (for the village lies all behind and to the north of the station) looked an ordinary heath. The gloomy five-o'clock sky was such as you might see on any autumn afternoon. The few houses and the clumps of red or yellowish trees were in no way remarkable. Who could imagine that a little farther on in that quiet landscape I should meet and shake by the hand a man who had lived and eaten and drunk in a world forty million miles distant from London, who had seen this Earth from where it looks like a mere point of green fire, and who had spoken face to face with a creature whose life began before our own planet was inhabitable?

For Ransom had met other things in Mars besides the Martians. He had met the creatures called *eldila,* and specially that great eldil who is the ruler of Mars or, in their speech, the *Oyarsa* of *Malacandra.* The eldila are very different from any planetary creatures. Their physical organism, if organism it can be called, is quite unlike either the human or the Martian. They do not eat, breed, breathe, or suffer natural death, and to that extent resemble thinking minerals more than they resemble anything we should recognise as an animal. Though they appear on planets and may even seem to our senses to be sometimes resident in them, the precise spatial location of an eldil at any moment presents great problems. They themselves regard space (or "Deep Heaven") as their true habitat, and the planets are to them not closed worlds but merely moving points—perhaps even interruptions—in what we know as the Solar System and they as the Field of Arbol.

At present I was going to see Ransom in answer to a wire which had said "Come down Thursday if possible. Business." I guessed what sort of business he meant, and that was why I kept on telling myself that it would be perfectly delightful to spend a night with Ransom and also kept on feeling that I was not enjoying the prospect as much as I ought to. It was the eldila that were my trouble. I could just get used to the fact that Ransom had been to Mars . . . but to have met an eldil, to have spoken with something whose life appeared to be practically unending. . . . Even the journey to Mars was bad enough. A man who has been in another world does not come back unchanged. One can't put the difference into words. When the man is a friend it may become painful: the old footing is not easy to recover. But much worse my growing conviction that, since his return, the eldila were not leaving him alone. Little things in his conversation, little mannerisms, accidental allusions which he made and then drew back with an awkward apology, all suggested that he was keeping strange company; that there were—well, Visitors—at that cottage.

As I plodded along the empty, unfenced road which runs across the middle of Worchester Common I tried to dispel my growing sense of *malaise* by analysing it. What, after all, was I afraid of? The moment I had put this question I regretted it. I was shocked to find that I had mentally used the word "afraid." Up till then I had tried to pretend that I was feeling only distaste, or embarrassment, or even boredom. But the mere word *afraid* had let the cat out of the bag. I realised now that my emotion was neither more, nor less, nor other, than Fear. And I realised that I was afraid of two things—afraid that sooner or later I myself might meet an eldil, and afraid that I might get "drawn in." I suppose every one knows this fear of getting "drawn in"—the moment at which a man realises that what had seemed mere speculations are on the point of landing him in the Communist Party or the Christian Church—the sense that a door has just slammed and left him on the inside. The thing was such sheer bad luck. Ransom himself had been taken to Mars (or Malacandra) against his will and almost by accident, and I had become connected with his affair by another accident. Yet here we were both getting more and more involved in what I could only describe as interplanetary politics. As to my intense wish never to come into contact with the eldila myself, I am not sure whether I can make you understand it. It was something more than a prudent desire to avoid creatures alien in kind, very powerful, and very intelligent. The truth was that all I heard about them served to connect two things which one's mind tends to keep separate, and that connecting gave one a sort of shock. We tend to think about non-human intelligences in two distinct categories which we label "scientific" and "supernatural" respectively. We think, in one mood, of Mr. Wells' Martians (very unlike the real Malacandrians, by the bye), or his Selenites. In quite a different mood we let our minds loose on the possibility of angels, ghosts, fairies, and the like. But the very moment we are compelled to recognise a creature in either class as *real* the distinction begins to get blurred: and when it is a creature like an eldil the distinction vanishes altogether. These things were not animals—to that extent one had to classify them with the second group; but they had some kind of material vehicle whose presence could (in principle) be scientifically verified. To that extent they belonged to the first group. The distinction between natural and supernatural, in fact, broke down; and when it had done so, one realised how great a comfort it had been—how it had eased the burden of intolerable strangeness which this universe imposes on us by dividing it into two halves and encouraging the mind never to think of both in the same context. What price we may have paid for this comfort in the way of false security and accepted confusion of thought is another matter.

"This is a long, dreary road," I thought to myself. "Thank goodness I haven't anything to carry." And then, with a start of realisation, I remembered that I ought to be carrying a pack, containing my things for the night. I swore to myself. I must have left the thing in the train. Will you believe me when I say that my immediate impulse was to turn back to the station and "do something about it"? Of course there was nothing to be done which could not equally well be done by ringing up from the cottage. That train, with my pack in it, must by this time be miles away.

I realise that now as clearly as you do. But at the moment it seemed perfectly obvious that I must retrace my steps, and I had indeed begun to do so before reason or conscience awoke and set me once more plodding forwards. In doing this I discovered more clearly than before how very little I wanted to do it. It was such hard work that I felt as if I were walking against a headwind; but in fact it was one of those still, dead evenings when no twig stirs, and beginning to be a little foggy.

The farther I went the more impossible I found it to think about anything except these eldila. What, after all, did Ransom really know about them? By his own account the sorts which he had met did not usually visit our own planet—or had only begun to do so since his return from Mars. We had eldila of our own, he said, Tellurian eldils, but they were of a different kind and mostly hostile to man. That, in fact, was why our world was cut off from communication with the other planets. He described us as being in a state of siege, as being, in fact, an enemy-occupied territory, held down by eldils who were at war both with us and with the eldils of "Deep Heaven," or "space." Like the bacteria on the microscopic level, so these co-inhabiting pests on the macroscopic permeate our whole life invisibly and are the real explanation of that fatal bent which is the main lesson of history. If all this were true, then, of course, we should welcome the fact that eldila of a better kind had at last broken the frontier (it is, they say, at the Moon's orbit) and were beginning to visit us. Always assuming that Ransom's account was the correct one.

A nasty idea occurred to me. Why should not Ransom be a dupe? If something from outer space were trying to invade our planet, what better smoke-screen could it put up than this very story of Ransom's? Was there the slightest evidence, after all, for the existence of the supposed maleficent eldils on this earth? How if my friend were the unwitting bridge, the Trojan Horse, whereby some possible invader were effecting its landing on Tellus? And then once more, just as when I had discovered that I had no pack, the impulse to go no farther returned to me. "Go back, go back," it whispered to me, "send him a wire, tell him you were ill, say you'll come some other time—anything." The strength of the feeling astonished me. I stood still for a few moments telling myself not to be a fool, and when I finally resumed my walk I was wondering whether this might be the beginning of a nervous breakdown. No sooner had this idea occurred to me than it also became a new reason for not visiting Ransom. Obviously, I wasn't fit for any such jumpy "business" as his telegram almost certainly referred to. I wasn't even fit to spend an ordinary week-end away from home. My only sensible course was to turn back at once and get safe home, before I lost my memory or became hysterical, and to put myself in the hands of a doctor. It was sheer madness to go on.

I was now coming to the end of the heath and going down a small hill, with a copse on my left and some apparently deserted industrial buildings on my right. At the bottom the evening mist was partly thick. "They call it a breakdown *at first*," I thought. Wasn't there some mental disease in which quite ordinary objects looked to the patient unbelievably ominous? . . . looked, in fact, just as that abandoned factory looks to me now? Great bulbous shapes of cement, strange brickwork bogeys, glowered at me over dry scrubby grass pock-marked with grey pools and intersected with the remains of a light railway. I was reminded of things which Ransom had seen in that other world: only there, they were people. Long spindle-like giants whom he called Sorns. What made it worse was that he regarded them as good people—very much nicer, in fact, than our own race. He was in league with them! How did I know he was even a dupe? He might be something worse . . . and again I came to a standstill.

The reader, not knowing Ransom, will not understand how contrary to all reason this idea was. The rational part of my mind, even at that moment, knew perfectly well that even if the whole universe were crazy and hostile, Ransom was sane and wholesome and honest. And this part of my mind in the end sent me forward—but with a reluctance and a difficulty I can hardly put into words. What enabled me to go on was the knowledge (deep down inside me) that I was getting nearer at every stride to the one friend: but I *felt* that I was getting nearer to the one enemy—the traitor, the sorcerer, the man in league with "them" . . . walking into the trap with my eyes open, like a fool. "They call it a breakdown at first," said my mind, "and send you to a nursing home; later on they move you to an asylum."

I was past the dead factory now, down in the fog, where it was very cold. Then came a moment—the first one—of absolute terror and I had to bite my lips to keep myself from screaming. It was only a cat that had run across the road, but I found myself completely unnerved. "Soon you will really be screaming," said my inner tormentor, "running round and round, screaming, and you won't be able to stop it."

There was a little empty house by the side of the road, with most of the windows boarded up and one staring like the eye of a dead fish. Please understand that at ordinary times the idea of a "haunted house" means no more to me than it does to you. No more; but also, no less. At that moment it was nothing so definite as the thought of a ghost that came to me. It was just the *word* "haunted." "Haunted" . . . "haunting" . . . what a quality there is in that first syllable! Would not a child who had never heard the word before and did not know its meaning shudder at the mere sound if, as the day was closing in, it heard one of its elders say to another "This house is haunted"?

At last I came to the cross-roads by the little Wesleyan chapel where I had to turn to the left under the beech trees. I ought to be seeing the lights from Ransom's windows by now—or was it past black-out time? My watch had stopped, and I didn't know. It was dark enough but that might be due to the fog and the trees. It wasn't the dark I was afraid of, you understand. We have all known times when inanimate objects seemed to have almost a facial expression, and it was the expression of this bit of road which I did not like. "It's not true," said my mind, "that people who are really going mad never think they're going mad." Suppose that real insanity had chosen this place in which to begin? In that case, of course, the black enmity of those dripping trees—their horrible expectancy—would be a hallucination. But that did not make it any better. To think that the spectre you see is an illusion does not rob him of his terrors: it simply adds the further terror of madness itself—and then on top of that the horrible surmise that those whom the rest call mad have, all along, been the only people who see the world as it really is.

This was upon me now. I staggered on into the cold and the darkness, already half convinced that I must be entering what is called Madness. But each moment my opinion about sanity changed. Had it ever been more than a convention—a comfortable set of blinkers, an agreed mode of wishful thinking, which excluded from our view the full strangeness and malevolence of the universe we are compelled to inhabit? The things I had begun to know during the last few months of my acquaintance with Ransom already amounted to more than "sanity" would admit; but I had come much too far to dismiss them as unreal. I doubted his interpretation, or his good faith. I did not doubt the existence of the things he had met in Mars—the Pfifltriggi, the Hrossa, and the Sorns—nor of these interplanetary eldila. I did not even doubt the reality of that mysterious being whom the eldila call Maleldil and to whom they appear to give a total obedience such as no Tellurian dictator can command. I knew what Ransom supposed Maleldil to be.

Surely that was the cottage. It was very well blacked-out. A childish, whining thought arose on my mind: why was he not out at the gate to welcome me? An even more childish thought followed it. Perhaps he *was* in the garden waiting for me, hiding. Perhaps he would jump on me from behind. Perhaps I should see a figure that looked like Ransom standing with its back to me and when I spoke to it, it would turn round and show a face that was not human at all. . . .

I have naturally no wish to enlarge on this phase of my story. The state of mind I was in was one which I look back on with humiliation. I would have passed it over if I did not think that some account of it was necessary for a full understanding of what follows—and, perhaps, of some other things as well. At all events, I *can't* really describe how I reached the front door of the cottage. Somehow or other, despite the loathing and dismay that pulled me back and a sort of invisible wall of resistance that met me in the face, fighting for each step, and almost shrieking as a harmless spray of the hedge touched my face, I managed to get through the gate and up the little path. And there I was, drumming on the door and wringing the handle and shouting to him to let me in as if my life depended on it.

There was no reply—not a sound except the echo of the sounds I had been making myself. There was only something white fluttering on the knocker. I guessed, of course, that it was a note. In striking a match to read it by, I discovered how very shaky my hands had become; and when the match went out I realised how dark the evening had grown. After several attempts I read the thing. "Sorry. Had to go up to Cambridge. Shan't be back till the late train. Eatables in larder and bed made up in your usual room. Don't wait supper for me unless you feel like it— E. R." And immediately the impulse to retreat, which had already assailed me several times, leaped upon me with a sort of demoniac violence. Here was my retreat left open, positively inviting me. Now was my chance. If anyone expected me to go into that house and sit there alone for several hours, they were mistaken! But then, as the thought of the return journey began to take shape in my mind, I faltered. The idea of setting out to traverse the avenue of beech trees again (it was really dark now) with this house behind me (one had the absurd feeling that it could follow one) was not attractive. And then, I hope, something better came into my mind—some rag of sanity and some reluctance to let Ransom down. At least I could try the door to see if it were really unlocked. I did. And it was. Next moment, I hardly know how, I found myself inside and let it slam behind me.

It was quite dark, and warm. I groped a few paces forward, hit my shin violently against something, and fell. I sat still for a few seconds nursing my leg. I thought I knew the layout of Ransom's hall-sitting-room pretty well and couldn't imagine what I had blundered into. Presently I groped in my pocket, got out my matches, and tried to strike a light. The head of the match flew off. I stamped on it and sniffed to make sure it was not smouldering on the carpet. As soon as I sniffed I became aware of a strange smell in the room. I could not for the life of me make out what it was. It had an unlikeness to ordinary domestic smells as great as that of some chemicals, but it was not a chemical kind of smell at all. Then I struck another match. It flickered and went out almost at once—not unnaturally, since I was sitting on the door-mat and there are few front doors even in better built houses than Ransom's country cottage which do not admit a draught. I had seen nothing by it except the palm of my own hand hollowed in an attempt to guard the flame. Obviously I must get away from the door. I rose gingerly and felt my way forward. I came at once to an obstacle—something smooth and very cold that rose a little higher than my knees. As I touched it I realised that it was the source of the smell. I groped my way along this to the left and finally came to the end of it. It seemed to present several surfaces and I couldn't picture the shape. It was not a table, for it had no top. One's hand groped along the rim of a kind of low wall—the thumb on the outside and the fingers down inside the enclosed space. If it had felt like wood I should have supposed it to be a large packing-case. But it was not wood. I thought for a moment that it was wet, but soon decided that I was mistaking coldness for moisture. When I reached the end of it I struck my third match.

I saw something white and semi-transparent—rather like ice. A great big thing, very long: a kind of box, an open box: and of a disquieting shape which I did not immediately recognise. It was big enough to put a man into. Then I took a step back, lifting the lighted match higher to get a more comprehensive view, and instantly tripped over something behind me. I found myself sprawling in darkness, not on the carpet, but on more of the cold substance with the odd smell. How many of the infernal things were there?

I was just preparing to rise again and hunt systematically round the room for a candle when I heard Ransom's name pronounced; and almost, but not quite, simultaneously I saw the thing I had feared so long to see. I heard Ransom's name pronounced: but I should not like to say I heard a voice pronounce it. The sound was quite astonishingly unlike a voice. It was perfectly articulate: it was even, I suppose, rather beautiful. But it was, if you understand me, inorganic. We feel the difference between animal voices (including those of the human animal) and all other noises pretty clearly, I fancy, though it is hard to define. Blood and lungs and the warm, moist cavity of the mouth are somehow indicated in every Voice. Here they were not. The two syllables sounded more as if they were played on an instrument than as if they were spoken: and yet they did not sound mechanical either. A machine is something we make out of natural materials; this was more as if rock or crystal or light had spoken of itself. And it went through me from chest to groin like the thrill that goes through you when you think you have lost your hold while climbing a cliff.

That was what I heard. What I saw was simply a very faint rod or pillar of light. I don't think it made a circle of light either on the floor or the ceiling, but I am not sure of this. It certainly had very little power of illuminating its surroundings. So far, all is plain sailing. But it had two other characteristics which are less easy to grasp. One was its colour. Since I saw the thing I must obviously have seen it either white or coloured; but no efforts of my memory can conjure up the faintest image of what that colour was. I try blue, and gold, and violet, and red, but none of them will fit. How it is possible to have a visual experience which immediately and ever after becomes impossible to remember, I do not attempt to explain. The other was its angle. It was not at right angles to the floor. But as soon as I have said this, I hasten to add that this way of putting it is a later reconstruction. What one actually felt at the moment was that the column of light was vertical but the floor was not horizontal—the whole room seemed to have heeled over as if it were on board ship. The impression, however produced, was that this creature had reference to some horizontal, to some whole system of directions, based outside the Earth, and that its mere presence imposed that alien system on me and abolished the terrestrial horizontal.

I had no doubt at all that I was seeing an eldil, and little doubt that I was seeing the archon of Mars, the Oyarsa of Malacandra. And now that the thing had happened I was no longer in a condition of abject panic. My sensations were, it is true, in some ways very unpleasant. The fact that it was quite obviously not organic—the knowledge that intelligence was somehow located in this homogeneous cylinder of light but not related to it as our consciousness is related to our brains and nerves—was profoundly disturbing.[1] It would not fit into our categories. The response which we ordinarily make to a living creature and that which we make to an inanimate object were here both equally inappropriate. On the other hand, all those doubts which I had felt before I entered the cottage as to whether these creatures were friend or foe, and whether Ransom were a pioneer or a dupe, had for the moment vanished. My fear was now of another kind. I felt sure that the creature was what we call "good," but I wasn't sure whether I liked "goodness" so much as I had supposed. This is a very terrible experience. As long as what you are afraid of is something evil, you may still hope that the good may come to your rescue. But suppose you struggle through to the good and find that it also is dreadful? How if food itself turns out to be the very thing you can't eat, and home the very place you can't live, and your very comforter the person who makes you uncomfortable? Then, indeed, there is no rescue possible: the last card has been played. For a

1. In the text I naturally keep to what I thought and felt at the time, since this alone is first-hand evidence: but there is obviously room for much further speculation about the form in which *eldila* appear to our senses. The only serious considerations of the problem so far are to be sought in the early seventeenth century. As a starting point for future investigation I recommend the following from Natvilcius (*De Aethereo at aerio Corpore*, Basel. 1627, II. xii.); *liquet simplicem flammam sensibus nostris subjectam non esse corpus proprie dictum angeli vel daemonis, sed potius aut illius corporis sensorium aut superficiem corporis in coelesti dispositione locorum supra cogitationes humanas existentis.* ("It appears that the homogeneous flame perceived by our senses is not the body, properly so called, of an angel or daemon, but rather either the sensorium of that body or the surface of a body which exists after a manner beyond our conception in the celestial frame of special references.") By the "celestial frame of references" I take him to mean what we should now call "multi-dimensional space." Not, of course, that Natvilcius knew anything about multi-dimensional geometry, but that he had reached empirically what mathematics has since reached on theoretical grounds.

second or two I was nearly in that condition. Here at last was a bit of that world from beyond the world, which I had always supposed that I loved and desired, breaking through and appearing to my senses: and I didn't like it, I wanted it to go away. I wanted every possible distance, gulf, curtain, blanket, and barrier to be placed between it and me. But I did not fall quite into the gulf. Oddly enough my very sense of helplessness saved me and steadied me. For now I was quite obviously "drawn in." The struggle was over. The next decision did not lie with me.

Then, like a noise from a different world, came the opening of the door and the sound of boots on the door-mat, and I saw, silhouetted against the greyness of the night in the open doorway, a figure which I recognised as Ransom. The speaking which was not a voice came again out of the rod of light, and Ransom, instead of moving, stood still and answered it. Both speeches were in a strange polysyllabic language which I had not heard before. I make no attempt to excuse the feelings which awoke in me when I heard the unhuman sound addressing my friend and my friend answering it in the unhuman language. They are, in fact, inexcusable; but if you think they are improbable at such a juncture, I must tell you plainly that you have read neither history nor your own heart to much effect. They were feelings of resentment, horror, and jealousy. It was in my mind to shout out, "Leave your familiar alone, you damned magician, and attend to Me."

What I actually said was, "Oh, Ransom. Thank God you've come."

2

The door was slammed (for the second time that night) and after a moment's groping Ransom had found and lit a candle. I glanced quickly round and could see no one but ourselves. The most noticeable thing in the room was the big white object. I recognised the shape well enough this time. It was a large coffin-shaped casket, open. On the floor beside it lay its lid, and it was doubtless this that I had tripped over. Both were made of the same white material, like ice, but more cloudy and less shining.

"By Jove, I'm glad to see you," said Ransom, advancing and shaking hands with me. "I'd hoped to be able to meet you at the station, but everything has had to be arranged in such a hurry and I found at the last moment that I'd got to go up to Cambridge. I never intended to leave you to make *that* journey alone." Then, seeing, I suppose, that I was still staring at him rather stupidly, he added, "I say—you're *all right*, aren't you? You got through the barrage without any damage?"

"The barrage?—I don't understand."

"I was thinking you would have met some difficulties in getting here."

"Oh, *that!*" said I. "You mean it wasn't just my nerves? There really was something in the way?"

"Yes. They didn't want you to get here. I was afraid something of the sort might happen but there was no time to do anything about it. I was pretty sure you'd get through somehow."

"By *they* you mean the others—our own eldila?"

"Of course. They've got wind of what's on hand. . . ."

I interrupted him. "To tell you the truth, Ransom," I said, "I'm getting more worried every day about the whole business. It came into my head as I was on my way here——"

"Oh, they'll put all sorts of things into your head if you let them," said Ransom lightly. "The best plan is to take no notice and keep straight on. Don't try to answer them. They like drawing you into an interminable argument."

"But, look here," said I. "This isn't child's play. Are you quite certain that this Dark Lord, this depraved Oyarsa of Tellus, really exists? Do you know for certain either that there are two sides, or which side is ours?"

He fixed me suddenly with one of his mild, but strangely formidable, glances.

"You are in *real* doubt about either, are you?" he asked.

"No," said I, after a pause, and felt rather ashamed.

"That's all right, then," said Ransom cheerfully. "Now let's get some supper and I'll explain as we go along."

"What's that coffin affair?" I asked as we moved into the kitchen.

"That is what I'm to travel in."

"Ransom!" I exclaimed. "He—it—the eldil—is not going to take you back to Malacandra?"

"Don't!" said he. "Oh, Lewis, you don't understand. Take me back to Malacandra? If only he would! I'd give anything I possess . . . just to look down one of those gorges again and see the blue, blue water winding in and out among the woods. Or to be up on top—to see a Sorn go gliding along the slopes. Or to be back there of an evening when Jupiter was rising, too bright to look at, and all the asteroids like a Milky Way, with each star in it as bright as Venus looks from Earth! And the smells! It is hardly ever out of my mind. You'd expect it to be worse at night when Malacandra is up and I can actually see it. But it isn't then that I get the real twinge. It's on hot summer days—looking up at the deep blue and that thinking that *in there,* millions of miles deep where I can never, never get back to it, there's a place I know, and flowers at that very moment growing over Meldilorn, and friends of mine, going about their business, who would welcome me back. No. No such luck. It's not Malacandra I'm being sent to. It's Perelandra."

"That's what we call Venus, isn't it?"

"Yes."

"And you say you're being sent."

"Yes. If you remember, before I left Malacandra the Oyarsa hinted to me that my going there at all might be the beginning of a whole new phase in the life of the Solar System—the Field of Arbol. It might mean, he said, that the isolation of our world, the siege, was beginning to draw to an end."

"Yes. I remember."

"Well, it really does look as if something of the sort were afoot. For one thing, the two sides, as you call them, have begun to appear much more clearly, much less mixed, here on Earth, in our own human affairs—to show in something a little more like their true colours."

"I see that all right."

"The other thing is this. The black archon—our own bent Oyarsa—is meditating some sort of attack on Perelandra."

"But is he at large like that in the Solar System? Can he get there?"

"That's just the point. He can't get there in his own person, in his own photosome or whatever we should call it. As you know, he was driven back within these bounds centuries before any human life existed on our planet. If he ventured to show himself outside the Moon's orbit he'd be driven back again—by main force. That would be a different kind of war. You or I could contribute no more to it than a flea could contribute to the defence of Moscow. No. He must be attempting Perelandra in some different way."

"And where do you come in?"

"Well—simply I've been ordered there."

"By the—by Oyarsa, you mean?"

"No. The order comes from much higher up. They all do, you know, in the long run."

"And what have you got to do when you get there?"

"I haven't been told."

"You are just part of the Oyarsa's *entourage?*"

"Oh, no. He isn't going to be there. He is to transport me to Venus—to deliver me there. After that, as far as I know, I shall be alone."

"But, look here, Ransom—I mean . . ." my voice trailed away.

"I know!" said he with one of his singularly disarming smiles. "You are feeling the absurdity of it. Dr. Elwin Ransom setting out single-handed to combat powers and principalities. You may even be wondering if I've got megalomania."

"I didn't mean that quite," said I.

"Oh, but I think you did. At any rate that is what I have been feeling myself ever since that thing was sprung on me. But when you come to think of it, is it odder than what all of us have to do every day? When the Bible used that very expression about fighting with principalities and powers and depraved hypersomatic beings at great heights (our translation is very misleading at that point, by the way) it meant that quite ordinary people were to do the fighting."

"Oh, I dare say," said I. "But that's rather different. That refers to a moral conflict."

Ransom threw back his head and laughed. "Oh, Lewis, Lewis," he said, "you are inimitable, simply inimitable!"

"Say what you like, Ransom, there *is* a difference."

"Yes. There is. But not a difference that makes it megalomania to think that any of us might have to fight either way. I'll tell you how I look at it. Haven't you noticed how in our own little war here on earth, there are different phases, and while any one phase is going on people get into the habit of thinking and behaving as if it was going to be permanent? But really the thing is changing under your hands all the time, and neither your assets nor your dangers this year are the same as the year before. Now your idea that ordinary people will never have to meet the Dark Eldila in any form except a psychological or moral form—as temptations or the like—is simply an idea that held good for a certain phase of the cosmic war: the phase of the great siege, the phase which gave to our planet its name of Thulcandra, the *silent* planet. But supposing that phase is passing? In the next phase it may be anyone's job to meet them . . . well, in some quite different mode."

"I see."

"Don't imagine I've been selected to go to Perelandra because I'm anyone in particular. One never can see, or not till long afterwards, why *any* one was selected for *any* job. And when one does, it is usually some reason that leaves no room for vanity. Certainly, it is never for what the man himself would have regarded as his chief qualifications. I rather fancy I am being sent because those two blackguards who kidnapped me and took me to Malacandra, did something which they never intended: namely, gave a human being a chance to learn that language."

"What language do you mean?"

"*Hressa-Hlab*, of course. The language I learned in Malacandra."

"But surely you don't imagine they will speak the same language on Venus?"

"Didn't I tell you about that?" said Ransom, leaning forward. We were now at table and had nearly finished our cold meat and beer and tea. "I'm surprised I didn't, for I found out two or three months ago, and scientifically it is one of the most interesting things about the whole affair. It appears we were quite mistaken in thinking *Hressa-Hlab* the peculiar speech of Mars. It is really what may be called Old Solar, *Hlab-Eribol-ef-Cordi*."

"What on earth do you mean?"

"I mean that there was originally a common speech for all rational creatures inhabiting the planets of our system: those that were ever inhabited, I mean—what the eldils call the Low Worlds. Most of them, of course, have never been inhabited and never will be. At least not what we'd call inhabited. That original speech was lost on Thulcandra, our own world, when our whole tragedy took place. No human language now known in the world is descended from it."

"But what about the other two languages on Mars?"

"I admit I don't understand about them. One thing I do know, and I believe I could prove it on purely philological grounds. They are incomparably less ancient than *Hressa-Hlab,* specially *Surnibur,* the speech of the Sorns. I believe it could be shown that *Surnibur* is, by Malacandrian standards, quite a modern development. I doubt if its birth can be put further back than a date which would fall within our Cambrian Period."

"And you think you will find *Hressa-Hlab,* or Old Solar, spoken on Venus?"

"Yes. I shall arrive knowing the language. It saves a lot of trouble—though, as a philologist I find it rather disappointing."

"But you've no idea what you are to do, or what conditions you will find?"

"No idea at all what I'm to do. There are jobs, you know, where it is essential that one should *not* know too much beforehand . . . things one might have to say which one couldn't say effectively if one had prepared them. As to conditions, well, I don't know much. It will be warm: I'm to go naked. Our astronomers don't know anything about the surface of Perelandra at all. The outer layer of her atmosphere is too thick. The main problem, apparently, is whether she revolves on her own axis or not, and at what speed. There are two schools of thought. There's a man called Schiaparelli who thinks she revolves once on herself in the same time it takes her to go once round Arbol—I mean, the Sun. The other people think she revolves on her own axis once in every twenty-three hours. That's one of the things I shall find out."

"If Schiaparelli is right there'd be perpetual day on one side of her and perpetual night on the other?"

He nodded, musing. "It'd be a funny frontier," he said presently. "Just think of it. You'd come to a country of eternal twilight, getting colder and darker every mile you went. And then presently you wouldn't be able to go further because there'd be no more air. I wonder can you stand in the day, just on the right side of the frontier, and look *into* the night which you can never reach? And perhaps see a star or two—the only place you *could* see them, for of course in the Day-Lands they would never be visible. . . . Of course if they have a scientific civilisation they may have diving-suits or things like submarines on wheels for going into the Night."

His eyes sparkled, and even I who had been mainly thinking of how I should miss him and wondering what chances there were of my ever seeing him again, felt a vicarious thrill of wonder and of longing to know. Presently he spoke again.

"You haven't yet asked me where *you* come in," he said.

"Do you mean I'm to go too?" said I, with a thrill of exactly the opposite kind.

"Not at all. I mean you are to pack me up, and to stand by to unpack me when I return—if all goes well."

"Pack you? Oh, I'd forgotten about that coffin affair. Ransom, how on earth are you going to travel in that thing? What's the motive power? What about air—and food—and water? There's only just room for you to lie in it."

"The Oyarsa of Malacandra himself will be the motive power. He will simply move it to Venus. Don't ask me how. I have no idea what organs or instruments they use. But a creature who has kept a planet in its orbit for several billions of years will be able to manage a packing-case!"

"But what will you eat? How will you breathe?"

"He tells me I shall need to do neither. I shall be in some state of suspended animation, as far as I can make out. I can't understand him when he tries to describe it. But that's his affair."

"Do you feel quite happy about it?" said I, for a sort of horror was beginning once more to creep over me.

"If you mean, Does my reason accept the view that he will (accidents apart) deliver me safe on the surface of Perelandra?—the answer is Yes," said Ransom. "If you mean, Do my nerves and my imagination respond to this view?—I'm afraid the answer is No. One can believe in anæsthetics and yet feel in a panic when they actually put the mask over your face. I think I feel as a man who believes in the future life feels when he is taken out to face a firing party. Perhaps it's good practice."

"And I'm to pack you into that accursed thing?" said I.

"Yes," said Ransom. "That's the first step. We must get out into the garden as soon as the sun is up and point it so that there are no trees or buildings in the way. Across the cabbage bed will do. Then I get in—with a bandage across my eyes, for those walls won't keep out all the sunlight once I'm beyond the air—and you screw me down. After that, I think you'll just see it glide off."

"And then?"

"Well, then comes the difficult part. You must hold yourself in readiness to come down here again the moment you are summoned, to take off the lid and let me out when I return."

"When do you expect to return?"

"Nobody can say. Six months—a year—twenty years. That's the trouble. I'm afraid I'm laying a pretty heavy burden on you."

"I might be dead."

"I know. I'm afraid part of your burden is to select a successor: at once, too. There are four or five people whom we can trust."

"What will the summons be?"

"Oyarsa will give it. It won't be mistakable for anything else. You needn't bother about that side of it. One other point. I've no particular reason to suppose I shall come back wounded. But just in case—if you can find a doctor whom we can let into the secret, it might be just as well to bring him with you when you come down to let me out."

"Would Humphrey do?"

"The very man. And now for some more personal matters. I've had to leave you out of my will, and I'd like you to know why."

"My dear chap, I never thought about your will till this moment."

"Of course not. But I'd like to have left you something. The reason I haven't, is this. I'm going to disappear. It is possible I may not come back. It's just conceivable there might be a murder trial, and if so one can't be too careful. I mean, for your sake. And now for one or two other private arrangements."

We laid our heads together and for a long time we talked about those matters which one usually discusses with relatives and not with friends. I got to know a lot more about Ransom than I had known before, and from the number of odd people whom he recommended to my care, "If ever I happened to be able to do anything," I came to realise the extent and intimacy of his charities. With every sentence the shadow of approaching separation and a kind of graveyard gloom began to settle more emphatically upon us. I found myself noticing and loving all sorts of little mannerisms and expressions in him such as we notice always in a woman we love, but notice in a man only as the last hours of his leave run out or the date of the probably fatal operation draws near. I felt our nature's incurable incredulity; and could hardly believe that what was now so close, so tangible and (in a sense) so much at my command, would in a few hours be wholly inaccessible, an image—soon, even an elusive image—in my memory. And finally a sort of shyness fell between us because each knew what the other was feeling. It had got very cold.

"We must be going soon," said Ransom.

"Not till he—the Oyarsa—comes back," said I—though, indeed, now that the thing was so near I wished it to be over.

"He has never left us," said Ransom, "he has been in the cottage all the time."

"You mean he has been waiting in the next room all these hours?"

"Not waiting. They never have that experience. You and I are conscious of waiting, because we have a body that grows tired or restless, and therefore a sense of cumulative duration. Also we can distinguish duties and spare time and therefore have a conception of leisure. It is not like that with him. He has been here all this time, but you can no more call it *waiting* than you can call the whole of his existence *waiting*. You might as well say that a tree in a wood was waiting, or the sunlight waiting on the side of a hill." Ransom yawned. "I'm tired," he said, "and so are you. I shall sleep well in that coffin of mine. Come. Let us lug it out."

We went in to the next room and I was made to stand before the featureless flame which did not wait but just was, and there, with Ransom as our interpreter, I was in some fashion presented and with my own tongue sworn in to this great business. Then we took down the blackout and let in the grey, comfortless morning. Between us we carried out the casket and the lid, so cold they seemed to burn our fingers. There was a heavy dew on the grass and my feet were soaked through at once. The eldil was with us, outside there, on the little lawn; hardly visible to my eyes at all in the daylight. Ransom showed me the clasps of the lid and how it was to be fastened on, and then there was some miserable hanging about, and then the final moment when he went back into the house and reappeared, naked; a tall, white, shivering, weary scarecrow of a man at that pale, raw hour. When he had got into the hideous box he made me tie a thick black bandage round his eyes and head. Then he lay down. I had no thoughts of the planet Venus now and no real belief that I should see him again. If I had dared I would have gone back on the whole scheme: but the other thing—the creature that did not wait—was there, and the fear of it was upon me. With feelings that have since often returned to me in nightmare I fastened the cold lid down on top of the living man and stood back. Next moment I was alone. I didn't see how it went. I went back indoors and was sick. A few hours later I shut up the cottage and returned to Oxford.

Then the months went past and grew to a year and a little more than a year, and we had raids and bad news and hopes deferred and all the earth became full of darkness and cruel habitations, till the night when Oyarsa came to me again. After that there was a journey in haste for Humphrey and me, standings in crowded corridors and waitings at small hours on windy platforms, and finally the moment when we stood in clear early sunlight in the little wilderness of deep weeds which Ransom's garden had now become and saw a black speck against the sunrise and then, almost silently, the casket had glided down between us. We flung ourselves upon it and had the lid off in about a minute and a half.

"Good God! All smashed to bits," I cried at my first glance of the interior.

"Wait a moment," said Humphrey. And as he spoke the figure in the coffin began to stir and then sat up, shaking off as it did so a mass of red things which had covered its head and shoulders and which I had momentarily mistaken for ruin and blood. As they streamed off him and were caught in the wind I perceived them to be flowers. He blinked for a second or so, then called us by our names, gave each of us a hand, and stepped out on the grass.

"How are you both?" he said. "You're looking rather knocked up."

I was silent for a moment, astonished at the form which had risen from that narrow house—almost a new Ransom, glowing with health and rounded with muscle and seemingly ten years younger. In the old days he had been beginning to show a few grey hairs; but now the beard which swept his chest was pure gold.

"Hullo, you've cut your foot," said Humphrey: and I saw now that Ransom was bleeding from the heel.

"Ugh, it's cold down here," said Ransom. "I hope you've got the boiler going and some hot water—and some clothes."

"Yes," said I, as we followed him into the house. "Humphrey thought of all that. I'm afraid I shouldn't have."

Ransom was now in the bathroom, with the door open, veiled in clouds of steam, and Humphrey and I were talking to him from the landing. Our questions were more numerous than he could answer.

"That idea of Schiaparelli's is all wrong," he shouted. "They have an ordinary day and night there," and "No, my heel doesn't hurt—or, at least, it's only just begun to," and "Thanks, any old clothes. Leave them on the chair" and "No thanks. I don't somehow feel like bacon or eggs or anything of that kind. No fruit, you say? Oh well, no matter. Bread or porridge or something" and "I'll be down in five minutes now."

He kept on asking if we were really all right and seemed to think we looked ill. I went down to get the breakfast, and Humphrey said he would stay and examine and dress the cut on Ransom's heel. When he rejoined me I was looking at one of the red petals which had come in the casket.

"That's rather a beautiful flower," said I, handing it to him.

"Yes," said Humphrey, studying it with the hands and eyes of a scientist. "What extraordinary delicacy! It makes an English violet seem like a coarse weed."

"Let's put some of them in water."

"Not much good. Look—it's withered already."

"How do you think he is?"

"Tip-top general. But I don't quite like that heel. He says the hæmorrhage has been going on for a long time."

Ransom joined us, fully dressed, and I poured out the tea. And all that day and far into the night he told us the story that follows.

3

What it is like to travel in a celestial coffin was a thing that Ransom never described. He said he couldn't. But odd hints about that journey have come out at one time or another when he was talking of quite different matters.

According to his own account he was not what we call conscious, and yet at the same time the experience was a very positive one with a quality of its own. On one occasion, someone had been talking about "seeing life" in the popular sense of knocking about the world and getting to know people, and B. who was present (and who is an Anthroposophist) said something I can't quite remember about "seeing life" in a very different sense. I think he was referring to some system of meditation which claimed to make "the form of Life itself" visible to the inner eye. At any rate Ransom let himself in for a long cross-examination by failing to conceal the fact that he attached some very definite idea to this. He even went so far—under extreme pressure—as to say that life appeared to him, in that condition, as a "coloured shape." Asked "what colour," he gave a curious look and could only say "what colours! yes, what colours!" But then he spoiled it all by adding, "of course it wasn't colour at all really. I mean, not what we'd call colour," and shutting up completely for the rest of the evening. Another hint came out when a sceptical friend of ours called McPhee was arguing against the Christian doctrine of the resurrection of the human body. I was his victim at the moment and he was pressing on me in his Scots way with such questions as "So you think you're going to have guts and palate for ever in a world where there'll be no eating, and genital organs in a world without copulation? Man, ye'll have a grand time of it!" when Ransom suddenly burst out with great excitement, "Oh, don't you see, you ass, that there's a difference between a trans-sensuous life and a non-sensuous life?" That, of course, directed McPhee's fire to him. What emerged was that in Ransom's opinion the present functions and appetites of the body would disappear, not because they were atrophied but because they were, as he said, "engulfed." He used the word "trans-sexual" I remember and began to hunt about for some similar words to apply to eating (after rejecting "trans-gastronomic"), and since he was not the only philologist present, that diverted the conversation into different channels. But I am pretty sure he was thinking of something he had experienced on his voyage to Venus. But perhaps the most mysterious thing he ever said about it was this. I was questioning him on the subject—which he doesn't often allow—and had incautiously said, "Of course I realise it's all rather too vague for you to put into words," when he took me up rather sharply, for such a patient man, by saying, "On the contrary, it is words that are vague. The reason why the thing can't be expressed is that it's too *definite* for language." And that is about all I can tell you of his journey. One thing is certain, that he came back from Venus even more changed than he had come back from Mars. But of course that may have been because of what happened to him after his landing.

To that landing, as Ransom narrated it to me, I will now proceed. He seems to have been awakened (if that is the right word) from his indescribable celestial state by the sensation of falling—in other words, when he was near enough to Venus to feel Venus as something in the downward direction. The next thing he noticed was that he was very warm on one side and very cold on the other, though neither sensation was so extreme as to be really painful. Anyway, both were soon swallowed up in the prodigious white light from below which began to penetrate through the semi-opaque walls of the casket. This steadily increased and became distressing in spite of the fact that his eyes were protected. There is no doubt this was the *albedo,* the outer veil of very dense atmosphere with which Venus is surrounded and which reflects the sun's rays with intense power. For some obscure reason he was not conscious, as he had been on his approach to Mars, of his own rapidly increasing weight. When the white light was just about to become unbearable, it disappeared altogether, and very soon after the cold on his left side and the heat on his right began to decrease and to be replaced by an equable warmth. I take it he was now in the outer layer of the Perelandrian atmosphere—at first in a pale, and later in a tinted, twilight. The prevailing colour, as far as he could see through the sides of the casket, was golden or coppery. By this time he must have been very near the surface of the planet, with the length of the casket at right angles to that surface—falling feet downwards like a man in a lift. The sensation of falling—helpless as he was and unable to move his arms—became frightening. Then suddenly there came a great green darkness, an unidentifiable noise—the first message from the new world—and a marked drop in temperature. He seemed now to have assumed a horizontal position and also, to his great surprise, to be moving not downwards but upwards; though, at the moment, he judged this to be an illusion. All this time he must have been making faint, unconscious efforts to move his limbs, for now he suddenly found that the sides of his prison-house yielded to pressure. He *was* moving his limbs, encumbered with some viscous substance. Where was the casket? His sensations were very confused. Sometimes he seemed to be falling, sometimes to be soaring upwards, and then again to be moving in the horizontal plane. The viscous substance was white. There seemed to be less of it every moment . . . white, cloudy stuff just like the casket, only not solid. With a horrible shock he realised that it *was* the casket, the casket melting, dissolving away, giving place to an indescribable confusion of colour—a rich, varied world in which nothing, for the moment, seemed palpable. There was no casket now. He was turned out—deposited—solitary. He was in Perelandra.

His first impression was of nothing more definite than of something slanted—as though he were looking at a photograph which had been taken when the camera was not held level. And even this lasted only for an instant. The slant was replaced by a different slant; then two slants rushed together and made a peak, and the peak flattened suddenly into a horizontal line, and the horizontal line tilted and became the edge of a vast gleaming slope which rushed furiously towards him. At the same moment he felt that he was being lifted. Up and up he soared till it seemed as if he must reach the burning dome of gold that hung above him instead of a sky. Then he was at a summit; but almost before his glance had taken in a huge valley that yawned beneath him—shining green like glass and marbled with streaks of scummy white—he was rushing down into that valley at perhaps thirty miles an hour. And now he realised that there was a delicious coolness over every part of him except his head, that his feet rested on nothing, and that he had for some time been performing unconsciously the actions of a swimmer. He was riding the foamless swell of an ocean, fresh and cool after the fierce temperatures of Heaven, but warm by earthly standards—as warm as a shallow bay with sandy bottom in a sub-tropical climate. As he rushed smoothly up the great convex hillside of the next wave he got a mouth-

ful of the water. It was hardly at all flavoured with salt; it was drinkable—like fresh water and only, by an infinitesimal degree, less insipid.
Though he had not been aware of thirst till now, his drink gave him a
quite astonishing pleasure. It was almost like meeting Pleasure itself for
the first time. He buried his flushed face in the green translucence, and
when he withdrew it, found himself once more on the top of a wave.

There was no land in sight. The sky was pure, flat gold like the background of a medieval picture. It looked very distant—as far off as a cir-
rhus cloud looks from earth. The ocean was gold too, in the offing,
flecked with innumerable shadows. The nearer waves, though golden
where their summits caught the light, were green on their slopes: first
emerald, and lower down a lustrous bottle green, deepening to blue
where they passed beneath the shadow of other waves.

All this he saw in a flash; then he was speeding down once more into
the trough. He had somehow turned on his back. He saw the golden
roof of that world quivering with a rapid variation of paler lights as a
ceiling quivers at the reflected sunlight from the bath-water when you
step into your bath on a summer morning. He guessed that this was the
reflection of the waves wherein he swam. It is a phenomenon observable
three days out of five in the planet of love. The queen of those seas views
herself continually in a celestial mirror.

Up again to the crest, and still no sight of land. Something that
looked like clouds—or could it be ships?—far away on his left. Then
down, down, down—he thought he would never reach the end of it . . .
this time he noticed how dim the light was. Such tepid revelry in water—
such glorious bathing, as one would have called it on earth, suggested as
its natural accompaniment a blazing sun. But here there was no such
thing. The water gleamed, the sky burned with gold, but all was rich and
dim, and his eyes fed upon it undazzled and unaching. The very names
of green and gold, which he used perforce in describing the scene, are
too harsh for the tenderness, the muted iridescence, of that warm,
maternal, delicately gorgeous world. It was mild to look upon as
evening, warm like summer noon, gentle and winning like early dawn. It
was altogether pleasurable. He sighed.

There was a wave ahead of him now so high that it was dreadful. We
speak idly in our own world of seas mountain high when they are not
much more than mast high. But this was the real thing. If the huge shape
had been a hill of land and not of water he might have spent a whole
forenoon or longer walking the slope before he reached the summit. It
gathered him into itself and hurled him up to that elevation in a matter
of seconds. But before he reached the top, he almost cried out in terror.
For this wave had not a smooth top like the others. A horrible crest

appeared; jagged and billowy and fantastic shapes, unnatural, even unliquid, in appearance, sprouted from the ridge. Rocks? Foam? Beasts? The question hardly had time to flash through his mind before the thing was upon him. Involuntarily he shut his eyes. Then he found himself once more rushing downhill. Whatever it was, it had gone past him. But it had been something. He had been struck in the face. Dabbing with his hands he found no blood. He had been struck by something soft which did him no harm but merely stung like a lash because of the speed at which he met it. He turned round on his back again—already, as he did so, soaring thousands of feet aloft to the high water of the next ridge. Far down below him in a vast momentary valley he saw the thing that had missed him. It was an irregularly shaped object with many curves and re-entrants. It was variegated in colours like a patch-work quilt—flame-colour, ultramarine, crimson, orange, gamboge, and violet. He could not say more about it for the whole glimpse lasted so short a time. Whatever the thing was, it was floating, for it rushed up the slope of the opposite wave and over the summit and out of sight. It sat to the water like a skin, curving as the water curved. It took the wave's shape at the top, so that for a moment half of it was already out of sight beyond the ridge and the other half still lying on the hither slope. It behaved rather like a mat of weeds on a river—a mat of weeds that takes on every contour of the little ripples you make by rowing past it—but on a very different scale. This thing might have been thirty acres or more in area.

Words are slow. You must not lose sight of the fact that his whole life on Venus up till now had lasted less than five minutes. He was not in the least tired, and not yet seriously alarmed as to his power of surviving in such a world. He had confidence in those who had sent him there, and for the meantime the coolness of the water and the freedom of his limbs were still a novelty and a delight; but more than all these was something else at which I have already hinted and which can hardly be put into words—the strange sense of excessive pleasure which seemed somehow to be communicated to him through all his senses at once. I use the word "excessive" because Ransom himself could only describe it by saying that for his first few days on Perelandra he was haunted, not by a feeling of guilt, but by surprise that he had no such feeling. There was an exuberance or prodigality of sweetness about the mere act of living which our race finds it difficult not to associate with forbidden and extravagant actions. Yet it is a violent world too. Hardly had he lost sight of the floating object when his eyes were stabbed by an unendurable light. A grading, blue-to-violet illumination made the golden sky seem dark by comparison and in a moment of time revealed more of the new planet than he had yet seen. He saw the waste of waves spread illimitably before him, and far away, at the very end of the world, against the sky, a single smooth column of ghastly green standing up, the one thing fixed and vertical in this universe of shifting slopes. Then the rich twilight rushed back (now seeming almost darkness) and he heard thunder. But it has a different *timbre* from terrestrial thunder, more resonance, and even, when distant, a kind of tinkling. It is the laugh, rather than the roar, of heaven. Another flash followed, and another, and then the storm was all about him. Enormous purple clouds came driving between him and the golden sky, and with no preliminary drops a rain such as he never experienced began to fall. There were no lines in it; the water above him seemed only less continuous than the sea, and he found it difficult to breathe. The flashes were incessant. In between them, when he looked in any direction except that of the clouds, he saw a completely changed world. It was like being at the centre of a rainbow, or in a cloud of multi-coloured steam. The water which now filled the air was turning sea and sky into a bedlam of flaming and writhing transparencies. He was dazzled and now for the first time a little frightened. In the flashes he saw, as before, only the endless sea and the still green column at the end of the world. No land anywhere—not the suggestion of a shore from one horizon to the other.

The thunder was ear-splitting and it was difficult to get enough air. All sorts of things seemed to be coming down in the rain—living things apparently. They looked like preternaturally airy and graceful frogs—sublimated frogs—and had the colour of dragon-flies, but he was in no plight to make careful observations. He was beginning to feel the first symptoms of exhaustion and was completely confused by the riot of colours in the atmosphere. How long this state of affairs lasted he could not say, but the next thing that he remembers noticing with any accuracy was that the swell was decreasing. He got the impression of being near the end of a range of water-mountains and looking down into lower country. For a long time he never reached this lower country; what had seemed, by comparison with the seas which he had met on his first arrival, to be calm water, always turned out to be only slightly smaller waves when he rushed down into them. There seemed to be a good many of the big floating objects about. And these, again, from some distance looked like an archipelago, but always, as he drew nearer and found the roughness of the water they were riding, they became more like a fleet. But in the end there was no doubt that the swell was subsiding. The rain stopped. The waves were merely of Atlantic height. The rainbow colours grew fainter and more transparent and the golden sky first showed timidly through them and then established itself again from horizon to horizon. The waves grew smaller still. He began to breathe freely. But he was now really tired, and beginning to find leisure to be afraid.

One of the great patches of floating stuff was sidling down a wave not more than a few hundred yards away. He eyed it eagerly, wondering whether he could climb on to one of these things for rest. He strongly suspected that they would prove mere mats of weed, or the topmost branches of submarine forests, incapable of supporting him. But while he thought this, the particular one on which his eyes were fixed crept up a wave and came between him and the sky. It was not flat. From its tawny surface a whole series of feathery and billowy shapes arose, very unequal in height; they looked darkish against the dim glow of the golden roof. Then they all tilted one way as the thing which carried them curled over the crown of the water and dipped out of sight. But here was another, not thirty yards away and bearing down on him. He struck out towards it, noticing as he did so how sore and feeble his arms were and feeling his first thrill of true fear. As he approached it he saw that it ended in a fringe of undoubtedly vegetable matter; it trailed, in fact, a dark red skirt of tubes and strings and bladders. He grabbed at them and found he was not yet near enough. He began swimming desperately, for the thing was gliding past him at some ten miles an hour. He grabbed again and got a handful of whip-like red strings, but they pulled out of his hand and almost cut him. Then he thrust himself right in among them, snatching wildly straight before him. For one second he was in a kind of vegetable broth of gurgling tubes and exploding bladders; next moment his hands caught something firmer ahead, something almost like very soft wood. Then, with the breath nearly knocked out of him and a bruised knee, he found himself lying face downward on a resistant surface. He pulled himself an inch or so further. Yes—there was no doubt now; one did not go through; it was something one could lie on.

It seems that he must have remained lying on his face, doing nothing and thinking nothing for a very long time. When he next began to take any notice of his surroundings he was, at all events, well rested. His first discovery was that he lay on a dry surface, which on examination turned out to consist of something very like heather, except for the colour which was coppery. Burrowing idly with his fingers he found something friable like dry soil, but very little of it, for almost at once he came upon a base of tough interlocked fibres. Then he rolled round on his back, and in doing so discovered the extreme resilience of the surface on which he lay. It was something much more than the pliancy of the heatherlike vegetation, and felt more as if the whole floating island beneath the vegetation were a kind of mattress. He turned and looked "inland"—if that is the right word—and for one instant what he saw looked very like a country.

He was looking up a long lonely valley with a copper-coloured floor bordered on each side by gentle slopes clothed in a kind of many-coloured forest. But even as he took this in, it became a long copper-coloured ridge with the forest sloping *down* on each side of it. Of course he ought to have been prepared for this, but he says that it gave him an almost sickening shock. The thing had looked, in that first glance, so like a real country that he had forgotten it was floating—an island if you like, with hills and valleys, but hills and valleys which changed places every minute so that only a cinematograph could make a contour map of it. And that is the nature of the floating islands of Perelandra. A photograph, omitting the colours and the perpetual variation of shape, would make them look deceptively like landscapes in our own world, but the reality is very different; for they are dry and fruitful like land but their only shape is the inconstant shape of the water beneath them. Yet the land-like appearance proved hard to resist. Although he had now grasped with his brain what was happening, Ransom had not yet grasped it with his muscles and nerves. He rose to take a few paces inland—and downhill, as it was at the moment of his rising—and immediately found himself flung down on his face, unhurt because of the softness of the weed. He scrambled to his feet—saw that he now had a steep slope to ascend—and fell a second time. A blessed relaxation of the strain in which he had been living since his arrival dissolved him into weak laughter. He rolled to and fro on the soft fragrant surface in a real schoolboy fit of the giggles.

This passed. And then for the next hour or two he was teaching himself to walk. It was much harder than getting your sea-legs on a ship, for whatever the sea is doing the deck of the ship remains a plane. But this was like learning to walk on water itself. It took him several hours to get a hundred yards away from the edge, or coast, of the floating island; and he was proud when he could go five paces without a fall, arms outstretched, knees bent in readiness for sudden change of balance, his whole body swaying and tense like that of one who is learning to walk the tightrope. Perhaps he would have learned more quickly if his falls had not been so soft, if it had not been so pleasant, having fallen, to lie still and gaze at the golden roof and hear the endless soothing noise of the water and breathe in the curiously delightful smell of the herbage. And then, too, it was so strange, after rolling head over heels down into some little dell, to open his eyes and find himself seated on the central mountain peak of the whole island looking down like Robinson Crusoe on field and forest to the shores in every direction, that a man could hardly help sitting there a few minutes longer—and then being detained again because, even as he made to rise, mountain and valley alike had been obliterated and the whole island had become a level plain.

At long last he reached the wooded part. There was an undergrowth of feathery vegetation, about the height of gooseberry bushes, coloured like sea anemones. Above this were the taller growths—strange trees with tube-like trunks of grey and purple spreading rich canopies above his head, in which orange, silver, and blue were the predominant colours. Here, with the aid of the tree trunks, he could keep his feet more easily. The smells in the forest were beyond all that he had ever conceived. To say that they made him feel hungry and thirsty would be misleading; almost, they created a new kind of hunger and thirst, a longing that seemed to flow over from the body into the soul and which was a heaven to feel. Again and again he stood still, clinging to some branch to steady himself, and breathed it all in, as if breathing had become a kind of ritual. And at the same time the forest landscape furnished what would have been a dozen landscapes on earth—now level wood with trees as vertical as towers, now a deep bottom where it was surprising not to find a stream, now a wood growing on a hillside, and now again, a hilltop whence one looked down through slanted boles at the distant sea. Save for the inorganic sound of waves there was utter silence about him. The sense of his solitude became intense without becoming at all painful—only adding, as it were, a last touch of wildness to the unearthly pleasures that surrounded him. If he had any fear now, it was a faint apprehension that his reason might be in danger. There was something in Perelandra that might overload a human brain.

Now he had come to a part of the wood where great globes of yellow fruit hung from the trees—clustered as toy-balloons are clustered on the back of the balloon-man and about the same size. He picked one of them and turned it over and over. The rind was smooth and firm and seemed impossible to tear open. Then by accident one of his fingers punctured it and went through into coldness. After a moment's hesitation he put the little aperture to his lips. He had meant to extract the smallest, experimental sip, but the first taste put his caution all to flight. It was, of course, a taste, just as his thirst and hunger had been thirst and hunger. But then it was so different from every other taste that it seemed mere pedantry to call it a taste at all. It was like the discovery of a totally new *genus* of pleasures, something unheard of among men, out of all reckoning, beyond all covenant. For one draught of this on earth wars would be fought and nations betrayed. It could not be classified. He could never tell us, when he came back to the world of men, whether it was sharp or sweet, savoury or voluptuous, creamy or piercing. "Not like that" was all he could ever say to such inquiries. As he let the empty gourd fall from his hand and was about to pluck a second one, it came into his head that he was now neither hungry nor thirsty.

And yet to repeat a pleasure so intense and almost so spiritual seemed an obvious thing to do. His reason, or what we commonly take to be reason in our own world, was all in favour of tasting this miracle again; the childlike innocence of fruit, the labours he had undergone, the uncertainty of the future, all seemed to commend the action. Yet something seemed opposed to this "reason." It is difficult to suppose that this opposition came from desire, for what desire would turn from so much deliciousness? But for whatever cause, it appeared to him better not to taste again. Perhaps the experience had been so complete that repetition would be a vulgarity—like asking to hear the same symphony twice in a day.

As he stood pondering over this and wondering how often in his life on earth he had reiterated pleasures not through desire, but in the teeth of desire and in obedience to a spurious rationalism, he noticed that the light was changing. It was darker behind him than it had been; ahead, the sky and sea shone through the wood with a changed intensity. To step out of the forest would have been a minute's work on earth; on this undulating island it took him longer, and when he finally emerged into the open an extraordinary spectacle met his eyes. All day there had been no variation at any point in the golden roof to mark the sun's position, but now the whole of one half-heaven revealed it. The orb itself remained invisible, but on the rim of the sea rested an arc of green so luminous that he could not look at it, and beyond that, spreading almost to the zenith, a great fan of colour like a peacock's tail. Looking over his shoulder he saw the whole island ablaze with blue, and across it and beyond it, even to the ends of the world, his own enormous shadow. The sea, far calmer now than he had yet seen it, smoked towards heaven in huge dolomites and elephants of blue and purple vapour, and a light wind, full of sweetness, lifted the hair on his forehead. The day was burning to death. Each moment the waters grew more level; something not far removed from silence began to be felt. He sat down cross-legged on the edge of the island, the desolate lord, it seemed, of this solemnity. For the first time it crossed his mind that he might have been sent to an uninhabited world, and the terror added, as it were, a razor-edge to all that profusion of pleasure.

Once more, a phenomenon which reason might have anticipated took him by surprise. To be naked yet warm, to wander among summer fruits and lie in sweet heather—all this had led him to count on a twilit night, a mild midsummer greyness. But before the great apocalyptic colours had died out in the west, the eastern heaven was black. A few moments, and the blackness had reached the western horizon. A little reddish light lingered at the zenith for a time, during which he crawled back to the woods. It was already, in common parlance, "too dark to see your way." But before he had lain down among the trees the real night had come—seamless darkness, not like night but like being in a coal-cellar, darkness in which his own hand held before his face was totally invisible. Absolute blackness, the undimensioned, the impenetrable, pressed on his eyeballs. There is no moon in that land, no star pierces the golden roof. But the darkness was warm. Sweet new scents came stealing out of it. The world had no size now. Its boundaries were the length and breadth of his own body and the little patch of soft fragrance which made his hammock, swaying ever more and more gently. Night covered him like a blanket and kept all loneliness from him. The blackness might have been his own room. Sleep came like a fruit which falls into the hand almost before you have touched the stem.

4

At Ransom's waking something happened to him which perhaps never happens to a man until he is out of his own world: he saw reality, and thought it was a dream. He opened his eyes and saw a strange heraldically coloured tree loaded with yellow fruits and silver leaves. Round the base of the indigo stem was coiled a small dragon covered with scales of red gold. He recognised the garden of the Hesperides at once. "This is the most vivid dream I have ever had," he thought. By some means or other he then realised that he was awake; but extreme comfort and some trance-like quality, both in the sleep which had just left him and in the experience to which he had awaked, kept him lying motionless. He remembered how in the very different world called Malacandra—that cold, archaic world, as it now seemed to him—he had met the original of the Cyclops, a giant in a cave and a shepherd. Were all the things which appeared as mythology on earth scattered through other worlds as realities? Then the realisation came to him "You are in an unknown planet, naked and alone, and that may be a dangerous animal." But he was not badly frightened. He knew that the ferocity of terrestrial animals was, by cosmic standards, an exception, and had found kindness in stranger creatures than this. But he lay quiet a little longer and looked at it. It was a creature of the lizard type, about the size of a St. Bernard dog, with a serrated back. Its eyes were open.

Presently he ventured to rise on one elbow. The creature went on looking at him. He noticed that the island was perfectly level. He sat up and saw, between the stems of the trees, that they were in calm water. The sea looked like gilded glass. He resumed his study of the dragon.

Could this be a rational animal—a *hnau* as they said in Malacandra—
and the very thing he had been sent there to meet? It did not look like
one, but it was worth trying. Speaking in the Old Solar tongue he
formed his first sentence—and his own voice sounded to him unfamiliar.

"Stranger," he said, "I have been sent to your world through the
Heaven by the servants of Maleldil. Do you give me welcome?"

The thing looked at him very hard and perhaps very wisely. Then,
for the first time, it shut its eyes. This seemed an unpromising start. Ransom decided to rise to his feet. The dragon reopened its eyes. He stood
looking at it while you could count to twenty, very uncertain how to
proceed. Then he saw that it was beginning to uncoil itself. By a great
effort of will he stood his ground; whether the thing were rational or
irrational, flight could hardly help him for long. It detached itself from
the tree, gave itself a shake, and opened two shining reptilian wings—
bluish gold and bat-like. When it had shaken these and closed them
again, it gave Ransom another long stare, and at last, half waddling and
half crawling, made its way to the edge of the island and buried its long
metallic-looking snout in the water. When it had drunk it raised its head
and gave a kind of croaking bleat which was not entirely unmusical.
Then it turned, looked yet again at Ransom, and finally approached
him. "It's madness to *wait* for it," said the false reason, but Ransom set
his teeth and stood. It came right up and began nudging him with its
cold snout about his knees. He was in great perplexity. Was it rational
and was this how it talked? Was it irrational but friendly—and if so,
how should he respond? You could hardly stroke a creature with scales!
Or was it merely scratching itself against him? At that moment, with a
suddenness which convinced him it was only a beast, it seemed to forget
all about him, turned away, and began tearing up the herbage with great
avidity. Feeling that honour was now satisfied, he also turned away back
to the woods.

There were trees near him loaded with the fruit which he had
already tasted, but his attention was diverted by a strange appearance a
little farther off. Amid the darker foliage of a greenish-grey thicket
something seemed to be sparkling. The impression, caught out of the
corner of his eye, had been that of a greenhouse roof with the sun on it.
Now that he looked at it squarely it still suggested glass, but glass in perpetual motion. Light seemed to be coming and going in a spasmodic
fashion. Just as he was moving to investigate this phenomenon he was
startled by a touch on his left leg. The beast had followed him. It was
once more nosing and nudging. Ransom quickened his pace. So did the
dragon. He stopped; so did it. When he went on again it accompanied
him so closely that its side pressed against his thighs and sometimes its

cold, hard, heavy foot descended on his. The arrangement was so little to his satisfaction that he was beginning to wonder seriously how he could put an end to it when suddenly his whole attention was attracted by something else. Over his head there hung from a hairy tube-like branch a great spherical object, almost transparent, and shining. It held an area of reflected light in it and at one place a suggestion of rainbow colouring. So this was the explanation of the glass-like appearance in the wood. And looking round he perceived innumerable shimmering globes of the same kind in every direction. He began to examine the nearest one attentively. At first he thought it was moving, then he thought it was not. Moved by a natural impulse he put out his hand to touch it. Immediately his head, face, and shoulders were drenched with what seemed (in that warm world) an ice-cold shower bath, and his nostrils filled with a sharp, shrill, exquisite scent that somehow brought to his mind the verse in Pope, "die of a rose in aromatic pain." Such was the refreshment that he seemed to himself to have been, till now, but half awake. When he opened his eyes—which had closed involuntarily at the shock of mois-ture—all the colours about him seemed richer and the dimness of that world seemed clarified. A re-enchantment fell upon him. The golden beast at his side seemed no longer either a danger or a nuisance. If a naked man and a wise dragon were indeed the sole inhabitants of this floating paradise, then this also was fitting, for at that moment he had a sensation not of following an adventure but of enacting a myth. To be the figure that he was in this unearthly pattern appeared sufficient.

He turned again to the tree. The thing that had drenched him was quite vanished. The tube or branch, deprived of its pendent globe, now ended in a little quivering orifice from which there hung a bead of crys-tal moisture. He looked round in some bewilderment. The grove was still full of its iridescent fruit but now he perceived that there was a slow continual movement. A second later he had mastered the phenomenon. Each of the bright spheres was very gradually increasing in size, and each, on reaching a certain dimension, vanished with a faint noise, and in its place there was a momentary dampness on the soil and a soon-fading, delicious fragrance and coldness in the air. In fact, the things were not fruit at all but bubbles. The trees (he christened them at that moment) were bubble-trees. Their life, apparently, consisted in drawing up water from the ocean and then expelling it in this form, but enriched by its short sojourn in their sappy innards. He sat down to feed his eyes upon the spectacle. Now that he knew the secret he could explain to himself why this wood looked and felt so different from every other part of the island. Each bubble, looked at individually, could be seen to emerge from its parent-branch as a mere bead, the size of a pea, and swell and burst; but looking at the wood as a whole, one was conscious only of a continual faint disturbance of light, an elusive interference with the prevailing Perelandrian silence, an unusual coolness in the air, and a fresher quality in the perfume. To a man born in our world it felt a more out-door place than the open parts of the island, or even the sea. Looking at a fine cluster of the bubbles which hung above his head he thought how easy it would be to get up and plunge oneself through the whole lot of them and to feel, all at once, that magical refreshment multiplied tenfold. But he was restrained by the same sort of feeling which had restrained him over-night from tasting a second gourd. He had always disliked the people who encored a favourite air in the opera—"That just spoils it" had been his comment. But this now appeared to him as a principle of far wider application and deeper moment. This itch to have things over again, as if life were a film that could be unrolled twice or even made to work backwards . . . was it possibly the root of all evil? No: of course the love of money was called that. But money itself—perhaps one valued it chiefly as a defence against chance, a security for being able to have things over again, a means of arresting the unrolling of the film.

He was startled from his meditation by the physical discomfort of some weight on his knees. The dragon had lain down and deposited its long, heavy head across them. "Do you know," he said to it in English, "that you are a considerable nuisance?" It never moved. He decided that he had better try and make friends with it. He stroked the hard dry head, but the creature took no notice. Then his hand passed lower down and found softer surface, or even a chink in the mail. Ah . . . that was where it liked being tickled. It grunted and shot out a long cylindrical slate-coloured tongue to lick him. It rolled round on its back revealing an almost white belly, which Ransom kneaded with his toes. His acquaintance with the dragon prospered exceedingly. In the end it went to sleep.

He rose and got a second shower from a bubble-tree. This made him feel so fresh and alert that he began to think of food. He had forgotten whereabouts on the island the yellow gourds were to be found, and so as he set out to look for them he discovered that it was difficult to walk. For a moment he wondered whether the liquid in the bubbles had some intoxicating quality, but a glance around assured him of the real reason. The plain of copper-coloured heather before him, even as he watched, swelled into a low hill and the low hill moved in his direction. Spellbound anew at the sight of land rolling towards him, like water, in a wave, he forgot to adjust himself to the movement and lost his feet. Picking himself up, he proceeded more carefully. This time there was no doubt about it. The sea was rising. Where two neighbouring woods made a vista to the edge of this living raft he could see troubled water, and the warm wind was now strong enough to ruffle his hair. He made his way gingerly towards the coast, but before he reached it he passed some bushes which carried a rich crop of oval green berries, about three times the size of almonds. He picked one and broke it in two. The flesh was dryish and bread-like, something of the same kind as a banana. It turned out to be good to eat. It did not give the orgiastic and almost alarming pleasure of the gourds, but rather the specific pleasure of plain food—the delight of munching and being nourished, a "Sober certainty of waking bliss." A man, or at least a man like Ransom, felt he ought to say grace over it; and so he presently did. The gourds would have required rather an oratorio or a mystical meditation. But the meal had its unexpected high lights. Every now and then one struck a berry which had a bright red centre: and these were so savoury, so memorable among a thousand tastes, that he would have begun to look for them and to feed on them only, but that he was once more forbidden by that same inner adviser which had already spoken to him twice since he came to Perelandra. "Now on earth," thought Ransom, "they'd soon discover how to breed these redhearts, and they'd cost a great deal more than the others." Money, in fact, would provide the means of saying *encore* in a voice that could not be disobeyed.

When he had finished his meal he went down to the water's edge to drink, but before he arrived there it was already "up" to the water's edge. The island at that moment was a little valley of bright land nestling between hills of green water, and as he lay on his belly to drink he had the extraordinary experience of dipping his mouth in a sea that was higher than the shore. Then he sat upright for a bit with his legs dangling over the edge among the red weeds that fringed this little country. His solitude became a more persistent element in his consciousness. What had he been brought here to do? A wild fancy came into his head that this empty world had been waiting for him as for its first inhabitant, that he was singled out to be the founder, the beginner. It was strange that the utter loneliness through all these hours had not troubled him so much as one night of it on Malacandra. He thought the difference lay in this, that mere chance, or what he took for chance, had turned him adrift in Mars, but here he knew that he was part of a plan. He was no longer unattached, no longer on the outside.

As his country climbed the smooth mountains of dimly lustrous water he had frequent opportunity to see that many other islands were close at hand. They varied from his own island and from one another in their colouring more than he would have thought possible. It was a wonder to see these big mats or carpets of land tossing all around him like yachts in harbour on a rough day—their trees each moment at a different angle just as the masts of the yachts would be. It was a wonder to see some edge of vivid green or velvety crimson come creeping over the top of a wave far above him and then wait till the whole country unrolled itself down the wave's side for him to study. Sometimes his own land and a neighbouring land would be on opposite slopes of a trough, with only a narrow strait of water between them; and then, for the moment, you were cheated with the semblance of a terrestrial landscape. It looked exactly as though you were in a well-wooded valley with a river at the bottom of it. But while you watched, that seeming river did the impossible. It thrust itself up so that the land on either side sloped downwards from it; and then up farther still and shouldered half the landscape out of sight beyond its ridge; and became a huge greeny-gold hog's back of water hanging in the sky and threatening to engulf your own land, which now was concave and reeled backwards to the next roller, and rushing upwards, became convex again.

A clanging, whirring noise startled him. For a moment he fancied he was in Europe and that a plane was flying low over his head. Then he recognised his friend the dragon. Its tail was streaked out straight behind it so that it looked like a flying worm, and it was heading for an island about half a mile away. Following its course with his eyes, he saw two long lines of winged objects, dark against the gold firmament, approaching the same island from the left and the right. But they were not bat-winged reptiles. Peering hard into the distance, he decided that they were birds, and a musical chattering noise, presently wafted to him by a change of the wind, confirmed this belief. They must have been a little larger than swans. Their steady approach to the same island for which the dragon was heading fixed his attention and filled him with a vague feeling of expectation. What followed next raised this to positive excitement. He became aware of some creamily foamed disturbance in the water, much nearer, and making for the same island. A whole fleet of objects was moving in formation. He rose to his feet. Then the lift of a wave cut them off from his sight. Next moment they were visible again, hundreds of feet below him. Silver-coloured objects, all alive with circling and frisking movements . . . he lost them again, and swore. In such a very uneventful world they had become important. Ah . . . ! here they were again. Fish certainly. Very large, obese, dolphin-like fish, two long lines together, some of them spouting columns of rainbow-coloured water from their noses, and one leader. There was something queer about the leader, some sort of projection or malformation on the back. If only the things would remain visible for more than fifty seconds at a time! They had almost reached that other island now, and the birds were all descending to meet them at its edge. There was the leader again, with his hump or pillar on his back. A moment of wild incredulity followed, and then Ransom was balanced, with legs wide apart, on the utmost fringe of his own island and shouting for all he was worth. For at the very moment when the leading fish had reached that neighbouring land, the land had risen up on a wave between him and the sky; and he had seen, in perfect and unmistakable silhouette, the thing on the fish's back reveal itself as a human form—a human form which stepped ashore, turned with a slight inclination of its body towards the fish and then vanished from sight as the whole island slid over the shoulder of the billow. With beating heart Ransom waited till it was in view again. This time it was not between him and the sky. For a second or so the human figure was undiscoverable. A stab of something like despair pierced him. Then he picked it out again—a tiny darkish shape moving slowly between him and a patch of blue vegetation. He waved and gesticulated and shouted till his throat was hoarse, but it took no notice of him. Every now and then he lost sight of it. Even when he found it again, he sometimes doubted whether it were not an optical illusion—some chance figuration of foliage which his intense desire had assimilated to the shape of a man. But always, just before he had despaired, it would become unmistakable again. Then his eyes began to grow tired and he knew that the longer he looked the less he would see. But he went on looking none the less.

At last, from mere exhaustion, he sat down. The solitude, which up till now had been scarcely painful, had become a horror. Any return to it was a possibility he dared not face. The drugging and entrancing beauty had vanished from his surroundings; take that one human form away and all the rest of this world was now pure nightmare, a horrible cell or trap in which he was imprisoned. The suspicion that he was beginning to suffer from hallucinations crossed his mind. He had a picture of living for ever and ever on this hideous island, always really alone but always haunted by the phantoms of human beings, who would come up to him with smiles and outstretched hands, and then fade away as he approached them. Bowing his head on his knees, he set his teeth and endeavoured to restore some order in his mind. At first he found he was merely listening to his own breathing and counting the beats of his heart; but he tried again and presently succeeded. And then, like revelation, came the very simple idea that if he wished to attract the attention of this man-like creature he must wait till he was on the crest of a wave and then stand up so that it would see him outlined against the sky.

Three times he waited till the shore whereon he stood became a ridge, and rose, swaying to the movement of his strange country, gesticulating. The fourth time he succeeded. The neighbouring island was, of course, lying for the moment beneath him like a valley. Quite unmistakably the small dark figure waved back. It detached itself from a confusing background of greenish vegetation and began running towards him—that is, towards the nearer coast of its own island—across an orange-coloured field. It ran easily: the heaving surface of the field did not seem to trouble it. Then his own land reeled downwards and backwards and a great wall of water pushed its way up between the two countries and cut each off from sight of the other. A moment later, and Ransom, from the valley in which he now stood, saw the orange-coloured land pouring itself like a moving hillside down the slightly convex slope of a wave far above him. The creature was still running. The width of water between the two islands was about thirty feet, and the creature was less than a hundred yards away from him. He knew now that it was not merely man-like, but a man—a green man on an orange field, green like the beautifully coloured green beetle in an English garden, running downhill towards him with easy strides and very swiftly. Then the seas lifted his own land and the green man became a foreshortened figure far below him, like an actor seen from the gallery at Covent Garden. Ransom stood on the very brink of his island, straining his body forward and shouting. The green man looked up. He was apparently shouting too, with his hands arched about his mouth; but the roar of the seas smothered the noise and the next moment Ransom's island dropped into the trough of the wave and the high green ridge of sea cut off his view. It was maddening. He was tortured with the fear that the distance between the islands might be increasing. Thank God: here came the orange land over the crest following him down into the pit. And there was the stranger, now on the very shore, face to face with him. For one second the alien eyes looked at his full of love and welcome. Then the whole face changed: a shock as of disappointment and astonishment passed over it. Ransom realised, not without a disappointment of his own, that he had been mistaken for someone else. The running, the waving, the shouts, had not been intended for him. And the green man was not a man at all, but a woman.

It is difficult to say why this surprised him so. Granted the human form, he was presumably as likely to meet a female as a male. But it did surprise him, so that only when the two islands once more began to fall apart into separate wave-valleys did he realise that he had said nothing to her, but stood staring like a fool. And now that she was out of sight he found his brain on fire with doubts. Was *this* what he had been sent to meet? He had been expecting wonders, had been prepared for wonders, but not prepared for a goddess carved apparently out of green stone, yet alive. And then it flashed across his mind—he had not noticed it while the scene was before him—that she had been strangely accompanied. She had stood up amidst a throng of beasts and birds as a tall sapling stands among bushes—big pigeon-coloured birds and flame-coloured birds, and dragons, and beaver-like creatures about the size of rats, and heraldic-looking fish in the sea at her feet. Or had he imagined that? Was this the beginning of the hallucinations he had feared? Or another myth coming out into the world of fact—perhaps a more terrible myth, of Circe or Alcina? And the expression on her face . . . what had she expected to find that made the finding of him such a disappointment?

The other island became visible again. He had been right about the animals. They surrounded her ten or twenty deep, all facing her, most of them motionless, but some of them finding their places, as at a ceremony, with delicate noiseless movements. The birds were in long lines and more of them seemed to be alighting on the island every moment and joining these lines. From a wood of bubble-trees behind her half a dozen creatures like very short-legged and elongated pigs—the dachshunds of the pig world—were waddling up to join the assembly. Tiny frog-like beasts, like those he had seen falling in the rain, kept leaping about her, sometimes higher than her head, sometimes alighting on her shoulders; their colours were so vivid that at first he mistook them for kingfishers. Amidst all this she stood looking at him; her feet together, her arms hanging at her sides, her stare level and unafraid, communicating nothing. Ransom determined to speak, using the Old Solar tongue. "I am from another world," he began and then stopped. The Green Lady had done something for which he was quite unprepared. She raised her arm and pointed at him: not as in menace, but as though inviting the other creatures to behold him. At the same moment her face changed again, and for a second he thought she was going to cry. Instead she burst into laughter—peal upon peal of laughter till her whole body shook with it, till she bent almost double, with her hands resting on her knees, still laughing and repeatedly pointing at him. The animals, like our own dogs in similar circumstances, dimly understood that there was merriment afoot; all manner of gambolling, wing-clapping, snorting, and standing upon hind legs began to be displayed. And still the Green Lady laughed till yet again the wave divided them and she was out of sight.

Ransom was thunderstruck. Had the eldila sent him to meet an idiot? Or an evil spirit that mocked men? Or was it after all a hallucination?—for this was just how a hallucination might be expected to behave. Then an idea occurred to him which would have taken much longer, perhaps, to occur to me or you. It might not be she who was mad but he who was ridiculous. He glanced down at himself. Certainly his legs presented an odd spectacle, for one was brownish-red (like the flanks of a Titian satyr) and the other was white—by comparison, almost a leprous white. As far as self-inspection could go, he had the same parti-coloured appearance all over—no unnatural result of his one-sided exposure to the sun during the voyage. Had this been the joke? He felt a momentary impatience with the creature who could mar the meeting of two worlds with laughter at such a triviality. Then he smiled in spite of himself at the very undistinguished career he was having on Perelandra. For dangers he had been prepared; but to be first a disappointment and then an absurdity . . . Hullo! Here were the Lady and her island in sight again.

She had recovered from her laughter and sat with her legs trailing in the sea, half unconsciously caressing a gazelle-like creature which had thrust its soft nose under her arm. It was difficult to believe that she had ever laughed, ever done anything but sit on the shore of her floating isle. Never had Ransom seen a face so calm, and so unearthly, despite the full humanity of every feature. He decided afterwards that the unearthly quality was due to the complete absence of that element of resignation which mixes, in however slight a degree, with all profound stillness in terrestrial faces. This was a calm which no storm had ever preceded. It might be idiocy, it might be immortality, it might be some condition of mind to which terrestrial experience offered no clue at all. A curious and rather horrifying sensation crept over him. On the ancient planet Malacandra he had met creatures who were not even remotely human in form but who had turned out, on further acquaintance, to be rational and friendly. Under an alien exterior he had discovered a heart like his own. Was he now to have the reverse experience? For now he realised that the word "human" refers to something more than the bodily form or even to the rational mind. It refers also to that community of blood and experience which unites all men and women on the Earth. But this creature was not of his race; no windings, however intricate, of any genealogical tree, could ever establish a connection between himself and her. In that sense, not one drop in her veins was "human." The universe had produced her species and his quite independently.

All this passed through his mind very quickly, and was speedily interrupted by his consciousness that the light was changing. At first he thought that the green Creature had, of herself, begun to turn bluish and to shine with a strange electric radiance. Then he noticed that the whole landscape was a blaze of blue and purple—and almost at the same time that the two islands were not so close together as they had been. He glanced at the sky. The many-coloured furnace of the short-lived evening was kindled all about him. In a few minutes it would be pitch black . . . and the islands were drifting apart. Speaking slowly in that ancient language, he cried out to her, "I am a stranger. I come in peace. Is it your will that I swim over to your land?"

The Green Lady looked quickly at him with an expression of curiosity.

"What is 'peace'?" she asked.

Ransom could have danced with impatience. Already it was visibly darker and there was no doubt now that the distance between the islands was increasing. Just as he was about to speak again a wave rose between them and once more she was out of sight; and as that wave hung above him, shining purple in the light of the sunset, he noticed how dark the sky beyond it had become. It was already through a kind of twilight that he looked down from the next ridge upon the other island far below him. He flung himself into the water. For some seconds he found a difficulty in getting clear of the shore. Then he seemed to succeed and struck out. Almost at once he found himself back again among the red weeds and bladders. A moment or two of violent struggling followed and then he was free—and swimming steadily—and then, almost without warning, swimming in total darkness. He swam on, but despair of finding the other land, or even of saving his life, now gripped him. The perpetual change of the great swell abolished all sense of direction. It could only be by chance that he would land anywhere. Indeed, he judged from the time he had already been in the water that he must have been swimming *along* the space between the islands instead of across it. He tried to alter his course; then doubted the wisdom of this, tried to return to his original course, and became so confused that he could not be sure he had done either. He kept on telling himself that he must keep his head. He was beginning to be tired. He gave up all attempts to guide himself. Suddenly, a long time after, he felt vegetation sliding past him. He gripped and pulled. Delicious smells of fruit and flowers came to him out of the darkness. He pulled harder still on his aching arms. Finally, he found himself, safe and panting, on the dry, sweet-scented, undulating surface of an island.

5

Ransom must have fallen asleep almost as soon as he landed, for he remembered nothing more till what seemed the song of a bird broke in upon his dreams. Opening his eyes, he saw that it was a bird indeed, a long-legged bird like a very small stork, singing rather like a canary. Full daylight—or what passes for such in Perelandra—was all about him, and in his heart such a premonition of good adventure as made him sit up forthwith and brought him, a moment later, to his feet. He stretched his arms and looked around. He was not on the orange-coloured island, but on the same island which had been his home ever since he came to this planet. He was floating in a dead calm and therefore had no difficulty in making his way to the shore. And there he stopped in astonishment. The Lady's island was floating beside his, divided only by five feet or so of water. The whole look of the world had changed. There was no expanse of sea now visible—only a flat wooded landscape as far as the eye could reach in every direction. Some ten or twelve of the islands, in fact, were here lying together and making a short-lived continent. And there walking before him, as if on the other side of a brook, was the Lady herself—walking with her head a little bowed and her hands occupied in plaiting together some blue flowers. She was singing to herself in a low voice but stopped and turned as he hailed her and looked him full in the face.

"I was young yesterday," she began, but he did not hear the rest of her speech. The meeting, now that it had actually come about, proved overwhelming. You must not misunderstand the story at this point. What overwhelmed him was not in the least the fact that she, like himself, was totally naked. Embarrassment and desire were both a thousand miles away from his experience: and if he was a little ashamed of his own body, that was a shame which had nothing to do with difference of sex and turned only on the fact that he knew his body to be a little ugly and a little ridiculous. Still less was her colour a source of horror to him. In her own world that green was beautiful and fitting; it was his pasty white and angry sunburn which were the monstrosity. It was neither of these; but he found himself unnerved. He had to ask her presently to repeat what she had been saying.

"I was young yesterday," she said. "When I laughed at you. Now I know that the people in your world do not like to be laughed at."

"You say you were young?"

"Yes."

"Are you not young to-day also?"

She appeared to be thinking for a few moments, so intently that the flowers dropped, unregarded, from her hand.

"I see it now," she said presently. "It is very strange to say one is young at the moment one is speaking. But to-morrow I shall be older. And then I shall say I was young to-day. You are quite right. This is great wisdom you are bringing, O Piebald Man."

"What do you mean?"

"This looking backward and forward along the line and seeing how a day has one appearance as it comes to you, and another when you are in it, and a third when it has gone past. Like the waves."

"But you are very little older than yesterday."

"How do you know that?"

"I mean," said Ransom, "a night is not a very long time."

She thought again, and then spoke suddenly, her face lightening. "I see it now," she said. "You think times have lengths. A night is always a night whatever you do in it, as from this tree to that is always so many paces whether you take them quickly or slowly. I suppose that is true in a way. But the waves do not always come at equal distances. I see that you come from a wise world . . . if this is wise. I have never done it before—stepping out of life into the Alongside and looking at oneself living as if one were not alive. Do they all do that in your world, Piebald?"

"What do you know about other worlds?" said Ransom.

"I know this. Beyond the roof it is all Deep Heaven, the high place. And the low is not really spread out as it seems to be" (here she indicated the whole landscape) "but is rolled up into little balls: little lumps of the low swimming in the high. And the oldest and greatest of them have on

them that which we have never seen nor heard and cannot at all understand. But on the younger Maleldil has made to grow the things like us,
that breathe and breed."

"How have you found all this out? Your roof is so dense that your
people cannot see through into Deep Heaven and look at the other
worlds."

Up till now her face had been grave. At this point she clapped her
hands and a smile such as Ransom had never seen changed her. One does
not see that smile here except in children, but there was nothing of the
child about it there.

"Oh, I see it," she said. "I am older now. Your world has no roof.
You look right out into the high place and see the great dance with your
own eyes. You live always in that terror and that delight, and what we
must only believe you can behold. Is not this a wonderful invention of
Maleldil's? When I was young I could imagine no beauty but this of our
own world. But He can think of all, and all different."

"That is one of the things that is bewildering me," said Ransom.
"That you are not different. You are shaped like the women of my own
kind. I had not expected that. I have been in one other world beside my
own. But the creatures there are not at all like you and me."

"What is bewildering about it?"

"I do not see why different worlds should bring forth like creatures.
Do different trees bring forth like fruit?"

"But that other world was older than yours," she said.

"How do you know that?" asked Ransom in amazement.

"Maleldil is telling me," answered the woman. And as she spoke the
landscape had become different, though with a difference none of the
senses would identify. The light was dim, the air gentle, and all Ransom's
body was bathed in bliss, but the garden world where he stood seemed
to be packed quite full, and as if an unendurable pressure had been laid
upon his shoulders, his legs failed him and he half sank, half fell, into a
sitting position.

"It all comes into my mind now," she continued. "I see the big furry
creatures, and the white giants—what is it you called them?—the Sorns,
and the blue rivers. Oh, what a strong pleasure it would be to see them
with my outward eyes, to touch them, and the stronger because there
are no more of that kind to come. It is only in the ancient worlds they
linger yet."

"Why?" said Ransom in a whisper, looking up at her.

"You must know that better than I," she said. "For was it not in
your own world that all this happened?"

"All what?"

"I thought it would be you who would tell me of it," said the woman, now in her turn bewildered.

"What are you talking about?" said Ransom.

"I mean," said she, "that in your world Maleldil first took Himself this form, the form of your race and mine."

"You know that?" said Ransom sharply. Those who have had a dream which is very beautiful but from which, nevertheless, they have ardently desired to awake, will understand his sensations.

"Yes, I know that Maleldil has made me older to that amount since we began speaking." The expression on her face was such as he had never seen, and could not steadily look at. The whole of this adventure seemed to be slipping out of his hands. There was a long silence. He stooped down to the water and drank before he spoke again.

"Oh, my Lady," he said, "why do you say that such creatures linger only in the ancient worlds?"

"Are you so young?" she answered. "How could they come again? Since our Beloved became a man, how should Reason in any world take on another form? Do you not understand? That is all over. Among times there is a time that turns a corner and everything this side of it is new. Times do not go backward."

"And can one little world like mine be the corner?"

"I do not understand. Corner with us is not the name of a size."

"And do you," said Ransom with some hesitation—"and do you know *why* He came thus to my world?"

All through this part of the conversation he found it difficult to look higher than her feet, so that her answer was merely a voice in the air above him. "Yes," said the voice. "I know the reason. But it is not the reason you know. There was more than one reason, and there is one I know and cannot tell to you, and another that you know and cannot tell to me."

"And after this," said Ransom, "it will all be men."

"You say it as if you were sorry."

"I think," said Ransom, "I have no more understanding than a beast. I do not well know what I am saying. But I loved the furry people whom I met in Malacandra, that old world. Are they to be swept away? Are they only rubbish in the Deep Heaven?"

"I do not know what *rubbish* means," she answered, "nor what you are saying. You do not mean they are worse because they come early in the history and do not come again? They are their own part of the history and not another. We are on this side of the wave and they on the far side. All is new."

One of Ransom's difficulties was an inability to be quite sure who was speaking at any moment in this conversation. It may (or may not) have been due to the fact that he could not look long at her face. And now he wanted the conversation to end. He had "had enough"—not in the half-comic sense whereby we use those words to mean that a man has had too much, but in the plain sense. He had had his fill, like a man who has slept or eaten enough. Even an hour ago, he would have found it difficult to express this quite bluntly; but now it came naturally to him to say:

"I do not wish to talk any more. But I would like to come over to your island so that we may meet again when we wish."

"Which do you call my island?" said the Lady.

"The one you are on," said Ransom. "What else?"

"Come," she said, with a gesture that made that whole world a house and her a hostess. He slid into the water and scrambled out beside her. Then he bowed, a little clumsily as all modern men do, and walked away from her into a neighbouring wood. He found his legs unsteady and they ached a little; in fact a curious physical exhaustion possessed him. He sat down to rest for a few minutes and fell immediately into dreamless sleep.

He awoke completely refreshed but with a sense of insecurity. This had nothing to do with the fact that he found himself, on waking, strangely attended. At his feet, and with its snout partially resting upon them, lay the dragon; it had one eye shut and one open. As he rose on his elbow and looked about him he found that he had another custodian at his head: a furred animal something like a wallaby but yellow. It was the yellowest thing he had ever seen. As soon as he moved both beasts began nudging him. They would not leave him alone till he rose, and when he had risen they would not let him walk in any direction but one. The dragon was much too heavy for him to shove it out of the way, and the yellow beast danced round him in a fashion that headed him off every direction but the one it wanted him to go. He yielded to their pressure and allowed himself to be shepherded, first through a wood of higher and browner trees than he had yet seen and then across a small open space and into a kind of alley of bubble-trees and beyond that into large fields of silver flowers that grew waist-high. And then he saw that they had been bringing him to be shown to their mistress. She was standing a few yards away, motionless but not apparently disengaged—doing something with her mind, perhaps even with her muscles, that he did not understand. It was the first time he had looked steadily at her, himself unobserved, and she seemed more strange to him than before. There was no category in the terrestrial mind which would fit her.

Opposites met in her and were fused in a fashion for which we have no images. One way of putting it would be to say that neither our sacred nor our profane art could make her portrait. Beautiful, naked, shameless, young—she was obviously a goddess: but then the face, the face so calm that it escaped insipidity by the very concentration of its mildness, the face that was like the sudden coldness and stillness of a church when we enter it from a hot street—that made her a Madonna. The alert, inner silence which looked out from those eyes overawed him; yet at any moment she might laugh like a child, or run like Artemis or dance like a Mænad. All this against the golden sky which looked as if it were only an arm's length above her head. The beasts raced forward to greet her, and as they rushed through the feathery vegetation they startled from it masses of the frogs, so that it looked as if huge drops of vividly coloured dew were being tossed in the air. She turned as they approached her and welcomed them, and once again the picture was half like many earthly scenes but in its total effect unlike them all. It was not really like a woman making much of a horse, nor yet a child playing with a puppy. There was in her face an authority, in her caresses a condescension, which by taking seriously the inferiority of her adorers made them somehow less inferior—raised them from the status of pets to that of slaves. As Ransom reached her she stooped and whispered something in the ear of the yellow creature, and then, addressing the dragon, bleated to it almost in its own voice. Both of them, having received their congé, darted back into the woods.

"The beasts in your world seem almost rational," said Ransom.

"We make them older every day," she answered. "Is not that what it means to be a beast?"

But Ransom clung to her use of the word *we*.

"That is what I have come to speak to you about," he said. "Maleldil has sent me to your world for some purpose. Do you know what it is?"

She stood for a moment almost like one listening and then answered "No."

"Then you must take me to your home and show me to your people."

"People? I do not know what you are saying."

"Your kindred—the others of your kind."

"Do you mean the King?"

"Yes. If you have a King, I had better be brought before him."

"I cannot do that," she answered. "I do not know where to find him."

"To your own home then."

"What is *home*?"

"The place where people live together and have their possessions and bring up their children."

She spread out her hands to indicate all that was in sight. "This is my home," she said.

"Do you live here alone?" asked Ransom.

"What is *alone*?"

Ransom tried a fresh start. "Bring me where I shall meet others of your kind."

"If you mean the King, I have already told you I do not know where he is. When we were young—many days ago—we were leaping from island to island, and when he was on one and I was on another the waves rose and we were driven apart."

"But can you take me to some other of your kind? The King cannot be the only one."

"He is the only one. Did you not know?"

"But there must be others of your kind—your brothers and sisters, your kindred, your friends."

"I do not know what these words mean."

"Who is this King?" said Ransom in desperation.

"He is himself, he is the King," said she. "How can one answer such a question?"

"Look here," said Ransom. "You must have had a mother. Is she alive? Where is she? When did you see her last?"

"I have a mother?" said the Green Lady, looking full at him with eyes of untroubled wonder. "What do you mean? I *am* the Mother." And once again there fell upon Ransom the feeling that it was not she, or not she only, who had spoken. No other sound came to his ears, for the sea and the air were still, but a phantom sense of vast choral music was all about him. The awe which her apparently witless replies had been dissipating for the last few minutes returned upon him.

"I do not understand," he said.

"Nor I," answered the Lady. "Only my spirit praises Maleldil who comes down from Deep Heaven into this lowness and will make me to be blessed by all the times that are rolling towards us. It is He who is strong and makes me strong and fills empty worlds with good creatures."

"If you are a mother, where are your children?"

"Not yet," she answered.

"Who will be their father?"

"The King—who else?"

"But the King—had he no father?"

"He *is* the Father."

"You mean," said Ransom slowly, "that you and he are the only two of your kind in the whole world?"

"Of course." Then presently her face changed. "Oh, how young I have been," she said. "I see it now. I had known that there were many creatures in that ancient world of the Hrossa and the Sorns. But I had forgotten that yours also was an older world than ours. I see—there are many of you by now. I had been thinking that of you also there were only two. I thought you were the King and Father of your world. But there are children of children of children by now, and you perhaps are one of these."

"Yes," said Ransom.

"Greet your Lady and Mother well from me when you return to your own world," said the Green Woman. And now for the first time there was a note of deliberate courtesy, even of ceremony, in her speech. Ransom understood. She knew now at last that she was not addressing an equal. She was a queen sending a message to a queen through a commoner, and her manner to him was henceforward more gracious. He found it difficult to make his next answer.

"Our Mother and Lady is dead," he said.

"What is *dead*?"

"With us they go away after a time. Maleldil takes the soul out of them and puts it somewhere else—in Deep Heaven, we hope. They call it death."

"Do not wonder, O Piebald Man, that your world should have been chosen for time's corner. You live looking out always on heaven itself, and as if this were not enough Maleldil takes you all thither in the end. You are favoured beyond all worlds."

Ransom shook his head. "No. It is not like that," he said.

"I wonder," said the woman, "if you were sent here to teach us *death*."

"You don't understand," he said. "It is not like that. It is horrible. It has a foul smell. Maleldil Himself wept when He saw it." Both his voice and his facial expression were apparently something new to her. He saw the shock, not of horror, but of utter bewilderment, on her face for one instant and then, without effort, the ocean of her peace swallowed it up as if it had never been, and she asked him what he meant.

"You could never understand, Lady," he replied. "But in our world not all events are pleasing or welcome. There may be such a thing that you would cut off both your arms and your legs to prevent it happening—and yet it happens: with us."

"But how can one wish any of those waves not to reach us which Maleldil is rolling towards us?"

Against his better judgment Ransom found himself goaded into argument.

"But even you," he said, "when you first saw me, I know now you were expecting and hoping that I was the King. When you found I was not, your face changed. Was *that* event not unwelcome? Did you not wish it to be otherwise?"

"Oh," said the Lady. She turned aside with her head bowed and her hands clasped in an intensity of thought. She looked up and said, "You make me grow older more quickly than I can bear," and walked a little farther off. Ransom wondered what he had done. It was suddenly borne in upon him that her purity and peace were not, as they had seemed, things settled and inevitable like the purity and peace of an animal—that they were alive and therefore breakable, a balance maintained by a mind and therefore, at least in theory, able to be lost. There is no reason why a man on a smooth road should lose his balance on a bicycle; but he could. There was no reason why she should step out of her happiness into the psychology of our own race; but neither was there any wall between to prevent her doing so. The sense of precariousness terrified him: but when she looked at him again he changed that word to Adventure, and then all words died out of his mind. Once more he could not look steadily at her. He knew now what the old painters were trying to represent when they invented the halo. Gaiety and gravity together, a splendour as of martyrdom yet with no pain in it at all, seemed to pour from her countenance. Yet when she spoke her words were a disappointment.

"I have been so young till this moment that all my life now seems to have been a kind of sleep. I have thought that I was being carried, and behold, I was walking."

Ransom asked what she meant.

"What you have made me see," answered the Lady, "is as plain as the sky, but I never saw it before. Yet it has happened every day. One goes into the forest to pick food and already the thought of one fruit rather than another has grown up in one's mind. Then, it may be, one finds a different fruit and not the fruit one thought of. One joy was expected and another is given. But this I had never noticed before—that the very moment of the finding there is in the mind a kind of thrusting back, or setting aside. The picture of the fruit you have *not* found is still, for a moment, before you. And if you wished—if it were possible to wish—you could keep it there. You could send your soul after the good you had expected, instead of turning it to the good you had got. You could refuse the real good; you could make the real fruit taste insipid by thinking of the other."

Ransom interrupted. "That is hardly the same thing as finding a stranger when you wanted your husband."

"Oh, that is how I came to understand the whole thing. You and the King differ more than two kinds of fruit. The joy of finding him again and the joy of all the new knowledge I have had from you are more unlike than two tastes; and when the difference is as great as that, and each of the two things so great, then the first picture does stay in the mind quite a long time—many beats of the heart—after the other good has come. And this, O Piebald, is the glory and wonder you have made me see; that it is I, I myself, who turn from the good expected to the given good. Out of my own heart I do it. One can conceive a heart which did not: which clung to the good it had first thought of and turned the good which was given it into no good."

"I don't see the wonder and the glory of it," said Ransom.

Her eyes flashed upon him such a triumphant flight above his thoughts as would have been scorn in earthly eyes; but in that world it was not scorn.

"I thought," she said, "that I was carried in the will of Him I love, but now I see that I walk with it. I thought that the good things He sent me drew me into them as the waves lift the islands; but now I see that it is I who plunge into them with my own legs and arms, as when we go swimming. I feel as if I were living in that roofless world of yours where men walk undefended beneath naked heaven. It is a delight with terror in it! One's own self to be walking from one good to another, walking beside Him as Himself may walk, not even holding hands. How has He made me so separate from Himself? How did it enter His mind to conceive such a thing? The world is so much larger than I thought. I thought we went along paths—but it seems there are no paths. The going itself is the path."

"And have you no fear," said Ransom, "that it will ever be hard to turn your heart from the thing you wanted to the thing Maleldil sends?"

"I see," said the Lady presently. "The wave you plunge into may be very swift and great. You may need all your force to swim into it. You mean, He might send me a good like that?"

"Yes—or like a wave so swift and great that all your force was too little."

"It often happens that way in swimming," said the Lady. "Is not that part of the delight?"

"But are you happy without the King? Do you not *want* the King?"

"Want him?" she said. "How could there be anything I did not want?"

There was something in her replies that began to repel Ransom.

"You can't want him very much if you are happy without him," he said: and was immediately surprised at the sulkiness of his own voice.

"Why?" asked the Lady. "And why, O Piebald, are you making little hills and valleys in your forehead and why do you give a little lift of your shoulders? Are these the signs of something in your world?"

"They mean nothing," said Ransom hastily. It was a small lie; but there it would not do. It tore him as he uttered it, like a vomit. It became of infinite importance. The silver meadow and the golden sky seemed to fling it back at him. As if stunned by some measureless anger in the very air he stammered an emendation: "They mean nothing I could explain to you." The Lady was looking at him with a new and more judicial expression. Perhaps in the presence of the first mother's son she had ever seen, she was already dimly forecasting the problems that might arise when she had children of her own.

"We have talked enough now," she said at last. At first he thought she was going to turn away and leave him. Then, when she did not move, he bowed and drew back a step or two. She still said nothing and seemed to have forgotten about him. He turned and retraced his way through the deep vegetation until they were out of sight of each other. The audience was at an end.

6

As soon as the Lady was out of sight Ransom's first impulse was to run his hands through his hair, to expel the breath from his lungs in a long whistle, to light a cigarette, to put his hands in his pockets, and in general, to go through all that ritual of relaxation which a man performs on finding himself alone after a rather trying interview. But he had no cigarettes and no pockets: nor indeed did he feel himself alone. That sense of being in Someone's Presence which had descended on him with such unbearable pressure during the very first moments of his conversation with the Lady did not disappear when he had left her. It was, if anything, increased. Her society had been, in some degree, a protection against it, and her absence left him not to solitude but to a more formidable kind of privacy. At first it was almost intolerable; as he put it to us, in telling the story, "There seemed no *room*." But later on, he discovered that it was intolerable only at certain moments—at just those moments in fact (symbolised by his impulse to smoke and to put his hands in his pockets) when a man asserts his independence and feels that now at last he's on his own. When you felt like that, then the very air seemed too crowded to breathe; a complete fulness seemed to be excluding you from a place which, nevertheless, you were unable to leave. But when you gave in to the thing, gave yourself up to it, there was no burden to be borne. It became not a load but a medium, a sort of splendour as of eatable, drinkable, breathable gold, which fed and carried you and not only poured into you but out from you as well. Taken the wrong way, it suffocated; taken the right way, it made terrestrial life seem, by comparison, a vacuum. At first, of course, the wrong moments occurred pretty often. But like a man who has a wound that hurts him in certain positions and who gradually learns to avoid those positions, Ransom learned not to make that inner gesture. His day became better and better as the hours passed.

During the course of the day he explored the island pretty thoroughly. The sea was still calm and it would have been possible in many directions to have reached neighbouring islands by a mere jump. He was placed, however, at the edge of this temporary archipelago, and from one shore he found himself looking out on the open sea. They were lying, or else very slowly drifting, in the neighbourhood of the huge green column which he had seen a few moments after his arrival in Perelandra. He had an excellent view of this object at about a mile's distance. It was clearly a mountainous island. The column turned out to be really a cluster of columns—that is, of crags much higher than they were broad, rather like exaggerated dolomites, but smoother; so much smoother in fact that it might be truer to describe them as pillars from the Giant's Causeway magnified to the height of mountains. This huge upright mass did not, however, rise directly from the sea. The island had a base of rough country, but with smoother land at the coast, and a hint of valleys with vegetation in them between the ridges, and even of steeper and narrower valleys which ran some way up between the central crags. It was certainly land, real fixed land with its roots in the solid surface of the planet. He could dimly make out the texture of true rock from where he sat. Some of it was inhabitable land. He felt a great desire to explore it. It looked as if a landing would present no difficulties, and even the great mountain itself might turn out to be climbable.

He did not see the Lady again that day. Early next morning, after he had amused himself by swimming for a little and eaten his first meal, he was again seated on the shore looking out towards the Fixed Land. Suddenly he heard her voice behind him and looked around. She had come forth from the woods with some beasts, as usual, following her. Her words had been words of greeting, but she showed no disposition to talk. She came and stood on the edge of the floating island beside him and looked with him towards the Fixed Land.

"I will go there," she said at last.

"May I go with you?" asked Ransom.

"If you will," said the Lady. "But you see it is the Fixed Land."

"That is why I wish to tread on it," said Ransom. "In my world all the lands are fixed, and it would give me pleasure to walk in such a land again."

She gave a sudden exclamation of surprise and stared at him.

"Where, then, do you live in your world?" she asked.

"On the lands."

"But you said they are all fixed."

"Yes. We live on the fixed lands."

For the first time since they had met, something not quite unlike an expression of horror or disgust passed over her face.

"But what do you do during the nights?"

"During the nights?" said Ransom in bewilderment. "Why, we sleep, of course."

"But where?"

"Where we live. On the land."

She remained in deep thought so long that Ransom feared she was never going to speak again. When she did, her voice was hushed and once more tranquil, though the note of joy had not yet returned to it.

"He has never bidden you not to," she said, less as a question than as a statement.

"No," said Ransom.

"There can, then, be different laws in different worlds."

"Is there a law in your world not to sleep in a Fixed Land?"

"Yes," said the Lady. "He does not wish us to dwell there. We may land on them and walk on them, for the world is ours. But to stay there—to sleep and awake there . . ." she ended with a shudder.

"You couldn't have that law in our world," said Ransom. "There *are* no floating lands with us."

"How many of you are there?" asked the Lady suddenly.

Ransom found that he didn't know the population of the Earth, but contrived to give her some idea of many millions. He had expected her to be astonished, but it appeared that numbers did not interest her. "How do you all find room on your Fixed Land?" she asked.

"There is not one fixed land, but many," he answered. "And they are big: almost as big as the sea."

"How do you endure it?" she burst out. "Almost half your world empty and dead. Loads and loads of land, all tied down. Does not the very thought of it crush you?"

"Not at all," said Ransom. "The very thought of a world which was all sea like yours would make my people unhappy and afraid."

"Where will this end?" said the Lady, speaking more to herself than to him. "I have grown so old in these last few hours that all my life before seems only like the stem of a tree, and now I am like the branches shooting out in every direction. They are getting so wide apart that I can hardly bear it. First to have learned that I walk from good to good with my own feet . . . that was a stretch enough. But now it seems that good is not the same in all worlds; that Maleldil has forbidden in one what He allows in another."

"Perhaps my world is wrong about this," said Ransom rather feebly, for he was dismayed at what he had done.

"It is not so," said she. "Maleldil Himself has told me now. And it could not be so, if your world has no floating lands. But He is not telling me why He has forbidden it to us."

"There's probably some good reason," began Ransom, when he was interrupted by her sudden laughter.

"Oh, Piebald, Piebald," she said, still laughing. "How often the people of your race speak!"

"I'm sorry," said Ransom, a little put out.

"What are you sorry for?"

"I am sorry if you think I talk too much."

"Too much? How can I tell what would be too much for you to talk?"

"In our world when they say a man talks much they mean they wish him to be silent."

"If that is what they mean, why do they not say it?"

"What made you laugh?" asked Ransom, finding her question too hard.

"I laughed, Piebald, because you were wondering, as I was, about this law which Maleldil has made for one world and not for another. And you had nothing to say about it and yet made the nothing up into words."

"I *had* something to say, though," said Ransom almost under his breath. "At least," he added in a louder voice, "this forbidding is no hardship in such a world as yours."

"That also is a strange thing to say," replied the Lady. "Who thought of its being hard? The beasts would not think it hard if I told them to walk on their heads. It would become their delight to walk on their heads. I am His beast, and all His biddings are joys. It is not that which makes me thoughtful. But it was coming into my mind to wonder whether there are two kinds of bidding."

"Some of our wise men have said . . ." began Ransom, when she interrupted him.

"Let us wait and ask the King," she said. "For I think, Piebald, you do not know much more about this than I do."

"Yes, the King, by all means," said Ransom. "If only we can find him." Then, quite involuntarily, he added in English, "By Jove! What was that?" She also had exclaimed. Something like a shooting star seemed to have streaked across the sky, far away on their left, and some seconds later an indeterminate noise reached their ears.

"What was that?" he asked again, this time in Old Solar.

"Something has fallen out of Deep Heaven," said the Lady. Her face showed wonder and curiosity: but on earth we so rarely see these emotions without some admixture of defensive fear that her expression seemed strange to him.

"I think you're right," said he. "Hullo! What's this?" The calm sea had swelled and all the weeds at the edge of their island were in movement. A single wave passed under their island and all was still again.

"Something has certainly fallen into the sea," said the Lady. Then she resumed the conversation as if nothing had happened.

"It was to look for the King that I had resolved to go over to-day to the Fixed Land. He is on none of these islands here, for I have searched them all. But if we climbed high up on the Fixed Land and looked about, then we should see a long way. We could see if there are any other islands near us."

"Let us do this," said Ransom. "If we can swim so far."

"We shall ride," said the Lady. Then she knelt down on the shore—and such grace was in all her movements that it was a wonder to see her kneel—and gave three low calls all on the same note. At first no result was visible. But soon Ransom saw broken water coming rapidly towards them. A moment later and the sea beside the island was a mass of the large silver fishes: spouting, curling their bodies, pressing upon one another to get nearer, and the nearest ones nosing the land. They had not only the colour but the smoothness of silver. The biggest were about nine feet long and all were thick-set and powerful-looking. They were very unlike any terrestrial species, for the base of the head was noticeably wider than the foremost part of the trunk. But then the trunk itself grew thicker again towards the tail. Without this tailward bulge they would have looked like giant tadpoles. As it was, they suggested rather pot-bellied and narrow-chested old men with very big heads. The Lady seemed to take a long time in selecting two of them. But the moment she had done so the others all fell back for a few yards and the two successful candidates wheeled round and lay still with their tails to the shore, gently moving their fins. "Now, Piebald, like this," she said, and seated herself astride the narrow part of the right-hand fish. Ransom followed her example. The great head in front of him served instead of shoulders so that there was no danger of sliding off. He watched his hostess. She gave her fish a slight kick with her heels. He did the same to his. A moment later they were gliding out to sea at about six miles an hour. The air over the water was cooler and the breeze lifted his hair. In a world where he had as yet only swum and walked, the fish's progress gave the impression of quite an exhilarating speed. He glanced back and saw the feathery and billowy mass of the islands receding and the sky growing larger and more emphatically golden. Ahead, the fantastically shaped and coloured mountain dominated his whole field of vision. He noticed with interest that the whole school of rejected fish were still with them—some following, but the majority gambolling in wide extended wings to left and right.

"Do they always follow like this?" he asked.

"Do the beasts not follow in your world?" she replied. "We cannot ride more than two. It would be hard if those we did not choose were not even allowed to follow."

"Was that why you took so long to choose the two fish, Lady?"

"Of course," said the Lady. "I try not to choose the same fish too often."

The land came towards them apace and what had seemed level coastline began to open into bays and thrust itself forward into promontories. And now they were near enough to see that in this apparently calm ocean there was an invisible swell, a very faint rise and fall of water on the beach. A moment later the fishes lacked depth to swim any further, and following the Green Lady's example, Ransom slipped both his legs to one side of his fish and groped down with his toes. Oh, ecstasy!—they touched solid pebbles. He had not realised till now that he was pining for "fixed land." He looked up. Down to the bay in which they were landing ran a steep narrow valley with low cliffs and outcroppings of a reddish rock and, lower down, banks of some kind of moss and a few trees. The trees might almost have been terrestrial: planted in any southern country of our own world they would not have seemed remarkable to anyone except a trained botanist. Best of all, down the middle of the valley—and welcome to Ransom's eyes and ears as a glimpse of home or of heaven—ran a little stream, a dark translucent stream where a man might hope for trout.

"You love this land, Piebald?" said the Lady, glancing at him.

"Yes," said he, "it is like my own world."

They began to walk up the valley to its head. When they were under the trees the resemblance of an earthly country was diminished, for there is so much less light in that world that the glade which would have cast only a little shadow cast a forest gloom. It was about a quarter of a mile to the top of the valley, where it narrowed into a mere cleft between low rocks. With one or two grips and a leap the Lady was up these, and Ransom followed. He was amazed at her strength. They emerged into a steep upland covered with a kind of turf which would have been very like grass but that there was more blue in it. It seemed to be closely cropped and dotted with white fluffy objects as far as the eye could reach.

"Flowers?" asked Ransom. The Lady laughed.

"No. These are the Piebalds. I named you after them." He was puzzled for a moment but presently the objects began to move, and soon to move quickly towards the human pair whom they had apparently winded—for they were already so high that there was a strong breeze. In a moment they were bounding all about the Lady and welcoming her. They were white beasts with black spots—about the size of sheep but with ears so much larger, noses so much mobile, and tails so much longer, that the general impression was rather of enormous mice. Their claw-like or almost hand-like paws were clearly built for climbing, and the bluish turf was their food. After a proper interchange of courtesies with these creatures, Ransom and the Lady continued their journey. The circle of golden sea below them was now spread out in an enormous expanse and the green rock pillars above seemed almost to overhang. But it was a long and stiff climb to their base. The temperature here was much lower, though it was still warm. The silence was also noticeable. Down below, on the islands, though one had not remarked it at the time, there must have been a continual background of water noises, bubble noises, and the movement of beasts.

They were now entering into a kind of bay or re-entrant of turf between two of the green pillars. Seen from below these had appeared to touch one another; but now, though they had gone in so deep between two of them that most of the view was cut off on either hand, there was still room for a battalion to march in line. The slope grew steeper every moment; and as it grew steeper the space between the pillars also grew narrower. Soon they were scrambling on hands and knees in a place where the green walls hemmed them in so that they must go in single file, and Ransom, looking up, could hardly see the sky overhead. Finally they were faced with a little bit of real rock work—a neck of stone about eight feet high which joined, like a gum of rock, the roots of the two monstrous teeth of the mountain. "I'd give a good deal to have a pair of trousers on," thought Ransom to himself as he looked at it. The Lady, who was ahead, stood on tiptoe and raised her arms to catch a projection on the lip of the ridge. Then he saw her pull, apparently intending to lift her whole weight on her arms and swing herself to the top in a single movement. "Look here, you can't do it that way," he began, speaking inadvertently in English, but before he had time to correct himself she was standing on the edge above him. He did not see exactly how it was done, but there was no sign that she had taken any unusual exertion. His own climb was a less dignified affair, and it was a panting and perspiring man with a smudge of blood on his knee who finally stood beside her. She was inquisitive about the blood, and when he had explained the phenomenon to her as well as he could, wanted to scrape a little skin off her own knee to see if the same would happen. This led him to try to explain to her what was meant by pain, which only made her more anxious to try the experiment. But at the last moment Maleldil apparently told her not to.

Ransom now turned to survey their surroundings. High overhead, and seeming by perspective to lean inwards towards each other at the top and almost to shut out the sky, rose the immense piers of rock—not two or three of them, but nine. Some of them, like those two between which they had entered the circle, were close together. Others were many yards apart. They surrounded a roughly oval plateau of perhaps seven acres, covered with a finer turf than any known on our planet and dotted with tiny crimson flowers. A high, singing wind carried, as it were, a cooled and refined quintessence of all the scents from the richer world below, and kept these in continual agitation. Glimpses of the far-spread sea, visible between pillars, made one continually conscious of great height; and Ransom's eyes, long accustomed to the medley of curves and colours in the floating islands, rested on the pure lines and stable masses of this place with great refreshment. He took a few paces forward into the cathedral spaciousness of the plateau, and when he spoke his voice woke echoes.

"Oh, this is good," he said. "But perhaps you—you to whom it is forbidden—do not feel it so." But a glance at the Lady's face told him he was wrong. He did not know what was in her mind; but her face, as once or twice before, seemed to shine with something before which he dropped his eyes. "Let us examine the sea," she said presently.

They made the circle of the plateau methodically. Behind them lay the group of islands from which they had set out that morning. Seen from this altitude it was larger even than Ransom had supposed. The richness of its colours—its orange, its silver, its purple and (to his surprise) its glossy blacks—made it seem almost heraldic. It was from this direction that the wind came; the smell of those islands, though faint, was like the sound of running water to a thirsty man. But on every other side they saw nothing but the ocean. At least, they saw no islands. But when they had made almost the whole circuit, Ransom shouted and the Lady pointed almost at the same moment. About two miles off, dark against the coppery-green of the water, there was some small round object. If he had been looking down on an earthly sea Ransom would have taken it, at first sight, for a buoy.

"I do not know what it is," said the Lady. "Unless it is the thing that fell out of Deep Heaven this morning."

"I wish I had a pair of field glasses," thought Ransom, for the Lady's words had awakened in him a sudden suspicion. And the longer he stared at the dark blob the more his suspicion was confirmed. It appeared to be perfectly spherical; and he thought he had seen something like it before.

You have already heard that Ransom had been in that world which men call Mars but whose true name is Malacandra. But he had not been taken thither by the eldila. He had been taken by men, and taken in a space-ship, a hollow sphere of glass and steel. He had, in fact, been kidnapped by men who thought that the ruling powers of Malacandra demanded a human sacrifice. The whole thing had been a misunderstanding. The great Oyarsa who has governed Mars from the beginning (and whom my own eyes beheld, in a sense, in the hall of Ransom's cottage) had done him no harm and meant him none. But his chief captor, Professor Weston, had meant plenty of harm. He was a man obsessed with the idea which is at this moment circulating all over our planet in obscure works of "scientifiction," in little Interplanetary Societies and Rocketry Clubs, and between the covers of monstrous magazines, ignored or mocked by the intellectuals, but ready, if ever the power is put into its hands, to open a new chapter of misery for the universe. It is the idea that humanity, having now sufficiently corrupted the planet where it arose, must at all costs contrive to seed itself over a larger area: that the vast astronomical distances which are God's quarantine regulations, must somehow be overcome. This for a start. But beyond this lies the sweet poison of the false infinite—the wild dream that planet after planet, system after system, in the end galaxy after galaxy, can be forced to sustain, everywhere and for ever, the sort of life which is contained in the loins of our own species—a dream begotten by the hatred of death upon the fear of true immortality, fondled in secret by thousands of ignorant men and hundreds who are not ignorant. The destruction or enslavement of other species in the universe, if such there are, is to these minds a welcome corollary. In Professor Weston the power had at last met the dream. The great physicist had discovered a motive power for his space-ship. And that little black object, now floating beneath him on the sinless waters of Perelandra, looked to Ransom more like the spaceship every moment. "So that," he thought, "that is why I have been sent here. He failed on Malacandra and now he is coming here. And it's up to me to do something about it." A terrible sense of inadequacy swept over him. Last time—in Mars—Weston had had only one accomplice. But he had had firearms. And how many accomplices might he have this time? And in Mars he had been foiled not by Ransom but by the eldila, and specially the great eldil, the Oyarsa, of that world. He turned quickly to the Lady.

"I have seen no eldila in your world," he said.

"Eldila?" she repeated as if it were a new name to her.

"Yes. Elidila," said Ransom, "the great and ancient servants of Maleldil. The creatures that neither breed nor breathe. Whose bodies are made of light. Whom we can hardly see. Who ought to be obeyed."

She mused for a moment and then spoke. "Sweetly and gently this time Maleldil makes me older. He shows me all the natures of these blessed creatures. But there is no obeying them *now*, not in this world. That is all the old order, Piebald, the far side of the wave that has rolled past us and will not come again. That very ancient world to which you journeyed was put under the eldila. In your own world also they ruled once: but not since our Beloved became a Man. In your world they linger still. But in our world, which is the first of worlds to wake after the great change, they have no power. There is nothing now between us and Him. They have grown less and we have increased. And now Maleldil puts it into my mind that this is their glory and their joy. They received us—us things of the low worlds, who breed and breathe—as weak and small beasts whom their lightest touch could destroy; and their glory was to cherish us and make us older till we were older than they—till they could fall at our feet. It is a joy we shall not have. However I teach the beasts they will never be better than I. But it is a joy beyond all. Not that it is better joy than ours. Every joy is beyond all others. The fruit we are eating is always the best fruit of all."

"There have been eldila who did not think it a joy," said Ransom.

"How?"

"You spoke yesterday, Lady, of clinging to the old good instead of taking the good that came."

"Yes—for a few heart-beats."

"There was an eldil who clung longer—who has been clinging since before the worlds were made."

"But the old good would cease to be a good at all if he did that."

"Yes. It has ceased. And still he clings."

She stared at him in wonder and was about to speak, but he interrupted her.

"There is no time to explain," he said.

"No time? What has happened to the time?" she asked.

"Listen," he said. "That thing down there has come through Deep Heaven from my world. There is a man in it: perhaps many men——"

"Look," she said, "it is turning into two—one big and one small."

Ransom saw that a small black object had detached itself from the space-ship and was beginning to move uncertainly away from it. It puzzled him for a moment. Then it dawned on him that Weston—if it was Weston—probably knew the watery surface he had to expect on Venus and had brought some kind of collapsible boat. But could it be that he had not reckoned with tides or storms and did not foresee that it might be impossible for him ever to recover the space-ship? It was not like Weston to cut off his own retreat. And Ransom certainly did not wish Weston's retreat to be cut off. A Weston who could not, even if he chose, return to Earth, was an insoluble problem. Anyway, what could he, Ransom, possibly do without support from the eldila? He began to smart under a sense of injustice. What was the good of sending him—a mere scholar—to cope with a situation of this sort? Any ordinary pugilist, or, better still, any man who could make good use of a tommy-gun, would have been more to the purpose. If only they could find this King whom the Green Woman kept on talking about. . . .

But while these thoughts were passing through his mind he became aware of a dim murmuring or growling sound which had gradually been encroaching on the silence for some time. "Look," said the Lady suddenly, and pointed to the mass of islands. Their surface was no longer level. At the same moment he realised that the noise was that of waves: small waves as yet, but definitely beginning to foam on the rocky headlands of the Fixed Island. "The sea is rising," said the Lady. "We must go down and leave this land at once. Soon the waves will be too great—and I must not be here by night."

"Not that way," shouted Ransom. "Not where you will meet the man from my world."

"Why?" said the Lady. "I am Lady and Mother of this world. If the King is not here, who else should greet a stranger?"

"I will meet him."

"It is not your world, Piebald," she replied.

"You do not understand," said Ransom. "This man—he is a friend of that eldil of whom I told you—one of those who cling to the wrong good."

"Then I must explain it to him," said the Lady. "Let us go and make him older," and with that she slung herself down the rocky edge of the plateau and began descending the mountain slope. Ransom took longer to manage the rocks; but once his feet were again on the turf he began running as fast as he could. The Lady cried out in surprise as he flashed past her, but he took no notice. He could now see clearly which bay the little boat was making for and his attention was fully occupied in directing his course and making sure of his feet. There was only one man in the boat. Down and down the long slope he raced. Now he was in a fold: now in a winding valley which momentarily cut off the sight of the sea. Now at last he was in the cove itself. He glanced back and saw to his dismay that the Lady had also been running and was only a few yards behind. He glanced forward again. There were waves, though not yet very large ones, breaking on the pebbly beach. A man in shirt and shorts and a pith helmet was ankle-deep in the water, wading ashore and pulling after him a little canvas punt. It was certainly Weston, though his face had something about it which seemed subtly unfamiliar. It seemed to Ransom of vital importance to prevent a meeting between Weston and the Lady. He had seen Weston murder an inhabitant of Malacandra. He turned back, stretching out both arms to bar her way and shouting "Go back!" She was too near. For a second she was almost in his arms. Then she stood back from him, panting from the race, surprised, her mouth opened to speak. But at that moment he heard Weston's voice, from behind him, saying in English, "May I ask you, Dr. Ransom, what is the meaning of this?"

7

In all the circumstances it would have been reasonable to expect that Weston would be much more taken aback at Ransom's presence than Ransom could be at his. But if he were, he showed no sign of it, and Ransom could hardly help admiring the massive egoism which enabled this man in the very moment of his arrival on an unknown world to stand there unmoved in all his authoritative vulgarity, his arms akimbo, his face scowling, and his feet planted as solidly on that unearthly soil as if he had been standing with his back to the fire in his own study. Then, with a shock, he noticed that Weston was speaking to the Lady in the Old Solar language with perfect fluency. On Malacandra, partly from incapacity, and much more from his contempt for the inhabitants, he had never acquired more than a smattering of it. Here was an inexplicable and disquieting novelty. Ransom felt that his only advantage had been taken from him. He felt that he was now in the presence of the incalculable. If the scales had been suddenly weighted in this one respect, what might come next?

He awoke from his abstraction to find that Weston and the Lady had been conversing fluently, but without mutual understanding. "It is no use," she was saying. "You and I are not old enough to speak together, it seems. The sea is rising; let us go back to the islands. Will he come with us, Piebald?"

"Where are the two fishes?" said Ransom.

"They will be waiting in the next bay," said the Lady.

"Quick, then," said Ransom to her; and then, in answer to her look: "No, he will not come." She did not, presumably, understand his urgency, but her eye was on the sea and she understood her own reason for haste. She had already begun to ascend the side of the valley, with Ransom following her, when Weston shouted, "No, you don't." Ransom turned and found himself covered by a revolver. The sudden heat which swept over his body was the only sign by which he knew that he was frightened. His head remained clear.

"Are you going to begin in this world also by murdering one of its inhabitants?" he asked.

"What are you saying?" asked the Lady, pausing and looking back at the two men with a puzzled, tranquil face.

"Stay where you are, Ransom," said the Professor. "That native can go where she likes; the sooner the better."

Ransom was about to implore her to make good her escape when he realised that no imploring was needed. He had irrationally supposed that she would understand the situation; but apparently she saw nothing more than two strangers talking about something which she did not at the moment understand—that, and her own necessity of leaving the Fixed Land at once.

"You and he do not come with me, Piebald?" she asked.

"No," said Ransom, without turning round. "It may be that you and I shall not meet soon again. Greet the King for me if you find him and speak of me always to Maleldil. I stay here."

"We shall meet when Maleldil pleases," she answered, "or if not, some greater good will happen to us instead." Then he heard her footsteps behind him for a few seconds, and then he heard them no more and knew he was alone with Weston.

"You allowed yourself to use the word Murder just now, Dr. Ransom," said the Professor, "in reference to an accident that occurred when we were in Malacandra. In any case, the creature killed was not a human being. Allow me to tell you that I consider the seduction of a native girl as an almost equally unfortunate way of introducing civilisation to a new planet."

"Seduction?" said Ransom. "Oh, I see. You thought I was making love to her."

"When I find a naked civilised man embracing a naked savage woman in a solitary place, that is the name I give to it."

"I wasn't embracing her," said Ransom dully, for the whole business of defending himself on this score seemed at that moment a mere weariness of the spirit. "And no one wears clothes here. But what does it matter? Get on with the job that brings you to Perelandra."

"You ask me to believe that you have been living here with that woman under these conditions in a state of sexless innocence?"

"Oh, sexless!" said Ransom disgustedly. "All right, if you like. It's about as good a description of living in Perelandra as it would be to say that a man had forgotten water because Niagara Falls didn't immediately give him the idea of making it into cups of tea. But you're right enough if you mean that I have had no more thought of desiring her than—than . . ." Comparisons failed him and his voice died. Then he began again: "But don't say I'm asking you to believe it, or to believe anything. I am asking you nothing but to begin and end as soon as possible whatever butcheries and robberies you have come to do."

Weston eyed him for a moment with a curious expression: then, unexpectedly, he returned his revolver to its holster.

"Ransom," he said, "you do me a great injustice."

For several seconds there was silence between them. Long breakers with white woolpacks of foam on them were now rolling into the cove exactly as on earth.

"Yes," said Weston at last, "and I will begin with a frank admission. You may make what capital of it you please. I shall not be deterred. I deliberately say that I was, in some respects, mistaken—seriously mistaken—in my conception of the whole interplanetary problem when I went to Malacandra."

Partly from the relaxation which followed the disappearance of the pistol, and partly from the elaborate air of magnanimity with which the great scientist spoke, Ransom felt very much inclined to laugh. But it occurred to him that this was possibly the first occasion in his whole life in which Weston had ever acknowledged himself in the wrong, and that even the false dawn of humility, which is still ninety-nine per cent of arrogance, ought not to be rebuffed—or not by him.

"Well, that's very handsome," he said. "How do you mean?"

"I'll tell you presently," said Weston. "In the meantime I must get my things ashore." Between them they beached the punt, and began carrying Weston's primus-stove and tins and tent and other packages to a spot about two hundred yards inland. Ransom, who knew all the paraphernalia to be needless, made no objection, and in about a quarter of an hour something like an encampment had been established in a mossy place under some blue-trunked silver-leaved trees beside a rivulet. Both men sat down and Ransom listened at first with interest, then with amazement, and finally with incredulity. Weston cleared his throat, threw out his chest, and assumed his lecturing manner. Throughout the conversation that followed, Ransom was filled with a sense of crazy irrelevance. Here were two human beings, thrown together in an alien world under conditions of inconceivable strangeness: the one separated from his spaceship, the other newly released from the threat of instant death. Was it sane—was it imaginable—that they should find themselves at once engaged in a philosophical argument which might just as well have occurred in a Cambridge combination room? Yet that, apparently, was what Weston insisted upon. He showed no interest in the fate of his space-ship; he even seemed to feel no curiosity about Ransom's presence on Venus. Could it be that he had travelled more than thirty million miles of space in search of—conversation? But as he went on talking, Ransom felt himself more and more in the presence of a monomaniac. Like an actor who cannot think of anything but his celebrity, or a lover who can think of nothing but his mistress, tense, tedious, and unescapable, the scientist pursued his fixed idea.

"The tragedy of my life," he said, "and indeed of the modern intellectual world in general, is the rigid specialisation of knowledge entailed by the growing complexity of what is known. It is my own share in that tragedy that an early devotion to physics has prevented me from paying any proper attention to Biology until I reached the fifties. To do myself justice, I should make it clear that the false humanist ideal of knowledge as an end in itself never appealed to me. I always wanted to know in order to achieve utility. At first, that utility naturally appeared to me in a personal form—I wanted scholarships, an income, and that generally recognised position in the world without which a man has no leverage. When those were attained, I began to look farther: to the utility of the human race!"

He paused as he rounded his period and Ransom nodded to him to proceed.

"The utility of the human race," continued Weston, "in the long run depends rigidly on the possibility of interplanetary, and even inter-sidereal, travel. That problem I solved. The key of human destiny was placed in my hands. It would be unnecessary—and painful to us both—to remind you how it was wrenched from me in Malacandra by a member of a hostile intelligent species whose existence, I admit, I had not anticipated."

"Not hostile exactly," said Ransom, "but go on."

"The rigours of our return journey from Malacandra led to a serious breakdown in my health——"

"Mine too," said Ransom.

Weston looked somewhat taken aback at the interruption and went on. "During my convalescence I had that leisure for reflection which I had denied myself for many years. In particular I reflected on the objections you had felt to that liquidation of the non-human inhabitants of Malacandra which was, of course, the necessary preliminary to its occupation by our own species. The traditional and, if I may say so, the humanitarian form in which you advanced those objections had till then concealed from me their true strength. That strength I now began to perceive. I began to see that my own exclusive devotion to human utility was really based on an unconscious dualism."

"What do you mean?"

"I mean that all my life I had been making a wholly unscientific dichotomy or antithesis between Man and Nature—had conceived myself fighting *for* Man against his non-human environment. During my illness I plunged into Biology, and particularly into what may be called biological philosophy. Hitherto, as a physicist, I had been content to regard Life as a subject outside my scope. The conflicting views of those who drew a sharp line between the organic and the inorganic and those who held that what we call Life was inherent in matter from the very beginning had not interested me. Now it did. I saw almost at once that I could admit no break, no discontinuity, in the unfolding of the cosmic process. I became a convinced believer in emergent evolution. All is one. The stuff of mind, the unconsciously purposive dynamism, is present from the very beginning."

Here he paused. Ransom had heard this sort of thing pretty often before and wondered when his companion was coming to the point. When Weston resumed it was with an even deeper solemnity of tone.

"The majestic spectacle of this blind, inarticulate purposiveness thrusting its way upward and ever upward in an endless unity of differentiated achievements towards an ever-increasing complexity of organisation, towards spontaneity and spirituality, swept away all my old conception of a duty to Man as such. Man in himself is nothing. The forward movement of Life—the growing spirituality—is everything. I say to you quite freely, Ransom, that I should have been wrong in liquidating the Malacandrians. It was a mere prejudice that made me prefer our own race to theirs. To spread spirituality, not to spread the human race, is henceforth my mission. This sets the coping-stone on my career. I worked first for myself; then for science; then for humanity; but now at last for Spirit itself—I might say, borrowing language which will be more familiar to you, the Holy Spirit."

"Now what exactly do you mean by that?" asked Ransom.

"I mean," said Weston, "that nothing now divides you and me except a few outworn theological technicalities with which organised religion has unhappily allowed itself to get incrusted. But I have penetrated that crust. The Meaning beneath it is as true and living as ever. If you will excuse me for putting it that way, the essential truth of the religious view of life finds a remarkable witness in the fact that it enabled you, on Malacandra, to grasp, in your own mythical and imaginative fashion, a truth which was hidden from me."

"I don't know much about what people call the religious view of life," said Ransom, wrinkling his brow. "You see, I'm a Christian. And what we mean by the Holy Ghost is *not* a blind, inarticulate purposiveness."

"My dear Ransom," said Weston, "I understand you perfectly. I have no doubt that my phraseology will seem strange to you, and perhaps even shocking. Early and revered associations may have put it out of your power to recognise in this new form the very same truths which religion has so long preserved and which science is now at last rediscovering. But whether you can see it or not, believe me, we are talking about exactly the same thing."

"I'm not at all sure that we are."

"That, if you will permit me to say so, is one of the real weaknesses of organised religion—that adherence to formulæ, that failure to recognise one's own friends. God is a spirit, Ransom. Get hold of that. You're familiar with that already. Stick to it. God is a spirit."

"Well, of course. But what then?"

"What then? Why, spirit—mind—freedom—spontaneity—that's what I'm talking about. That is the goal towards which the whole cosmic process is moving. The final disengagement of that freedom, that spirituality, is the work to which I dedicate my own life and the life of humanity. The goal, Ransom, the goal: think of it! *Pure* spirit: the final vortex of self-thinking, self-originating activity."

"Final?" said Ransom. "You mean it doesn't yet exist?"

"Ah," said Weston, "I see what's bothering you. Of course I know. Religion pictures it as being there from the beginning. But surely that is not a real difference? To make it one, would be to take time too seriously. When it has once been attained, you might then say it had been at the beginning just as well as at the end. Time is one of the things it will transcend."

"By the way," said Ransom, "is it in any sense at all personal—is it alive?"

An indescribable expression passed over Weston's face. He moved a little nearer to Ransom and began speaking in a lower voice.

"That's what none of them understand," he said. It was such a gangster's or a schoolboy's whisper and so unlike his usual orotund lecturing style that Ransom for a moment felt a sensation almost of disgust.

"Yes," said Weston, "I couldn't have believed, myself, till recently. Not a person, of course. Anthropomorphism is one of the childish diseases of popular religion" (here he had resumed his public manner), "but the opposite extreme of excessive abstraction has perhaps in the aggregate proved more disastrous. Call it a Force. A great, inscrutable

Force, pouring up into us from the dark bases of being. A Force that can choose its instruments. It is only lately, Ransom, that I've learned from actual experience something which you have believed all your life as part of your religion." Here he suddenly subsided again into a whisper—a croaking whisper unlike his usual voice. "Guided," he said. "Chosen. Guided. I've become conscious that I'm a man set apart. Why did I do physics? Why did I discover the Weston rays? Why did I go to Malacandra? It—the Force—has pushed me on all the time. I'm being guided. I know now that I am the greatest scientist the world has yet produced. I've been made so for a purpose. It is through me that Spirit itself is at this moment pushing on to its goal."

"Look here," said Ransom, "one wants to be careful about this sort of thing. There are spirits and spirits you know."

"Eh?" said Weston. "What are you talking about?"

"I mean a thing might be a spirit and not good for you."

"But I thought you agreed that Spirit was the good—the end of the whole process? I thought you religious people were all out for spirituality? What is the point of asceticism—fasts and celibacy and all that? Didn't we agree that God is a spirit? Don't you worship Him because He is pure spirit?"

"Good heavens, no! We worship Him because He is wise and good. There's nothing specially fine about simply being a spirit. The Devil is a spirit."

"Now your mentioning the Devil is very interesting," said Weston, who had by this time quite recovered his normal manner. "It is a most interesting thing in popular religion, this tendency to fissiparate, to breed pairs of opposites: heaven and hell, God and Devil. I need hardly say that in my view no real dualism in the universe is admissible; and on that ground I should have been disposed, even a few weeks ago, to reject these pairs of doublets as pure mythology. It would have been a profound error. The cause of this universal religious tendency is to be sought much deeper. The doublets are really portraits of Spirit, of cosmic energy—self-portraits, indeed, for it is the Life-Force itself which has deposited them in our brains."

"What on earth do you mean?" said Ransom. As he spoke he rose to his feet and began pacing to and fro. A quite appalling weariness and malaise had descended upon him.

"*Your* Devil and *your* God," said Weston, "are both pictures of the same Force. Your heaven is a picture of the perfect spirituality ahead; your hell a picture of the urge or *nisus* which is driving us on to it from behind. Hence the static peace of the one and the fire and darkness of the other. The next stage of emergent evolution, beckoning us forward, is

God; the transcended stage behind, ejecting us, is the Devil. Your own religion, after all, says that the devils are fallen angels."

"And you are saying precisely the opposite, as far as I can make out—that angels are devils who've risen in the world."

"It comes to the same thing," said Weston.

There was another long pause. "Look here," said Ransom, "it's easy to misunderstand one another on a point like this. What you are saying sounds to me like the most horrible mistake a man could fall into. But that may be because in the effort to accommodate it to my supposed 'religious views,' you're saying a good deal more than you mean. It's only a metaphor, isn't it, all this about spirits and forces? I expect all you really mean is that you feel it your duty to work for the spread of civilisation and knowledge and that kind of thing." He had tried to keep out of his voice the involuntary anxiety which he had begun to feel. Next moment he recoiled in horror at the cackling laughter, almost an infantile or senile laughter, with which Weston replied.

"There you go, there you go," he said. "Like all you religious people. You talk and talk about these things all your life, and the moment you meet the reality you get frightened."

"What proof," said Ransom (who indeed did feel frightened), "what proof have you that you are being guided or supported by anything except your own individual mind and other people's books?"

"You didn't notice, dear Ransom," said Weston, "that I'd improved a bit since we last met in my knowledge of extraterrestrial language. You are a philologist, they tell me."

Ransom started. "How did you do it?" he blurted out.

"Guidance, you know, guidance," croaked Weston. He was squatting at the roots of his tree with his knees drawn up, and his face, now the colour of putty, wore a fixed and even slightly twisted grin. "Guidance. Guidance," he went on. "Things coming into my head. I'm being prepared all the time. Being made a fit receptacle for it."

"That ought to be fairly easy," said Ransom impatiently. "If this Life-Force is something so ambiguous that God and the Devil are equally good portraits of it, I suppose any receptacle is equally fit, and anything you can do is equally an expression of it."

"There's such a thing as the main current," said Weston. "It's a question of surrendering yourself to that—making yourself the conductor of the live, fiery, central purpose—becoming the very finger with which it reaches forward."

"But I thought that was the Devil aspect of it, a moment ago."

"That is the fundamental paradox. The thing we are reaching forward to is what you would call God. The reaching forward, the dynamism, is what people like you always call the Devil. The people like me, who do the reaching forward, are always martyrs. You revile us, and by us come to your goal."

"Does that mean in plainer language that the things the Force wants you to do are what ordinary people call diabolical?"

"My dear Ransom, I wish you would not keep relapsing on to the popular level. The two things are only moments in the single, unique reality. The world leaps forward through great men and greatness always transcends mere moralism. When the leap has been made our 'diabolism' as you would call it becomes the morality of the next stage; but while we are making it, we are called criminals, heretics, blasphemers. . . ."

"How far does it go? Would you still obey the Life-Force if you found it prompting you to murder me?"

"Yes."

"Or to sell England to the Germans?"

"Yes."

"Or to print lies as serious research in a scientific periodical?"

"Yes."

"God help you!" said Ransom.

"You are still wedded to your conventionalities," said Weston. "Still dealing in abstractions. Can you not even conceive a total commitment—a commitment to something which utterly overrides all our petty ethical pigeon-holes?"

Ransom grasped at the straw. "Wait, Weston," he said abruptly. "That may be a point of contact. You say it's a total commitment. That is, you're giving up yourself. You're not out for your own advantage. No, wait half a second. This *is* the point of contact between your morality and mine. We both acknowledge——"

"Idiot," said Weston. His voice was almost a howl and he had risen to his feet. "Idiot," he repeated. "Can you understand nothing? Will you always try to press everything back into the miserable framework of your old jargon about self and self-sacrifice? That is the old accursed dualism in another form. There is no possible distinction in concrete thought between me and the universe. In so far as I am the conductor of the central forward pressure of the universe, I am it. Do you see, you timid, scruple-mongering fool? I *am* the Universe. I, Weston, am your God and your Devil. I call that Force into me completely. . . ."

Then horrible things began happening. A spasm like that preceding a deadly vomit twisted Weston's face out of recognition. As it passed, for one second something like the old Weston reappeared—the old Weston, staring with eyes of horror and howling, "Ransom, Ransom! For

Christ's sake don't let them——" and instantly his whole body spun round as if he had been hit by a revolver-bullet and he fell to the earth, and was there rolling at Ransom's feet, slavering and chattering and tearing up the moss by handfuls. Gradually the convulsions decreased. He lay still, breathing heavily, his eyes open but without expression. Ransom was kneeling beside him now. It was obvious that the body was alive, and Ransom wondered whether this were a stroke or an epileptic fit, for he had never seen either. He rummaged among the packages and found a bottle of brandy which he uncorked and applied to the patient's mouth. To his consternation the teeth opened, closed on the neck of the bottle and bit it through. No glass was spat out. "O God, I've killed him," said Ransom. But beyond a spurt of blood at the lips there was no change in his appearance. The face suggested that either he was in no pain or in pain beyond all human comprehension. Ransom rose at last, but before doing so he plucked the revolver from Weston's belt, then, walking down to the beach, he threw it as far as he could into the sea.

He stood for some moments gazing out upon the bay and undecided what to do. Presently he turned and climbed up the turfy ridge that bordered the little valley on his left hand. He found himself on a fairly level upland with a good view of the sea, now running high and teased out of its level gold into a continually changing pattern of lights and shadows. For a second or two he could catch no sight of the islands. Then suddenly their tree-tops appeared, hanging high up against the sky, and widely separated. The weather, apparently, was already driving them apart—and even as he thought this they vanished once more into some unseen valley of the waves. What was his chance, he wondered, of ever finding them again? A sense of loneliness smote him, and then a feeling of angry frustration. If Weston were dying, or even if Weston were to live, imprisoned here with him on an island they could not leave, what had been the danger he was sent to avert from Perelandra? And so, having begun to think of himself, he realised that he was hungry. He had seen neither fruit nor gourd on the Fixed Land. Perhaps it was a death trap. He smiled bitterly at the folly which had made him so glad, that morning, to exchange those floating paradises, where every grove dropped sweetness, for this barren rock. But perhaps it was not barren after all. Determined, despite the weariness which was every moment descending upon him, to make a search for food, he was just turning inland when the swift changes of colour that announce the evening of that world overtook him. Uselessly he quickened his pace. Before he had got down into the valley, the grove where he had left Weston was a mere cloud of darkness. Before he had reached it he was in seamless, undimensioned night. An effort or two to grope his way to the place where

Weston's stores had been deposited only served to abolish his sense of direction altogether. He sat down perforce. He called Weston's name aloud once or twice but, as he expected, received no answer. "I'm glad I removed his gun, all the same," thought Ransom; and then, "Well, *qui dort dîne* and I suppose I must make the best of it till the morning." When he lay down he discovered that the solid earth and moss of the Fixed Land was very much less comfortable than the surfaces to which he had lately been accustomed. That, and the thought of the other human being lying, no doubt, close at hand with open eyes and teeth clenched on splintered glass, and the sullen recurring pound of breakers on the beach, all made the night comfortless. "If I lived on Perelandra," he muttered, "Maleldil wouldn't need to *forbid* this island. I wish I'd never set eyes on it."

8

He woke, after a disturbed and dreamful sleep, in full daylight. He had a dry mouth, a crick in his neck, and a soreness in his limbs. It was so unlike all previous wakings in the world of Venus, that for a moment he supposed himself back on Earth: and the dream (for so it seemed to him) of having lived and walked on the oceans of the Morning Star rushed through his memory with a sense of lost sweetness that was well-nigh unbearable. Then he sat up and the facts came back to him. "It's jolly nearly the same as having waked from a dream, though," he thought. Hunger and thirst became at once his dominant sensations, but he conceived it a duty to look first at the sick man—though with very little hope that he could help him. He gazed round. There was the grove of silvery trees all right, but he could not see Weston. Then he glanced at the bay; there was no punt either. Assuming that in the darkness he had blundered into the wrong valley, he rose and approached the stream for a drink. As he lifted his face from the water with a long sigh of satisfaction, his eyes suddenly fell on a little wooden box—and then beyond it on a couple of tins. His brain was working rather slowly and it took him a few seconds to realise that he was in the right valley after all, and a few more to draw conclusions from the fact that the box was open and empty, and that some of the stores had been removed and others left behind. But was it possible that a man in Weston's physical condition could have recovered sufficiently during the night to strike camp and to go away laden with some kind of pack? Was it possible that any man could have faced a sea like that in a collapsible punt? It was true, as he now noticed for the first time, that the storm (which had been a mere squall by Perelandrian standards) appeared to have blown itself out during the night; but there was still a quite formidable swell and it seemed out of the question that the Professor could have left the island. Much more probably he had left the valley on foot and carried the punt with him. Ransom decided that he must find Weston at once: he must keep in touch with his enemy. For if Weston had recovered, there was no doubt he meant mischief of some kind. Ransom was not at all certain that he had understood all his wild talk on the previous day; but what he did understand he disliked very much, and suspected that this vague mysticism about "spirituality" would turn out to be something even nastier than his old and comparatively simple programme of planetary imperialism. It would be unfair to take seriously the things the man had said immediately before his seizure, no doubt; but there was enough without that.

The next few hours Ransom passed in searching the island for food and for Weston. As far as food was concerned, he was rewarded. Some fruit like bilberries could be gathered in handfuls on the upper slopes, and the wooded valleys abounded in a kind of oval nut. The kernel had a toughly soft consistency, rather like cork or kidneys, and the flavour, though somewhat austere and prosaic after the fruit of the floating islands, was not unsatisfactory. The giant mice were as tame as other Perelandrian beasts but seemed stupider. Ransom ascended to the central plateau. The sea was dotted with islands in every direction, rising and falling with the swell, and all separated from one another by wide stretches of water. His eye at once picked out an orange-coloured island, but did not know whether it was that on which he had been living, for he saw at least two others in which the same colour predominated. At one time he counted twenty-three floating islands in all. That, he thought, was more than the temporary archipelago had contained, and allowed him to hope that any one of those he saw might hide the King— or that the King might even at this moment be re-united to the Lady. Without thinking it out very clearly, he had come to rest almost all his hopes on the King.

Of Weston he could find no trace. It really did seem, in spite of all improbabilities, that he had somehow contrived to leave the Fixed Island; and Ransom's anxiety was very great. What Weston, in his new vein, might do, he had no idea. The best to hope for was that he would simply ignore the master and mistress of Perelandra as mere savages or "natives."

Late in the day, being tired, he sat down on the shore. There was very little swell now and the waves, just before they broke, were less than knee-deep. His feet, made soft by the mattress-like surface which one walks on in those floating islands, were hot and sore. Presently he decided to refresh them by a little wading. The delicious quality of the water drew him out till he was waist-deep. As he stood there, deep in thought, he suddenly perceived that what he had taken to be an effect of light on the water was really the back of one of the great silvery fish. "I wonder would it let me ride it?" he thought; and then, watching how the beast nosed towards him and kept itself as near the shallows as it dared, it was borne in upon him that it was trying to attract his attention. Could it have been *sent?* The thought had no sooner darted through his mind than he decided to make the experiment. He laid his hand across the creature's back, and it did not flinch from his touch. Then with some difficulty he scrambled into a sitting position across the narrow part behind its head, and while he was doing this it remained as nearly stationary as it could; but as soon as he was firmly in the saddle it whisked itself about and headed for the sea.

If he had wished to withdraw, it was very soon impossible to do so. Already the green pinnacles of the mountain, as he looked back, had withdrawn their summits from the sky and the coastline of the island had begun to conceal its bays and nesses. The breakers were no longer audible—only the prolonged sibilant or chattering noises of the water about him. Many floating islands were visible, though seen from this level they were mere feathery silhouettes. But the fish seemed to be heading for none of these. Straight on, as if it well knew its way, the beat of the great fins carried him for more than an hour. Then green and purple splashed the whole world, and after that darkness.

Somehow he felt hardly any uneasiness when he found himself swiftly climbing and descending the low hills of water through the black night. And here it was not all black. The heavens had vanished, and the surface of the sea; but far, far below him in the heart of the vacancy through which he appeared to be travelling, strange bursting star shells and writhing streaks of a bluish-green luminosity appeared. At first they were very remote, but soon, as far as he could judge, they were nearer. A whole world of phosphorescent creatures seemed to be at play not far from the surface—coiling eels and darting things in complete armour, and then heraldically fantastic shapes to which the sea-horse of our own waters would be commonplace. They were all round him—twenty or thirty of them often in sight at once. And mixed with all this riot of sea-centaurs and sea-dragons he saw yet stranger forms: fishes, if fishes they were, whose forward part was so nearly human in shape that when he first caught sight of them he thought he had fallen into a dream and shook himself to awake. But it was no dream. There—and there again—it was unmistakable: now a shoulder, now a profile, and then for one second a full face: veritable mermen or mermaids. The resemblance to humanity was indeed greater, not less, than he had first supposed. What had for a moment concealed it from him was the total absence of human expression. Yet the faces were not idiotic; they were not even brutal parodies of humanity like those of our terrestrial apes. They were more like human faces asleep, or faces in which humanity slept while some other life, neither bestial nor diabolic, but merely elvish, out of our orbit, was irrelevantly awake. He remembered his old suspicion that what was myth in one world might always be fact in some other. He wondered also whether the King and Queen of Perelandra, though doubtless the first human pair of this planet, might on the physical side have a marine ancestry. And if so, what then of the man-like things before men in our own world? Must they in truth have been the wistful brutalities whose pictures we see in popular books on evolution? Or were the old myths truer than the modern myths? Had there in truth been a time when satyrs danced in the Italian woods? But he said "Hush" to his mind at this stage, for the mere pleasure of breathing in the fragrance which now began to steal towards him from the blackness ahead. Warm and sweet, and every moment sweeter and purer, and every moment stronger and more filled with all delights, it came to him. He knew well what it was. He would know it henceforward out of the whole universe—the night-breath of a floating island in the star Venus. It was strange to be filled with homesickness for places where his sojourn had been so brief and which were, by any objective standard, so alien to all our race. Or were they? The cord of longing which drew him to the invisible isle seemed to him at that moment to have been fastened long, long before his coming to Perelandra, long before the earliest times that memory could recover in his childhood, before birth, before the birth of man himself, before the origins of time. It was sharp, sweet, wild, and holy, all in one, and in any world where men's nerves have ceased to obey their central desires would doubtless have been aphrodisiac too, but not in Perelandra. The fish was no longer moving. Ransom put out his hand. He found he was touching weed. He crawled forward over the head of the monstrous fish, and levered himself on to the gently moving surface of the island. Short as his absence from such places had been, his earth-trained habits of walking had reasserted themselves, and he fell more than once as he groped his way on the heaving lawn. But it did no harm falling here; good luck to it! There were trees all about him in the dark and when a smooth, cool, rounded object came away in his hand he put it, unfearing, to his lips. It was none of the fruits he had tasted before. It was better than any of them. Well might the Lady say of her world that the fruit you ate at any moment was, at that moment, the best. Wearied with his day's walking and climbing, and, still more, borne down by absolute satisfaction, he sank into dreamless sleep.

He felt that it was several hours later when he awoke and found himself still in darkness. He knew, too, that he had been suddenly waked: and a moment later he was listening to the sound that had waked him. It was the sound of voices—a man's voice and a woman's in earnest conversation. He judged that they were very close to him—for in a Perelandrian night an object is no more visible six inches than six miles away. He perceived at once who the speakers were: but the voices sounded strange, and the emotions of the speakers were obscure to him, with no facial expression to eke them out.

"I am wondering," said the woman's voice, "whether all the people of your world have the habit of talking about the same thing more than once. I have said already that we are forbidden to dwell on the Fixed Land. Why do you not either talk of something else or stop talking?"

"Because this forbidding is such a strange one," said the Man's voice. "And so unlike the ways of Maleldil in my world. And He has not forbidden you to think about dwelling on the Fixed Land."

"That would be a strange thing—to think about what will never happen."

"Nay, in our world we do it all the time. We put words together to mean things that have never happened and places that never were: beautiful words, well put together. And then tell them to one another. We call it stories or poetry. In that old world you spoke of, Malacandra, they did the same. It is for mirth and wonder and wisdom."

"What is the wisdom in it?"

"Because the world is made up not only of what is but of what might be. Maleldil knows both and wants us to know both."

"This is more than I ever thought of. The other—the Piebald one—has already told me things which made me feel like a tree whose branches were growing wider and wider apart. But this goes beyond all. Stepping out of what is into what might be and talking and making things out there . . . alongside the world. I will ask the King what he thinks of it."

"You see, that is what we always come back to. If only you had not been parted from the King."

"Oh, I see. That also is one of the things that might be. The world might be so made that the King and I were never parted."

"The world would not have to be different—only the way you live. In a world where people live on the Fixed Lands they do not become suddenly separated."

"But you remember we are not to live on the Fixed Land."

"No, but He has never forbidden you to think about it. Might not that be one of the reasons why you are forbidden to do it—so that you may have a Might Be to think about, to make Story about as we call it?"

"I will think more of this. I will get the King to make me older about it."

"How greatly I desire to meet this King of yours! But in the matter of Stories he may be no older than you himself."

"That saying of yours is like a tree with no fruit. The King is always older than I, and about all things."

"But Piebald and I have already made you older about certain matters which the King never mentioned to you. That is the new good which you never expected. You thought you would always learn all things from the King; but now Maleldil has sent you other men whom it had never entered your mind to think of and they have told you things the King himself could not know."

"I begin to see now why the King and I were parted at this time. This is a strange and great good He intended for me."

"And if you refused to learn things from me and kept on saying you would wait and ask the King, would that not be like turning away from the fruit you had found to the fruit you had expected?"

"These are deep questions, Stranger. Maleldil is not putting much into my mind about them."

"Do you not see why?"

"No."

"Since Piebald and I have come to your world we have put many things into your mind which Maleldil has not. Do you not see that He is letting go of your hand a little?"

"How could He? He is wherever we go."

"Yes, but in another way. He is making you older—making you to learn things not straight from Him but by your own meetings with other people and your own questions and thoughts."

"He is certainly doing that."

"Yes. He is making you a full woman, for up till now you were only half made—like the beasts who do nothing of themselves. This time, when you meet the King again, it is you who will have things to tell him. It is you who will be older than he and who will make him older."

"Maleldil would not make a thing like that happen. It would be like a fruit with no taste."

"But it would have a taste for *him*. Do you not think the King must sometimes be tired of being the older? Would he not love you more if you were wiser than he?"

"Is this what you call a Poetry or do you mean that it really is?"

"I mean a thing that really is."

"But how could anyone love anything more? It is like saying a thing could be bigger than itself."

"I only meant you could become more like the women of my world."

"What are they like?"

"They are of a great spirit. They always reach out their hands for the new and unexpected good, and see that it is good long before the men understand it. Their minds run ahead of what Maleldil has told them. They do not need to wait for Him to tell them what is good, but know it for themselves as He does. They are, as it were, little Maleldils. And because of their wisdom, their beauty is as much greater than yours as the sweetness of these gourds surpasses the taste of water. And because of their beauty the love which the men have for them is as much greater than the King's love for you as the naked burning of Deep Heaven seen from my world is more wonderful than the golden roof of yours."

"I wish I could see them."

"I wish you could."

"How beautiful is Maleldil and how wonderful are all His works: perhaps He will bring out of me daughters as much greater than I as I am greater than the beasts. It will be better than I thought. I had thought I was to be always Queen and Lady. But I see now that I may be as the eldila. I may be appointed to cherish when they are small and weak children who will grow up and overtop me and at whose feet I shall fall. I see it is not only questions and thoughts that grow out wider and wider like branches. Joy also widens out and comes where we had never thought."

"I will sleep now," said the other voice. As it said this it became, for the first time, unmistakably the voice of Weston—and of Weston disgruntled and snappish. Up till now Ransom, though constantly resolving to join the conversation, had been kept silent in a kind of suspense between two conflicting states of mind. On the one hand he was certain, both from the voice and from many of the things it said, that the male speaker was Weston. On the other hand, the voice, divided from the man's appearance, sounded curiously unlike itself. Still more, the patient persistent manner in which it was used was very unlike the Professor's usual alternation between pompous lecturing and abrupt bullying. And how could a man fresh from such a physical crisis as he had seen Weston undergo have recovered such mastery of himself in a few hours? And how could he have reached the floating island? Ransom had found himself throughout their dialogue confronted with an intolerable contradiction. Something which was and was not Weston was talking: and the sense of this monstrosity, only a few feet away in the darkness, had sent thrills of exquisite horror tingling along his spine, and raised questions in his mind which he tried to dismiss as fantastic. Now that the conversation was over he realised, too, with what intense anxiety he had followed it. At the same moment he was conscious of a sense of triumph. But it was not he who was triumphant. The whole darkness about him rang with victory. He started and half raised himself. Had there been any actual sound? Listening hard he could hear nothing but the low murmurous noise of warm wind and gentle swell. The suggestion of music must have been from within. But as soon as he lay down again he felt assured that it was not. From without, most certainly from without, but not by the sense of hearing, festal revelry and dance and splendour poured into him—no sound, yet in such fashion that it could not be remembered or thought of except as music. It was like having a new sense. It was like being present when the morning stars sang together. It was as if Perelandra had that moment been created—and perhaps in some sense it had. The feeling of a great disaster averted was forced upon his mind, and with it came the hope that there would be no second attempt; and then, sweeter than all, the suggestion that he had been brought there not to do anything but only as a spectator or a witness. A few minutes later he was asleep.

9

The weather had changed during the night. Ransom sat looking out from the edge of the forest in which he had slept, on a flat sea where there were no other islands in view. He had waked a few minutes before and found himself lying alone in a close thicket of stems that were rather reed-like in character but stout as those of birch trees and which carried an almost flat roof of thick foliage. From this there hung fruits as smooth and bright and round as holly-berries, some of which he ate. Then he found his way to open country near the skirts of the island and looked about him. Neither Weston nor the Lady was in sight, and he began walking in a leisurely fashion beside the sea. His bare feet sank a little into a carpet of saffron-coloured vegetation, which covered them with an aromatic dust. As he was looking down at this he suddenly noticed something else. At first he thought it was a creature of more fantastic shape than he had yet seen on Perelandra. Its shape was not only fantastic but hideous. Then he dropped on one knee to examine it. Finally he touched it, with reluctance. A moment later he drew back his hands like a man who had touched a snake.

It was a damaged animal. It was, or had been, one of the brightly coloured frogs. But some accident had happened to it. The whole back had been ripped open in a sort of V-shaped gash, the point of the V being a little behind the head. Something had torn a widening wound backward—as we do in opening an envelope—along the trunk and pulled it out so far behind the animal that the hoppers or hind legs had been almost torn off with it. They were so damaged that the frog could not leap. On earth it would have been merely a nasty sight, but up to this moment Ransom had as yet seen nothing dead or spoiled in Perelandra, and it was like a blow in the face. It was like the first spasm of well-remembered pain warning a man who had thought he was cured that his family have deceived him and he is dying after all. It was like the first lie from the mouth of a friend on whose truth one was willing to stake a thousand pounds. It was irrevocable. The milk-warm wind blowing over the golden sea, the blues and silvers and greens of the floating garden, the sky itself—all these had become, in one instant, merely the illuminated margin of a book whose text was the struggling little horror at his feet, and he himself, in that same instant, had passed into a state of emotion which he could neither control nor understand. He told himself that a creature of that kind probably had very little sensation. But it did not much mend matters. It was not merely pity for pain that had suddenly changed the rhythm of his heart-beats. The thing was an intolerable obscenity which afflicted him with shame. It would have been better, or so he thought at that moment, for the whole universe never to have existed than for this one thing to have happened. Then he decided, in spite of his theoretical belief that it was an organism too low for much pain, that it had better be killed. He had neither boots nor stone nor stick. The frog proved remarkably hard to kill. When it was far too late to desist he saw clearly that he had been a fool to make the attempt. Whatever its sufferings might be he had certainly increased and not diminished them. But he had to go through with it. The job seemed to take nearly an hour. And when at last the mangled result was quite still and he went down to the water's edge to wash, he was sick and shaken. It seems odd to say this of a man who had been on the Somme; but the architects tell us that nothing is great or small save by position.

At last he got up and resumed his walk. Next moment he started and looked at the ground again. He quickened his pace, and then once more stopped and looked. He stood stock-still and covered his face. He called aloud upon heaven to break the nightmare or to let him understand what was happening. A trail of mutilated frogs lay along the edge of the island. Picking his footsteps with care, he followed it. He counted ten, fifteen, twenty: and the twenty-first brought him to a place where the wood came down to the water's edge. He went into the wood and came out on the other side. There he stopped dead and stared. Weston, still clothed but without his pith helmet, was standing about thirty feet away: and as Ransom watched he was tearing a frog—quietly and almost surgically inserting his forefinger, with its long sharp nail, under the skin behind the creature's head and ripping it open. Ransom had not noticed before that Weston had such remarkable nails. Then he finished the operation, threw the bleeding ruin away, and looked up. Their eyes met.

If Ransom said nothing, it was because he could not speak. He saw a man who was certainly not ill, to judge from his easy stance and the powerful use he had just been making of his fingers. He saw a man who was certainly Weston, to judge from his height and build and colouring and features. In that sense he was quite recognisable. But the terror was that he was also unrecognisable. He did not look like a sick man: but he looked very like a dead one. The face which he raised from torturing the frog had that terrible power which the face of a corpse sometimes has of simply rebuffing every conceivable human attitude one can adopt towards it. The expressionless mouth, the unwinking stare of the eyes, something heavy and inorganic in the very folds of the cheek, said clearly: "I have features as you have, but there is nothing in common between you and me." It was this that kept Ransom speechless. What could you say—what appeal or threat could have any meaning—to *that*? And now, forcing its way up into consciousness, thrusting aside every mental habit and every longing not to believe, came the conviction that this, in fact, was not a man: that Weston's body was kept, walking and undecaying, in Perelandra by some wholly different kind of life, and that Weston himself was gone.

It looked at Ransom in silence and at last began to smile. We have all often spoken—Ransom himself had often spoken—of a devilish smile. Now he realised that he had never taken the words seriously. The smile was not bitter, nor raging, nor, in an ordinary sense, sinister; it was not even mocking. It seemed to summon Ransom, with horrible naïveté of welcome, into the world of its own pleasures, as if all men were at one in those pleasures, as if they were the most natural thing in the world and no dispute could ever have occurred about them. It was not furtive, nor ashamed, it had nothing of the conspirator in it. It did not defy goodness, it ignored it to the point of annihilation. Ransom perceived that he had never before seen anything but half-hearted and uneasy attempts at evil. This creature was whole-hearted. The extremity of its evil had passed beyond all struggle into some state which bore a horrible similarity to innocence. It was beyond vice as the Lady was beyond virtue.

The stillness and the smiling lasted for perhaps two whole minutes: certainly not less. Then Ransom made to take a step towards the thing, with no very clear notion of what he would do when he reached it. He stumbled and fell. He had a curious difficulty in getting to his feet again, and when he got to them he overbalanced and fell for the second time. Then there was a moment of darkness with a noise of roaring express trains. After that the golden sky and coloured waves returned and he knew he was alone and recovering from a faint. As he lay there, still unable and perhaps unwilling to rise, it came into his mind that in certain old philosophers and poets he had read that the mere sight of the devils was one of the greatest among the torments of Hell. It had seemed to him till now merely a quaint fancy. And yet (as he now saw) even the children know better: no child would have any difficulty in understanding that there might be a face the mere beholding of which was final calamity. The children, the poets, and the philosophers were right. As there is one Face above all worlds merely to see which is irrevocable joy, so at the bottom of all worlds that face is waiting whose sight alone is the misery from which none who beholds it can recover. And though there seemed to be, and indeed were, a thousand roads by which a man could walk through the world, there was not a single one which did not lead sooner or later either to the Beatific or the Miserific Vision. He himself had, of course, seen only a mask or faint adumbration of it; even so, he was not quite sure that he would live.

When he was able, he got up and set out to search for the thing. He must either try to prevent it from meeting the Lady or at least be present when they met. What he could do, he did not know; but it was clear beyond all evasion that this was what he had been sent for. Weston's body, travelling in a space-ship, had been the bridge by which something else had invaded Perelandra—whether that supreme and original evil whom in Mars they call The Bent One, or one of his lesser followers, made no difference. Ransom was all gooseflesh, and his knees kept getting in each other's way. It surprised him that he could experience so extreme a terror and yet be walking and thinking—as men in war or sickness are surprised to find how much can be borne: "It will drive us mad," "It will kill us outright," we say; and then it happens and we find ourselves neither mad nor dead, still held to the task.

The weather changed. The plain on which he was walking swelled to a wave of land. The sky grew paler: it was soon rather primrose than gold. The sea grew darker, almost the colour of bronze. Soon the island was climbing considerable hills of water. Once or twice he had to sit down and rest. After several hours (for his progress was very slow) he suddenly saw two human figures on what was for the moment a skyline. Next moment they were out of sight as the country heaved up between them and him. It took about half an hour to reach them. Weston's body was standing—swaying and balancing itself to meet each change of the ground in a manner of which the real Weston would have been incapable. It was talking to the Lady. And what surprised Ransom most was that she continued to listen to it without turning to welcome him or even to comment on his arrival when he came and sat down beside her on the soft turf.

"It *is* a great branching out," it was saying. "This making of story or poetry about things that might be but are not. If you shrink back from it, are you not drawing back from the fruit that is offered you?"

"It is not from the making of a story that I shrink back, O Stranger," she answered, "but from this one story that you have put into my head. I can make myself stories about my children or the King. I can make it that the fish fly and the land beasts swim. But if I try to make the story about living on the Fixed Island I do not know how to make it about Maleldil. For if I make it that He has changed His command, that will not go. And if I make it that we are living there against His command, that is like making the sky all black and the water so that we cannot drink it and the air so that we cannot breathe it. But also, I do not see what is the pleasure of trying to make these things."

"To make you wiser, older," said Weston's body.

"Do you know for certain that it will do that?" she asked.

"Yes, for certain," it replied. "That is how the women of my world have become so great and so beautiful."

"Do not listen to him," broke in Ransom; "send him away. Do not hear what he says, do not think of it."

She turned to Ransom for the first time. There had been some very slight change in her face since he had last seen her. It was not sad, nor deeply bewildered, but the hint of something precarious had increased. On the other hand she was clearly pleased to see him, though surprised at his interruption; and her first words revealed that her failure to greet him at his arrival had resulted from her never having envisaged the possibility of a conversation between more than two speakers. And throughout the rest of their talk, her ignorance of the technique of general conversation gave a curious and disquieting quality to the whole scene. She had no notion of how to glance rapidly from one face to another or to disentangle two remarks at once. Sometimes she listened wholly to Ransom, sometimes wholly to the other, but never to both.

"Why do you start speaking before this man has finished, Piebald?" she inquired. "How do they do in your world where you are many and more than two must often be together? Do they not talk in turns; or have you an art to understand even when all speak together? I am not old enough for that."

"I do not want you to hear him at all," said Ransom. "He is——" and then he hesitated. "Bad," "liar," "enemy," none of these words would, as yet, have any meaning for her. Racking his brains he thought of their previous conversation about the great eldil who had held on to the old good and refused the new one. Yes; that would be her only approach to the idea of badness. He was just about to speak but it was too late. Weston's voice anticipated him.

"This Piebald," it said, "does not want you to hear me, because he wants to keep you young. He does not want you to go on to the new fruits that you have never tasted before."

"But how could he want to keep me younger?"

"Have you not seen already," said Weston's body, "that Piebald is one who always shrinks back from the wave that is coming towards us and would like, if he could, to bring back the wave that is past? In the very first hour of his talking with you, did he not betray this? He did not know that all was new since Maleldil became a man and that now all creatures with reason will be men. You had to teach him this. And when he had learned it he did not welcome it. He was sorry that there would be no more of the old furry people. He would bring back that old world if he could. And when you asked him to teach you Death, he would not. He wanted you to remain young, not to learn Death. Was it not he who first put into your mind the very thought that it was possible not to desire the wave that Maleldil was rolling towards us; to shrink so much that you would cut off your arms and legs to prevent it coming?"

"You mean he is so young?"

"He is what in my world we call Bad," said Weston's body. "One who rejects the fruit he is given for the sake of the fruit he expected or the fruit he found last time."

"We must make him older, then," said the Lady, and though she did not look at Ransom, all the Queen and Mother in her were revealed to him and he knew that she wished him, and all things, infinitely well. And he—he could do nothing. His weapon had been knocked out of his hand.

"And will you teach us Death?" said the Lady to Weston's shape, where it stood above her.

"Yes," it said, "it is for this that I came here, that you may have Death in abundance. But you must be very courageous."

"*Courageous.* What is that?"

"It is what makes you to swim on a day when the waves are so great and swift that something inside you bids you to stay on land."

"I know. And those are the best days of all for swimming."

"Yes. But to find Death, and with Death the real oldness and the strong beauty and the uttermost branching out, you must plunge into things greater than waves."

"Go on. Your words are like no other words that I have ever heard.

They are like the bubble breaking on the tree. They make me think of—
of—I do not know what they make me think of."

"I will speak greater words than these; but I must wait till you are
older."

"Make me older."

"Lady, Lady," broke in Ransom, "will not Maleldil make you older
in His own time and His own way, and will not that be far better?"

Weston's face did not turn in his direction either at this point or at
any other time during the conversation, but his voice, addressed wholly
to the Lady, answered Ransom's interruption.

"You see?" it said. "He himself, though he did not mean nor wish to
do so, made you see a few days ago that Maleldil is beginning to teach
you to walk by yourself, without holding you by the hand. That was the
first branching out. When you came to know that, you were becoming
really old. And since then Maleldil has let you learn much—not from
His own voice, but from mine. You are becoming your own. That is
what Maleldil wants you to do. That is why He has let you be separated
from the King and even, in a way, from Himself. His way of making you
older is to make you make yourself older. And yet this Piebald would
have you sit still and wait for Maleldil to do it all."

"What must we do to Piebald to make him older?" said the Lady.

"I do not think you can help him till you are older yourself," said the
voice of Weston. "You cannot help anyone yet. You are as a tree without fruit."

"It is very true," said the Lady. "Go on."

"Then listen," said Weston's body. "Have you understood that to
wait for Maleldil's voice when Maleldil wishes you to walk on your own
is a kind of disobedience?"

"I think I have."

"The wrong kind of obeying itself can be a disobeying."

The Lady thought for a few moments and then clapped her hands.
"I see," she said, "I see! Oh, how old you make me. Before now I have
chased a beast for mirth. And it has understood and run away from me.
If it had stood still and let me catch it, that would have been a sort of
obeying—but not the best sort."

"You understand very well. When you are fully grown you will be
even wiser and more beautiful than the women of my own world. And
you see that it might be so with Maleldil's biddings."

"I think I do not see quite clearly."

"Are you certain that He really wishes to be always obeyed?"

"How can we not obey what we love?"

"The beast that ran away loved you."

"I wonder," said the Lady, "if that is the same. The beast knows very well when I mean it to run away and when I want it to come to me. But Maleldil has never said to us that any word or work of His was a jest. How could our Beloved need to jest or frolic as we do? He is all a burning joy and a strength. It is like thinking that He needed sleep or food."

"No, it would not be a jest. That is only a thing like it, not the thing itself. But could the taking away of your hand from His—the full growing up—the walking in your own way—could that ever be perfect unless you had, if only once, *seemed* to disobey Him?"

"How could one *seem* to disobey?"

"By doing what He only *seemed* to forbid. There might be a commanding which He wished you to break."

"But if He told us we were to break it, then it would be no command. And if He did not, how should we know?"

"How wise you are growing, beautiful one," said Weston's mouth. "No. If He told you to break what He commanded, it would be no true command, as you have seen. For you are right, He makes no jests. A real disobeying, a real branching out, this is what He secretly longs for: secretly, because to tell you would spoil all."

"I begin to wonder," said the Lady after a pause, "whether you are so much older than I. Surely what you are saying is like fruit with no taste! How can I step out of His will save into something that cannot be wished? Shall I start trying not to love Him—or the King—or the beasts? It would be like trying to walk on water or swim through islands. Shall I try not to sleep or to drink or to laugh? I thought your words had a meaning. But now it seems they have none. To walk out of His will is to walk into nowhere."

"That is true of all His commands except one."

"But can that one be different?"

"Nay, you see of yourself that it is different. These other commands of His—to love, to sleep, to fill this world with your children—you see for yourself that they are good. And they are the same in all worlds. But the command against living on the Fixed Island is not so. You have already learned that He gave no such command to my world. And you cannot see where the goodness of it is. No wonder. If it were really good, must He not have commanded it to all worlds alike? For how could Maleldil not command what was good? There is *no* good in it. Maleldil Himself is showing you that, this moment, through your own reason. It is mere command. It is forbidding for the mere sake of forbidding."

"But why . . . ?"

"In order that you may break it. What other reason can there be? It is not good. It is not the same for other worlds. It stands between you and all settled life, all command of your own days. Is not Maleldil show-ing you as plainly as He can that it was set up as a test—as a great wave you have to go over, that you may become really old, really separate from Him."

"But if this concerns me so deeply, why does He put none of this into my mind? It is all coming from you, Stranger. There is no whisper, even, of the Voice saying Yes to your words."

"But do you not see that there cannot be? He longs—oh, how greatly He longs—to see His creature become fully itself, to stand up in its own reason and its own courage even against Him. But how can He *tell* it to do this? That would spoil all. Whatever it did after that would only be one more step taken *with* Him. This is the one thing of all the things He desires in which He must have no finger. Do you think He is not weary of seeing nothing but Himself in all that He has made? If that contented Him, why should He create at all? To find the Other—the thing whose will is no longer His—that is Maleldil's desire."

"If I could but know this——"

"He must not tell you. He cannot tell you. The nearest He can come to telling you is to let some other creature tell it for Him. And behold, He has done so. Is it for nothing, or without His will, that I have jour-neyed through Deep Heaven to teach you what He would have you know but must not teach you Himself?"

"Lady," said Ransom, "if I speak, will you hear me?"

"Gladly, Piebald."

"This man has said that the law against living on the Fixed Island is different from the other Laws, because it is not the same for all worlds and because we cannot see the goodness in it. And so far he says well. But then he says that it is thus different in order that you may disobey it. But there might be another reason."

"Say it, Piebald."

"I think He made one law of that kind in order that there might be obedience. In all these other matters what you call obeying Him is but doing what seems good in your own eyes also. Is love content with that? You do them, indeed, because they are His will, but not only because they are His will. Where can you taste the joy of obeying unless He bids you do something for which His bidding is the *only* reason? When we spoke last you said that if you told the beasts to walk on their heads, they would delight to do so. So I know that you understand well what I am saying."

"Oh, brave Piebald," said the Green Lady, "this is the best you have said yet. This makes me older far: yet it does not feel like the oldness this other is giving me. Oh, how well I see it! We cannot walk out of

Maleldil's will: but He has given us a way to walk out of *our* will. And
there could be no such way except a command like this. Out of our own
will. It is like passing out through the world's roof into Deep Heaven. All
beyond is Love Himself. I knew there was joy in looking upon the Fixed
Island and laying down all thought of ever living there, but I did not till
now understand." Her face was radiant as she spoke, but then a shade
of bewilderment crossed it. "Piebald," she said, "if you are so young, as
this other says, how do you know these things?"

"He says I am young, but I say not."

The voice of Weston's face spoke suddenly, and it was louder and
deeper than before and less like Weston's voice.

"I am older than he," it said, "and he dare not deny it. Before the
mothers of the mothers of his mother were conceived, I was already
older than he could reckon. I have been with Maleldil in Deep Heaven
where he never came and heard the eternal councils. And in the order of
creation I am greater than he, and before me he is of no account. Is it not
so?" The corpse-like face did not even now turn towards him, but the
speaker and the Lady both seemed to wait for Ransom to reply. The
falsehood which sprang to his mind died on his lips. In that air, even
when truth seemed fatal, only truth would serve. Licking his lips and
choking down a feeling of nausea, he answered:

"In our world to be older is not always to be wiser."

"Look at him," said Weston's body to the Lady; "consider how
white his cheeks have turned and how his forehead is wet. You have not
seen such things before: you will see them more often hereafter. It is
what happens—it is the beginning of what happens—to little creatures
when they set themselves against great ones."

An exquisite thrill of fear travelled along Ransom's spine. What
saved him was the face of the Lady. Untouched by the evil so close to her,
removed as it were ten years' journey deep within the region of her own
innocence, and by that innocence at once protected and so endangered,
she looked up at the standing Death above her, puzzled indeed, but not
beyond the bounds of cheerful curiosity, and said:

"But he was right, Stranger, about this forbidding. It is you who
need to be made older. Can you not see?"

"I have always seen the whole whereof he sees but the half. It is most
true that Maleldil has given you a way of walking out of your own
will—but out of your deepest will."

"And what is that?"

"Your deepest will, at present, is to obey Him—to be always as you
are now, only His beast or His very young child. The way out of that is
hard. It was made hard that only the very great, the very wise, the very

courageous should dare to walk in it, to go on—on out of this smallness in which you now live—through the dark wave of His forbidding, into the real life, Deep Life, with all its joy and splendour and hardness."

"Listen, Lady," said Ransom. "There is something he is not telling you. All this that we are now talking has been talked before. The thing he wants you to try has been tried before. Long ago, when our world began, there was only one man and one woman in it, as you and the King are in this. And there once before he stood, as he stands now, talking to the woman. He had found her alone as he has found you alone. And she listened, and did the thing Maleldil had forbidden her to do. But no joy and splendour came of it. What came of it I cannot tell you because you have no image of it in your mind. But all love was troubled and made cold, and Maleldil's voice became hard to hear so that wisdom grew little among them; and the woman was against the man and the mother against the child; and when they looked to eat there was no fruit on their trees, and hunting for food took all their time, so that their life became narrower, not wider."

"He has hidden the half of what happened," said Weston's corpse-like mouth. "Hardness came out of it but also splendour. They made with their own hands mountains higher than your Fixed Island. They made for themselves Floating Islands greater than yours which they could move at will through the ocean faster than any bird can fly. Because there was not always food enough, a woman could give the only fruit to her child or her husband and eat death instead—could give them all, as you in your little narrow life of playing and kissing and riding fishes have never done, nor shall do till you break the commandment. Because knowledge was harder to find, those few who found it became more beautiful and excelled their fellows as you excel the beasts; and thousands were striving for their love . . ."

"I think I will go to sleep now," said the Lady quite suddenly. Up to this point she had been listening to Weston's body with open mouth and wide eyes, but as he spoke of the women with the thousands of lovers she yawned, with the unconcealed and unpremeditated yawn of a young cat.

"Not yet," said the other. "There is more. He has not told you that it was this breaking of the commandment which brought Maleldil to our world and because of which He was made man. He dare not deny it."

"Do you say this, Piebald?" asked the Lady.

Ransom was sitting with his fingers locked so tightly that his knuckles were white. The unfairness of it all was wounding him like barbed wire. Unfair . . . unfair. How could Maleldil expect him to fight against this, to fight with every weapon taken from him, forbidden to lie and yet brought to places where truth seemed fatal? It was unfair! A sudden impulse of hot rebellion arose in him. A second later, doubt, like a huge wave, came breaking over him. How if the enemy were right after all? *Felix peccatum Adae.* Even the Church would tell him that good came of disobedience in the end. Yes, and it was true too that he, Ransom, was a timid creature, a man who shrank back from new and hard things. On which side, after all, did the temptation lie? Progress passed before his eyes in a great momentary vision: cities, armies, tall ships, and libraries and fame, and the grandeur of poetry spurting like a fountain out of the labours and ambitions of men. Who could be certain that Creative Evolution was not the deepest truth? From all sorts of secret crannies in his own mind whose very existence he had never before suspected, something wild and heady and delicious began to rise, to pour itself towards the shape of Weston. "It is a spirit, it is a spirit," said this inner voice, "and you are only a man. It goes on from century to century. You are only a man. . . ."

"Do you say this, Piebald?" asked the Lady a second time.

The spell was broken.

"I will tell you what I say," answered Ransom, jumping to his feet. "Of course good came of it. Is Maleldil a beast that we can stop His path, or a leaf that we can twist His shape? Whatever you do, He will make good of it. But not the good He had prepared for you if you had obeyed Him. That is lost for ever. The first King and first Mother of our world did the forbidden thing; and He brought good of it in the end. But what they did was not good; and what they lost we have not seen. And there were some to whom no good came nor ever will come." He turned to the body of Weston. "You," he said, "tell her all. What good came to you? Do *you* rejoice that Maleldil became a man? Tell her of *your* joys, and of what profit you had when you made Maleldil and death acquainted."

In that moment that followed this speech two things happened that were utterly unlike terrestrial experience. The body that had been Weston's threw up its head and opened its mouth and gave a long melancholy howl like a dog; and the Lady lay down, wholly unconcerned, and closed her eyes and was instantly asleep. And while these two things were happening the piece of ground on which the two men stood and the woman lay was rushing down a great hillside of water.

Ransom kept his eyes fixed upon the enemy, but it took no notice of him. Its eyes moved like the eyes of a living man but it was hard to be sure what it was looking at, or whether it really used the eyes as organs of vision at all. One got the impression of a force that cleverly kept the pupils of those eyes fixed in a suitable direction while the mouth talked

but which, for its own purpose, used wholly different modes of percep-
tion. The thing sat down close to the Lady's head on the far side of her
from Ransom. If you could call it sitting down. The body did not reach
its squatting position by the normal movements of a man: it was more as
if some external force manœuvred it into the right position and then let
it drop. It was impossible to point to any particular motion which was
definitely non-human. Ransom had the sense of watching an imitation
of living motions which had been very well studied and was technically
correct: but somehow it lacked the master touch. And he was chilled
with an inarticulate, night-nursery horror of the thing he had to deal
with—the man-aged corpse, the bogey, the Un-man.

There was nothing to do but to watch: to sit there, for ever if need
be, guarding the Lady from the Un-man while their island climbed inter-
minably over the Alps and Andes of burnished water. All three were very
still. Beasts and birds came often and looked upon them. Hours later the
Un-man began to speak. It did not even look in Ransom's direction;
slowly and cumbrously, as if by some machinery that needed oiling, it
made its mouth and lips pronounce his name.

"Ransom," it said.

"Well?" said Ransom.

"Nothing," said the Un-man. He shot an inquisitive glance at it. Was
the creature mad? But it looked, as before, dead rather than mad, sitting
there with the head bowed and the mouth a little open, and some yellow
dust from the moss settled in the creases of its cheeks, and the legs
crossed tailor-wise, and the hands, with their long metallic-looking nails,
pressed flat together on the ground before it. He dismissed the problem
from his mind and returned to his own uncomfortable thoughts.

"Ransom," it said again.

"What is it?" said Ransom sharply.

"Nothing," it answered.

Again there was silence; and again, about a minute later, the horrible mouth said:

"Ransom!" This time he made no reply. Another minute and it
uttered his name again; and then, like a minute gun, "Ransom . . . Ransom . . . Ransom," perhaps a hundred times.

"What the Hell do you want?" he roared at last.

"Nothing," said the voice. Next time he determined not to answer;
but when it had called on him a thousand times he found himself
answering whether he would or no, and "Nothing," came the reply. He
taught himself to keep silent in the end: not that the torture of resisting
his impulse to speak was less than the torture of response but because
something within him rose up to combat the tormentor's assurance that

he must yield in the end. If the attack had been of some more violent kind it might have been easier to resist. What chilled and almost cowed him was the union of malice with something nearly childish. For temptation, for blasphemy, for a whole battery of horrors, he was in some sort prepared: but hardly for this petty, indefatigable nagging as of a nasty little boy at a preparatory school. Indeed no imagined horror could have surpassed the sense which grew within him as the slow hours passed, that this creature was, by all human standards, inside out—its heart on the surface and its shallowness at the heart. On the surface, great designs and an antagonism to Heaven which involved the fate of worlds: but deep within, when every veil had been pierced, was there, after all, nothing but a black puerility, an aimless empty spitefulness content to sate itself with the tiniest cruelties, as love does not disdain the smallest kindness? What kept him steady, long after all possibility of thinking about something else had disappeared, was the decision that if he must hear either the word Ransom or the word Nothing a million times, he would prefer the word Ransom.

And all the time the little jewel-coloured land went soaring up into the yellow firmament and hung there a moment and tilted its woods and went racing down into the warm lustrous depths between the waves: and the Lady lay sleeping with one arm bent beneath her head and her lips a little parted. Sleeping, assuredly—for her eyes were shut and her breathing regular—yet not looking quite like those who sleep in our world, for her face was full of expression and intelligence, and the limbs looked as if they were ready at any moment to leap up, and altogether she gave the impression that sleep was not a thing that happened to her but an action which she performed.

Then all at once it was night. "Ransom . . . Ransom . . . Ransom . . . Ransom" went on the voice. And suddenly it crossed his mind that though he would some time require sleep, the Un-man might not.

IO

Sleep proved to be indeed the problem. For what seemed a great time, cramped and wearied, and soon hungry and thirsty as well, he sat still in the darkness trying not to attend to the unflagging repetition of "Ransom—Ransom—Ransom." But presently he found himself listening to a conversation of which he knew he had not heard the beginning and realised he had slept. The Lady seemed to be saying very little. Weston's voice was speaking gently and continuously. It was not talking about the Fixed Land nor even about Maleldil. It appeared to be telling, with extreme beauty and pathos, a number of stories, and at first Ransom could not perceive any connecting link between them. They were all about women, but women who had apparently lived at different periods of the world's history and in quite different circumstances. From the Lady's replies it appeared that the stories contained much that she did not understand; but oddly enough the Un-man did not mind. If the questions aroused by any one story proved at all difficult to answer, the speaker simply dropped that story and instantly began another. The heroines of the stories seemed all to have suffered a great deal—they had been oppressed by fathers, cast off by husbands, deserted by lovers. Their children had risen up against them and society had driven them out. But the stories all ended, in a sense, happily: sometimes with honours and praises to a heroine still living, more often with tardy acknowledgment and unavailing tears after her death. As the endless speech proceeded, the Lady's questions grew always fewer; some meaning for the words Death and Sorrow—though what kind of meaning Ransom could not even guess—was apparently being created in her mind by mere repetition. At last it dawned upon him what all these stories were about. Each one of these women had stood forth alone and braved a terrible risk for her child, her lover, or her people. Each had been misunderstood, reviled, and persecuted: but each also magnificently vindicated by the event. The precise details were often not very easy to follow. Ransom had more than a suspicion that many of these noble pioneers had been what in ordinary terrestrial speech we call witches or perverts. But that was all in the background. What emerged from the stories was rather an image than an idea—the picture of the tall, slender form, unbowed though the world's weight rested upon its shoulders, stepping forth fearless and friendless into the dark to do for others what those others forbade it to do yet needed to have done. And all the time, as a sort of background to these goddess shapes, the speaker was building up a picture of the other sex. No word was directly spoken on the subject: but one felt them there as a huge, dim multitude of creatures pitifully childish and complacently arrogant; timid, meticulous, unoriginating; sluggish and ox-like, rooted to the earth almost in their indolence, prepared to try nothing, to risk nothing, to make no exertion, and capable of being raised into full life only by the unthanked and rebellious virtue of their females. It was very well done. Ransom, who had little of the pride of sex, found himself for a few moments all but believing it.

In the midst of this the darkness was suddenly torn by a flash of lightning; a few seconds later came a revel of Perelandrian thunder, like the playing of a heavenly tambourine, and after that warm rain. Ransom did not much regard it. The flash had shown him the Un-man sitting bolt upright, the Lady raised on one elbow, the dragon lying awake at her head, a grove of trees beyond, and great waves against the horizon. He was thinking of what he had seen. He was wondering how the Lady could see that face—those jaws monotonously moving as if they were rather munching than talking—and not know the creature to be evil. He saw, of course, that this was unreasonable of him. He himself was doubtless an uncouth figure in her eyes; she could have no knowledge either about evil or about the normal appearance of terrestrial man to guide her. The expression on her face, revealed in the sudden light, was one that he had not seen there before. Her eyes were not fixed on the narrator: as far as that went, her thoughts might have been a thousand miles away. Her lips were shut and a little pursed. Her eyebrows were slightly raised. He had not yet seen her look so like a woman of our own race; and yet her expression was one he had not very often met on earth—except, as he realised with a shock, on the stage. "Like a tragedy queen" was the disgusting comparison that arose in his mind. Of course it was a gross exaggeration. It was an insult for which he could not forgive himself. And yet . . . and yet . . . the tableau revealed by the lightning had photographed itself on his brain. Do what he would, he found it impossible not to think of that new look in her face. A very *good* tragedy queen, no doubt. The heroine of a very great tragedy, very nobly played by an actress who was a good woman in real life. By earthly standards, an expression to be praised, even to be revered: but remembering all that he had read in her countenance before, the unselfconscious radiance, the frolic sanctity, the depth of stillness that reminded him sometimes of infancy and sometimes of extreme old age while the hard youth and valiancy of face and body denied both, he found this new expression horrifying. The fatal touch of invited grandeur, of enjoyed pathos—the assumption, however slight, of a rôle—seemed a hateful vulgarity. Perhaps she was doing no more—he had good hope that she was doing no more—than responding in a purely imaginative fashion to this new art of Story or Poetry. But by God she'd better not! And for the first time the thought "This can't go on" formulated itself in his mind.

"I will go where the leaves cover us from the rain," said her voice in the darkness. Ransom had hardly noticed that he was getting wet—in a world without clothes it is less important. But he rose when he heard her move and followed her as well as he could by ear. The Un-man seemed to be doing the same. They progressed in total darkness on a surface as variable as that of water. Every now and then there was another flash. One saw the Lady walking erect, the Un-man slouching by her side with Weston's shirt and shorts now sodden and clinging to it, and the dragon puffing and waddling behind. At last they came to a place where the carpet under their feet was dry and there was a drumming noise of rain on firm leaves above their heads. They lay down again. "And another time," began the Un-man at once, "there was a queen in our world who ruled over a little land——"

"Hush!" said the Lady, "let us listen to the rain." Then, after a moment, she added, "What was that? It was some beast I never heard before"—and indeed, there had been something very like a low growl close beside them.

"I do not know," said the voice of Weston.

"I think I do," said Ransom.

"Hush!" said the Lady again, and no more was said that night.

This was the beginning of a series of days and nights which Ransom remembered with loathing for the rest of his life. He had been only too correct in supposing that his enemy required no sleep. Fortunately the Lady did, but she needed a good deal less than Ransom and possibly, as the days passed, came to take less than she needed. It seemed to Ransom that whenever he dozed he awoke to find the Un-man already in conversation with her. He was dead tired. He could hardly have endured it at all but for the fact that their hostess quite frequently dismissed them both from her presence. On such occasions Ransom kept close to the Un-man. It was a rest from the main battle, but it was a very imperfect rest. He did not dare to let the enemy out of his sight for a moment, and every day its society became more unendurable. He had full opportunity to learn the falsity of the maxim that the Prince of Darkness is a gentleman. Again and again he felt that a suave and subtle Mephistopheles with red cloak and rapier and a feather in his cap, or even a sombre tragic Satan out of *Paradise Lost,* would have been a welcome release from the thing he was actually doomed to watch. It was not like dealing with a wicked politician at all: it was much more like being set to guard an imbecile or a monkey or a very nasty child. What had staggered and disgusted him when it first began saying, "Ransom . . . Ransom . . ." continued to disgust him every day and every hour. It showed plenty of subtlety and intelligence when talking to the Lady; but Ransom soon perceived that it regarded intelligence simply and solely as a weapon, which it had no more wish to employ in its off-duty hours than a soldier has to do bayonet practice when he is on leave. Thought was for it a device necessary to certain ends, but thought in itself did not interest it. It assumed reason as externally and inorganically as it had assumed Weston's body. The moment the Lady was out of sight it seemed to relapse. A great deal of his time was spent in protecting the animals from it. Whenever it got out of sight, or even a few yards ahead, it would make a grab at any beast or bird within its reach and pull out some fur or feathers. Ransom tried whenever possible to get between it and its victim. On such occasions there were nasty moments when the two stood facing each other. It never came to a fight, for the Un-man merely grinned and perhaps spat and fell back a little, but before that happened Ransom usually had opportunity to discover how terribly he feared it. For side by side with his disgust, the more childlike terror of living with a ghost or a mechanised corpse never left him for many minutes together. The fact of being *alone* with it sometimes rushed upon his mind with such dismay that it took all his reason to resist his longing for society—his impulse to rush madly over the island until he found the Lady and to beg her protection. When the Un-man could not get animals it was content with plants. It was fond of cutting their outer rinds through with its nails, or grubbing up roots, or pulling off leaves, or even tearing up handfuls of turf. With Ransom himself it had innumerable games to play. It had a whole repertory of obscenities to perform with its own— or rather with Weston's—body: and the mere silliness of them was almost worse than the dirtiness. It would sit making grimaces at him for hours together; and then, for hours more, it would go back to its old repetition of "Ransom . . . Ransom." Often its grimaces achieved a horrible resemblance to people whom Ransom had known and loved in our own world. But worst of all were those moments when it allowed Weston to come back into its countenance. Then its voice, which was always Weston's voice, would begin a pitiful, hesitant mumbling, "You be very careful, Ransom. I'm down in the bottom of a big black hole. No I'm not, though. I'm on Perelandra. I can't think very well now, but that doesn't matter, he does all my thinking for me. It'll get quite easy presently. That boy keeps on shutting the windows. That's all right, they've taken off my head and put someone else's on me. I'll soon be all right now. They won't let me see my press cuttings. So then I went and told him that if they didn't want me in the first Fifteen they could jolly well do without me, see. We'll tell that young whelp it's an insult to the examiners to show up this kind of work. What I want to know is why I should pay for a first-class ticket and then be crowded out like this. It's not fair. Not fair. I never meant any harm. Could you take some of this weight off my chest, I don't want all those clothes. Let me alone. Let me alone. It's not fair. It's not fair. What enormous bluebottles. They say you get used to them"—and then it would end in the canine howl. Ransom never could make up his mind whether it was a trick or whether a decaying psychic energy that had once been Weston were indeed fitfully and miserably alive within the body that sat there beside him. He discovered that any hatred he had once felt for the Professor was dead. He found it natural to pray fervently for his soul. Yet what he felt for Weston was not exactly pity. Up till that moment, whenever he had thought of Hell, he had pictured the lost souls as being still human; now, as the frightful abyss which parts ghosthood from manhood yawned before him, pity was almost swallowed up in horror—in the unconquerable revulsion of the life within him from positive and self-consuming Death. If the remains of Weston were, at such moments, speaking through the lips of the Un-man, then Weston was not now a man at all. The forces which had begun, perhaps years ago, to eat away his humanity had now completed their work. The intoxicated will which had been slowly poisoning the intelligence and the affections had now at last poisoned itself and the whole psychic organism had fallen to pieces. Only a ghost was left—an everlasting unrest, a crumbling, a ruin, an odour of decay. "And this," thought Ransom, "might be my destination; or hers."

But of course the hours spent alone with the Un-man were like hours in a back area. The real business of life was the interminable conversation between the Tempter and the Green Lady. Taken hour by hour the progress was hard to estimate; but as the days passed Ransom could not resist the conviction that the general development was in the enemy's favour. There were, of course, ups and downs. Often the Un-man was unexpectedly repulsed by some simplicity which it seemed not to have anticipated. Often, too, Ransom's own contributions to the terrible debate were for the moment successful. There were times when he thought, "Thank God! We've won at last." But the enemy was never tired, and Ransom grew more weary all the time; and presently he thought he could see signs that the Lady was becoming tired too. In the end he taxed her with it and begged her to send them both away. But she rebuked him, and her rebuke revealed how dangerous the situation had already become. "Shall I go and rest and play," she asked, "while all this lies on our hands? Not till I am certain that there is no great deed to be done by me for the King and for the children of our children."

It was on those lines that the enemy now worked almost exclusively. Though the Lady had no word for Duty he had made it appear to her in the light of a Duty that she should continue to fondle the idea of disobedience, and convinced her that it would be a cowardice if she repulsed him. The ideas of the Great Deed, of the Great Risk, of a kind of martyrdom, were presented to her every day, varied in a thousand forms. The notion of waiting to ask the King before a decision was made had been unobtrusively shuffled aside. Any such "cowardice" was now not to be thought of. The whole point of her action—the whole grandeur—would lie in taking it without the King's knowledge, in leaving him utterly free to repudiate it, so that all the benefits should be his, and all the risks hers; and with the risk, of course, all the magnanimity, the pathos, the tragedy, and the originality. And also, the Tempter hinted, it would be no use asking the King, for he would certainly *not* approve the action: men were like that. The King must be forced to be free. Now, while she was on her own—now or never—the noble thing must be achieved; and with that "Now or never" he began to play on a fear which the Lady apparently shared with the women of earth—the fear that life might be wasted, some great opportunity let slip. "How if I were as a tree that could have born gourds and yet bore none," she said. Ransom tried to convince her that children were fruit enough. But the Un-man asked whether this elaborate division of the human race into two sexes could possibly be meant for no other purpose than offspring?—a matter which might have been more simply provided for, as it was in many of the plants. A moment later it was explaining that men like Ransom in his own world—men of that intensely male and backward-looking type who always shrank away from the new good—had continuously laboured to keep women down to mere childbearing and to ignore the high destiny for which Maleldil had actually created her. It told her that such men had already done incalculable harm. Let her look to it that nothing of the sort happened on Perelandra. It was at this stage that it began to teach her many new words: words like Creative and Intuition and Spiritual. But that was one of its false steps. When she had at last been made to understand what "creative" meant she forgot all about the Great Risk and the tragic loneliness and laughed for a whole minute on end. Finally she told the Un-man that it was younger even than Piebald, and sent them both away.

Ransom gained ground over that; but on the following day he lost it all by losing his temper. The enemy had been pressing on her with more than usual ardour the nobility of self-sacrifice and self-dedication, and the enchantment seemed to be deepening in her mind every moment, when Ransom, goaded beyond all patience, had leaped to his feet and really turned upon her, talking far too quickly and almost shouting, and even forgetting his Old Solar and intermixing English words. He tried to tell her that he'd seen this kind of "unselfishness" in action: to tell her of women making themselves sick with hunger rather than begin the meal before the man of the house returned, though they knew perfectly well that there was nothing he disliked more; of mothers wearing themselves to a ravelling to marry some daughter to a man whom she detested; of Agrippina and of Lady Macbeth. "Can you not see," he shouted, "that he is making you say words that mean nothing? What is the good of saying you would do this for the King's sake when you know it is what the King would hate most? Are you Maleldil that you should determine what is good for the King?" But she understood only a very small part of what he said and was bewildered by his manner. The Un-man made capital out of this speech.

But through all these ups and downs, all changes of the front line, all counter-attacks and stands and withdrawals, Ransom came to see more and more clearly the strategy of the whole affair. The Lady's response to the suggestion of becoming a risk-bearer, a tragic pioneer, was still a response made chiefly out of her love for the King and for her unborn children, and even, in a sense, of Maleldil Himself. The idea that He might not really wish to be obeyed to the letter was the sluice through which the whole flood of suggestion had been admitted to her mind. But mixed with this response, from the moment when the Un-man began its tragic stories, there was the faintest touch of theatricality, the first hint of a self-admiring inclination to seize a grand rôle in the drama of her world. It was clear that the Un-man's whole effort was to increase this element. As long as this was but one drop, so to speak, in the sea of her mind, he would not really succeed. Perhaps, while it remained so, she was protected from actual disobedience: perhaps no rational creature, until such a motive became dominant, could really throw away happiness for anything quite so vague as the Tempter's chatter about Deeper Life and the Upward Path. The veiled egoism in the conception of noble revolt must be increased. And Ransom thought, despite many rallies on her part and many setbacks suffered by the enemy, that it was, very slowly and yet perceptibly, increasing. The matter was, of course, cruelly, cruelly complicated. What the Un-man said was always very nearly true. Certainly it must be part of the Divine plan that this happy creature should mature, should become more and more a creature of free choice, should become, in a sense, more distinct from God and from her husband in order thereby to be at one with them in a richer fashion. In fact, he had seen this very process going on from the moment at which he met her, and had, unconsciously, assisted it. This present temptation, if conquered, would itself be the next, and greatest, step in the same direction: an obedience freer, more reasoned, more conscious than any she had known before, was being put in her power. But for that very reason the fatal false step which, once taken, would thrust her down into the terrible slavery of appetite and hate and economics and government which our race knows so well, could be made to sound so like the true one. What made him feel sure that the dangerous element in her interest was growing was her progressive disregard of the plain intellectual bones of the problem. It became harder to recall her mind to the *data*—a command from Maleldil, a complete uncertainty about the results of breaking it, and a present happiness so great that hardly any change could be for the better. The turgid swell of indistinctly splendid images which the Un-man aroused, and the transcendent importance of the central image, carried all this away. She was still in her innocence. No evil intention had been formed in her mind. But if her will was uncorrupted, half her imagination was already filled with bright, poisonous shapes. "This can't go on," thought Ransom for the second time. But all his arguments proved in the long run unavailing, and it did go on.

There came a night when he was so tired that towards morning he fell into a leaden sleep and slept far into the following day. He woke to find himself alone. A great horror came over him. "What could I have done? What could I have done?" he cried out, for he thought that all was lost. With sick heart and sore head he staggered to the edge of the island: his idea was to find a fish and to pursue the truants to the Fixed Land where he felt little doubt that they had gone. In the bitterness and confusion of his mind he forgot that he had no notion in which direction that land now lay nor how far it was distant. Hurrying through the woods, he emerged into an open place and suddenly found that he was not alone. Two human figures, robed to their feet, stood before him, silent under the yellow sky. Their clothes were of purple and blue, their heads wore chaplets of silver leaves, and their feet were bare. They seemed to him to be, the one the ugliest, and the other the most beautiful, of the children of men. Then one of them spoke and he realised that they were none other than the Green Lady herself and the haunted body of Weston. The robes were of feathers, and he knew well the Perelandrian birds from which they had been derived; the art of the weaving it could be called, was beyond his comprehension.

"Welcome, Piebald," said the Lady. "You have slept long. What do you think of us in our leaves?"

"The birds," said Ransom. "The poor birds! What has he done to them?"

"He has found the feathers somewhere," said the Lady carelessly. "They drop them."

"Why have you done this, Lady?"

"He has been making me older again. Why did you never tell me, Piebald?"

"Tell you what?"

"We never knew. This one showed me that the trees have leaves and the beasts have fur, and said that in your world the men and women also hung beautiful things about them. Why do you not tell us how we look? Oh, Piebald, Piebald, I hope this is not going to be another of the new goods from which you draw back your hand. It cannot be new to you if they all do it in your world."

"Ah," said Ransom, "but it is different there. It is cold."

"So the Stranger said," she answered. "But not in all parts of your world. He says they do it even where it is warm."

"Has he said why they do it?"

"To be beautiful. Why else?" said the Lady, with some wonder in her face.

"Thank Heaven," thought Ransom, "he is only teaching her vanity"; for he had feared something worse. Yet could it be possible, in the long run, to wear clothes without learning modesty, and through modesty lasciviousness?

"Do you think we are more beautiful?" said the Lady, interrupting his thoughts.

"No," said Ransom; and then, correcting himself, "I don't know." It was, indeed, not easy to reply. The Un-man, now that Weston's prosaic shirt and shorts were concealed, looked a more exotic and therefore a more imaginatively, less squalidly, hideous figure. As for the Lady—that she looked in some way worse was not doubtful. Yet there is a plainness in nudity—as we speak of "plain" bread. A sort of richness, a flamboyancy, a concession, as it were, to lower conceptions of the beautiful, had come with the purple robe. For the first (and last) time she appeared to him at that moment as a woman whom an earth-born man might conceivably love. And this was intolerable. The ghastly inappropriateness of the idea had, all in one moment, stolen something from the colours of the landscape and the scent of the flowers.

"Do you think we are more beautiful?" repeated the Lady.

"What does it matter?" said Ransom dully.

"Everyone should wish to be as beautiful as they can," she answered. "And we cannot see ourselves."

"We can," said Weston's body.

"How can this be?" said the Lady, turning to it. "Even if you could roll your eyes right round to look inside they would see only blackness."

"Not that way," it answered. "I will show you." It walked a few paces away to where Weston's pack lay in the yellow turf. With that curious distinctness which often falls upon us when we are anxious and preoccupied Ransom noticed the exact make and pattern of the pack. It must have been from the same shop in London where he had bought his own: and that little fact, suddenly reminding him that Weston had once been a man, that he too had once had pleasures and pains and a human mind, almost brought the tears into his eyes. The horrible fingers which Weston would never use again worked at the buckles and brought out a small bright object—an English pocket mirror that might have cost three-and-six. He handed it to the Green Lady. She turned it over in her hands.

"What is it? What am I to do with it?" she said.

"Look in it," said the Un-man.

"How?"

"Look!" he said. Then taking it from her he held it up to her face. She stared for quite an appreciable time without apparently making anything of it. Then she started back with a cry and covered her face. Ransom started too. It was the first time he had seen her the mere passive recipient of any emotion. The world about him was big with change.

"Oh—oh," she cried. "What is it? I saw a face."

"Only your own face, beautiful one," said the Un-man.

"I know," said the Lady, still averting her eyes from the mirror. "My face—out there—looking at me. Am I growing older or is it something else? I feel . . . I feel . . . my heart is beating too hard. I am not warm. What is it?" She glanced from one of them to the other. The mysteries had all vanished from her face. It was as easy to read as that of a man in a shelter when a bomb is coming.

"What is it?" she repeated.

"It is called Fear," said Weston's mouth. Then the creature turned its face full on Ransom and grinned.

"Fear," she said. "This is Fear," pondering the discovery; then, with abrupt finality, "I do not like it."

"It will go away," said the Un-man, when Ransom interrupted.

"It will never go away if you do what he wishes. It is into more and more fear that he is leading you."

"It is," said the Un-man, "into the great waves and through them and beyond. Now that you know Fear, you see that it must be you who shall taste it on behalf of your race. You know the King will not. You do not wish him to. But there is no cause for fear in this little thing: rather of joy. What is fearful in it?"

"Things being two when they are one," replied the Lady decisively. "That thing" (she pointed at the mirror) "is me and not me."

"But if you do not look you will never know how beautiful you are."

"It comes into my mind, Stranger," she answered, "that a fruit does not eat itself, and a man cannot be together with himself."

"A fruit cannot do that because it is only a fruit," said the Un-man. "But we can do it. We call this thing a mirror. A man can love himself, and be together with himself. That is what it means to be a man or a woman—to walk alongside oneself as if one were a second person and to delight in one's own beauty. Mirrors were made to teach this art."

"Is it a good?" said the Lady.

"No," said Ransom.

"How can you find out without trying?" said the Un-man.

"If you try it and it is not good," said Ransom, "how do you know whether you will be able to stop doing it?"

"I am walking alongside myself already," said the Lady. "But I do not yet know what I look like. If I have become two I had better know what the other is. As for you, Piebald, one look will show me this woman's face and why should I look more than once?"

She took the mirror, timidly but firmly, from the Un-man and looked into it in silence for the better part of a minute. Then she let it sink and stood holding it at her side.

"It is very strange," she said at last.

"It is very beautiful," said the Un-man. "Do you not think so?"

"Yes."

"But you have not yet found what you set out to find."

"What was that? I have forgotten."

"Whether the robe of feathers made you more beautiful or less."

"I saw only a face."

"Hold it further away and you will see the whole of the alongside woman—the other who is yourself. Or no—I will hold it."

The commonplace suggestions of the scene became grotesque at this stage. She looked at herself first with the robe, then without it, then with it again; finally she decided against it and threw it away. The Un-man picked it up.

"Will you not keep it?" he said: "you might wish to carry it on some days even if you do not wish for it on all days."

"*Keep* it?" she asked, not clearly understanding.

"I had forgotten," said the Un-man. "I had forgotten that you would not live on the Fixed Land nor build a house nor in any way become mistress of your own days. *Keeping* means putting a thing where you know you can always find it again, and where rain, and beasts, and other people cannot reach it. I would give you this mirror to keep. It would be the Queen's mirror, a gift brought into the world from Deep Heaven: the other women would not have it. But you have reminded me. There can be no gifts, no keeping, no foresight while you live as you do—from day to day, like the beasts."

But the Lady did not appear to be listening to him. She stood like one almost dazed with the richness of a day-dream. She did not look in the least like a woman who is thinking about a new dress. The expression of her face was noble. It was a great deal too noble. Greatness, tragedy, high sentiment—these were obviously what occupied her thoughts. Ransom perceived that the affair of the robes and the mirror had been only superficially concerned with what is commonly called female vanity. The image of her beautiful body had been offered to her only as a means to awake the far more perilous image of her great soul. The external and, as it were, dramatic conception of the self was the enemy's true aim. He was making her mind a theatre in which that phantom self should hold the stage. He had already written the play.

II

Because he had slept so late that morning Ransom found it easy to keep awake the following night. The sea had become calm and there was no rain. He sat upright in the darkness with his back against a tree. The others were close beside him—the Lady, to judge by her breathing, asleep and the Un-man doubtless waiting to arouse her and resume its solicitations the moment Ransom should doze. For the third time, more strongly than ever before, it came into his head, "This can't go on."

The Enemy was using Third Degree methods. It seemed to Ransom that, but for a miracle, the Lady's resistance was bound to be worn away in the end. Why did no miracle come? Or rather, why no miracle on the right side? For the presence of the Enemy was in itself a kind of Miracle. Had Hell a prerogative to work wonders? Why did Heaven work none? Not for the first time he found himself questioning Divine Justice. He could not understand why Maleldil should remain absent when the Enemy was there in person.

But while he was thinking this, as suddenly and sharply as if the solid darkness about him had spoken with articulate voice, he knew that Maleldil was not absent. That sense—so very welcome yet never welcomed without the overcoming of a certain resistance—that sense of the Presence which he had once or twice before experienced on Perelandra, returned to him. The darkness was packed quite full. It seemed to press upon his trunk so that he could hardly use his lungs: it seemed to close in on his skull like a crown of intolerable weight so that for a space he could hardly think. Moreover, he became aware in some indefinable fashion that it had never been absent, that only some unconscious activity of his own had succeeded in ignoring it for the past few days.

Inner silence is for our race a difficult achievement. There is a chattering part of the mind which continues, until it is corrected, to chatter on even in the holiest places. Thus, while one part of Ransom remained, as it were, prostrated in a hush of fear and love that resembled a kind of death, something else inside him, wholly unaffected by reverence, continued to pour queries and objections into his brain. "It's all very well," said this voluble critic, "a presence of *that* sort! But the Enemy is really here, really saying and doing things. Where is Maleldil's representative?"

The answer which came back to him, quick as a fencer's or a tennis player's *riposte*, out of the silence and the darkness, almost took his breath away. It seemed Blasphemous. "Anyway, what can I do?" babbled the voluble self. "I've done all I can. I've talked till I'm sick of it. It's no good, I tell you." He tried to persuade himself that he, Ransom, could not possibly be Maleldil's representative as the Un-man was the representative of Hell. The suggestion was, he argued, itself diabolical— a temptation to fatuous pride, to megalomania. He was horrified when the darkness simply flung back this argument in his face, almost impatiently. And then—he wondered how it had escaped him till now—he was forced to perceive that his own coming to Perelandra was at least as much of a marvel as the Enemy's. That miracle on the right side, which he had demanded, had in fact occurred. He himself was the miracle.

"Oh, but this is nonsense," said the voluble self. He, Ransom, with his ridiculous piebald body and his ten times defeated arguments—what sort of a miracle was that? His mind darted hopefully down a side-alley that seemed to promise escape. Very well then. He *had* been brought here miraculously. He was in God's hands. As long as he did his best— and he *had* done his best—God would see to the final issue. He had not succeeded. But he had done his best. No one could do more. "'Tis not in mortals to command success." He must not be worried about the final result. Maleldil would see to that. And Maleldil would bring him safe back to earth after his very real, though unsuccessful, efforts. Probably Maleldil's real intention was that he should publish to the human race the truths he had learned on the planet Venus. As for the fate of Venus, that could not really rest upon his shoulders. It was in God's hands. One must be content to leave it there. One must have Faith. . . .

It snapped like a violin string. Not one rag of all this evasion was left. Relentlessly, unmistakably, the Darkness pressed down upon him the knowledge that this picture of the situation was utterly false. His journey to Perelandra was not a moral exercise, nor a sham fight. If the issue lay in Maleldil's hands, Ransom and the Lady *were* those hands. The fate of a world really depended on how they behaved in the next few hours. The thing was irreducibly, nakedly real. They could, if they chose, decline to save the innocence of this new race, and if they declined its innocence would not be saved. It rested with no other creature in all time or all space. This he saw clearly, though as yet he had no inkling of what he could do.

The voluble self protested, wildly, swiftly, like the propeller of a ship racing when it is out of the water. The imprudence, the unfairness, the absurdity of it! Did Maleldil *want* to lose worlds? What was the sense of so arranging things that anything really important should finally and absolutely depend on such a man of straw as himself? And at that moment, far away on Earth, as he now could not help remembering, men were at war, and white-faced subalterns and freckled corporals who had but lately begun to shave, stood in horrible gaps or crawled forward in deadly darkness, awaking, like him, to the preposterous truth that all really depended on their actions; and far away in time Horatius stood on the bridge, and Constantine settled in his mind whether he would or would not embrace the new religion, and Eve herself stood looking upon the forbidden fruit and the Heaven of Heavens waited for her decision. He writhed and ground his teeth, but could not help seeing. Thus, and not otherwise, the world was made. Either something or nothing must depend on individual choices. And if something, who could set bounds to it? A stone may determine the course of a river. He was that stone at this horrible moment which had become the centre of the whole universe. The eldila of all worlds, the sinless organisms of everlasting light, were silent in Deep Heaven to see what Elwin Ransom of Cambridge would do.

Then came blessed relief. He suddenly realised that he did not know what he *could* do. He almost laughed with joy. All this horror had been premature. No definite task was before him. All that was being demanded of him was a general and preliminary resolution to oppose the Enemy in any mode which circumstances might show to be desirable: in fact—and he flew back to the comforting words as a child flies back to its mother's arms—"to do his best"—or rather, to go on doing his best, for he had really been doing it all along. "What bug-bears we make of things unnecessarily!" he murmured, settling himself in a slightly more comfortable position. A mild flood of what appeared to him to be cheerful and rational piety rose and engulfed him.

Hullo! What was this? He sat straight upright again, his heart beating wildly against his side. His thoughts had stumbled on an idea from which they started back as a man starts back when he has touched a hot poker. But this time the idea was really too childish to entertain. This time it *must* be a deception, risen from his own mind. It stood to reason that a struggle with the Devil meant a *spiritual* struggle . . . the notion of a physical combat was only fit for a savage. If only it *were* as simple as that . . . but here the voluble self had made a fatal mistake. The habit of imaginative honesty was too deeply engrained in Ransom to let him toy for more than a second with the pretence that he feared bodily strife with the Un-man less than he feared anything else. Vivid pictures crowded upon him . . . the deadly cold of those hands (he had touched the creature accidentally some hours before) . . . the long metallic nails . . . ripping off narrow strips of flesh, pulling out tendons. One would die slowly. Up to the very end that cruel idiocy would smile into one's face. One would give way long before one died—beg for mercy, promise it help, worship, anything.

It was fortunate that something so horrible should be so obviously out of the question. Almost, but not quite, Ransom decreed that whatever the Silence and the Darkness seemed to be saying about this, no such crude, materialistic struggle could possibly be what Maleldil really intended. Any suggestion to the contrary must be only his own morbid fancy. It would degrade the spiritual warfare to the condition of mere mythology. But here he got another check. Long since on Mars, and more strongly since he came to Perelandra, Ransom had been perceiving that the triple distinction of truth from myth and of both from fact was purely terrestrial—was part and parcel of that unhappy division between soul and body which resulted from the Fall. Even on earth the sacraments existed as a permanent reminder that the division was neither wholesome nor final. The Incarnation had been the beginning of its disappearance. In Perelandra it would have no meaning at all. Whatever happened here would be of such a nature that earth-men would call it mythological. All this he had thought before. Now he knew it. The Presence in the darkness, never before so formidable, was putting these truths into his hands, like terrible jewels.

The voluble self was almost thrown out of its argumentative stride— became for some seconds as the voice of a mere whimpering child begging to be let off, to be allowed to go home. Then it rallied. It explained precisely where the absurdity of a physical battle with the Un-man lay. It would be quite irrelevant to the spiritual issue. If the Lady were to be kept in obedience only by the forcible removal of the Tempter, what was the use of that? What would it prove? And if the temptation were not a proving or testing, why was it allowed to happen at all? Did Maleldil suggest that our own world might have been saved if the elephant had accidentally trodden on the serpent a moment before Eve was about to yield? Was it as easy and as un-moral as that? The thing was patently absurd!

The terrible silence went on. It became more and more like a face, a face not without sadness, that looks upon you while you are telling lies, and never interrupts, but gradually you know that it knows, and falter, and contradict yourself, and lapse into silence. The voluble self petered out in the end. Almost the Darkness said to Ransom, "You know you are only wasting time." Every minute it became clearer to him that the parallel he had tried to draw between Eden and Perelandra was crude and imperfect. What had happened on Earth, when Maleldil was born a man at Bethlehem, had altered the universe for ever. The new world of Perelandra was not a mere repetition of the old world Tellus. Maleldil never repeated Himself. As the Lady had said, the same wave never came twice. When Eve fell, God was not Man. He had not yet made men members of His body: since then He had, and through them henceforward He would save and suffer. One of the purposes for which He had done all this was to save Perelandra not through Himself but through Himself in Ransom. If Ransom refused, the plan, so far, miscarried. For that point in the story, a story far more complicated than he had conceived, it was he who had been selected. With a strange sense of "fallings from him, vanishings," he perceived that you might just as well call Perelandra, not Tellus, the centre. You might look upon the Perelandrian story as merely an indirect consequence of the Incarnation on earth: or you might look on the Earth story as mere preparation for the new worlds of which Perelandra was the first. The one was neither more nor less true than the other. Nothing was more or less important than anything else, nothing was a copy or model of anything else.

At the same time he also perceived that his voluble self had begged the question. Up to this point the Lady had repelled her assailant. She was shaken and weary, and there were some stains perhaps in her imagination, but she had stood. In that respect the story already differed from anything that he certainly knew about the mother of our own race. He did not know whether Eve had resisted at all, or if so, for how long. Still less did he know how the story would have ended if she had. If the "serpent" had been foiled, and returned the next day, and the next . . . what then? Would the trial have lasted for ever? How would Maleldil have stopped it? Here on Perelandra his own intuition had been not that no temptation must occur but that "This can't go on." This stopping of a third-degree solicitation, already more than once refused, was a problem to which the terrestrial Fall offered no clue—a new task, and for that new task a new character in the drama, who appeared (most unfortunately) to be himself. In vain did his mind hark back, time after time, to the Book of Genesis, asking "What would have happened?" But to this the Darkness gave him no answer. Patiently and inexorably it brought him back to the here and the now, and to the growing certainty of what was here and now demanded. Almost he felt that the words "would have happened" were meaningless—mere invitations to wander in what the Lady would have called an "alongside world" which had no reality. Only the actual was real: and every actual situation was new. Here in Perelandra the temptation would be stopped by Ransom, or it would not be stopped at all. The Voice—for it was almost with a Voice that he was now contending—seemed to create around this alternative an infinite vacancy. This chapter, this page, this very sentence, in the cosmic story was utterly and eternally itself; no other passage that had occurred or ever would occur could be substituted for it.

He fell back on a different line of defence. How *could* he fight the immortal enemy? Even if he were a fighting man—instead of a sedentary scholar with weak eyes and a baddish wound from the last war—what use was there in fighting it? It couldn't be killed, could it? But the answer was almost immediately plain. Weston's body could be destroyed; and presumably that body was the Enemy's only foothold in Perelandra. By that body, when that body still obeyed a human will, it had entered the new world: expelled from it, it would doubtless have no other habitation. It had entered that body at Weston's own invitation, and without such invitation could enter no other. Ransom remembered that the unclean spirits, in the Bible, had a horror of being cast out into the "deep." And thinking of these things he perceived at last, with a sinking of heart, that if physical action were indeed demanded of him, it was an action, by ordinary standards, neither impossible nor hopeless. On the physical plane it was one middle-aged, sedentary body against another, and both unarmed save for fists and teeth and nails. At the thought of these details, terror and disgust overcame him. To kill the thing with such weapons (he remembered his killing of the frog) would be a nightmare; to be killed—who knew how slowly?—was more than he could face. That he would be killed he felt certain. "When," he asked, "did I ever win a fight in all my life?"

He was no longer making efforts to resist the conviction of what he must do. He had exhausted all his efforts. The answer was plain beyond all subterfuge. The Voice out of the night spoke it to him in such unanswerable fashion that, though there was no noise, he almost felt it must wake the woman who slept close by. He was faced with the impossible. This he must do: this he could not do. In vain he reminded himself of the things that unbelieving boys might at this moment be doing on Earth for a lesser cause. His will was in that valley where the appeal to shame becomes useless—nay, makes the valley darker and deeper. He believed he could face the Un-man with firearms: even that he could stand up unarmed and face certain death if the creature had retained Weston's revolver. But to come to grips with it, to go voluntarily into those dead yet living arms, to grapple with it, naked chest to naked chest. . . . Terrible follies came into his mind. He would fail to obey the Voice, but it would be all right because he would repent later on, when he was back on Earth. He would lose his nerve as St. Peter had done, and be, like St. Peter, forgiven. Intellectually, of course, he knew the answer to these temptations perfectly well; but he was at one of those moments when all the utterances of intellect sound like twice-told tales. Then some crosswind of the mind changed his mood. Perhaps he would fight and win, perhaps not even be badly mauled. But no faintest hint of a guarantee in that direction came to him from the darkness. The future was black as the night itself.

"It is not for nothing that you are named Ransom," said the Voice.

And he knew that this was no fancy of his own. He knew it for a very curious reason—because he had known for many years that his surname was derived not from *ransom* but from *Ranolf's son*. It would never have occurred to him thus to associate the two words. To connect the name Ransom with the act of ransoming would have been for him a mere pun. But even his voluble self did not now dare to suggest that the Voice was making a play upon words. All in a moment of time he perceived that what was, to human philologists, a merely accidental resemblance of two sounds, was in truth no accident. The whole distinction between things accidental and things designed, like the distinction between fact and myth, was purely terrestrial. The pattern is so large that within the little frame of earthly experience there appear pieces of it between which we can see no connection, and other pieces between which we can. Hence we rightly, for our use, distinguish the accidental from the essential. But step outside that frame and the distinction drops down into the void, fluttering useless wings. He had been forced out of the frame, caught up into the larger pattern. He knew now why the old philosophers had said that there is no such thing as chance or fortune beyond the Moon. Before his Mother had born him, before his ancestors had been called Ransoms, before *ransom* had been the name for a payment that delivers, before the world was made, all these things had so stood together in eternity that the very significance of the pattern at this point lay in their coming together in just this fashion. And he bowed his head and groaned and repined against his fate—to be still a man and yet to be forced up into the metaphysical world, to enact what philosophy only thinks.

"My name also is Ransom," said the Voice.

It was some time before the purport of this saying dawned upon him. He whom the other worlds call Maleldil, was the world's ransom, his own ransom, well he knew. But to what purpose was it said now? Before the answer came to him he felt its insufferable approach and held out his arms before him as if he could keep it from forcing open the door of his mind. But it came. So *that* was the real issue. If he now failed, this world also would hereafter be redeemed. If he were not the ransom, Another would be. Yet nothing was ever repeated. Not a second crucifixion: perhaps—who knows—not even a second Incarnation . . . some act of even more appalling love, some glory of yet deeper humility. For he had seen already how the pattern grows and how from each world it sprouts into the next through some other dimension. The small external evil which Satan had done in Malacandra was only as a line: the deeper evil he had done in Earth was as a square: if Venus fell, her evil would be a cube—her Redemption beyond conceiving. Yet redeemed she would be. He had long known that great issues hung on his choice; but as he now realised the true width of the frightful freedom that was being put into his hands—a width to which all merely spatial infinity seemed narrow—he felt like a man brought out under naked heaven, on the edge of a precipice, into the teeth of a wind that came howling from the Pole. He had pictured himself, till now, standing before the Lord, like Peter. But it was worse. He sat before Him like Pilate. It lay with him to save or to spill. His hands had been reddened, as all men's hands have been, in the slaying before the foundation of the world; now, if he chose, he could dip them again in the same blood. "Mercy," he groaned; and then, "Lord, why me?" But there was no answer.

The thing still seemed impossible. But gradually something happened to him which had happened to him only twice before in his life. It had happened once while he was trying to make up his mind to do a very dangerous job in the last war. It had happened again while he was screwing his resolution to go and see a certain man in London and make to him an excessively embarrassing confession which justice demanded. In both cases the thing had seemed a sheer impossibility: he had not thought but known that, being what he was, he was psychologically incapable of doing it; and then, without any apparent movement of the will, as objective and unemotional as the reading on a dial, there had arisen before him, with perfect certitude, the knowledge "about this time tomorrow you will have done the impossible." The same thing happened now. His fear, his shame, his love, all his arguments, were not altered in the least. The thing was neither more nor less dreadful than it had been before. The only difference was that he knew—almost as a historical proposition—that it was going to be done. He might beg, weep, or rebel—might curse or adore—sing like a martyr or blaspheme like a devil. It made not the slightest difference. The thing was going to be done. There was going to arrive, in the course of time, a moment at which he would have done it. The future act stood there, fixed and unaltered as if he had already performed it. It was a mere irrelevant detail that it happened to occupy the position we call future instead of that which we call past. The whole struggle was over, and yet there seemed to have been no moment of victory. You might say, if you liked, that the power of choice had been simply set aside and an inflexible destiny substituted for it. On the other hand, you might say that he had delivered from the rhetoric of his passions and had emerged into unassailable freedom. Ransom could not, for the life of him, see any difference between these two statements. Predestination and freedom were apparently identical. He could no longer see any meaning in the many arguments he had heard on this subject.

No sooner had he discovered that he would certainly try to kill the Un-man to-morrow than the doing of it appeared to him a smaller matter than he had supposed. He could hardly remember why he had accused himself of megalomania when the idea first occurred to him. It was true that if he left it undone, Maleldil Himself would do some greater thing instead. In that sense, he stood for Maleldil: but no more than Eve would have stood for Him by simply not eating the apple, or than any man stands for Him in doing any good action. As there was no comparison in person, so there was none in suffering—or only such comparison as may be between a man who burns his finger putting out a spark and a fireman who loses his life in fighting a conflagration because that spark was not put out. He asked no longer "Why me?" It might as well be he as another. It might as well be any other choice as this. The fierce light which he had seen resting on this moment of decision rested in reality on all.

"I have cast your Enemy into sleep," said the Voice. "He will not wake till morning. Get up. Walk twenty paces back into the wood; there sleep. Your sister sleeps also."

12

When some dreaded morning comes we usually wake fully to it at once. Ransom passed with no intermediate stages from dreamless sleep to a full consciousness of his task. He found himself alone—the island gently rocking on a sea that was neither calm nor stormy. The golden light, glinting through indigo trunks of trees, told him in which direction the water lay. He went to it and bathed. Then, having landed again, he lay down and drank. He stood for a few minutes running his hands through his wet hair and stroking his limbs. Looking down at his own body he noticed how greatly the sunburn on one side and the pallor on the other had decreased. He would hardly be christened Piebald if the Lady were now to meet him for the first time. His colour had become more like ivory: and his toes, after so many days of nakedness, had begun to lose the cramped, squalid shape imposed by boots. Altogether he thought better of himself as a human animal than he had done before. He felt pretty certain that he would never again wield an un-maimed body until a greater morning came for the whole universe, and he was glad that the instrument had been thus tuned up to concert pitch before he had to surrender it. "When I wake up after Thy image, I shall be satisfied," he said to himself.

Presently he walked into the woods. Accidentally—for he was at the moment intent on food—he blundered through a whole cloud of the arboreal bubbles. The pleasure was as sharp as when he had first experienced it, and his very stride was different as he emerged from them. Although this was to be his last meal, he did not even now feel it proper to look for any favorite fruit. But what met him was gourds. "A good breakfast on the morning you're hanged," he thought whimsically as he let the empty shell drop from his hand—filled for the moment with such pleasure as seemed to make the whole world a dance. "All said and done," he thought, "it's been worth it. I have had a time. I have lived in Paradise."

He went a little farther in the wood, which grew thickly hereabout, and almost tripped over the sleeping form of the Lady. It was unusual for her to be sleeping at this time of the day, and he assumed it was Maleldil's doing. "I shall never see her again," he thought; and then, "I shall never again look on a female body in quite the same way as I look on this." As he stood looking down on her, what was most with him was an intense and orphaned longing that he might, if only for once, have seen the great Mother of his own race thus, in her innocence and splendour. "Other things, other blessings, other glories," he murmured. "But never that. Never in all worlds, that. God can make good use of all that happens. But the loss is real." He looked at her once again and then walked abruptly past the place where she lay. "I was right," he thought, "it couldn't have gone on. It was time to stop it."

It took him a long time, wandering like this, in and out of the dark yet coloured thickets, before he found his Enemy. He came on his old friend the dragon, just as he had first seen it, coiled about the trunk of a tree, but it also was asleep; and now he noticed that ever since he awoke he had perceived no chattering of birds, no rustling of sleek bodies or peering of brown eyes through the leafage, nor heard any noise but that of water. It seemed that the Lord God had cast that whole island or perhaps that whole world into deep sleep. For a moment this gave him a sense of desolation, but almost at once he rejoiced that no memory of blood and rage should be left imprinted in these happy minds.

After about an hour, suddenly rounding a little clump of bubble-trees he found himself face to face with the Un-man. "Is it wounded already?" he thought as the first vision of a blood-stained chest broke on him. Then he saw that of course it was not its own blood. A bird, already half plucked and with beak wide open in the soundless yell of strangulation, was feebly struggling in its long clever hands. Ransom found himself acting before he knew what he had done. Some memory of boxing at his preparatory school must have awaked, for he found he had delivered a straight left with all his might on the Un-man's jaw. But he had forgotten that he was not fighting with gloves; what recalled him to himself was the pain as his fist crashed against the jaw-bone—it seemed almost to have broken his knuckles—and the sickening jar all up his arm. He stood still for a second under the shock of it and this gave the Un-man time to fall back about six paces. It too had not liked the first taste of the encounter. It had apparently bitten its tongue, for blood came bubbling out of the mouth when it tried to speak. It was still holding the bird.

"So you mean to try strength," it said in English, speaking thick.

"Put down that bird," said Ransom.

"But this is very foolish," said the Un-man. "Do you not know who I am?"

"I know *what* you are," said Ransom. "Which of them doesn't matter."

"And you think, little one," it answered, "that you can fight with me? You think He will help you, perhaps? Many thought that. I've known Him longer than you, little one. They all think He's going to help them—till they come to their senses screaming recantations too late in the middle of the fire, mouldering in concentration camps, writhing under saws, jibbering in mad-houses, or nailed on to crosses. Could He help Himself?"—and the creature suddenly threw back its head and cried in a voice so loud that it seemed the golden sky-roof must break, "*Eloi, Eloi, lama sabachthani.*"

And the moment it had done so, Ransom felt certain that the sounds it had made were perfect Aramaic of the First Century. The Un-man was not quoting; it was remembering. These were the very words spoken from the Cross, treasured through all those years in the burning memory of the outcast creature which had heard them, and now brought forward in hideous parody; the horror made him momentarily sick. Befor he had recovered the Un-man was upon him, howling like a gale, with eyes so wide opened that they seemed to have no lids, and with all its hair rising on its scalp. It had him caught tightly to its chest, with its arms about him, and its nails were ripping great strips off his back. His own arms were inside its embrace and, pummelling wildly, he could get no blow at it. He turned his head and bit deeply into the muscle of its right arm, at first without success, then deeper. It gave a howl, tried to hold on, and then suddenly he was free. Its defence was for an instant unready and he found himself raining punches about the region of its heart, faster and harder than he had supposed possible. He could hear through its open mouth the great gusts of breath that he was knocking out of it. Then its hands came up again, fingers arched like claws. It was not trying to box. It wanted to grapple. He knocked its right arm aside with a horrible shock of bone against bone and caught it a jab on the fleshy part of the chin: at the same moment its nails tore his right. He grabbed at its arms. More by luck than by skill he got it held by both wrists.

What followed for the next minute or so would hardly have looked like a fight at all to any spectator. The Un-man was trying with every ounce of power it could find in Weston's body to wrench its arms free from Ransom's hands, and he, with every ounce of his power, was trying to retain his manacle hold round its wrists. But this effort, which sent streams of sweat down the backs of both combatants, resulted in a slow and seemingly leisurely, and even aimless, movement of both pairs of arms. Neither could for the moment hurt the other. The Un-man bent forward its head and tried to bite, but Ransom straightened his arms and kept it at arm's length. There seemed no reason why this should ever end.

Then suddenly it shot out its leg and crooked it behind his knee. He was nearly taken off his feet. Movements became quick and flurried on both sides. Ransom in his turn tried to trip, and failed. He started bending the enemy's left arm back by main force with some idea of breaking or at least spraining it. But in the effort to do so he must have weakened his hold on the other wrist. It got its right free. He had just time to close his eyes before the nails tore fiercely down his cheek and the pain put an end to the blows his left was already raining on its ribs. A second later—he did not know how it happened—they were standing apart, their chests heaving in great gasps, each staring at the other.

Both were doubtless sorry spectacles. Ransom could not see his own wounds but he seemed to be covered with blood. The enemy's eyes were nearly closed and the body, wherever the remains of Weston's shirt did not conceal it, was a mass of what would soon be bruises. This, and its laboured breathing, and the very taste of its strength in their grapples, had altered Ransom's state of mind completely. He had been astonished to find it no stronger. He had all along, despite what reason told him, expected that the strength of its body would be superhuman, diabolical. He had reckoned on arms that could no more be caught and stopped than the blades of an aeroplane's propeller. But now he knew, by actual experience, that its bodily strength was merely that of Weston. On the physical plane it was one middle-aged scholar against another. Weston had been the more powerfully built of the two men, but he was fat; his body would not take punishment well. Ransom was nimbler and better breathed. His former certainty of death now seemed to him ridiculous. It was a very fair match. There was no reason why he should not win—and live.

This time it was Ransom who attacked, and the second bout was much the same as the first. What it came to was that whenever he could box Ransom was superior; whenever he came under tooth and claw he was beaten. His mind, even in the thick of it, was now quite clear. He saw that the issue of the day hung on a very simple question—whether loss of blood would undo him before heavy blows on heart and kidneys undid the other.

All that rich world was asleep about them. There were no rules, no umpire, no spectators; but mere exhaustion, constantly compelling them to fall apart, divided the grotesque duel into rounds as accurately as could be wished. Ransom could never remember how many of these rounds were fought. The thing became like the frantic repetitions of delirium, and thirst a greater pain than any the adversary could inflict. Sometimes they were both on the ground together. Once he was actually astride the enemy's chest, squeezing its throat with both hands and—he found to his surprise—shouting a line out of *The Battle of Maldon*: but it tore his arms so with its nails and so pounded his back with its knees that he was thrown off.

Then he remembers—as one remembers an island of consciousness preceded and followed by long anæsthesia—going forward to meet the Un-man for what seemed the thousandth time and knowing clearly that he could not fight much more. He remembers seeing the Enemy for a moment looking not like Weston but like a mandrill, and realising almost at once that this was delirium. He wavered. Then an experience that perhaps no good man can ever have in our world came over him— a torrent of perfectly unmixed and lawful hatred. The energy of hating, never before felt without some guilt, without some dim knowledge that he was failing fully to distinguish the sinner from the sin, rose into his arms and legs till he felt that they were pillars of burning blood. What was before him appeared no longer a creature of corrupted will. It was corruption itself to which will was attached only as an instrument. Ages ago it had been a Person: but the ruins of personality now survived in it only as weapons at the disposal of a furious self-exiled negation. It is perhaps difficult to understand why this filled Ransom not with horror but with a kind of joy. The joy came from finding at last what hatred was made for. As a boy with an axe rejoices on finding a tree, or a boy with a box of coloured chalks rejoices on finding a pile of perfectly white paper, so he rejoiced in the perfect congruity between his emotion and its object. Bleeding and trembling with weariness as he was, he felt that nothing was beyond his power, and when he flung himself upon the living Death, the eternal Surd in the universal mathematic, he was astonished, and yet (on a deeper level) not astonished at all, at his own strength. His arms seemed to move quicker than his thought. His hands taught him terrible things. He felt its ribs break, he heard its jaw-bone crack. The whole creature seemed to be cracking and splitting under his blows. His own pains, where it tore him, somehow failed to matter. He felt that he could so fight, so hate with a perfect hatred, for a whole year.

All at once he found he was beating the air. He was in such a state that at first he could not understand what was happening—could not believe that the Un-man had fled. His momentary stupidity gave it a start; and when he came to his senses he was just in time to see it vanishing into the wood, with a limping uneven stride, with one arm hanging useless, and with its dog-like howl. He dashed after it. For a second or so it was concealed from him by the tree trunks. Then it was once more in sight. He began running with all his power, but it kept its lead.

It was a fantastic chase, in and out of the lights and shadows and up and down the slowly moving ridges and valleys. They passed the dragon where it slept. They passed the Lady, sleeping with a smile on her face. The Un-man stooped low as it passed her with the fingers of its left hand crooked for scratching. It would have torn her if it dared, but Ransom was close behind and it could not risk the delay. They passed through a flock of large orange-coloured birds all fast asleep, each on one leg, each with its head beneath its wing, so that they looked like a grove of formal and flowery shrubs. They picked their steps where pairs and families of the yellow wallabies lay on their backs with eyes fast shut and their small forepaws folded on their breasts as if they were crusaders carved on tombs. They stooped beneath branches which were bowed down because on them lay the tree-pigs, making a comfortable noise like a child's snore. They crashed through thickets of bubble-trees and forgot, for the moment, their weariness. It was a large island. They came out of the woods and rushed across wide fields of saffron or of silver, sometimes deep to their ankles and sometimes to their waists in the cool or poignant scents. They rushed down into yet other woods which lay, as they approached them, at the bottom of secret valleys, but rose before they reached them to crown the summits of lonely hills. Ransom could not gain on his quarry. It was a wonder that any creature so maimed as its uneven strides showed it to be, could maintain that pace. If the ankle were really sprained, as he suspected, it must suffer indescribably at every step. Then the horrible thought came into his mind that perhaps it could somehow hand over the pain to be borne by whatever remnants of Weston's consciousness yet survived in its body. The idea that something which had once been of his own kind and fed at a human breast might even now be imprisoned in the thing he was pursuing redoubled his hatred, which was unlike nearly all other hatreds he had ever known, for it increased his strength.

As they emerged from about the fourth wood he saw the sea before them not thirty yards away. The Un-man rushed on as if it made no distinction between land and water and plunged in with a great splash. He could see its head, dark against the coppery sea, as it swam. Ransom rejoiced, for swimming was the only sport in which he had ever approached excellence. As he took the water he lost sight of the Un-man for a moment; then, looking up and shaking the wet hair from his face as he struck out in pursuit (his hair was very long by now), he saw its whole body upright and above the surface as though it were sitting on the sea. A second glance and he realised that it had mounted a fish. Apparently the charm'd slumber extended only to the island, for the Unman on his mount was making good speed. It was stooping down doing something to its fish, Ransom could not see what. Doubtless it would have many ways of urging the animal to quicken its pace.

For a moment he was in despair: but he had forgotten the man-loving nature of these sea-horses. He found almost at once that he was in a complete shoal of the creatures, leaping and frisking to attract his attention. In spite of their good will it was no easy matter to get himself on to the slippery surface of the fine specimen which his grabbing hands first reached: while he was struggling to mount, the distance widened between him and the fugitive. But at last it was done. Settling himself behind the great goggle-eyed head he nudged the animal with his knees, kicked it with his heels, whispered words of praise and encouragement, and in general did all he could to awake its mettle. It began threshing its way forward. But looking ahead Ransom could no longer see any sign of the Un-man, but only the long empty ridge of the next wave coming towards him. Doubtless the quarry was beyond the ridge. Then he noticed that he had no cause to be bothered about the direction. The slope of water was dotted all over with the great fish, each marked by a heap of yellow foam and some of them spouting as well. The Un-man possibly had not reckoned on the instinct which made them follow as leader any of their company on whom a human being sat. They were all forging straight ahead, no more uncertain of their course than homing rooks or bloodhounds on a scent. As Ransom and his fish rose to the top of the wave, he found himself looking down on a wide shallow trough shaped much like a valley in the home counties. Far away and now approaching the opposite slope was the little, dark puppet-like silhouette of the Un-man: and between it and him the whole school of fish was spread out in three or four lines. Clearly there was no danger of losing touch. Ransom was hunting him with the fish and they would not cease to follow. He laughed aloud. "My hounds are bred out of the Spartan kind, so flew'd so sanded," he roared.

Now for the first time the blessed fact that he was no longer fighting nor even standing thrust itself upon his attention. He made to assume a more relaxed position and was pulled up sharp by a grinding pain across his back. He foolishly put back his hand to explore his shoulders, and almost screamed at the pain of his own touch. His back seemed to be in shreds and the shreds seemed to be all stuck together. At the same time he noticed that he had lost a tooth and that nearly all the skin was gone from his knuckles; and underneath the smarting surface pains, deeper and more ominous aches racked him from head to foot. He had not known he was so knocked up.

Then he remembered that he was thirsty. Now that he had begun to cool and stiffen he found the task of getting a drink from the water that raced by him extremely difficult. His first idea had been to stoop low till his head was almost upside down and bury his face in the water: but a single attempt cured him of that. He was reduced to putting down his cupped hands, and even this, as his stiffness grew upon him, had to be done with infinite caution and with many groans and gasps. It took many minutes to get a tiny sip which merely mocked his thirst. The quenching of that thirst kept him employed for what seemed to be half an hour—a half-hour of sharp pains and insane pleasures. Nothing had ever tasted so good. Even when he had done drinking he went on taking up water and splashing it over himself. This would have been among the happiest moments of his life—if only the smarting of his back did not seem to be getting worse and if only he were not afraid that there was poison in the cuts. His legs kept on getting stuck to the fish and having to be unstuck with pain and care. Every now and then blackness threatened to come over him. He could easily have fainted, but he thought "This will never do" and fixed his eyes on objects close at hand and thought plain thoughts and so retained his consciousness.

All this time the Un-man rode on before him, up-wave and down-wave, and the fishes followed and Ransom followed the fishes. There seemed to be more of them now, as if the chase had met other shoals and gathered them up into itself in snowball fashion: and soon there were creatures other than fish. Birds with long necks like swans—he could not tell their colour for they looked black against the sky—came, wheeling at first, overhead, but afterwards they settled in long straight files—all following the Un-man. The crying of these birds was often audible, and it was the wildest sound that Ransom had ever heard, the loneliest, and the one that had least to do with Man. No land was in sight, nor had been for many hours. He was on the high seas, the waste places of Perelandra, as he had not been since his first arrival. The sea-noises continuously filled his ear: the sea-smell, unmistakable and stirring as that of our Tellurian oceans, but quite different in its warmth and golden sweetness, entered into his brain. It also was wild and strange. It was not hostile: if it had been, its wildness and strangeness would have been the less, for hostility is a relation and an enemy is not a total stranger. It came into his head that he knew nothing at all about this world. Some day, no doubt, it would be peopled by the descendants of the King and Queen. But all its millions of years in the unpeopled past, all its uncounted miles of laughing water in the lonely present . . . did they exist solely for that? It was strange that he to whom a wood or a morning sky on earth had sometimes been a kind of meal, should have had to come to another planet in order to realise Nature as a thing in her own right. The diffused meaning, the inscrutable character, which had been both in Tellus and Perelandra since they split off from the Sun, and which would be, in one sense, displaced by the advent of imperial man, yet, in some other sense, not displaced at all, enfolded him on every side and caught him into itself.

Darkness fell upon the waves as suddenly as if it had been poured out of a bottle. As soon as the colours and the distances were thus taken away, sound and pain became more emphatic. The world was reduced to a dull ache, and sudden stabs, and the beating of the fish's fins, and the monotonous yet infinitely varied noises of the water. Then he found himself almost falling off the fish, recovered his seat with difficulty, and realised that he had been asleep, perhaps for hours. He foresaw that this danger would continually recur. After some consideration he levered himself painfully out of the narrow saddle behind its head and stretched his body at full length along the fish's back. He parted his legs and wound them about the creature as far as he could and did the same with his arms, hoping that thus he could retain his mount even while sleeping. It was the best he could do. A strange thrilling sensation crept over him, communicated doubtless from the movement of its muscles. It gave him the illusion of sharing in its strong bestial life, as if he were himself becoming a fish.

Long after this he found himself staring into something like a human face. It ought to have terrified him but, as sometimes happens to us in a dream, it did not. It was a bluish-greenish face shining apparently by its own light. The eyes were much larger than those of a man and gave it a goblin appearance. A fringe of corrugated membranes at the sides suggested whiskers. With a shock he realised that he was not dreaming, but awake. The thing was real. He was still lying, sore and wearied, on the body of the fish and this face belonged to something that was swimming alongside him. He remembered the swimming submen or mermen whom he had seen before. He was not at all frightened, and he guessed that the creature's reaction to him was the very same as his to it—an uneasy, though not hostile, bewilderment. Each was wholly irrelevant to the other. They met as the branches of different trees meet when the wind brings them together.

Ransom now raised himself once more to a sitting position. He found that the darkness was not complete. His own fish swam in a bath of phosphorescence and so did the stranger at his side. All about him were other blobs and daggers of blue light and he could dimly make out from the shapes which were fish and which were the water-people. Their movements faintly indicated the contours of the waves and introduced some hint of perspective into the night. He noticed presently that several of the water-people in his immediate neighbourhood seemed to be feeding. They were picking dark masses of something off the water with their webbed frog-like hands and devouring it. As they munched, it hung out of their mouths in bushy and shredded bundles and looked like moustaches. It is significant that it never occurred to him to try to establish any contact with these beings, as he had done with every other animal on Perelandra, nor did they try to establish any with him. They did not seem to be the natural subjects of man as the other creatures were. He got the impression that they simply shared a planet with him as sheep and horses share a field, each species ignoring the other. Later, this came to be a trouble in his mind: but for the moment he was occupied with a more practical problem. The sight of their eating had reminded him that he was hungry, and he was wondering whether the stuff they ate were eatable by him. It took him a long time, scooping the water with his fingers, to catch any of it. When at last he did it turned out to be of the same general structure as one of our smaller sea-weeds, and to have little bladders that popped when one pressed them. It was tough and slippery, but not salt like the weed of a Tellurian sea. What it tasted like, he could never properly describe. It is to be noted all through this story that while Ransom was on Perelandra his sense of taste had become something more than it was on Earth: it gave knowledge as well as pleasure, though not a knowledge that can be reduced to words. As soon as he had eaten a few mouthfuls of the seaweed he felt his mind oddly changed. He felt the surface of the sea to be the top of the world. He thought of the floating islands as we think of clouds; he saw them in imagination as they would appear from below—mats of fibre with long streamers hanging down from them, and became startlingly conscious of his own experience in walking on the topside of them as a miracle or a myth. He felt his memory of the Green Lady and all her promised descendants and all the issues which had occupied him ever since he came to Perelandra rapidly fading from his mind, as a dream fades when we wake, or as if it were shouldered aside by a whole world of interests and emotions to which he could give no name. It terrified him. In spite of his hunger he threw the rest of the weed away.

He must have slept again, for the next scene that he remembers was in daylight. The Un-man was still visible ahead, and the shoal of fishes was still spread out between it and him. The birds had abandoned the chase. And now at last a full and prosaic sense of his position descended upon him. It is a curious flaw in the reason, to judge from Ransom's experience, that when a man comes to a strange planet he at first quite forgets its size. That whole world is so small in comparison with his journey through space that he forgets the distances within it: any two places in Mars, or in Venus, appear to him like places in the same town. But now, as Ransom looked round once more and saw nothing in every direction but golden sky and tumbling waves, the full absurdity of this delusion was borne in upon him. Even if there were continents in Perelandra, he might well be divided from the nearest of them by the breadth of the Pacific or more. But he had no reason to suppose that there were any. He had no reason to suppose that even the floating islands were very numerous, or that they were equally distributed over the surface of the planet. Even if their loose archipelago spread over a thousand square miles, what would that be but a negligible freckling in a landless ocean that rolled for ever round a globe not much smaller than the World of Men? Soon his fish would be tired. Already, he fancied, it was not swimming at its original speed. The Un-man would doubtless torture its mount to swim till it died. But he could not do that. As he was thinking of these things and staring ahead, he saw something that turned his heart cold. One of the other fish deliberately turned out of line, spurted a little column of foam, dived, and reappeared some yards away, apparently drifting. In a few minutes it was out of sight. It had had enough.

And now the experiences of the past day and night began to make a direct assault upon his faith. The solitude of the seas and, still more, the experiences which had followed his taste of the seaweed, had insinuated a doubt as to whether this world in any real sense belonged to those who called themselves its King and Queen. How could it be made for them when most of it, in fact, was uninhabitable by them? Was not the very idea naïve and anthropomorphic in the highest degree? As for the great prohibition, on which so much had seemed to hang—was it really so important? What did these roarers with the yellow foam, and these strange people who lived in them, care whether two little creatures, now far away, lived or did not live on one particular rock? The parallelism between the scenes he had lately witnessed and those recorded in the

Book of Genesis, and which had hitherto given him the feeling of knowing by experience what other men only believe, now began to shrink in importance. Need it prove anything more than that similar irrational *taboos* had accompanied the dawn of reason in two different worlds? It was all very well to talk of Maleldil: but where was Maleldil now? If this illimitable ocean said anything, it said something very different. Like all solitudes it was, indeed, haunted: but not by an anthropomorphic Deity, rather by the wholly inscrutable to which man and his life remained eternally irrelevant. And beyond this ocean was space itself. In vain did Ransom try to remember that he had been in "space" and found it Heaven, tingling with a fulness of life for which infinity itself was not one cubic inch too large. All that seemed like a dream. That opposite mode of thought which he had often mocked and called in mockery The Empirical Bogey, came surging into his mind—the great myth of our century with its gases and galaxies, its light years and evolutions, its nightmare perspectives of simple arithmetic in which everything that can possibly hold significance for the mind becomes the mere by-product of essential disorder. Always till now he had belittled it, had treated with a certain disdain its flat superlatives, its clownish amazement that different things should be of different sizes, its glib munificence of ciphers. Even now, his reason was not quite subdued, though his heart would not listen to his reason. Part of him still knew that the size of a thing is its least important characteristic, that the material universe derived from the comparing and mythopœic power within him that very majesty before which he was now asked to abase himself, and that mere numbers could not overawe us unless we lent them, from our own resources, that awfulness which they themselves could no more supply than a banker's ledger. But this knowledge remained an abstraction. Mere bigness and loneliness overbore him.

These thoughts must have taken several hours and absorbed all his attention. He was aroused by what he least expected—the sound of a human voice. Emerging from his reverie he saw that all the fishes had deserted him. His own was swimming feebly: and there a few yards away, no longer fleeing him but moving slowly towards him, was the Unman. It sat hugging itself, its eyes almost shut up with bruises, its flesh the colour of liver, its leg apparently broken, its mouth twisted with pain.

"Ransom," it said feebly.

Ransom held his tongue. He was not going to encourage it to start that game again.

"Ransom," it said again in a broken voice, "for God's sake speak to me."

He glanced at it in surprise. Tears were on its cheeks.

"Ransom, don't cold-shoulder me," it said. "Tell me what has happened. What have they done to us? You—you're all bleeding. My leg's broken . . ." its voice died away in a whimper.

"Who are you?" he asked sharply.

"Oh, don't pretend you don't know me," mumbled Weston's voice. "I'm Weston. You're Ransom—Elwin Ransom of Leicester, Cambridge, the philologist. We've had our quarrels, I know. I'm sorry. I dare say I've been in the wrong. Ransom, you'll not leave me to die in this horrible place, will you?"

"Where did you learn Aramaic?" asked Ransom, keeping his eyes on the other.

"Aramaic?" said Weston's voice. "I don't know what you're talking about. It's not much of a game to make fun of a dying man."

"But are you really Weston?" said Ransom, for he began to think that Weston had actually come back.

"Who else should I be?" came the answer, with a burst of weak temper, on the verge of tears.

"Where have you been?" asked Ransom.

Weston—if it was Weston—shuddered. "Where are we now?" he asked presently.

"In Perelandra—Venus, you know," answered Ransom.

"Have you found the space-ship?" asked Weston.

"I never saw it except at a distance," said Ransom. "And I've no idea where it is now—a couple of hundred miles away for all I know."

"You mean we're trapped?" said Weston, almost in a scream. Ransom said nothing and the other bowed his head and cried like a baby.

"Come," said Ransom at last, "there's no good taking it like that. Hang it all, you'd not be much better off if you were on Earth. You remember they're having a war there. The Germans may be bombing London to bits at this moment!" Then seeing the creature still crying, he added, "Buck up, Weston. It's only death, all said and done. We should have to die some day, you know. We shan't lack water, and hunger—without thirst—isn't too bad. As for drowning—well, a bayonet wound, or cancer, would be worse."

"You mean to say you're going to leave me," said Weston.

"I can't, even if I wanted to," said Ransom. "Don't you see I'm in the same position as yourself?"

"You'll promise not to go off and leave me in the lurch?" said Weston.

"All right, I'll promise if you like. Where could I go to?"

Weston looked very slowly all round and then urged his fish a little nearer to Ransom's.

"Where is . . . *it?*" he asked in a whisper. "You know," and he made meaningless gestures.

"I might ask you the same question," said Ransom.

"Me?" said Weston. His face was, in one way and another, so disfigured that it was hard to be sure of its expression.

"Have you any idea of what's been happening to you for the last few days?" said Ransom.

Weston once more looked all round him uneasily.

"It's all true, you know," he said at last.

"What's all true?" said Ransom.

Suddenly Weston turned on him with a snarl of rage. "It's all very well for *you*," he said. "Drowning doesn't hurt and death is bound to come anyway, and all that nonsense. What do *you* know about death? It's all true, I tell you."

"What are you talking about?"

"I've been stuffing myself up with a lot of nonsense all my life," said Weston. "Trying to persuade myself that it matters what happens to the human race . . . trying to believe that anything you can do will make the universe bearable. It's all rot, do you see?"

"And something else is truer!"

"Yes," said Weston, and then was silent for a long time.

"We'd better turn our fishes head on to this," said Ransom presently, his eyes on the seas, "or we'll be driven apart." Weston obeyed without seeming to notice what he did, and for a time the two men were riding very slowly side by side.

"I'll tell you what's truer," said Weston presently.

"What?"

"A little child that creeps upstairs when nobody's looking and very slowly turns the handle to take one peep into the room where its grandmother's dead body is laid out—and then runs away and has bad dreams. An enormous grandmother, you understand."

"What do you mean by saying that's truer?"

"I mean that child knows something about the universe which all science and all religion is trying to hide."

Ransom said nothing.

"Lots of things," said Weston presently. "Children are afraid to go through a churchyard at night, and the grown-ups tell them not to be silly: but the children know better than the grown-ups. People in Central Africa doing beastly things with masks on in the middle of the night— and missionaries and civil servants say it's all superstition. Well, the blacks know more about the universe than the white people. Dirty priests in back streets in Dublin frightening half-witted children to death with stories about it. You'd say they are unenlightened. They're not: except that they think there is a way of escape. There isn't. That is the real universe, always will be. That's what it all *means*."

"I'm not quite clear——" began Ransom, when Weston interrupted him.

"That's why it's so important to live as long as you can. All the good things are now—a thin little rind of what we call life, put on for show, and then—the *real* universe for ever and ever. To thicken the rind by one centimetre—to live one week, one day, one half-hour longer—that's the only thing that matters. Of course you don't know it: but every man who is waiting to be hanged knows it. You say, 'What difference does a short reprieve make?' What difference!!"

"But nobody need go there," said Ransom.

"I know that's what you believe," said Weston. "But you're wrong. It's only a small parcel of civilised people who think that. Humanity as a whole knows better. It knows—Homer knew—that *all* the dead have sunk down into the inner darkness: under the rind. All witless, all twittering, gibbering, decaying. Bogeymen. Every savage knows that *all* ghosts hate the living who are still enjoying the rind: just as old women hate girls who still have their good looks. It's quite right to be afraid of the ghosts. You're going to be one all the same."

"You don't believe in God," said Ransom.

"Well, now, that's another point," said Weston. "I've been to church as well as you when I was a boy. There's more sense in parts of the Bible than you religious people know. Doesn't it say He's the God of the living, not of the dead? That's just it. Perhaps your God does exist—but it makes no difference whether He does or not. No, of course you wouldn't see it; but one day you will. I don't think you've got the idea of the rind—the thin outer skin which we call life—really clear. Picture the universe as an infinite globe with this very thin crust on the outside. But remember its thickness is a thickness of *time*. It's about seventy years thick in the best places. We are born on the surface of it and all our lives we are sinking through it. When we've got all the way through then we are what's called Dead: we've got into the dark part inside, the real globe. If your God exists, He's not in the globe—He's outside, like a moon. As we pass into the interior we pass out of His ken. He doesn't follow us in. You would express it by saying He's not in time—which you think comforting! In other words He stays put: out in the light and air, outside. But we are in time. We 'move with the times.' That is, from His point of view, we move *away*, into what He regards as nonentity, where He never follows. That is all there is to us, all there ever was. He may be there in what you call 'Life,' or He may not. What difference does it make? *We're* not going to be there for long!"

"That could hardly be the whole story," said Ransom. "If the whole universe were like that, then we, being parts of it, would feel at home in such a universe. The very fact that it strikes us as monstrous——"

"Yes," interrupted Weston, "that would be all very well if it wasn't that reasoning itself is only valid as long as you stay in the rind. It has nothing to do with the real universe. Even the ordinary scientists—like what I used to be myself—are beginning to find that out. Haven't you seen the real meaning of all this modern stuff about the dangers of extrapolation and bent space and the indeterminacy of the atom? They don't say in so many words, of course, but what they're getting to, even before they die nowadays, is what all men get to when they're dead—the knowledge that reality is neither rational nor consistent nor anything else. In a sense you might say it isn't there. 'Real' and 'Unreal,' 'true' and 'false'—they're all only on the surface. They give way the moment you press them."

"If all this were true," said Ransom, "what would be the point of saying it?"

"Or of anything else?" replied Weston. "The only point in anything is that there isn't any point. Why do ghosts want to frighten? Because they *are* ghosts. What else is there to do?"

"I get the idea," said Ransom. "That the account a man gives of the universe, or of any other building, depends very much on where he is standing."

"But specially," said Weston, "on whether he's inside or out. All the things you like to dwell upon are outsides. A planet like our own, or like Perelandra, for instance. Or a beautiful human body. All the colours and pleasant shapes are merely where it ends, where it ceases to be. Inside, what do you get? Darkness, worms, heat, pressure, salt, suffocation, stink."

They ploughed forward for a few minutes in silence over waves which were now growing larger. The fish seemed to be making little headway.

"Of course you don't care," said Weston. "What do you people in the rind care about us? You haven't been pulled down yet. It's like a dream I once had, though I didn't know then how true it was. I dreamed I was lying dead—you know, nicely laid out in the ward in a nursing home with my face settled by the undertaker and big lilies in the room. And then a sort of person who was all falling to bits—like a tramp, you know, only it was himself not his clothes that was coming to pieces—

came and stood at the foot of the bed, just hating me. 'All right,' he said, 'all right. You think you're mighty fine with your clean sheet and your shiny coffin being got ready. I began like that. We all did. Just wait and see what you come down to in the end.' "

"Really," said Ransom, "I think you might just as well shut up."

"Then there's Spiritualism," said Weston, ignoring this suggestion. "I used to think it all nonsense. But it isn't. It's all true. You've noticed that all *pleasant* accounts of the dead are traditional or philosophical? What actual experiment discovers is quite different. Ectoplasm—slimy films coming out of a medium's belly and making great, chaotic, tumbledown faces. Automatic writing producing reams of rubbish."

"*Are* you Weston?" said Ransom, suddenly turning upon his companion. The persistent mumbling voice, so articulate that you had to listen to it and yet so inarticulate that you had to strain your ears to follow what it said, was beginning to madden him.

"Don't be angry," said the voice. "There's no good being angry with me. I thought you might be sorry. My God, Ransom, it's awful. You don't understand. Right down under layers and layers. Buried alive. You try to connect things and can't. They take your head off . . . and you can't even look back on what life was like in the rind, because you know it never did mean anything even from the beginning."

"What are you?" cried Ransom. "How do you know what death is like? God knows, I'd help you if I could. But give me the facts. Where have you been these few days?"

"Hush," said the other suddenly, "what's that?"

Ransom listened. Certainly there did seem to be a new element in the great concourse of noises with which they were surrounded. At first he could not define it. The seas were very big now and the wind was strong. All at once his companion reached out his hand and clutched Ransom's arm.

"Oh, my God!" he cried. "Oh, Ransom, Ransom! We shall be killed. Killed and put back under the rind. Ransom, you promised to help me. Don't let them get me again."

"Shut up," said Ransom in disgust, for the creature was wailing and blubbering so that he could hear nothing else: and he wanted very much to identify the deeper note that had mingled with the piping wind and roar of water.

"Breakers," said Weston, "breakers, you fool! Can't you hear? There's a country over there! There's a rocky coast. Look there—no, to your right. We shall be smashed into a jelly. Look—O God, here comes the dark!"

And the dark came. Horror of death such as he had never known, horror of the terrified creature at his side, descended upon Ransom: finally, horror with no definite object. In a few minutes he could see through the jet-black night the luminous cloud of foam. From the way in which it shot steeply upward he judged it was breaking on cliffs. Invisible birds, with a shriek and flurry, passed low overhead.

"Are you there, Weston?" he shouted. "What cheer? Pull yourself together. All that stuff you've been talking is lunacy. Say a child's prayer if you can't say a man's. Repent your sins. Take my hand. There are hundreds of mere boys on Earth facing death this moment. We'll do very well."

His hand was clutched in the darkness, rather more firmly than he wished. "I can't bear it, I can't bear it," came Weston's voice.

"Steady now. None of that," he shouted back, for Weston had suddenly gripped his arm with both hands.

"I can't bear it," came the voice again.

"Hi!" said Ransom. "Let go. What the devil are you doing?"—and as he spoke strong arms had plucked him from the saddle, had wrapped him round in a terrible embrace just below his thighs, and, clutching uselessly at the smooth surface of the fish's body, he was dragged down. The waters closed over his head: and still his enemy pulled him down into the warm depth, and down farther yet to where it was no longer warm.

14

can't hold my breath any longer," thought Ransom. "I can't. I can't."
Cold slimy things slid upwards over his agonised body. He decided to
stop holding his breath, to open his mouth and die, but his will did not
obey this decision. Not only his chest but his temples felt as if they were
going to burst. It was idle to struggle. His arms met no adversary and his
legs were pinioned. He became aware that they were moving upwards.
But this gave him no hope. The surface was too far away, he could not
hold out till they reached it. In the immediate presence of death all ideas
of the after life were withdrawn from his mind. The mere abstract
proposition, "This is a man dying," floated before him in an unemotional way. Suddenly a roar of sound rushed back upon his ears—intolerable boomings and clangings. His mouth opened automatically. He
was breathing again. In a pitch darkness full of echoes he was clutching
what seemed to be gravel and kicking wildly to throw off the grip that
still held his legs. Then he was free and fighting once more: a blind
struggle half in and half out of the water on what seemed to be a pebbly
beach, with sharper rocks here and there that cut his feet and elbows.
The blackness was filled with gasping curses, now in his own voice, now
in Weston's, with yelps of pain, thudding concussions, and the noise of
laboured breath. In the end he was astride of the enemy. He pressed its
sides between his knees till its ribs cracked and clasped his hands round
its throat. Somehow he was able to resist its fierce tearing at his arms—
to keep on pressing. Once before he had had to press like this, but that
had been on an artery, to save life, not to kill. It seemed to last for ages.
Long after the creature's struggles had ceased he did not dare to relax his

grip. Even when he was quite sure that it breathed no longer he retained his seat on its chest and kept his tired hands, though now loosely, on its throat. He was nearly fainting himself, but he counted a thousand before he would shift his posture. Even then he continued to sit on its body. He did not know whether in the last few hours the spirit which had spoken to him was really Weston's or whether he had been the victim of a ruse. Indeed, it made little difference. There was, no doubt, a confusion of persons in damnation: what Pantheists falsely hoped of Heaven bad men really received in Hell. They were melted down into their Master, as a lead soldier slips down and loses his shape in the ladle held over the gas ring. The question whether Satan, or one whom Satan has digested, is acting on any given occasion, has in the long run no clear significance. In the meantime, the great thing was not to be tricked again.

There was nothing to be done, then, except to wait for the morning. From the roar of echoes all about him he concluded that they were in a very narrow bay between cliffs. How they had ever made it was a mystery. The morning must be many hours distant. This was a considerable nuisance. He determined not to leave the body till he had examined it by daylight and perhaps taken further steps to make sure that it could not be re-animated. Till then he must pass the time as best he could. The pebbly beach was not very comfortable, and when he tried to lean back he found a jagged wall. Fortunately he was so tired that for a time the mere fact of sitting still contented him. But this phase passed.

He tried to make the best of it. He determined to give up guessing how the time was going. "The only safe answer," he told himself, "is to think of the earliest hour you can suppose possible, and then assume the real time is two hours earlier than that." He beguiled himself by recapitulating the whole story of his adventure in Perelandra. He recited all that he could remember of the *Iliad*, the *Odyssey*, the *Æneid*, the *Chanson de Roland*, *Paradise Lost*, the *Kalevala*, the *Hunting of the Snark*, and a rhyme about Germanic sound-laws which he had composed as a freshman. He tried to spend as long as he could hunting for the lines he could not remember. He set himself a chess problem. He tried to rough out a chapter for a book he was writing. But it was all rather a failure.

These things went on, alternating with periods of dogged inactivity, until it seemed to him that he could hardly remember a time before that night. He could scarcely believe that even to a bored and wakeful man twelve hours could appear so long. And the noise—the gritty, slippery discomfort! It was very odd, now he came to think it, that this country should have none of those sweet night breezes which he had met everywhere else in Perelandra. It was odd too (but this thought came to him what seemed hours later) that he had not even the phosphorescent wave-crests to feed his eyes on. Very slowly a possible explanation of both facts dawned upon him: and it would also explain why the darkness lasted so long. The idea was too terrible for any indulgence of fear. Controlling himself, he rose stiffly to his feet and began picking his steps along the beach. His progress was very slow: but presently his outstretched arms touched perpendicular rock. He stood on tiptoe and stretched his hands up as far as he could. They found nothing but rock. "Don't get the wind up," he said to himself. He started groping his way back. He came to the Un-man's body, passed it, and went beyond it round the opposite beach. It curved rapidly, and here, before he had gone twenty steps his hands—which he was holding above his head—met not a wall, but a roof, of rock. A few paces farther and it was lower. Then he had to stoop. A little later and he had to go on his hands and knees. It was obvious that the roof came down and finally met the beach.

Sick with despair he felt his way back to the body and sat down. The truth was now beyond doubt. There was no good waiting for the morning. There would be no morning here till the end of the world, and perhaps he had already waited a night and a day. The clanging echoes, the dead air, the very smell of the place, all confirmed this. He and his enemy when they sank had clearly, by some hundredth chance, been carried through a hole in the cliffs well below water-level and come up on the beach of a cavern. Was it possible to reverse the process? He went down to the water's edge—or rather as he groped his way down to where the shingle was wet, the water came to meet him. It thundered over his head far up behind him, and then receded with a tug which he only resisted by spread-eagling himself on the beach and gripping the stones. It would be useless to plunge into *that*—he would merely have his ribs broken against the opposite wall of the cave. If one had light, and a high place to dive from, it was conceivable one might get down to the bottom and strike the exit . . . but very doubtful. And anyway, one had no light.

Although the air was not very good he supposed that this prison must be supplied with air from somewhere—but whether from any aperture that he could possibly reach was another matter. He turned at once and began exploring the rock behind the beach. At first it seemed hopeless, but the conviction that caves may lead you anywhere dies hard, and after some time his groping hands found a shelf about three feet high. He stepped up on it. He had expected it to be only a few inches deep but his hands could find no wall before him. Very cautiously he took some paces forward. His right foot touched something sharp. He whistled with the pain and went on even more cautiously. Then he found vertical rock—smooth as high as he could reach. He turned to his right and presently lost it. He turned left and began to go forward again and almost at once stubbed his toe. After nursing it for a moment he went down on hands and knees. He seemed to be among boulders, but the way was practicable. For ten minutes or so he made fairly good going, pretty steeply upward, sometimes on slippery shingle, sometimes over the tops of the big stones. Then he came to another cliff. There appeared to be a shelf on this about four feet up, but this time a really shallow one. He got on to it somehow and glued himself to the face, feeling out to left and right for further grips.

When he found one and realised that he was now about to attempt some real climbing, he hesitated. He remembered that what was above him might be a cliff which even in daylight and properly clothed he would never dare to attempt: but hope whispered that it might equally well be only seven feet high and that a few minutes of coolness might bring him into those gently winding passages up into the heart of the mountain which had, by now, won such a firm place in his imagination. He decided to go on. What worried him was not, in fact, the fear of falling, but the fear of cutting himself off from the water. Starvation he thought he could face: not thirst. But he went on. For some minutes he did things which he had never done on Earth. Doubtless he was in one way helped by the darkness: he had no real sensation of height and no giddiness. On the other hand, to work by touch alone made crazy climbing. Doubtless if anyone had seen him he would have appeared at one moment to take mad risks and at another to indulge in excessive caution. He tried to keep out of his mind the possibility that he might be climbing merely towards a roof.

After about quarter of an hour he found himself on a wide horizontal surface—either a much deeper shelf or the top of the precipice. He rested here for a while and licked his cuts. Then he got up and felt his way forwards, expecting every moment to meet another rock wall. When, after about thirty paces, he had not done so, he tried shouting and judged from the sound that he was in a fairly open place. Then he continued. The floor was of small pebble and ascended fairly steeply. There were some larger stones but he had learned to curl up his toes as his foot felt for the next pace and he seldom stubbed them now. One minor trouble was that even in this perfect blackness he could not help straining his eyes to see. It gave him a headache and created phantom lights and colours.

This slow uphill trek through darkness lasted so long that he began to fear he was going round in a circle, or that he had blundered into some gallery which ran on for ever beneath the surface of the planet. The steady ascent in some degree reassured him. The starvation for light became very painful. He found himself thinking about light as a hungry man thinks about food—picturing April hillsides with milky clouds racing over them in blue skies or quiet circles of lamp-light on tables pleasantly littered with books and pipes. By a curious confusion of mind he found it impossible not to imagine that the slope he walked on was not merely dark, but black in its own right, as if with soot. He felt that his feet and hands must be blackened by touching it. Whenever he pictured himself arriving at any light, he also pictured that light revealing a world of soot all around him.

He struck his head sharply against something and sat down half stunned. When he had collected himself he found by groping that the shingle slope had run up into a roof of smooth rock. His heart was very low as he sat there digesting this discovery. The sound of the waves came up faint and melancholy from below and told him that he was now at a great height. At last, though with very little hope, he began walking to his right, keeping contact with the roof by raising his arms. Presently it receded beyond his reach. A long time after that he heard a sound of water. He went on more slowly in great fear of encountering a waterfall. The shingle began to be wet and finally he stood in a little pool. Turning to his left he found, indeed, a waterfall, but it was a tiny stream with no force of water that could endanger him. He knelt in the rippling pool and drank from the fall and put his aching head and weary shoulders under it. Then, greatly refreshed, he tried to work his way up it.

Though the stones were slippery with some kind of moss and many of the pools were deep, it presented no serious difficulties. In about twenty minutes he had reached the top, and as far as he could judge by shouting and noticing the echoes he was now in a very large cave indeed. He took the stream for guidance and proceeded to follow it up. In that featureless dark it was some sort of company. Some real hope—distinct from that mere convention of hope which supports men in desperate situations—began to enter his mind.

It was shortly after this that he began to be worried by the noises. The last faint booming of the sea in the little hole whence he had set out so many hours ago had now died away and the predominant sound was the gentle tinkling of the stream. But he now began to think that he heard other noises mixed with it. Sometimes it would be a dull plump as if something had slipped into one of the pools behind him: sometimes, more mysteriously, a dry rattling sound as if metal were being dragged over the stones. At first he put it down to imagination. Then he stopped once or twice to listen and heard nothing; but each time when he went on it began again. At last, stopping once more, he heard it quite unmistakably. Could it be that the Un-man had after all come to life and was still following him? But that seemed improbable, for its whole plan had been to escape. It was not so easy to dispose of the other possibility—that these caverns might have inhabitants. All this experience, indeed, assured him that if there were such inhabitants they would probably be harmless, but somehow he could not quite believe that anything which lived in such a place would be agreeable, and a little echo of the Un-man's—or was it Weston's—talk came back to him. "All beautiful on the surface, but down inside—darkness, heat, horror, and stink." Then it occurred to him that if some creature were following him up the stream it might be well for him to leave its banks and wait till the creature had gone past. But if it were hunting him it would presumably hunt by scent; and in any case he would not risk losing the stream. In the end he went on.

Whether through weakness—for he was now very hungry indeed—or because the noises behind made him involuntarily quicken his pace, he found himself unpleasantly hot, and even the stream did not appear very refreshing when he put his feet in it. He began to think that whether he were pursued or not he must have a short rest—but just at that moment he saw the light. His eyes had been mocked so often before that he would not at first believe it. He shut them while he counted a hundred and looked again. He turned round and sat down for several minutes, praying that it might not be a delusion, and looked again. "Well," said Ransom, "if it is a delusion, it's a pretty stubborn one." A very dim, tiny, quivering luminosity, slightly red in colour, was before him. It was too weak to illuminate anything else and in that world of blackness he could not tell whether it was five feet or five miles away. He set out at once, with beating heart. Thank Heaven, the stream appeared to be leading him towards it.

While he thought it was still a long way off he found himself almost stepping into it. It was a circle of light lying on the surface of the water, which thereabouts formed a deepish trembling pool. It came from above. Stepping into the pool he looked up. An irregularly shaped patch of light, now quite distinctly red, was immediately above him. This time it was strong enough to show him the objects immediately around it, and when his eyes had mastered them he perceived that he was looking up a funnel or fissure. Its lower aperture lay in the roof of his own cavern which must here be only a few feet above his head: its upper aperture was obviously in the floor of a separate and higher chamber whence the light came. He could see the uneven side of the funnel, dimly illuminated, and clothed with pads and streamers of a jelly-like and rather unpleasing vegetation. Down this water was trickling and falling on his head and shoulders in a warm rain. This warmth, together with the red colour of the light, suggested that the upper cave was illuminated by subterranean fire. It will not be clear to the reader, and it was not clear to Ransom when he thought about it afterwards, why he immediately decided to get into the upper cave if he possibly could. What really moved him, he thinks, was the mere hunger for light. The very first glance at the funnel restored dimensions and perspective to his world, and this in itself was like delivery from prison. It seemed to tell him far more than it actually did of his surroundings: it gave him back that whole frame of spatial directions without which a man seems hardly able to call his body his own. After this, any return to the horrible black vacancy, the world of soot and grime, the world without size or distance, in which he had been wandering, was out of the question. Perhaps also he had some idea that whatever was following him would cease to follow if he could get into the lighted cave.

But it was not easy to do. He could not reach the opening of the funnel. Even when he jumped he only just touched the fringe of its vegetation. At last he hit upon an unlikely plan which was the best he could think of. There was just enough light here for him to see a number of larger stones among the gravel, and he set to work to build up a pile in the centre of the pool. He worked rather feverishly and often had to undo what he had done: and he tried it several times before it was really high enough. When at last it was completed and he stood sweating and shaky on the summit the real hazard was still to be run. He had to grip the vegetation on each side above his head, trusting to luck that it would hold, and half jump, half pull himself up as quickly as he could, since if it held at all it would, he felt sure, not hold for long. Somehow or other he managed it. He got himself wedged into the fissure with his back against one side and his feet against the other, like a mountaineer in what is called a chimney. The thick squashy growth protected his skin, and after a few upward struggles he found the walls of the passage so irregular that it could be climbed in the ordinary way. The heat increased rapidly. "I'm a fool to have come up here," said Ransom: but even as he said so, he was at the top.

At first he was blinded by the light. When at last he could take in his surroundings he found himself in a vast hall so filled with firelight that it gave him the impression of being hollowed out of red clay. He was looking along the length of it. The floor sloped down to the left side. On his right it sloped upward to what appeared a cliff edge, beyond which was an abyss of blinding brightness. A broad shallow river was flowing down the middle of the cavern. The roof was so high as to be invisible, but the walls soared up into darkness with broad curves like the roots of a beech tree.

He staggered to his feet, splashed across the river (which was hot to the touch) and approached the cliff edge. The fire appeared to be thousands of feet below him and he could not see the other side of the pit in which it swelled and roared and writhed. His eyes could only bear it for a second or so, and when he turned away the rest of the cavern seemed dark. The heat of his body was painful. He drew away from the cliff edge and sat down with his back to the fire to collect his thoughts.

They were collected in an unlooked-for way. Suddenly and irresistibly, like an attack by tanks, that whole view of the universe which Weston (if it were Weston) had so lately preached to him, took all but complete possession of his mind. He seemed to see that he had been living all his life in a world of illusion. The ghosts, the damned ghosts, were right. The beauty of Perelandra, the innocence of the Lady, the sufferings of saints, and the kindly affections of men, were all only an appearance and outward show. What he had called the worlds were but the skins of the worlds: a quarter of a mile beneath the surface, and from thence through thousands of miles of dark and silence and infernal fire, to the very heart of each, Reality lived—the meaningless, the un-made, the omnipotent idiocy to which all spirits were irrelevant and before which all efforts were vain. Whatever was following him would come up that wet, dark hole, would presently be excreted by that hideous duct, and then he would die. He fixed his eyes upon the dark opening from which he had himself just emerged. And then—"I thought as much," said Ransom.

Slowly, shakily, with unnatural and inhuman movements a human form, scarlet in the firelight, crawled out on to the floor of the cave. It was Un-man, of course: dragging its broken leg and with its lower jaw sagging open like that of a corpse, it raised itself to a standing position. And then, close behind it, something else came up out of the hole. First came what looked like branches of trees, and then seven or eight spots of light, irregularly grouped like a constellation. Then a tubular mass which reflected the red glow as if it were polished. His heart gave a great leap as the branches suddenly resolved themselves into long wiry feelers and the dotted lights became the many eyes of a shell-helmeted head and the mass that followed it was revealed as a large roughly cylindrical body. Horrible things followed—angular, many jointed legs, and presently, when he thought the whole body was in sight, a second body came following it and after that a third. The thing was in three parts, united only by a kind of wasp's waist structure—three parts that did not seem to be truly aligned and made it look as if it had been trodden on— a huge, many legged, quivering deformity, standing just behind the Un-man so that the horrible shadows of both danced in enormous and united menace on the wall of rock behind them.

"They want to frighten me," said something in Ransom's brain, and at the same moment he became convinced both that the Un-man had summoned this great crawler and also that the evil thoughts which had preceded the appearance of the enemy had been poured into his own mind by the enemy's will. The knowledge that his thoughts could be thus managed from without did not awake terror but rage. Ransom found that he had risen, that he was approaching the Un-man, that he was saying things, perhaps foolish things, in English. "Do you think I'm going to stand *this?*" he yelled. "Get out of my brain. It isn't yours, I tell you! Get out of it." As he shouted he had picked up a big, jagged stone from beside the stream. "Ransom," croaked the Un-man, "wait! We're both trapped . . ." but Ransom was already upon it.

"In the name of the Father and of the Son and of the Holy Ghost, here goes—I mean Amen," said Ransom, and hurled the stone as hard as he could into the Un-man's face. The Un-man fell as a pencil falls, the face smashed out of all recognition. Ransom did not give it a glance but turned to face the other horror. But where had the horror gone? The creature was there, a curiously shaped creature no doubt, but all loathing had vanished clean out of his mind, so that neither then nor at any other time could he remember it, nor ever understand again why one should quarrel with an animal for having more legs or eyes than oneself. All that he had felt from childhood about insects and reptiles died that moment: died utterly, as hideous music does when you switch off the wireless. Apparently it had all, even from the beginning, been a dark enchantment of the enemy's. Once, as he had sat writing near an open window in Cambridge, he had looked up and shuddered to see, as he supposed, a many coloured beetle of unusually hideous shape crawling across his paper. A second glance showed him that it was a dead leaf, moved by the breeze; and instantly the very curves and re-entrants which had made its ugliness turned into its beauties. At this moment he had almost the same sensation. He saw at once that the creature intended him no harm—had indeed no intentions at all. It had been drawn thither by the Un-man, and now stood still, tentatively moving its antennæ. Then, apparently not liking its surroundings, it turned laboriously round and began descending into the hole by which it had come. As he saw the last section of its tripartite body wobble on the edge of the aperture, and then finally tip upward with its torpedo-shaped tail in the air, Ransom almost laughed. "Like an animated corridor train" was his comment.

He turned to the Un-man. It had hardly anything left that you could call a head, but he thought it better to take no risks. He took it by its ankles and lugged it up to the edge of the cliff: then, after resting a few seconds, he shoved it over. He saw its shape black, for a second, against the sea of fire: and then that was the end of it.

He rolled rather than crawled back to the stream and drank deeply. "This may be the end of me or it may not," thought Ransom. "There may be a way out of these caves or there may not. But I won't go another step further to-day. Not if it was to save my life—not to save my life. That's flat. Glory be to God, I'm tired." A second later he was asleep.

15

For the rest of the subterranean journey after his long sleep in the firelit cave, Ransom was somewhat light-headed with hunger and fatigue. He remembers lying still after he woke for what seemed many hours and even debating with himself whether it was worth going on. The actual moment of decision has vanished from his mind. Pictures come back in a chaotic, disjointed fashion. There was a long gallery open to the fire-pit on one side and a terrible place where clouds of steam went up for ever and ever. Doubtless one of the many torrents that roared in the neighbourhood here fell into the depth of the fire. Beyond that were great halls still dimly illuminated and full of unknown mineral wealth that sparkled and danced in the light and mocked his eyes as if he were exploring a hall of mirrors by the help of a pocket torch. It seemed to him also, though this may have been delirium, that he came through a vast cathedral space which was more like the work of art than that of Nature, with two great thrones at one end and chairs on either hand too large for human occupants. If the things were real, he never found any explanation of them. There was a dark tunnel in which a wind from Heaven knows where was blowing and drove sand in his face. There was also a place where he himself walked in darkness and looked down through fathom below fathom of shafts and natural arches and winding gulfs on to a smooth floor lit with a cold green light. And as he stood and looked it seemed to him that four of the great earth-beetles, dwarfed by distance to the size of gnats, and crawling two by two, came slowly into sight. And they were drawing behind them a flat car, and on the car, upright, unshaken, stood a mantled form, huge and still and slender.

And driving its strange team it passed on with insufferable majesty and went out of sight. Assuredly the inside of this world was not for man. But it was for something. And it appeared to Ransom that there might, if a man could find it, be some way to renew the old Pagan practice of propitiating the local gods of unknown places in such fashion that it was no offence to God Himself but only a prudent and courteous apology for trespass. That thing, that swathed form in its chariot, was no doubt his fellow creature. It did not follow that they were equals or had an equal right in the under-land. A long time after this came the drumming—the *boom-ba-ba-ba-boom-boom* out of pitch darkness, distant at first, then all around him, then dying away after endless prolongation of echoes in the black labyrinth. Then came the fountain of cold light—a column, as of water, shining with some radiance of its own, and pulsating, and never any nearer however long he travelled and at last suddenly eclipsed. He did not find what it was. And so, after more strangeness and grandeur and labour than I can tell, there came a moment when his feet slid without warning on clay—a wild grasp—a spasm of terror—and he was spluttering and struggling in deep, swift-flowing water. He thought that even if he escaped being battered to death against the walls of the channel he would presently plunge along with the stream into the pit of fire. But the channel must have been very straight and the current per-haps was less violent than he had supposed. At all events he never touched the sides. He lay helpless, in the end, rushing forward through echoing darkness. It lasted a long time.

You will understand that what with expectation of death, and weari-ness, and the great noise, he was confused in mind. Looking back on the adventure afterwards it seemed to him that he floated out of blackness into greyness and then into an inexplicable chaos of semi-transparent blues and greens and whites. There was a hint of arches above his head and faintly shining columns, but all vague and all obliterating one another as soon as seen. It looked like a cave of ice, but it was too warm for that. And the roof above him seemed to be itself rippling like water, but this was doubtless a reflection. A moment later and he was rushed out into broad daylight and air and warmth, and rolled head over heels, and deposited, dazzled and breathless, in the shallows of a great pool.

He was now almost too weak to move. Something in the air, and the wide silence which made a background to the lonely crying of birds, told him that he was on a high mountain top. He rolled rather than crawled out of the pool on to sweet blue turf. Looking back whence he had come he saw a river pouring from the mouth of a cave, a cave that seemed indeed to be made of ice. Under it the water was spectral blue, but near where he lay it was warm amber. There was mist and freshness and dew all about him. At his side rose a cliff mantled with streamers of bright vegetation, but gleaming like glass where its own surface showed through. But this he heeded little. There were rich clusters of a grape-like fruit glowing under the little pointed leaves, and he could reach them without getting up. Eating passed into sleeping by a transition he could never remember.

At this point it becomes increasingly difficult to give Ransom's experiences in any certain order. How long he lay beside the river at the cavern mouth eating and sleeping and waking only to eat and sleep again, he has no idea. He thinks it was only a day or two, but from the state of his body when this period of convalescence ended I should imagine it must have been more like a fortnight or three weeks. It was a time to be remembered only in dreams as we remember infancy. Indeed it was a second infancy, in which he was breast-fed by the planet Venus herself: unweaned till he moved from that place. Three impressions of this long Sabbath remain. One is the endless sound of rejoicing water. Another is the delicious life that he sucked from the clusters which almost seemed to bow themselves unasked into his upstretched hands. The third is the song. Now high in air above him, now welling up as if from glens and valleys far below, it floated through his sleep and was the first sound at every waking. It was formless as the song of a bird, yet it was not a bird's voice. As a bird's voice is to a flute, so this was to a cello: low and ripe and tender, full-bellied, rich and golden-brown: passionate too, but not with the passions of men.

Because he was weaned so gradually from this state of rest I cannot give his impressions of the place he lay in, bit by bit, as he came to take it in. But when he was cured and his mind was clear again, this was what he saw. The cliffs out of which his river had broken through the cave were not of ice, but of some kind of translucent rock. Any little splinter broken off them was as transparent as glass, but the cliffs themselves, when you looked at them close, seemed to become opaque about six inches from the surface. If you waded up-stream into the cave and then turned back and looked towards the light, the edges of the arch which formed the cave's mouth were distinctly transparent: and everything looked blue inside the cave. He did not know what happened at the top of these cliffs.

Before him the lawn of blue turf continued level for about thirty paces, and then dropped with a steep slope, leading the river down in a series of cataracts. The slope was covered with flowers which shook continually in a light breeze. It went down a long way and ended in a winding and wooded valley which curled out of sight on his right hand round a majestic slope: but beyond that, lower down—so much lower down as to be almost incredible—one caught the point of mountain tops, and beyond that, fainter yet, the hint of still lower valleys, and then a vanishing of everything in golden haze. On the opposite side of this valley the earth leaped up in great sweeps and folds of almost Himalayan height to the red rocks. They were not red like Devonshire cliffs: they were true rose-red, as if they had been painted. Their brightness astonished him, and so did the needle-like sharpness of their spires, until it occurred to him that he was in a young world and that these mountains might, geologically speaking, be in their infancy. Also, they might be farther off than they looked.

To his left and behind him the crystal cliffs shut off his view. To his right they soon ended and beyond them the ground rose to another and nearer peak—a much lower one than those he saw across the valley. The fantastic steepness of all the slopes confirmed his idea that he was on a very young mountain.

Except for the song it was all very still. When he saw birds flying they were usually a long way below him. On the slopes to his right and, less distinctly, on the slope of the great *massif* which faced him, there was a continual rippling effect which he could not account for. It was like water flowing: but since, if it were a stream on the remoter mountain, it would have to be a stream two or three miles wide, this seemed improbable.

In trying to put the completed picture together I have omitted something which, in fact, made it a long job for Ransom to get that picture. The whole place was subject to mists. It kept on vanishing in a veil of saffron or very pale gold and reappearing again—almost as if the golden sky-roof, which indeed looked only a few feet above the mountain-tops, were opening and pouring down riches upon the world.

Day by day as he came to know more of the place, Ransom also came to know more of the state of his own body. For a long time he was too stiff almost to move and even an incautious breath made him wince. It healed, however, surprisingly quickly. But just as a man who has had a fall only discovers the real hurt when the minor bruises and cuts are less painful, so Ransom was nearly well before he detected his most serious injury. It was a wound in his heel. The shape made it quite clear that the wound had been inflicted by human teeth—the nasty, blunt teeth of our own species which crush and grind more than they cut. Oddly enough, he had no recollection of this particular bite in any of his innumerable tussles with the Un-man. It did not look unhealthy, but it was still bleeding. It was not bleeding at all fast, but nothing he could do would stop it. But he worried very little about this. Neither the future nor the past really concerned him at this period. Wishing and fearing were modes of consciousness for which he seemed to have lost the faculty.

Nevertheless there came a day when he felt the need of some activity and yet did not feel ready to leave the little lair between the pool and the cliff which had become like a home. He employed that day in doing something which may appear rather foolish and yet at the time it seemed to him that he could hardly omit it. He had discovered that the substance of the translucent cliffs was not very hard. Now he took a sharp stone of a different kind, and cleared a wide space on the cliff wall of vegetation. Then he made measurements and spaced it all out carefully and after a few hours had produced the following. The language was Old Solar but the letters were Roman.

WITHIN THESE CAVES WAS BURNED

THE BODY

OF

EDWARD ROLLES WESTON

A LEARNED HNAU OF THE WORLD WHICH THOSE WHO INHABIT IT

CALL TELLUS

BUT THE ELDILA

THULCANDRA

HE WAS BORN WHEN TELLUS HAD COMPLETED

ONE THOUSAND EIGHT HUNDRED AND NINETY-SIX REVOLUTIONS

ABOUT ARBOL

SINCE THE TIME WHEN

MALELDIL

BLESSED BE HE

WAS BORN AS A HNAU IN THULCANDRA

HE STUDIED THE PROPERTIES OF BODIES

AND FIRST OF THE TELLURIANS TRAVELLED THROUGH DEEP

HEAVEN TO MALACANDRA

AND TO PERELANDRA

WHERE HE GAVE UP HIS WILL AND REASON

TO THE BENT ELDIL

WHEN TELLUS WAS MAKING

THE ONE THOUSANDTH NINE HUNDREDTH AND FORTY-SECOND

REVOLUTION AFTER THE BIRTH OF MALELDIL

BLESSED BE HE

"That was a tomfool thing to do," said Ransom to himself contentedly as he lay down again. "No one will ever read it. But there ought to be some record. He was a great physicist after all. Anyway, it has given me some exercise." He yawned prodigiously and settled down to yet another twelve hours of sleep.

The next day he was better and began taking little walks, not going down but strolling to and fro on the hillside on each side of the cave. The following day he was better still. But on the third day he was well, and ready for adventures.

He set out very early in the morning and began to follow the water-course down the hill. The slope was very steep but there were no out-croppings of rock and the turf was soft and springy and to his surprise he found that the descent brought no weariness to his knees. When he had been going about half an hour and the peaks of the opposite mountain were now too high to see and the crystal cliffs behind him were only a dis-tant glare, he came to a new kind of vegetation. He was approaching a forest of little trees whose trunks were only about two and a half feet high; but from the top of each trunk there grew long streamers which did not rise in the air but flowed in the wind downhill and parallel to the ground. Thus, when he went in among them, he found himself wading knee deep and more in a continually rippling sea of them—a sea which presently tossed all about him as far as his eye could reach. It was blue in colour, but far lighter than the blue of the turf—almost a Cambridge blue at the centre of each streamer, but dying away at their tasselled and feathery edges into a delicacy of bluish grey which it would take the sub-tlest effects of smoke and cloud to rival in our world. The soft, almost impalpable, caresses of the long thin leaves on his flesh, the low, singing, rustling, whispering music, and the frolic movement all about him, began to set his heart beating with that almost formidable sense of delight which he had felt before in Perelandra. He realised that these dwarf forests—these ripple-trees as he now christened them—were the expla-nation of that water-like movement he had seen on the farther slopes.

When he was tired he sat down and found himself at once in a new world. The streamers now flowed above his head. He was in a forest made for dwarfs, a forest with a blue transparent roof, continually mov-ing and casting an endless dance of lights and shades upon its mossy floor. And presently he saw that it was indeed made for dwarfs. Through the moss, which here was of extraordinary fineness, he saw the hithering and thithering of what at first he took for insects but what proved, on closer inspection, to be tiny mammals. They were many mountain mice, exquisite scale models of those he had seen on the Forbidden Island, each about the size of a bumble bee. There were little miracles of grace which looked more like horses than anything he had yet seen on this world, though they resembled proto-hippos rather than his modern rep-resentative.

"How can I avoid treading on thousands of these?" he wondered. But they were not really very numerous and the main crowd of them seemed to be all moving away on his left. When he made to rise he noticed that there were already very few of them in sight.

He continued to wade down through the rippling streamers (it was like a sort of vegetable surf-bathing) for about an hour longer. Then he came into woods and presently to a river with a rocky course flowing across his path to the right. He had, in fact, reached the wooded valley, and knew that the ground which sloped upwards through trees on the far side of the water was the beginning of the great ascent. Here was amber shade and solemn height under the forest roof, and rocks wet with cataracts, and, over all, the noise of that deep singing. It was so loud now and so full of melody that he went downstream, a little out of his way, to look for its origin. This brought him almost at once out of stately aisles and open glades into a different kind of wood. Soon he was pressing his way through thornless thickets, all in bloom. His head was covered with the petals that showered on it, his sides gilded with pollen. Much that his fingers touched was gummy and at each pace his contact with soil and bush appeared to wake new odours that darted into his brain and there begot wild and enormous pleasures. The noise was very loud now and the thicket very dense so that he could not see a yard ahead, when the music stopped suddenly. There was a sound of rustling and broken twigs and he made hastily in that direction, but found nothing. He had almost decided to give up the search when the song began again a little farther away. Once more he made after it; once more the creature stopped singing and evaded him. He must have played thus at hide-and-seek with it for the best part of an hour before his search was rewarded.

Treading delicately during one of the loudest bursts of music he at last saw through the flowery branches a black something. Standing still whenever it stopped singing, and advancing with great caution whenever it began again, he stalked it for ten minutes. At last it was in full view, and singing, and ignorant that it was watched. It sat upright like a dog, black and sleek and shiny, but its shoulders were high above Ransom's head, and the forelegs on which they were pillared were like young trees and the wide soft pads on which they rested were large as those of a camel. The enormous rounded belly was white, and far up above the shoulders the neck rose like that of a horse. The head was in profile from where Ransom stood—the mouth wide open as it sang of joy in thick-coming trills, and the music almost visibly rippled in its glossy throat. He stared in wonder at the wide liquid eyes and the quivering, sensitive nostrils. Then the creature stopped, saw him, and darted away, and stood, now a few paces distant, on all four legs, not much smaller than a young elephant, swaying a long bushy tail. It was the first thing in Perelandra which seemed to show any fear of man. Yet it was not fear. When he called to it it came nearer. It put its velvet nose into his hand and endured his touch; but almost at once it darted back and, bending its long neck, buried its head in its paws. He could make no headway with it, and when at length it retreated out of sight he did not follow it. To do so would have seemed an injury to its fawn-like shyness, to the yielding softness of its expression, its evident wish to be for ever a sound and only a sound in the thickest centre of untravelled woods. He resumed his journey: a few seconds later the song broke out behind him, louder and lovelier than before, as if in a paean of rejoicing at its recovered privacy.

Ransom now addressed himself seriously to the ascent of the great mountain and in a few minutes emerged from the woods on to its lower slopes. He continued ascending so steeply that he used hands as well as feet for about half an hour and was puzzled to find himself doing it with almost no fatigue. Then he came once more into a region of ripple-trees. This time the wind was blowing the streamers not down the mountain-side but up it, so that his course had to the eye the astonishing appearance of lying through a wide blue waterfall which flowed the wrong way, curving and foaming towards the heights. Whenever the wind failed for a second or two the extreme ends of the streamers began to curl back under the influence of gravitation, so that it looked as if the heads of the waves were being flung back by a high wind. He continued going up through this for a long time, never feeling any real need for rest but resting occasionally none the less. He was now so high that the crystal cliffs from which he had set out appeared on a level with him as he looked across the valley. He now saw that the land leaped up beyond them into a whole waste of the same translucent formation which ended in a kind of glassy table-land. Under the naked sun of our own planet this would have been too bright to look at: here, it was a tremulous dazzle changing every moment under the undulations which the Perelandrian sky receives from the ocean. To the left of this table-land were some peaks of greenish rock. He went on. Little by little the peaks and the table-land sank and grew smaller, and presently there arose beyond them an exquisite haze like vaporised amethyst and emerald and gold, and the edge of this haze rose as he rose, and became at last the horizon of the sea, high lifted above the hills. And the sea grew ever larger and the mountains less, and the horizon of the sea rose and rose till all the lower mountains behind him seemed to be lying at the bottom of a great bowl of sea; but ahead, the interminable slope, now blue, now violet, now flickering with the smoke-like upward movement of the ripple-trees, soared up and up to the sky. And now the wooded valley in which he had met the singing beast was invisible and the mountain from which he had set out looked no more than a little swell on the slope of the great mountain, and there was not a bird in the air, nor any creature underneath the streamers, and still he went on unwearied, but always bleeding a little from his heel. He was not lonely nor afraid. He had no desires and did not even think about reaching the top nor why he should reach it. To be always climbing this was not, in his present mood, a process but a state, and in that state of life he was content. It did once cross his mind that he had died and felt no weariness because he had no body. The wound in his heel convinced him that this was not so; but if it had been so indeed, and these had been trans-mortal mountains, his journey could hardly have been more great and strange.

That night he lay on the slopes between the stems of the ripple-trees with the sweet-scented, wind-proof, delicately-whispering roof above his head, and when morning came he resumed his journey. At first he climbed through dense mists. When these parted, he found himself so high that the concave of the sea seemed to close him in on every side but one: and on that one he saw the rose-red peaks, no longer very distant, and a pass between the two nearest ones through which he caught a glimpse of something soft and flushed. And now he began to feel a strange mixture of sensations—a sense of perfect duty to enter that secret place which the peaks were guarding combined with an equal sense of trespass. He dared not go up that pass: he dared not do otherwise. He looked to see an angel with a flaming sword: he knew that Maleldil bade him go on. "This is the holiest and the most unholy thing I have ever done," he thought; but he went on. And now he was right in the pass. The peaks on either hand were not of red rock. Cores of rock they must have had; but what he saw were great matterhorns clothed in flowers—a flower shaped something like a lily but tinted like a rose. And soon the ground on which he trod was carpeted with the same flowers and he must crush them as he walked; and here at last his bleeding left no visible trace.

From the neck between the two peaks he looked a little down, for the top of the mountain was a shallow cup. He saw a valley, a few acres in size, as secret as a valley in the top of a cloud: a valley pure rose-red, with ten or twelve of the glowing peaks about it, and in the centre a pool, married in pure unrippled clearness to the gold of the sky. The lilies came down to its very edge and lined all its bays and headlands. Yielding without resistance to the awe which was gaining upon him, he walked forward with slow paces and bowed head. There was something white near the water's edge. An altar? A patch of white lilies among the red? A tomb? But whose tomb? No, it was not a tomb but a coffin, open and empty, and its lid lying beside it.

Then of course he understood. This thing was his own brother to the coffin-like chariot in which the strength of angels had brought him from Earth to Venus. It was prepared for his return. If he had said, "It is for my burial," his feelings would not have been very different. And while he thought of this he became gradually aware that there was something odd about the flowers at two places in his immediate neighbourhood. Next, he perceived that the oddity was an oddity in the light; thirdly, that it was in the air as well as on the ground. Then, as the blood pricked his veins and a familiar, yet strange, sense of diminished being possessed him, he knew that he was in the presence of two eldila. He stood still. It was not for him to speak.

clear voice like a chime of remote bells, a voice with no blood in it, spoke out of the air and sent a tingling through his frame.

"They have already set foot on the sand and are beginning to ascend," it said.

"The small one from Thulcandra is already here," said a second voice.

"Look on him, beloved, and love him," said the first. "He is indeed but breathing dust and a careless touch would unmake him. And in his best thoughts there are such things mingled as, if we thought them, our light would perish. But he is in the body of Maleldil and his sins are forgiven. His very name in his own tongue is Elwin, the friend of the eldila."

"How great is your knowledge!" said the second voice.

"I have been down into the air of Thulcandra," said the first, "which the small ones call Tellus. A thickened air is full of the Darkened as Deep Heaven is of the Light Ones. I have heard the prisoners there talking in their divided tongues and Elwin has taught me how it is with them."

From these words Ransom knew the speaker was the Oyarsa of Malacandra, the great archon of Mars. He did not, of course, recognise the voice, for there is no difference between one eldil's voice and another's. It is by art, not nature, that they affect human ear-drums and their words owe nothing to lungs or lips.

"If it is good, Oyarsa," said Ransom, "tell me who is this other."

"It is Oyarsa," said Oyarsa, "and here that is not my name. In my own sphere I am Oyarsa. Here I am only Malacandra."

"I am Perelandra," said the other voice.

"I do not understand," said Ransom. "The Woman told me there were no eldila in this world."

"They have not seen my face till to-day," said the second voice, "except as they see it in the water and the roof-heaven, the islands, the caves, and the trees. I was not set to rule them, but while they were young I ruled all else. I rounded this ball when it first arose from Arbol. I spun the air about it and wove the roof. I built the Fixed Island and this, the holy mountain, as Maleldil taught me. The beasts that sing and the beasts that fly and all that swims on my breast and all that creeps and tunnels within me down to the centre has been mine. And to-day all this is taken from me. Blessed be He."

"The small one will not understand you," said the Lord of Malacandra. "He will think that this is a grievous thing in your eyes."

"He does not say this, Malacandra."

"No. That is another strange thing about the children of Adam."

There was a moment's silence and then Malacandra addressed Ransom. "You will think of this best if you think of it in the likeness of certain things from your own world."

"I think I understand," said Ransom, "for one of Maleldil's sayers has told us. It is like when the children of a great house come to their full age. Then those who administered all their riches, and whom perhaps they have never seen, come and put all in their hands and give up their keys."

"You understand well," said Perelandra. "Or like when the singing beast leaves the dumb dam who suckled him."

"The singing beast?" said Ransom. "I would gladly hear more of this."

"The beasts of that kind have no milk and always what they bring forth is suckled by the she-beast of another kind. She is great and beautiful and dumb, and till the young singing beast is weaned it is among her whelps and is subject to her. But when it is grown it becomes the most delicate and glorious of all beasts and goes from her. And she wonders at its song."

"Why has Maleldil made such a thing?" said Ransom.

"That is to ask why Maleldil has made me," said Perelandra. "But now it is enough to say that from the habits of these two beasts much wisdom will come into the minds of my King and my Queen and their children. But the hour is upon us, and this is enough."

"What hour?" asked Ransom.

"Today is the morning day," said one or other or both the voices.

But there was something much more than sound about Ransom and his heart began beating fast.

"The morning . . . do you mean . . . ?" he asked. "Is all well? Has the Queen found the King?"

"The world is born to-day," said Malacandra. "To-day for the first time two creatures of the low worlds, two images of Maleldil that breathe and breed like the beasts, step up that step at which your parents fell, and sit in the throne of what they were meant to be. It was never seen before. Because it did not happen in your world a greater thing happened, but not this. Because the greater thing happened in Thulcandra, this and not the greater thing happens here."

"Elwin is falling to the ground," said the other voice.

"Be comforted," said Malacandra. "It is no doing of yours. You are not great, though you could have prevented a thing so great that Deep Heaven sees it with amazement. Be comforted, small one, in your smallness. He lays no merit on you. Receive and be glad. Have no fear, lest your shoulders be bearing this world. Look! it is beneath your head and carries you."

"Will they come here?" asked Ransom some time later.

"They are already well up the mountain's side," said Perelandra. "And our hour is upon us. Let us prepare our shapes. We are hard for them to see while we remain in ourselves."

"It is very well said," answered Malacandra. "But in what form shall we show ourselves to do them honour?"

"Let us appear to the small one here," said the other. "For he is a man and can tell us what is pleasing to their senses."

"I can see—I can see *something* even now," said Ransom.

"Would you have the King strain his eyes to see those who come to do him honour?" said the archon of Perelandra. "But look on this and tell us how it deals with you."

The very faint light—the almost imperceptible alteration in the visual field—which betokens an eldil vanished suddenly. The rosy peaks and the calm pool vanished also. A tornado of sheer monstrosities seemed to be pouring over Ransom. Darting pillars filled with eyes, lightning pulsations of flame, talons and beaks and billowy masses of what suggested snow, volleyed through cubes and heptagons into an infinite black void. "Stop it . . . stop it," he yelled, and the scene cleared. He gazed round blinking on the field of lilies, and presently gave the eldila to understand that this kind of appearance was not suited to human sensations. "Look then on this," said the voices again. And he looked with some reluctance, and far off between the peaks on the other side of the little valley there came rolling wheels. There was nothing but that—concentric wheels moving with a rather sickening slowness one inside the other. There was nothing terrible about them if you could get used to their appalling size, but there was also nothing significant. He bade them to try yet a third time. And suddenly two human figures stood before him on the opposite side of the lake.

They were taller than the Sorns, the giants whom he had met in Mars. They were perhaps thirty feet high. They were burning white like white-hot iron. The outline of their bodies when he looked at it steadily against the red landscape seemed to be faintly, swiftly undulating as though the permanence of their shape, like that of waterfalls or flames, co-existed with a rushing movement of the matter it contained. For a fraction of an inch inward from this outline the landscape was just visible through them: beyond that they were opaque.

Whenever he looked straight at them they appeared to be rushing towards him with enormous speed: whenever his eyes took in their surroundings he realised that they were stationary. This may have been due in part to the fact that their long and sparkling hair stood out straight behind them as if in a great wind. But if there were a wind it was not made of air, for no petal of the flowers was shaken. They were not standing quite vertically in relation to the floor of the valley: but to Ransom it appeared (as it had appeared to me on Earth when I saw one) that the eldils were vertical. It was the valley—it was the whole world of Perelandra—which was aslant. He remembered the words of Oyarsa long ago in Mars, "I am not *here* in the same way you are *here*." It was borne in upon him that the creatures were really moving, though not moving in relation to him. This planet which inevitably seemed to him while he was in it an unmoving world—*the* world, in fact—was to them a thing moving through the heavens. In relation to their own celestial frame of reference they were rushing forward to keep abreast of the mountain valley. Had they stood still, they would have flashed past him too quickly for him to see, doubly dropped behind by the planet's spin on its own axis and by its onward march around the Sun.

Their bodies, he said, were white. But a flush of diverse colours began at about the shoulders and streamed up the necks and flickered over face and head and stood out around the head like plumage or a halo. He told me he could in a sense remember these colours—that is, he would know them if he saw them again—but that he cannot by any effort call up a visual image of them nor give them any name. The very few people with whom he and I can discuss these matters all give the same explanation. We think that when creatures of the hypersomatic kind choose to "appear" to us, they are not in fact affecting our retina at all, but directly manipulating the relevant parts of our brain. If so, it is quite possible that they can produce there the sensations we *should* have if our eyes were capable of receiving those colours in the spectrum which are actually beyond their range. The "plumage" or halo of the one eldil was extremely different from that of the other. The Oyarsa of Mars shone with cold and morning colours, a little metallic—pure, hard, and bracing. The Oyarsa of Venus glowed with a warm splendour, full of the suggestion of teeming vegetable life.

The faces surprised him very much. Nothing less like the "angel" of popular art could well be imagined. The rich variety, the hint of undeveloped possibilities, which make the interest of human faces, were entirely absent. One single, changeless expression—so clear that it hurt and dazzled him—was stamped on each and there was nothing else there at all. In that sense their faces were as "primitive," as unnatural, if you like, as those of archaic statues from Ægina. What this one thing was he could not be certain. He concluded in the end that it was charity. But it was terrifyingly different from the expression of human charity, which we always see either blossoming out of, or hastening to descend into, natural affection. Here there was no affection at all: no least lingering memory of it even at ten million years' distance, no germ from which it could spring in any future, however remote. Pure, spiritual, intellectual love shot from their faces like barbed lightning. It was so unlike the love we experience that its expression could easily be mistaken for ferocity.

Both the bodies were naked, and both were free from any sexual characteristics, either primary or secondary. That, one would have expected. But whence came this curious difference between them? He found that he could point to no single feature wherein the difference resided, yet it was impossible to ignore. One could try—Ransom has tried a hundred times—to put it into words. He has said that Malacandra was like rhythm and Perelandra like melody. He has said that Malacandra affected him like a quantitative, Perelandra like an accentual, metre. He thinks that the first held in his hand something like a spear, but the hands of the other were open, with the palms towards him. But I don't know that any of these attempts has helped me much. At all events what Ransom saw at that moment was the real meaning of gender. Everyone must sometimes have wondered why in nearly all tongues certain inanimate objects are masculine and others feminine. What is masculine about a mountain or feminine about certain trees? Ransom has cured me of believing that this is a purely morphological phenomenon, depending on the form of the word. Still less is gender an imaginative extension of sex. Our ancestors did not make mountains masculine because they projected male characteristics into them. The real process is the reverse. Gender is a reality, and a more fundamental reality than sex. Sex is, in fact, merely the adaptation to organic life of a fundamental polarity which divides all created beings. Female sex is simply one of the things that have feminine gender; there are many others, and Masculine and Feminine meet us on planes of reality where male and female would be simply meaningless. Masculine is not attenuated male, nor feminine attenuated female. On the contrary, the male and female of organic creatures are rather faint and blurred reflections of masculine and feminine. Their reproductive functions, their differences in strength and size, partly exhibit, but partly also confuse and misrepresent, the real polarity. All this Ransom saw, as it were, with his own eyes. The two white creatures were sexless. But he of Malacandra was masculine (not male); she of Perelandra was feminine (not female). Malacandra seemed to him to have the look of one standing armed, at the ramparts of his own remote archaic world, in ceaseless vigilance, his eyes ever roaming the earth-ward horizon whence his danger came long ago. "A sailor's look," Ransom once said to me; "you know . . . eyes that are impregnated with distance." But the eyes of Perelandra opened, as it were, inward, as if they were the curtained gateway to a world of waves and murmurings and wandering airs, of life that rocked in winds and splashed on mossy stones and descended as the dew and arose sunward in thin-spun delicacy of mist. On Mars the very forests are of stone; in Venus the lands swim. For now he thought of them no more as Malacandra and Perelandra. He called them by their Tellurian names. With deep wonder he thought to himself, "My eyes have seen Mars and Venus. I have seen Ares and Aphrodite." He asked them how they were known to the old poets of Tellus. When and from whom had the children of Adam learned that Ares was a man of war and that Aphrodite rose from the sea foam? Earth has been besieged, an enemy-occupied territory, since before history began. The gods have had no commerce there. How then do we know of them? It comes, they told him, a long way round and through many stages. There is an environment of minds as well as of space. The universe is one—a spider's web wherein each mind lives along every line, a vast whispering gallery where (save for the direct action of Maleldil) though no news travels unchanged yet no secret can be rigorously kept. In the mind of the fallen Archon under whom our planet groans, the memory of Deep Heaven and the gods with whom he once consorted is still alive. Nay, in the very matter of our world, the traces of the celestial commonwealth are not quite lost. Memory passes through the womb and hovers in the air. The Muse is a real thing. A faint breath, as Virgil says, reaches even the late generations. Our mythology is based on a solider reality than we dream: but it is also

at an almost infinite distance from that base. And when they told him
this, Ransom at last understood why mythology was what it was—
gleams of celestial strength and beauty falling on a jungle of filth and
imbecility. His cheeks burned on behalf of our race when he looked on
the true Mars and Venus and remembered the follies that have been
talked of them on Earth. Then a doubt struck him.

"But do I see you as you really are?" he asked.

"Only Maleldil sees any creature as it really is," said Mars.

"How do you see one another?" asked Ransom.

"There are no holding places in your mind for an answer to that."

"Am I then seeing only an appearance? Is it not real at all?"

"You see only an appearance, small one. You have never seen more
than an appearance of anything—not of Arbol, nor of a stone, nor of
your own body. This appearance is as true as what you see of those."

"But . . . there were those other appearances."

"No. There was only the failure of appearance."

I don't understand," said Ransom. "Were all those other things—the
wheels and the eyes—more real than this or less?"

"There is no meaning in your question," said Mars. "You can see a
stone, if it is a fit distance from you and if you and it are moving at
speeds not too different. But if one throws the stone at your eye, what
then is the appearance?"

"I should feel pain and perhaps see splintered light," said Ransom.
"But I don't know that I should call that an appearance of the stone."

"Yet it would be the true operation of the stone. And there is your
question answered. We are now at the right distance from you."

"And were you nearer in what I first saw?"

"I do not mean that kind of distance."

"And then," said Ransom, still pondering, "there is what I had
thought was your wonted appearance—the very faint light, Oyarsa, as I
used to see it in your own world. What of that?"

"That is enough appearance for us to speak to you by. No more was
needed between us: no more is needed now. It is to honour the King that
we would now appear more. That light is the overflow or echo into the
world of your senses of vehicles made for appearance to one another and
to the greater eldila."

At this moment Ransom suddenly noticed an increasing disturbance
of sound behind his back—of unco-ordinated sound, husky and patter-
ing noises which broke in on the mountain silence and the crystal voices
of the gods with a delicious note of warm animality. He glanced round.
Romping, prancing, fluttering, gliding, crawling, waddling, with every
kind of movement—in every kind of shape and colour and size—a whole

zoo of beasts and birds was pouring into a flowery valley through the passes between the peaks at his back. They came mostly in their pairs, male and female together, fawning upon one another, climbing over one another, diving under one another's bellies, perching upon one another's backs. Flaming plumage, gilded beaks, glossy flanks, liquid eyes, great red caverns of whinneying or of bleating mouths, and thickets of switching tails, surrounded him on every side. "A regular Noah's Ark!" thought Ransom, and then, with sudden seriousness, "But there will be no ark needed in this world."

The song of four singing beasts rose in almost deafening triumph above the restless multitude. The great eldil of Perelandra kept back the creatures to the hither side of the pool, leaving the opposite side of the valley empty except for the coffin-like object. Ransom was not clear whether Venus spoke to the beasts or even whether they were conscious of her presence. Her connection with them was perhaps of some subtler kind—quite different from the relations he had observed between them and the Green Lady. Both the eldila were now on the same side of the pool with Ransom. He and they and all the beasts were facing in the same direction. The thing began to arrange itself. First, on the very brink of the pool, were the eldila, standing: between them, and a little back, was Ransom, still sitting among the lilies. Behind him the four singing beasts, sitting up on their haunches like fire-dogs, and proclaiming joy to all ears. Behind these again, the other animals. The sense of ceremony deepened. The expectation became intense. In our foolish human fashion he asked a question merely for the purpose of breaking it. "How can they climb to here and go down again and yet be off this island before nightfall?" Nobody answered him. He did not need an answer, for somehow he knew perfectly well that *this* island had never been forbidden them, and that one purpose in forbidding the other had been to lead them to this their destined throne. Instead of answering, the gods said, "Be still."

Ransom's eyes had grown so used to the tinted softness of Perelandrian daylight—and specially since his journey in the dark guts of the mountain—that he had quite ceased to notice its difference from the daylight of our own world. It was, therefore, with a shock of double amazement that he now suddenly saw the peaks on the far side of the valley showing really dark against what seemed a terrestrial dawn. A moment later sharp, well-defined shadows—long, like the shadows at early morning—were streaming back from every beast and every unevenness of the ground and each lily had its light and its dark side. Up and up came the light from the mountain slope. It filled the whole valley. The shadows disappeared again. All was in a pure daylight that seemed to come from nowhere in particular. He knew ever afterwards what is meant by a light "resting on" or "overshadowing" a holy thing, but not emanating from it. For as the light reached its perfection and settled itself, as it were, like a lord upon his throne or like wine in a bowl, and filled the whole flowery cup of the mountain top, every cranny, with its purity, the holy thing, Paradise itself in its two Persons, Paradise walking hand in hand, its two bodies shining in the light like emeralds yet not themselves too bright to look at, came in sight in the cleft between two peaks, and stood a moment with its male right hand lifted in regal and pontifical benediction, and they walked down and stood on the far side of the water. And the gods kneeled and bowed their huge bodies before the small forms of that young King and Queen.

17

There was great silence on the mountain top and Ransom also had fallen down before the human pair. When at last he raised his eyes from the four blessed feet, he found himself involuntarily speaking though his voice was broken and his eyes dimmed. "Do not move away, do not raise me up," he said. "I have never before seen a man or a woman. I have lived all my life among shadows and broken images. Oh, my Father and my Mother, my Lord and my Lady, do not move, do not answer me yet. My own father and mother I have never seen. Take me for your son. We have been alone in my world for a great time."

The eyes of the Queen looked upon him with love and recognition, but it was not of the Queen that he thought most. It was hard to think of anything but the King. And how shall I—I who have not seen him—tell you what he was like? It was hard even for Ransom to tell me of the King's face. But we dare not withhold the truth. It was that face which no man can say he does not know. You might ask how it was possible to look upon it and not to commit idolatry, not to mistake it for that of which it was the likeness. For the resemblance was, in its own fashion, infinite, so that almost you could wonder at finding no sorrows in his brow and no wounds in his hands and feet. Yet there was no danger of mistaking, not one moment of confusion, no least sally of the will towards forbidden reverence. Where likeness was greatest, mistake was least possible. Perhaps this is always so. A clever wax-work can be made so like a man that for a moment it deceives us: the great portrait which is far more deeply like him does not. Plaster images of the Holy One may before now have drawn to themselves the adoration they were meant to arouse for the reality. But here, where His live image, like Him within and without, made by His own bare hands out of the depth of divine artistry, His masterpiece of self-portraiture coming forth from His work-shop to delight all worlds, walked and spoke before Ransom's eyes, it could never be taken for more than an image. Nay, the very beauty of it lay in the certainty that it was a copy, like and not the same, an echo, a rhyme, an exquisite reverberation of the uncreated music prolonged in a created medium.

Ransom was lost for a while in the wonder of these things, so that when he came to himself he found that Perelandra was speaking, and what he heard seemed to be the end of a long oration. "The floating lands and the firm lands," she was saying, "the air and the curtains at the gates of Deep Heaven, the seas and the Holy Mountain, the rivers above and the rivers of underland, the fire, the fish, the birds, the beasts, and the others of the waves whom yet you know not; all these Maleldil puts into your hand from this day forth as far as you live in time and far-ther. My word henceforth is nothing: your word is law unchangeable and the very daughter of the Voice. In all that circle which this world runs about Arbol, you are Oyarsa. Enjoy it well. Give names to all crea-tures, guide all natures to perfection. Strengthen the feebler, lighten the darker, love all. Hail and be glad, oh man and woman, Oyarsa-Perelen-dri, the Adam, the Crown, Tor and Tinidril, Baru and Baru'ah, Ask and Embla, Yatsur and Yatsurah, dear to Maleldil. Blessed be He!"

When the King spoke in answer, Ransom looked up at him again. He saw that the human pair were now seated on a low bank that rose near the margin of the pool. So great was the light, that they cast clear reflections in the water as they might have done in our own world.

"We give you thanks, fair foster mother," said the King, "and spe-cially for this world in which you have laboured for long ages as Maleldil's very hand that all might be ready for us when we woke. We have not known you till to-day. We have often wondered whose hand it was that we saw in the long waves and the bright islands and whose breath delighted us in the wind at morning. For though we were young then, we saw dimly that to say 'It is Maleldil' was true, but not all the truth. This world we receive: our joy is the greater because we take it by your gift as well as by His. But what does He put into your mind to do henceforward?"

"It lies in your bidding, Tor-Oyarsa," said Perelandra, "whether I now converse in Deep Heaven only or also in that part of Deep Heaven which is to you a World."

"It is very much our will," said the King, "that you remain with us, both for the love we bear you and also that you may strengthen us with counsel and even with your operations. Not till we have gone many times about Arbol shall we grow up to the full management of the dominion which Maleldil puts into our hands: nor are we yet ripe to steer the world through Heaven nor to make rain and fair weather upon us. If it seems good to you, remain."

"I am content," said Perelandra.

While this dialogue proceeded, it was a wonder that the contrast between the Adam and the eldils was not a discord. On the one side, the crystal, bloodless voice, and the immutable expression of the snow-white face; on the other the blood coursing in the veins, the feeling trembling on the lips and sparkling in the eyes, the might of the man's shoulders, the wonder of the woman's breasts, a splendour of virility and richness of womanhood unknown on earth, a living torrent of perfect animality—yet when these met, the one did not seem rank nor the other spectral. *Animal rationale*—an animal, yet also a reasonable soul: such, he remembered, was the old definition of Man. But he had never till now seen the reality. For now he saw this living Paradise, the Lord and Lady, as the resolution of discords, the bridge that spans what would else be a chasm in creation, the keystone of the whole arch. By entering that mountain valley they had suddenly united the warm multitude of the brutes behind him with the transcorporeal intelligences at his side. They closed the circle, and with their coming all the separate notes of strength or beauty which that assembly had hitherto struck became one music. But now the King was speaking again.

"And as it is not Maleldil's gift simply," he said, "but also Maleldil's gift through you, and thereby the richer, so it is not through you only, but through a third, and thereby the richer again. And this is the first word I speak as Tor-Oyarsa-Perelendri; that in our world, as long as it is a world, neither shall morning come nor night but that we and all our children shall speak to Maleldil of Ransom the man of Thulcandra and praise him to one another. And to you, Ransom, I say this, that you have called us Lord and Father, Lady and Mother. And rightly, for this is our name. But in another fashion we call you Lord and Father. For it seems to us that Maleldil sent you into our world at that day when the time of our being young drew to its end, and from it we must now go up or go down, into corruption or into perfection. Maleldil has taken us where He meant us to be: but of Maleldil's instruments in this, you were the chief."

They made him go across the water to them, wading, for it came only to his knees. He would have fallen at their feet but they would not let him. They rose to meet him and both kissed him, mouth to mouth and heart to heart as equals embrace. They would have made him sit between them, but when they saw that this troubled him they let it be. He went and sat down on the level ground, below them, and a little to the left. From there he faced the assembly—the huge shapes of the gods and the concourse of beasts. And then the Queen spoke.

"As soon as you had taken away the Evil One," she said, "and I awoke from sleep, my mind was cleared. It is a wonder to me, Piebald, that for all those days you and I could have been so young. The reason for not yet living on the Fixed Land is now so plain. How could I wish to live there except because it was Fixed? And why should I desire the Fixed except to make sure—to be able on one day to command where I should be the next and what should happen to me? It was to reject the wave—to draw my hands out of Maleldil's, to say to Him, 'Not thus, but thus'—to put in our own power what times should roll towards us . . . as if you gathered fruits together to-day for to-morrow's eating instead of taking what came. That would have been cold love and feeble trust. And out of it how could we ever have climbed back into love and trust again?"

"I see it well," said Ransom. "Though in my world it would pass for folly. We have been evil so long"—and then he stopped, doubtful of being understood and surprised that he had used a word for *evil* which he had not hitherto known that he knew, and which he had not heard either in Mars or in Venus.

"We know these things now," said the King, seeing Ransom's hesitation. "All this, all that happened in your world, Maleldil has put into our mind. We have learned of evil, though not as the Evil One wished us to learn. We have learned better than that, and know it more, for it is waking that understands sleep and not sleep that understands waking. There is an ignorance of evil that comes from being young: there is a darker ignorance that comes from doing it, as men by sleeping lose the knowledge of sleep. You are more ignorant of evil in Thulcandra now than in the days before your Lord and Lady began to do it. But Maleldil has brought us out of the one ignorance, and we have not entered the other. It was by the Evil One himself that he brought us out of the first. Little did that dark mind know the errand on which he really came to Perelandra!"

"Forgive me, my Father, if I speak foolishly," said Ransom. "I see how evil has been made known to the Queen, but not how it was made known to you."

Then unexpectedly the King laughed. His body was very big and his laugh was like an earthquake in it, loud and deep and long, till in the end Ransom laughed too, though he had not seen the joke, and the Queen laughed as well. And the birds began clapping their wings and the beasts wagging their tails, and the light seemed brighter and the pulse of the whole assembly quickened, and new modes of joy that had nothing to do with mirth as we understand it passed into them all, as if it were from the very air, or as if there were dancing in Deep Heaven. Some say there always is.

"I know what he is thinking," said the King, looking upon the Queen. "He is thinking that you suffered and strove and I have a world for my reward." Then he turned to Ransom and continued. "You are right," he said, "I know now what they say in your world about justice. And perhaps they say well, for in that world things always fall below justice. But Maleldil always goes above it. All is gift. I am Oyarsa not by His gift alone but by our foster mother's, not by hers alone but by yours, not by yours alone but my wife's—nay, in some sort, by gift of the very beasts and birds. Through many hands, enriched with many different kinds of love and labour, the gift comes to me. It is the Law. The best fruits are plucked for each by some hand that is not his own."

"That is not the whole of what happened, Piebald," said the Queen. "The King has not told you all. Maleldil drove him far away into a green sea where forests grow up from the bottom through the waves. . . ."

"Its name is Lur," said the King.

"Its name is Lur," repeated the eldila. And Ransom realised that the King had uttered not an observation but an enactment.

"And there in Lur (it is far hence)," said the Queen, "strange things befell him."

"Is it good to ask about these things?" said Ransom.

"There were many things," said Tor the King. "For many hours I learned the properties of shapes by drawing lines in the turf of a little island on which I rode. For many hours I learned new things about Maleldil and about His Father and the Third One. We knew little of this while we were young. But after that He showed me in a darkness what was happening to the Queen. And I knew it was possible for her to be undone. And then I saw what had happened in your world, and how your Mother fell and how your Father went with her, doing her no good thereby and bringing the darkness upon all their children. And then it was before me like a thing coming towards my hand . . . what I should do in like case. There I learned of evil and good, of anguish and joy."

Ransom had expected the King to relate his decision, but when the King's voice died away into thoughtful silence he had not the assurance to question him.

"Yes . . ." said the King, musing. "Though a man were to be torn in two halves . . . though half of him turned into earth. . . . The living half must still follow Maleldil. For if it also lay down and became earth, what hope would there be for the whole? But while one half lived, through it He might send life back into the other." Here he paused for a long time, and then spoke again somewhat quickly. "He gave me no assurance. No fixed land. Always one must throw oneself into the wave." Then he cleared his brow and turned to the eldila and spoke in a new voice.

"Certainly, O foster mother," he said. "We have much need of counsel for already we feel that growing up within our bodies which our young wisdom can hardly overtake. They will not always be bodies bound to the low worlds. Hear the second word that I speak as Tor-Oyarsa-Perelendri. While this World goes about Arbol ten thousand times, we shall judge and hearten our people from this throne. Its name is Tai Harendrimar, The Hill of Life."

"Its name is Tai Harendrimar," said the eldila.

"On the Fixed Land which once was forbidden," said Tor the King, "we will make a great place to the splendour of Maleldil. Our sons shall bend the pillars of rock into arches——"

"What are arches?" said Tinidril the Queen.

"Arches," said Tor the King, "are when pillars of stone throw out branches like trees and knit their branches together and bear up a great dome as of leafage, but the leaves shall be shaped stones. And there our sons will make images."

"What are images?" said Tinidril.

"Splendour of Deep Heaven!" cried the King with a great laugh. "It seems there are too many new words in the air. I had thought these things were coming out of your mind into mine, and lo! you have not thought them at all. Yet I think Maleldil passed them to me through you, none the less. I will show you images, I will show you houses. It may be that in this matter our natures are reversed and it is you who beget and I who bear. But let us speak of plainer matters. We will fill this world with our children. We will know this world to the centre. We will make the nobler of the beasts so wise that they will become *hnau* and speak: their lives shall awake to a new life in us as we awake in Maleldil. When the time is ripe for it and the ten thousand circlings are nearly at an end, we will tear the sky curtain and Deep Heaven shall become familiar to the eyes of our sons as the trees and the waves to ours."

"And what after this, Tor-Oyarsa?" said Malacandra.

"Then it is Maleldil's purpose to make us free of Deep Heaven. Our bodies will be changed, but not all changed. We shall be as the eldila, but not all as eldila. And so will all our sons and daughters be changed in the time of this ripeness, until the number is made up which Maleldil read in His Father's mind before times flowed."

"And that," said Ransom, "will be the end?"

Tor the King stared at him.

"The end?" he said. "Who spoke of an end?"

"The end of your world, I mean," said Ransom.

"Splendour of Heaven!" said Tor. "Your thoughts are unlike ours. About that time we shall be not far from the beginning of all things. But there will be one matter to settle before the beginning rightly begins."

"What is that?" asked Ransom.

"Your own world," said Tor, "Thulcandra. The siege of your world shall be raised, the black spot cleared away, before the real beginning. In those days Maleldil will go to war—in us, and in many who once were *hnau* on your world, and in many from far off and in many eldila, and, last of all, in Himself unveiled, He will go down to Thulcandra. Some of us will go before. It is in my mind, Malacandra, that thou and I will be among those. We shall fall upon your moon, wherein there is a secret evil, and which is as the shield of the Dark Lord of Thulcandra—scarred with many a blow. We shall break her. Her light shall be put out. Her fragments shall fall into your world and the seas and the smoke shall arise so that the dwellers in Thulcandra will no longer see the light of Arbol. And as Maleldil Himself draws near, the evil things in your world shall show themselves stripped of disguise so that plagues and horrors shall cover your lands and seas. But in the end all shall be cleansed, and even the memory of your Black Oyarsa blotted out, and your world shall be fair and sweet and reunited to the field of Arbol and its true name shall be heard again. But can it be, Friend, that no rumour of all this is heard in Thulcandra? Do your people think that their Dark Lord will hold his prey forever?"

"Most of them," said Ransom, "have ceased to think of such things at all. Some of us still have the knowledge: but I did not at once see what you were talking of, because what you call the beginning we are accustomed to call the Last Things."

"I do not call it the beginning," said Tor the King. "It is but the wiping out of a false start in order that the world may *then* begin. As when a man lies down to sleep, if he finds a twisted root under his shoulder he will change his place—and after that his real sleep begins. Or as a man setting foot on an island, may make a false step. He steadies himself and after that his journey begins. You would not call that steadying of himself a last thing?"

"And is the whole story of my race no more than this?" said Ransom.

"I see no more than beginnings in the history of the Low Worlds," said Tor the King. "And in yours a failure to begin. You talk of evenings before the day has dawned. I set forth even now on ten thousand years of preparation—I, the first of my race, my race the first of races, to begin. I tell you that when the last of my children has ripened and ripeness has spread from them to all the Low Worlds, it will be whispered that the morning is at hand."

"I am full of doubts and ignorance," said Ransom. "In our world those who know Maleldil at all believe that His coming down to us and being a man is the central happening of all that happens. If you take that from me, Father, whither will you lead me? Surely not to the enemy's talk which thrusts my world and my race into a remote corner and gives me a universe, with no centre at all, but millions of worlds that lead nowhere or (what is worse) to more and more worlds for ever, and comes over me with numbers and empty spaces and repetitions and asks me to bow down before bigness. Or do you make your world the centre? But I am troubled. What of the people on Malacandra? Would they also think that their world was the centre? I do not even see how your world can rightly be called yours. You were made yesterday and it is from of old. The most of it is water where you cannot live. And what of the things beneath its crust? And of the great spaces with no world at all? Is the enemy easily answered when He says that all is without plan or meaning? As soon as we think we see one it melts away into nothing, or into some other plan that we never dreamed of, and what was the centre becomes the rim, till we doubt if any shape or plan or pattern was ever more than a trick of our own eyes, cheated with hope, or tired with too much looking. To what is all driving? What is the morning you speak of? What is it the beginning of?"

"The beginning of the Great Game, of the Great Dance," said Tor. "I know little of it as yet. Let the eldila speak."

The voice that spoke next seemed to be that of Mars, but Ransom was not certain. And who spoke after that, he does not know at all. For in the conversation that followed—if it can be called a conversation—though he believes that he himself was sometimes the speaker, he never knew which words were his or another's, or even whether a man or an eldil was talking. The speeches followed one another—if, indeed, they did not all take place at the same time—like the parts of a music into which all five of them had entered as instruments or like a wind blowing through five trees that stand together on a hilltop.

"We would not talk of it like that," said the first voice. "The Great Dance does not wait to be perfect until the peoples of the Low Worlds are gathered into it. We speak not of when it will begin. It has begun from before always. There was no time when we did not rejoice before His face as now. The dance which we dance is at the centre and for the dance all things were made. Blessed be He!"

Another said, "Never did He make two things the same; never did He utter one word twice. After earths, not better earths but beasts; after beasts, not better beasts, but spirits. After a falling, not a recovery but a new creation. Out of the new creation, not a third but the mode of change itself is changed for ever. Blessed is He!"

And another said, "It is loaded with justice as a tree bows down with fruit. All is righteousness and there is no equality. Not as when stones lie side by side, but as when stones support and are supported in an arch, such is His order; rule and obedience, begetting and bearing, heat glancing down, life growing up. Blessed be He!"

One said, "They who add years to years in lumpish aggregation, or miles to miles and galaxies to galaxies, shall not come near His greatness. The day of the fields of Arbol will fade and the days of Deep Heaven itself are numbered. Not thus is He great. He dwells (all of Him dwells) within the seed of the smallest flower and is not cramped: Deep Heaven is inside Him who is inside the seed and does not distend Him. Blessed be He!"

"The edge of each nature borders on that whereof it contains no shadow or similitude. Of many points one line; of many lines one shape; of many shapes one solid body; of many senses and thoughts one person; of three persons, Himself. As is the circle to the sphere, so are the ancient worlds that needed no redemption to that world wherein He was born and died. As is a point to a line, so is that world to the far-off fruits of its redeeming. Blessed be He!"

"Yet the circle is not less round than the sphere, and the sphere is the home and fatherland of circles. Infinite multitudes of circles lie enclosed in every sphere, and if they spoke they would say, For us were spheres created. Let no mouth open to gainsay them. Blessed be He!"

"The peoples of the ancient worlds who never sinned, for whom He never came down, are the peoples for whose sake the Low Worlds were made. For though the healing what was wounded and the straightening what was bent is a new dimension of glory, yet the straight was not made that it might be bent nor the whole that it might be wounded. The ancient peoples are at the centre. Blessed be He!"

"All which is not itself the Great Dance was made in order that He might come down into it. In the Fallen World He prepared for Himself a body and was united with the Dust and made it glorious for ever. This is the end and final cause of all creating, and the sin whereby it came is called Fortunate and the world where this was enacted is the centre of worlds. Blessed be He!"

"The Tree was planted in that world but the fruit has ripened in this. The fountain that sprang with mingled blood and life in the Dark World, flows here with life only. We have passed the first cataracts, and from here onward the stream flows deep and turns in the direction of the sea. This is the Morning Star which He promised to those who conquer; this is the centre of worlds. Till now all has waited. But now the trumpet has sounded and the army is on the move. Blessed be He!"

"Though men or angels rule them, the worlds are for themselves. The waters you have not floated on, the fruit you have not plucked, the caves into which you have not descended and the fire through which your bodies cannot pass, do not await your coming to put on perfection, though they will obey you when you come. Times without number I have circled Arbol while you were not alive, and those times were not desert. Their own voice was in them, not merely a dreaming of the day when you should awake. They also were at the centre. Be comforted, small immortals. You are not the voice that all things utter, nor is there eternal silence in the places where you cannot come. No feet have walked, nor shall, on the ice of Glund; no eye looked up from beneath on the Ring of Lurga, and Iron-plain in Neruval is chaste and empty. Yet it is not for nothing that the gods walk ceaselessly around the fields of Arbol. Blessed be He!"

"That Dust itself which is scattered so rare in Heaven, whereof all worlds, and the bodies that are not worlds, are made, is at the centre. It waits not till created eyes have seen it or hands handled it, to be in itself a strength and splendour of Maleldil. Only the least part has served, or ever shall, a beast, a man, or a god. But always, and beyond all distances, before they came and after they are gone and where they never come, it is what it is and utters the heart of the Holy One with its own voice. It is farthest from Him of all things, for it has no life, nor sense, nor reason; it is nearest to Him of all things for without intervening soul, as sparks fly out of fire, He utters in each grain of it the unmixed image of His energy. Each grain, if it spoke, would say, I am at the centre; for me all things were made. Let no mouth open to gainsay it. Blessed be He!"

"Each grain is at the centre. The Dust is at the centre. The Worlds are at the centre. The beasts are at the centre. The ancient peoples are there. The race that sinned is there. Tor and Tinidril are there. The gods are there also. Blessed be He!"

"Where Maleldil is, there is the centre. He is in every place. Not some of Him in one place and some in another, but in each place the whole Maleldil, even in the smallness beyond thought. There is no way out of the centre save into the Bent Will which casts itself into the Nowhere. Blessed be He!"

"Each thing was made for Him. He is the centre. Because we are with Him, each of us is at the centre. It is not as in a city of the Darkened World where they say that each must live for all. In His city all things are made for each. When He died in the Wounded World He died not for men, but for each man. If each man had been the only man made, He would have done no less. Each thing, from the single grain of Dust to the strongest eldil, is the end and the final cause of all creation and the mirror in which the beam of His brightness comes to rest and so returns to Him. Blessed be He!"

"In the plan of the Great Dance plans without number interlock, and each movement becomes in its season the breaking into flower of the whole design to which all else had been directed. Thus each is equally at the centre and none are there by being equals, but some by giving place and some by receiving it, the small things by their smallness and the great by their greatness, and all the patterns linked and looped together by the unions of a kneeling with a sceptred love. Blessed be He!"

"He has immeasurable use for each thing that is made, that His love and splendour may flow forth like a strong river which has need of a great watercourse and fills alike the deep pools and the little crannies, that are filled equally and remain unequal; and when it has filled them brim full it flows over and makes new channels. We also have need beyond measure of all that He has made. Love me, my brothers, for I am infinitely necessary to you and for your delight I was made. Blessed be He!"

"He has no need at all of anything that is made. An eldil is not more needful to Him than a grain of the Dust: a peopled world no more needful than a world that is empty: but all needless alike, and what all add to Him is nothing. We also have no need of anything that is made. Love me, my brothers, for I am infinitely superfluous, and your love shall be like His, born neither of your need nor of my deserving, but a plain bounty. Blessed be He!"

"All things are by Him and for Him. He utters Himself also for His own delight and sees that He is good. He is His own begotten and what proceeds from Him is Himself. Blessed be He!"

"All that is made seems planless to the darkened mind, because there are more plans than it looked for. In these seas there are islands where the hairs of the turf are so fine and so closely woven together that unless a man looked long at them he would see neither hairs nor weaving at all, but only the same and the flat. So with the Great Dance. Set your eyes on one movement and it will lead you through all patterns and it will seem to you the master movement. But the seeming will be true. Let no mouth open to gainsay it. There seems no plan because it is all plan: there seems no centre because it is all centre. Blessed be He!"

"Yet this seeming also is the end and final cause for which He spreads out Time so long and Heaven so deep; lest if we never met the dark, and the road that leads nowhither, and the question to which no answer is imaginable, we should have in our minds no likeness of the Abyss of the Father, into which if a creature drop down his thoughts for ever he shall hear no echo return to him. Blessed, blessed, blessed be He!"

And now, by a transition which he did not notice, it seemed that what had begun as speech was turned into sight, or into something that can be remembered only as if it were seeing. He thought he saw the Great Dance. It seemed to be woven out of the intertwining undulation of many cords or bands of light, leaping over and under one another and mutually embraced in arabesques and flower-like subtleties. Each figure as he looked at it became the master-figure or focus of the whole spectacle, by means of which his eye disentangled all else and brought it into unity—only to be itself entangled when he looked to what he had taken for mere marginal decorations and found that there also the same hegemony was claimed, and the claim made good, yet the former pattern not thereby dispossessed but finding in its new subordination a significance greater than that which it had abdicated. He could see also (but the word "seeing" is now plainly inadequate) wherever the ribbons or serpents of light intersected, minute corpuscles of momentary brightness: and he knew somehow that these particles were the secular generalities of which history tells—peoples, institutions, climates of opinion, civilisations, arts, sciences, and the like—ephemeral coruscations that piped their short song and vanished. The ribbons or cords themselves, in which millions of corpuscles lived and died, were things of some different kind. At first he could not say what. But he knew in the end that most of them were individual entities. If so, the time in which the Great Dance proceeds is very unlike time as we know it. Some of the thinner and more delicate cords were beings that we call short-lived: flowers and insects, a fruit or a storm of rain, and once (he thought) a wave of the sea. Others were such things as we also think lasting: crystals, rivers, mountains, or even stars. Far above these in girth and luminosity and flashing with colours from beyond our spectrum were the lines of the personal beings, yet as different from one another in splendour as all of them from the previous class. But not all the cords were individuals: some were universal truths or universal qualities. It did not surprise him then to find that these and the persons were both cords and both stood together as against the mere atoms of generality which lived and died in the clashing of their streams: but afterwards, when he came back to earth, he wondered. And by now the thing must have passed together out of the region of sight as we understand it. For he says that the whole solid figure of these enamoured and inter-inanimated circlings was suddenly revealed as the mere superficies of a far vaster pattern in four dimensions, and that figure as the boundary of yet others in other worlds: till suddenly as the movement grew yet swifter, the interweaving yet more ecstatic, the relevance of all to all yet more intense, as dimension was added to dimension and that part of him which could reason and remember was dropped farther and farther behind that part of him which saw, even then, at the very zenith of complexity, complexity was eaten up and faded, as a thin white cloud fades into the hard blue burning of the sky, and a simplicity beyond all comprehension, ancient and young as spring, illimitable, pellucid, drew him with cords of infinite desire into its own stillness. He went up into such a quietness, a privacy, and a freshness that at the very moment when he stood farthest from our ordinary mode of being he had the sense of stripping off encumbrances and awaking from trance, and coming to himself. With a gesture of relaxation he looked about him. . . .

The animals had gone. The two white figures had disappeared. Tor and Tinidril and he were alone, in ordinary Perelandrian daylight, early in the morning.

"Where are the beasts?" said Ransom.

"They have gone about their small affairs," said Tinidril. "They have gone to bring up their whelps and lay their eggs, to build their nests and spin their webs and dig their burrows, to sing and play and to eat and drink."

"They did not wait long," said Ransom, "for I feel it is still early in the morning."

"But not the same morning," said Tor.

"We have been here long, then?" asked Ransom.

"Yes," said Tor. "I did not know it till now. But we have accomplished one whole circle about Arbol since we met on this mountain top."

"A year?" said Ransom. "A whole year? O Heavens, what may by now have happened in my own dark world! Did you know, Father, that so much time was passing?"

"I did not feel it pass," said Tor. "I believe the waves of time will often change for us henceforward. We are coming to have it in our own choice whether we shall be above them and see many waves together or whether we shall reach them one by one as we used to."

"It comes into my mind," said Tinidril, "that to-day, now that the year has brought us back to the same place in Heaven, the eldila are coming for Piebald to take him back to his own world."

"You are right, Tinidril," said Tor. Then he looked at Ransom and said, "There is a red dew coming up out of your foot, like a little spring."

Ransom looked down and saw that his heel was still bleeding. "Yes," he said, "it is where the Evil One bit me. The redness is of *hrū* (blood)."

"Sit down, friend," said Tor, "and let me wash your foot in this pool." Ransom hesitated but the King compelled him. So presently he sat on the little bank and the King kneeled before him in the shallow water and took the injured foot in his hand. He paused as he looked at it.

"So this is *hrū* ," he said at last. "I have never seen such a fluid before. And this is the substance wherewith Maleldil remade the worlds before any world was made."

He washed the foot for a long time but the bleeding did not stop. "Does it mean Piebald will die?" said Tinidril at last.

"I do not think so," said Tor. "I think that any of his race who has breathed the air that he has breathed and drunk the waters that he has drunk since he came to the Holy Mountain will not find it easy to die. Tell me, Friend, was it not so in your world that after they had lost their paradise the men of your race did not learn to die quickly?"

"I had heard," said Ransom, "that those first generations were long livers, but most take it for only a Story or a Poetry and I had not thought of the cause."

"Oh!" said Tinidril suddenly. "The eldila are come to take him."

Ransom looked round and saw, not the white manlike forms in which he had last seen Mars and Venus, but only the almost invisible lights. The King and Queen apparently recognised the spirits in this guise also: as easily, he thought, as an earthly King would recognise his acquaintance even when they were not in court dress.

The King released Ransom's foot and all three of them went towards the white casket. Its covering lay beside it on the ground. All felt an impulse to delay.

"What is this that we feel, Tor?" said Tinidril.

"I don't know," said the King. "One day I will give it a name. This is not a day for making names."

"It is like a fruit with a very thick shell," said Tinidril. "The joy of our meeting when we meet again in the Great Dance is the sweet of it. But the rind is thick—more years thick than I can count."

"You see now," said Tor, "what that Evil One would have done to us. If we had listened to him we should now be trying to get at that sweet without biting through the shell."

"And so it would not be 'That sweet' at all," said Tinidril.

"It is now his time to go," said the tingling voice of an eldil. Ransom found no words to say as he laid himself down in the casket. The sides rose up high above him like walls: beyond them, as if framed in a coffin-shaped window, he saw the golden sky and the faces of Tor and Tinidril. "You must cover my eyes," he said presently: and the two human forms went out of sight for a moment and returned. Their arms were full of the rose-red lilies. Both bent down and kissed him. He saw the King's hand lifted in blessing and then never saw anything again in that world. They covered his face with the cool petals till he was blinded in a red sweet-smelling cloud.

"Is all ready?" said the King's voice. "Farewell, Friend and Saviour, farewell," said both voices. "Farewell till we three pass out of the dimensions of time. Speak of us always to Maleldil as we speak always of you. The splendour, the love, and the strength be upon you."

Then came the great cumbrous noise of the lid being fastened on above him. Then, for a few seconds, noises without, in the world from which he was eternally divided. Then his consciousness was engulfed.

BY C. S. LEWIS

The Abolition of Man

Mere Christianity

The Great Divorce

The Problem of Pain

The Weight of Glory and Other Addresses

The Screwtape Letters (with "Screwtape Proposes a Toast")

Miracles

The Case for Christianity

The Lion, the Witch and the Wardrobe

Prince Caspian

The Voyage of the Dawn Treader

The Silver Chair

The Magician's Nephew

The Horse and His Boy

The Last Battle

Perelandra

That Hideous Strength

Out of the Silent Planet

The Joyful Christian

George Macdonald: An Anthology

C. S. Lewis: Letters to Children

C. S. Lewis

THAT HIDEOUS STRENGTH

A Modern Fairy-Tale for Grown-Ups

THE SHADOW OF THAT HYDDEOUS STRENGTH
SAX MYLE AND MORE IT IS OF LENGTH.
(Sir David Lyndsay: from *Ane Dialog*, describing the Tower of Babel)

SCRIBNER
NEW YORK   LONDON   TORONTO   SYDNEY   NEW DELHI

SCRIBNER
1230 Avenue of the Americas
New York, NY 10020

First Scribner trade paperback edition 2003
SCRIBNER and design are trademarks
of Macmillan Library Reference USA, Inc., used under license
by Simon & Schuster, the publisher of this work.

For information about special discounts for bulk purchases,
please contact Simon & Schuster Special Sales:
1-800-456-6798 or business@simonandschuster.com

Designed by Brooke Koven
Set in Sabon

Manufactured in the United States of America

13 15 17 19 20 18 16 14

Library of Congress Cataloging-in-Publication Data is available.

ISBN-10: 978-0-684-83367-5
ISBN-10:   0-684-83367-0
ISBN-13: 978-0-7432-3492-4 (PBK)
ISBN-10:   0-7432-3492-8 (PBK)

To J. McNeill

PREFACE

I have called this a fairy-tale in the hope that no one who dislikes fantasy may be misled by the first two chapters into reading further, and then complain of his disappointment. If you ask why—intending to write about magicians, devils, pantomime animals, and planetary angels—I nevertheless begin with such hum-drum scenes and persons, I reply that I am following the traditional fairy-tale. We do not always notice its method, because the cottages, castles, woodcutters, and petty kings with which a fairy-tale opens have become for us as remote as the witches and ogres to which it proceeds. But they were not remote at all to the men who made and first enjoyed the stories. They were, indeed, more realistic and commonplace than Bracton College is to me: for many German peasants had actually met cruel stepmothers, whereas I have never, in any university, come across a college like Bracton. This is a "tall story" about devilry, though it has behind it a serious "point" which I have tried to make in my *Abolition of Man*. In the story, the outer rim of that devilry had to be shown touching the life of some ordinary and respectable profession. I selected my own profession, not, of course, because I think fellows of colleges more likely to be thus corrupted than anyone else, but because my own is the only profession I know well enough to write about. A very small university is imagined because that has certain conveniences for fiction. Edgestow has no resemblance, save for its smallness, to Durham—a university with which the only connection I have had was entirely pleasant.

I believe that one of the central ideas of this tale came into my head from conversations I had with a scientific colleague, some time before I met a rather similar suggestion in the works of Mr. Olaf Stapledon. If I am mistaken in this, Mr. Stapledon is so rich in invention that he can well afford to lend, and I admire his invention (though not his philosophy) so much that I should feel no shame to borrow.

Those who would like to learn further about Numinor and the True West must (alas!) await the publication of much that still exists only in the MSS. of my friend, Professor J. R. R. Tolkien.

The period of this story is vaguely "after the war." It concludes the Trilogy of which *Out of the Silent Planet* was the first part, and *Perelandra* the second, but can be read on its own.

C. S. LEWIS
Magdalen College,
Oxford.
Christmas Eve, 1943.

CONTENTS

1 Sale of College Property   11
2 Dinner with the Sub-Warden   32
3 Belbury and St. Anne's-on-the-Hill   50
4 The Liquidation of Anachronisms   72
5 Elasticity   92
6 Fog   116
7 The Pendragon   136
8 Moonlight at Belbury   157
9 The Saracen's Head   178
10 The Conquered City   202
11 Battle Begun   228
12 Wet and Windy Night   246
13 They Have Pulled Down Deep Heaven
     on Their Heads   268
14 "Real Life Is Meeting"   292
15 The Descent of the Gods   317
16 Banquet at Belbury   340
17 Venus at St. Anne's   357

I

Sale of College Property

I

"Matrimony was ordained, thirdly," said Jane Studdock to herself, "for the mutual society, help, and comfort that the one ought to have of the other." She had not been to church since her schooldays until she went there six months ago to be married, and the words of the service had stuck in her mind.

Through the open door she could see the tiny kitchen of the flat and hear the loud, ungentle tick tick of the clock. She had just left the kitchen and knew how tidy it was. The breakfast things were washed up, the tea towels were hanging above the stove, and the floor was mopped. The beds were made and the rooms "done." She had just returned from the only shopping she need do that day, and it was still a minute before eleven. Except for getting her own lunch and tea, there was nothing that had to be done till six o'clock, even supposing that Mark was really coming home for dinner. But there was a College Meeting today. Almost certainly Mark would ring up about teatime to say that the meeting was taking longer than he had expected and that he would have to dine in College. The hours before her were as empy as the flat. The sun shone and the clock ticked.

"Mutual society, help, and comfort," said Jane bitterly. In reality marriage had proved to be the door out of a world of work and comradeship and laughter and innumerable things to do, into something like solitary confinement. For some years before their marriage she had never seen so little of Mark as she had done in the last six months. Even when he was at home he hardly ever talked. He was always either sleepy or intellectually preoccupied. While they had been friends, and later when they were lovers, life itself had seemed too short for all they had to say to each other. But now . . . why had he married her? Was he still in love? If so, "being in love" must mean totally different things to men and women. Was it the crude truth that all the endless talks which had seemed to her, before they were married, the very medium of love itself, had never been to him more than a preliminary?

"Here I am, starting to waste another morning, mooning," said Jane to herself sharply. "I *must* do some work." By work she meant her doctorate thesis on Donne. She had always intended to continue her own career as a scholar after she was married: that was one of the reasons why they were to have no children, at any rate for a long time yet. Jane was not perhaps a very original thinker and her plan had been to lay great stress on Donne's "triumphant vindication of the body." She still believed that if she got out all her notebooks and editions and really sat down to the job, she could force herself back into her lost enthusiasm for the subject. But before she did so—perhaps in order to put off the moment of beginning—she turned over a newspaper which was lying on the table and glanced at a picture on the back page.

The moment she saw the picture, she remembered her dream. She remembered not only the dream but the measureless time after she had crept out of bed and sat waiting for the first hint of morning, afraid to put on the light for fear Mark should wake up and fuss, yet feeling offended by the sound of his regular breathing. He was an excellent sleeper. Only one thing ever seemed able to keep him awake after he had gone to bed, and even that did not keep him awake for long.

The terror of this dream, like the terror of most dreams, evaporates in the telling, but it must be set down for the sake of what came afterwards.

She had begun by dreaming simply of a face. It was a foreign-looking face, bearded and rather yellow, with a hooked nose. Its expression was frightening because it was frightened. The mouth sagged open and the eyes stared as she had seen other men's eyes stare for a second or two when some sudden shock had occurred. But this face seemed to be meeting a shock that lasted for hours. Then gradually she became aware of more. The face belonged to a man who was sitting hunched up in one corner of a little square room with white-washed walls—waiting, she thought, for those who had him in their power, to come in and do something horrible to him. At last the door was opened and a rather good-looking man with a pointed grey beard came in. The prisoner seemed to recognize him as an old acquaintance, and they sat down together and began to talk. In all the dreams which Jane had hitherto dreamed, one either understood what the dream-people were saying or else one did not hear it. But in this dream— and that helped to make its extraordinary realism—the conversation was in French and Jane understood bits of it, but by no means all, just as she would have done in real life. The visitor was telling the prisoner something which he apparently intended him to regard as good news. And the prisoner at first looked up with a gleam of hope in his eye and said, "*Tiens...ah...ça marche*"; but then he wavered and changed his mind. The visitor continued in a low, fluent voice to press his point. He was a good-looking man in his rather cold way, but he wore *pince-nez* and these kept on catching the light so as to make his eyes invisible. This, combined with the almost unnatural perfection of his teeth, somehow gave Jane a disagreeable impression. And this was increased by the growing distress, and finally the terror, of the prisoner. She could not make out what it was that the visitor was proposing to him, but she did discover that the prisoner was under sentence of death. Whatever the visitor was offering him was something that frightened him more than that. At this point the dream abandoned all pretence to realism and became ordinary nightmare. The visitor, adjusting his *pince-nez* and still smiling his cold smile, seized the prisoner's head between his two hands. He gave it a sharp turn—just as Jane had last summer seen men give a sharp turn to the helmet on a diver's head. The visitor unscrewed the prisoner's head and took it away. Then all became confused. The Head was still the centre of the dream but it was quite a different head now—a head with a flowing white beard all covered with earth. It belonged to an old man whom some people were digging up in a kind of churchyard—a sort of ancient British, druidical kind of man, in a long mantle. Jane didn't mind this much at first because she thought it was a corpse. Then suddenly she noticed that this ancient thing was coming to life. "Look out!" she cried in her dream. "He's alive. Stop! Stop! You're waking him." But they did not stop. The old, buried man sat up and began talking in something that sounded vaguely like Spanish. And this for some reason frightened Jane so badly that she woke up.

That was the dream—no worse, if also no better, than many another nightmare. But it was not the mere memory of a nightmare that made the sitting room of the flat swim before Jane's eyes and caused her to sit down quickly for fear she should fall. The trouble was elsewhere. There, on the back page of the newspaper, was the Head she had seen in the nightmare: the first head (if there had been two of them)—the head of the Prisoner. With extreme reluctance, she took up the paper. EXECU-TION OF ALCASAN was the headline, and beneath it SCIENTIST BLUEBEARD GOES TO GUILLOTINE. She remembered having vaguely followed the case. Alcasan was a distinguished radiologist in a neighbouring country—an Arab by descent, they said—who had cut short an otherwise brilliant career by poisoning his wife. So that was the origin of her dream. She must have looked at this photo in the paper—the man certainly had a very unpleasant face—before going to bed. But no: that couldn't be it. It was this morning's paper. But, of course, there must have been some earlier picture which she had seen and forgotten—probably weeks ago when the trial began. It was silly to have let it give her such a turn. And now for Donne. Let's see, where were we? The ambiguous passage at the end of *Love's Alchymie,*

> Hope not for minde in women; at their best
> Sweetnesse and wit, they are but Mummy possest.

"Hope not for mind in women." Did any man really *want* mind in women? But that wasn't the point. "I *must* get back my power of con-centrating," said Jane; and then, "was there a previous picture of Alcasan? Supposing . . ."

Five minutes later she swept all her books away, went to the mirror, put on her hat, and went out. She was not quite sure where she was going. Anywhere, to be out of that room, that flat, that whole house.

2

Mark himself, meanwhile, was walking down to Bracton College, and thinking of a very different matter. He did not notice at all the morning beauty of the little street that led him from the sandy hillside suburb where he and Jane lived down into the central and academic part of Edgestow.

Though I am Oxford-bred and very fond of Cambridge, I think that Edgestow is more beautiful than either. For one thing it is so small. No maker of cars or sausages or marmalades has yet come to industrialise the country town which is the setting of the University, and the University itself is tiny. Apart from Bracton and from the nineteenth-century women's college beyond the railway, there are only two colleges: Northumberland which stands below Bracton on the river Wynd, and Duke's opposite the Abbey. Bracton takes no undergraduates. It was founded in 1300 for the support of ten learned men whose duties were to pray for the soul of Henry de Bracton and to study the laws of England. The number of Fellows has gradually increased to forty, of whom only six (apart from the Bacon Professor) now study Law and of whom none, perhaps, prays for the soul of Bracton. Mark Studdock was himself a Sociologist and had been elected to a fellowship in that subject five years ago. He was beginning to find his feet. If he had felt any doubt on that point (which he did not) it would have been laid to rest when he found himself meeting Curry just outside the Post Office and seen how natural Curry found it that they should walk to College together and discuss the agenda for the meeting. Curry was the Sub-Warden of Bracton.

"Yes," said Curry, "it will take the hell of a time. Probably go on after dinner. We shall have all the obstructionists wasting time as hard as they can. But luckily that's the worst they can do."

You would never have guessed from the tone of Studdock's reply what intense pleasure he derived from Curry's use of the pronoun "we." So very recently he had been an outsider, watching the proceedings of what he then called "Curry and his gang" with awe and with little understanding, and making at College meetings short, nervous speeches which never influenced the course of events. Now he was inside and "Curry and his gang" had become "we" or "the Progressive Element in College." It had all happened quite suddenly and was still sweet in the mouth.

"You think it'll go through, then?" said Studdock.

"Sure to," said Curry. "We've got the Warden, and the Bursar, and all the chemical and bio-chemical people for a start. I've tackled Pelham and Ted and they're sound. I've made Sancho believe that he sees the point and that he's in favour of it. Bill the Blizzard will probably do something pretty devastating but he's bound to side with us if it comes to a vote. Besides, I haven't yet told you. Dick's going to be there. He came up in time for dinner last night and got busy at once."

Studdock's mind darted hither and thither in search of some safe way to conceal the fact that he did not know who Dick was. In the nick of time he remembered a very obscure colleague whose Christian name was Richard.

"Telford?" said Studdock in a puzzled voice. He knew very well that Telford could not be the Dick that Curry meant and therefore threw a slightly whimsical and ironical tone into his question.

"Good Lord! Telford!!" said Curry with a laugh. "No. I mean Lord Feverstone—Dick Devine as he used to be."

"I *was* a little baffled by the idea of Telford," said Studdock, joining in the laugh. "I'm glad Feverstone is coming. I've never met him, you know."

"Oh, but you must," said Curry. "Look here, come and dine in my rooms tonight. I've asked him."

"I should like to very much," said Studdock quite truly. And then, after a pause, "By the way, I suppose Feverstone's own position is quite secure?"

"How do you mean?" asked Curry.

"Well, there was some talk, if you remember, as to whether someone who was away quite so much could go on holding a fellowship."

"Oh, you mean Glossop and all that ramp. Nothing will come of that. Didn't you think it absolute blah?"

"As between ourselves, yes. But I confess if I were put up to explain *in public* exactly why a man who is nearly always in London should go on being a Fellow of Bracton, I shouldn't find it altogether easy. The real reasons are the sort that Watson would call imponderables."

"I don't agree. I shouldn't have the least objection to explaining the real reasons in public. Isn't it important for a college like this to have influential connections with the outer world? It's not in the least impossible that Dick will be in the next Cabinet. Even already Dick in London has been a damn sight more use to the College than Glossop and half a dozen others of that sort have been by sitting here all their lives."

"Yes. Of course, that's the real point. It would be a little difficult to put in that form at a College meeting, though!"

"There's one thing," said Curry in a slightly less intimate tone, "that perhaps you ought to know about Dick."

"What's that?"

"He got you your fellowship."

Mark was silent. He did not like things which reminded him that he had once been not only outside the Progressive Element but even outside the College. He did not always like Curry either. His pleasure in being with him was not that sort of pleasure.

"Yes," said Curry. "Denniston was your chief rival. Between ourselves, a good many people liked his papers better than yours. It was Dick who insisted all through that you were the sort of man we really wanted. He went around to Duke's and ferreted out all about you. He took the line that the one thing to consider is the type of man we need, and be damned to paper qualifications. And I must say he turned out to be right."

"Very kind of you," said Studdock, with a little mock bow. He was surprised at the turn the conversation had taken. It was an old rule at Bracton, as presumably in most colleges, that one never mentioned in the presence of a man the circumstances of his own election, and Studdock had not realised till now that this also was one of the traditions the Progressive Element was prepared to scrap. It had also never occurred to him that his own election had depended on anything but the excellence of his work in the fellowship examination: still less that it had been so narrow a thing. He was so accustomed to his position by now that this thought gave him the same curious sensation which a man has when he discovers that his father once very nearly married a different woman.

"Yes," continued Curry, pursuing another train of thought. "One sees now that Denniston would never have done. Most emphatically not. A brilliant man at that time, of course, but he seems to have gone quite off the rails since then with all his Distributivism and what not. They tell me he's likely to end up in a monastery."

"He's no fool, all the same," said Studdock.

"I'm glad you're going to meet Dick," said Curry. "We haven't time now, but there's one thing about him I wanted to discuss with you."

Studdock looked enquiringly at him.

"James and I and one or two others," said Curry in a somewhat lower voice, "have been thinking he ought to be the new Warden. But here we are."

"It's not yet twelve," said Studdock. "What about popping into the Bristol for a drink?"

Into the Bristol they accordingly went. It would not have been easy to preserve the atmosphere in which the Progressive Element operated without a good many of these little courtesies. This weighed harder on Studdock than on Curry who was unmarried and had a Sub-Warden's stipend. But the Bristol was a very pleasant place. Studdock bought a double whiskey for his companion and half a pint of beer for himself.

3

The only time I was a guest at Bracton I persuaded my host to let me into the Wood and leave me there alone for an hour. He apologised for locking me in.

Very few people were allowed into Bragdon Wood. The gate was by Inigo Jones and was the only entry: a high wall enclosed the Wood, which was perhaps a quarter of a mile broad and a mile from east to west. If you came in from the street and went through the College to reach it, the sense of gradual penetration into a holy of holies was very strong. First you went through the Newton quadrangle which is dry and gravelly; florid, but beautiful, Gregorian buildings look down upon it. Next you must enter a cool tunnel-like passage, nearly dark at mid-day unless either the door into Hall should be open on your right or the buttery hatch on your left, giving you a glimpse of indoor daylight falling on panels, and a whiff of the smell of fresh bread. When you emerged from this tunnel you would find yourself in the medieval College: in the cloister of the much smaller quadrangle called Republic. The grass here looks very green after the aridity of Newton and the very stone of the buttresses that rise from it gives the impression of being soft and alive. Chapel is not far off: the hoarse, heavy noise of the works of a great and old clock comes to you from somewhere overhead. You went along this cloister, past slabs and urns and busts that commemorate dead Bractonians, and then down shallow steps into the full daylight of the quadrangle called Lady Alice. The buildings to your left and right were seventeenth-century work: humble, almost domestic in character, with dormer windows, mossy and grey-tiled. You were in a sweet, Protestant world. You found yourself, perhaps, thinking of Bunyan or of Walton's *Lives*. There were no buildings straight ahead on the fourth side of Lady Alice: only a row of elms and a wall: and here first one became aware of the sound of running water and the cooing of wood pigeons. The street was so far off by now that there were no other noises. In the wall there was a door. It led you into a covered gallery pierced with narrow windows on either side. Looking out through these, you discovered that you were crossing a bridge and the dark brown dimpled Wynd was flowing under you. Now you were very near your goal. A wicket at the far end of the bridge brought you out on the Fellows' bowling green, and across that you saw the high wall of the Wood, and through the Inigo Jones gate you caught a glimpse of sunlit green and deep shadows.

I suppose the mere fact of being walled in gave the Wood part of its peculiar quality, for when a thing is enclosed, the mind does not willingly regard it as common. As I went forward over the quiet turf I had the sense of being received. The trees were just so wide apart that one saw uninterrupted foliage in the distance but the place where one stood seemed always to be a clearing; surrounded by a world of shadows, one walked in mild sunshine. Except for the sheep whose nibbling kept the grass so short and who sometimes raised their long, foolish faces to stare at me, I was quite alone; and it felt more like the loneliness of a very large room in a deserted house than like any ordinary solitude out of doors. I remember thinking, "This is the sort of place which, as a child, one would have been rather afraid of or else would have liked very much indeed." A moment later I thought, "But when alone—really alone—everyone is a child: or no one?" Youth and age touch only the surface of our lives.

Half a mile is a short walk. Yet it seemed a long time before I came to the centre of the Wood. I knew it was the centre, for there was the thing I had chiefly come to see. It was a well: a well with steps going down to it and the remains of an ancient pavement about it. It was very imperfect now. I did not step on it, but I lay down in the grass and touched it with my fingers. For this was the heart of Bracton or Bragdon Wood: out of this all the legends had come and on this, I suspected, the very existence of the College had originally depended. The archaeologists were agreed that the masonry was very late British-Roman work, done on the eve of the Anglo-Saxon invasion. How Bragdon the wood was connected with Bracton the lawyer was a mystery, but I fancy myself that the Bracton family had availed themselves of an accidental similarity in the names to believe, or make believe, that they had something to do with it. Certainly, if all that was told were true, or even half of it, the Wood was older than the Bractons. I suppose no one now would attach much importance to Strabo's *Balachthon* though it had led a sixteenth-century Warden of the College to say that, "We know not by ancientest report of any Britain without Bragdon." But the medieval song takes us back to the fourteenth century.

In Bragdon bricht this ende dai
Herde ich Merlin ther he lai
Singende woo and welawai.

It is good enough evidence that the well with the British-Roman pavement was already "Merlin's Well," though the name is not found till Queen Elizabeth's reign when good Warden Shovel surrounded the Wood with a wall "for the taking away of all profane and heathenish superstitions and the deterring of the vulgar sort from all wakes, may games, dancings, mummings, and baking of Morgan's bread, heretofore used about the fountain called in vanity Merlin's Well, and utterly to be renounced and abominated as a galli-maufrey of papistry, gentilism, lewdness and dunsicall folly." Not that the College had by this action renounced its own interest in the place. Old Dr. Shovel, who lived to be nearly a hundred, can scarcely have been cold in his grave when one of Cromwell's Major Generals, conceiving it his business to destroy "the groves and the high places," sent a few troopers with power to impress the country people for this pious work. The scheme came to nothing in the end; but there had been a bicker between the College and the troopers in the heart of Bragdon, and the fabulously learned and saintly Richard Crowe had been killed by a musket-ball on the very steps of the Well. He would be a brave man who would accuse Crowe either of popery or "gentilism"; yet the story is that his last words had been, "Marry, Sirs, if Merlin who was the Devil's son was a true King's man as ever ate bread, is it not a shame that you, being but the sons of bitches, must be rebels and regicides?" And always, through all changes, every Warden of Bracton, on the day of his election, had drunk a ceremonial draught of water from Merlin's Well in the great cup which, both for its antiquity and beauty, was the greatest of the Bracton treasures.

All of this I thought of, lying beside Merlin's Well, beside the well which must certainly date from Merlin's time if there had ever been a real Merlin: lying where Sir Kenelm Digby had lain all one summer night and seen a certain strange appearance: where Collins the poet had lain, and where George the Third had cried: where the brilliant and much-loved Nathaniel Fox had composed the famous poem three weeks before he was killed in France. The air was so still and the billows of foliage so heavy above me, that I fell asleep. I was wakened by my friend hallowing to me from a long way off.

4

The most controversial business before the College Meeting was the question of selling Bragdon Wood. The purchaser was the N.I.C.E., the National Institute of Co-ordinated Experiments. They wanted a site for the building which would worthily house this remarkable organisation. The N.I.C.E. was the first-fruits of that constructive fusion between the state and the laboratory on which so many thoughtful people base their hopes of a better world. It was to be free from almost all the tiresome restraints—"red tape" was the word its supporters used—which have hitherto hampered research in this country. It was also largely free from the restraints of economy, for, as it was argued, a nation which can spend so many millions a day on a war can surely afford a few millions a month on productive research in peacetime. The building proposed for it was one which would make a quite noticeable addition to the skyline of New York, the staff was to be enormous, and their salaries princely. Persistent pressure and endless diplomacy on the part of the Senate of Edgestow had lured the new Institute away from Oxford, from Cambridge, from London. It had thought of all these in turn as possible scenes for its labours. At times the Progressive Element in Edgestow had almost despaired. But success was now practically certain. If the N.I.C.E. could get the necessary land, it would come to Edgestow. And once it came, then, as everyone felt, things would at last begin to move. Curry had even expressed a doubt whether, eventually, Oxford and Cambridge could survive as major universities at all.

Three years ago, if Mark Studdock had come to a College Meeting at which such a question was to be decided, he would have expected to hear the claims of sentiment against progress and beauty against utility openly debated. Today, as he took his seat in the Soler, the long upper room on the south of Lady Alice, he expected no such matter. He knew now that that was not the way things are done.

The Progressive Element managed its business really very well. Most of the Fellows did not know when they came into the Soler that there was any question of selling the Wood. They saw, of course, from their agenda paper that item Fifteen was, "Sale of College land," but as that appeared at almost every College Meeting, they were not very interested. On the other hand, they did see that item One was, "Questions about

Bragdon Wood." These were not concerned with the proposed sale. Curry, who rose as Sub-Warden to introduce them, had a few letters to read to the College. The first was from a society concerned for the preservation of ancient monuments. I think myself that this society had been ill-advised to make two complaints in one letter. It would have been wiser if they had confined themselves to drawing the College's attention to the disrepair of the wall round the Wood. When they went on to urge the desirability of building some protection over the Well itself, and even to point out that they had urged this before, the College began to be restive. And when, as a kind of afterthought, they expressed a wish that the College could be a little more accommodating to serious antiquaries who wanted to examine the Well, the College became definitely ill-tempered. I would not like to accuse a man in Curry's position of mis-reading a letter; but his reading of this letter was certainly not such as to gloss over any defects in the tone of the original composition. Before he sat down, nearly every one in the room desired strongly to make the outer world understand that Bragdon Wood was the private property of Bracton College and that the outer world had better mind its own busi-ness. Then he rose again to read another letter. This was from a society of Spiritualists who wanted leave to investigate the "reported phenom-ena" in the Wood—a letter "connected," as Curry said, "with the next which, with the Warden's permission, I will now read to you." This was from a firm who had heard of the Spiritualists' proposal and wanted per-mission to make a film, not exactly of the phenomena, but of the Spiri-tualists looking for the phenomena. Curry was directed to write short refusals to all three letters.

Then came a new voice from quite a different part of the Soler. Lord Feverstone had risen. He fully agreed with the action which the College had taken about these impertinent letters from various busybodies out-side. But was it not, after all, a fact, that the wall of the Wood was in a very unsatisfactory condition? A good many Fellows—Studdock was not one of them—imagined they were watching a revolt on Feverstone's part against "Curry and his gang" and became intensely interested. Almost at once the Bursar, James Busby, was on his feet. He welcomed Lord Feverstone's question. In his Bursarial capacity he had recently taken expert advice about the wall of the Wood. "Unsatisfactory" was, he feared, much too mild a word to describe its condition. Nothing but a complete new wall would really meet the situation. With great diffi-culty the probable cost of this was elicited from him; and when the College heard the figure it gasped. Lord Feverstone inquired icily whether the Bursar was seriously proposing that the College should undertake such an expense. Busby (a very large ex-clergyman with a bushy black beard) replied with some temper that he had proposed nothing: if he *were* to make a suggestion, it would be that the question could not be treated in isolation from some important financial considerations which it would become his duty to lay before them later in the day. There was a pause at this ominous statement, until gradually, one by one, the "outsiders" and "obstructionists," the men not included in the Progressive Element, began coming into the debate. Most of these found it hard to believe that nothing short of a complete new wall would be any use. The Progressive Element let them talk for nearly ten minutes. Then it looked once again as if Lord Feverstone were actually leading the outsiders. He wanted to know whether it was possible that the Bursar and the Preservation Committee could really find no alternative between building a new wall and allowing Bragdon Wood to degenerate into a common. He pressed for an answer. Some of the outsiders even began to feel that he was being too rude to the Bursar. At last the Bursar answered in a low voice that he *had* in a purely theoretical way got some facts about possible alternatives. A barbed wire fence—but the rest was drowned in a roar of disapproval, during which old Canon Jewel was heard to say that he would sooner have every tree in the Wood felled to the ground than see it caged in barbed wire. Finally, the matter was postponed for consideration at the next meeting.

The next item was one of those which the majority of the Fellows could not understand. It involved the recapitulation (by Curry) of a long correspondence between the College and the Senate of the University about the proposed incorporation of the N.I.C.E. in the University of Edgestow. The words, "committed to," kept recurring in the debate that followed. "We appear," said Watson, "to have pledged ourselves as a college to the fullest possible support of the new Institute." "We appear," said Feverstone, "to have tied ourselves up hand and foot and given the University *carte blanche.*" What all this actually amounted to never became clear to any of the outsiders. They remembered fighting hard at a previous meeting against the N.I.C.E. and all its works, and being defeated; but every effort to find out what their defeat had meant, though answered with great lucidity by Curry, served only to entangle them further in the impenetrable mazes of the university constitution and the still darker mystery of the relations between University and College. The result of the discussion was to leave them under the impression that the honour of the College was not involved in the establishment of the N.I.C.E. at Edgestow.

During this item the thoughts of more than one Fellow had turned to lunch, and attention had wandered. But when Curry rose at five minutes to one to introduce item Three, there was a sharp revival of interest. It was called, "Rectification of an anomaly of the Stipends of Junior Fellows." I would not like to say what the most junior Fellows of Bracton were getting at this time, but I believe it hardly covered the expenses of their residence in College, which was compulsory. Studdock who had only recently emerged from this class felt great sympathy with them. He understood the look in their faces. The Rectification, if it went through, would mean to them clothes and holidays and meat for lunch and a chance to buy a half, instead of a fifth, of the books they needed. All their eyes were fixed on the Bursar when he rose to reply to Curry's proposals. He hoped that no one would imagine he approved the anomaly which had, in 1910, excluded the lowest class of the Fellows from the new clauses in the eighteenth paragraph of Statute 17. He felt sure that every one present would *wish* it to be rectified; but it was his duty, as Bursar, to point out that this was the second proposal involving very heavy expenditure which had come before them that morning. He could only say of this, as he had said of the previous proposal, that it could not be isolated from the whole problem of the present financial position of the College, which he hoped to lay before them during the course of the afternoon. A great deal more was said, but the Bursar remained unanswered, the matter was postponed, and when, at quarter to two, the Fellows came surging out of the Soler for lunch, hungry and headachy and ravenous for tobacco, every junior had it fixed in his mind that a new wall for the Wood and a rise in his own stipend were strictly exclusive alternatives. "That darn Wood has been in our way all morning," said one. "We're not out of it yet," answered another.

In this frame of mind, the College returned to the Soler after lunch to consider its finances. Busby, the Bursar, was naturally the principal speaker. It is very hot in the Soler on a sunny afternoon; and the smooth flow of the Bursar's exposition, and even the flashing of his level, white teeth above his beard (he had remarkably fine teeth) had a sort of hypnotic power. Fellows of colleges do not always find money matters easy to understand: if they did, they would probably not have been the sort of men who became Fellows of colleges. They gathered that the situation was bad, very bad, indeed. Some of the youngest and most inexperienced members ceased to wonder whether they would get a new wall or a rise of stipend and began to wonder instead whether the College would continue to function at all. The times, as the Bursar so truly said, were extraordinarily difficult. Older members had heard of such times very often before from dozens of previous Bursars and were less disturbed. I am not suggesting for a moment that the Bursar of Bracton was in any way misrepresenting the position. It is very seldom that the affairs of a large corporation, indefinitely committed to the advancement of learning, can be described as being, in a quite unambiguous sense, satisfactory. His delivery was excellent. Each sentence was a model of lucidity; and if his hearers found the gist of his whole statement less clear than the parts, that may have been their own fault. Some minor retrenchments and reinvestments which he suggested were unanimously approved and the College adjourned for tea in a chastened mood. Studdock rang up Jane and told her he would not be home for dinner.

It was not till six o'clock that all the converging lines of thought and feeling aroused by the earlier business came together upon the question of selling Bragdon Wood. It was not called, "the sale of Bragdon Wood." The Bursar called it the "sale of the area coloured pink on the plan which, with the Warden's permission, I will now pass round the table." He pointed out quite frankly that this involved the loss of *part* of the Wood. In fact, the proposed N.I.C.E. site still left to the College a strip about sixteen feet broad along the far half of the south side but there was no deception for the Fellows had the plan to look at with their own eyes. It was a small scale plan and not perhaps perfectly accurate—only meant to give one a general idea. In answer to questions he admitted that unfortunately—or perhaps fortunately—the Well itself was in the area which the N.I.C.E. wanted. The rights of the College to access would, of course, be guaranteed; and the Well and its pavement would be preserved by the Institute in a manner to satisfy all the archaeologists in the world. He refrained from offering any advice and merely mentioned the quite astonishing figure which the N.I.C.E. was offering. After that, the meeting became lively. The advantages of the sale discovered themselves one by one like ripe fruit dropping into the hand. It solved the problem of the wall; it solved the problem of protecting ancient monuments; it solved the financial problem; it looked like solving the problem of the junior Fellows' stipends. It appeared further that the N.I.C.E. regarded this as the only possible site in Edgestow; if by any chance

Bracton would not sell, the whole scheme miscarried and the Institute would undoubtedly go to Cambridge. It was even drawn out of the Bursar by much questioning that he knew of a Cambridge college very anxious to sell.

The few real "Die-hards" present, to whom Bragdon Wood was almost a basic assumption of life, could hardly bring themselves to realise what was happening. When they found their voices, they struck a discordant note amid the general buzz of cheerful comment. They were manoeuvered into the position of appearing as the party who passionately desired to see Bragdon surrounded with barbed wire. When at last old Jewel, blind and shaky and almost weeping, rose to his feet, his voice was hardly audible. Men turned round to gaze at, and some to admire, the clear-cut, half-childish face and the white hair which had become more conspicuous as the long room grew darker. But only those close to him could hear what he said. At this moment Lord Feverstone sprang to his feet, folded his arms, and looking straight at the old man said in a very loud, clear voice:

"If Canon Jewel wishes us *not* to hear his views, I suggest that his end could be better attained by silence."

Jewel had been already an old man in the days before the first war when old men were treated with kindness, and he had never succeeded in getting used to the modern world. For a moment as he stood with his head thrust forward, people thought he was going to reply. Then quite suddenly he spread out his hands with a gesture of helplessness, shrunk back, and began laboriously to resume his chair.

The motion was carried.

5

After leaving the flat that morning Jane also had gone down to Edgestow and bought a hat. She had before now expressed some contempt for the kind of woman who buys hats, as a man buys drinks, for a stimulant and a consolation. It did not occur to her that she was doing so herself on this occasion. She liked her clothes to be rather severe and in colours that were really good on serious aesthetic grounds—clothes which would make it plain to everyone that she was an intelligent adult and not a woman of the chocolate-box variety—and because of this preference, she did not know that she was interested in clothes at all. She was therefore a little annoyed when Mrs. Dimble met her coming out of Sparrow's and said, "Hullo dear! Been buying a hat? Come home to lunch and let's see it. Cecil has the car just round the corner."

Cecil Dimble, a Fellow of Northumberland, had been Jane's tutor for her last year as a student and Mrs. Dimble (one tended to call her Mother Dimble) had been a kind of unofficial aunt to all the girls of her year. A liking for the female pupils of one's husband is not, perhaps, so common as might be wished among dons' wives; but Mrs. Dimble appeared to like all Dr. Dimble's pupils of both sexes and the Dimbles' house, away on the far side of the river, was a kind of noisy *salon* all the term. She had been particularly fond of Jane with that kind of affection which a humorous, easy natured and childless woman sometimes feels for a girl whom she thinks pretty and rather absurd. For the last year or so Jane had been somewhat losing sight of the Dimbles and felt rather guilty about it. She accepted the invitation to lunch.

They drove over the bridge to the north of Bracton and then south along the bank of the Wynd, past the cottages, then left and eastward at the Norman church and down the straight road with the poplars on one side and the wall of Bragdon Wood on the other, and so finally to the Dimbles' front door.

"How lovely it's looking," said Jane quite sincerely as she got out of the car. The Dimbles' garden was famous.

"You'd better take a good look at it then," said Dr. Dimble.

"What do you mean?" asked Jane.

"Haven't you told her?" said Dr. Dimble to his wife.

"I haven't screwed myself up to it yet," said Mrs. Dimble. "Besides, poor dear, her husband is one of the villains of the piece. Anyway, I expect she knows."

"I've no idea what you're talking about," said Jane.

"Your own College is being so tiresome, dear. They're turning us out. They won't renew the lease."

"Oh, Mrs. Dimble!" exclaimed Jane. "And I didn't even know this was Bracton property."

"There you are!" said Mrs. Dimble. "One half of the world doesn't know how the other half lives. Here have I been imagining that you were using all your influence with Mr. Studdock to try to save us, whereas in reality—"

"Mark never talks to me about College business."

"Good husbands never do," said Dr. Dimble. "At least, only about the business of other people's colleges. That's why Margaret knows all about Bracton and nothing about Northumberland. Is no one coming in to have lunch?"

Dimble guessed that Bracton was going to sell the Wood and everything else it owned on that side of the river. The whole region seemed to him now even more of a paradise than when he first came to live there twenty-five years ago, and he felt much too strongly on the subject to wish to talk about it before the wife of one of the Bracton men.

"You'll have to wait for lunch till I've seen Jane's new hat," said Mother Dimble, and forthwith hurried Jane upstairs. Then followed some minutes of conversation which was strictly feminine in the old-fashioned sense. Jane, while preserving a certain sense of superiority, found it indefinably comforting; and though Mrs. Dimble had really the wrong point of view about such things, there was no denying that the one small alteration which she suggested did go to the root of the matter. When the hat was being put away again Mrs. Dimble suddenly said,

"There's nothing wrong, is there?"

"Wrong?" said Jane. "Why? What should there be?"

"You're not looking yourself."

"Oh, I'm all right," said Jane aloud. Mentally she added, "She's dying to know whether I'm going to have a baby. That sort of woman always is."

"Do you hate being kissed?" said Mrs. Dimble unexpectedly.

"Do I hate being kissed?" thought Jane to herself. "That indeed is the question. Do I hate being kissed? Hope not for mind in women—" She had intended to reply, "Of course not," but inexplicably, and to her great annoyance found herself crying instead. And then, for a moment, Mrs. Dimble became simply a grown-up as grown-ups had been when one was a very small child: large, warm, soft objects to whom one ran with bruised knees or broken toys. When she thought of her childhood, Jane usually remembered those occasions on which the voluminous embrace of Nurse or Mother had been unwelcome and resisted as an insult to one's maturity; now, for the moment, she was back in those forgotten, yet infrequent, times when fear or misery induced a willing surrender and surrender brought comfort. Not to detest being petted and pawed was contrary to her whole theory of life; yet, before they went downstairs, she had told Mrs. Dimble that she was not going to have a baby, but was a bit depressed from being very much alone, and from a nightmare.

During lunch Dr. Dimble talked about the Arthurian legend. "It's really wonderful," he said, "how the whole thing hangs together, even in a late version like Malory's. You've noticed how there are two sets of characters? There's Guinevere and Launcelot and all those people in the centre: all very courtly and nothing particularly British about them. But then in the background—on the other side of Arthur, so to speak—there are all those *dark* people like Morgan and Morgawse, who are very British indeed and usually more or less hostile though they are his own relatives. Mixed up with magic. You remember that wonderful phrase, how Queen Morgan 'set all the country on fire with ladies that were enchantresses.' Merlin too, of course, is British, though not hostile. Doesn't it look very like a picture of Britain as it must have been on the eve of the invasion?"

"How do you mean, Dr. Dimble?" said Jane.

"Well, wouldn't there have been one section of society that was almost purely Roman? People wearing togas and talking a Celticised Latin—something that would sound to us rather like Spanish: and fully Christian. But further up country, in the out-of-the-way places, cut off by the forests, there would have been little courts ruled by real old British under-kings, talking something like Welsh, and practising a certain amount of the Druidical religion."

"And what would Arthur himself have been?" said Jane. It was silly that her heart should have missed a beat at the words "rather like Spanish."

"That's just the point," said Dr. Dimble. "One can imagine a man of the old British line, but also a Christian and a fully-trained general with Roman technique, trying to pull this whole society together and almost succeeding. There'd be jealousy from his own British family, and the Romanised section—the Launcelots and Lionels—would look down on the Britons. That'd be why Kay is always represented as a boor: he is part of the native strain. And always that under-tow, that tug back to Druidism."

"And where would Merlin be?"

"Yes. . . . He's the really interesting figure. Did the whole thing fail because he died so soon? Has it ever struck you what an odd creation Merlin is? He's not evil; yet he's a magician. He is obviously a druid; yet he knows all about the Grail. He's 'the devil's son'; but then Layamon goes out of his way to tell you that the kind of being who fathered Merlin needn't have been bad after all. You remember, 'There dwell in the sky many kinds of wights. Some of them are good, and some work evil.'"

"It *is* rather puzzling. I hadn't thought of it before."

"I often wonder," said Dr. Dimble, "whether Merlin doesn't represent the last trace of something the later tradition has quite forgotten about—something that became impossible when the only people in touch with the supernatural were either white or black, either priests or sorcerers."

"What a horrid idea," said Mrs. Dimble, who had noticed that Jane seemed to be preoccupied. "Anyway, Merlin happened a long time ago if he happened at all and he's safely dead and buried under Bragdon Wood as every one of us knows."

"Buried but *not* dead, according to the story," corrected Dr. Dimble.

"Ugh!" said Jane involuntarily, but Dr. Dimble was musing aloud.

"I wonder what they *will find* if they start digging up that place for the foundations of their N.I.C.E.," he said.

"First mud and then water," said Mrs. Dimble. "That's why they can't really build it there."

"So you'd think," said her husband. "And if so, why should they want to come here at all? A little cockney like Jules is not likely to be influenced by any poetic fancy about Merlin's mantle having fallen on him!"

"Merlin's mantle indeed!" said Mrs. Dimble.

"Yes," said the Doctor, "it's a rum idea. I daresay some of his set would like to recover the mantle well enough. Whether they'll be big enough to fill it is another matter! I don't think they'd like it if the old man himself came back to life along with it."

"That child's going to faint," said Mrs. Dimble, suddenly jumping up.

"Hullo! What's the matter?" said Dr. Dimble, looking with amazement at Jane's face. "Is the room too hot for you?"

"Oh, it's too ridiculous," said Jane.

"Let's come into the drawing room," said Dr. Dimble. "Here. Lean on my arm."

A little later, in the drawing room, seated beside a window that opened onto the lawn, now strewn with bright yellow leaves, Jane attempted to excuse her absurd behaviour by telling the story of her dream. "I suppose I've given myself away dreadfully," she said. "You can both start psycho-analysing me now."

From Dr. Dimble's face, Jane might have indeed conjectured that her dream had shocked him exceedingly. "Extraordinary thing . . . most extraordinary," he kept muttering. "*Two* heads. And one of them Alcasan's. Now is that a false scent . . . ?"

"Don't, Cecil," said Mrs. Dimble.

"Do you think I ought to be analysed?" said Jane.

"Analysed?" said Dr. Dimble, glancing at her as if he had not quite understood. "Oh, I see. You mean going to Brizeacre or someone of that sort?" Jane realised that her question had recalled him from some quite different train of thought and even—disconcertingly—that the problem of her own health had been shouldered aside. The telling of her dream had raised some other problem, though what this was she could not even imagine.

Dr. Dimble looked out of the window. "There is my dullest pupil just ringing the bell," he said. "I must go to the study, and listen to an essay on Swift beginning, 'Swift was born.' Must try to keep my mind on it, too, which won't be easy." He rose and stood for a moment with his hand on Jane's shoulder. "Look here," he said, "I'm not going to give any advice. But if you do decide to go to anyone about that dream, I wish you would *first* consider going to someone whose address Margery or I will give you."

"You don't believe in Mr. Brizeacre?" said Jane.

"I can't explain," said Dr. Dimble. "Not now. It's all so complicated. Try not to bother about it. But if you *do,* just let us know first. Good-bye."

Almost immediately after his departure some other visitors arrived, so that there was no opportunity of further private conversation between Jane and her hostess. She left the Dimbles about half an hour later and walked home, not along the road with the poplars but by the footpath across the common, past the donkeys and the geese, with the towers and spires of Edgestow to her left and the old windmill on the horizon to her right.

2

Dinner with the Sub-Warden

I

"This is a blow!" said Curry standing in front of the fireplace in his magnificent rooms which overlooked Newton. They were the best set in College.

"Something from N.O.?" said James Busby. He and Lord Feverstone and Mark were all drinking sherry before dining with Curry. N.O., which stood for Non-Olet, was the nickname of Charles Place, the Warden of Bracton. His election to this post, some fifteen years before, had been one of the earliest triumphs of the Progressive Element. By dint of saying that the College needed "new blood" and must be shaken out of its "academic grooves," they had succeeded in bringing in an elderly civil servant who had certainly never been contaminated by academic weaknesses since he left his rather obscure Cambridge college in the previous century, but who had written a monumental report on National Sanitation. The subject had, if anything, rather recommended him to the Progressive Element. They regarded it as a slap in the face for the *dilettanti* and Die-hards, who replied by christening their new Warden Non-Olet. But gradually even Place's supporters had adopted the name. For Place had not answered their expectations, having turned out to be a dyspeptic with a taste for philately, whose voice was so seldom heard that some of the junior Fellows did not know what it sounded like.

"Yes, blast him," said Curry, "wishes to see me on a most important matter as soon as I can conveniently call on him after dinner."

"That means," said the Bursar, "that Jewel and Co. have been getting at him and want to find some way of going back on the whole business."

"I don't give a damn for that," said Curry. "How can you go back on a Resolution? It isn't that. But it's enough to muck up the whole evening."

"Only *your* evening," said Feverstone. "Don't forget to leave out that very special brandy of yours before you go."

"Jewel! Good God!" said Busby, burying his left hand in his beard.

"I was rather sorry for old Jewel," said Mark. His motives for saying this were very mixed. To do him justice, it must be said that the quite unexpected and apparently unnecessary brutality of Feverstone's behaviour to the old man had disgusted him. And then, too, the whole idea of his debt to Feverstone in the matter of his own fellowship had been rankling all day. Who was this man Feverstone? But paradoxically, even while he felt that the time had come for asserting his own independence and showing that his agreement with all the methods of the Progressive Element must not be taken for granted, he also felt that a little independence would raise him to a higher position within that Element itself. If the idea, "Feverstone will think all the more of you for showing your teeth," had occurred to him in so many words, he would probably have rejected it as servile; but it didn't.

"Sorry for Jewel?" said Curry wheeling round. "You wouldn't say that if you knew what he was like in his prime."

"I agree with you," said Feverstone to Mark, "but then I take the Clausewitz view. Total war is the most humane in the long run. I shut him up instantaneously. Now that he's got over the shock, he's quite enjoying himself because I've fully confirmed everything he's been saying about the Younger Generation for the last forty years. What was the alternative? To let him drivel on until he'd worked himself into a coughing fit or a heart attack, and give him in addition the disappointment of finding that he was treated civilly."

"That's a point of view, certainly," said Mark.

"Damn it all," continued Feverstone, "no man likes to have his stock in trade taken away. What would poor Curry, here, do if the Diehards one day all refused to do any Die-harding? Othello's occupation would be gone."

"Dinner is served, Sir," said Curry's "Shooter"—for that is what they call a College servant at Bracton.

"That's all rot, Dick," said Curry as they sat down. "There's nothing I should like better than to see the end of all these Die-hards and obstructionists and be able to get on with the job. You don't suppose I *like* having to spend all my time merely getting the road clear?" Mark noticed that his host was a little nettled at Lord Feverstone's banter. The latter had an extremely virile and infectious laugh. Mark felt he was beginning to like him.

"The job being . . . ?" said Feverstone, not exactly glancing, much less winking, at Mark, but making him feel that he was somehow being included in the fun.

"Well, some of us have got work of our own to do," replied Curry, dropping his voice to give it a more serious tone, almost as some people drop their voices to speak of medical or religious matters.

"I never knew you were *that* sort of person," said Feverstone.

"That's the worst of the whole system," said Curry. "In a place like this you've either got to be content to see everything go to pieces—I mean, become stagnant—or else to sacrifice your own career as a scholar to all these infernal college politics. One of these days I *shall* chuck that side of it and get down to my book. The stuff's all there, you know, Feverstone. One long vacation clear and I really believe I could put it into shape."

Mark, who had never seen Curry baited before, was beginning to enjoy himself.

"I see," said Feverstone. "In order to keep the place going as a learned society, all the best brains in it have to give up doing anything about learning."

"Exactly!" said Curry. "That's just—" and then stopped, uncertain whether he was being taken quite seriously. Feverstone burst into laughter. The Bursar who had up till now been busily engaged in eating, wiped his beard carefully and spoke seriously.

"All that's very well in theory," he said, "but I think Curry's quite right. Supposing he resigned his office as Sub-Warden and retired into his cave. He might give us a thundering good book on economics—"

"Economics?" said Feverstone lifting his eyebrows.

"I happen to be a military historian, James," said Curry. He was often somewhat annoyed at the difficulty which his colleagues seemed to find in remembering what particular branch of learning he had been elected to pursue.

"I mean military history, of course," said Busby. "As I say, he might give us a thundering good book on military history. But it would be superseded in twenty years. Whereas the work he is actually doing for the College will benefit it for centuries. This whole business, now, of bringing the N.I.C.E. to Edgestow. What about a thing like that, Feverstone? I'm not speaking merely of the financial side of it, though as Bursar I naturally rate that pretty high. But think of the new life, the awakening of new vision, the stirring of dormant impulses. What would any book on economics—"

"Military history," said Feverstone gently, but this time Busby did not hear him.

"What would any book on economics be, compared with a thing like that?" he continued. "I look upon it as the greatest triumph of practical idealism that this century has yet seen."

The good wine was beginning to do its good office. We have all known the kind of clergyman who tends to forget his clerical collar after the third glass; but Busby's habit was the reverse. It was after the third glass that he began to remember his collar. As wine and candlelight loosened his tongue, the parson still latent within him after thirty years' apostasy began to wake into a strange galvanic life.

"As you chaps know," he said, "I make no claim to orthodoxy. But if religion is understood in the deepest sense, I have no hesitation in saying that Curry, by bringing the N.I.C.E. to Edgestow, has done more for it in one year than Jewel has done in his whole life."

"Well," said Curry modestly, "that's rather the sort of thing one had hoped. I mightn't put it exactly as you do, James—"

"No, no," said the Bursar, "of course not. We all have our different languages; but we all really mean the same thing."

"Has anyone discovered," asked Feverstone, "what, precisely, the N.I.C.E. is, or what it intends to do?"

Curry looked at him with a slightly startled expression. "That comes oddly from you, Dick," he said. "I thought you were in on it, yourself."

"Isn't it a little naïf," said Feverstone, "to suppose that being in on a thing involves any distinct knowledge of its official programme?"

"Oh well, if you mean *details*," said Curry, and then stopped.

"Surely, Feverstone," said Busby, "you're making a great mystery about nothing. I should have thought the objects of the N.I.C.E. were pretty clear. It's the first attempt to take applied science seriously from the national point of view. The difference in scale between it and anything we've had before amounts to a difference in kind. The buildings alone, the apparatus alone—! Think what it has done already for industry. Think how it is going to mobilise all the talent of the country; and not only scientific talent in the narrower sense. Fifteen departmental directors at fifteen thousand a year each! Its own legal staff! Its own police, I'm told! Its own permanent staff of architects, surveyors, engineers! The thing's stupendous!"

"Careers for our sons," said Feverstone. "I see."

"What do you mean by that, Lord Feverstone?" said Busby putting down his glass.

"Lord!" said Feverstone, his eyes laughing, "what a brick to drop. I'd quite forgotten you had a family, James."

"I agree with James," said Curry, who had been waiting somewhat impatiently to speak. "The N.I.C.E. marks the beginning of a new era— the *really* scientific era. Up to now, everything has been haphazard. This is going to put science itself on a scientific basis. There are to be forty interlocking committees sitting every day and they've got a wonderful gadget—I was shown the model last time I was in town—by which the findings of each committee print themselves off in their own little compartment on the Analytical Notice-Board every half hour. Then, that report slides itself into the right position where it's connected up by little arrows with all the relevant parts of the other reports. A glance at the Board shows you the policy of the whole Institute actually taking shape under your own eyes. There'll be a staff of at least twenty experts at the top of the building working this Notice-Board in a room rather like the Tube control rooms. It's a marvellous gadget. The different kinds of business all come out in the Board in different coloured lights. It must have cost half a million. They call it a Pragmatometer."

"And there," said Busby, "you see again what the Institute is already doing for the country. Pragmatometry is going to be a big thing. Hundreds of people are going in for it. Why this Analytical Notice-Board will probably be out of date before the building is finished!"

"Yes, by Jove," said Feverstone, "and N.O. himself told me this morning that the sanitation of the Institute was going to be something quite out of the ordinary."

"So it is," said Busby sturdily. "I don't see why one should think that unimportant."

"And what do you think about it, Studdock?" said Feverstone.

"I think," said Mark, "that James touched on the most important point when he said that it would have its own legal staff and its own police. I don't give a fig for Pragmatometers and sanitation *de luxe*. The real thing is that this time we're going to get science applied to social problems and backed by the whole force of the state, just as war has been backed by the whole force of the state in the past. One hopes, of course, that it'll find out more than the old free-lance science did; but what's certain is that it can *do* more."

"Damn," said Curry, looking at his watch. "I'll have to go and talk to N.O. now. If you people would like any brandy when you've finished your wine, it's in that cupboard. You'll find balloon glasses on the shelf above. I'll be back as soon as I can. You're not going, James, are you?"

"Yes," said the Bursar. "I'm going to bed early. Don't let me break up the party for you two. I've been on my legs nearly all day, you know. A man's a fool to hold any office in this College. Continual anxiety. Crushing responsibility. And then you get people suggesting that all the little research-beetles who never poke their noses outside their libraries and laboratories are the real workers! I'd like to see Glossop or any of that lot face the sort of day's work I've had today. Curry, my lad, you'd have had an easier life if you'd stuck to economics."

"I've told you before," began Curry, but the Bursar, now risen, was bending over Lord Feverstone and telling him a funny story.

As soon as the two men had got out of the room, Lord Feverstone looked steadily at Mark for some seconds with an enigmatic expression. Then he chuckled. Then the chuckle developed into a laugh. He threw his lean, muscular body well back into his chair and laughed louder and louder. He was very infectious in his laughter and Mark found himself laughing too—quite sincerely and even helplessly, like a child. "Pragmatometers—palatial lavatories—practical idealism," gasped Feverstone. It was a moment of extraordinary liberation for Mark. All sorts of things about Curry and Busby which he had not previously noticed, or else, noticing, had slurred over in his reverence for the Progressive Element, came back to his mind. He wondered how he could have been so blind to the funny side of them.

"It really is rather devastating," said Feverstone when he had partially recovered, "that the people one has to use for getting things done should talk such drivel the moment you ask them about the things themselves."

"And yet they *are*, in a sense, the brains of Bracton," said Mark.

"Good Lord no! Glossop and Bill the Blizzard, and even old Jewel, have ten times their intelligence."

"I didn't know you took that view."

"I think Glossop, etc., are quite mistaken. I think their idea of culture and knowledge and what not is unrealistic. I don't think it fits the world we're living in. It's a mere fantasy. But it is quite a clear idea and they follow it out consistently. They know what they want. But our two poor friends, though they can be persuaded to take the right train, or even to drive it, haven't a ghost of a notion where it's going to, or why. They'll sweat blood to bring the N.I.C.E. to Edgestow: that's why they're indispensable. But what the point of the N.I.C.E. is, what the point of anything is—ask them another. Pragmatometry! Fifteen sub-directors!"

"Well, perhaps I'm in the same boat myself."

"Not at all. You saw the point at once. I knew you would. I've read everything you've written since you were in for your fellowship. That's what I wanted to talk to you about."

Mark was silent. The giddy sensation of being suddenly whirled up from one plane of secrecy to another, coupled with the growing effect of Curry's excellent port, prevented him from speaking.

"I want you to come into the Institute," said Feverstone.

"You mean—to leave Bracton?"

"That makes no odds. Anyway, I don't suppose there's anything you want here. We'd make Curry Warden when N.O. retires and—"

"They were talking of making you Warden."

"God!" said Feverstone and stared. Mark realised that from Feverstone's point of view this was like the suggestion that he should become Headmaster of a small idiots' school, and thanked his stars that his own remark had not been uttered in a tone that made it obviously serious. Then they both laughed again.

"You," said Feverstone, "would be absolutely wasted as Warden. That's the job for Curry. He'll do it very well. You want a man who loves business and wire-pulling for their own sake and doesn't really ask what it's all about. If he did, he'd start bringing in his own—well, I suppose he'd call them 'ideas.' As it is, we've only got to tell him that he thinks so-and-so is a man the College wants, and he *will* think it. And then he'll never rest till so-and-so gets a fellowship. That's what we want the College for: a drag net, a recruiting office."

"A recruiting office for the N.I.C.E., you mean?"

"Yes, in the first instance. But it's only part of the general show."

"I'm not sure that I know what you mean."

"You soon will. The Home Side, and all that, you know! It sounds rather in Busby's style to say that Humanity is at the cross-roads. But it is the main question at the moment: which side one's on—obscurantism or Order. It does really look as if we now had the power to dig ourselves in as a species for a pretty staggering period, to take control of our own destiny. If Science is really given a free hand it can now take over the human race and re-condition it: make man a really efficient animal. If it doesn't—well, we're done."

"Go on."

"There are three main problems. First, the interplanetary problem—"

"What on earth do you mean?"

"Well, that doesn't really matter. We can't do anything about that at present. The only man who could help was Weston."

"He was killed in a blitz, wasn't he?"

"He was murdered."

"Murdered?"

"I'm pretty sure of it, and I've a shrewd idea who the murderer was."

"Good God! Can nothing be done?"

"There's no evidence. The murderer is a respectable Cambridge don with weak eyes, a game leg, and a fair beard. He's dined in this College."

"What was Weston murdered for?"

"For being on our side. The murderer is one of the enemy."

"You don't mean to say he murdered him for that?"

"Yes," said Feverstone, bringing his hand down smartly on the table. "That's just the point. You'll hear people like Curry or James burbling away about the 'war' against reaction. It never enters their heads that it might be a real war with real casualties. They think the violent resistance of the other side ended with the persecution of Galileo and all that. But don't believe it. It is just seriously beginning. They know now that we have at last got *real* powers: that the question of what humanity is to be is going to be decided in the next sixty years. They're going to fight every inch. They'll stop at nothing."

"They can't win," said Mark.

"We'll hope not," said Lord Feverstone. "I think they can't. That is why it is of such immense importance to each of us to choose the right side. If you try to be neutral you become simply a pawn."

"Oh, I haven't any doubt which is *my* side," said Mark. "Hang it all—the preservation of the human race—it's a pretty rock-bottom obligation."

"Well, personally," said Feverstone, "I'm not indulging in any Busbyisms about that. It's a little fantastic to base one's actions on a supposed concern for what's going to happen millions of years hence; and you must remember that the other side would claim to be preserving humanity, too. Both can be explained psycho-analytically if they take that line. The practical point is that you and I don't like being pawns, and we do rather like fighting—specially on the winning side."

"And what is the first practical step?"

"Yes, that's the real question. As I said, the interplanetary problem must be left on one side for the moment. The second problem is our rivals on this planet. I don't mean only insects and bacteria. There's far too much life of every kind about, animal and vegetable. We haven't really cleared the place yet. First we couldn't; and then we had aesthetic and humanitarian scruples; and we still haven't short-circuited the question of the balance of nature. All that is to be gone into. The third problem is Man himself."

"Go on. This interests me very much."

"Man has got to take charge of Man. That means, remember, that some men have got to take charge of the rest—which is another reason for cashing in on it as soon as one can. You and I want to be the people who do the taking charge, not the ones who are taken charge of. Quite."

"What sort of thing have you in mind?"

"Quite simple and obvious things, at first—sterilization of the unfit, liquidation of backward races (we don't want any dead weights), selective breeding. Then real education, including pre-natal education. By real education I mean one that has no 'take-it-or-leave-it' nonsense. A real education makes the patient what it wants infallibly: whatever he or his parents try to do about it. Of course, it'll have to be mainly psychological at first. But we'll get on to biochemical conditioning in the end and direct manipulation of the brain. . . ."

"But this is stupendous, Feverstone."

"It's the real thing at last. A new type of man: and it's people like you who've got to begin to make him."

"That's my trouble. Don't think it's false modesty, but I haven't yet seen how I can contribute."

"No, but *we* have. You are what we need: a trained sociologist with a radically realistic outlook, not afraid of responsibility. Also, a sociologist who can write."

"You don't mean you want me to write up all this?"

"No. We want you to write it *down*—to camouflage it. Only for the present, of course. Once the thing gets going we shan't have to bother about the great heart of the British public. We'll make the great heart what we want it to be. But in the meantime, it *does* make a difference how things are put. For instance, if it were even whispered that the N.I.C.E. wanted powers to experiment on criminals, you'd have all the old women of both sexes up in arms and yapping about humanity. Call it re-education of the mal-adjusted, and you have them all slobbering with delight that the brutal era of retributive punishment has at last come to an end. Odd thing it is—the word 'experiment' is unpopular, but not the word 'experimental.' You musn't experiment on children; but offer the dear little kiddies free education in an experimental school attached to the N.I.C.E. and it's all correct!"

"You don't mean that this—er—journalistic side would be my main job?"

"It's nothing to do with journalism. Your readers in the first instance would be Committees of the House of Commons, not the public. But that would only be a side line. As for the job itself—why, it's impossible to say how it might develop. Talking to a man like you, I don't stress the financial side. You'd start at something quite modest: say about fifteen hundred a year."

"I wasn't thinking about that," said Mark, flushing with pure excitement.

"Of course," said Feverstone, "I ought to warn you, there is the danger. Not yet, perhaps. But when things really begin to hum, it's quite on the cards they may try to bump you off, like poor old Weston."

"I don't think I was thinking about that either," said Mark.

"Look here," said Feverstone. "Let me run you across tomorrow to see John Wither. He told me to bring you for the week-end if you were interested. You'll meet all the important people there and it'll give you a chance to make up your mind."

"How does Wither come into it? I thought Jules was the head of the N.I.C.E." Jules was a distinguished novelist and scientific populariser whose name always appeared before the public in connection with the new Institute.

"Jules! Hell's bells!" said Feverstone. "You don't imagine that little mascot has anything to say to what really goes on? He's all right for selling the Institute to the great British public in the Sunday papers and he draws a whacking salary. He's no use for work. There's nothing inside his head except some nineteenth-century socialist stuff, and blah about the rights of man. He's just about got as far as Darwin!"

"Oh quite," said Mark. "I was always rather puzzled at his being in the show at all. Do you know, since you're so kind, I think I'd better accept your offer and go over to Wither's for the week-end. What time would you be starting?"

"About quarter to eleven. They tell me you live out Sandawn way. I could call and pick you up."

"Thanks very much. Now tell me about Wither."

"John Wither," began Feverstone, but suddenly broke off. "Damn!" he said. "Here comes Curry. Now we shall have to hear everything N.O. said and how wonderfully the arch-politician has managed him. Don't run away. I shall need your moral support."

2

The last bus had gone long before Mark left College and he walked home up the hill in brilliant moonlight. Something happened to him the moment he had let himself into the flat which was very unusual. He found himself, on the doormat, embracing a frightened, half-sobbing Jane—even a humble Jane—who was saying, "Oh Mark, I've been so frightened."

There was a quality in the very muscles of his wife's body which took him by surprise. A certain indefinable defensiveness had momentarily deserted her. He had known such occasions before, but they were rare. They were already becoming rarer. And they tended, in his experience, to be followed next day by inexplicable quarrels. This puzzled him greatly, but he had never put his bewilderment into words.

It is doubtful whether he could have understood her feelings even if they had been explained to him; and Jane, in any case, could not have explained them. She was in extreme confusion. But the reasons for her unusual behavior on this particular evening were simple enough. She had got back from the Dimbles at about half-past four, feeling much exhilarated by her walk, and hungry, and quite sure that her experiences on the previous night and at lunch were over and done with. She had had to light up and draw the curtains before she had finished tea, for the days were getting short. While doing so, the thought had come into her mind that her fright at the dream and at the mere mention of a mantle, an old man, an old man buried but not dead, and a language like Spanish, had really been as irrational as a child's fear of the dark. This had led her to remember moments when she had feared the dark as a child. Perhaps, she allowed herself to remember them too long. At any rate, when she sat down to drink her last cup of tea, the evening had somehow deteriorated. It never recovered. First, she found it rather difficult to keep her mind on her book. Then, when she had acknowledged this difficulty, she found it difficult to fix on any book. Then she realised that she was restless. From being restless, she became nervous. Then followed a long time when she was not frightened, but knew that she would be very frightened indeed if she did not keep herself in hand. Then came a curious reluctance to go into the kitchen to get herself some supper, and a difficulty—indeed, an impossibility—of eating anything when she had got it. And now, there was no disguising the fact that she was frightened. In desperation she rang up the Dimbles. "I think I might go and see the person you suggested, after all," she said. Mrs. Dimble's voice came back, after a curious little pause, giving her the address. Ironwood was the name—Miss Ironwood, apparently. Jane had assumed it would be a man and was rather repelled. Miss Ironwood lived out at St. Anne's on the Hill. Jane asked if she should make an appointment. "No," said Mrs. Dimble, "they'll be—you needn't make an appointment." Jane kept the conversation going as long as she could. She had rung up not chiefly to get the address but to hear Mother Dimble's voice. Secretly she had had a wild hope that Mother Dimble would recognise her distress and say at once, "I'll come straight up to you by car." Instead, she got the mere information and a hurried "Good-night." It seemed to Jane that there was something queer about Mrs. Dimble's voice. She felt that by ringing up she had interrupted a conversation about herself—or no—not about herself but about something else more important, with which she was somehow connected. And what had Mrs. Dimble meant by, "They'll be—" "They'll be expecting you"? Horrible, childish night-nursery visions of *They* "expecting her" passed before her mind. She saw Miss Ironwood, dressed all in black, sitting with her hands folded on her knees and then someone leading her into Miss Ironwood's presence and saying, "She's come," and leaving her there.

"Damn the Dimbles!" said Jane to herself, and then unsaid it, more in fear than in remorse. And now that the life-line had been used and brought no comfort, the terror, as if insulted by her futile attempt to escape it, rushed back on her with no possibility of disguise, and she could never afterwards remember whether the horrible old man and the mantle had actually appeared to her in a dream or whether she had merely sat there, huddled and wild eyed, hoping, hoping, hoping (even praying, though she believed in no one to pray to) that they would not.

And that is why Mark found such an unexpected Jane on the door mat. It was a pity, he thought, that this should have happened on a night when he was so late and so tired and, to tell the truth, not perfectly sober.

3

"Do you feel quite all right this morning?" said Mark.

"Yes, thank you," said Jane shortly.

Mark was lying in bed and drinking a cup of tea. Jane was seated at the dressing table, partially dressed, and doing her hair. Mark's eyes rested on her with indolent, early-morning pleasure. If he guessed very little of the mal-adjustment between them, this was partly due to our race's incurable habit of "projection." We think the lamb gentle because its wool is soft to our hands: men call a woman voluptuous when she arouses voluptuous feelings in them. Jane's body, soft though firm and slim though rounded, was so exactly to Mark's mind that it was all but impossible for him not to attribute to her the same sensations which she excited in him.

"You're quite sure you're all right?" he asked again.

"Quite," said Jane more shortly still.

Jane thought she was annoyed because her hair was not going up to her liking and because Mark was fussing. She also knew, of course, that she was deeply angry with herself for the collapse which had betrayed her last night, into being what she most detested—the fluttering, tearful "little woman" of sentimental fiction running for comfort to male arms. But she thought this anger was only in the back of her mind, and had no suspicion that it was pulsing through every vein and producing at that very moment the clumsiness in her fingers which made her hair seem intractable.

"Because," continued Mark, "if you felt the least bit uncomfortable, I *could* put off going to see this man Wither."

Jane said nothing.

"If I did go," said Mark, "I'd certainly have to be away for the night, perhaps two."

Jane closed her lips a little more firmly and still said nothing.

"Supposing I did," said Mark, "you wouldn't think of asking Myrtle over to stay?"

"No thank you," said Jane emphatically, and then, "I'm quite accustomed to being alone."

"I know," said Mark in a rather defensive voice. "That's the devil of the way things are in College at present. That's one of the chief reasons I'm thinking of another job."

Jane was still silent.

"Look here, old thing," said Mark, suddenly sitting up and throwing his legs out of bed. "There's no good beating about the bush. I don't feel comfortable about going away while you're in your present state—"

"What state?" said Jane, turning round and facing him for the first time.

"Well—I mean—just a bit nervy—as anyone may be temporarily."

"Because I happened to be having a nightmare when you came home last night—or rather this morning—there's no need to talk as if I was a neurasthenic." This was not in the least what Jane had intended or expected to say.

"Now there's no good going on like that . . ." began Mark.

"Like what?" said Jane icily, and then, before he had time to reply, "If you've decided that I'm going mad you'd better get Brizeacre to come down and certify me. It would be convenient to do it while you're away. They could get me packed off while you are at Mr. Wither's without any fuss. I'm going to see about the breakfast now. If you don't shave and dress pretty quickly, you'll not be ready when Lord Feverstone calls."

The upshot of it was that Mark gave himself a very bad cut while shaving (and saw, at once, a picture of himself talking to the all-important Wither with a great blob of cotton-wool on his upper lip) while Jane decided, from a mixture of motives, to cook Mark an unusually elaborate breakfast—of which she would rather die than eat any herself—and did so with the swift efficiency of an angry woman, only to upset it all over the new stove at the last moment. They were still at the table and both pretending to read newspapers when Lord Feverstone arrived. Most unfortunately Mrs. Maggs arrived at the same moment. Mrs. Maggs was that element in Jane's economy represented by the phrase "I have a woman who comes in twice a week." Twenty years earlier Jane's mother would have addressed such a functionary as "Maggs" and been addressed by her as "Mum." But Jane and her "woman who came in" called one another Mrs. Maggs and Mrs. Studdock. They were about the same age and to a bachelor's eye there was no very noticeable difference in the clothes they wore. It was therefore perhaps not inexcusable that when Mark attempted to introduce Feverstone to his wife Feverstone should have shaken Mrs. Maggs by the hand; but it did not sweeten the last few minutes before the two men departed.

Jane left the flat under pretence of shopping almost at once. "I really couldn't stand Mrs. Maggs today," she said to herself. "She's a terrible talker." So that was Lord Feverstone—that man with the loud, unnatural laugh and the mouth like a shark, and no manners. Apparently a perfect fool too! What good could it do Mark to go about with a man like that? Jane had distrusted his face. She could always tell—there was something shifty about him. Probably he was making a fool of Mark. Mark was so easily taken in. If only he wasn't at Bracton! It was a horrible college. What did Mark see in people like Mr. Curry and the odious old clergyman with the beard? And meanwhile, what of the day that awaited her, and the night, and the next night, and beyond that—for when men say they may be away for two nights, it means that two nights is the minimum, and they hope to be away for a week. A telegram (never a trunk call) puts it all right, as far as they are concerned.

She must do something. She even thought of following Mark's advice and getting Myrtle to come and stay. But Myrtle was her sister-in-law, Mark's twin sister, with much too much of the adoring sister's attitude to the brilliant brother. She would talk about Mark's health and his shirts and socks with a continual undercurrent of unexpressed yet unmistakable astonishment at Jane's good luck in marrying him. No, certainly not Myrtle. Then she thought of going to see Dr. Brizeacre as a patient. He was a Bracton man and would therefore probably charge her nothing. But when she came to think of answering, to Brizeacre of all people, the sort of questions which Brizeacre would certainly ask, this turned out to be impossible. She must do something. In the end, somewhat to her own surprise, she found that she had decided to go out to St. Anne's and see Miss Ironwood. She thought herself a fool for doing so.

4

An observer placed at the right altitude above Edgestow that day might have seen far to the south a moving spot on a main road and later, to the east, much nearer the silver thread of the Wynd, and much more slowly moving, the smoke of a train.

The spot would have been the car which was carrying Mark Studdock towards the Blood Transfusion Office at Belbury, where the nucleus of the N.I.C.E. had taken up its temporary abode. The very size and style of the car had made a favorable impression on him the moment he saw it. The upholstery was of such quality that one felt it ought to be good to eat. And what fine, male energy (Mark felt sick of women at the moment) revealed itself in the very gestures with which Feverstone settled himself at the wheel and put his elbow on the horn, and clasped his pipe firmly between his teeth! The speed of the car, even in the narrow streets of Edgestow, was impressive, and so were the laconic criticisms of Feverstone on other drivers and pedestrians. Once over the level crossing and beyond Jane's old college (St. Elizabeth's), he began to show what his car could do. Their speed became so great that even on a rather empty road the inexcusably bad drivers, the manifestly half-witted pedestrians and men with horses, the hen that they actually ran over and the dogs and hens that Feverstone pronounced "damned lucky," seemed to follow one another almost without intermission. Telegraph posts raced by, bridges rushed overhead with a roar, villages streamed backward to join the country already devoured, and Mark, drunk with air and at once fascinated and repelled by the insolence of Feverstone's driving sat saying, "Yes," and "Quite," and "It was *their* fault," and stealing side-long glances at his companion. Certainly, he was a change from the fussy importance of Curry and the Bursar! The long, straight nose and the clenched teeth, the hard bony outlines beneath the face, the very way he wore his clothes, all spoke of a big man driving a big car to somewhere where they would find big stuff going on. And he, Mark, was to be in it all. At one or two moments when his heart came into his mouth he wondered whether the quality of Lord Feverstone's driving quite justified its speed. "You need never take a cross-road like that seriously," yelled Feverstone as they plunged on after the narrowest of these escapes. "Quite," bawled Mark. "No good making a fetish of them!" "Drive much yourself?" said Feverstone. "Used to a good deal," said Mark.

The smoke which our imaginary observer might have seen to the east of Edgestow would have indicated the train in which Jane Studdock was progressing slowly towards the village of St. Anne's. Edgestow itself, for those who had reached it from London, had all the appearance of a terminus; but if you looked about you, you might see presently, in a bay, a little train of two or three coaches and a tank engine—a train that sizzled and exuded steam from beneath the footboards and in which most of the passengers seemed to know one another. On some days, instead of the third coach, there might be a horse-box, and on the platform there would be hampers containing dead rabbits or live poultry, and men in brown bowler hats and gaiters, and perhaps a terrier or a sheepdog that seemed to be used to travelling. In this train, which started at half-past one, Jane jerked and rattled along an embankment whence she looked down through some bare branches and some branches freckled with red and yellow leaves into Bragdon Wood itself and thence through the cutting and over the level crossing at Bragdon Camp and along the edge of Brawl Park (the great house was just visible at one point) and so to the first stop at Duke's Eaton. Here, as at Woolham and Cure Hardy and Fourstones, the train settled back, when it stopped, with a little jerk and something like a sigh. And then there would be a noise of milk cans rolling and coarse boots treading on the platform and after that a pause which seemed to last long, during which the autumn sunlight grew warm on the window pane and smells of wood and field from beyond the tiny station floated in and seemed to claim the railway as part of the land. Passengers got in and out of her carriage at every stop; apple-faced men, and women with elastic-side boots and imitation fruit on their hats, and schoolboys. Jane hardly noticed them: for though she was theoretically an extreme democrat, no social class save her own had yet become a reality to her in any place except the printed page. And in between the stations things flitted past, so isolated from their context that each seemed to promise some unearthly happiness if one could but have descended from the train at that very moment to seize it: a house backed with a group of haystacks and wide brown fields about it, two aged horses standing head to tail, a little orchard with washing hanging on a line, and a rabbit staring at the train, whose two eyes looked like the dots, and his ears like the uprights, of a double exclamation mark. At quarter-past two she came to St. Anne's, which was the real terminus of the branch, and the end of everything. The air struck her as cold and tonic when she left the station.

Although the train had been chugging and wheezing up-hill for the latter half of her journey, there was still a climb to be done on foot, for St. Anne's is one of those villages perched on a hilltop which are commoner in Ireland than in England, and the station is some way from the village. A winding road between high banks led her up to it. As soon as she had passed the church she turned left, as she had been instructed, at the Saxon Cross. There were no houses on her left—only a row of beech trees and unfenced ploughland falling steeply away, and beyond that the timbered midland plain spreading as far as she could see and blue in the distance. She was on the highest ground in all that region. Presently, she came to a high wall on her right that seemed to run on for a great way: there was a door in it and beside the door an old iron bell-pull. A kind of flatness of spirit was on her. She felt sure she had come on a fool's errand; nevertheless she rang. When the jangling noise had ceased there followed a silence so long, and in that upland place so chilly, that Jane began to wonder whether the house were inhabited. Then, just as she was debating whether to ring again or to turn away, she heard the noise of someone's feet approaching briskly on the inside of the wall.

Meanwhile Lord Feverstone's car had long since arrived at Belbury—a florid Edwardian mansion which had been built for a millionaire who admired Versailles. At the sides, it seemed to have sprouted into a widespread outgrowth of newer cement buildings, which housed the Blood Transfusion Office.

3

Belbury and St. Anne's-on-the-Hill

On his way up the wide staircase Mark caught sight of himself and his companion in a mirror. Feverstone looked, as always, master of his clothes, his face, and of the whole situation. The blob of cotton wool on Mark's upper lip had been blown awry during the journey so that it looked like one-half of a fiercely up-turned false moustache and revealed a patch of blackened blood beneath it. A moment later he found himself in a big-windowed room with a blazing fire, being introduced to Mr. John Wither, Deputy Director of the N.I.C.E.

Wither was a white-haired old man with a courtly manner. His face was clean shaven and very large indeed, with watery blue eyes and something rather vague and chaotic about it. He did not appear to be giving them his whole attention and this impression must, I think, have been due to the eyes, for his actual words and gestures were polite to the point of effusiveness. He said it was a great, a very great pleasure, to welcome Mr. Studdock among them. It added to the deep obligations under which Lord Feverstone had already laid him. He hoped they had had an agreeable journey. Mr. Wither appeared to be under the impression that they had come by air and, when this was corrected, that they had come from London by train. Then he began enquiring whether Mr. Studdock found his quarters perfectly comfortable and had to be reminded that they had only that moment arrived. "I suppose," thought Mark, "the old chap is trying to put me at my ease." In fact, Mr. Wither's conversation was having precisely the opposite effect. Mark wished he would offer him a cigarette. His growing conviction that this man really knew nothing about him and even that all the well-knit schemes and promises of Feverstone were at this moment dissolving into some sort of mist, was extremely uncomfortable. At last he took his courage in both hands and endeavoured to bring Mr. Wither to the point by saying that he was still not quite clear in what capacity he would be able to assist the Institute.

"I assure you, Mr. Studdock," said the Deputy Director with an unusually far away look in his eye, "that you needn't anticipate the slightest—er—the slightest difficulty on that point. There was never any idea of circumscribing your activities and your general influence on policy, much less your relations with your colleagues and what I might call in general the terms of reference under which you would be collaborating with us, without the fullest possible consideration of your own views and, indeed, your own advice. You will find us, Mr. Studdock, if I might express myself in that way, a very happy family."

"Oh, don't misunderstand me, Sir," said Mark. "I didn't mean that at all. I only meant that I felt I should like some sort of idea of what exactly I should be doing if I came to you."

"Well now, when you speak of coming to us," said the Deputy Director, "that raises a point on which I hope there is no misunderstanding. I think we all agreed that no question of residence need be raised—I mean, at this stage. We thought, we all thought, that you should be left entirely free to carry on your work wherever you pleased. If you care to live in London or Cambridge—"

"Edgestow," prompted Lord Feverstone.

"Ah yes, Edgestow," here the Deputy Director turned round and addressed Feverstone. "I was just explaining to Mr.—er—Studdock, and I feel sure you will fully agree with me, that nothing was further from the mind of the Committee than to dictate in any way, or even to advise, where Mr.—where your friend should live. Of course, wherever he lives we should naturally place air transport and road transport at his disposal. I daresay, Lord Feverstone, you have already explained to him that he will find all questions of that sort will adjust themselves without the smallest difficulty."

"Really, Sir," said Mark, "I wasn't thinking about that at all. I

haven't—I mean I shouldn't have the smallest objection to living anywhere: I only—"

The Deputy Director interrupted him, if anything so gentle as
Wither's voice can be called an interruption. "But I assure you, Mr.—
er—I assure you, Sir, that there is not the smallest objection to your
residing wherever you may find it convenient. There was never, at any
stage, the slightest suggestion—" But here Mark, almost in desperation,
ventured to interrupt himself.

"It is the exact nature of the work," he said, "and of my qualifications for it that I wanted to get clear."

"My dear friend," said the Deputy Director, "you need not have the
slightest uneasiness in that direction. As I said before, you will find us a
very happy family, and may feel perfectly satisfied that no questions as
to your entire suitability have been agitating anyone's mind in the least.
I should not be offering you a position among us if there were the slightest danger of your not being completely welcome to all, or the least suspicion that your very valuable qualities were not fully appreciated. You
are—you are among *friends* here, Mr. Studdock. I should be the last person to advise you to connect yourself with any organisation where you
ran the risk of being exposed—er—to disagreeable personal contacts."

Mark did not ask again in so many words what the N.I.C.E. wanted
him to do; partly because he began to be afraid that he was supposed to
know this already, and partly because a perfectly direct question would
have sounded a crudity in that room—a crudity which might suddenly
exclude him from the warm and almost drugged atmosphere of vague,
yet heavily important, confidence in which he was gradually being
enfolded.

"You are very kind," he said. "The only thing I should like to get just
a little clearer is the exact—well, the exact scope of the appointment."

"Well," said Mr. Wither in a voice so low and rich that it was almost
a sigh, "I am very glad you have raised this issue now in a quite informal
way. Obviously neither you nor I would wish to commit ourselves, in
this room, in any sense which was at all injurious to the powers of the
Committee. I quite understand your motives and—er—respect them. We
are not, of course, speaking of an Appointment in the quasi-technical
sense of the term; it would be improper for both of us (though, you may
well remind me, in different ways) to do so—or at least it might lead to
certain inconveniences. But I think I can most definitely assure you that
nobody wants to force you into any kind of straight waistcoat or bed of

Procrustes. We do not really think, among ourselves, in terms of strictly demarcated functions, of course. I take it that men like you and me are—well, to put it frankly, hardly in the habit of using concepts of that type. Everyone in the Institute feels that his own work is not so much a departmental contribution to an end already defined as a moment or grade in the progressive self-definition of an organic whole."

And Mark said—God forgive him, for he was young and shy and vain and timid, all in one—"I do think that is so important. The elasticity of your organisation is one of the things that attracts me." After that, he had no further chance of bringing the Director to the point and whenever the slow, gentle voice ceased he found himself answering it in its own style, and apparently helpless to do otherwise despite the torturing recurrence of the question, "What are we both talking *about?*" At the very end of the interview there came one moment of clarity. Mr. Wither supposed that he, Mark, would find it convenient to join the N.I.C.E. club: even for the next few days he would be freer as a member than as someone's guest. Mark agreed and then flushed crimson like a small boy on learning that the easiest course was to become a life member at the cost of £200. He had not that amount in the bank. Of course if he had got the new job with its fifteen hundred a year, all would be well. But had he got it? Was there a job at all?

"How silly," he said aloud, "I haven't got my cheque book with me."

A moment later he found himself on the stairs with Feverstone.

"Well?" asked Mark eagerly. Feverstone did not seem to hear him.

"Well?" repeated Mark. "When shall I know my fate? I mean, have I got the job?"

'Hullo Guy!' bawled Feverstone suddenly to a man in the hall beneath. Next moment he had trotted down to the foot of the stairs, grasped his friend warmly by the hand, and disappeared. Mark, following him more slowly, found himself in the hall, silent, alone, and self-conscious, among the groups and pairs of chattering men, who were all crossing it towards the big folding doors on his left.

2

It seemed to last long, this standing, this wondering what to do, this effort to look natural and not to catch the eyes of strangers. The noise and the agreeable smells which came from the folding doors made it obvious that people were going to lunch. Mark hesitated, uncertain of his own status. In the end, he decided that he couldn't stand there looking like a fool any longer, and went in.

He had hoped that there would be several small tables at one of which he could have sat alone. But there was only a single long table, already so nearly filled that, after looking in vain for Feverstone, he had to sit down beside a stranger. "I suppose one sits where one likes?" he murmured as he did so; but the stranger apparently did not hear. He was a bustling sort of man who was eating very quickly and talking at the same time to his neighbour on the other side.

"That's just it," he was saying. "As I told him, it makes no difference to me which way they settle it. I've no objection to the I.J.P. people taking over the whole thing if that's what the D.D. wants but what I dislike is one man being responsible for it when half the work is being done by someone else. As I said to him, you've now got three H.D.'s all tumbling over one another about some job that could really be done by a clerk. It's becoming ridiculous. Look at what happened this morning." Conversation on these lines continued throughout the meal.

Although the food and the drinks were excellent, it was a relief to Mark when people began getting up from table. Following the general movement, he recrossed the hall and came into a large room furnished as a lounge where coffee was being served. Here at last he saw Feverstone. Indeed, it would have been difficult not to notice him for he was the centre of a group and laughing prodigiously. Mark wished to approach him, if only to find out whether he were expected to stay the night and, if so, whether a room had been assigned to him. But the knot of men round Feverstone was of that confidential kind which it is difficult to join. He moved towards one of the many tables and began turning over the glossy pages of an illustrated weekly. Every few seconds he looked up to see if there were any chance of getting a word with Feverstone alone. The fifth time he did so, he found himself looking into the face of one of his own colleagues, a Fellow of Bracton called William Hingest. The Progressive Element called him, though not to his face, Bill the Blizzard.

Hingest had not, as Curry anticipated, been present at the College Meeting and was hardly on speaking terms with Lord Feverstone. Mark realised with a certain awe that here was a man *directly* in touch with the N.I.C.E.—one who started, so to speak, at a point beyond Feverstone. Hingest, who was a physical chemist, was one of the two scientists at Bracton who had a reputation outside England. I hope the reader has not been misled into supposing that the Fellows of Bracton were a specially distinguished body. It was certainly not the intention of the Progressive Element to elect mediocrities to fellowships, but their determination to elect "sound men" cruelly limited their field of choice and, as Busby had once said, "You can't have everything." Bill the Blizzard had an old-fashioned curly moustache in which white had almost, but not completely, triumphed over yellow, a large beak-like nose, and a bald head.

"This is an unexpected pleasure," said Mark with a hint of formality. He was always a little afraid of Hingest.

"Huh?" grunted Bill. "Eh? Oh, it's you, Studdock? Didn't know they'd secured your services here."

"I was sorry not to see you at the College Meeting yesterday," said Mark.

This was a lie. The Progressive Element always found Hingest's presence an embarrassment. As a scientist—and the only really eminent scientist they had—he was their rightful property; but he was that hateful anomaly, the wrong sort of scientist. Glossop, who was a classic, was his chief friend in College. He had the air (the "affectation" Curry called it) of not attaching much importance to his own revolutionary discoveries in chemistry and of valuing himself much more on being a Hingest: the family was of almost mythical antiquity, "never contaminated," as its Nineteenth-Century historian had said, "by traitor, placeman or baronetcy." He had given particular offence on the occasion of de Broglie's visit to Edgestow. The Frenchman had spent his spare time exclusively in Bill the Blizzard's society, but when an enthusiastic junior Fellow had thrown out a feeler about the rich feast of science which the two *savants* must have shared, Bill the Blizzard had appeared to search his memory for a moment and then replied that he didn't think they had got onto that subject. "Gassing Almanac de Gotha nonsense, I suppose," was Curry's comment, though not in Hingest's presence.

"Eh? What's that? College Meeting?" said the Blizzard. "What were they talking about?"

"About the sale of Bragdon Wood."

"All nonsense," muttered the Blizzard.

"I hope you would have agreed with the decision we came to."

"It made no difference what decision they came to."

"Oh!" said Mark with some surprise.

"It was all nonsense. The N.I.C.E. would have had the Wood in any case. They had powers to compel a sale."

"What an extraordinary thing! I was given to understand they were going to Cambridge if we didn't sell."

Hingest sniffed loudly.

"Not a word of truth in it. As to its being an extraordinary thing, that depends on what you mean. There's nothing extraordinary in the Fellows of Bracton talking all afternoon about an unreal issue. And there's nothing extraordinary in the fact that the N.I.C.E. should wish, if possible, to hand over to Bracton the odium of turning the heart of England into a cross between an abortive American hotel and a glorified gas works. The only real puzzle is why the N.I.C.E. should want that bit of land."

"I suppose we shall find out as things go on."

"You may. I shan't."

"Oh?" said Mark interrogatively.

"I've had enough of it," said Hingest, lowering his voice, "I'm leaving tonight. I don't know what you were doing at Bracton, but if it was any good I'd advise you to go back and stick to it."

"Really!" said Mark. "Why do you say that?"

"Doesn't matter for an old fellow like me," said Hingest, "but they could play the devil with *you*. Of course it all depends on what a man likes."

"As a matter of fact," said Mark, "I haven't fully made up my mind." He had been taught to regard Hingest as a warped reactionary. "I don't even know yet what my job would be if I stayed."

"What's your subject?"

"Sociology."

"Huh," said Hingest. "In that case I can soon point you out the man you'd be under. A fellow called Steele. Over there by the window, do you see?"

"Perhaps you could introduce me."

"You're determined to stay then?"

"Well, I suppose I ought at least to see him."

"All right," said Hingest. "No business of mine." Then he added in a louder voice, "Steele."

Steele turned round. He was a tall, unsmiling man with that kind of face which, though long and horse-like, has nevertheless rather thick and pouting lips.

"This is Studdock," said Hingest, "the new man for your department." Then he turned away.

"Oh," said Steele. Then after a pause, "Did he say *my* department?"

"That's what he *said*," replied Mark with an attempt at a smile, "but perhaps he's got it wrong. I'm supposed to be a sociologist—if that throws any light on it."

"I'm H.D. for Sociology all right," said Steele, "but this is the first I've heard about you. Who told you you were to be there?"

"Well, as a matter of fact," said Mark, "the whole thing is rather vague. I've just had a talk with the Deputy Director but we didn't actually go into any details."

"How did you manage to see *him*?"

"Lord Feverstone introduced me."

Steele whistled. "I say, Cosser," he called out to a freckle-faced man who was passing by, "listen to this. Feverstone has just unloaded this chap on our department. Taken him straight to the D.D. without saying a word to me about it. What do you think of that?"

"Well, I'm damned!" said Cosser, hardly glancing at Mark but looking very hard at Steele.

"I'm sorry," said Mark, a little more loudly and a little more stiffly than he had yet spoken. "Don't be alarmed. I seem to have been put in rather a false position. There must have been some misunderstanding. As a matter of fact I am, at the moment, merely having a look round. I'm not at all certain that I intend to stay in any case."

Neither of the other two took any notice of this last suggestion.

"That's Feverstone all over," said Cosser to Steele.

Steele turned to Mark. "I shouldn't advise you to take much notice of what Lord Feverstone says here," he remarked. "This isn't his business at all."

"All I object to," said Mark, wishing that he could prevent his face from turning red, "is being put in a false position. I only came over as an experiment. It is a matter of indifference to me whether I take a job in the N.I.C.E. or not."

"You see," said Steele to Cosser, "there isn't really any room for a man in our show—specially for someone who doesn't know the work. Unless they put him on the U.L."

"That's right," said Cosser.

"Mr. Studdock, I think," said a new voice at Mark's elbow, a treble voice which seemed disproportionate to the huge hill of a man whom he saw when he turned his head. He recognised the speaker at once. His dark, smooth face and black hair were unmistakable, and so was the foreign accent. This was Professor Filostrato, the great physiologist, whom Mark had sat next to at a dinner about two years before. He was fat to that degree which is comic on the stage, but the effect was not funny in real life. Mark was charmed that such a man should have remembered him.

"I am very glad you have come to join us," said Filostrato taking hold of Mark's arm and gently piloting him away from Steele and Cosser.

"To tell you the truth," said Mark, "I'm not sure that I have. I was brought over by Feverstone but he has disappeared, and Steele—I'd have been in his Department I suppose—doesn't seem to know anything about me."

"Bah! Steele!" said the Professor. "That is all a bagatelle. He get too big for his boots. He will be put in his place one of these days. It may be you who will put him. I have read all your work, *si si*. Do not consider him."

"I have a strong objection to being put in a false position—" began Mark.

"Listen, my friend," interrupted Filostrato, "you must put all such ideas out of your head. The first thing to realise is that the N.I.C.E. is serious. It is nothing less than the existence of the human race that depends on our work: our *real* work, you comprehend? You will find frictions and impertinences among this *canaglia*, this rabble. They are no more to be regarded than your dislike of a brother officer when the battle is at its crisis."

"As long as I'm given something to do that is worth doing," said Mark, "I shouldn't allow anything of that sort to interfere with it."

"Yes, yes, that is right. The work is more important than you can yet understand. You will see. These Steeles and Feverstones—they are of no consequence. As long as you have the good will of the Deputy Director, you snap your fingers at them. You need listen to no one but him, you comprehend? Ah—and there is one other. Do not have the Fairy for your enemy. For the rest—you laugh at them."

"The Fairy?"

"Yes. Her they call the Fairy. Oh my God, a terrible *Inglesaccia!* She is the head of our police, the Institutional Police. *Ecco,* she come. I will present you. Miss Hardcastle, permit that I present to you Mr. Studdock."

Mark found himself writhing from the stoker's or carter's hand-grip of a big woman in a black, short-skirted uniform. Despite a bust that would have done credit to a Victorian barmaid, she was rather thickly built than fat and her iron-grey hair was cropped short. Her face was square, stern, and pale, and her voice deep. A smudge of lipstick laid on with violent inattention to the real shape of her mouth was her only concession to fashion and she rolled or chewed a long black cheroot, unlit, between her teeth. As she talked she had a habit of removing this, staring intently at the mixture of lipstick and saliva on its mangled end, and then replacing it more firmly than before. She sat down immediately in a chair close to where Mark was standing, flung her right leg over one of the arms, and fixed him with a gaze of cold intimacy.

3

Click—clack, distinct in the silence, where Jane stood waiting, came the tread of the person on the other side of the wall. Then the door opened and Jane found herself facing a tall woman of about her own age. This person looked at her with keen, non-committal eyes.

"Does a Miss Ironwood live here?" said Jane.

"Yes," said the other girl, neither opening the door any further nor standing aside.

"I want to see her, please," said Jane.

"Have you an appointment?" said the tall woman.

"Well, not exactly," said Jane. "I was directed here by Dr. Dimble who knows Miss Ironwood. He said I shouldn't need an appointment."

"Oh, if you're from Dr. Dimble that is another matter," said the woman. "Come in. Now wait a moment while I attend to this lock. That's better. Now we're all right. There's not room for two on this path so you must excuse me if I go first."

The woman led her along a brick path beside a wall on which fruit trees were growing, and then to the left along a mossy path with gooseberry bushes on each side. Then came a little lawn with a see-saw in the middle of it, and beyond that a greenhouse. Here they found themselves in the sort of hamlet that sometimes occurs in the purlieus of a large garden—walking in fact down a little street which had a barn and a stable on one side and, on the other, a second greenhouse, and a potting shed and a pigstye—inhabited, as the grunts and the not wholly agreeable smell informed her. After that were narrow paths across a vegetable garden that seemed to be on a fairly steep hillside, and then, rose bushes, all stiff and prickly in their winter garb. At one place, they were going along a path made of single planks. This reminded Jane of something. It was a very large garden. It was like—like—yes, now she had it: it was like the garden in *Peter Rabbit*. Or was it like the garden in the *Romance of the Rose*? No, not in the least like really. Or like Klingsor's garden? Or the garden in *Alice*? Or like the garden on the top of some Mesopotamian ziggurat which had probably given rise to the whole legend of Paradise? Or simply like all walled gardens? Freud said we liked gardens because they were symbols of the female body. But that must be a man's point of view. Presumably gardens meant something different in women's dreams. Or did they? Did men and women both feel interested in the female body and even, though it sounded ridiculous, in almost the same way? A sentence rose to her memory. "The beauty of the female is the root of joy to the female as well as to the male, and it is no accident that the goddess of Love is older and stronger than the god." Where on earth had she read that? And, incidentally, what frightful nonsense she had been thinking for the last minute or so! She shook off all these ideas about gardens and determined to pull herself together. A curious feeling that she was now on hostile, or at least alien, ground warned her to keep all her wits about her. At that moment, they suddenly emerged from between plantations of rhododendron and laurel, and found themselves at a small side door, flanked by a water butt, in the long wall of a large house. Just as they did so a window clapped shut upstairs.

A minute or two later Jane was sitting waiting in a large sparely furnished room with a shut stove to warm it. Most of the floor was bare, and the walls, above the waist-high wainscotting, were of greyish white plaster, so that the whole effect was faintly austere and conventual. The tall woman's tread died away in the passages and the room became very quiet when it had done so. Occasionally the cawing of rooks could be heard. "I've let myself in for it now," thought Jane. "I shall have to tell this woman that dream and she'll ask all sorts of questions." She considered herself, in general, a modern person who could talk without embarrassment of anything, but it began to look quite different as she sat in that room. All sorts of secret reservations in her programme of frankness—things which, she now realised, she had set apart as never to be told—came creeping back into consciousness. It was surprising that very few of them were connected with sex. "In dentists'," said Jane, "they at least leave illustrated papers in the waiting room." She got up and opened the one book that lay on the table in the middle of the room. Instantly her eyes lit on the following words: "The beauty of the female is the root of joy to the female as well as to the male, and it is no accident that the goddess of Love is older and stronger than the god. To desire the desiring of her own beauty is the vanity of Lilith, but to desire the enjoying of her own beauty is the obedience of Eve, and to both it is in the lover that the beloved tastes her own delightfulness. As obedience is the stairway of pleasure, so humility is the—"

At that moment the door was suddenly opened. Jane turned crimson as she shut the book and looked up. The same girl who had first let her in had apparently just opened the door and was still standing in the doorway. Jane now conceived for her that almost passionate admiration which women, more often than is supposed, feel for other women whose beauty is not of their own type. It would be nice, Jane thought, to be like that—so straight, so forthright, so valiant, so fit to be mounted on a horse, and so divinely tall.

"Is—is Miss Ironwood in?" said Jane.

"Are you Mrs. Studdock?" said the girl.

"Yes," said Jane.

"I will bring you to her at once," said the other. "We have been expecting you. My name is Camilla—Camilla Denniston."

Jane followed her. From the narrowness and plainness of the passages, Jane judged that they were still in the back parts of the house, and that, if so, it must be a very large house indeed. They went a long way before Camilla knocked at a door and stood aside for Jane to enter, after saying in a low, clear voice ("like a servant," Jane thought) "She has come." And Jane went in; and there was Miss Ironwood dressed all in black and sitting with her hands folded on her knees, just as Jane had seen her when dreaming—if she were dreaming—last night in the flat.

"Sit down, young lady," said Miss Ironwood.

The hands which were folded on her knees were very big and bony though they did not suggest coarseness, and even when seated Miss Ironwood was extremely tall. Everything about her was big—the nose, the unsmiling lips, and the grey eyes. She was perhaps nearer sixty than fifty. There was an atmosphere in the room which Jane found uncongenial.

"What is your name, young lady?" said Miss Ironwood, taking up a pencil and a notebook.

"Jane Studdock."

"Are you married?"

"Yes."

"Does your husband know you have come to us?"

"No."

"And your age, if you please?"

"Twenty-three."

"And now," said Miss Ironwood, "what have you to tell me?"

Jane took a deep breath. "I've been having bad dreams and—and feeling depressed lately," she said.

"What were the dreams?" asked Miss Ironwood.

Jane's narrative—she did not do it very well—took some time. While she was speaking she kept her eyes fixed on Miss Ironwood's large hands and her black skirt and the pencil and the notebook. And that was why she suddenly stopped. For as she proceeded she saw Miss Ironwood's hand cease to write and the fingers wrap themselves round the pencil: immensely strong fingers they seemed. And every moment they tightened, till the knuckles grew white and the veins stood out on the backs of the hands and at last, as if under the influence of some stifled emotion, they broke the pencil in two. It was then that Jane stopped in astonishment and looked up at Miss Ironwood's face. The wide grey eyes were still looking at her with no change of expression.

"Pray continue, young lady," said Miss Ironwood.

Jane resumed her story. When she had finished Miss Ironwood put a number of questions. After that she became silent for so long that Jane said,

"Is there, do you think, anything very seriously wrong with me?"

"There is nothing wrong with you," said Miss Ironwood.

"You mean it will go away?"

"I have no means of telling. I should say probably not."

Disappointment shadowed Jane's face.

"Then—can't anything be done about it? They were horrible dreams—horribly vivid, not like dreams at all."

"I can quite understand that."

"Is it something that can't be cured?"

"The reason you cannot be cured is that you are not ill."

"But there must be something wrong. It's surely not natural to have dreams like that."

There was a pause. "I think," said Miss Ironwood, "I had better tell you the whole truth."

"Yes, do," said Jane in a strained voice. The other's words had frightened her.

"And I will begin by saying this," continued Miss Ironwood. "You are a more important person than you imagine."

Jane said nothing, but thought inwardly, "She is humouring me. She thinks I am mad."

"What was your maiden name?" asked Miss Ironwood.

"Tudor," said Jane. At any other moment she would have said it rather self-consciously, for she was very anxious not to be supposed vain of her ancient ancestry.

"The Warwickshire branch of the family?"

"Yes."

"Did you ever read a little book—it is only forty pages long—written by an ancestor of yours about the battle of Worcester?"

"No. Father had a copy—the only copy, I think he said. But I never read it. It was lost when the house was broken up after his death."

"Your father was mistaken in thinking it the only copy. There are at least two others: one is in America, and the other is in this house."

"Well?"

"Your ancestor gave a full and, on the whole, correct account of the battle, which he says he completed on the same day on which it was fought. But he was not at it. He was in York at the time."

Jane, who had not really been following this, looked at Miss Ironwood.

"If he was speaking the truth," said Miss Ironwood, "and we believe that he was, he dreamed it. Do you understand?"

"Dreamed about the battle?"

"Yes. But dreamed it right. He saw the real battle in his dream."

"I don't see the connection."

"Vision—the power of dreaming realities—is sometimes hereditary," said Miss Ironwood.

Something seemed to be interfering with Jane's breathing. She felt a sense of injury—this was just the sort of thing she hated: something out of the past, something irrational and utterly uncalled for, coming up from its den and interfering with her.

"Can it be proved?" she asked. "I mean, we have only his word for it."

"We have your dreams," said Miss Ironwood. Her voice, always grave, had become stern. A fantastic thought crossed Jane's mind. Could this old woman have some idea that one ought not to call even one's remote ancestors liars?

"My dreams?" she said a little sharply.

"Yes," said Miss Ironwood.

"What do you mean?"

"My opinion is that you have seen real things in your dreams. You have seen Alcasan as he really sat in the condemned cell, and you have seen a visitor whom he really had."

"But—but—oh, this is ridiculous," said Jane. "*That* part was a mere coincidence. The rest was just a nightmare. It was all impossible. He screwed off his head, I tell you. And they—dug up the horrible old man. They made him come to life."

"There are some confusions there, no doubt. But in my opinion there are realities behind even those episodes."

"I am afraid I don't believe in that sort of thing," said Jane coldly.

"Your upbringing makes it natural that you should not," replied Miss Ironwood. "Unless, or course, you have discovered for yourself that you have a tendency to dream real things."

Jane thought of the book on the table which she had apparently remembered before she saw it, and then there was Miss Ironwood's own appearance—that too she had seen before she saw it. But it must be non-sense.

"Can you then do nothing for me?"

"I can tell you the truth," said Miss Ironwood. "I have tried to do so."

"I mean, can you not stop it—cure it?"

"Vision is not a disease."

"But I don't *want* it," said Jane passionately. "I must stop it. I hate this sort of thing." Miss Ironwood said nothing.

"Don't you even know anyone who could stop it?" said Jane. "Can't you recommend anyone?"

"If you go to an ordinary psychotherapist," said Miss Ironwood, "he will proceed on the assumption that the dreams merely reflect your own sub-conscious. He would try to treat you. I do not know what would be the results of treatment based on that assumption. I am afraid they might be very serious. And—it would certainly not remove the dreams."

"But what is this all about?" said Jane. "I want to lead an ordinary life. I want to do my own work. It's unbearable! Why should I be selected for this horrible thing?"

"The answer to that is known only to authorities much higher than myself."

There was a short silence. Jane made a vague movement and said, rather sulkily, "Well, if you can do nothing for me, perhaps I'd better be going—" Then suddenly she added, "But how can you *know* all this? I mean—what realities are you talking about?"

"I think," said Miss Ironwood, "that you yourself have probably more reason to suspect the truth of your dreams than you have yet told me. If not, you soon will have. In the meantime, I will answer your question. We know your dreams to be partly true because they fit in with information we already possess. It was because he saw their importance that Dr. Dimble sent you to us."

"Do you mean he sent me here not to be cured but to give information?" said Jane. The idea fitted in with things she had observed in his manner when she first told him.

"Exactly."

"I wish I had known that a little earlier," said Jane coldly, and now definitely getting up to go. "I'm afraid it has been a misunderstanding. I had imagined Dr. Dimble was trying to help me."

"He was. But he was also trying to do something more important at the same time."

"I suppose I should be grateful for being considered at all," said Jane drily, "and how, exactly, was I to be helped by—by all this sort of thing?" The attempt at icy irony collapsed as she said these last words and red, undisguised anger rushed back into her face. In some ways she was very young.

"Young lady," said Miss Ironwood, "you do not at all realise the seriousness of this matter. The things you have seen concern something compared with which the happiness, or even the life, of you and me, *is* of no importance. I must beg you to face the situation. You cannot get rid of your gift. You can try to suppress it, but you will fail, and you will be very badly frightened. On the other hand, you can put it at our disposal. If you do so, you will be much less frightened in the long run and you will be helping to save the human race from a very great disaster. Or thirdly, you may tell someone else about it. If you do that, I warn you that you will almost certainly fall into the hands of other people who are at least as anxious as we to make use of your faculty and who will care no more about your life and happiness than about those of a fly. The people you have seen in your dreams are real people. It is not at all unlikely that they know you have, involuntarily, been spying on them. And, if so, they will not rest till they have got hold of you. I would advise you, even for your own sake, to join our side."

"You keep on talking of *We* and *Us*. Are you some kind of company?"

"Yes. You may call it a company."

Jane had been standing for the last few minutes; and she had almost been believing what she heard. Then suddenly, all her repugnance came over her again—all her wounded vanity, her resentment of the meaningless complication in which she seemed to be caught, and her general dislike of the mysterious and the unfamiliar. At that moment, nothing seemed to matter but to get out of that room and away from the grave, patient voice of Miss Ironwood. "She's made me worse already," thought Jane, still regarding herself as a patient. Aloud, she said,

"I must go home now. I don't know what you are talking about. I don't want to have anything to do with it."

4

Mark discovered in the end that he was expected to stay, at least for the night, and when he went up to dress for dinner he was feeling more cheerful. This was partly due to a whisky and soda taken with "Fairy" Hardcastle immediately before and partly to the fact that by a glance at the mirror he saw that he could now remove the objectionable piece of cotton wool from his lip. The bedroom with its bright fire and its private bathroom attached had also something to do with it. Thank goodness, he had allowed Jane to talk him into buying that new dress suit! It looked very well, laid out on the bed; and he saw now that the old one really would not have done. But what had reassured him most of all was his conversation with the Fairy.

It would be misleading to say that he liked her. She had indeed excited in him all the distaste which a young man feels at the proximity of something rankly, even insolently sexed, and at the same time wholly unattractive. And something in her cold eye had told him that she was well aware of this reaction and found it amusing. She had told him a good many smoking-room stories. Often before now Mark had shuddered at the clumsy efforts of the emancipated female to indulge in this kind of humour, but his shudders had always been consoled by a sense of superiority. This time he had the feeling that he was the butt; this woman was exasperating male prudery for her diversion. Later on, she drifted into police reminiscences. In spite of some initial scepticism, Mark was gradually horrified by her assumption that about thirty per cent of our murder trials ended by the hanging of an innocent man. There were details, too, about the execution shed which had not occurred to him before.

All this was disagreeable. But it was made up for by the deliciously esoteric character of the conversation. Several times that day he had been made to feel himself an outsider; that feeling completely disappeared while Miss Hardcastle was talking to him. He had the sense of getting *in*. Miss Hardcastle had apparently lived an exciting life. She had been, at different times, a suffragette, a pacifist, and a British Fascist. She had been manhandled by the police and imprisoned. On the other hand, she had met Prime Ministers, Dictators, and famous film stars; all her history was secret history. She knew from both ends what a police force could do and what it could not, and there were in her opinion very few things it could not do. "Specially now," she said. "Here in the Institute, we're backing the crusade against Red Tape."

Mark gathered that, for the Fairy, the police side of the Institute was the really important side. It existed to relieve the ordinary executive of what might be called all sanitary cases—a category which ranged from vaccination to charges of unnatural vice—from which, as she pointed out, it was only a step to bringing in all cases of blackmail. As regards crime in general, they had already popularised in the press the idea that the Institute should be allowed to experiment pretty largely in the hope of discovering how far humane, remedial treatment could be substituted for the old notion of "retributive" or "vindictive" punishment. That was where a lot of legal Red Tape stood in their way. "But there are only two papers we don't control," said the Fairy. "And we'll smash them. You've got to get the ordinary man into the state in which he says 'Sadism' automatically when he hears the word Punishment." And then one would have *carte blanche*. Mark did not immediately follow this. But the Fairy pointed out that what had hampered every English police force up to date was precisely the idea of deserved punishment. For desert was always finite: you could do so much to the criminal and no more. Remedial treatment, on the other hand, need have no fixed limit; it could go on till it had effected a cure, and those who were carrying it out would decide when *that* was. And if cure were humane and desirable, how much more prevention? Soon anyone who had ever been in the hands of the police at all would come under the control of the N.I.C.E.; in the end, every citizen. "And that's where you and I come in, Sonny," added the Fairy, tapping Mark's chest with her forefinger. "There's no distinction in the long run between police work and sociology. You and I've got to work hand in hand."

This had brought Mark back to his doubts as to whether he were really being given a job and, if so, what it was. The Fairy had warned him that Steele was a dangerous man. "There are two people you want to be very cautious about," she said. "One is Frost and the other is old Wither." But she had laughed at his fears in general. "You're in all right, Sonny," she said. "Only don't be too particular about what exactly you've got to do. You'll find out as it comes along. Wither doesn't like people who try to pin him down. There's no good saying you've come here to do *this* and you won't do *that*. The game's too fast just at present for that sort of thing. You've got to make yourself useful. And don't believe everything you're told."

At dinner Mark found himself seated next to Hingest.

"Well," said Hingest, "have they finally roped you into it, eh?"

"I rather believe they have," said Mark.

"Because," said Hingest, "if you thought the better of it, I'm motoring back tonight and I could give you a lift."

"You haven't yet told me why you are leaving us yourself," said Mark.

"Oh well, it all depends what a man likes. If you enjoy the society of that Italian eunuch and the mad parson and that Hardcastle girl—her grandmother would have boxed her ears if she were alive—of course, there's nothing more to be said."

"I suppose it's hardly to be judged on purely social grounds—I mean, it's something more than a club."

"Eh? Judged? Never judged anything in my life, to the best of my knowledge, except at a flower show. It's all a question of taste. I came here because I thought it had something to do with science. Now that I find it's something more like a political conspiracy, I shall go home. I'm too old for that kind of thing, and if I wanted to join a conspiracy, this one wouldn't be my choice."

"You mean, I suppose, that the element of social planning doesn't appeal to you? I can quite understand that it doesn't fit in with your work as it does with sciences like Sociology, but—"

"There *are* no sciences like Sociology. And if I found chemistry beginning to fit in with a secret police run by a middle-aged virago who doesn't wear corsets and a scheme for taking away his farm and his shop and his children from every Englishman, I'd let chemistry go to the devil and take up gardening again."

"I think I *do* understand the sentiment that still attaches to the small man, but when you come to study the reality as I have to do—"

"I should want to pull it to bits and put something else in its place. Of course. That's what happens when you study men: you find mare's nests. I happen to believe that you can't study men; you can only get to know them, which is quite a different thing. Because you study them, you want to make the lower orders govern the country and listen to classical music, which is balderdash. You also want to take away from them everything which makes life worth living and not only from them but from everyone except a parcel of prigs and professors."

"Bill!" said Fairy Hardcastle suddenly, from the far side of the table, in a voice so loud that even he could not ignore it. Hingest fixed his eyes upon her and his face grew a dark red.

"Is it true," bawled the Fairy, "that you're going off by car immediately after dinner?"

"Yes, Miss Hardcastle, it is."

"I was wondering if you could give me a lift."

"I should be happy to do so," said Hingest in a voice not intended to deceive, "if we are going in the same direction."

"Where are you going?"

"I am going to Edgestow."

"Will you be passing Brenstock?"

"No. I leave the by-pass at the crossroads just beyond Lord Holywood's front gate and go down what they used to call Potter's Lane."

"Oh, damn! No good to me. I may as well wait till the morning."

After this Mark found himself engaged by his left hand neighbour and did not see Bill the Blizzard again until he met him in the hall after dinner. He was in his overcoat and just ready to go to his car.

He began talking as he opened the door and thus Mark was drawn into accompanying him across the gravel sweep to where his car was parked.

"Take my advice, Studdock," he said. "Or at least think it over. I don't believe in Sociology myself, but you've got quite a decent career before you if you stay at Bracton. You'll do yourself no good by getting mixed up with the N.I.C.E.—and, by God, you'll do nobody else any good either."

"I suppose there are two views about everything," said Mark.

"Eh? Two views? There are a dozen views about everything until you know the answer. Then there's never more than one. But it's no affair of mine. Good night."

"Good night, Hingest," said Mark. The other started up the car and drove off.

There was a touch of frost in the air. The shoulder of Orion, though Mark did not know even that earnest constellation, flamed at him above the tree-tops. He felt a hesitation about going back into the house. It might mean further talk with interesting and influential people; but it might also mean feeling once more an outsider, hanging about and watching conversations which he could not join. Anyway, he was tired. Strolling along the front of the house he came presently to another and smaller door by which, he judged, one could enter without passing through the hall or the public rooms. He did so, and went upstairs for the night immediately.

5

Camilla Denniston showed Jane out—not by the little door in the wall at which she had come in but by the main gate which opened on the same road about a hundred yards further on. Yellow light from a westward gap in the grey sky was pouring a short-lived and chilly brightness over the whole landscape. Jane had been ashamed to show either temper or anxiety before Camilla; as a result both had in reality been diminished when she said goodbye. But a settled distaste for what she called, "all this nonsense," remained. She was not indeed sure that it was nonsense; but she had already resolved to treat it as if it were. She would not get "mixed up in it," would not be drawn in. One had to live one's own life. To avoid entanglements and interferences had long been one of her first principles. Even when she had discovered that she was going to marry Mark if he asked her, the thought, "But I must still keep up my own life," had arisen at once and had never for more than a few minutes at a stretch been absent from her mind. Some resentment against love itself, and therefore against Mark, for thus invading her life, remained. She was at least very vividly aware how much a woman gives up in getting married. Mark seemed to her insufficiently aware of this. Though she did not formulate it, this fear of being invaded and entangled was the deepest ground of her determination not to have a child—or not for a long time yet. One had one's own life to live.

Almost as soon as she got back to the flat the telephone went. "Is that you, Jane?" came a voice. "It's me, Margaret Dimble. Such a dreadful thing's happened. I'll tell you when I come. I'm too angry to speak at the moment. Have you a spare bed by any chance? What? Mr. Studdock's away? Not a bit, if *you* don't mind. I've sent Cecil to sleep in College. You're sure it won't be a nuisance? Thanks most awfully. I'll be round in half an hour."

4

The Liquidation of Anachronisms

I

Almost before Jane had finished putting clean sheets on Mark's bed, Mrs. Dimble, with a great many parcels, arrived. "You're an angel to have me for the night," she said. "We'd tried every hotel in Edgestow, I believe. This place is going to become unendurable. The same answer everywhere! All full up with the hangers-on and camp-followers of this detestable N.I.C.E. Secretaries here—typists there—commissioners of works—the thing's outrageous. If Cecil hadn't had a room in College I really believe he'd have had to sleep in the waiting room at the station. I only hope that man in College has aired the bed."

"But what on earth's happened?" asked Jane.

"Turned out, my dear!"

"But it isn't possible, Mrs. Dimble. I mean, it can't be legal."

"That's what Cecil said . . . Just think of it, Jane. The first thing we saw when we poked our heads out of the window this morning was a lorry on the drive with its back wheels in the middle of the rose bed, unloading a small army of what looked like criminals, with picks and spades. Right in our own garden! There was an odious little man in a peaked cap who talked to Cecil with a cigarette in his mouth, at least it wasn't in his mouth but seccotined onto his upper lip—you know—and guess what he said? He said they'd have no objection to our remaining in possession (of the *house,* mind you, not the garden) till 8 o'clock tomorrow morning. No objection!"

"But surely—surely—it must be some mistake."

"Of course, Cecil rang up your Bursar. And, of course, your Bursar was out. That took nearly all morning, ringing up again and again, and by that time, the big beech that you used to be so fond of had been cut down, and all the plum trees. If I hadn't been so angry, I'd have sat down and cried my eyes out. That's what I felt like. At last Cecil did get onto your Mr. Busby, who was perfectly useless. Said there must be some misunderstanding but it was out of his hands now and we'd better get onto the N.I.C.E. at Belbury. Of course, it turned out to be quite impossible to get *them.* But by lunchtime we saw that one simply *couldn't* stay there for the night, whatever happened."

"Why not?"

"My dear, you've no conception what it was like. Great lorries and traction engines roaring past all the time, and a crane on a thing like a railway truck. Why, our own tradesmen couldn't get through it. The milk didn't arrive till eleven o'clock. The meat never arrived at all; they rang up in the afternoon to say their people hadn't been able to reach us by either road. We'd the greatest difficulty in getting into town ourselves. It took us half an hour from our house to the bridge. It was like a nightmare. Flares and noise everywhere and the road practically ruined and a sort of great tin camp already going up on the Common. And the people! Such horrid men. I didn't know we *had* workpeople like that in England. Oh, horrible, horrible!" Mrs. Dimble fanned herself with the hat she had just taken off.

"And what are you going to do?" asked Jane.

"Heaven knows!" said Mrs. Dimble. "For the moment, we have shut up the house and Cecil has been at Rumbold, the solicitor's, to see if we can at least have it sealed and left alone until we've got our things out of it. Rumbold doesn't seem to know where he is. He keeps on saying the N.I.C.E. are in a very peculiar position legally. After that, I'm sure I don't know. As far as I can see, there won't be *any* houses in Edgestow. There's no question of trying to live on the far side of the river any longer, even if they'd let us. What did you say? Oh, indescribable. All the poplars are going down. All those nice little cottages by the church are going down. I found poor Ivy—that's your Mrs. Maggs, you know—in tears. Poor things! They do look dreadful when they cry on top of powder. She's being turned out too. Poor little woman; she's had enough troubles in her life without this. I was glad to get away. The men were so horrible. Three big brutes came to the back door asking for hot water and went on so that they frightened Martha out of her wits and Cecil had to go and speak to them. I thought they were going to strike Cecil, really I did. It was most horribly unpleasant. But a sort of special constable sent them away. What? Oh yes, there are dozens of what look like policemen all over the place, and I didn't like the look of *them* either. Swinging some kind of truncheon things, like what you'd see in an American film. Do you know, Jane, Cecil and I both thought the same thing: we thought, it's almost as if we'd lost the war. Oh, good girl—tea! That's just what I wanted."

"You must stay here as long as you like, Mrs. Dimble," said Jane. "Mark'll just have to sleep in College."

"Well, really," said Mother Dimble, "I feel at the moment that no Fellow of Bracton ought to be allowed to sleep anywhere! But I'd make an exception in favour of Mr. Studdock. As a matter of fact, I shan't have to behave like the sword of Siegfried—and, incidentally, a nasty fat stodgy sword I should be! But that side of it is all fixed up. Cecil and I are to go out to the Manor at St. Anne's. We have to be there so much at present, you see."

"Oh," said Jane, involuntarily prolonging the exclamation as the whole of her own story flowed back on her mind.

"Why, what a selfish pig I've been," said Mother Dimble. "Here have I been chattering away about my own troubles and quite forgetting that you've been out there and are full of things to tell me. Did you see Grace? And did you like her?"

"Is 'Grace' Miss Ironwood?" asked Jane.

"Yes."

"I saw her. I don't know if I liked her or not. But I don't want to talk about all that. I can't think about anything except this outrageous business of yours. It's you who are the real martyr, not me."

"No, my dear," said Mrs. Dimble, "I'm not a martyr. I'm only an angry old woman with sore feet and a splitting head (but that's beginning to be better) who's trying to talk herself into a good temper. After all, Cecil and I haven't lost our livelihood as poor Ivy Maggs has. It doesn't *really* matter leaving the old house. Do you know, the pleasure of living there was in a way a melancholy pleasure. (I wonder, by the bye, do human beings really *like* being happy?) A little melancholy, yes. All those big upper rooms which we thought we should want because we thought we were going to have lots of children, and then we never had. Perhaps I was getting too fond of mooning about them on long afternoons when Cecil was away. Pitying oneself. I shall be better away from it, I daresay. I might have got like that frightful woman in Ibsen who was always maundering about dolls. It's really worse for Cecil. He did so love having all his pupils about the place. Jane, that's the third time you've yawned. You're dropping asleep and I've talked your head off. It comes of being married thirty years. Husbands were made to be talked to. It helps them to concentrate their minds on what they're reading— like the sound of a weir. There!—you're yawning again."

Jane found Mother Dimble an embarrassing person to share a room with because she said prayers. It was quite extraordinary, Jane thought, how this put one out. One didn't know where to look, and it was so difficult to talk naturally again for several minutes after Mrs. Dimble had risen from her knees.

2

"Are you awake now?" said Mrs. Dimble's voice, quietly, in the middle of the night.

"Yes," said Jane. "I'm sorry. Did I wake you up? Was I shouting?"

"Yes. You were shouting out about someone being hit on the head."

"I saw them killing a man—a man in a big car driving along a country road. Then he came to a crossroads and turned off to the right past some trees, and there was someone standing in the middle of the road waving a light to stop him. I couldn't hear what they said; I was too far away. They must have persuaded him to get out of the car somehow, and there he was talking to one of them. The light fell full on his face. He wasn't the same old man I saw in my other dream. He hadn't a beard, only a moustache. And he had a very quick, kind of proud, way. He didn't like what the man said to him and presently he put up his fists and knocked him down. Another man behind him tried to hit him on the head with something but the old man was too quick and turned round in time. Then it was rather horrible, but rather fine. There were three of them at him and he was fighting them all. I've read about that kind of thing in books but I never realised how one would feel about it. Of course, they got him in the end. They beat his head about terribly with the things in their hands. They were quite cool about it and stooped down to examine him and make sure he was really dead. The light from the lantern seemed all funny. It looked as if it made long uprights of light—sort of rods—all round the place. But perhaps I was waking up by then. No thanks, I'm all right. It was horrid, of course, but I'm not really frightened—not the way I would have been before. I'm more sorry for the old man."

"You feel you can go to sleep again?"

"Oh rather! Is your headache better, Mrs. Dimble?"

"Quite gone, thank you. Good night."

3

"Without a doubt," thought Mark, "this must be the Mad Parson that Bill the Blizzard was talking of." The Committee at Belbury did not meet till ten-thirty, and ever since breakfast he had been walking with the Reverend Straik in the garden, despite the raw and misty weather of the morning. At the very moment when the man had first buttonholed him, the threadbare clothes and clumsy boots, the frayed clerical collar, the dark, lean, tragic face, gashed and ill-shaved and seamed, and the bitter sincerity of his manner, had struck a discordant note. It was not a type Mark had expected to meet in the N.I.C.E.

"Do not imagine," said Mr. Straik, "that I indulge in any dreams of carrying out our programme without violence. There will be resistance. They will gnaw their tongues and not repent. We are not to be deterred. We face these disorders with a firmness which will lead traducers to say that we have desired them. Let them say so. In a sense we have. It is no part of our witness to preserve that organisation of ordered sin which is called Society. To that organisation the message which we have to deliver is a message of absolute despair."

"Now that is what I meant," said Mark, "when I said that your point of view and mine must, in the long run, be incompatible. The preservation, which involves the thorough planning, of Society is just precisely the end I have in view. I do not think there is or can be any other end. The problem is quite different for you because you look forward to something else, something better than human society, in some other world."

"With every thought and vibration of my heart, with every drop of my blood," said Mr. Straik, "I repudiate that damnable doctrine. That is precisely the subterfuge by which the World, the organization and body of Death, has sidetracked and emasculated the teaching of Jesus, and turned into priestcraft and mysticism the plain demand of the Lord for righteousness and judgment here and now. The Kingdom of God is to be realised here—in this world. And it will be. At the name of Jesus every knee shall bow. In that name I dissociate myself completely from all the organised religion that has yet been seen in the world."

And at the name of Jesus, Mark, who would have lectured on abortion or perversion to an audience of young women without a qualm, felt himself so embarrassed that he knew his cheeks were slightly reddening; and he became so angry with himself and Mr. Straik at this discovery that they then proceeded to redden very much indeed. This was exactly the kind of conversation he could not endure; and never since the well remembered misery of scripture lessons at school had he felt so uncomfortable. He muttered something about his ignorance of theology.

"Theology!" said Mr. Straik with profound contempt. "It's not theology I'm talking about, young man, but the Lord Jesus. Theology is talk—eyewash—a smoke screen—a game for rich men. It wasn't in lecture rooms I found the Lord Jesus. It was in the coal pits, and beside the coffin of my daughter. If they think that Theology is a sort of cotton wool which will keep them safe in the great and terrible day, they'll find their mistake. For, mark my words, this thing is going to happen. The Kingdom is going to arrive: in this world: in this country. The powers of science are an instrument. An irresistible instrument, as all of us in the N.I.C.E. know. And why are they an irresistible instrument?"

"Because science is based on observation," suggested Mark.

"They are an irresistible instrument," shouted Straik, "because they are an instrument in His hand. An instrument of judgment as well as of healing. That is what I couldn't get any of the Churches to see. They are blinded. Blinded by their filthy rags of humanism, their culture and humanitarianism and liberalism, as well as by their sins, or what they think their sins, though they are really the least sinful thing about them. That is why I have come to stand alone: a poor, weak, unworthy man, but the only prophet left. I knew that He was coming in power. And therefore, where we see power, we see the sign of His coming. And that is why I find myself joining with communists and materialists and anyone else who is really ready to expedite the coming. The feeblest of these people here has the tragic sense of life, the ruthlessness, the total commitment, the readiness to sacrifice all merely human values, which I could not find amid all the nauseating cant of the organised religions."

"You mean, do you," said Mark, "that as far as immediate practice is concerned, there are no limits to your co-operation with the programme?"

"Sweep away all idea of co-operation!" said the other. "Does clay *co-operate* with the potter? Did Cyrus *co-operate* with the Lord? These people will be used. I shall be used too. Instruments. Vehicles. But here comes the point that concerns you, young man. You have no choice whether you will be used or not. There is no turning back once you have set your hand to the plough. No one goes *out* of the N.I.C.E. Those who try to turn back will perish in the wilderness. But the question is, whether you are content to be one of the instruments which is thrown aside when it has served His turn—one which having executed judgment on others, is reserved for judgment itself—or will you be among those who enter on the inheritance? For it's all true, you know. It is the Saints who are going to inherit the Earth—here in England, perhaps within the next twelve months—the Saints and no one else. Know you not that we shall judge angels?" Then, suddenly lowering his voice, Straik added: "The *real* resurrection is even now taking place. The real life everlasting. Here in this world. You will see it."

"I say," said Mark, "it's nearly twenty past. Oughtn't we to be going to the Committee?"

Straik turned with him in silence. Partly to avoid further conversation along the same lines, and partly because he really wanted to know the answer, Mark said presently, "A rather annoying thing has happened. I've lost my wallet. There wasn't much money in it—only about three pounds. But there were letters and things, and it's a nuisance. Ought I to tell someone about it?"

"You could tell the Steward," said Straik.

4

The Committee sat for about two hours and the Deputy Director was in the chair. His method of conducting business was slow and involved and to Mark, with his Bracton experience to guide him, it soon became obvious that the real work of the N.I.C.E. must go on somewhere else. This, indeed, was what he had expected, and he was too reasonable to suppose that he should find himself, at this early stage, in the Inner Ring or whatever at Belbury corresponded to the Progressive Element at Bracton. But he hoped he would not be kept marking time on phantom committees for too long. This morning the business mainly concerned the details of the work which had already begun at Edgestow. The N.I.C.E. had apparently won some sort of victory which gave it the right to pull down the little Norman church at the corner. "The usual objections were, of course, tabled," said Wither. Mark, who was not interested in architecture and who did not know the other side of the Wynd nearly so well as his wife, allowed his attention to wander. It was only at the end of the meeting that Wither opened a much more sensational subject. He believed that most of those present had already heard ("Why do chairmen always begin that way?" thought Mark) the very distressing piece of news which it was, nevertheless, his duty now to communicate to them in a semi-official manner. He was referring, of course, to the murder of William Hingest. As far as Mark could discover from the chairman's tortuous and allusive narrative, Bill the Blizzard had been discovered with his head beaten in by some blunt instrument, lying near his car in Potter's Lane at about four o'clock that morning. He had been dead for several hours. Mr. Wither ventured to suppose that it would be a melancholy pleasure to the committee to know that the N.I.C.E. police had been on the scene of the crime before five and that neither the local authorities nor Scotland Yard were making any objections to the fullest collaboration. He felt that if the occasion were more appropriate he would have welcomed a motion for some expression of the gratitude they must all feel to Miss Hardcastle and possibly of congratulations to her on the smooth interaction between her own forces and those of the state. This was a most gratifying feature in the sad story and, he suggested, a good omen for the future. Some decently subdued applause went round the table at this. Mr. Wither then proceeded to speak at some length about the dead man. They had all much regretted Mr. Hingest's resolution to withdraw from the N.I.C.E., while fully appreciating his motives; they had all felt that this official severance would not in the least alter the cordial relations which existed between the deceased and almost all—he thought he could even say all without exception—of his former colleagues in the Institute. The obituary (in Raleigh's fine phrase) was an instrument which the Deputy Director's talents well fitted him to play, and he spoke at great length. He concluded by suggesting that they should all stand in silence for one minute as a token of respect for the memory of William Hingest.

And they did—a world-without-end minute in which odd creakings and breathings became audible, and behind the mask of each glazed and tight-lipped face, shy, irrelevant thoughts of this and that came creeping out as birds and mice creep out again in the clearing of a wood when the picnickers have gone, and everyone silently assured himself that he, at least, was not being morbid and not thinking about death.

Then there was a stir and a bustle and the Committee broke up.

5

The whole process of getting up and doing the "morning jobs" was more cheerful, Jane found, because she had Mrs. Dimble with her. Mark often helped; but as he always took the view—and Jane could feel it even if he did not express it in words—that "anything would do" and that Jane made a lot of unnecessary work and that men could keep house with a tithe of the fuss and trouble which women made about it, Mark's help was one of the commonest causes of quarrels between them. Mrs. Dimble, on the other hand, fell in with her ways. It was a bright sunny morning and as they sat down to breakfast in the kitchen Jane was feeling bright herself. During the night her mind had evolved a comfortable theory that the mere fact of having seen Miss Ironwood and "had it all out" would probably stop the dreams altogether. The episode would be closed. And now—there was all the exciting possibility of Mark's new job to look forward to. She began to see pictures in her mind.

Mrs. Dimble was anxious to know what had happened to Jane at St. Anne's and when she was going there again. Jane answered evasively on the first question and Mrs. Dimble was too polite to press it. As to the second, Jane thought she wouldn't "bother" Miss Ironwood again, or wouldn't "bother" any further about the dreams. She said she had been "silly" but felt sure she'd be all right now. And she glanced at the clock and wondered why Mrs. Maggs hadn't yet turned up.

"My dear, I'm afraid you've lost Ivy Maggs," said Mrs. Dimble. "Didn't I tell you they'd taken her house too? I thought you'd understand she wouldn't be coming to you in the future. You see there's nowhere for her to live in Edgestow."

"Bother!" said Jane, and added, without much interest in the reply, "What is she doing, do you know?"

"She's gone out to St. Anne's."

"Has she got friends there?"

"She's gone to the Manor, along with Cecil and me."

"Do you mean she's got a job there?"

"Well, yes. I suppose it is a job."

Mrs. Dimble left at about eleven. She also, it appeared, was going to St. Anne's, but was first to meet her husband and lunch with him at Northumberland. Jane walked down to the town with her to do a little shopping and they parted at the bottom of Market Street. It was just after this that Jane met Mr. Curry.

"Have you heard the news, Mrs. Studdock?" said Curry. His manner was always important and his tone always vaguely confidential, but this morning they seemed more so than usual.

"No. What's wrong?" said Jane. She thought Mr. Curry a pompous fool and Mark a fool for being impressed by him. But as soon as Curry began speaking, her face showed all the wonder and consternation he could have wished. Nor were they, this time, feigned. He told her that Mr. Hingest had been murdered, sometime during the night, or in the small hours of that morning. The body had been found lying beside his car, in Potter's Lane, badly beaten about the head. He had been driving from Belbury to Edgestow. Curry was at the moment hastening back to college to talk to the Warden about it; he had just been at the police station. One saw that the murder had already become Curry's property. The "matter" was, in some indefinable sense, "in his hands," and he was heavy with responsibility. At another time Jane would have found this amusing. She escaped from him as soon as possible and went into Blackie's for a cup of coffee. She felt she must sit down.

The death of Hingest in itself meant nothing to her. She had met him only once and she had accepted from Mark the view that he was a disagreeable old man and rather a snob. But the certainty that she herself in her dream had witnessed a real murder shattered at one blow all the consoling pretences with which she had begun the morning. It came over her with sickening clarity that the affair of her dreams, far from being ended, was only beginning. The bright, narrow little life which she had proposed to live was being irremediably broken into. Windows into huge, dark landscapes were opening on every side and she was powerless to shut them. It would drive her mad, she thought, to face it alone. The other alternative was to go back to Miss Ironwood. But that seemed to be only a way of going deeper into all this darkness. This Manor at St. Anne's—this "kind of company"—was "mixed up in it." She didn't want to get drawn in. It was unfair. It wasn't as if she had asked much of

life. All she wanted was to be left alone. And the thing was so preposterous! The sort of thing which, according to all the authorities she had
hitherto accepted, could not really happen.

6

Cosser—the frecklefaced man with the little wisp of black moustache—
approached Mark as he was coming away from the Committee.

"You and I have a job to do," he said. "Got to get out a report about
Cure Hardy."

Mark was very relieved to hear of a job. But he was a little on his
dignity, not having liked Cosser much when he had met him yesterday,
and he answered:

"Does that mean I *am* to be in Steele's department after all?"

"That's right," said Cosser.

"The reason I ask," said Mark, "is that neither he nor you seemed
particularly keen on having me. I don't want to push myself in, you
know. I don't need to stay at the N.I.C.E. at all if it comes to that."

"Well, don't start talking about it here," said Cosser. "Come
upstairs."

They were talking in the hall and Mark noticed Wither pacing
thoughtfully towards them. "Wouldn't it be as well to speak to *him* and
get the whole thing thrashed out?" he suggested. But the Deputy Director, after coming within ten feet of them, had turned in another direction. He was humming to himself under his breath and seemed so deep
in thought that Mark felt the moment unsuitable for an interview.
Cosser, though he said nothing, apparently thought the same and so
Mark followed him up to an office on the third floor.

"It's about the village of Cure Hardy," said Cosser when they were
seated. "You see, all that land at Bragdon Wood is going to be little better than a swamp once they get to work. Why the hell we wanted to go
there I don't know. Anyway, the latest plan is to divert the Wynd: block
up the old channel through Edgestow altogether. Look. Here's Shilling-
bridge, ten miles north of the town. It's to be diverted there and brought
down an artificial channel—here, to the east, where the blue line is—and
rejoin the old bed down here."

"The university will hardly agree to that," said Mark. "What would
Edgestow be without the river?"

"We've got the university by the short hairs," said Cosser. "You needn't worry about that. Anyway it's not our job. The point is that the new Wynd must come right through Cure Hardy. Now look at your contours. Cure Hardy is in this narrow little valley. Eh? Oh, you've been there, have you? That makes it all the easier. I don't know these parts myself. Well, the idea is to dam the valley at the southern end and make a big reservoir. You'll need a new water supply for Edgestow now that it's to be the second city in the country."

"But what happens to Cure Hardy?"

"That's another advantage. We build a new model village (it's to be called Jules Hardy or Wither Hardy) four miles away. Over here, on the railway."

"I say, you know, there'll be the devil of a stink about this. Cure Hardy is famous. It's a beauty spot. There are the sixteenth-century almshouses, and a Norman church, and all that."

"Exactly. That's where you and I come in. We've got to make a report on Cure Hardy. We'll run out and have a look round tomorrow, but we can write most of the report today. It ought to be pretty easy. If it's a beauty spot, you can bet it's insanitary. That's the first point to stress. Then we've got to get out some facts about the population. I think you'll find it consists almost entirely of the two most undesirable elements—small *rentiers* and agricultural labourers."

"The small *rentier* is a bad element, I agree," said Mark. "I suppose the agricultural labourer is more controversial."

"The Institute doesn't approve of him. He's a very recalcitrant element in a planned community, and he's always backward. We're not going in for English agriculture. So you see, all we have to do is to verify a few facts. Otherwise the report writes itself."

Mark was silent for a moment or two.

"That's easy enough," he said. "But before I get down to it, I'd just like to be a bit clearer about my own position. Oughtn't I go and see Steele? I don't fancy settling down to work in this department if he doesn't want to have me."

"I wouldn't do that," said Cosser.

"Why not?"

"Well, for one thing, Steele can't prevent you if the D.D. backs you up, as he seems to be doing for the moment. For another, Steele is rather a dangerous man. If you just go quietly on with the job, he may get used to you in the end; but if you go and see him it might lead to a bust-up.

There's another thing too." Cosser paused, picked his nose thoughtfully, and proceeded. "Between ourselves, I don't think things can go on indefinitely in this department in the way they are at present."

The excellent training which Mark had had at Bracton enabled him to understand this. Cosser was hoping to get Steele out of the department altogether. He thought he saw the whole situation. Steele was dangerous while he lasted, but he might not last.

"I got the impression yesterday," said Mark, "that you and Steele hit it off together rather well."

"The great thing here," said Cosser, "is never to quarrel with anyone. I hate quarrels myself. I can get on with anybody—as long as the work gets done."

"Of course," said Mark. "By the way, if we go to Cure Hardy tomorrow I might as well run in to Edgestow and spend the night at home."

For Mark a good deal hung on the answer to this. He might find out whether he were actually under orders from Cosser. If Cosser said, "you can't do that," he would at least know where he stood. If Cosser said that Mark couldn't be spared, that would be better still. Or Cosser might reply that he'd better consult the D.D. That also would have made Mark feel surer of his position. But Cosser merely said "Oh," leaving Mark in doubt whether no one needed leave of absence or whether Mark was not sufficiently established as a member of the Institute for his absence to be of any consequence. Then they went to work on their report.

It took them the rest of the day, so that Cosser and he came in to dinner late and without dressing. This gave Mark a most agreeable sensation. And he enjoyed the meal too. Although he was among men he had not met before, he seemed to know everyone within the first five minutes and to be joining naturally in the conversation. He was learning how to talk their shop.

"How nice it is!" said Mark to himself next morning as the car left the main road at Duke's Eaton and began descending the bumpy little lane into the long valley where Cure Hardy lay. Mark was not as a rule very sensitive to beauty, but Jane and his love for Jane had already awakened him a little in this respect. Perhaps the winter morning sunlight affected him all the more because he had never been taught to regard it as specially beautiful and it therefore worked on his senses without interference. The earth and sky had the look of things recently washed. The brown fields looked as if they would be good to eat, and those in grass set off the curves of the little hills as close clipped hair sets off the body of a horse. The sky looked further away than usual, but also clearer, so that the long slender streaks of cloud (dark slate colour against the pale blue) had edges as clear as if they were cut out of cardboard. Every little copse was black and bristling as a hairbrush, and when the car stopped in Cure Hardy itself the silence that followed the turning off of the engine was filled with the noise of rooks that seemed to be calling "Wake! Wake!"

"Bloody awful noise those birds make," said Cosser. "Got your map? Now . . ." He plunged at once into business.

They walked about that village for two hours and saw with their own eyes all the abuses and anachronisms they came to destroy. They saw the recalcitrant and backward labourer and heard his views on the weather. They met the wastefully supported pauper in the person of an old man shuffling across the courtyard of the almshouses to fill a kettle, and the elderly *rentier* (to make matters worse, she had a fat old dog with her) in earnest conversation with the postman. It made Mark feel as he were on a holiday, for it was only on holidays that he had ever wandered about an English village. For that reason he felt pleasure in it. It did not quite escape him that the face of the backward labourer was rather more interesting than Cosser's and his voice a great deal more pleasing to the ear. The resemblance between the elderly *rentier* and Aunt Gilly (When had he last thought of *her?* Good Lord, that took one back.) did make him understand how it was possible to like that kind of person. All this did not in the least influence his sociological convictions. Even if he had been free from Belbury and wholly unambitious, it could not have done so, for his education had had the curious effect of making things that he read and wrote more real to him than things he saw. Statistics about agricultural labourers were the substance; any real ditcher, ploughman, or farmer's boy, was the shadow. Though he had never noticed it himself, he had a great reluctance, in his work, ever to use such words as "man" or "woman." He preferred to write about "vocational groups," "elements," "classes" and "populations": for, in his own way, he believed as firmly as any mystic in the superior reality of the things that are not seen.

And yet, he could not help rather liking this village. When, at one o'clock, he persuaded Cosser to turn into the Two Bells, he even said so. They had both brought sandwiches with them, but Mark felt he would like a pint of beer. In the Two Bells it was very warm and dark, for the window was small. Two labourers (no doubt recalcitrant and backward) were sitting with earthenware mugs at their elbows, munching very thick sandwiches, and a third was standing up at the counter conducting a conversation with the landlord.

"No beer for me, thanks," said Cosser, "and we don't want to muck about here too long. What were you saying?"

"I was saying that on a fine morning there is something rather attractive about a place like this, in spite of all its obvious absurdities."

"Yes, it *is* a fine morning. Makes a real difference to one's health, a bit of sunlight."

"I was thinking of the place."

"You mean *this?*" said Cosser glancing round the room. "I should have thought it was just the sort of thing we wanted to get rid of. No sunlight, no ventilation. Haven't much use for alcohol myself (read the Miller Report) but if people have got to have their stimulants, I'd like to see them administered in a more hygienic way."

"I don't know that the stimulant is quite the whole point," said Mark, looking at his beer. The whole scene was reminding him of drinks and talks long ago—of laughter and arguments in undergraduate days. Somehow one had made friends more easily then. He wondered what had become of all that set—of Carey and Wadsden and Denniston, who had so nearly got his own Fellowship.

"Don't know, I'm sure," said Cosser, in answer to his last remark. "Nutrition isn't my subject. You'd want to ask Stock about that."

"What I'm really thinking about," said Mark, "is not this pub, but the whole village. Of course, you're quite right: that sort of thing has to go. But it had its pleasant side. We'll have to be careful that whatever we're building up in its place will really be able to beat it on all levels— not merely in efficiency."

"Oh, architecture and all that," said Cosser. "Well, that's hardly my line, you know. That's more for someone like Wither. Have you nearly finished?"

All at once it came over Mark what a terrible bore this little man was, and in the same moment he felt utterly sick of the N.I.C.E. But he reminded himself that one could not expect to be in the interesting set at once; there would be better things later on. Anyway, he had not burnt his boats. Perhaps he would chuck up the whole thing and go back to Bracton in a day or two. But not at once. It would be only sensible to hang on for a bit and see how things shaped.

On their way back Cosser dropped him near Edgestow station, and as he walked home Mark began to think of what he would say to Jane about Belbury. You will quite misunderstand him if you think he was consciously inventing a lie. Almost involuntarily, as the picture of himself entering the flat, and of Jane's questioning face, arose in his mind, there arose also the imagination of his own voice answering her, hitting off the salient features of Belbury in amusing, confident phrases. This imaginary speech of his own gradually drove out of his mind the real experiences he had undergone. Those real experiences of misgivings and of uneasiness, indeed, quickened his desire to cut a good figure in the eyes of his wife. Almost without noticing it, he had decided not to mention the affair of Cure Hardy; Jane cared for old buildings and all that sort of thing. As a result, when Jane, who was at that moment drawing the curtains, heard the door opening and looked round and saw Mark, she saw a rather breezy and buoyant Mark. Yes, he was almost sure he'd got the job. The salary wasn't absolutely fixed, but he'd be going into that tomorrow. It was a very funny place: he'd explain all that later. But he had already got onto the real people there. Wither and Miss Hardcastle were the ones that mattered. "I *must* tell you about the Hardcastle woman," he said, "she's quite incredible."

Jane had to decide what she would say to Mark much more quickly than he had decided what he would say to her. And she decided to tell him nothing about the dreams or St. Anne's. Men hated women who had things wrong with them, specially queer, unusual things. Her resolution was easily kept for Mark, full of his own story, asked her no questions. She was not, perhaps, entirely convinced by what he said. There was a vagueness about all the details. Very early in the conversation she said in a sharp frightened voice (she had no idea how he disliked that voice), "Mark, you haven't given up your fellowship at Bracton?" He said, No, of course not, and went on. She listened only with half her mind. She knew he often had rather grandiose ideas, and from something in his face she divined that during his absence he had been drinking much more than he usually did. And so, all evening, the male bird displayed his plumage and the female played her part and asked questions and laughed and feigned more interest than she felt. Both were young, and if neither loved very much, each was still anxious to be admired.

7

That evening the Fellows of Bracton sat in Common Room over their wine and dessert. They had given up dressing for dinner, as an economy during the war, and not yet resumed the practice, so that their sports coats and cardigans struck a somewhat discordant note against the dark Jacobean panels, the candle light, and the silver of many different periods. Feverstone and Curry were sitting together. Until that night for about three hundred years this Common Room had been one of the pleasant quiet places of England. It was in Lady Alice, on the ground floor beneath the soler, and the windows at its eastern end looked out on the river and on Bragdon Wood, across a little terrace where the Fellows were in the habit of taking their dessert on summer evenings. At this hour and season these windows were of course shut and curtained. And from beyond them came such noises as had never been heard in that room before—shouts and curses and the sound of lorries heavily drumming past or harshly changing gear, rattling of chains, drumming of mechanical drills, clanging of iron, whistles, thuddings, and an all pervasive vibration. *Saeva sonare verbera, tum stridor ferri tractaeque catenae,* as Glossop, sitting on the far side of the fire, had observed to Jewel. For beyond those windows, scarcely thirty yards away on the other side of the Wynd, the conversion of an ancient woodland into an inferno of mud and noise and steel and concrete was already going on apace. Several members even of the Progressive Element—those who had rooms on this side of College—had already been grumbling about it. Curry himself had been a little surprised by the form which his dream had taken now that it was a reality, but he was doing his best to brazen it out, and though his conversation with Feverstone had to be conducted at the top of their voices, he made no allusion to this inconvenience.

"It's quite definite, then," he bawled, "that young Studdock is not coming back?"

"Oh quite," shouted Feverstone. "He sent me a message through a high official to tell me to let the College know."

"When will he send a formal resignation?"

"Haven't an earthly! Like all these youngsters, he's very casual about these things. As a matter of fact, the longer he delays the better."

"You mean it gives us a chance to look about us?"

"Quite. You see, nothing need come before the College till he writes. One wants to have the whole question of his successor taped *before* that."

"Obviously. That is most important. Once you present an open question to all these people who don't understand the field and don't know their own minds, you get anything happening."

"Exactly. That's what we want to avoid. The only way to manage a place like this is to produce your candidate—bring the rabbit out of a hat—two minutes after you've announced the vacancy."

"We must begin thinking about it at once."

"Does his successor have to be a sociologist? I mean is the fellowship tied to the subject?"

"Oh, not in the least. It's one of those Paston fellowships. Why? Had you any subject in mind?"

"It's a long time since we had anyone in Politics."

"Um—yes. There's still a considerable prejudice against Politics as an academic subject. I say, Feverstone, oughtn't we to give this new subject a leg up?"

"What new subject?"

"Pragmatometry."

"Well now, it's funny you should say that, because the man I was beginning to think of is a Politician who has also been going in a good deal for Pragmatometry. One could call it a fellowship in social Pragmatometry, or something like that."

"Who is the man?"

"Laird—from Leicester, Cambridge."

It was automatic for Curry to look very thoughtful, though he had never heard of Laird, and to say, "Ah, Laird. Just remind me of the details of his academic career."

"Well," said Feverstone, "as you remember, he was in bad health at the time of his finals, and came rather a cropper. The Cambridge examining is so bad nowadays that one hardly counts that. Everyone knew he was one of the most brilliant men of his year. He was President of the Sphinxes and used to edit *The Adult*. David Laird, you know."

"Yes, to be sure. David Laird. But I say, Dick . . ."

"Yes?"

"I'm not quite happy about his bad degree. Of course I don't attach a superstitious value to examination results any more than you do. Still . . . We have made one or two unfortunate elections lately." Almost involuntarily, as he said this, Curry glanced across the room to where Pelham sat—Pelham with his little button-like mouth and his pudding face. Pelham was a sound man; but even Curry found it difficult to remember anything that Pelham had ever done or said.

"Yes, I know," said Feverstone, "but even our worst elections aren't quite so dim as those the College makes when we leave it to itself."

Perhaps because the intolerable noise had frayed his nerves, Curry felt a momentary doubt about the "dimness" of these outsiders. He had dined recently at Northumberland and found Telford dining there the same night. The contrast between the alert and witty Telford whom everyone at Northumberland seemed to know, whom everyone listened to, and the "dim" Telford in Bracton Common Room had perplexed him. Could it be that the silences of all these "outsiders" in his own College, their monosyllabic replies when he condescended and their blank faces when he assumed his confidential manner, had an explanation which had never occurred to him? The fantastic suggestion that he, Curry, might be a bore, passed through his mind so swiftly that a second later he had forgotten it forever. The much less painful suggestion that these traditionalists and research beetles affected to look down on him was retained. But Feverstone was shouting at him again.

"I'm going to be at Cambridge next week," he said. "In fact I'm giving a dinner. I'd as soon it wasn't mentioned here, because, as a matter of fact, the P.M. may be coming, and one or two big newspaper people and Tony Dew. What? Oh, of course you know Tony. That little dark man from the Bank. Laird is going to be there. He's some kind of cousin of the P.M.'s. I was wondering if you could join us. I know David's very anxious to meet you. He's heard a lot about you from some chap who used to go to your lectures. I can't remember the name."

"Well, it would be very difficult. It rather depends on when old Bill's funeral is to be. I should have to be here for that of course. Was there anything about the inquest on the six o'clock news?"

"I didn't hear. But of course that raises a second question. Now that Blizzard has gone to blow in a better world, we have *two* vacancies."

"I can't hear," yelled Curry. "Is this noise getting worse? Or am I getting deaf?"

"I say, Sub-Warden," shouted Brizeacre from beyond Feverstone, "what the devil are your friends outside doing?"

"Can't they work without shouting?" asked someone else.

"It doesn't sound like work at all to me," said a third.

"Listen!" said Glossop suddenly, "that's not work. Listen to the feet. It's more like a game of rugger."

"It's getting worse every minute," said Raynor.

Next moment nearly everyone in the room was on his feet. "What was that?" shouted one. "They're murdering someone," said Glossop. "There's only one way of getting a noise like that out of a man's throat." "Where are you going?" asked Curry. "I'm going to see what's happening," said Glossop. "Curry, go and collect all the shooters in College. Someone ring up the police." "I shouldn't go out if I were you," said Feverstone who had remained seated and was pouring himself out another glass of wine. "It sounds as if the police, or something, was there already."

"What do you mean?"

"Listen. There!"

"I thought that was their infernal drill."

"Listen!"

"My God . . . you really think it's a machine gun?"

"Look out! Look out!" said a dozen voices at once as a splintering of glass became audible and a shower of stones fell onto the Common Room floor. A moment later several of the Fellows had made a rush for the windows and put up the shutters; and then they were all standing staring at one another, and silent but for the noise of their heavy breathing. Glossop had a cut on the forehead, and on the floor lay the fragments of that famous east window on which Henrietta Maria had once cut her name with a diamond.

5

Elasticity

I

Next morning Mark went back to Belbury by train. He had promised his wife to clear up a number of points about his salary and place of residence, and the memory of all these promises made a little cloud of uneasiness in his mind, but on the whole he was in good spirits. This return to Belbury—just sauntering in and hanging up his hat and ordering a drink—was a pleasant contrast to his first arrival. The servant who brought the drink knew him. Filostrato nodded to him. Women *would* fuss, but this was clearly the real world. After the drink he strolled upstairs to Cosser's office. He was there for only five minutes, and when he came out, his state of mind had been completely altered.

Steele and Cosser were both there and both looked up with the air of men who have been interrupted by a total stranger. Neither spoke.

"Ah—good morning," said Mark awkwardly.

Steele finished making a pencil note on some large document which was spread out before him.

"What is it, Mr. Studdock?" he said without looking up.

"I came to see Cosser," said Mark, and then, addressing Cosser, "I've just been thinking over the last section but one in that report—"

"What report's this?" said Steele to Cosser.

"Oh, I thought," replied Cosser with a little twisty smile at one corner of his mouth, "that it would be a good thing to put together a report on Cure Hardy in my spare time, and as there was nothing particular to do yesterday I drew it up. Mr. Studdock helped me."

"Well, never mind about that now," said Steele. "You can talk to Mr. Cosser about it some other time, Mr. Studdock. I'm afraid he's busy at present."

"Look here," said Mark, "I think we'd better understand one another. Am I to take it that this report was simply a private hobby of Cosser's? And if so, I should like to have known that before I spent eight hours' work on it. And whose orders am I under?"

Steele, playing with his pencil, looked at Cosser.

"I asked you a question about my position, Mr. Steele," said Mark.

"I haven't time for this sort of thing," said Steele. "If you haven't any work to do, I have. I know nothing about your position."

Mark thought, for a moment, of turning to Cosser; but Cosser's smooth, freckled face and non-committal eyes suddenly filled him with such contempt that he turned on his heel and left the room, slamming the door behind him. He was going to see the Deputy Director.

At the door of Wither's room he hesitated for a moment because he heard voices from within. But he was too angry to wait. He knocked and entered without noticing whether the knock had been answered.

"My dear boy," said the Deputy Director looking up but not quite fixing his eyes on Mark's face. "I'm delighted to see you." As he heard these words Mark noticed that there was a third person in the room. It was a man called Stone whom he had met at dinner the day before yesterday. Stone was standing in front of Wither's table, rolling and unrolling a piece of blotting paper with his fingers. His mouth was open, his eyes fixed on the Deputy Director.

"Delighted to see you," repeated Wither. "All the more so because you—er—interrupted me in what I am afraid I must call a rather painful interview. As I was just saying to poor Mr. Stone when you came in, nothing is nearer to my heart than the wish that this great Institute should all work together like one family . . . the greatest unity of will and purpose, Mr. Stone, the fullest mutual confidence . . . that is what I expect of my colleagues. But then as you may remind me, Mr.—ah—Studdock, even in family life, there are occasionally strains and frictions and misunderstandings. And that is why, my dear boy, I am not at the moment quite at leisure—don't go, Mr. Stone. I have a great deal more to say to you."

"Perhaps I'd better come back later?" said Mark.

"Well, perhaps in all the circumstances . . . it is *your* feelings that I am considering, Mr. Stone . . . perhaps . . . the usual method of seeing me, Mr. Studdock, is to apply to my secretary and make an appointment. Not, you will understand, that I have the least wish to insist on any formalities or would be other than pleased to see you whenever you looked in. It is the waste of *your* time that I am anxious to avoid."

"Thank you, Sir," said Mark. "I'll go and see your secretary."

The secretary's office was next door. When one went in, one found not the secretary himself, but a number of subordinates who were cut off from their visitors behind a sort of counter. Mark made an appointment for ten o'clock tomorrow which was the earliest hour they could offer him. As he came out he ran into Fairy Hardcastle.

"Hullo, Studdock," said the Fairy. "Hanging round the D.D.'s office? That won't do, you know."

"I have decided," said Mark, "that I must either get my position definitely fixed once and for all or else leave the Institute."

She looked at him with an ambiguous expression in which amusement seemed to predominate. Then she suddenly slipped her arm through his.

"Look, Sonny," she said, "you drop all that, see? It isn't going to do you any good. You come along and have a talk with me."

"There's really nothing to talk about, Miss Hardcastle," said Mark. "I'm quite clear in my mind. Either I get a real job here, or I go back to Bracton. That's simple enough: I don't even particularly mind which, so long as I know."

To this, the Fairy made no answer, and the steady pressure of her arm compelled Mark, unless he was prepared to struggle, to go with her along the passage. The intimacy and authority of her grip was ludicrously ambiguous and would have fitted almost equally well the relations of policeman and prisoner, mistress and lover, nurse and child. Mark felt that he would look a fool if they met anyone.

She brought him to her own offices which were on the second floor. The outer office was full of what he had already learned to call Waips, the girls of the Women's Auxiliary Institutional Police. The men of the force, though very much more numerous, were not so often met with indoors, but Waips were constantly seen flitting to and from wherever Miss Hardcastle appeared. Far from sharing the masculine characteristics of their chief they were (as Feverstone once said) "feminine to the point of imbecility"—small and slight and fluffy and full of giggles. Miss

Hardcastle behaved to them as if she were a man, and addressed them in tones of half-breezy, half-ferocious, gallantry. "Cocktails, Dolly," she bawled as they entered the outer office. When they reached the inner office she made Mark sit down but remained standing herself with her back to the fire and her legs wide apart. The drinks were brought and Dolly retired closing the door behind her. Mark had grumblingly told his grievance on the way.

"Cut it all out, Studdock," said Miss Hardcastle. "And whatever you do, don't go bothering the D.D. I told you before that you needn't worry about all those little third floor people provided you've got him on your side. Which you have at present. But you won't have if you keep on going to him with complaints."

"That might be very good advice, Miss Hardcastle," said Mark, "if I were committed to staying here at all. But I'm not. And from what I've seen I don't like the place. I've very nearly made up my mind to go home. Only I thought I'd just have a talk with him first, to make everything clear."

"Making things clear is the one thing the D.D. can't stand," replied Miss Hardcastle. "That's not how he runs the place. And mind you, he knows what he's about. It works, Sonny. You've no idea yet how well it works. As for leaving . . . you're not superstitious, are you? I am. I don't think it's lucky to leave the N.I.C.E. You needn't bother your head about all the Steeles and Cossers. That's part of your apprenticeship. You're being put through it at the moment, but if you hold on you'll come out above them. All you've got to do is to sit tight. Not one of them is going to be left when we get going."

"That's just the sort of line Cosser took about Steele," said Mark, "and it didn't seem to do me much good when it came to the point."

"Do you know, Studdock," said Miss Hardcastle, "I've taken a fancy to you. And it's just as well I have. Because if I hadn't, I'd be disposed to resent that last remark."

"I don't mean to be offensive," said Mark. "But—damn it all—look at it from my point of view."

"No good, Sonny," said Miss Hardcastle shaking her head. "You don't know enough facts yet for your point of view to be worth sixpence. You haven't yet realized what you're in on. You're being offered a chance of something far bigger than a seat in the cabinet. And there are only two alternatives, you know. Either to be in the N.I.C.E. or to be out of it. And I know better than you which is going to be most fun."

"I *do* understand that," said Mark. "But anything is better than being nominally in and having nothing to do. Give me a real place in the Sociological Department and I'll . . ."

"Rats! That whole Department is going to be scrapped. It had to be there at the beginning for propaganda purposes. But they're all going to be weeded out."

"But what assurance have I that I'm going to be one of their successors?"

"You aren't. They're not going to have any successors. The real work has nothing to do with all these departments. The kind of sociology we're interested in will be done by my people—the police."

"Then where do I come in?"

"If you'll trust me," said the Fairy, putting down her empty glass and producing a cheroot, "I can put you onto a bit of your real work— what you were really brought here to do—straight away."

"What's that?"

"Alcasan," said Miss Hardcastle between her teeth. She had started one of her interminable dry smokes. Then, glancing at Mark with a hint of contempt, "You know who I'm talking about, don't you?"

"You mean the radiologist—the man who was guillotined?" asked Mark who was completely bewildered. The Fairy nodded.

"He's to be rehabilitated," she said. "Gradually. I've got all the facts in the dossier. You begin with a quiet little article—not questioning his guilt, not at first, but just hinting that of course he *was* a member of their Quisling government and there was a prejudice against him. Say you don't doubt the verdict was just, but it's disquieting to realize that it would almost certainly have been the same even if he'd been innocent. Then you follow it up in a day or two with an article of quite a different kind. Popular account of the value of his work. You can mug up the facts— enough for *that* kind of article—in an afternoon. Then a letter, rather indignant, to the paper that printed the first article, and going much further. The execution *was* a miscarriage of justice. By that time—"

"What on earth is the point of all this?"

"I'm telling you, Studdock. Alcasan is to be rehabilitated. Made into a martyr. An irreparable loss to the human race."

"But what for?"

"There you go again! You grumble about being given nothing to do, and as soon as I suggest a bit of real work you expect to have the whole plan of campaign told you before you do it. It doesn't make sense. That's not the way to get on here. The great thing is to do what you're told. If you turn out to be any good you'll soon understand what's going on. But you've got to begin by doing the work. You don't seem to realize what we are. We're an army."

"Anyway," said Mark, "I'm not a journalist. I didn't come here to write newspaper articles. I tried to make that clear to Feverstone at the very beginning."

"The sooner you drop all that talk about what you came here to do, the better you'll get on. I'm speaking for your own good, Studdock. You *can* write. That's one of the things you're wanted for."

"Then I've come here under a misunderstanding," said Mark. The sop to his literary vanity, at that period of his career, by no means compensated for the implication that his Sociology was of no importance. "I've no notion of spending my life writing newspaper articles," he said. "And if I had, I'd want to know a good deal more about the politics of the N.I.C.E. before I went in for that sort of thing."

"Haven't you been told that it's strictly non-political?"

"I've been told so many things that I don't know whether I'm on my head or my heels," said Mark. "But I don't see how one's going to start a newspaper stunt (which is about what this comes to) without being political. Is it Left or Right papers that are going to print all this rot about Alcasan?"

"Both, honey, both," said Miss Hardcastle. "Don't you understand *anything*? Isn't it absolutely essential to keep a fierce Left and a fierce Right, both on their toes and each terrified of the other? That's how we get things done. Any opposition to the N.I.C.E. is represented as a Left racket in the Right papers and a Right racket in the Left papers. If it's properly done, you get each side outbidding the other in support of us— to refute the enemy slanders. *Of course* we're non-political. The real power always is."

"I don't believe you can do that," said Mark. "Not with the papers that are read by educated people."

"That shows you're still in the nursery, lovey," said Miss Hardcastle. "Haven't you yet realised that it's the other way round?"

"How do you mean?"

"Why you fool, it's the educated reader who *can* be gulled. All our difficulty comes with the others. When did you meet a workman who believes the papers? He takes it for granted that they're all propaganda and skips the leading articles. He buys his paper for the football results and the little paragraphs about girls falling out of windows and corpses found in Mayfair flats. He is our problem. We have to recondition him. But the educated public, the people who read the high-brow weeklies, don't need reconditioning. They're all right already. They'll believe anything."

"As one of the class you mention," said Mark with a smile, "I just don't believe it."

"Good Lord!" said the Fairy, "where are your eyes? Look at what the weeklies have got away with! Look at the *Weekly Question*. There's a paper for you. When Basic English came in simply as the invention of a free-thinking Cambridge don, nothing was too good for it; as soon as it was taken up by a Tory Prime Minister it became a menace to the purity of our language. And wasn't the Monarchy an expensive absurdity for ten years? And then, when the Duke of Windsor abdicated, didn't the *Question* go all monarchist and legitimist for about a fortnight? Did they drop a single reader? Don't you see that the educated reader *can't* stop reading the high-brow weeklies whatever they do? He can't. He's been conditioned."

"Well," said Mark, "this is all very interesting, Miss Hardcastle, but it has nothing to do with me. In the first place, I don't want to become a journalist at all, and if I did, I should like to be an honest journalist."

"Very well," said Miss Hardcastle. "All you'll do is help to ruin this country, and perhaps the whole human race. Besides dishing your own career."

The confidential tone in which she had been speaking up till now had disappeared and there was a threatening finality in her voice. The citizen and the honest man which had been awakened in Mark by the conversation, quailed a little; his other and far stronger self, the self that was anxious at all costs not to be placed among the outsiders, leaped up, fully alarmed.

"I don't mean," he said, "that I don't see your point. I was only wondering . . ."

"It's all one to me, Studdock," said Miss Hardcastle seating herself at last at her table. "If you don't like the job, of course, that's your affair. Go and settle it with the D.D. He doesn't *like* people resigning, but of course you can. He'll have something to say to Feverstone for bringing you here. We'd assumed you understood."

The mention of Feverstone brought sharply before Mark as a reality the plan, which had up till now been slightly unreal, of going back to Edgestow and satisfying himself with the career of a Fellow of Bracton.

On what terms would he go back? Would he still be a member of the Inner Circle even at Bracton? To find himself no longer in the confidence of the Progressive Element, to be thrust down among the Telfords and Jewels, seemed to him unendurable. And the salary of a mere don looked a poor thing after the dreams he had been dreaming for the last few days. Married life was already turning out more expensive than he had reckoned. Then came a sharp doubt about that two hundred pounds for membership of the N.I.C.E. club. But no—that was absurd. They couldn't possibly dun him for that.

"Well obviously," he said in a vague voice, "the first thing is to see the D.D."

"Now that you're leaving," said the Fairy, "there's one thing I've got to say, I've laid all the cards on the table. If it should ever enter your head that it would be fun to repeat any of this conversation in the outer world, take my advice and don't. It wouldn't be at all healthy for your future career."

"Oh but of course," began Mark.

"You'd better run along now," said Miss Hardcastle. "Have a nice talk with the D.D. Be careful not to annoy the old man. He does so hate resignations."

Mark made an attempt to prolong the interview but the Fairy did not permit this and in a few seconds he was outside the door.

The rest of that day he passed miserably enough, keeping out of people's way as much as possible lest his lack of occupation should be noticed. He went out before lunch for one of those short, unsatisfactory walks which a man takes in a strange neighborhood when he has brought with him neither old clothes nor a walking stick. After lunch he explored the grounds. But they were not the sort of grounds that anyone could walk in for pleasure. The Edwardian millionaire who had built Belbury had enclosed about twenty acres with a low brick wall surmounted by an iron railing, and laid it all out in what his contractor called Ornamental Pleasure Grounds. There were trees dotted about and winding paths covered so thickly with round white pebbles that you could hardly walk on them. There were immense flower beds, some oblong, some lozenge-shaped, and some crescents. There were plantations—slabs would be almost a better word—of that kind of laurel which looks as if it were made of cleverly painted and varnished metal. Massive summer seats of bright green stood at regular intervals along the paths. The whole effect was like that of a municipal cemetery. Yet, unattractive as it was, he sought it again after tea, smoking though the wind blew the lit part down the side of his cigarette and his tongue was already burning. This time he wandered round to the back parts of the house where the newer and lower buildings joined it. Here he was surprised by a stable-like smell and a medley of growls, grunts and whimpers—all the signs, in fact, of a considerable zoo. At first he did not understand, but presently he remembered that an immense programme of vivisection, freed at last from Red Tape and from niggling economy, was one of the plans of the N.I.C.E. He had not been particularly interested and had thought vaguely of rats, rabbits, and an occasional dog. The confused noises from within suggested something very different. As he stood there a loud melancholy howl arose and then, as if it had set the key, all manner of trumpetings, bayings, screams, laughter even, which shuddered and protested for a moment and then died away into mutterings and whines. Mark had no scruples about vivisection. What the noise meant to him was the greatness and grandiosity of this whole undertaking from which, apparently, he was likely to be excluded. There were all sorts of things in there: thousands of pounds' worth of living animality, which the Institute could afford to cut up like paper on the mere chance of some interesting discovery. He *must* get the job: he must somehow solve the problem of Steele. But the noise was disagreeable and he moved away.

2

Mark woke next morning with the feeling that there would certainly be one fence and perhaps two fences for him to get over during the day. The first was his interview with the Deputy Director. Unless he could get a very definite assurance about a post and a salary, he would cut his connection with the Institute. And then, when he reached home, the second fence would be his explanation to Jane of how the whole dream had faded away.

The first real fog of the autumn had descended on Belbury that morning. Mark ate his breakfast by artificial light, and neither post nor newspaper had arrived. It was a Friday and a servant handed him his bill for the portion of a week, which he had already spent in the Institute. He put it in his pocket after a hasty glance with a resolution that this, at any rate, should never be mentioned to Jane. Neither the total nor the items were of the sort that wives easily understand. He himself doubted whether there were not some mistake, but he was still at that age when a man would rather be fleeced to his last penny than dispute a bill. Then he finished his second cup of tea, felt for cigarettes, found none, and ordered a new packet.

The odd half hour which he had waited before keeping his appointment with the Deputy Director passed slowly. No one spoke to him. Everyone else seemed to be hasting away on some important and well-defined purpose. For part of the time he was alone in the lounge and felt that the servants looked at him as if he ought not to be there. He was glad when he was able to go upstairs and knock on Wither's door.

He was admitted at once, but the conversation was not easy to begin because Wither said nothing, and though he looked up as soon as Mark entered, with an expression of dreamy courtesy, he did not look exactly at Mark, nor did he ask him to sit down. The room, as usual, was extremely hot, and Mark, divided between his desire to make it clear that he had fully resolved to be left hanging about no longer and his equally keen desire not to lose the job if there were any real job going, did not perhaps speak very well. At all events, the Deputy Director left him to run down—to pass into disjointed repetitions and thence into complete silence. That silence lasted for some time. Wither sat with his lips pouted and slightly open as though he were humming a tune.

"So I think, Sir, I'd better go," said Mark at last with vague reference to what he had been saying.

"You are Mr. Studdock, I think?" said Wither tentatively after another prolonged silence.

"Yes," said Mark impatiently. "I called on you with Lord Feverstone a few days ago. You gave me to understand that you were offering me a position on the sociological side of the N.I.C.E. But as I was saying—"

"One moment, Mr. Studdock," interrupted the Deputy Director. "It is so important to be perfectly clear what we are doing. You are no doubt aware that in certain senses of the words it would be most unfortunate to speak of my offering anyone a post in the Institute. You must not imagine for a moment that I hold any kind of autocratic position, nor, on the other hand, that the relation between my own sphere of influence and the powers—I am speaking of their temporary powers, you understand—of the Permanent Committee or those of the Director himself are defined by any hard and fast system of what—er—one might call a constitutional, or even a constitutive, character. For example—"

"Then, Sir, can you tell me whether anyone has offered me a post, and, if so, who?"

"Oh," said Wither suddenly, changing both his position and his tone, as if a new idea had struck him. "There has never been the least question of that sort. It was always understood that your co-operation with the Institute would be entirely acceptable—would be of the greatest value."

"Well, can I—I mean, oughtn't we to discuss the details? I mean the salary for example and—who should I be working under?"

"My dear friend," said Wither with a smile, "I do not anticipate that there will be any difficulty about the—er—the financial side of the matter. As for—"

"What would the salary be, Sir?" said Mark.

"Well, there you touch on a point which it is hardly for me to decide. I believe that members in the position which we had envisaged you as occupying usually draw some sum like fifteen hundred a year, allowing for fluctuations calculated on a very liberal basis. You will find that all questions of that sort will adjust themselves with the greatest of ease."

"But when should I know, Sir? Who ought I go to about it?"

"You mustn't suppose, Mr. Studdock, that when I mention fifteen hundred I am at all excluding the possibility of some higher figure. I don't think any of us here would allow a disagreement on that point—"

"I should be perfectly satisfied with fifteen hundred," said Mark. "I wasn't thinking of that at all. But—but—" The Deputy Director's expression became more and more courtly and confidential as Mark stammered, so that when he finally blurted out, "I suppose there'd be a contract or something of the kind," he felt he had committed an unutterable vulgarity.

"Well," said the Deputy Director fixing his eyes on the ceiling and sinking his voice to a whisper as though he too were profoundly embarrassed, "that is not exactly the sort of procedure . . . it would, no doubt, be possible. . . ."

"And that isn't the main point, Sir," said Mark reddening. "There's the question of my status. Am I to work under Mr. Steele?"

"I have here a form," said Wither opening a drawer, "which has not, I believe, been ever actually used but which was designed for such agreements. You might care to study it at your leisure and if you are satisfied we could sign it at any time."

"But about Mr. Steele?"

At that moment a secretary entered and placed some letters on the Deputy Director's table.

"Ah! The post at last!" said Wither. "Perhaps, Mr. Studdock, er— you will have letters of your own to attend to. You are, I believe, married?" A smile of fatherly indulgence overspread his face as he said these words.

"I'm sorry to delay you, Sir," said Mark, "but about Mr. Steele? There is no good my looking at the form of agreement until that question is settled. I should feel compelled to refuse any position which involved working under Mr. Steele."

"That opens up a very interesting question about which I should like to have a quite informal and confidential chat with you on some future occasion," said Wither. "For the moment, Mr. Studdock, I shall not regard anything you have said as final. If you cared to call on me tomorrow . . ." He became absorbed in the letter he had opened, and Mark, feeling that he had achieved enough for one interview, left the room. Apparently, they did really want him at the N.I.C.E. and were prepared to pay a high price for him. He would fight it out about Steele later; meanwhile, he would study the form of agreement.

He came downstairs again and found the following letter waiting for him.

Bracton College,
Edgestow,
Oct. 20th, 19—

My dear Mark.

We were all sorry to hear from Dick that you are resigning your fellowship, but feel quite certain you've made the right decision as far as your own career is concerned. Once the N.I.C.E. is settled in here I shall expect to see almost as much of you as before. If you have not yet sent a formal resignation to N.O., I shouldn't be in any hurry to do so. If you wrote early next term, the vacancy would come up at the February meeting, and we should have time to get ready a suitable candidate as your successor. Have you any ideas on the subject yourself? I was talking to James and Dick the other night about David Laird (James hadn't heard of him before). No doubt, you know his work: could you let me have a line about it, and about his more general qualifications? I may see him next week when I'm running over to Cambridge to dine with the Prime Minister and one or two others, and I think Dick might be induced to ask Laird as well. You'll have heard that we had rather a shindy here the other night. There was apparently some sort of *fracas* between the new workmen and the local inhabitants. The N.I.C.E. police, who seem to be a nervy lot, made the mistake of firing a few rounds over the head of the crowd. We had the Henrietta Maria window smashed and several stones came into Common Room. Glossop lost his head and wanted to go out and harangue the mob, but I managed to quiet him down. This is in strict confidence. There are lots of people ready to make capital out of it here and to get up a hue and cry against us for selling the wood. In haste—I must run off and make arrangements about Hingest's funeral.

Yours,

G. C. CURRY

At the first words of this letter a stab of fear ran through Mark. He tried to reassure himself. An explanation of the misunderstanding—which he would write and post immediately—would be bound to put everything right. They couldn't shove a man out of his fellowship simply on a chance word spoken by Lord Feverstone in Common Room. It came back to him with miserable insight that what he was now calling, "a chance word," was exactly what he had learned, in the Progressive Element, to describe as, "settling real business in private," or "cutting out the Red Tape," but he tried to thrust this out of his mind. It came back to him that poor Conington had actually lost his job in a way very similar to this, but he explained to himself that the circumstances had been quite different. Conington had been an outsider; he was inside, even more inside than Curry himself. But was he? If he were not "inside" at Belbury (and it began to look as if he were not), was he still in Feverstone's confidence? If he had to go back to Bracton, would he find that he retained even his old status there? *Could* he go to Bracton? Yes, of course. He must write a letter at once explaining that he had not resigned, and would not resign, his fellowship. He sat down at a table in the writing room and took out his pen. Then another thought struck him. A letter to Curry, saying plainly that he meant to stay at Bracton, would be shown to Feverstone. Feverstone would tell Wither. Such a letter could be regarded as a refusal of any post at Belbury. Well—let it be! He would give up this shortlived dream and fall back on his fellowship. But how if that were impossible? The whole thing might have been arranged simply to let him fall between the two stools—kicked out of Belbury because he was retaining the Bracton fellowship and kicked out of Bracton because he was supposed to be taking a job at Belbury—then he and Jane left to sink or swim with not a *sou* between them—perhaps, with Feverstone's influence against him when he tried to get another job. And where *was* Feverstone?

Obviously, he must play his cards very carefully. He rang the bell and ordered a large whisky. At home he would not have drunk till twelve and even then would have drunk only beer. But now—and anyway, he felt curiously chilly. There was no point in catching a cold on top of all his other troubles.

He decided that he must write a very careful and rather elusive letter. His first draught was, he thought, not vague enough: it could be used as a proof that he had abandoned all idea of a job at Belbury. He must make it vaguer. But then, if it were too vague, it would do no good. Oh damn, damn, damn the whole thing. The two hundred pounds entrance fee, the bill for his first week, and snatches of imagined attempts to make Jane see the whole episode in the proper light, kept coming between him and his task. In the end, with the aid of the whisky and of a great many cigarettes, he produced the following letter:

THE NATIONAL INSTITUTE FOR CO-ORDINATED
EXPERIMENTS, BELBURY.

Oct. 21st, 19—

My dear Curry,

Feverstone must have got me wrong. I never made the slightest suggestion of resigning my fellowship and don't in the least wish to do so. As a matter of fact, I have almost made up my mind not to take a full time job with the N.I.C.E. and hope to be back in college in a day or two. For one thing, I am rather worried about my wife's health and don't like to commit myself to being much away at present. In the second place, though everyone here has been extremely flattering and all press me to stay, the kind of job they want me for is more on the administrative and publicity side and less scientific than I had expected. So be sure and contradict it if you hear anyone saying I am thinking of leaving Edgestow. I hope you'll enjoy your jaunt to Cambridge: what circles you do move in!

Yours,

Mark G. Studdock

P.S. Laird wouldn't have done in any case. He got a third, and the only published work he's ventured on has been treated as a joke by serious reviewers. In particular, he has no *critical* faculty at all. You can always depend on him for admiring anything that is thoroughly bogus.

The relief of having finished the letter was only momentary, for almost as soon as he had sealed it the problem of how to pass the rest of this day returned to him. He decided to go and sit in his own room; but when he went up there he found the bed stripped and a vacuum cleaner in the middle of the floor. Apparently, members were not expected to be in their bedrooms at this time of day. He came down and tried the lounge; the servants were tidying it. He looked into the library. It was empty but for two men who were talking with their heads close together. They stopped and looked up as soon as he entered, obviously waiting for him to go. He pretended that he had come to get a book and retired. In the hall he saw Steele himself standing by the notice board and talking to a man with a pointed beard. Neither looked at Mark but as he passed them they became silent. He dawdled across the hall and pretended to examine the barometer. Wherever he went he heard doors opening and shutting, the tread of rapid feet, occasional ringing of telephones; all the signs of a busy institution carrying on a vigorous life from which he was excluded. He opened the front door and looked out; the fog was thick, wet, and cold.

There is one sense in which every narrative is false; it dare not attempt, even if it could, to express the actual movement of time. This day was so long to Mark that a faithful account of it would be unreadable. Sometimes he sat upstairs—for at last they finished "doing" his bedroom—sometimes he went out into the fog, sometimes he hung about the public rooms. Every now and then these would be unaccountably filled up by crowds of talking people and for a few minutes the strain of trying not to look unoccupied, not to seem miserable and embarrassed, would be imposed on him; then suddenly, as if summoned by their next engagement, all these people would hurry away.

Some time after lunch he met Stone in one of the passages. Mark had not thought of him since yesterday morning, but now, looking at the expression on his face and something furtive in his whole manner, he realised that here, at any rate, was someone who felt as uncomfortable as himself. Stone had the look which Mark had often seen before in unpopular boys or new boys at school, in "outsiders" at Bracton—the look which was for Mark the symbol of all his worst fears, for to be one who must wear that look was, in his scale of values, the greatest evil. His instinct was not to speak to this man Stone. He knew by experience how dangerous it is to be friends with a sinking man or even to be seen with him: you cannot keep him afloat and he may pull you under. But his own craving for companionship was now acute, so that against his better judgment he smiled a sickly smile and said "Hullo!"

Stone gave a start as if to be spoken to were almost a frightening experience. "Good afternoon," he said nervously and made to pass on.

"Let's come and talk somewhere, if you're not busy," said Mark.

"I am—that is to say—I'm not quite sure how long I shall be free," said Stone.

"Tell me about this place," said Mark. "It seems to me perfectly bloody, but I haven't yet made up my mind. Come to my room."

"I don't think that at all. Not at all. Who said I thought that?" answered Stone very quickly. And Mark did not answer because at that moment he saw the Deputy Director approaching them. He was to discover during the next few weeks that no passage and no public room at Belbury was ever safe from the prolonged indoor walks of the Deputy Director. They could not be regarded as a form of espionage for the creak of Wither's boots and the dreary little tune which he was nearly always humming would have defeated any such purpose. One heard him quite a long way off. Often one saw him a long way off as well, for he was a tall man (without his stoop he would have been very tall indeed) and often, even in a crowd, one saw that face at a distance staring vaguely towards one. But this was Mark's first experience of that ubiquity and he felt that the D.D. could not have appeared at a more unfortunate moment. Very slowly he came towards them, looked in their direction though it was not plain from his face whether he recognised them or not, and passed on. Neither of the young men attempted to resume their conversation.

At tea Mark saw Feverstone and went at once to sit beside him. He knew that the worst thing a man in his position could do was to try to force himself on anyone, but he was now feeling desperate.

"I say, Feverstone," he began gaily, "I'm in search of information"— and was relieved to see Feverstone smile in reply.

"Yes," said Mark. "I haven't had exactly what you'd call a glowing reception from Steele. But the D.D. won't hear of my leaving. And the Fairy seems to want me to write newspaper articles. What the hell *am* I supposed to be doing?"

Feverstone laughed long and loud.

"Because," concluded Mark, "I'm damned if I can find out. I've tried to tackle the old boy direct—"

"God!" said Feverstone laughing even louder.

"Can one *never* get anything out of him?"

"Not what *you* want," said Feverstone with a chuckle.

"Well, how the devil is one to find out what's wanted if nobody offers any information?"

"Quite."

"Oh, and by the way, that reminds me of something else. How on earth did Curry get hold of the idea that I'm resigning my fellowship?"

"Aren't you?"

"I never had the faintest notion of resigning it."

"Really! I was told distinctly by the Fairy that you weren't coming back."

"You don't suppose I'd do it through her if I *was* going to resign?"

Feverstone's smile brightened and widened. "It doesn't make any odds, you know," he said. "If the N.I.C.E. want you to have a nominal job somewhere outside Belbury, you'll have one; and if they don't, you won't. Just like that."

"Damn the N.I.C.E. I'm merely trying to retain the fellowship I already had, which is no concern of theirs. One doesn't want to fall between two stools."

"One doesn't *want* to."

"You mean?"

"Take my advice and get into Wither's good books again as soon as you can. I gave you a good start but you seem to have rubbed him up the wrong way. His attitude has changed since this morning. You need to humour him, you know. And just between ourselves, I wouldn't be too thick with the Fairy: it won't do you any good higher up. There are wheels within wheels."

"In the meantime," said Mark, "I've written to Curry to explain that it's all rot about my resignation."

"No harm if it amuses you," said Feverstone, still smiling.

"Well, I don't suppose College wants to kick me out simply because Curry misunderstood something Miss Hardcastle said to you."

"You *can't* be deprived of a fellowship under any statute I know, except for gross immorality."

"No, of course not. I didn't mean that. I meant not being re-elected when I come up for re-electon next term."

"Oh. I see."

"And that's why I must rely on you to get that idea out of Curry's head."

Feverstone said nothing.

"You will be sure," urged Mark against his own better judgment, "to make it quite clear to him that the whole thing was a misunderstanding."

"Don't you know Curry? He will have got his whole wangling-machine going on the problem of your successor long ago."

"That's why I am relying on you to stop him."

"Me?"

"Yes."

"Why me?"

"Well—damn it all, Feverstone, it was you who first put the idea into his head."

"Do you know," said Feverstone, helping himself to a muffin, "I find your style of conversation rather difficult. You will come up for re-election in a few months. The College may decide to re-elect you; or, of course, it may not. As far as I can make out, you are at present attempting to canvass my vote in advance. To which the proper answer is the one I now give—go to Hell!"

"You know perfectly well that there was no doubt about my re-election until you spoke a word in Curry's ear."

Feverstone eyed the muffin critically. "You make me rather tired," he said. "If you don't know how to steer your own course in a place like Bracton, why come and pester me? I'm not a bucking nurse. And for your own good, I would advise you, in talking to people here, to adopt a more agreeable manner than you are using now. Otherwise your life may be, in the famous words, 'nasty, poor, brutish, and short' "!

"Short?" said Mark. "Is that a threat? Do you mean my life at Bracton or at the N.I.C.E.?"

"I shouldn't stress the distinction too much if I were you," said Feverstone.

"I shall remember that," said Mark, rising from his chair. As he made to move away, he could not help turning to this smiling man once again and saying, "It was you who brought me here. I thought you at least were my friend."

"Incurable romantic!" said Lord Feverstone, deftly extending his mouth to an even wider grin and popping the muffin into it entire.

And thus Mark knew that if he lost the Belbury job he would lose his fellowship at Bracton as well.

3

During these days Jane spent as little time as possible in the flat and kept herself awake reading in bed, as long as she could, each night. Sleep had become her enemy. In the daytime she kept on going to Edgestow—nominally in the attempt to find another "woman who would come in twice a week" instead of Mrs. Maggs. On one of these occasions she was delighted to find herself suddenly addressed by Camilla Denniston. Camilla had just stepped out of a car and next moment she introduced a tall dark man as her husband. Jane saw at once that both the Dennistons were the sort of people she liked. She knew that Mr. Denniston had once been a friend of Mark's but she had never met him; and her first thought was to wonder, as she had wondered before, why Mark's present friends were so inferior to those he once had. Carey and Wadsden and the Taylors, who had all been members of the set in which she first got to know him, had been nicer than Curry and Busby, not to mention the Feverstone man—and this Mr. Denniston was obviously much nicer indeed.

"We were just coming to see you," said Camilla. "Look here, we have lunch with us. Let's drive you up to the woods beyond Sandown and all feed together in the car. There's lots to talk about."

"Or what about your coming to the flat and lunching with me?" said Jane, inwardly wondering how she could manage this. "It's hardly a day for picnicking."

"That only means extra washing up for you," said Camilla. "Had we better go somewhere in town, Frank?—if Mrs. Studdock thinks it's too cold and foggy."

"A restaurant would hardly do, Mrs. Studdock," said Denniston. "We want to be private." The "we" obviously meant "we three" and established at once a pleasant, business-like unity between them. "As well," he continued, "don't you like a rather foggy day in a wood in autumn? You'll find we shall be perfectly warm sitting in the car."

Jane said she'd never heard of anyone liking fogs before but she didn't mind trying. All three got in.

"That's why Camilla and I got married," said Denniston as they drove off. "We both like Weather. Not this or that kind of weather, but just Weather. It's a useful taste if one lives in England."

"How ever did you learn to do that, Mr. Denniston?" said Jane. "I don't think I should ever learn to like rain and snow."

"It's the other way round," said Denniston. "Everyone begins as a child by liking Weather. You learn the art of disliking it as you grow up. Haven't you ever noticed it on a snowy day? The grown-ups are all going about with long faces, but look at the children—and the dogs? *They* know what snow's made for."

"I'm sure I hated wet days as a child," said Jane.

"That's because the grown-ups kept you in," said Camilla. "Any child loves rain if it's allowed to go out and paddle about in it."

Presently, they left the unfenced road beyond Sandown and went bumping across grass and among trees and finally came to rest in a sort of little grassy bay with a fir thicket on one side and a group of beeches on the other. There were wet cobwebs and a rich autumnal smell all round them. Then all three sat together in the back of the car and there was some unstrapping of baskets, and then sandwiches and a little flask of sherry and finally hot coffee and cigarettes. Jane was beginning to enjoy herself.

"Now!" said Camilla.

"Well," said Denniston, "I suppose I'd better begin. You know of course where we've come from, Mrs. Studdock?"

"From Miss Ironwood's," said Jane.

"Well, from the same house. But we don't belong to Grace Ironwood. She and we both belong to someone else."

"Yes?" said Jane.

"Our little household, or company, or society, or whatever you like to call it is run by a Mr. Fisher-King. At least that is the name he has recently taken. You might or might not know his original name if I told it to you. He is a great traveller but now an invalid. He got a wound in his foot, on his last journey, which won't heal."

"How did he come to change his name?"

"He had a married sister in India, a Mrs. Fisher-King. She has just died and left him a large fortune on condition that he took the name. She was a remarkable woman in her way; a friend of the great native Christian mystic whom you may have heard of—the Sura. And that's the point. The Sura had reason to believe, or thought he had reason to believe, that a great danger was hanging over the human race. And just before the end—just before he disappeared—he became convinced that it would actually come to a head in this island. And after he'd gone—"

"Is he dead?" asked Jane.

"That we don't know," answered Denniston. "Some people think he's alive, others not. At any rate he disappeared. And Mrs. Fisher-King more or less handed over the problem to her brother, to our chief. That in fact was why she gave him the money. He was to collect a company round him to watch for this danger, and to strike when it came."

"That's not quite right, Arthur," said Camilla. "He was told that a company would in fact collect round him and he was to be its Head."

"I don't think we need go into that," said Arthur. "But I agree. And now, Mrs. Studdock, this is where you come in."

Jane waited.

"The Sura said that when the time came we should find what he called a seer: a person with second sight."

"Not that we'd *get* a seer, Arthur," said Camilla, "that a seer would turn up. Either we or the other side would get her."

"And it looks," said Denniston to Jane, "as if you were the seer."

"But, please," said Jane smiling, "I don't want to be anything so exciting."

"No," said Denniston. "It's rough luck on you." There was just the right amount of sympathy in his tone.

Camilla turned to Jane and said, "I gathered from Grace Ironwood that you weren't quite convinced you *were* a seer. I mean you thought it might be just ordinary dreams. Do you still think that?"

"It's all so strange and—*beastly*," said Jane. She liked these people, but her habitual inner prompter was whispering, "Take care. Don't get drawn in. Don't commit yourself to anything. You've got your own life to live." Then an impulse of honesty forced her to add:

"As a matter of fact, I've had another dream since then. And it turns out to have been true. I saw the murder—Mr. Hingest's murder."

"There you are," said Camilla. "Oh, Mrs. Studdock, you *must* come in. You must, you must. That means we're right on top of it now. Don't you see? We've been wondering all this time exactly where the trouble is going to begin, and now your dream gives us a clue. You've seen something within a few miles of Edgestow. In fact, we are apparently in the thick of it already—whatever it is. And we can't move an inch without your help. You are our secret service, our eyes. It's all been arranged long before we were born. Don't spoil everything. Do join us."

"No, Cam, don't," said Denniston. "The Pendragon—the Head, I mean, wouldn't like us to do that. Mrs. Studdock must come in freely."

"But," said Jane, "I don't know anything about all this. Do I? I don't want to take sides in something I don't understand."

"But don't you see," broke in Camilla, "that you can't be neutral? If you don't give yourself to us, the enemy will use you."

The words, "give yourself to us," were ill-chosen. The very muscles of Jane's body stiffened a little: if the speaker had been anyone who attracted her less than Camilla she would have become like stone to any further appeal. Denniston laid a hand on his wife's arm.

"You must see it from Mrs. Studdock's point of view, dear," he said. "You forget she knows practically nothing at all about us. And that is the real difficulty. We can't tell her much until she has joined. We are in fact asking her to take a leap in the dark." He turned to Jane with a slightly quizzical smile on his face which was, nevertheless, grave. "It *is* like that," he said, "like getting married, or going into the Navy as a boy, or becoming a monk, or trying a new thing to eat. You can't know what it's like until you take the plunge." He did not perhaps know (or again perhaps he did) the complicated resentments and resistances which his choice of illustrations awoke in Jane, nor could she herself analyse them. She merely replied in a colder voice than she had yet used:

"In that case, it is rather difficult to see why one should take it at all."

"I admit frankly," said Denniston, "that you can only take it on trust. It all depends really, I suppose, what impression the Dimbles and Grace and we two have made on you: and, of course, the Head himself, when you meet *him*."

Jane softened again.

"What exactly are you asking me to do?" she said.

"To come and see our chief, first of all. And then—well, to join. It would involve making certain promises to him. He is really a Head, you see. We have all agreed to take his orders. Oh—there's one other thing. What view would Mark take about it?—he and I are old friends, you know."

"I wonder," said Camilla. "Need we go into that for the moment?"

"It's bound to come up sooner or later," said her husband.

There was a little pause.

"Mark?" said Jane. "How does he come into it? I can't imagine what he'd say about all this. He'd probably think we were all off our heads."

"Would he object, though?" said Denniston. "I mean, would he object to your joining us?"

"If he were at home, I suppose he'd be rather surprised if I announced I was going to stay indefinitely at St. Anne's. Does 'joining you' mean that?"

"Isn't Mark at home?" asked Denniston with some surprise.

"No," said Jane. "He's at Belbury. I think he's going to have a job in the N.I.C.E." She was rather pleased to be able to say this for she was well aware of the distinction it implied. If Denniston was impressed he did not show it.

"I don't think," he said, "that 'joining us' would mean, at the moment, coming to live at St. Anne's, specially in the case of a married woman. Unless old Mark got really interested and came himself—"

"That is quite out of the question," said Jane.

("He doesn't know Mark," she thought.)

"Anyway," continued Denniston, "that is hardly the real point at the moment. Would he object to your joining—putting yourself under the Head's orders and making the promises and all that?"

"Would he object?" asked Jane. "What on earth would it have to do with him?"

"Well," said Denniston, hesitating a little, "the Head—or the authorities he obeys—have rather old-fashioned notions. He wouldn't like a married woman to come in, if it could be avoided, without her husband's—without consulting—"

"Do you mean I'm to ask Mark's *permission?*" said Jane with a strained little laugh. The resentment which had been rising and ebbing, but rising each time a little more than it ebbed, for several minutes, had now overflowed. All this talk of promises and obedience to an unknown Mr. Fisher-King had already repelled her. But the idea of this same person sending her back to get Mark's permission—as if she were a child asking leave to go to a party—was the climax. For a moment she looked on Mr. Denniston with real dislike. She saw him, and Mark, and the Fisher-King man and this preposterous Indian fakir simply as Men—complacent, patriarchal figures making arrangements for women as if women were children or bartering them like cattle. ("And so the king promised that if anyone killed the dragon he would *give* him his daughter in marriage.") She was very angry.

"Arthur," said Camilla, "I see a light over there. Do you think it's a bonfire?"

"Yes, I should say it was."

"My feet are getting cold. Let's go for a little walk and look at the fire. I wish we had some chestnuts."

"Oh, do let's," said Jane.

They got out. It was warmer in the open than it had by now become in the car—warm and full of heavy smells, and dampness, and the small noise of dripping branches. The fire was big and in its middle life—a smoking hillside of leaves on one side and great caves and cliffs of glowing red on the other. They stood round it and chatted of indifferent matters for a time.

"I'll tell you what I'll do," said Jane presently. "I won't join your—your—whatever it is. But I'll promise to let you know if I have any more dreams of that sort."

"That is splendid," said Denniston. "And I think it is as much as we had a right to expect. I quite see your point of view. May I ask for one more promise?"

"What is that?"

"Not to mention us to anyone."

"Oh, certainly."

Later, when they had returned to the car and were driving back, Mr. Denniston said, "I hope the dreams will not *worry* you much, now, Mrs. Studdock. No: I don't mean I hope they'll stop: and I don't think they will either. But now that you know they are not something in yourself but only things going on in the outer world (nasty things, no doubt, but no worse than lots you read in the papers), I believe you'll find them quite bearable. The less you think of them as *your dreams* and the more you think of them—well, as News—the better you'll feel about them."

6

Fog

I

A night (with little sleep) and half another day dragged past before Mark was able to see the Deputy Director again. He went to him in a chastened frame of mind, anxious to get the job on almost any terms.

"I have brought back the Form, Sir," he said.

"What Form?" asked the Deputy Director. Mark found he was talking to a new and different Wither. The absent-mindedness was still there, but the courtliness was gone. The man looked at him as if out of a dream, as if divided from him by an immense distance, but with a sort of dreamy distaste which might turn into active hatred if ever that distance were diminished. He still smiled, but there was something cat-like in the smile; an occasional alteration of the lines about the mouth which even hinted at a snarl. Mark in his hands was as a mouse. At Bracton the Progressive Element, having to face only scholars, had passed for very knowing fellows, but here at Belbury, one felt quite different. Wither said he had understood that Mark had already refused the job. He could not, in any event, renew the offer. He spoke vaguely and alarmingly of strains and frictions, of injudicious behaviour, of the danger of making enemies, of the impossibility that the N.I.C.E. could harbour a person who appeared to have quarreled with all its members in the first week. He spoke even more vaguely and alarmingly of conversations he had

had with "your colleagues at Bracton" which entirely confirmed this view. He doubted if Mark were really suited to a learned career, but disclaimed any intention of giving advice. Only after he had hinted and murmured Mark into a sufficient state of dejection did he throw him, like a bone to a dog, the suggestion of an appointment for a probationary period at (roughly—he could not commit the Institute) six hundred a year. And Mark took it. He attempted to get answers even then to some of his questions. From whom was he to take orders? Was he to reside at Belbury?

Wither replied, "I think, Mr. Studdock, we have already mentioned elasticity as the keynote of the Institute. Unless you are prepared to treat membership as—er—a vocation rather than a mere appointment, I could not conscientiously advise you to come to us. There are no watertight compartments. I fear I could not persuade the Committee to invent for your benefit some cut and dried position in which you would discharge artificially limited duties and, apart from those, regard your time as your own. Pray allow me to finish, Mr. Studdock. We are, as I have said before, more like a family, or even, perhaps, like a single personality. There must be no question of 'taking your orders,' as you (rather unfortunately) suggest, from some specified official and considering yourself free to adopt an intransigent attitude to your other colleagues. (I must ask you not to interrupt me, please.) That is not the spirit in which I would wish you to approach your duties. You must make yourself useful, Mr. Studdock—generally useful. I do not think the Institute could allow anyone to remain in it who showed a disposition to stand on his rights—who grudged this or that piece of service because it fell outside some function which he had chosen to circumscribe by a rigid definition. On the other hand, it would be quite equally disastrous—I mean for yourself, Mr. Studdock: I am thinking throughout of your own interests—quite equally disastrous if you allowed yourself ever to be distracted from your real work by unauthorised collaboration—or, worse still, interference—with the work of other members. Do not let casual suggestions distract you or dissipate your energies. Concentration, Mr. Studdock, concentration. And the free spirit of give and take. If you avoid both the errors I have mentioned then—ah, I do not think I need despair of correcting on your behalf certain unfortunate impressions which (we must admit) your behaviour has already produced. No, Mr. Studdock, I can allow no further discussion. My time is already fully occupied. I cannot be continually harassed by conversations of this sort.

You must find your own level, Mr. Studdock. Good morning, Mr. Studdock, good morning. Remember what I have said. I am trying to do all I can for you. Good morning."

Mark reimbursed himself for the humiliation of this interview by reflecting that if he were not a married man he would not have borne it for a moment. This seemed to him (though he did not put it into words) to throw the burden upon Jane. It also set him free to think of all the things he would have said to Wither if he hadn't had Jane to bother about—and would still say if ever he got a chance. This kept him in a sort of twilight happiness for several minutes; and when he went to tea he found that the reward for his submission had already begun. The Fairy signed to him to come and sit beside her.

"You haven't done anything about Alcasan yet?" she asked.

"No," said Mark, "because I hadn't really decided to stay, not until this morning. I could come up and look at your materials this afternoon—at least as far as I know, for I haven't yet really found out what I'm supposed to be doing."

"Elasticity, Sonny, elasticity," said Miss Hardcastle. "You never will. Your line is to do whatever you're told and above all not to bother the old man."

2

During the next few days several processes, which afterwards came to seem important, were steadily going on.

The fog, which covered Edgestow as well as Belbury, continued and grew denser. At Edgestow one regarded it as "coming up from the river," but in reality it lay all over the heart of England. It blanketed the whole town so that walls dripped and you could write your name in the dampness on tables and men worked by artificial light at midday. The workings, where Bragdon Wood had been, ceased to offend conservative eyes and become mere clangings, thuddings, hootings, shouts, curses, and metallic screams in an invisible world.

Some felt glad that the obscenity should thus be covered for all beyond the Wynd was now an abomination. The grip of the N.I.C.E. on Edgestow was tightening. The river itself which had once been brownish green and amber and smooth-skinned silver, tugging at the reeds and playing with the red roots, now flowed opaque, thick with mud, sailed on by endless fleets of empty tins, sheets of paper, cigarette ends and fragments of wood, sometimes varied by rainbow patches of oil. Then, the invasion actually crossed it. The Institute had bought the land up to the left or eastern bank. But now Busby was summoned to meet Feverstone and a Professor Frost as the representatives of the N.I.C.E., and learned for the first time that the Wynd itself was to be diverted: there was to be no river in Edgestow. This was still strictly confidential, but the Institute had already powers to force it. This being so, a new adjustment of boundaries between it and the College was clearly needed. Busby's jaw fell when he realised that the Institute wanted to come right up to the College walls. He refused of course. And it was then that he first heard a hint of requisitioning. The College could sell today and the Institute offered a good price: if they did not, compulsion and a merely nominal compensation awaited them. Relations between Feverstone and the Bursar deteriorated during this interview. An extraordinary College Meeting had to be summoned, and Busby had to put the best face he could on things to his colleagues. He was almost physically shocked by the storm of hatred which met him. In vain did he point out that those who were now abusing him had themselves voted for the sale of the wood; but equally in vain did they abuse him. The College was caught in the net of necessity. They sold the little strip on their side of the Wynd which meant so much. It was no more than a terrace between the eastern walls and the water. Twenty-four hours later the N.I.C.E. boarded over the doomed Wynd and converted the terrace into a dump. All day long workmen were trampling across the planks with heavy loads which they flung down against the very walls of Bracton till the pile had covered the boarded blindness which had once been the Henrietta Maria window and reached almost to the east window of chapel.

In these days many members of the Progressive Element dropped off and joined the opposition. Those who were left were hammered closer together by the unpopularity they had to face. And though the College was thus sharply divided within, yet for the very same reason it also took on a new unity perforce in its relations to the outer world. Bracton as a whole bore the blame for bringing the N.I.C.E. to Edgestow at all. This was unfair, for many high authorities in the University had thoroughly approved Bracton's action in doing so, but now that the result was becoming apparent people refused to remember this. Busby, though he had heard the hint of requisitioning in confidence, lost no time in spreading it through Edgestow common rooms—"It would have done no good if we *had* refused to sell," he said. But nobody believed that this was why Bracton had sold, and the unpopularity of that College steadily increased. The undergraduates got wind of it, and stopped attending the lectures of Bracton dons. Busby, and even the wholly innocent Warden, were mobbed in the streets.

The Town, which did not usually share the opinions of the University, was also in an unsettled condition. The disturbance in which the Bracton windows had been broken was taken little notice of in the London papers or even in the *Edgestow Telegraph*. But it was followed by other episodes. There was an indecent assault in one of the mean streets down by the station. There were two "beatings up" in a public house. There were increasing complaints of threatening and disorderly behaviour on the part of the N.I.C.E. workmen. But these complaints never appeared in the papers. Those who had actually seen ugly incidents were surprised to read in the *Telegraph* that the new Institute was settling down very comfortably in Edgestow and the most cordial relations developing between it and the natives. Those who had not seen them but only heard of them, finding nothing in the *Telegraph*, dismissed the stories as rumours or exaggerations. Those who had seen them wrote letters to it, but it did not print their letters.

But if episodes could be doubted, no one could doubt that nearly all the hotels of the town had passed into the hands of the Institute, so that a man could no longer drink with a friend in his accustomed bar; that familiar shops were crowded with strangers who seemed to have plenty of money, and that prices were higher; that there was a queue for every omnibus and a difficulty in getting into every cinema. Quiet houses that had looked out on quiet streets were shaken all day long by heavy and unaccustomed traffic: wherever one went one was jostled by crowds of strangers. To a little midland market town like Edgestow even visitors from the other side of the county had hitherto ranked as aliens: the day-long clamour of Northern, Welsh, and even Irish voices, the shouts, the cat-calls, the songs, the wild faces passing in the fog, were utterly detestable. "There's going to be trouble here," was the comment of many a citizen; and in a few days, "You'd think they *wanted* trouble." It is not recorded who first said, "We need more police." And then at last the *Edgestow Telegraph* took notice. A shy little article—a cloud no bigger than a man's hand—appeared suggesting that the local police were quite incapable of dealing with the new population.

Of all these things Jane took little notice. She was, during these days, merely "hanging on." Perhaps Mark would summon her to Belbury. Perhaps he would give up the whole Belbury scheme and come home—his letters were vague and unsatisfactory. Perhaps she would go out to St. Anne's and see the Dennistons. The dreams continued. But Mr. Denniston had been right: it was better when one had given in to regarding them as "news." If it had not been, she could hardly have endured her nights. There was one recurrent dream in which nothing exactly happened. She seemed indeed to be lying in her own bed. But there was someone beside the bed—someone who had apparently drawn a chair up to the bedside and then sat down to watch. He had a notebook in which he occasionally made an entry. Otherwise he sat perfectly still and patiently attentive—like a doctor. She knew his face already, and came to know it infinitely well: the *pince-nez,* the well chiselled, rather white, features, and the little pointed beard. And presumably—if he could see her—he must by now know hers equally well: it was certainly herself whom he appeared to be studying. Jane did not write about this to the Dennistons the first time it occurred. Even after the second she delayed until it was too late to post the letter that day. She had a sort of hope that the longer she kept silent the more likely they would be to come in and see her again. She wanted comfort but she wanted it, if possible, without going out to St. Anne's, without meeting this Fisher-King man and getting drawn into his orbit.

Mark meanwhile was working at the rehabilitation of Alcasan. He had never seen a police dossier before and found it difficult to understand. In spite of his efforts to conceal his ignorance, the Fairy soon discovered it. "I'll put you onto the Captain," she said. "He'll show you the ropes." That was how Mark came to spend most of his working hours with her second in command, Captain O'Hara, a big white-haired man with a handsome face, talking in what English people called a Southern brogue and Irish people, "a Dublin accent you could cut with a knife." He claimed to be of ancient family and had a seat at Castlemortle. Mark did not really understand his explanations of the dossier, the Q Register, the Sliding File system, and what the Captain called "weeding." But he was ashamed to confess this and so it came about that the whole selection of facts really remained in O'Hara's hands and Mark found himself working merely as a writer. He did his best to conceal this from O'Hara and to make it appear that they were really working together; this naturally made it impossible for him to repeat his original protests against being treated as a mere journalist. He had, indeed, a taking style (which had helped his academic career much more than he would have liked to acknowledge) and his journalism was a success. His articles and letters about Alcasan appeared in papers where he would never have had the *entree* over his own signature: papers read by millions. He could not help feeling a little thrill of pleasurable excitement.

He also confided to Captain O'Hara his minor financial anxieties. When was one paid? And in the meantime, he was short of petty cash. He had lost his wallet on his very first night at Belbury and it had never been recovered. O'Hara roared with laughter. "Sure you can have any money you like by asking the Steward."

"You mean it's then deducted from one's next cheque?" asked Mark.

"Man," said the Captain, "once you're in the Institute, God bless it, you needn't bother your head about that. Aren't we going to take over the whole currency question? It's we that *make* money."

"Do you mean?" gasped Mark and then paused and added, "But they'd come down on you for the lot if you left."

"What do you want to be talking about leaving for at all?" said O'Hara. "No one leaves the Institute. At least, the only one that ever I heard of was old Hingest."

About this time Hingest's inquest came to an end with a verdict of murder by a person or persons unknown. The funeral service was held in the college chapel at Bracton.

It was the third and thickest day of the fog, which was now so dense and white that men's eyes smarted from looking at it and all distant sounds were annihilated; only the drip from eaves and trees and the shouts of the workmen outside chapel were audible within the College. Inside the chapel the candles burned with straight flames, each flame the centre of a globe of greasy luminosity, and cast almost no light on the building as a whole; but for the coughing and shuffling of feet, one would not have known that the stalls were quite full. Curry, black-suited and black-gowned and looming unnaturally large, went to and fro at the western end of the chapel, whispering and peering, anxious lest the fog might delay the arrival of what he called the Remains, and not unpleasingly conscious of the weight wherewith his responsibility for the whole ceremony pressed upon his shoulders. Curry was very great at College funerals. There was no taint of the undertaker about him; he was the restrained, manly friend, stricken by a heavy blow but still mindful that he was (in some undefined sense) the father of the College and that amid all the spoils of mutability he, at any rate, must not give way. Strangers who had been present on such occasions often said to one another as they drove off, "You could see that Sub-Warden chap felt it, though he wasn't going to show it." There was no hypocrisy in this. Curry was so used to superintending the lives of his colleagues that it came naturally to him to superintend their deaths; and possibly, if he had possessed an analytic mind, he might have discovered in himself a vague feeling that his influence, his power of smoothing paths and pulling suitable wires, could not really quite cease once the breath was out of the body.

The organ began to play and drowned both the coughing within and the harsher noises without—the monotonously ill-tempered voices, the rattle of iron, and the vibrating shocks with which loads were flung from time to time against the chapel wall. But the fog had, as Curry feared, delayed the coffin, and the organist had been playing for half an hour before there came a stir about the door and the family mourners, the black-clad Hingests of both sexes with their ram-rod backs and country faces, began to be ushered into the stalls reserved for them. Then came maces and beadles and censors and the Grand Rector of Edgestow; then, singing, the choir, and finally the coffin—an island of flowers drifting indistinctly through the fog, which seemed to have poured in, thicker, colder, and wetter, with the opening of the door. The service began.

Canon Storey took it. His voice was still beautiful, and there was beauty too in his isolation from all that company. He was isolated both by his faith and by his deafness. He felt no qualm about the appropriateness of the words which he read over the corpse of the proud old unbeliever, for he had never suspected his unbelief; and he was wholly unconscious of the strange antiphony between his own voice reading and the other voices from without. Glossop might wince when one of those voices, impossible to ignore in the silence of the chapel, was heard shouting, "Take your bucking great foot out of the light or I'll let you have the whole lot on top of it"; but Storey, unmoved and unaware, replied, "Thou fool, that which thou sowest is not quickened unless it die."

"I'll give you one across your ugly face in a moment, see if I don't," said the voice again.

"It is sown a natural body; it is raised a spiritual body," said Storey.

"Disgraceful, disgraceful," muttered Curry to the Bursar who sat next to him. But some of the junior Fellows saw, as they said, the funny side of it and thought how Feverstone (who had been unable to be present) would enjoy the story.

3

The pleasantest of the rewards which fell to Mark for his obedience was admission to the library. Shortly after his brief intrusion into it on that miserable morning he had discovered that this room, though nominally public, was in practice reserved for what one had learned, at school, to call "bloods" and, at Bracton, "the Progressive Element." It was on the library hearthrug and during the hours between ten and midnight that the important and confidential talks took place; and that was why, when Feverstone one evening sidled up to Mark in the lounge and said, "What about a drink in the library?" Mark smiled and agreed and harboured no resentment for the last conversation he had had with Feverstone. If he felt a little contempt of himself for doing so, he repressed and forgot it: that sort of thing was childish and unrealistic.

The circle in the library usually consisted of Feverstone, the Fairy, Filostrato, and—more surprising—Straik. It was balm to Mark's wounds to find that Steele never appeared there. He had apparently got in beyond, or behind, Steele, as they had promised him he would; all was working according to programme. The one person whose frequent appearance in the library he did not understand was the silent man with the *pince-nez* and the pointed beard, Professor Frost. The Deputy Direc- tor—or, as Mark now called him, the D.D., or the Old Man—was often there, but in a peculiar mode. He had a habit of drifting in and saunter- ing about the room, creaking and humming as usual. Sometimes he came up to the circle by the fire and listened and looked on with a vaguely parental expression on his face; but he seldom said anything and he never joined the party. He drifted away again, and then, perhaps, would return an hour later and once more potter about the empty parts of the room and once more go away. He had never spoken to Mark since the humili- ating interview in his study, and Mark learned from the Fairy that he was still out of favour. "The Old Man will thaw in time," she said. "But I told you he didn't like people to talk about leaving."

The least satisfactory member of the circle in Mark's eyes was Straik. Straik made no effort to adapt himself to the ribald and realistic tone in which his colleagues spoke. He never drank nor smoked. He would sit silent, nursing a threadbare knee with a lean hand and turning his large unhappy eyes from one speaker to another, without attempting to combat them or to join in the joke when they laughed. Then—perhaps once in the whole evening—something said would start him off: usually something about the opposition of reactionaries in the outer world and the measures which the N.I.C.E. would take to deal with it. At such moments he would burst into loud and prolonged speech, threatening, denouncing, prophesying. The strange thing was that the others neither interrupted him nor laughed. There was some deeper unity between this uncouth man and them which apparently held in check the obvious lack of sympathy, but what it was Mark did not discover. Sometimes Straik addressed him in particular, talking, to Mark's great discomfort and bewilderment, about resurrection. "Neither a historical fact nor a fable, young man," he said, "but a prophecy. All the miracles—shadows of things to come. Get rid of false spirituality. It is all going to happen, here in this world, in the only world there is. What did the Master tell us? Heal the sick, cast out devils, raise the dead. We shall. The Son of Man— that is, Man himself, full grown—has power to judge the world—to distribute life without end, and punishment without end. You shall see. Here and now." It was all very unpleasant.

It was on the day after Hingest's funeral that Mark first ventured to walk into the library on his own: hitherto he had always been supported by Feverstone or Filostrato. He was a little uncertain of his reception, and yet also afraid that if he did not soon assert his right to the *entree*, this modesty might damage him. He knew that in such matters the error in either direction is equally fatal; one has to guess and take the risk.

It was a brilliant success. The circle were all there, and before he had closed the door behind him, all had turned with welcoming faces, and Filostrato had said, "*Ecco*," and the Fairy, "Here's the very man." A glow of sheer pleasure passed over Mark's whole body. Never had the fire seemed to burn more brightly nor the smell of the drinks to be more attractive. He was actually being waited for. He was wanted.

"How quick can you write two leading articles, Mark?" said Feverstone.

"Can you work all night?" asked Miss Hardcastle.

"I *have* done," said Mark. "What's it all about?"

"You are satisfied," asked Filostrato, "that it—the disturbance— must go forward at once, yes?"

"That's the joke of it," said Feverstone. "She's done her work too well. She hasn't read her Ovid. *Ad metam properate simul.*"

"We cannot delay it if we wished," said Straik.

"What are we talking about?" said Mark.

"The disturbances at Edgestow," answered Feverstone.

"Oh . . . I haven't been following them very much. Are they becoming serious?"

"They're going to become serious, Sonny," said the Fairy. "And that's the point. The real riot was timed for next week. All this little stuff was only meant to prepare the ground. But it's been going on too well, damn it. The balloon will have to go up tomorrow, or the day after, at latest."

Mark glanced in bewilderment from her face to Feverstone's. The latter doubled himself up with laughter and Mark, almost automatically, gave a jocular turn to his own bewilderment.

"I think the penny hasn't dropped, Fairy," he said.

"You surely didn't imagine," grinned Feverstone, "that the Fairy left the initiative with the natives?"

"You mean she herself is the Disturbance?" said Mark.

"Yes, yes," said Filostrato, his little eyes glistening above his fat cheeks.

"It's all fair and square," said Miss Hardcastle. "You can't put a few hundred thousand imported workmen—"

"Not the sort you enrolled!" interjected Feverstone.

"Into a sleepy little hole like Edgestow," Miss Hardcastle continued, "without having trouble. I mean there'd have been trouble anyway. As it turns out, I don't believe my boys needed to do anything. But, since the trouble was bound to come, there was no harm in seeing it came at the right moment."

"You mean you've *engineered* the disturbances?" said Mark. To do him justice, his mind was reeling from this new revelation. Nor was he aware of any decision to conceal his state of mind: in the snugness and intimacy of that circle he found his facial muscles and his voice, without any conscious volition, taking on the tone of his colleagues.

"That's a crude way of putting it," said Feverstone.

"It makes no difference," said Filostrato. "This is how things have to be managed."

"Quite," said Miss Hardcastle. "It's always done. Anyone who knows police work will tell you. And as I say, the real thing—the big riot—must take place within the next forty-eight hours."

"It's nice to get the tip straight from the horse's mouth!" said Mark. "I wish I'd got my wife out of the town, though."

"Where does she live?" said the Fairy.

"Up at Sandown."

"Ah. It'll hardly affect her. In the meantime, you and I have got to get busy about the account of the riot."

"But—what's it all for?"

"Emergency regulations," said Feverstone. "You'll never get the powers we want at Edgestow until the Government declares that a state of emergency exists there."

"Exactly," said Filostrato. "It is folly to talk of peaceful revolutions. Not that the *canaglia* would always resist—often they have to be prodded into it—but until there is the disturbance, the firing, the barricades—no one gets powers to act effectively. There is not enough what you call weight on the boat to steer him."

"And the stuff must be all ready to appear in the papers the very day after the riot," said Miss Hardcastle. "That means it must be handed in to the D.D. by six tomorrow morning, at latest."

"But how are we to write it tonight if the thing doesn't even happen till tomorrow at the earliest?"

Everyone burst out laughing.

"You'll never manage publicity that way, Mark," said Feverstone. "You surely don't need to wait for a thing to happen before you tell the story of it!"

"Well, I admit," said Mark, and his face was full of laughter, "I had a faint prejudice for doing so, not living in Mr. Dunne's sort of time nor in looking-glass land."

"No good, Sonny," said Miss Hardcastle. "We've got to get on with it at once. Time for one more drink and you and I'd better go upstairs and begin. We'll get them to give us devilled bones and coffee at three."

This was the first thing Mark had been asked to do which he himself, before he did it, clearly knew to be criminal. But the moment of his consent almost escaped his notice; certainly, there was no struggle, no sense of turning a corner. There may have been a time in the world's history when such moments fully revealed their gravity, with witches prophesying on a blasted heath or visible Rubicons to be crossed. But, for him, it all slipped past in a chatter of laughter, of that intimate laughter between fellow professionals, which of all earthly powers is strongest to make men do very bad things before they are yet, individually, very bad men. A few moments later he was trotting upstairs with the Fairy. They passed Cosser on the way and Mark, talking busily to his companion, saw out of the corner of his eye that Cosser was watching them. To think that he had once been afraid of Cosser!

"Who has the job of waking the D.D. up at six?" asked Mark.

"Probably not necessary," said the Fairy. "I suppose the old man must sleep sometime. But I've never discovered when he does it."

4

At four o'clock Mark sat in the Fairy's office re-reading the last two articles he had written—one for the most respectable of our papers, the other for a more popular organ. This was the only part of the night's work which had anything in it to flatter literary vanity. The earlier hours had been spent in the sterner labour of concocting the news itself. These two Leaders had been kept for the end, and the ink was still wet. The first was as follows:

> While it would be premature to make any final comment on last night's riot at Edgestow, two conclusions seem to emerge from the first accounts (which we publish elsewhere) with a clarity which is not likely to be shaken by subsequent developments. In the first place, the whole episode will administer a rude shock to any complacency which may still lurk among us as to the enlightenment of our own civilisation. It must, of course, be admitted that the transformation of a small university town into a centre of national research cannot be carried out without some friction and some cases of hardship to the local inhabitants. But the Englishman has always had his own quiet and humourous way of dealing with frictions and has never showed himself unwilling, when the issue is properly put before him, to make sacrifices much greater than those small alterations of habit and sentiment which progress demands of the people of Edgestow. It is gratifying to note that there is no suggestion in any authoritative quarter that the N.I.C.E. has in any way exceeded its powers or failed in that consideration and courtesy which was expected of it; and there is little doubt that the actual starting point of the disturbances was some quarrel, probably in a public house, between one of the N.I.C.E. workmen and some local Sir Oracle. But as the Stagyrite said long ago, disorders which

have trivial occasions have deeper causes, and there seems little doubt that this petty *fracas* must have been inflamed, if not exploited, by sectional interests or widespread prejudice.

It is disquieting to be forced to suspect that the old distrust of planned efficiency and the old jealousy of what is ambiguously called "Bureaucracy" can be so easily (though, we hope, temporarily) revived; though at the same time, this very suspicion, by revealing the gaps and weaknesses in our national level of education, emphasises one of the very diseases which the National Institute exists to cure. That it will cure it we need have no doubt. The will of the nation is behind this magnificent "peace-effort," as Mr. Jules so happily described the Institute, and any ill-informed opposition which ventures to try conclusions with it will be, we hope, gently, but certainly firmly, resisted.

The second moral to be drawn from last night's events is a more cheering one. The original proposal to provide the N.I.C.E. with what is misleadingly called its own "police force" was viewed with distrust in many quarters. Our readers will remember that while not sharing that distrust, we extended to it a certain sympathy. Even the false fears of those who love liberty should be respected as we respect even the ill-grounded anxieties of a mother. At the same time we insisted that the complexity of modern society rendered it an anachronism to confine the actual execution of the will of society to a body of men whose real function was the prevention and detection of crime: that the police, in fact, must be relieved sooner or later of that growing body of coercive functions which do not properly fall within their sphere. That this problem has been solved by other countries in a manner which proved fatal to liberty and justice, by creating a real *imperium in imperio,* is a fact which no one is likely to forget. The so-called "Police" of the N.I.C.E.—who should rather be called its "Sanitary Executive"—is the characteristically English solution. Its relation to the National Police cannot, perhaps, be defined with perfect logical accuracy; but, as a nation, we have never been much enamoured of logic. The executive of the N.I.C.E. has no connection with politics; and if it ever comes into relation with criminal justice, it does so in the gracious role of a rescuer—a rescuer who can remove the criminal from the harsh sphere of punishment into that of remedial treatment. If any doubt as to the value of such a force existed, it has been amply set at rest by the episodes at Edgestow. The happiest relations seem to have been maintained throughout between the officers of the Institute and the National Police, who, but for the assistance of the Institute, would have found themselves faced with an impossible situation. As an eminent police officer observed to one of our representatives this morning, "But for the N.I.C.E. Police, things would have taken quite a different turn." If in the light of these events it is found convenient to place the whole Edgestow area under the exclusive control of the Institutional "police" for some limited period, we do not believe that the British people— always realists at heart—will have the slightest objection. A special tribute is due to the female members of the force, who appear to have acted throughout with that mixture of courage and common sense which the last few years have taught us to expect of English women almost as a matter of course. The wild rumours, current in London this morning, of machine-gun fire in the streets and casualties by the hundred, remain to be sifted. Probably, when accurate details are available, it will be found (in the words of a recent Prime Minister) that "when blood flowed, it was generally from the nose."

The second ran thus:

What is happening at Edgestow?

That is the question which John Citizen wants to have answered. The Institute which has settled at Edgestow is a *National* Institute. That means it is yours and mine. We are not scientists and we do not pretend to know what the master-brains of the Institute are thinking. We do know what each man or woman expects of it. We expect a solution of the unemployment problem, the cancer problem, the housing problem, the problems of currency, of war, of education. We expect from it a brighter, cleaner and fuller life for our children, in which we and they can march ever onward and onward and develop to the full urge of life which God has given each one of us. The N.I.C.E. is the people's instrument for bringing about all the things we fought for.

Meanwhile—what is happening at Edgestow?

Do you believe this riot arose simply because Mrs. Snooks or Mr. Buggins found that the landlord had sold their shop or their allotment to the N.I.C.E.? Mrs. Snooks and Mr. Buggins know better. They know that the Institute means more trade in Edgestow, more public amenities, a larger population, a burst of undreamed-of prosperity. I say these disturbances have been ENGINEERED.

This charge may sound strange, but it is true.

Therefore I ask yet again: What is happening at Edgestow?

There are traitors in the camp. I am not afraid to say so, whoever they may be. They may be so-called religious people. They may be financial interests. They may be the old cobweb-spinning professors and philosophers of Edgestow University itself. They may be Jews. They may be lawyers. I don't care who they are, but I have one thing to tell them. Take care. The people of England are not going to stand this. We are not going to have the Institute sabotaged.

What is to be done at Edgestow?

I say, put the whole place under the Institutional Police. Some of you may have been to Edgestow for a holiday. If so, you'll know as well as I do what it is like—a little, sleepy, country town with half a dozen policemen who have had nothing to do for ten years but stop cyclists because their lamps have gone out. It doesn't make sense to expect these poor old Bobbies to deal with an ENGINEERED RIOT. Last night the N.I.C.E. police showed that they could. What I say is—Hats off to Miss Hardcastle and her brave boys, yes, and her brave girls too. Give them a free hand and let them get on with the job. Cut out the Red Tape.

I've one bit of advice. If you hear anyone backbiting the N.I.C.E. police, tell him where he gets off. If you hear anyone comparing them to the Gestapo or the Ogpu, tell him you've heard that one before. If you hear anyone talking about the liberties of England (by which he means the liberties of the obscurantists, the Mrs. Grundies, the Bishops, and the capitalists), watch that man. He's the enemy. Tell him from me that the N.I.C.E. is the boxing glove on the democracy's fist, and if he doesn't like it, he'd best get out of the way.

Meanwhile—WATCH EDGESTOW.

It might be supposed that after enjoying these articles in the heat of composition, Mark would awake to reason, and with it to disgust, when reading through the finished product. Unfortunately the process had been almost the reverse. He had become more and more reconciled to the job the longer he worked at it.

The complete reconciliation came when he fair-copied both articles. When a man has crossed the T's and dotted the I's, and likes the look of his work, he does not wish it to be committed to the wastepaper basket. The more often he re-read the articles the better he liked them. And, anyway, the thing was a kind of joke. He had in his mind a picture of himself, old and rich (probably with a peerage, certainly very distinguished) when all this—all the unpleasant side of the N.I.C.E.—was over, regaling his juniors with wild, unbelievable tales of this present time. ("Ah . . . it was a rum show in those early days. I remember once . . .") And then, too, for a man whose writings had hitherto appeared only in learned periodicals or at best in books which only other dons would read, there was an all but irresistible lure in the thought of the daily press—editors waiting for copy—readers all over Europe—something really depending on his words. The idea of the immense dynamo which had been placed for the moment at his disposal, thrilled through his whole being. It was, after all, not so long ago that he had been excited by admission to the Progressive Element at Bracton. But what was the Progressive Element to this? It wasn't as if he were taken in by the articles himself. He was writing with his tongue in his cheek—a phrase that somehow comforted him by making the whole thing appear like a practical joke. And anyway, if he didn't do it, someone else would. And all the while the child inside him whispered how splendid and how triumphantly grown up it was to be sitting like this, so full of alcohol and yet not drunk, writing (with his tongue in his cheek) articles for great newspapers, against time, "with the printer's devil at the door" and all the inner ring of the N.I.C.E. depending on him, and nobody ever again having the least right to consider him a nonentity or cipher.

5

Jane stretched out her hand in the darkness but did not feel the table which ought to have been there at her bed's head. Then with a shock of surprise she discovered that she was not in bed at all, but standing.

There was utter darkness all about her and it was intensely cold. Groping, she touched what appeared to be uneven surfaces of stone. The air, also, had some odd quality about it—dead air, imprisoned air, it seemed. Somewhere far away, possibly overhead, there were noises which came to her muffled and shuddering as if through earth. So the worst had happened—a bomb had fallen on the house and she was buried alive. But before she had time to feel the full impact of this idea she remembered that the war was over . . . oh, and all sorts of things had happened since then . . . she had married Mark . . . she had seen Alcasan in his cell . . . she had met Camilla. Then, with great and swift relief she thought, "It is one of my dreams. It is a piece of news. It'll stop presently. There's nothing to be frightened of."

The place, whatever it was, did not seem to be very large. She groped all along one of the rough walls and then, turning at the corner, struck her foot against something hard. She stooped down and felt. There was a sort of raised platform or table of stone, about three feet high. And on it? Did she dare to explore? But it would be worse not to. She began trying the surface of the table with her hand, and next moment bit her lip to save herself from screaming, for she had touched a human foot. It was a naked foot, and dead to judge by its coldness. To go on groping seemed the hardest thing she had ever done but somehow she was impelled to do it. The corpse was clothed in some very coarse stuff which was also uneven, as though it were heavily embroidered, and very voluminous. It must be a very large man, she thought, still groping upwards towards his head. On his chest the texture suddenly changed—as if the skin of some hairy animal had been laid over the coarse robe. So she thought at first; then she realised that the hair really belonged to a beard. She hesitated about feeling the face; she had a fear lest the man should stir or wake or speak if she did so. She therefore became still for a moment. It was only a dream; she could bear it; but it was so dreary and it all seemed to be happening so long ago, as if she had slipped through a cleft in the present, down into some cold, sunless pit of the remote past. She hoped they wouldn't leave her here long. If only someone would come quickly and let her out. And immediately she had a picture of someone, someone bearded but also (it was odd) divinely young, someone all golden and strong and warm coming with a mighty earth-shaking tread down into that black place. The dream became chaotic at this point. Jane had an impression that she ought to courtsy to this person (who never actually arrived though the impression of him lay bright and heavy on her mind), and felt great consternation on realising that some dim memories of dancing lessons at school were not sufficient to show her how to do so. At this point she woke.

She went into Edgestow immediately after breakfast to hunt, as she now hunted every day, for someone who would replace Mrs. Maggs. At the top of Market Street something happened which finally determined her to go to St. Anne's that very day and by the ten-twenty-three train. She came to a place where a big car was standing beside the pavement, a N.I.C.E. car. Just as she reached it a man came out of a shop, cut across her path to speak to the chauffeur of the car, and then got in. He was so close to her that, despite the fog, she saw him very clearly, in isolation from all other objects: the background was all grey fog and passing feet and the harsh sounds of that unaccustomed traffic which now never ceased in Edgestow. She would have known him, anywhere: not Mark's face, not her own face in a mirror, was by now more familiar. She saw the pointed beard, the *pince-nez,* the face which somehow reminded her of a waxworks face. She had no need to think what she would do. Her body, walking quickly past, seemed of itself to have decided that it was heading for the station and thence for St. Anne's. It was something different from fear (though she was frightened too, almost to the point of nausea) that drove her so unerringly forward. It was a total rejection of, or revulsion from, this man on all levels of her being at once. Dreams sank into insignificance compared with the blinding reality of the man's presence. She shuddered to think that their hands might have touched as she passed him.

The train was blessedly warm, her compartment empty, the fact of sitting down delightful. The slow journey through the fog almost sent her to sleep. She hardly thought about St. Anne's until she found herself there: even as she walked up the steep hill she made no plans, rehearsed nothing that she meant to say, but only thought of Camilla and Mrs. Dimble. The childish levels, the undersoil of the mind, had been turned up. She wanted to be with Nice people, away from Nasty people—that nursery distinction seeming at the moment more important than any later categories of Good and Bad or Friend and Enemy.

She was roused from this state by noticing that it was lighter. She looked ahead: surely that bend in the road was more visible than it ought to be in such a fog? Or was it only that a country fog was different from a town one? Certainly what had been grey was becoming white, almost dazzlingly white. A few yards further and luminous blue was showing overhead and trees cast shadows (she had not seen a shadow for days), and then all of a sudden the enormous spaces of the sky had become visible and the pale golden sun, and looking back, as she took the turn to the Manor, Jane saw that she was standing on the shore of a little green sun-lit island looking down on a sea of white fog, fur-rowed and ridged yet level on the whole, which spread as far as she could see. There were other islands too. That dark one to the west was the wooded hills above Sandown where she had picnicked with the Den-nistons; and the far bigger and brighter one to the north was the many caverned hills—mountains one could nearly call them—in which the Wynd had its source. She took a deep breath. It was the *size* of this world above the fog which impressed her. Down in Edgestow all these days one had lived, even when out-of-doors, as if in a room, for only objects close at hand were visible. She felt she had come near to forgetting how big the sky is, how remote the horizon.

7

The Pendragon

I

Before she reached the door in the wall Jane met Mr. Denniston and he guided her into the Manor, not by that door but by the main gate which opened on the same road a few hundred yards further on. She told him her story as they walked. In his company she had that curious sensation which most married people know of being with someone whom (for the final but wholly mysterious reason) one could never have married but who is nevertheless more of one's own world than the person one has married in fact. As they entered the house they met Mrs. Maggs.

"What? Mrs. Studdock! Fancy!" said Mrs. Maggs.

"Yes, Ivy," said Denniston, "and bringing great news. Things are beginning to move. We must see Grace at once. And is MacPhee about?"

"He's out gardening hours ago," said Mrs. Maggs. "And Dr. Dimble's gone in to College. And Camilla's in the kitchen. Shall I send her along?"

"Yes, do. And if you can prevent Mr. Bultitude from butting in—"

"That's right. I'll keep him out of mischief all right. You'd like a cup of tea, Mrs. Studdock, wouldn't you? Coming by train and all that."

A few minutes later Jane found herself once more in Grace Ironwood's room. Miss Ironwood and the Dennistons all sat facing her so that she felt as if she were the candidate in a *viva voce* examination. And when Ivy Maggs brought in the tea she did not go away again but sat down as if she also were one of the examiners.

"Now!" said Camilla, her eyes and nostrils widened with a sort of fresh mental hunger—it was too concentrated to be called excitement.

Jane glanced round the room.

"You need not mind Ivy, young lady," said Miss Ironwood. "She is one of our company."

There was a pause. "We have your letter of the 10th," continued Miss Ironwood, "describing your dream of the man with the pointed beard sitting making notes in your bedroom. Perhaps I ought to tell you that he wasn't really there: at least, the Director does not think it possible. But he was really studying *you*. He was getting information about you from some other source which, unfortunately, was not visible to you in the dream."

"Will you tell us, if you don't mind," said Mr. Denniston, "what you were telling me as we came along?"

Jane told them about the dream of the corpse (if it was a corpse) in the dark place and how she had met the bearded man that morning in Market Street; and at once she was aware of having created intense interest.

"Fancy!" said Ivy Maggs. "So we were right about Bragdon Wood!" said Camilla. "It *is* really Belbury," said her husband. "But in that case, where does Alcasan come in?"

"Excuse me," said Miss Ironwood in her level voice, and the others became instantly silent. "We must not discuss the matter here. Mrs. Studdock has not yet joined us."

"Am I to be told nothing?" asked Jane.

"Young lady," said Miss Ironwood. "You must excuse me. It would not be wise at the moment: indeed, we are not at liberty to do so. Will you allow me to ask you two more questions?"

"If you like," said Jane, a little sulkily, but only a very little. The presence of Camilla and Camilla's husband somehow put her on her best behaviour.

Miss Ironwood had opened a drawer and for a few moments there was silence while she hunted in it. Then she handed a photograph across to Jane and asked,

"Do you recognise that person?"

"Yes," said Jane in a low voice. "That is the man I've dreamed of and the man I saw this morning in Edgestow."

It was a good photograph and beneath it was the name Augustus Frost, with a few other details which Jane did not at the moment take in.

"In the second place," continued Miss Ironwood, holding out her hand for Jane to return the photograph, "are you prepared to see the Director—*now?*"

"Well—yes, if you like."

"In that case, Arthur," said Miss Ironwood to Denniston, "you had better go and tell him what we have just heard and find out if he is well enough to meet Mrs. Studdock."

Denniston at once rose.

"In the meantime," said Miss Ironwood, "I would like a word with Mrs. Studdock alone." At this the others rose also and preceded Denniston out of the room. A very large cat which Jane had not noticed before jumped up and occupied the chair which Ivy Maggs had just vacated.

"I have very little doubt," said Miss Ironwood, "that the Director will see you."

Jane said nothing.

"And at that interview," continued the other, "you will, I presume, be called upon to make a final decision."

Jane gave a little cough which had no other purpose than to dispel a certain air of unwelcome solemnity which seemed to have settled on the room as soon as she and Miss Ironwood were left alone.

"There are also certain things," said Miss Ironwood, "which you ought to know about the Director before you see him. He will appear to you, Mrs. Studdock, to be a very young man: younger than yourself. You will please understand that this is not the case. He is nearer fifty than forty. He is a man of very great experience, who has travelled where no other human being ever travelled before and mixed in societies of which you and I have no conception."

"That is very interesting," said Jane, though displaying no interest.

"And thirdly," said Miss Ironwood, "I must ask you to remember that he is often in great pain. Whatever decision you come to, I trust you will not say or do anything that may put an unnecessary strain upon him."

"If Mr. Fisher-King is not well enough to see visitors . . ." said Jane vaguely.

"You must excuse me," said Miss Ironwood, "for impressing these points upon you. I am a doctor, and I am the only doctor in our company. I am therefore responsible for protecting him as far as I can. If you will now come with me I will show you to the Blue Room."

She rose and held the door open for Jane. They passed out into the plain, narrow passage and thence up shallow steps into a large entrance hall whence a fine Georgian staircase led to the upper floors. The house, larger than Jane had at first supposed, was warm and very silent, and after so many days spent in fog, the autumn sunlight, falling on soft carpets and on walls, seemed to her bright and golden. On the first floor, but raised above it by six steps, they found a little square place with white pillars where Camilla, quiet and alert, sat waiting for them. There was a door behind her.

"He will see her," she said to Miss Ironwood, getting up.

"Is he in much pain this morning?"

"It is not continuous. It is one of his good days."

As Miss Ironwood raised her hand to knock on the door, Jane thought to herself, "Be careful. Don't get let in for anything. All these long passages and low voices will make a fool of you, if you don't look out. You'll become another of this man's female adorers." Next moment she found herself going in. It was light—it seemed all windows. And it was warm—a fire blazed on the hearth. And blue was the prevailing colour. Before her eyes had taken it in she was annoyed, and in a way ashamed, to see that Miss Ironwood was courtsying. "I won't," contended in Jane's mind with "I can't": for it had been true in her dream, she couldn't.

"This is the young lady, Sir," said Miss Ironwood.

Jane looked; and instantly her world was unmade.

On a sofa before her, with one foot bandaged as if he had a wound, lay what appeared to be a boy, twenty years old.

On one of the long window sills a tame jackdaw was walking up and down. The light of the fire with its weak reflection, and the light of the sun with its stronger reflection, contended on the ceiling. But all the light in the room seemed to run towards the gold hair and the gold beard of the wounded man.

Of course he was not a boy—how could she have thought so? The fresh skin on his forehead and cheeks and, above all, on his hands, had suggested the idea. But no boy could have so full a beard. And no boy could be so strong. She had expected to see an invalid. Now it was manifest that the grip of those hands would be inescapable, and imagination suggested that those arms and shoulders could support the whole house.

Miss Ironwood at her side struck her as a little old woman, shrivelled and pale—a thing you could have blown away.

The sofa was placed on a kind of dais divided from the rest of the room by a step. She had an impression of massed hangings of blue—later, she saw that it was only a screen—behind the man, so that the effect was that of a throne room. She would have called it silly if, instead of seeing it, she had been told of it by another. Through the window she saw no trees nor hills nor shapes of other houses: only the level floor of mist, as if this man and she were perched in a blue tower overlooking the world.

Pain came and went in his face: sudden jabs of sickening and burning pain. But as lightning goes through the darkness and the darkness closes up again and shows no trace, so the tranquillity of his countenance swallowed up each shock of torture. How could she have thought him young? Or old either? It came over her, with a sensation of quick fear, that this face was of no age at all. She had (or so she had believed) disliked bearded faces except for old men with white hair. But that was because she had long since forgotten the imagined Arthur of her childhood—and the imagined Solomon too. Solomon—for the first time in many years the bright solar blend of king and lover and magician which hangs about that name stole back upon her mind. For the first time in all those years she tasted the word *King* itself with all linked associations of battle, marriage, priesthood, mercy, and power. At that moment, as her eyes first rested on his face, Jane forgot who she was, and where, and her faint grudge against Grace Ironwood, and her more obscure grudge against Mark, and her childhood and her father's house. It was, of course, only for a flash. Next moment she was once more the ordinary social Jane, flushed and confused to find that she had been staring rudely (at least she hoped that rudeness would be the main impression produced) at a total stranger. But her world was unmade; she knew that. Anything might happen now.

"Thank you, Grace," the man was saying. "Is this Mrs. Studdock?"

And the voice also seemed to be like sunlight and gold. Like gold not only as gold is beautiful but as it is heavy: like sunlight not only as it falls gently on English walls in autumn but as it beats down on the jungle or the desert to engender life or destroy it. And now it was addressing her.

"You must forgive me for not getting up, Mrs. Studdock," it said. "My foot is hurt."

And Jane heard her own voice saying, "Yes, sir," soft and chastened like Miss Ironwood's voice. She had meant to say, "Good morning, Mr. Fisher-King," in an easy tone that would have counteracted the absurdity of her behaviour on first entering the room. But the other was what actually came out of her mouth. Shortly after this she found herself seated before the Director. She was shaken: she was even shaking. She hoped intensely that she was not going to cry, or be unable to speak, or do anything silly. For her world was unmade: anything might happen now. If only the conversation were over!—so that she could get out of that room without disgrace, and go away, not for good, but for a long time.

"Do you wish me to remain, Sir?" said Miss Ironwood.

"No, Grace," said the Director, "I don't think you need stay. Thank you."

"And now," thought Jane, "it's coming—it's coming—it's coming now." All the most intolerable questions he might ask, all the most extravagant things he might make her do, flashed through her mind in a fatuous medley. For all power of resistance seemed to have been drained away from her and she was left without protection.

2

For the first few minutes after Grace Ironwood had left them alone, Jane hardly took in what the Director was saying. It was not that her attention wandered; on the contrary, her attention was so fixed on him that it defeated itself. Every tone, every look (how could they have supposed she would think him young?), every gesture, was printing itself upon her memory; and it was not until she found that he had ceased speaking and was apparently awaiting an answer, that she realized she had taken in so little of what he had been saying.

"I—I beg your pardon," she said, wishing that she did not keep on turning red like a schoolgirl.

"I was saying," he answered, "that you have already done us the greatest possible service. We knew that one of the most dangerous attacks ever made upon the human race was coming very soon and in this island. We had an idea that Belbury might be connected with it. But we were not certain. We certainly did not know that Belbury was so important. That is why your information is so valuable. But in another way, it presents us with a difficulty. I mean a difficulty as far as you are concerned. We had hoped you would be able to join us—to become one of our army."

"Can I not, Sir?" said Jane.

"It is difficult," said the Director after a pause. "You see, your husband is in Belbury."

Jane glanced up. It had been on the tip of her tongue to say, "Do you mean that Mark is in any danger?" But she had realised that anxiety about Mark did not, in fact, make any part of the complex emotions she was feeling, and that to reply thus would be hypocrisy. It was a sort of scruple she had not often felt before. Finally, she said, "What do you mean?"

"Why," said the Director, "it would be hard for the same person to be the wife of an official in the N.I.C.E. and also a member of my company."

"You mean you couldn't trust me?"

"I mean nothing we need be afraid to speak of. I mean that, in the circumstances, you and I and your husband could not all be trusting one another."

Jane bit her lip in anger, not at the Director but at Mark. Why should he and his affairs with the Feverstone man intrude themselves at such a moment as this?

"I must do what I think right, mustn't I?" she said softly. "I mean— if Mark—if my husband—is on the wrong side, I can't let that make any difference to what *I* do. Can I?"

"You are thinking about what is *right?*" said the Director. Jane started, and flushed. She had not, she realised, been thinking about that.

"Of course," said the Director, "things might come to such a point that you would be justified in coming here, even wholly against his will, even secretly. It depends on how close the danger is—the danger to us all, and to you personally."

"I thought the danger was right on top of us now—from the way Mrs. Denniston talked."

"That is just the question," said the Director, with a smile. "I am not allowed to be *too* prudent. I am not allowed to use desperate remedies until desperate diseases are really apparent. Otherwise we become just like our enemies—breaking all the rules whenever we imagine that it might possibly do some vague good to humanity in the remote future."

"But will it do anyone any harm if I come here?" asked Jane.

He did not directly answer this. Presently he spoke again.

"It looks as if you will have to go back; at least for the present. You will, no doubt, be seeing your husband again fairly soon. I think you must make at least one effort to detach him from the N.I.C.E."

"But how can I, Sir?" said Jane. "What have I to say to him. He'd think it all nonsense. He wouldn't believe all that about an attack on the human race." As soon as she had said it she wondered, "Did that sound cunning?" then, more disconcertingly, "*Was* it cunning?"

"No," said the Director. "And you must not tell him. You must not mention me nor the company at all. We have put our lives in your hands. You must simply ask him to leave Belbury. You must put it on your own wishes. You are his wife."

"Mark never takes any notice of what I say," answered Jane. She and Mark each thought that of the other.

"Perhaps," said the Director, "you have never asked anything as you will be able to ask this. Do you not *want* to save him as well as yourself?"

Jane ignored this question. Now that the threat of expulsion from the house was imminent, she felt a kind of desperation. Heedless of that inner commentator, who had more than once during this conversation shown her her own words and wishes in such a novel light, she began speaking rapidly.

"Don't send me back," she said, "I am all alone at home, with terrible dreams. It isn't as if Mark and I saw much of one another at the best of times. I am so unhappy. He won't care whether I come here or not. He'd only laugh at it all if he knew. Is it fair that my whole life should be spoiled just because he's got mixed up with some horrible people? You don't think a woman is to have no life of her own just because she's married?"

"Are you unhappy *now*?" said the Director. A dozen affirmatives died on Jane's lips as she looked up in answer to his question. Then suddenly, in a kind of deep calm, like the stillness at the centre of a whirlpool, she saw the truth, and ceased at last to think how her words might make him think of her, and answered, "No."

"But," she added after a short pause, "it will be worse now, if I go back."

"Will it?"

"I don't know. No. I suppose not." And for a little time Jane was hardly conscious of anything but peace and well-being, the comfort of her own body in the chair where she sat, and a sort of clear beauty in the colours and proportions of the room. But soon she began thinking to herself, "This is the end. In a moment he will send for the Ironwood woman to take you away." It seemed to her that her fate depended on what she said in the next minute.

"But is it really necessary?" she began. "I don't think I look on marriage quite as you do. It seems to me extraordinary that everything should hang on what Mark says . . . about something he doesn't understand."

"Child," said the Director, "it is not a question of how you or I look on marriage but how my Masters look on it."

"Someone said they were very old fashioned. But—"

"That was a joke. They are not old fashioned; but they are very, very old."

"They would never think of finding out first whether Mark and I believed in their ideas of marriage?"

"Well—no," said the Director with a curious smile. "No. Quite definitely they wouldn't think of doing that."

"And would it make no difference to them what a marriage was actually like—whether it was a success? Whether the woman loved her husband?"

Jane had not exactly intended to say this: much less to say it in the cheaply pathetic tone which, it now seemed to her, she had used. Hating herself, and fearing the Director's silence, she added, "But I suppose you will say I oughtn't to have told you that."

"My dear child," said the Director, "you have been telling me that ever since your husband was mentioned."

"Does it make no difference?"

"I suppose," said the Director, "it would depend on how he lost your love."

Jane was silent. Though she could not tell the Director the truth, and indeed did not know it herself, yet when she tried to explore her inarticulate grievance against Mark, a novel sense of her own injustice and even of pity for her husband, arose in her mind. And her heart sank, for now it seemed to her that this conversation, to which she had vaguely looked for some sort of deliverance from all problems was in fact involving her in new ones.

"It was not his fault," she said at last. "I suppose our marriage was just a mistake."

The Director said nothing.

"What would you—what would the people you are talking of—say about a case like that?"

"I will tell you if you really want to know," said the Director.

"Please," said Jane reluctantly.

"They would say," he answered, "that you do not fail in obedience through lack of love, but have lost love because you never attempted obedience."

Something in Jane that would normally have reacted to such a remark with anger or laughter was banished to a remote distance (where she could still, but only just, hear its voice) by the fact that the word Obedience—but certainly not obedience to Mark—came over her, in that room and in that presence, like a strange oriental perfume, perilous, seductive, and ambiguous . . .

"Stop it!" said the Director, sharply.

Jane stared at him, open mouthed. There were a few moments of silence during which the exotic fragrance faded away.

"You were saying, my dear?" resumed the Director.

"I thought love meant equality," she said, "and free companionship."

"Ah, equality!" said the Director. "We must talk of that some other time. Yes, we must all be guarded by equal rights from one another's greed, because we are fallen. Just as we must all wear clothes for the same reason. But the naked body should be there underneath the clothes, ripening for the day when we shall need them no longer. Equality is not the deepest thing, you know."

"I always thought that was just what it was. I thought it was in their souls that people were equal."

"You were mistaken," said he gravely. "That is the last place where they are equal. Equality before the law, equality of incomes—that is very well. Equality guards life; it doesn't make it. It is medicine, not food. You might as well try to warm yourself with a blue-book."

"But surely in marriage . . . ?"

"Worse and worse," said the Director. "Courtship knows nothing of it; nor does fruition. What has free companionship to do with that? Those who are enjoying something, or suffering something together, are companions. Those who enjoy or suffer one another, are not. Do you not know how bashful friendship is? Friends—comrades—do not look *at* each other. Friendship would be ashamed . . ."

"I thought," said Jane and stopped.

"I see," said the Director. "It is not your fault. They never warned you. No one has ever told you that obedience—humility—is an erotic necessity. You are putting equality just where it ought not to be. As to your coming here, that may admit of some doubt. For the present, I must send you back. You can come out and see us. In the meantime, talk to your husband and I will talk to my authorities."

"When will you be seeing them?"

"They come to me when they please. But we've been talking too solemnly about obedience all this time. I'd like to show you some of its drolleries. You are not afraid of mice, are you?"

"Afraid of what?" said Jane in astonishment.

"Mice," said the Director.

"No," said Jane in a puzzled voice.

The Director struck a little bell beside his sofa which was almost immediately answered by Mrs. Maggs.

"I think," said the Director, "I should like my lunch now, if you please. They will give you lunch downstairs, Mrs. Studdock—something more substantial than mine. But if you will sit with me while I eat and drink, I will show you some of the amenities of our house."

Mrs. Maggs presently returned with a tray, bearing a glass, a small flacon of red wine, and a roll of bread. She set it down on a table at the Director's side and left the room.

"You see," said the Director, "I live like the King in *Curdie*. It is a surprisingly pleasant diet." With these words he broke the bread and poured himself out a glass of wine.

"I never read the book you are speaking of," said Jane.

They talked of the book a little while the Director ate and drank; but presently he took up the plate and tipped the crumbs off onto the floor. "Now, Mrs. Studdock," he said, "you shall see a diversion. But you must be perfectly still." With these words he took from his pocket a little silver whistle and blew a note on it. And Jane sat still till the room became filled with silence like a solid thing and there was first a scratching and then a rustling and presently she saw three plump mice working their passage across what was to them the thick undergrowth of the carpet, nosing this way and that so that if their course had been drawn it would have resembled that of a winding river, until they were so close that she could see the twinkling of their eyes and even the palpitation of their noses. In spite of what she had said she did not really care for mice in the neighbourhood of her feet and it was with an effort that she sat still. Thanks to this effort she saw mice for the first time as they really are—not as creeping things but as dainty quadrupeds, almost, when they sat up, like tiny kangaroos, with sensitive kid-gloved forepaws and transparent ears. With quick, inaudible movements they ranged to and fro till not a crumb was left on the floor. Then he blew a second time on his whistle and with a sudden whisk of tails all three of them were racing for home and in a few seconds had disappeared behind the coal box. The Director looked at her with laughter in his eyes ("It is impossible," thought Jane, "to regard him as old"). "There," he said, "a very simple adjustment. Humans want crumbs removed; mice are anxious to remove them. It ought never to have been a cause of war. But you see that obedience and rule are more like a dance than a drill—specially between man and woman where the roles are always changing."

"How huge we must seem to them," said Jane.

This inconsequent remark had a very curious cause. Hugeness was what she was thinking of and for one moment it had seemed she was thinking of her own hugeness in comparison with the mice. But almost at once this identification collapsed. She was really thinking simply of hugeness. Or rather, she was not thinking of it. She was, in some strange fashion, experiencing it. Something intolerably big, something from Brobdingnag was pressing on her, was approaching, was almost in the room. She felt herself shrinking, suffocated, emptied of all power and virtue. She darted a glance at the Director which was really a cry for help, and that glance, in some inexplicable way, revealed him as being, like herself, a very small object. The whole room was a tiny place, a mouse's hole, and it seemed to her to be tilted aslant—as though the insupportable mass and splendour of this formless hugeness, in approaching, had knocked it askew. She heard the Director's voice.

"Quick," he said gently, "you must leave me now. This is no place for us small ones, but I am inured. Go!"

3

When Jane left the hill-top village of St. Anne's and came down to the station she found that, even down there, the fog had begun to lift. Great windows had opened in it, and as the train carried her on it passed repeatedly through pools of afternoon sunlight.

During this journey she was so divided against herself that one might say there were three, if not four, Janes in the compartment.

The first was a Jane simply receptive of the Director, recalling every word and every look, and delighting in them—a Jane taken utterly off her guard, shaken out of the modest little outfit of contemporary ideas which had hitherto made her portion of wisdom, and swept away on the flood tide of an experience which she did not understand and could not control. For she was trying to control it; that was the function of the second Jane. This second Jane regarded the first with disgust, as the kind of woman, in fact, whom she had always particularly despised. Once, coming out of a cinema, she had heard a little shop girl say to her friend, "Oh, wasn't he lovely! If he'd looked at me the way he looked at her, I'd have followed him to the end of the world." A little, tawdry, made-up girl, sucking a peppermint. Whether the second Jane was right in equating the first Jane with that girl, may be questioned, but she did. And she found her intolerable. To have surrendered without terms at the mere voice and look of this stranger, to have abandoned (without noticing it) that prim little grasp on her own destiny, that perpetual reservation, which she thought essential to her status as a grown-up, integrated, intelligent person . . . the thing was utterly degrading, vulgar, uncivilised.

The third Jane was a new and unexpected visitant. Of the first there had been traces in girlhood, and the second was what Jane took to be her "real" or normal self. But the third one, this moral Jane, was one whose existence she had never suspected. Risen from some unknown region of grace or heredity, it uttered all sorts of things which Jane had often heard before but which had never, till that moment, seemed to be connected with real life. If it had simply told her that her feelings about the Director were wrong, she would not have been very surprised, and would have discounted it as the voice of tradition. But it did not. It kept on blaming her for not having similar feelings about Mark. It kept on pressing into her mind those new feelings about Mark, feelings of guilt and pity, which she had first experienced in the Director's room. It was Mark who had made the fatal mistake; she must, must, must be "nice" to Mark. The Director obviously insisted on it. At the very moment when her mind was most filled with another man there arose, clouded with some undefined emotion, a resolution to give Mark much more than she had ever given him before, and a feeling that in so doing she would be really giving it to the Director. And this produced in her such a confusion of sensations that the whole inner debate became indistinct and flowed over into the larger experience of the fourth Jane, who was

Jane herself and dominated all the rest at every moment without effort and even without choice.

This fourth and supreme Jane was simply in the state of joy. The other three had no power upon her, for she was in the sphere of Jove, amid light and music and festal pomp, brimmed with life and radiant in health, jocund and clothed in shining garments. She thought scarcely at all of the curious sensations which had immediately preceded the Director's dismissal of her and made that dismissal almost a relief. When she tried to, it immediately led her thoughts back to the Director himself. Whatever she tried to think of led back to the Director himself and, in him, to joy. She saw from the windows of the train the outlined beams of sunlight pouring over stubble or burnished woods and felt that they were like the notes of a trumpet. Her eyes rested on the rabbits and cows as they flitted by and she embraced them in heart with merry, holiday love. She delighted in the occasional speech of the one wizened old man who shared her compartment and saw, as never before, the beauty of his shrewd and sunny old mind, sweet as a nut and English as a chalk down. She reflected with surprise how long it was since music had played any part in her life, and resolved to listen to many chorales by Bach on the gramophone that evening. Or else—perhaps—she would read a great many Shakespeare sonnets. She rejoiced also in her hunger and thirst and decided that she would make herself buttered toast for tea—a great deal of buttered toast. And she rejoiced also in the consciousness of her own beauty; for she had the sensation—it may have been false in fact, but it had nothing to do with vanity—that it was growing and expanding like a magic flower with every minute that passed. In such a mood it was only natural, after the old countryman had got out at Cure Hardy, to stand up and look at herself in the mirror which confronted her on the wall of the compartment. Certainly she was looking well: she was looking unusually well. And, once more, there was little vanity in this. For beauty was made for others. Her beauty belonged to the Director. It belonged to him so completely that he could even decide not to keep it for himself but to order that it be given to another, by an act of obedience lower, and therefore higher, more unconditional and therefore more delighting, than if he had demanded it for himself.

As the train came into Edgestow Station Jane was just deciding that she would not try to get a 'bus. She would enjoy the walk up to Sandown. And then—what on earth was all this? The platform, usually almost deserted at this hour, was like a London platform on a bank holiday. "Here you are, mate!" cried a voice as she opened the door, and half a dozen men crowded into her carriage so roughly that for a moment she could not get out. She found difficulty in crossing the platform. People seemed to be going in all directions at once—angry, rough, and excited people. "Get back into the train, quick!" shouted someone. "Get out of the station, if you're not travelling," bawled another voice. "What the devil?" asked a third just beside her, and then a woman's voice said, "Oh dear, oh dear! Why don't they *stop* it!" And from outside, beyond the station came a great roaring noise like the noise of a football crowd. There seemed to be a lot of unfamiliar lights about.

4

Hours later, bruised, frightened, and tired to death, Jane found herself in a street she did not even know, surrounded by N.I.C.E. policemen and a few of their females, the Waips. Her course had been like that of a man trying to get home along the beach when the tide is coming in. She had been driven out of her natural route along Warwick Street—they were looting shops and making bonfires there—and forced to take a much wider circle, up by the Asylum, which would have brought her home in the end. Then even that wider circle had proved impracticable, for the same reason. She had been forced to try a still longer way round; and each time the tide had got there before her. Finally she had seen Bone Lane, straight and empty and still, and apparently her last chance of getting home that night at all. A couple of N.I.C.E. police—one seemed to meet them everywhere except where the rioting was most violent—had shouted out, "You can't go down there, Miss." But as they then turned their backs on her, and it was poorly lit, and because she was now desperate, Jane had made a bolt for it. They caught her. And that was how she found herself being taken into a lighted room and questioned by a uniformed woman with short grey hair, a square face, and an unlighted cheroot. The room was in disorder—as if a private house had been suddenly and roughly converted into a temporary police station. The woman with the cheroot took no particular interest until Jane had given her name. Then Miss Hardcastle looked her in the face for the first time. And Jane felt quite a new sensation. She was already tired and frightened, but this was different. The face of the other woman affected her as the face of some men—fat men with small greedy eyes and strange disquieting smiles—had affected her when she was in her 'teens. It was dreadfully quiet and yet dreadfully interested in her. And Jane saw that some quite new idea was dawning on the woman as she stared at her: some idea that the woman found attractive, and then tried to put aside, and then returned to dally with, and then finally, with a little sigh of contentment, accepted. Miss Hardcastle lit her cheroot and blew a cloud of smoke towards her. If Jane had known how seldom Miss Hardcastle actually smoked she would have been even more alarmed. The policemen and policewomen who surrounded her probably did. The whole atmosphere of the room became a little different.

"Jane Studdock," said the Fairy. "I know all about you, honey. You'll be the wife of my friend Mark." While she spoke she was writing something on a green form.

"*That's* all right," said Miss Hardcastle. "You'll be able to see Hubby again now. We'll take you out to Belbury tonight. Now just one question, dear. What were you doing down here at this time of night?"

"I had just come off a train."

"And where had you been, honey?"

Jane said nothing.

"You hadn't been getting up to mischief while Hubby was away, had you?"

"Will you please let me go?" said Jane. "I want to get home. I am very tired and it's very late."

"But you're not going home," said Miss Hardcastle. "You're coming out to Belbury."

"My husband has said nothing about my joining him there."

Miss Hardcastle nodded. "That was one of his mistakes. But you're coming with *us*."

"What do you mean?"

"It's an arrest, honey," said Miss Hardcastle, holding out the piece of green paper on which she had been writing. It appeared to Jane as all official forms always appeared—a mass of compartments, some empty, some full of small print, some scrawled with signatures in pencil, and one bearing her own name; all meaningless.

"Oh!" screamed Jane suddenly, overcome with a sensation of nightmare, and made a dash for the door. Of course she never reached it. A moment later she came to her senses and found herself held by the two policewomen.

"What a naughty temper!" said Miss Hardcastle playfully. "But we'll put the nasty men outside, shall we?" She said something and the policemen removed themselves and shut the door behind them. As soon as they were gone Jane felt that a protection had been withdrawn from her.

"Well," said Miss Hardcastle, addressing the two uniformed girls. "Let's see. Quarter to one . . . and all going nicely. I think, Daisy, we can afford ourselves a little stand-easy. Be careful, Kitty, make your top grip under her shoulder just a little tighter. That's right." While she was speaking Miss Hardcastle was undoing her belt, and when she had finished she removed her tunic and flung it on the sofa, revealing a huge torso, uncorseted (as Bill the Blizzard had complained), rank, floppy and thinly clad: such things as Rubens might have painted in delirium. Then she resumed her seat, removed the cheroot from her mouth, blew another cloud of smoke in Jane's direction, and addressed her.

"Where had you been by that train?" she said.

And Jane said nothing, partly because she could not speak, and partly because she now knew beyond all doubt that these were the enemies of the human race whom the Director was fighting against and one must tell them nothing. She did not feel heroic in making this decision. The whole scene was becoming unreal to her; and it was as if between sleeping and waking that she heard Miss Hardcastle say, "I think, Kitty dear, you and Daisy had better bring her round here." And it was still only half real when the two women forced her round to the other side of the table, and she saw Miss Hardcastle sitting with her legs wide apart and settling herself in the chair as if in the saddle; long leather-clad legs projecting from beneath her short skirt. The women forced her on, with a skilled, quiet increase of pressure whenever she resisted, until she stood between Miss Hardcastle's feet, whereupon Miss Hardcastle brought her feet together so that she had Jane's ankles pinioned between her own. This proximity to the ogress affected Jane with such horror that she had no fears left for what they might be going to do with her. And for what seemed an endless time Miss Hardcastle stared at her, smiling a little and blowing smoke in her face.

"Do you know," said Miss Hardcastle at last, "you're rather a pretty little thing in your way."

There was another silence.

"Where had you been by that train?" said Miss Hardcastle.

And Jane stared as if her eyes would start out of her head and said nothing. Then suddenly Miss Hardcastle leant forward and, after very carefully turning down the edge of Jane's dress, thrust the lighted end of the cheroot against her shoulder. After that there was another pause and another silence.

"Where had you been by that train?" said Miss Hardcastle.

How many times this happened Jane could never remember. But somehow or other there came a time when Miss Hardcastle was talking not to her but to one of the women. "What *are* you fussing about, Daisy?" she was saying.

"I was only saying, Ma'am, it was five past one."

"How time flies, doesn't it, Daisy? But what if it is? Aren't you comfortable, Daisy? You're not getting tired, holding a little bit of a thing like her?"

"No Ma'am, thank you. But you did say, Ma'am, you'd meet Captain O'Hara at one sharp."

"Captain O'Hara?" said Miss Hardcastle dreamily at first, and then louder, like one waking from a dream. Next moment she had jumped up and was putting on her tunic. "Bless the girl!" she said. "What a pair of blockheads you are! Why didn't you remind me before?"

"Well, Ma'am, I didn't exactly like to."

"Like to! What do you think you're there for?"

"You don't like us to interrupt, Ma'am, sometimes, when you're examining," said the girl sulkily.

"Don't argue!" shouted Miss Hardcastle, wheeling round and hitting her cheek a resounding blow with the palm of her hand. "Look sharp. Get the prisoner into the car. Don't wait to button up her dress, idiots. I'll be after you the moment I've dipped my face in cold water."

A few seconds later, pinioned between Daisy and Kitty, but still close to Miss Hardcastle (there seemed to be room for five in the back of the car), Jane found herself gliding through the darkness. "Better go through the town as little as possible, Joe," said Miss Hardcastle's voice. "It'll be pretty lively by now. Go on to the Asylum and work down those little streets at the back of the close." There seemed to be all sorts of strange noises and lights about. At places, too, there seemed to be a great many people. Then there came a moment when Jane found that the car had drawn up. "What the hell are you stopping for?" said Miss Hardcastle. For a second or two there was no answer from the driver except grunts and the noise of unsuccessful attempts to start up the engine. "What's the matter?" repeated Miss Hardcastle sharply. "Don't know, Ma'am," said the driver, still working away. "God!" said Miss Hardcastle, "can't you even look after a car? Some of you people want a little humane remedial treatment yourselves." The street in which they were was empty but, to judge by the noise, it was near some other street which was very full and very angry. The man got out, swearing under his breath, and opened the bonnet of the car. "Here," said Miss Hardcastle. "You two hop out. Look round for another car—anywhere within five minutes' walk—commandeer it. If you don't find one, be back here in ten minutes whatever happens. Sharp." The two other policemen alighted, and disappeared at the double. Miss Hardcastle continued pouring abuse on the driver and the driver continued working at the engine. The noise grew louder. Suddenly the driver straightened himself and turned his face (Jane saw the sweat shining on it in the lamplight) towards Miss Hardcastle. "Look here, Miss," he said, "that's about enough, see? You keep a civil tongue in your head, or else come and mend the bloody car yourself if you're so bloody clever." "Don't you try taking that line with me, Joe," said Miss Hardcastle, "or you'll find me saying a little word about you to the ordinary police." "Well, suppose you do?" said Joe, "I'm beginning to think I might as well be in clink as in your bucking tea-party. 'Struth! I've been in the military police and I've been in the Black and Tans and I've been in the B.U.F., but they were all ruddy picnics to this lot. A man got some decent treatment there. And he had men over him, not a bloody lot of old women." "Yes, Joe," said Miss Hardcastle, "but it wouldn't be clink for you this time if I passed the word to the ordinary cops."

"Oh, it wouldn't, wouldn't it? I might have a story or two to tell about yourself if it came to that."

"For the lord's sake, speak to him nicely, Ma'am," wailed Kitty. "They're coming. We'll catch it proper." And in fact men running, by twos and threes, had begun to trickle into the street.

"Foot it, girls," said Miss Hardcastle. "Sharp's the word. This way."

Jane found herself hustled out of the car and hurried along between Daisy and Kitty. Miss Hardcastle moved in front. The little party darted across the street and up an alley on the far side.

"Any of you know the way here?" asked Miss Hardcastle when they had walked a few steps.

"Don't know, I'm sure, Ma'am," said Daisy.

"I'm a stranger here myself, Ma'am," said Kitty.

"Nice useful lot I've got," said Miss Hardcastle. "Is there anything you do know?"

"It doesn't seem to go no further, Ma'am," said Kitty.

The alley had indeed turned out to be a dead end. Miss Hardcastle stood still for a moment. Unlike her subordinates, she did not seem to be frightened, but only pleasantly excited, and rather amused at the white faces and shaky voices of the girls.

"Well," she said, "this is what I call a night out. You're seeing life, Daisy, aren't you? I wonder are any of these houses empty? All locked anyway. Perhaps we'd best stay where we are."

The shouting in the street they had left had grown louder and they could see a confused mass of humanity surging vaguely in a westward direction. Suddenly it became much louder still and angrier.

"They've caught Joe," said Miss Hardcastle. "If he can make·himself heard he'll send them up here. Blast! This means losing the prisoner. Stop blubbering, Daisy, you little fool. Quick. We must go down into the crowd separately. We've a very good chance of getting through. Keep your heads. Don't shoot, whatever you do. Try to get to Billingham at the crossroads. Ta-ta, Babs! The quieter you keep the less likely we are to meet again."

Miss Hardcastle set off at once. Jane saw her stand for a few seconds on the fringes of the crowd and then disappear into it. The two girls hesitated and then followed. Jane sat down on a doorstep. The burns were painful where her dress had rubbed against them, but what chiefly troubled her was extreme weariness. She was also deadly cold and a little sick. But above all tired; so tired she could drop asleep almost . . .

She shook herself. There was complete silence all about her: she was colder than she had ever been before and her limbs ached. "I believe I *have* been asleep," she thought. She rose, stretched herself, and walked down the desolate lamp lit alley into the larger street. It was quite empty except for one man in a railway uniform who said, "Good morning, Miss," as he walked smartly past. She stood for a moment, undecided and then began to walk slowly to her right. She put her hand in the pocket of the coat which Daisy and Kitty had flung round her before leaving the flat and found three quarters of a large slab of chocolate. She was ravenous and began munching it. Just as she finished she was overtaken by a car which drew up shortly after it had passed her. "Are you all right?" said a man, poking his head out.

"Were you hurt in the riot?" said a woman's voice from within.

"No . . . not much . . . I don't know," said Jane stupidly.

The man stared at her and then got out. "I say," he said, "you don't look too good. Are you sure you're quite well?" Then he turned and spoke to the woman inside. It seemed so long to Jane since she had heard kind, or even sane, voices that she felt like crying. The unknown couple made her sit in the car and gave her brandy and after that sandwiches. Finally they asked if they could give her a lift home. Where was home? And Jane, somewhat to her surprise, heard her own voice very sleepily answering, "The Manor, at St. Anne's." "That's fine," said the man, "we're making for Birmingham and we have to pass it." Then Jane fell asleep at once again, and awoke only to find herself entering a lighted doorway and being received by a woman in pyjamas and an overcoat who turned out to be Mrs. Maggs. But she was too tired to remember how or where she got to bed.

8

Moonlight at Belbury

I

"I am the last person, Miss Hardcastle," said the Deputy Director, "to wish to interfere with your—er—private pleasures. But really . . . !" It was some hours before breakfast time and the old gentleman was fully dressed and unshaved. But if he had been up all night, it was odd that he had let his fire out. He and the Fairy were standing by a cold and blackened grate in his study.

"She can't be far away," said Fairy Hardcastle. "We'll pick her up some other time. It was well worth trying. If I'd got out of her where she'd been—and I should have got it if I'd had a few minutes longer—why, it might have turned out to be enemy headquarters. We might have rounded up the whole gang."

"It was hardly a suitable occasion . . ." began Wither, but she interrupted him.

"We haven't so much time to waste, you know. You tell me Frost is already complaining that the woman's mind is less accessible. And according to your own metapsychology, or whatever you call the damned jargon, that means she's falling under the influence of the other side. You told me that yourself! Where'll we be if you lose touch with her mind before I've got her body locked up here?"

"I am always, of course," said Wither, "most ready and—er—interested to hear expressions of your own opinions and would not for a moment deny that they are (in certain respects, of course, if not in all) of a very real value. On the other hand, there are matters on which your— ah—necessarily specialised experience does not entirely qualify you . . . An arrest was not contemplated at this stage. The Head will, I fear, take the view that you have exceeded your authority. Trespassed beyond your proper sphere, Miss Hardcastle. I do not say that I necessarily agree with him. But we must *all* agree that unauthorized action—"

"Oh, cut it out, Wither!" said the Fairy, seating herself on the side of the table. "Try that game on the Steeles and Stones. I know too much about it. It's no bloody good trying the elasticity stunt on me. It was a golden opportunity, running into that girl. If I hadn't taken it, you'd have talked about lack of initiative; as I did, you talk about exceeding my authority. You can't frighten me. I know bloody well we're all for it if the N.I.C.E. fails; and in the meantime, I'd like to see you do without me. We've got to get the girl, haven't we?"

"But not by an arrest. We have always deprecated anything like violence. If a mere arrest could have secured the—er—good will and collaboration of Mrs. Studdock, we should hardly have embarrassed ourselves with the presence of her husband. And even supposing (merely, of course, for the purpose of argument) that your action in arresting her could be justified, I am afraid your conduct of the affair after that is open to serious criticism."

"I couldn't tell that the bucking car was going to break down, could I?"

"I do not think," said Wither, "the Head could be induced to regard that as the only miscarriage. Once the slightest resistance on this woman's part developed, it was not, in my opinion, reasonable to expect success by the method you employed. As you are aware, I always deplore anything that is not perfectly humane; but that is quite consistent with the position that if more drastic expedients have to be used then they must be used thoroughly. *Moderate* pain, such as any ordinary degree of endurance can resist, is always a mistake. It is no true kindness to the prisoner. The more scientific and, may I add, more civilised facilities for coercive examination which we have placed at your disposal here, might have been successful. I am not speaking officially, Miss Hardcastle, and I would not in any sense attempt to anticipate the reactions of our Head. But I should not be doing my duty if I failed to remind you that complaints from that quarter have already been made (though not, of course, minuted) as to your tendency to allow a certain—er—emotional excitement in the disciplinary or remedial side of your work to distract you from the demands of policy."

"You won't find anyone can do a job like mine well unless they get some kick out of it," said the Fairy sulkily.

The Deputy Director looked at his watch.

"Anyway," said the Fairy, "what does the Head want to see me *now* for? I've been on my feet the whole bloody night. I might be allowed a bath and some breakfast."

"The path of duty, Miss Hardcastle," said Wither, "can never be an easy one. You will not forget that punctuality is one of the points on which emphasis has sometimes been laid."

Miss Hardcastle got up and rubbed her face with her hands. "Well, I must have something to drink before I go in," she said. Wither held out his hands in deprecation.

"Come on, Wither. I *must,*" said Miss Hardcastle.

"You don't think he'll smell it?" said Wither.

"I'm not going in without it, anyway," said she.

The old man unlocked his cupboard and gave her whisky. Then the two left the study and went a long way, right over to the other side of the house where it joined onto the actual Blood Transfusion offices. It was all dark at this hour in the morning and they went by the light of Miss Hardcastle's torch—on through carpeted and pictured passages into blank passages with rubberoid floors and distempered walls and then through a door they had to unlock, and then through another. All the way Miss Hardcastle's booted feet made a noise but the slippered feet of the Deputy Director made no noise at all. At last they came to a place where the lights were on and there was a mixture of animal and chemical smells, and then to a door which was opened to them after they had parleyed through a speaking tube. Filostrato, wearing a white coat, confronted them in the doorway.

"Enter," said Filostrato. "He expect you for some time."

"Is it in a bad temper?" said Miss Hardcastle.

"Sh!" said Wither. "And in any case, my dear lady, I don't think that is quite the way in which one should speak of our Head. His sufferings—in his peculiar condition, you know—"

"You are to go in at once," said Filostrato, "as soon as you have made yourselves ready."

"Stop. Half a moment," said Miss Hardcastle suddenly.

"What is it? Be quick, please," said Filostrato.

"I'm going to be sick."

"You cannot be sick here. Go back. I will give you some X54 at once."

"It's all right now," said Miss Hardcastle. "It was only momentary. It'd take more than this to upset me."

"Silence, please," said the Italian. "Do not attempt to open the second door until my assistant has shut the first one behind you. Do not speak more than you can help. Do not even say yes when you are given an order. The Head will assume your obedience. Do not make sudden movements, do not get too close, do not shout, and above all do not argue. Now."

2

Long after sunrise there came into Jane's sleeping mind a sensation which, had she put it into words, would have sung, "Be glad thou sleeper and thy sorrow offcast. I am the gate to all good adventure." And after she had wakened and found herself lying in pleasant langour with winter morning sunlight falling across her bed, the mood continued. "He *must* let me stay here now," she thought. Sometime after this Mrs. Maggs came in and lit the fire and brought the breakfast. Jane winced as she sat up in bed for some of the burns had stuck to the strange nightdress (rather too large for her) in which she found herself clad. There was an indefinable difference in Mrs. Maggs' behaviour. "It's ever so nice us both being here, isn't it, Mrs. Studdock?" she said, and somehow the tone seemed to imply a closer relation than Jane had envisaged between them. But she was too lazy to wonder much about it. Shortly after breakfast came Miss Ironwood. She examined and dressed the burns, which were not serious. "You can get up in the afternoon if you like, Mrs. Studdock," she said. "I should just take a quiet day till then. What would you like to read? There's a pretty large library." "I'd like the *Curdie* books, please," said Jane, "and *Mansfield Park* and Shakespeare's *Sonnets*." Having thus been provided with reading matter for several hours, she very comfortably went to sleep again.

When Mrs. Maggs looked in at about four o'clock to see if Jane was awake, Jane said she would like to get up. "All right, Mrs. Studdock," said Mrs. Maggs, "just as you like. I'll bring you along a nice cup of tea in a minute and then I'll get the bathroom ready for you. There's a bathroom next door almost, only I'll have to get that Mr. Bultitude out of it. He's that lazy and he *will* go in and sit there all day when it's cold weather."

As soon as Mrs. Maggs had gone however, Jane decided to get up. She felt that her social abilities were quite equal to dealing with the eccentric Mr. Bultitude and she did not want to waste any more time in bed. She had an idea that if once she were "up and about" all sorts of pleasant and interesting things might happen. Accordingly she put on her coat, took her towel, and proceeded to explore; and that was why Mrs. Maggs, coming upstairs with tea a moment later, heard a suppressed shriek and saw Jane emerge from the bathroom with a white face and slam the door behind her.

"Oh dear!" said Mrs. Maggs bursting into laughter. "I ought to have told you. Never mind. I'll soon have him out of that." She set the tea tray down on the passage floor and turned to the bathroom.

"Is it safe?" asked Jane.

"Oh yes, he's *safe* all right," said Mrs. Maggs. "But he's not that easy to shift. Not for you or me, Mrs. Studdock. Of course if it was Miss Ironwood or the Director it would be another matter." With that she opened the bathroom door. Inside, sitting up on its hunkers beside the bath and occupying most of the room was a great, snuffly, wheezy, beady-eyed, loose-skinned, gor-bellied brown bear, which, after a great many reproaches, appeals, exhortations, pushes, and blows from Mrs. Maggs, heaved up its enormous bulk and came very slowly out into the passage.

"Why don't you go out and take some exercise that lovely afternoon, you great lazy thing?" said Mrs. Maggs. "You ought to be ashamed of yourself, sitting there getting in everyone's way. Don't be frightened, Mrs. Studdock. He's as tame as tame. He'll let you stroke him. Go on, Mr. Bultitude. Go and say how do you do to the lady!"

Jane extended a hesitant and unconvincing hand to touch the animal's back, but Mr. Bultitude was sulking and without a glance at Jane continued his slow walk along the passage to a point about ten yards away where he quite suddenly sat down. The tea things rattled at Jane's feet, and everyone on the floor below must have known that Mr. Bultitude had sat down.

"Is it really safe to have a creature like that loose about the house?" said Jane.

"Mrs. Studdock," said Ivy Maggs with some solemnity, "if the

Director wanted to have a tiger about the house it would be safe. That's the way he has with animals. There isn't a creature in the place that would go for another or for us once he's had his little talk with them. Just the same as he does with us. You'll see."

"If you would put the tea in my room . . ." said Jane rather coldly and went into the bathroom. "Yes," said Mrs. Maggs, standing in the open doorway, "you might have had your bath with Mr. Bultitude sitting there beside you—though he's that big and that human I don't somehow feel it would be Nice myself."

Jane made to shut the door.

"Well, I'll leave you *to* it, then," said Mrs. Maggs without moving.

"Thank you," said Jane.

"Sure you got everything you want?" said Mrs. Maggs.

"Quite sure," said Jane.

"Well, I'll be getting along, then," said Mrs. Maggs, turning as if to go, but almost instantly turning back again to say, "you'll find us in the kitchen, I expect, Mother Dimble and me and the rest."

"Is Mrs. Dimble staying in the house?" asked Jane with a slight emphasis on the *Mrs.*

"*Mother* Dimble, we all call her here," said Mrs. Maggs. "And I'm sure she won't mind you doing the same. You'll get used to our ways in a day or two, *I'm* sure. It's a funny house really, when you come to think of it. Well. I'll be getting along then. Don't take too long or your tea won't be worth drinking. But I daresay you'd better not have a bath, not with those nasty places on your chest. Got all you want?"

When Jane had washed and had tea and dressed herself with as much care as strange hairbrushes and a strange mirror allowed, she set out to look for the inhabited rooms. She passed down one long passage, through that silence which is not quite like any other in the world—the silence upstairs, in a big house, on a winter afternoon. Presently, she came to a place where two passages met, and here the silence was broken by a faint irregular noise—*pob-pob-pob-pob*. Looking to her right she saw the explanation, for where the passage ended in a bay window stood Mr. Bultitude, this time on his hind legs, meditatively boxing a punch-ball. Jane chose the way to her left and came to a gallery whence she looked down the staircase into a large hall where daylight mixed with firelight. On the same level with herself, but only to be reached by descending to a landing and ascending again, were shadowy regions which she recognised as leading to the Director's room. A sort of solemnity seemed to her to emanate from them and she went down into the hall almost on tiptoes, and now, for the first time, her memory of that last and curious experience in the blue room came back to her with a weight which even the thought of the Director himself could not counteract. When she reached the hall she saw at once where the back premises of the house must lie—down two steps and along a paved passage, past a stuffed pike in a glass case and then past a grandfather clock, and then, guided by voices and other sounds, to the kitchen itself.

A wide, open hearth glowing with burning wood lit up the comfortable form of Mrs. Dimble who was seated in a kitchen chair at one side of it, apparently, from the basin in her lap and other indications on a table beside her, engaged in preparing vegetables. Mrs. Maggs and Camilla were doing something at a stove—the hearth was apparently not used for cooking—and in a doorway which doubtless led to the scullery a tall grizzle-headed man who wore gum-boots and seemed to have just come from the garden, was drying his hands.

"Come in, Jane," said Mother Dimble, cordially. "We're not expecting you to do any work today. Come and sit on the other side of the fire and talk to me. This is Mr. MacPhee—who has no right to be here, but he'd better be introduced to you."

Mr. MacPhee, having finished the drying process and carefully hung the towel behind the door, advanced rather ceremoniously and shook hands with Jane. His own hand was very large and coarse in texture and he had a shrewd hard-featured face.

"I am very glad to see you, Mrs. Studdock," he said in what Jane took to be a Scotch accent, though it was really that of an Ulsterman.

"Don't believe a word he says, Jane," said Mother Dimble. "He's your prime enemy in this House. He doesn't believe in your dreams."

"Mrs. Dimble!" said MacPhee, "I have repeatedly explained to you the distinction between a personal feeling of confidence and a logical satisfaction of the claims of evidence. The one is a psychological event—"

"And the other a perpetual nuisance," said Mrs. Dimble.

"Never mind her, Mrs. Studdock," said MacPhee. "I am, as I was saying, very glad to welcome you among us. The fact that I have found it my duty on several occasions to point out that no *experimentum crucis* has yet confirmed the hypothesis that your dreams are veridical, has no connection in the world with my personal attitude."

"Of course," said Jane vaguely, and a little confused. "I'm sure you have a right to your own opinions."

All the women laughed as MacPhee in a somewhat louder tone replied, "Mrs. Studdock, I have *no* opinions—on any subject in the world. I state the facts and exhibit the implications. If everyone indulged in fewer opinions" (he pronounced the word with emphatic disgust), "there'd be less silly talking and printing in the world."

"I know who talks most in this house," said Mrs. Maggs, somewhat to Jane's surprise. The Ulsterman eyed the last speaker with an unaltered face while producing a small pewter box from his pocket and helping himself to a pinch of snuff.

"What are you waiting for anyway?" said Mrs. Maggs. "Women's day in the kitchen today."

"I was wondering," said MacPhee, "whether you had a cup of tea saved for me."

"And why didn't you come in at the right time, then?" said Mrs. Maggs. Jane noticed that she talked to him much as she talked to the bear.

"I was busy," said the other seating himself at one end of the table; and added after a pause, "trenching celery. The wee woman does the best she can but she has a poor notion of what needs doing in a garden."

"What is 'women's day' in the kitchen?" asked Jane of Mother Dimble.

"There are no servants here," said Mother Dimble, "and we all do the work. The women do it one day and the men the next. What? No, it's a very sensible arrangement. The Director's idea is that men and women can't do housework together without quarreling. There's something in it. Of course, it doesn't do to look at the cups too closely on the men's day, but on the whole we get along pretty well."

"But why should they quarrel?" asked Jane.

"Different methods, my dear. Men can't *help* in a job, you know. They can be induced to do it: not to help while you're doing it. At least, it makes them grumpy."

"The cardinal difficulty," said MacPhee, "in collaboration between the sexes is that women speak a language without nouns. If two men are doing a bit of work, one will say to the other, 'Put this bowl inside the bigger bowl which you'll find on the top shelf of the green cupboard.' The female for this is, 'Put that in the other one in there.' And then if you ask them, 'in where?' they say, 'in *there*, of course.' There is consequently a phatic hiatus." He pronounced this so as to rhyme with "get *at* us."

"There's your tea now," said Ivy Maggs, "and I'll go and get you a piece of cake, which is more than you deserve. And when you've had it you can go upstairs and talk about nouns for the rest of the evening."

"Not *about* nouns: *by means of* nouns," said MacPhee, but Mrs. Maggs had already left the room. Jane took advantage of this to say to Mother Dimble in a lower voice, "Mrs. Maggs seems to make herself very much at home here."

"My dear, she *is* at home here."

"As a maid, you mean?"

"Well, no more than anyone else. She's here chiefly because her house has been taken from her. She had nowhere else to go."

"You mean she is—one of the Director's charities."

"Certainly that. Why do you ask?"

"Well—I don't know. It *did* seem a little odd that she should call you Mother Dimble. I hope I'm not being snobbish . . ."

"You're forgetting that Cecil and I are another of the Director's charities."

"Isn't that rather playing on words?"

"Not a bit. Ivy and Cecil and I are all here because we were turned out of our homes. At least Ivy and I are. It may be rather different for Cecil."

"And does the Director know that Mrs. Maggs talks to everyone like that?"

"My dear child, don't ask me what the Director knows."

"I think what's puzzling me is that when I saw him he said something about equality not being the important thing. But his own house seems to be run on—well, on very democratic lines indeed."

"I never attempt to understand what he says on that subject," said Mother Dimble. "He's usually talking either about spiritual ranks—and you were never goose enough to think yourself *spiritually* superior to Ivy—or else he's talking about marriage."

"Did you understand his views on marriage?"

"My dear, the Director is a very wise man. But he *is* a man, after all, and an unmarried man at that. Some of what he says, or what the Masters say, about marriage does seem to me to be a lot of fuss about something so simple and natural that it oughtn't to need saying at all. But I suppose there are young women now-a-days who need to be told it."

"You haven't got much use for young women who do, I see."

"Well, perhaps I'm unfair. Things were easier for us. We were brought up on stories with happy endings and on the Prayer Book. We always intended to love, honour and obey, and we had figures and we wore petticoats and we liked waltzes . . ."

"Waltzes are ever so nice," said Mrs. Maggs who had just returned and given MacPhee his slab of cake, "so old fashioned."

At that moment the door opened and a voice from behind it said, "Well, go in then, if you're going." Thus admonished, a very fine jackdaw hopped into the room, followed firstly by Mr. Bultitude and secondly by Arthur Denniston.

"I've told you before, Arthur," said Ivy Maggs, "not to bring that bear in here when we're cooking the dinner." While she was speaking Mr. Bultitude, who was apparently himself uncertain of his welcome, walked across the room in what he believed (erroneously) to be an unobtrusive manner and sat down behind Mrs. Dimble's chair.

"Dr. Dimble's just come back, Mother Dimble," said Denniston. "But he's had to go straight to the Blue Room. And the Director wants you to go to him too, MacPhee."

3

Mark sat down to lunch that day in good spirits. Everyone reported that the riot had gone off most satisfactorily and he had enjoyed reading his own accounts of it in the morning papers. He enjoyed it even more when he heard Steele and Cosser talking about it in a way which showed that they did not even know how it had been engineered, much less who had written it up in the newspapers. And he had enjoyed his morning too. It had involved a conversation with Frost, the Fairy, and Wither himself, about the future of Edgestow. All were agreed that the government would follow the almost unanimous opinion of the nation (as expressed in the newspapers) and put it temporarily under the control of the Institutional Police. An emergency governor of Edgestow must be appointed. Feverstone was the obvious man. As a member of Parliament he represented the Nation, as a Fellow of Bracton he represented the University, as a member of the Institute he represented the Institute. All the competing claims that might otherwise have come into collision were reconciled in the person of Lord Feverstone; the articles on this subject which Mark was to write that afternoon would almost write themselves! But that had not been all. As the conversation proceeded it had become clear that there was really a double object in getting this invidious post for Feverstone. When the time came, and the local unpopularity of the N.I.C.E. rose to its height, he could be sacrificed. This of course was not said in so many words, but Mark realised perfectly clearly that even Feverstone was no longer quite in the Inner Ring. The Fairy said that old Dick was a mere politician at heart and always would be. Wither, deeply sighing, confessed that his talents had been perhaps more useful at an earlier stage of the movement than they were likely to be in the period on which they were now entering. There was in Mark's mind no plan for undermining Feverstone nor even a fully formed wish that he should be undermined; but the whole atmosphere of the discussion became somehow more agreeable to him as he began to understand the real situation. He was also pleased that he had (as he would have put it) "got to know" Frost. He knew by experience that there is in almost every organization some quiet, inconspicuous person whom the small fry suppose to be of no importance but who is really one of the mainsprings of the whole machine. Even to recognize such people for what they are shows that one had made considerable progress. There was, to be sure, a cold fish-like quality about Frost which Mark did not like and something even repulsive about the regularity of his features. But every word he spoke (he did not speak many) went to the root of what was being discussed, and Mark found it delightful to speak to him. The pleasures of conversation were coming, for Mark, to have less and less connection with his spontaneous liking or disliking of the people he talked to. He was aware of this change—which had begun when he joined the Progressive Element in College—and welcomed it as a sign of maturity.

Wither had thawed in a most encouraging manner. At the end of the conversation he had taken Mark aside, spoken vaguely but paternally of the great work he was doing, and finally asked after his wife. The D.D. hoped there was no truth in the rumour which had reached him that she was suffering from—er—some nervous disorder. "Who the devil has been telling him that?" thought Mark. "Because," said Wither, "it had occurred to me, in view of the great pressure of work which rests on you at present and the difficulty, therefore, of your being at home as much as we should all (for your sake) wish, that in *your* case the Institute might be induced . . . I am speaking in a quite informal way . . . that we should all be delighted to welcome Mrs. Studdock here."

Until the D.D. had said this Mark had not realised that there was nothing he would dislike so much as having Jane at Belbury. There were so many things that Jane would not understand: not only the pretty heavy drinking which was becoming his habit but—oh, everything from morning to night. For it is only justice both to Mark and to Jane to record that he would have found it impossible to conduct in her hearing any one of the hundred conversations which his life at Belbury involved. Her mere presence would have made all the laughter of the Inner Ring sound metallic, unreal; and what he now regarded as common prudence would seem to her, and through her to himself, mere flattery, back-biting and toad-eating. Jane in the middle of Belbury would turn the whole of Belbury into a vast vulgarity, flashy and yet furtive. His mind sickened at the thought of trying to teach Jane that she must help to keep Wither in a good temper and must play up to Fairy Hardcastle. He excused himself vaguely to the D.D., with profuse thanks, and got away as quickly as he could.

That afternoon, while he was having tea, Fairy Hardcastle came and leaned over the back of his chair and said in his ear,

"*You've* torn it, Studdock."

"What's the matter now, Fairy?" said he.

"I can't make out what's the matter with *you*, young Studdock, and that's a fact. Have you made up your mind to annoy the Old Man? Because it's a dangerous game, you know."

"What on earth are you talking about?"

"Well, here we've all been working on your behalf and soothing him down and this morning we thought we'd finally succeeded. He was talking about giving you the appointment originally intended for you and waiving the probationary period. Not a cloud in the sky: and then you have five minutes' chat with him—barely five minutes, in fact—and in that time you've managed to undo it all. I begin to think you are mental."

"What the devil's wrong with him this time?"

"Well *you* ought to know! Didn't he say something about bringing your wife here?"

"Yes, he did. What about it?"

"And what did you say?"

"I said not to bother about it—and, of course, thanked him very much and all that." The Fairy whistled.

"Don't you see, honey," she said, gently rapping Mark's scalp with her knuckles, "that you could hardly have made a worse bloomer? It was a most terrific concession for him to make. He's never done it to anyone else. You might have known he'd be offended if you cold-shouldered him. He's burbling away now about lack of confidence. Says he's 'hurt': which means that somebody else soon will be! He takes your refusal as a sign that you are not really 'settled' here."

"But that is sheer madness. I mean . . ."

"Why the blazes couldn't you tell him you'd have your wife here?"

"Isn't that my own business?"

"Don't you want to have her? You're not very polite to little wifie, Studdock. And they tell me she's a damned pretty girl."

At that moment the form of Wither, slowly sauntering in their direction, became apparent to both and the conversation ended.

At dinner he sat next to Filostrato. There were no other members of the inner circle within earshot. The Italian was in good spirits and talkative. He had just given orders for the cutting down of some fine beech trees in the grounds.

"Why have you done that, Professor?" said a Mr. Winter who sat opposite. "I shouldn't have thought they did much harm at that distance from the house. I'm rather fond of trees myself."

"Oh, yes, yes," replied Filostrato. "The pretty trees, the garden trees. But not the savages. I put the rose in my garden, but not the brier. The forest tree is a weed. But I tell you I have seen the civilised tree in Persia. It was a French *attaché* who had it because he was in a place where trees do not grow. It was made of metal. A poor, crude thing. But how if it were perfected? Light, made of aluminium. So natural, it would even deceive."

"It would hardly be the same as a real tree," said Winter.

"But consider the advantages! You get tired of him in one place: two workmen carry him somewhere else: wherever you please. It never dies. No leaves to fall, no twigs, no birds building nests, no muck and mess."

"I suppose one or two, as curiosities, might be rather amusing."

"Why one or two? At present, I allow, we must have forests, for the atmosphere. Presently we find a chemical substitute. And then, why *any* natural trees? I foresee nothing but the *art* tree all over the earth. In fact, we *clean* the planet."

"Do you mean," put in a man called Gould, "that we are to have no vegetation at all?"

"Exactly. You shave your face: even, in the English fashion, you shave him every day. One day we shave the planet."

"I wonder what the birds will make of it?"

"I would not have any birds either. On the art tree I would have the art birds all singing when you press a switch inside the house. When you are tired of the singing you switch them off. Consider again the improvement. No feathers dropped about, no nests, no eggs, no dirt."

"It sounds," said Mark, "like abolishing pretty well all organic life."

"And why not? It is simple hygiene. Listen, my friends. If you pick up some rotten thing and find this organic life crawling over it, do you not say, 'Oh, the horrid thing. It is alive,' and then drop it?"

"Go on," said Winter.

"And you, especially you English, are you not hostile to any organic life except your own on your own body? Rather than permit it you have invented the daily bath."

"That's true."

"And what do you call dirty dirt? Is it not precisely the organic? Minerals are clean dirt. But the real filth is what comes from organisms—sweat, spittles, excretions. Is not your whole idea of purity one huge example? The impure and the organic are interchangeable conceptions."

"What are you driving at, Professor?" said Gould. "After all we are organisms ourselves."

"I grant it. That is the point. In us organic life has produced Mind. It has done its work. After that we want no more of it. We do not want the world any longer furred over with organic life, like what you call the blue mould—all sprouting and budding and breeding and decaying. We must get rid of it. By little and little, of course. Slowly we learn how. Learn to make our brains live with less and less body: learn to build our bodies directly with chemicals, no longer have to stuff them full of dead brutes and weeds. Learn how to reproduce ourselves without copulation."

"I don't think that would be much fun," said Winter.

"My friend, you have already separated the Fun, as you call it, from fertility. The Fun itself begins to pass away. Bah! I know that is not what you think. But look at your English women. Six out of ten are frigid, are they not? You see? Nature herself begins to throw away the anachronism. When she has thrown it away, then real civilisation becomes possible. You would understand if you were peasants. Who would try to work with stallions and bulls? No, no; we want geldings and oxen. There will never be peace and order and discipline so long as there is sex. When man has thrown it away, then he will become finally governable."

This brought them to the end of dinner and as they rose from the table Filostrato whispered in Mark's ear, "I would not advise the Library for you tonight. You understand? You are not in favour. Come and have a little conversation with me in my room."

Mark rose and followed him, glad and surprised that in this new crisis with the D.D. Filostrato was apparently still his friend. They went up to the Italian's sitting-room on the first floor. There Mark sat down before the fire, but his host continued to walk up and down the room.

"I am very sorry, my young friend," said Filostrato, "to hear of this new trouble between you and the Deputy Director. It must be stopped, you understand? If he invites you to bring your wife here, why do you not bring her?"

"Well, really," said Mark, "I never knew he attached so much importance to it. I thought he was merely being polite."

His objection to having Jane at Belbury had been, if not removed, at least temporarily deadened by the wine he had drunk at dinner and by the sharp pang he had felt at the threat of expulsion from the library circle.

"It is of no importance in itself," said Filostrato. "But I have reason to believe it came not from Wither but from the Head himself."

"The Head? You mean Jules?" said Mark in surprise. "I thought he was a mere figurehead. And why should *he* care whether I bring my wife here or not?"

"You were mistaken," said Filostrato. "Our Head is no figurehead." There was something odd about his manner, Mark thought. For some time neither man spoke.

"It is all true," said Filostrato at last, "what I said at dinner."

"But about Jules," said Mark. "What business is it of his?"

"Jules?" said Filostrato. "Why do you speak of him? I say it was all true. The world I look forward to is the world of perfect purity. The clean mind and the clean minerals. What are the things that most offend the dignity of man? Birth and breeding and death. How if we are about to discover that man can live without any of the three?"

Mark stared. Filostrato's conversation appeared so disjointed and his manner so unusual that he began to wonder if he were quite sane or quite sober.

"As for your wife," resumed Filostrato, "I attach no importance to it. What have I to do with men's wives? The whole subject disgusts me. But if they make a point of it . . . Look, my friend, the real question is whether you mean to be truly at one with us or not."

"I don't quite follow," said Mark.

"Do you want to be a mere hireling? But you have already come too far in for that. You are at the turning point of your career, Mr. Studdock. If you try to go back you will be as unfortunate as the fool Hingest. If you come really in—the world . . . bah, what do I say? . . . the universe is at your feet."

"But of course I want to come in," said Mark. A certain excitement was stealing over him.

"The Head thinks that you cannot be really one of us if you will not bring your wife here. He will have all of you, and all that is yours—or nothing. You must bring the woman in too. She also must be one of us."

This remark was like a shock of cold water in Mark's face. And yet . . . and yet . . . in that room and at that moment, fixed with the little, bright eyes of the Professor, he could hardly make the thought of Jane quite real to himself.

"You shall hear it from the lips of the Head himself," said Filostrato suddenly.

"Is Jules *here?*" said Mark.

Instead of answering, Filostrato turned sharply from him and with a great scraping movement flung back the window curtains. Then he switched off the light. The fog had all gone, the wind had risen. Small clouds were scudding across the stars and the full Moon—Mark had never seen her so bright—stared down upon them. As the clouds passed her she looked like a ball that was rolling through them. Her bloodless light filled the room.

"There is a world for you, no?" said Filostrato. "There is cleanness, purity. Thousands of square miles of polished rock with not one blade of grass, not one fibre of lichen, not one grain of dust. Not even air. Have you thought what it would be like, my friend, if you could walk on that land? No crumbling, no erosion. The peaks of those mountains are real peaks: sharp as needles, they would go through your hand. Cliffs as high as Everest and as straight as the wall of a house. And cast by those cliffs, acres of shadow black as ebony, and in the shadow hundreds of degrees of frost. And then, one step beyond the shadow, light that would pierce your eyeballs like steel and rock that would burn your feet. The temperature is at boiling point. You would die, no? But even then you would not become filth. In a few moments you are a little heap of ash; clean, white powder. And mark, no wind to blow that powder about. Every grain in the little heap would remain in its place, just where you died, till the end of the world . . . but that is nonsense. The universe will have no end."

"Yes. A dead world," said Mark gazing at the Moon.

"No!" said Filostrato. He had come close to Mark and spoke almost in a whisper, the bat-like whisper of a voice that is naturally high-pitched. "No. There is life there."

"Do we *know* that?" asked Mark.

"Oh, *si*. Intelligent life. Under the surface. A great race, further advanced than we. An inspiration. A *pure* race. They have cleaned their world, broken free (almost) from the organic."

"But how—?"

"They do not need to be born and breed and die; only their common people, their *canaglia* do that. The Masters live on. They retain their intelligence: they can keep it artificially alive after the organic body has been dispensed with—a miracle of applied biochemistry. They do not need organic food. You understand? They are almost free of Nature, attached to her only by the thinnest, finest cord."

"Do you mean that all *that*," Mark pointed to the mottled globe of the Moon, "is their own doing?"

"Why not? If you remove all the vegetation, presently you have no atmosphere, no water."

"But what was the purpose?"

"Hygiene. Why should they have their world all crawling with organisms? And specially, they would banish one organism. Her surface is not all as you see. There are still surface-dwellers—savages. One great dirty patch on the far side of her where there is still water and air and forests—yes, and germs and death. They are slowly spreading their hygiene over their whole globe. Disinfecting her. The savages fight against them. There are frontiers, and fierce wars, in the caves and galleries down below. But the great race presses on. If you could see the other side you would see year by year the clean rock—like this side of the Moon—encroaching: the organic stain, all the green and blue and mist, growing smaller. Like cleaning tarnished silver."

"But how do we know all this?"

"I will tell you all that another time. The Head has many sources of information. For the moment, I speak only to inspire you. I speak that you may know what can be done: what shall be done here. This Institute—*Dio meo*, it is for something better than housing and vaccinations and faster trains and curing the people of cancer. It is for the conquest of death: or for the conquest of organic life, if you prefer. They are the same thing. It is to bring out of that cocoon of organic life which sheltered the babyhood of mind the New Man, the man who will not die, the artificial man, free from Nature. Nature is the ladder we have climbed up by, now we kick her away."

"And you think that some day we shall really find a means of keeping the brain alive indefinitely?"

"We have begun already. The Head himself . . ."

"Go on," said Mark. His heart was beating wildly and he had forgotten both Jane and Wither. This at last was the real thing.

"The Head himself has already survived death, and you shall speak to him this night."

"Do you mean that Jules has died?"

"Bah! Jules is nothing. He is not the Head."

"Then who is?"

At this moment there was a knock on the door. Someone, without waiting for an answer came in.

"Is the young man ready?" asked the voice of Straik.

"Oh yes. You are ready, are you not, Mr. Studdock?"

"You have explained it to him, then?" said Straik. He turned to Mark and the moonlight in the room was so bright that Mark could now partially recognise his face—its harsh furrows emphasised by that cold light and shade.

"Do you mean really to join us, young man?" said Straik. "There is no turning back once you have set your hand to the plough. And there are no reservations. The Head has sent for you. Do you understand—*the Head?* You will look upon one who was killed and is still alive. The resurrection of Jesus in the Bible was a symbol: tonight you shall see what it symbolised. This is real Man at last, and it claims all our allegiance."

"What the devil are you talking about?" said Mark. The tension of his nerves distorted his voice into a hoarse blustering cry.

"My friend is quite right," said Filostrato. "Our Head is the first of the New Men—the first that lives beyond animal life. As far as Nature is concerned he is already dead: if Nature had her way his brain would now be mouldering in the grave. But he will speak to you within this hour, and—a word in your ear, my friend—you will obey his orders."

"But who *is* it?" said Mark.

"It is François Alcasan," said Filostrato.

"You mean the man who was guillotined?" gasped Mark. Both the heads nodded. Both faces were close to him: in that disastrous light they looked like masks hanging in the air.

"You are frightened?" said Filostrato. "You will get over that. We are offering to make you one of us. *Ahi*—if you were outside, if you were mere *canaglia* you would have reason to be frightened. It is the beginning of all power. He lives forever. The giant time is conquered. And the giant space—he was already conquered too. One of our company has already travelled in space. True, he was betrayed and murdered and his manuscripts are imperfect: we have not yet been able to reconstruct his space ship. But that will come."

"It is the beginning of Man Immortal and Man Ubiquitous," said Straik. "Man on the throne of the universe. It is what all the prophecies really meant."

"At first, of course," said Filostrato, "the power will be confined to a number—a small number—of individual men. Those who are selected for eternal life."

"And you mean," said Mark, "it will then be extended to all men?"

"No," said Filostrato. "I mean it will then be reduced to one man. You are not a fool, are you, my young friend? All that talk about the power of Man over Nature—Man in the abstract—is only for the *canaglia*. You know as well as I do that Man's power over Nature means the power of some men over other men with Nature as the instrument. There is no such thing as Man—it is a word. There are only men. No! It is not Man who will be omnipotent, it is some one man, some immortal man. Alcasan, our Head, is the first sketch of it. The completed product may be someone else. It may be you. It may be me."

"A king cometh," said Straik, "who shall rule the universe with righteousness and the heavens with judgment. You thought all that was mythology, no doubt. You thought because fables had clustered about the phrase, 'Son of Man,' that Man would never really have a son who will wield all power. But he will."

"I don't understand, I don't understand," said Mark.

"But it is very easy," said Filostrato. "We have found how to make a dead man live. He was a wise man even in his natural life. He lives now forever; he gets wiser. Later, we make them live better—for at present, one must concede, this second life is probably not very agreeable to him who has it. You see? Later we make it pleasant for some—perhaps not so pleasant for others. For we can make the dead live whether they wish it or not. He who shall be finally king of the universe can give this life to whom he pleases. They cannot refuse the little present."

"And so," said Straik, "the lessons you learned at your mother's knee return. God will have power to give eternal reward and eternal punishment."

"God?" said Mark. "How does He come into it? I don't believe in God."

"But, my friend," said Filostrato, "does it follow that because there was no God in the past that there will be no God also in the future?"

"Don't you see," said Straik, "that we are offering you the unspeakable glory of being present at the creation of God Almighty? Here, in this house, you shall meet the first sketch of the real God. It is a man—or a being made by man—who will finally ascend the throne of the universe. And rule forever."

"You will come with us?" said Filostrato. "He has sent for you!"

"Of course, he will come," said Straik. "Does he think he could hold back and live?"

"And that little affair of the wife," added Filostrato. "You will not mention a triviality like that. You will do as you are told. One does not argue with the Head."

Mark had nothing now to help him but the rapidly ebbing exhilaration of the alcohol taken at dinner time and some faint gleams of memory from hours with Jane and with friends made before he went to Bracton, during which the world had had a different taste from this exciting horror which now pressed upon him. These, and a merely instinctive dislike for both the moonlit faces which so held his attention. On the other side was fear. What would they do to him if he refused? And aiding fear was his young man's belief that if one gave in for the present things would somehow right themselves "in the morning." And, aiding the fear and the hope, there was still, even then, a not wholly disagreeable thrill at the thought of sharing so stupendous a secret.

"Yes," he said, halting in his speech as if he were out of breath, "Yes—of course—I'll come."

They led him out. The passages were already still and the sound of talk and laughter from the public rooms on the ground floor had ceased. He stumbled, and they linked arms with him. The journey seemed long: passage after passage, passages he had never seen before, doors to unlock, and then into a place where all the lights were on, and there were strange smells. Then Filostrato spoke through a speaking tube and a door was opened to them.

Mark found himself in a surgical-looking room with glaring lights, and sinks, and bottles, and glittering instruments. A young man whom he hardly knew, dressed in a white coat, received them.

"Strip to your underclothes," said Filostrato. While Mark was obeying he noticed that the opposite wall of the room was covered with dials. Numbers of flexible tubes came out of the floor and went into the wall just beneath the dials. The staring dial faces and the bunches of tubes beneath them, which seemed to be faintly pulsating, gave one the impression of looking at some creature with many eyes and many tentacles. The young man kept his eyes fixed on the vibrating needles of the dials. When the three newcomers had removed their outer clothes, they washed their hands and faces, and after that Filostrato plucked white clothes for them out of a glass container with a pair of forceps. When they had put these on he gave them also gloves and masks such as surgeons wear. There followed a moment's silence while Filostrato studied the dials. "Yes, yes," he said. "A little more air. Not much: point nought three. Turn on the chamber air—slowly—to full. Now the lights. Now air in the lock. A little less of the solution. And now" (here he turned to Straik and Studdock) "are you ready to go in?"

He led them to a door in the same wall as the dials.

9

The Saracen's Head

"It was the worst dream I've had yet," said Jane next morning. She was seated in the Blue Room with the Director and Grace Ironwood.

"Yes," said the Director. "Yours is perhaps the hardest post: until the real struggle begins."

"I dreamed I was in a dark room," said Jane, "with queer smells in it and a sort of low humming noise. Then the light came on—but not very much light, and for a long time I didn't realise what I was looking at. And when I made it out . . . I should have waked up if I hadn't made a great effort not to. I thought I saw a face floating in front of me. A face, not a head, if you understand what I mean. That is, there was a beard and nose and eyes—at least, you couldn't see the eyes because it had coloured glasses on, but there didn't seem to be anything above the eyes. Not at first. But as I got used to the light, I got a horrible shock. I thought the face was a mask tied on to a kind of balloon thing. But it wasn't, exactly. Perhaps it looked a bit like a man wearing a sort of turban . . . I'm telling this dreadfully badly. What it really was, was a head (the rest of a head) which had had the top part of the skull taken off and then . . . then . . . as if something inside had boiled over. A great big mass which bulged out from inside what was left of the skull. Wrapped in some kind of composition stuff, but very thin stuff. You could see it twitch. Even in my fright I remember thinking, 'Oh kill it, kill it. Put it out of its pain.' But only for a second because I thought the thing was real, really. It was green looking and the mouth was wide open and quite dry. You realise I was a long time, looking at it, before anything else happened. And soon I saw that it wasn't exactly floating. It was fixed up on some kind of bracket, or shelf, or pedestal—I don't know quite what, and there were things hanging from it. From the neck, I mean. Yes, it had a neck and a sort of collar thing round it, but nothing below the collar; no shoulders or body. Only these hanging things. In the dream I thought it was some kind of new man that had only head and entrails: I thought all those tubes were its insides. But presently—I don't quite know how, I saw that they were artificial. Little rubber tubes and bulbs and little metal things too. I couldn't understand them. All the tubes went into the wall. Then at last something happened."

"You're all right, Jane, are you?" said Miss Ironwood.

"Oh yes," said Jane, "as far as that goes. Only one somehow doesn't *want* to tell it. Well, quite suddenly, like when an engine is started, there came a puff of air out of its mouth, with a hard dry rasping sound. And then there came another, and it settled down into a sort of rhythm—*huff, huff, huff*—like an imitation of breathing. Then came a most horrible thing: the mouth began to dribble. I know it sounds silly but in a way I felt sorry for it because it had no hands and couldn't wipe its mouth. It seems a small thing compared with all the rest but that is how I felt. Then it began working its mouth about and even licking its lips. It was like someone getting a machine into working order. To see it doing that just as if it was alive, and at the same time dribbling over the beard which was all stiff and dead looking . . . Then three people came into the room, all dressed up in white, with masks on, walking as carefully as cats on the top of a wall. One was a great fat man, and another was lanky and bony. The third . . ." here Jane paused involuntarily. "The third . . . I think it was Mark . . . I mean my husband."

"You are uncertain?" said the Director.

"No," said Jane. "It was Mark. I knew his walk. And I knew the shoes he was wearing. And his voice. It *was* Mark."

"I am sorry," said the Director.

"And then," said Jane, "all three of them came round and stood in front of the Head. They bowed to it. You couldn't tell if it was looking at them because of its dark glasses. It kept on with that rhythmical huffing noise. Then it spoke."

"In English?" said Grace Ironwood.

"No, in French."

"What did it say?"

"Well, my French wasn't quite good enough to follow it. It spoke in a queer way. In starts—like a man who's out of breath. With no proper expression. And of course it couldn't turn itself this way or that way as a—a real person—does."

The Director spoke again.

"Did you understand any of what was said?"

"Not very much. The fat man seemed to be introducing Mark to it. It said something to him. Then Mark tried to answer. I could follow him all right: his French isn't much better than mine."

"What did he say?"

He said something about 'doing it in a few days if it was possible.' "

"Was that all?"

"Very nearly. You see Mark couldn't stand it. I knew he wouldn't be able to: I remember, idiotically, in the dream I wanted to tell him. I saw he was going to fall. I think I tried to shout out to the other two 'He's going to fall.' But of course I couldn't. He was sick too. Then they got him out of the room."

All three were silent for a few seconds.

"Was that all?" said Miss Ironwood.

"Yes," said Jane. "That's all I remember. I think I woke up then."

The Director took a deep breath. "Well," he said, glancing at Miss Ironwood, "it becomes plainer and plainer. We must hold a council at once. Is everyone here?"

"No. Dr. Dimble has had to go into Edgestow, into College, to take pupils. He won't be back till evening."

"Then we must hold the council this evening. Make all arrangements." He paused for a moment and then turned to Jane.

"I am afraid this is very bad for you, my dear," he said—"and worse for him."

"You mean for Mark, Sir?"

The Director nodded.

"Yes. Don't think hardly of him. He is suffering. If we are defeated we shall all go down with him. If we win we will rescue him; he cannot be far gone yet." He paused, smiled, and added, "We are quite used to trouble about husbands here, you know. Poor Ivy's is in jail."

"In jail?"

"Oh, yes—for ordinary theft. But quite a good fellow. He'll be all right again."

Though Jane felt horror, even to the point of nausea, at the sight (in her dream) of Mark's real surroundings and associates, it had been horror that carried a certain grandeur and mystery with it. The sudden equation between his predicament and that of a common convict whipped the blood to her cheeks. She said nothing.

"One other thing," continued the Director. "You will not misunderstand it if I exclude you from our council tonight."

"Of course not, Sir," said Jane, in fact misunderstanding it very much.

"You see," he said, "MacPhee takes the line that if you hear things talked of, you will carry ideas of them into your sleep and that will destroy the evidential value of your dreams. And it's not very easy to refute him. He is our sceptic; a very important office."

"I quite understand," said Jane.

"That applies, of course," said the Director, "only to things we don't know yet. You mustn't hear our guesses, you mustn't be there when we're puzzling over the evidence. But we have no secrets from you about the earlier history of our family. In fact MacPhee himself will insist on being the one who tells you all that. He'd be afraid Grace's account, or mine, wouldn't be objective enough."

"I see."

"I want you to like him if you can. He's one of my oldest friends. And he'll be about our best man if we're going to be defeated. You couldn't have a better man at your side in a losing battle. What he'll do if we win, I can't imagine."

2

Mark woke next morning to the consciousness that his head ached all over but specially at the back. He remembered that he had fallen—that was how he had hurt his head—fallen in that other room, with Filostrato and Straik . . . and then, as one of the poets says, he "discov-

ered in his mind an inflammation swollen and deformed, his memory."
Oh, but impossible, not to be accepted for a moment: it had been a
nightmare, it must be shoved away, it would vanish away now that he
was fully awake. It was an absurdity. Once in delirium he had seen the
front part of a horse, by itself, with no body or hind legs, running across
a lawn, had felt it ridiculous at the very moment of seeing it, but not the
less horrible for that. This was an absurdity of the same sort. A Head
without any body underneath. A Head that could speak when they
turned on the air and the artificial saliva with taps in the next room. His
own head began to throb so hard that he had to stop thinking.

But he knew it was true. And he could not, as they say, "take it." He
was very ashamed of this, for he wished to be considered one of the
tough ones. But the truth is that his toughness was only of the will, not
of the nerves, and the virtues he had almost succeeded in banishing from
his mind still lived, if only negatively and as weaknesses, in his body. He
approved of vivisection, but had never worked in a dissecting room. He
recommended that certain classes of people should be gradually elimi-
nated: but he had never been there when a small shopkeeper went to the
workhouse or a starved old woman of the governess type came to the
very last day and hour and minute in the cold attic. He knew nothing
about the last half cup of cocoa drunk slowly ten days before.

Meantime he must get up. He must do something about Jane.
Apparently he would *have* to bring her to Belbury. His mind had made
this decision for him at some moment he did not remember. He must
get her, to save his life. All his anxieties about being in the inner ring or
getting a job had shrunk into insignificance. It was a question of life
or death. They would kill him if he annoyed them; perhaps behead him
. . . oh God, if only they would really kill that monstrous little lump of
torture, that lump with a face, which they kept there talking on its steel
bracket. All the minor fears at Belbury—for he knew now that all except
the leaders were always afraid—were only emanations from that central
fear. He must get Jane; he wasn't fighting against that now.

It must be remembered that in Mark's mind hardly one rag of noble
thought, either Christian or Pagan, had a secure lodging. His education
had been neither scientific nor classical—merely "Modern." The severi-
ties both of abstraction and of high human tradition had passed him by:
and he had neither peasant shrewdness nor aristocratic honour to help
him. He was a man of straw, a glib examinee in subjects that require no
exact knowledge (he had always done well on Essays and General

Papers) and the first hint of a real threat to his bodily life knocked him sprawling. And his head ached so terribly and he felt so sick. Luckily he now kept a bottle of whisky in his room. A stiff one enabled him to shave and dress.

He was late for breakfast, but that made little difference for he could not eat. He drank several cups of black coffee and then went into the writing room. Here he sat for a long time drawing things on the blotting paper. This letter to Jane proved almost impossible now that it came to the point. And why did they want Jane? Formless fears stirred in his mind. And Jane of all people! Would they take her to the Head? For almost the first time in his life a gleam of something like disinterested love came into his mind; he wished he had never married her, never dragged her into this whole outfit of horrors which was, apparently, to be his life.

"Hello, Studdock!" said a voice. "Writing to little wifie, eh?"

"Damn!" said Mark, "You've made me drop my pen."

"Then pick it up, Sonny," said Miss Hardcastle, seating herself on the table. Mark did so, and then sat still without looking up at her. Not since he had been bullied at school had he known what it was to hate and dread anyone with every nerve of his body as he now hated and dreaded this woman.

"I've got bad news for you, Sonny," she said presently. His heart gave a jump.

"Take it like a man, Studdock," said the Fairy.

"What is it?"

She did not answer quite at once and he knew she was studying him, watching how the instrument responded to her playing.

"I'm worried about little wifie, and that's a fact," she said at last.

"What do you mean?" said Mark sharply, this time looking up. The cheroot between her teeth was still unlit but she had got as far as taking out her matches.

"I looked her up," said Miss Hardcastle, "all on your account, too. I thought Edgestow wasn't too healthy a place for her to be at present."

"What's wrong with her?" shouted Mark.

"Ssh!" said Miss Hardcastle. "You don't want everyone to hear."

"Can't you tell me what's wrong?"

She waited for a few seconds before replying. "How much do you know about her family, Studdock?"

"Lots. What's that got to do with it?"

"Nothing . . . queer . . . on either side?"

"What the devil do you mean?"

"Don't be rude, honey. I'm doing all I can for you. It's only—well, I thought she was behaving pretty oddly when I saw her."

Mark well remembered his conversation with his wife on the morning he left for Belbury. A new stab of fear pierced him. Might not this detestable woman be speaking the truth?

"What did she say?" he asked.

"If there is anything wrong with her in that way," said the Fairy, "take my advice, Studdock, and have her over here at once. She'll be properly looked after here."

"You haven't yet told me what she said or did."

"I wouldn't like to have anyone belonging to me popped into Edgestow Asylum. Specially now that we're getting our emergency powers. They'll be using the ordinary patients experimentally, you know. Whereas if you'll just sign this form I'll run over after lunch and have her here this evening."

Mark threw his pen on the desk.

"I shall do nothing of the sort. Specially as you haven't given me the slightest notion what's wrong with her."

"I've been trying to tell you but you don't let me. She kept on talking about someone who'd broken into your flat—or else met her at the station (one couldn't make out which) and burned her with cigars. Then, most unfortunately, she noticed my cheroot, and, if you please, she identified *me* with this imaginary persecutor. Of course after that I could do no good."

"I must go home at once," said Mark getting up.

"Here—whoa! You can't do that," said the Fairy also rising.

"Can't go home? I've bloody well got to, if all this is true."

"Don't be a fool, lovey," said Miss Hardcastle. "Honest! I know what I'm talking about. You're in a damn dangerous position already. You'll about do yourself in if you're absent without leave now. Send me. Sign the form. That's the sensible way to do it."

"But a moment ago you said she couldn't stand you at any price."

"Oh, that wouldn't make any odds. Of course, it would be easier if she hadn't taken a dislike to me. I say, Studdock, you don't think little wifie could be jealous, do you?"

"Jealous? Of you?" said Mark with uncontrollable disgust.

"Where are you off to?" said the Fairy sharply.

"To see the D.D. and then home."

"Stop. You won't do that unless you mean to make me your enemy for life—and let me tell you, you can't afford many more enemies."

"Oh, go to the devil," said Mark.

"Come back, Studdock," shouted the Fairy. "Wait! Don't be a bloody fool." But Mark was already in the hall. For the moment everything seemed to have become clear. He would look in on Wither, not to ask for leave but simply to announce that he had to go home at once because his wife was dangerously ill; he would be out of the room before Wither could reply—and then off. The further future was vague, but that did not seem to matter. He put on his hat and coat, ran upstairs and knocked at the door of the Deputy Director's office.

There was no answer. Then Mark noticed that the door was not quite shut. He ventured to push it open a little further and saw the Deputy Director sitting inside with his back to the door. "Excuse me, Sir," said Mark. "Might I speak to you for a few minutes?" There was no answer. "Excuse me, Sir," said Mark in a louder voice, but the figure neither spoke nor moved. With some hesitation, Mark went into the room and walked around to the other side of the desk; but when he turned to look at Wither he caught his breath, for he thought he was looking into the face of a corpse. A moment later he recognised his mistake. In the stillness of the room he could hear the man breathing. He was not even asleep, for his eyes were open. He was not unconscious, for his eyes rested momentarily on Mark and then looked away. "I beg your pardon, Sir," began Mark and then stopped. The Deputy Director was not listening. He was so far from listening that Mark felt an insane doubt whether he was there at all, whether the soul of the Deputy Director were not floating far away, spreading and dissipating itself like a gas through formless and lightless worlds, waste lands and lumber rooms of the universe. What looked out of those pale watery eyes was, in a sense, infinity—the shapeless and the interminable. The room was still and cold: there was no clock and the fire had gone out. It was impossible to speak to a face like that. Yet it seemed impossible also to get out of the room, for the man had seen him. Mark was afraid; it was so unlike any experience he had ever had before.

When at last Mr. Wither spoke, his eyes were not fixed on Mark but on some remote point beyond him, beyond the window, perhaps in the sky.

"I know who it is," said Wither. "Your name is Studdock. What do you mean by coming here? You had better have stayed outside. Go away."

It was then that Mark's nerve suddenly broke. All the slowly mounting fears of the last few days ran together into one fixed determination and a few seconds later he was going downstairs three steps at a time. Then he was crossing the hall. Then he was out, and walking down the drive. Once again, his immediate course seemed quite plain to him. Opposite the entrance was a thick belt of trees pierced by a field path. That path would bring him in half an hour to Courthampton and there he could get a country bus to Edgestow. About the future he did not think at all. Only two things mattered: firstly, to get out of that house, and, secondly, to get back to Jane. He was devoured with a longing for Jane which was physical without being at all sensual: as if comfort and fortitude would flow from her body, as if her very skin would clean away all the filth that seemed to hang about him. The idea that she might be really mad had somehow dropped out of his mind. And he was still young enough to be incredulous of misery. He could not quite rid himself of the belief that if only he made a dash for it the net must somehow break, the sky must clear, and it would all end up with Jane and Mark having tea together as if none of all this had happened.

He was out of the grounds now; he was crossing the road: he had entered a belt of trees. He stopped suddenly. Something impossible was happening. There was a figure before him on the path: a tall, very tall, slightly stooping figure, sauntering and humming a little dreary tune: the Deputy Director himself. And in one moment all that brittle hardihood was gone from Mark's mood. He turned back. He stood in the road; this seemed to him the worst pain that he ever felt. Then, tired, so tired that he felt the weak tears filling his eyes, he walked very slowly back into Belbury.

3

Mr. MacPhee had a little room on the ground floor at the Manor which he called his office and to which no woman was ever admitted except under his own conduct; and in this tidy but dusty apartment he sat with Jane Studdock shortly before dinner that evening, having invited her there to give her what he called "a brief, objective outline of the situation."

"I should premise at the outset, Mrs. Studdock," he said, "that I have known the Director for a great many years and that for most of his life he was a philologist. I'm not just satisfied myself that philology can be regarded as an exact science, but I mention the fact as a testimony to his general intellectual capacity. And, not to forejudge any issue, I will not say, as I would in ordinary conversation, that he has always been a man of what you might call an imaginative turn. His original name was Ransom."

"Not Ransom's *Dialect and Semantics?*" said Jane.

"Aye. That's the man," said MacPhee. "Well, about six years ago—I have all the dates in a wee book there, but it doesn't concern us at the moment—came his first disappearance. He was clean gone—not a trace of him—for about nine months. I thought he'd most likely been drowned bathing or something of the kind. And then one day what does he do but turn up again in his rooms at Cambridge and go down sick and into hospital for three months more. And he wouldn't say where he'd been except privately to a few friends."

"Well?" said Jane eagerly.

"He said," answered MacPhee, producing his snuff-box and laying great emphasis on the word *said,* "he said he'd been to the planet Mars."

"You mean he said this . . . while he was ill?"

"No, no. He says so still. Make what you can of it; that's his story."

"I believe it," said Jane.

MacPhee selected a pinch of snuff with as much care as if those particular grains had differed from all the others in his box and spoke before applying them to his nostrils.

"I'm giving you the facts," he said. "He told us he'd been to Mars, kidnapped, by Professor Weston and Mr. Devine—Lord Feverstone as he now is. And by his own account he'd escaped from them—on Mars, you'll understand—and been wandering about there alone for a bit. Alone."

"It's uninhabited, I suppose?"

"We have no evidence on that point except his own story. You are doubtless aware, Mrs. Studdock, that a man in complete solitude even on this earth—an explorer, for example—gets into very remarkable states of consciousness. I'm told a man might forget his own identity."

"You mean he might have imagined things on Mars that weren't there?"

"I'm making no comments," said MacPhee. "I'm merely recording. By his own accounts there are all kinds of creatures walking about there;

that's maybe why he has turned his house into a sort of menagerie, but no matter for that. But he also says he met one kind of creature there which specially concerns us at this moment. He called them *eldils.*"

"A kind of animal, do you mean?"

"Did ever you try to define the word Animal, Mrs. Studdock?"

"Not that I remember. I meant, were these things . . . well, intelligent? Could they talk?"

"Aye. They could talk. They were intelligent, for-bye, which is not always the same thing."

"In fact, these were the Martians?"

"That's just what they weren't, according to his account. They were on Mars but they didn't rightly belong there. He says they are creatures that live in empty space."

"But there's no air."

"I'm telling you his story. He says they don't breathe. He said also that they don't reproduce their species and don't die. But you'll observe that even if we assume the rest of his story to be correct this last statement could not rest on observation."

"What on earth are they like?"

"I'm telling you how he described them."

"I mean, what do they look like?"

"I'm not just exactly prepared to answer that question," said MacPhee.

"Are they perfectly *huge?*" said Jane almost involuntarily. MacPhee blew his nose and continued.

"The point, Mrs. Studdock," he said, "is this: Dr. Ransom claims that he has received continual visits from these creatures since he returned to Earth. So much for his first disappearance. Then came the second. He was away for more than a year and that time he said he'd been in the planet Venus—taken there by these *eldils.*"

"Venus is inhabited by them too?"

"You'll forgive me observing that this remark shows you have not grasped what I'm telling you. These creatures are not planetary creatures at all. Supposing them to exist, you are to conceive them floating about the depth of space, though they may alight on a planet here and there, like a bird alighting on a tree, you understand. There's some of them, he says, are more or less permanently attached to particular planets, but they're not native there. They're just a clean different kind of thing."

There were a few seconds of silence, and then Jane asked, "They are, I gather, more or less friendly?"

"That is certainly the Director's idea about them, with one important exception."

"What's that?"

"The eldils that have for many centuries concentrated on our own planet. We seem to have had no luck at all in choosing our particular complement of parasites. And that, Mrs. Studdock, brings me to the point."

Jane waited. It was extraordinary how MacPhee's manner almost neutralised the strangeness of what he was telling her.

"The long and short of it is," said he, "that this house is dominated either by the creatures I'm talking about, or by a sheer delusion. It is by advices he thinks he has received from eldils that the Director has discovered the conspiracy against the human race; and what's more, it's on instructions from eldils that he's conducting the campaign—if you can call it conducting! It may have occurred to you to wonder, Mrs. Studdock, how any man in his senses thinks we're going to defeat a powerful conspiracy by sitting here growing winter vegetables and training performing bears. It is a question I have propounded on more than one occasion. The answer is always the same; we're waiting for orders."

"From the eldils? It was they he meant when he spoke of his Masters?"

"I doubt it would be, though he doesn't use that word in speaking to me."

"But, Mr. MacPhee, I don't understand. I thought you said the ones on our planet were hostile."

"That's a very good question," said MacPhee, "but it's not our own ones that the Director claims to be in communication with. It's his friends from outer space. Our own crew, the terrestrial eldils, are at the back of the whole conspiracy. You are to imagine us, Mrs. Studdock, living on a world where the criminal classes of the eldils have established their headquarters. And what's happening now, if the Director's views are correct, is that their own respectable kith and kin are visiting this planet to red the place up."

"You mean that the other eldils out of space actually come here—to this house?"

"That is what the Director thinks."

"But you must know whether it's true or not."

"How?"

"Have you seen them?"

"That's not a question to be answered Aye or No. I've seen a good many things in my time that weren't there or weren't what they were letting on to be: rainbows and reflections and sunsets, not to mention dreams. And there's heterosuggestion too. I will not deny that I have observed a class of phenomena in this house that I have not yet fully accounted for. But they never occurred at a moment when I had a notebook handy or any facilities for verification."

"Isn't seeing believing?"

"It may be—for children or beasts," said MacPhee.

"But not for sensible people, you mean?"

"My uncle, Dr. Duncanson," said MacPhee, "whose name may be familiar to you—he was Moderator of the General Assembly over the water, in Scotland—used to say, 'Show it to me in the word of God.' And then he'd slap the big Bible on the table. It was a way he had of shutting up people that came to him blathering about religious experiences. And granting his premises, he was quite right. I don't hold his views, Mrs. Studdock, you understand, but I work on the same principles. If anything wants Andrew MacPhee to believe in its existence, I'll be obliged if it will present itself in full daylight, with a sufficient number of witnesses present, and not get shy if you hold up a camera or a thermometer."

MacPhee regarded his snuff-box meditatively.

"You have seen something, then."

"Aye. But we must keep an open mind. It might be a hallucination. It might be a conjuring trick . . ."

"By the Director?" asked Jane angrily. Mr. MacPhee once more had recourse to his snuff-box. "Do you really expect me," said Jane, "to believe that the Director is that sort of man? A charlatan?"

"I wish, Ma'am," said MacPhee, "you could see your way to consider the matter without constantly using such terms as *believe*. Obviously, conjuring is one of the hypotheses that any impartial investigator must take into account. The fact that it is a hypothesis specially uncongenial to the emotions of this investigator or that, is neither here nor there. Unless, maybe, it is an extra ground for emphasising the hypothesis in question, just because there is a strong psychological danger of neglecting it."

"There's such a thing as loyalty," said Jane. MacPhee, who had been carefully shutting up the snuff-box, suddenly looked up with a hundred covenanters in his eyes.

"There is, Ma'am," he said. "As you get older you will learn that it is a virtue too important to be lavished on individual personalities."

At that moment there was a knock at the door. "Come in," said MacPhee, and Camilla entered.

"Have you finished with Jane, Mr. MacPhee?" she said. "She promised to come out for a breath of air with me before dinner."

"Och, breath of air your grandmother!" said MacPhee with a gesture of despair. "Very well, ladies, very well. Away out to the garden. I doubt they're doing something more to the purpose on the enemy's side. They'll have all this country under their hands before we move, at this rate."

"I wish you'd read the poem I'm reading," said Camilla. "For it says in one line just what I feel about this waiting:
Fool,
All lies in a passion of patience, my lord's rule."

"What's that from?" asked Jane.

"*Taliessin through Logres.*"

"Mr. MacPhee probably approves of no poets except Burns."

"Burns!" said MacPhee with profound contempt, opening the drawer of his table with great energy and producing a formidable sheaf of papers. "If you're going to the garden, don't let me delay you, ladies."

"He's been telling you?" said Camilla, as the two girls went together down the passage. Moved by a kind of impulse which was rare to her experience, Jane seized her friend's hand as she answered, "Yes!" Both were filled with some passion, but what passion they did not know. They came to the front door and as they opened it a sight met their eyes which, though natural, seemed at the moment apocalyptic.

All day the wind had been rising and they found themselves looking out on a sky swept almost clean. The air was intensely cold, the stars severe and bright. High above the last rags of scurrying clouds hung the Moon in all her wildness—not the voluptuous Moon of a thousand southern love-songs, but the huntress, the untameable virgin, the spearhead of madness. If that cold satellite had just then joined our planet for the first time, it could hardly have looked more like an omen. The wildness crept into Jane's blood.

"That Mr. MacPhee . . ." said Jane as they walked steeply uphill to the very summit of the garden.

"I know," said Camilla. And then, "*You* believed it?"

"Of course."

"How does Mr. MacPhee explain the Director's age?"

"You mean his looking—or being—so young—if you call it young?"

"Yes. That is what people are like who come back from the stars. Or at least from Perelandra. Paradise is still going on there; make him tell you about it some time. He will never grow a year or a month older again."

"Will he die?"

"He will be taken away, I believe. Back into Deep Heaven. It has happened to one or two people, perhaps about six, since the world began."

"Camilla!"

"Yes."

"What—what *is* he?"

"He's a man, my dear. And he is the Pendragon of Logres. This house, all of us here, and Mr. Bultitude and Pinch, are all that's left of the Logres: all the rest has become merely Britain. Go on. Let's go right to the top. How it's blowing! They might come to him tonight."

4

That evening Jane washed up under the attentive eye of Baron Corvo, the jackdaw, while the others held council in the Blue Room.

"Well," said Ransom as Grace Ironwood concluded reading from her notes. "That is the dream, and everything in it seems to be objective."

"Objective?" said Dimble. "I don't understand, Sir. You don't mean they could really have a thing like that?"

"What do you think, MacPhee?" asked Ransom.

"Oh aye, it's possible," said MacPhee. "You see it's an old experiment with animals' heads. They do it often in laboratories. You cut off a cat's head, maybe, and throw the body away. You can keep the head going a bit if you supply it with blood at the right pressure."

"Fancy!" said Ivy Maggs.

"Do you mean, keep it *alive*," said Dimble.

"*Alive* is an ambiguous word. You can keep all the functions. It's what would be popularly called alive. But a human head—and consciousness—I don't know what would happen if you tried that."

"It has been tried," said Miss Ironwood. "A German tried it before the first war. With the head of a criminal."

"Is that a fact?" said MacPhee with great interest. "And do you know what result he got?"

"It failed. The head simply decayed in the ordinary way."

"I've had enough of this, I have," said Ivy Maggs rising and abruptly leaving the room.

"Then this filthy abomination," said Dr. Dimble, "is real—not only a dream." His face was white and his expression strained. His wife's face, on the other hand, showed nothing more than that controlled distaste with which a lady of the old school listens to any disgusting detail when its mention becomes unavoidable.

"We have no evidence of that," said MacPhee. "I'm only stating facts. What the girl has dreamed is possible."

"And what about this turban business," said Denniston, "this sort of swelling on top of the head?"

"You see what it *might* be," said the Director.

"I'm not sure that I do, Sir," said Dimble.

"Supposing the dream to be veridical," said MacPhee. "You can guess what it would be. Once they'd got it kept alive, the first thing that would occur to boys like them would be to increase its brain. They'd try all sorts of stimulants. And then, maybe, they'd ease open the skull-cap and just—well, just let it boil over as you might say. That's the idea, I don't doubt. A cerebral hypertrophy artificially induced to support a superhuman power of ideation."

"Is it at all probable," said the Director, "that a hypertrophy like that would increase thinking power?"

"That seems to me the weak point," said Miss Ironwood. "I should have thought it was just as likely to produce lunacy—or nothing at all. But it *might* have the opposite effect."

There was a thoughtful silence.

"Then what we are up against," said Dimble, "is a criminal's brain swollen to super-human proportions and experiencing a mode of consciousness which we can't imagine, but which is presumably a consciousness of agony and hatred."

"It's not certain," said Miss Ironwood, "that there would be very much actual pain. Some from the neck, perhaps, at first."

"What concerns us much more immediately," said MacPhee, "is to determine what conclusions we can draw from these carryings on with

Alcasan's head and what practical steps should be taken on our part—always and simply as a working hypothesis, assuming the dream to be veridical."

"It tells us one thing straight away," said Denniston.

"What's that?" asked MacPhee.

"That the enemy movement is international. To get that head they must have been hand in glove with at least one foreign police force."

MacPhee rubbed his hands. "Man," he said, "you have the makings of a logical thinker. But the deduction's not all that certain. Bribery might account for it without actual consolidation."

"It tells us something in the long run even more important," said the Director. "It means that if this technique is really successful, the Belbury people have for all practical purposes discovered a way of making themselves immortal." There was a moment's silence, and then he continued: "It is the beginning of what is really a new species—the Chosen Heads who never die. They will call it the next step in evolution. And henceforward, all the creatures that you and I call human are mere candidates for admission to the new species or else its slaves—perhaps its food."

"The emergence of the Bodiless Men!" said Dimble.

"Very likely, very likely," said MacPhee, extending his snuff-box to the last speaker. It was refused and he took a very deliberate pinch before proceeding. "But there's no good at all applying the forces of rhetoric to make ourselves skeery or daffing our own heads off our shoulders because some other fellows have had the shoulders taken from under their heads. I'll back the Director's Head, and yours, Dr. Dimble, and my own, against this lad's whether the brains is boiling out of it or no. Provided we use them. I should be glad to hear what practical measures on our side are suggested."

With these words he tapped his knuckles gently on his knee and stared hard at the Director.

"It is," said MacPhee, "a question I have ventured to propound before."

A sudden transformation, like the leaping up of a flame in embers, passed over Grace Ironwood's face. "Can the Director not be trusted to produce his own plan in his own time, Mr. MacPhee?" she said fiercely.

"By the same token, Doctor," said he, "can the Director's council not be trusted to hear his plan?"

"What do you mean, MacPhee?" asked Dimble.

"Mr. Director," said MacPhee. "You'll excuse me for speaking frankly. Your enemies have provided themselves with this Head. They have taken possession of Edgestow and they're in a fair way to suspend the laws of England. And still you tell us it is not time to move. If you had taken my advice six months ago we would have had an organisation all over this island by now and maybe a party in the House of Commons. I know well what you'll say—that those are not the right methods. And maybe no. But if you can neither take our advice nor give us anything to do, what are we all sitting here for? Have you seriously considered sending us away and getting some other colleagues that you *can* work with?"

"Dissolve the Company, do you mean?" said Dimble.

"Aye, I do," said MacPhee.

The Director looked up with a smile. "But," he said, "I have no power to dissolve it."

"In that case," said MacPhee, "I must ask what authority you had to bring it together?"

"I never brought it together," said the Director. Then, after glancing round the company he added: "There is some strange misunderstanding here! Were you all under the impression I had *selected* you?"

"Were you?" he repeated, when no one answered.

"Well," said Dimble, "as regards myself I fully realise that the thing has come about more or less unconsciously . . . even accidentally. There was no moment at which you asked me to join a definite movement, or anything of that kind. That is why I have always regarded myself as a sort of camp follower. I had assumed that the others were in a more regular position."

"You know why Camilla and I are here, Sir," said Denniston. "We certainly didn't intend or foresee how we were going to be employed."

Grace Ironwood looked up with a set expression on her face which had grown rather pale. "Do you wish . . . ?" she began. The Director laid his hand on her arm. "No," he said, "No. There is no need for all these stories to be told."

MacPhee's stern features relaxed into a broad grin. "I see what you're driving at," he said. "We've all been playing blind man's buff, I doubt. But I'll take leave to observe, Dr. Ransom, that you carry things a wee bit high. I don't just remember how you came to be called Director: but from that title and from one or two other indications a man would have thought you behaved more like the leader of an organisation than the host at a house-party."

"I am the Director," said Ransom, smiling. "Do you think I would claim the authority I do if the relation between us depended either on your choice or mine? You never chose me. I never chose you. Even the great Oyéresu whom I serve never chose me. I came into their worlds by what seemed, at first, a chance; as you came to me—as the very animals in this house first came to it. You and I have not started or devised this: it has descended on us—sucked us into itself, if you like. It is, no doubt, an organisation: but we are not the organisers. And that is why I have no authority to give any one of you permission to leave my household."

For a time there was complete silence in the Blue Room, except for the crackling of the fire.

"If there is nothing more to discuss," said Grace Ironwood presently, "perhaps we had better leave the Director to rest."

MacPhee rose and dusted some snuff off the baggy knees of his trousers—thus preparing a wholly novel adventure for the mice when they next came out in obedience to the Director's whistle.

"I have no notion," he said, "of leaving this house if anyone wishes me to stay. But as regards the general hypothesis on which the Director appears to be acting and the very peculiar authority he claims, I absolutely reserve my judgment. You know well, Mr. Director, in what sense I have, and in what sense I have not, complete confidence in yourself."

The Director laughed. "Heaven forbid," he said, "that I should claim to know what goes on in the two halves of your head, MacPhee, much less how you connect them. But I know (what matters much more) the kind of confidence I have in you. But won't you sit down? There is much more to be said."

MacPhee resumed his chair; Grace Ironwood, who had been sitting bolt upright in hers, relaxed; and the Director spoke.

"We have learned tonight," he said, "if not what the real power behind our enemies is doing, at least the form in which it is embodied at Belbury. We therefore know something about one of the two attacks which are about to be made on our race. But I'm thinking of the other."

"Yes," said Camilla earnestly. "The other."

"Meaning by that?" asked MacPhee.

"Meaning," said Ransom, "whatever is under Bragdon Wood."

"You're still thinking about *that*?" said the Ulsterman.

A moment of silence ensued.

"I am thinking of almost nothing else," said the Director. "We knew already that the enemy wanted the wood. Some of us guessed why. Now Jane has seen—or rather felt—in a vision what it is they are looking for in Bragdon. It may be the greater danger of the two. But what is certain is that the greatest danger of all is the junction of the enemies' forces. He is staking everything on that. When the new power from Belbury joins up with the old power under Bragdon Wood, Logres—indeed Man— will be almost surrounded. For us everything turns on preventing that junction. That is the point at which we must be ready both to kill and die. But we cannot strike yet. We cannot get into Bragdon and start excavating for ourselves. There must be a moment when they find him— it. I have no doubt we shall be told in one way or another. Till then we must wait."

"I don't believe a word of all that other story," said MacPhee.

"I thought," said Miss Ironwood, "we weren't to use words like *believe*. I thought we were only to state facts and exhibit implications."

"If you two quarrel much more," said the Director, "I think I'll make you marry one another."

5

At the beginning the grand mystery for the Company had been why the enemy wanted Bragdon Wood. The land was unsuitable and could be made fit to bear a building on the scale they proposed only by the costliest preliminary work; and Edgestow itself was not an obviously convenient place. By intense study in collaboration with Dr. Dimble, and despite the continued scepticism of MacPhee, the Director had at last come to a certain conclusion. Dimble and he and the Dennistons shared between them a knowledge of Arthurian Britain which orthodox scholarship will probably not reach for some centuries. They knew that Edgestow lay in what had been the very heart of ancient Logres, that the village of Cure Hardy preserved the name of Ozana le Coeur Hardi, and that a historical Merlin had once worked in what was now Bragdon Wood.

What exactly he had done there they did not know; but they had all, by various routes, come too far either to consider his art mere legend and imposture, or to equate it exactly with what the Renaissance called Magic. Dimble even maintained that a good critic, by his sensibility alone, could detect the difference between the traces which the two things had left on literature. "What common measure is there," he would ask, "between ceremonial occultists like Faustus and Prospero and Archimago with their midnight studies, their forbidden books, their attendant fiends or elementals, and a figure like Merlin who seems to produce his results simply by being Merlin?" And Ransom agreed. He thought that Merlin's art was the last survival of something older and different—something brought to Western Europe after the fall of Numinor and going back to an era in which the general relations of mind and matter on this planet had been other than those we know. It had probably differed from Renaissance Magic profoundly. It had possibly (though this was doubtful) been less guilty: it had certainly been more effective. For Paracelsus and Agrippa and the rest had achieved little or nothing: Bacon himself—no enemy to magic except on this account—reported that the magicians "attained not to greatness and certainty of works." The whole Renaissance outburst of forbidden arts had, it seemed, been a method of losing one's soul on singularly unfavourable terms. But the older Art had been a different proposition.

But if the only possible attraction of Bragdon lay in its association with the last vestiges of Atlantean magic, this told the Company something else. It told them that the N.I.C.E., at its core, was not concerned solely with modern or materialistic forms of power. It told the Director, in fact, that there was eldilic energy and eldilic knowledge behind it. It was, of course, another question whether its human members knew of the dark powers who were their real organisers. And in the long run this question was not perhaps important. As Ransom himself had said more than once, "Whether they know it or whether they don't, much the same sort of things are going to happen. It's not a question of how the Belbury people are going to act (the dark-eldils will see to that) but of how they will think about their actions. They'll go to Bragdon: it remains to be seen whether any of them will know the real reason why they're going there, or whether they'll all fudge up some theory of soils, or air, or etheric tensions, to explain it."

Up to a certain point the Director had supposed that the powers for which the enemy hankered were resident in the mere site at Bragdon—for there is an old and wide-spread belief that locality itself is of importance in such matters. But from Jane's dream of the cold sleeper he had learned better. It was something much more definite, something located under the soil of Bragdon Wood, something to be discovered by digging. It was, in fact the body of Merlin. What the eldils had told him about the possibility of such discovery he had received, while they were with him, almost without wonder. It was no wonder to them. In their eyes the normal Tellurian modes of being—engendering and birth and death and decay—which are to us the framework of thought, were no less wonderful than the countless other patterns of being which were continually present to their unsleeping minds. To those high creatures whose activity builds what we call Nature, nothing is "natural." From their station the essential arbitrariness (so to call it) of every actual creation is ceaselessly visible; for them there are no basic assumptions: all springs with the willful beauty of a jest or a tune from that miraculous moment of self-limitation wherein the Infinite, rejecting a myriad possibilities, throws out of Himself the positive and elected invention. That a body should lie uncorrupted for fifteen hundred years, did not seem strange to them; they knew worlds where there was no corruption at all. That its individual life should remain latent in it all that time, was to them no more strange: they had seen innumerable different modes in which soul and matter could be combined and separated, separated without loss of reciprocal influence, combined without true incarnation, fused so utterly as to be a third thing, or periodically brought together in a union as short, and as momentous, as the nuptial embrace. It was not as a marvel in natural philosophy, but as an information in time of war, that they brought the Director their tidings. Merlin had not died. His life had been hidden, sidetracked, moved out of our one-dimensioned time, for fifteen centuries. But under certain conditions it would return to his body.

They had not told him this till recently because they had not known it. One of Ransom's greatest difficulties in disputing with MacPhee (who consistently professed to disbelieve the very existence of the eldils) was that MacPhee made the common, but curious assumption that if there are creatures wiser and stronger than man they must be forthwith omniscient and omnipotent. In vain did Ransom endeavor to explain the truth. Doubtless, the great beings who now so often came to him had power sufficient to sweep Belbury from the face of England and England from the face of the globe; perhaps, to blot the globe itself out of existence. But no power of that kind would be used. Nor had they any direct vision into the minds of men. It was in a different place, and approaching their knowledge from the other side, that they had discovered the state of Merlin: not from inspection of the thing that slept under Bragdon Wood, but from observing a certain unique configuration in that place where those things remain that are taken off time's mainroad, behind the invisible hedges, into the unimaginable fields. Not all the times that are outside the present are therefore past or future.

It was this that kept the Director wakeful, with knitted brow, in the small cold hours of that morning when the others had left him. There was no doubt in his mind now that the enemy had bought Bragdon to find Merlin: and if they found him they would re-awake him. The old Druid would inevitably cast his lot with the new planners—what could prevent his doing so? A junction would be effected between two kinds of power which between them would determine the fate of our planet. Doubtless that had been the will of the dark-eldils for centuries. The physical sciences, good and innocent in themselves, had already, even in Ransom's own time, begun to be warped, had been subtly manœuvred in a certain direction. Despair of objective truth had been increasingly insinuated into the scientists; indiffererence to it, and a concentration upon mere power, had been the result. Babble about the *élan vital* and flirtations with panpsychism were bidding fair to restore the *Anima Mundi* of the magicians. Dreams of the far future destiny of man were dragging up from its shallow and unquiet grave the old dream of Man as God. The very experiences of the dissecting room and the pathological laboratory were breeding a conviction that the stifling of all deep-set repugnances was the first essential for progess. And now, all this had reached the stage at which its dark contrivers thought they could safely begin to bend it back so that it would meet that other and earlier kind of power. Indeed they were choosing the first moment at which this could have been done. You could not have done it with Nineteenth-Century scientists. Their firm objective materialism would have excluded it from their minds; and even if they could have been made to believe, their inherited morality would have kept them from touching dirt. MacPhee was a survivor from that tradition. It was different now. Perhaps few or none of the people at Belbury knew what was happening; but once it happened, they would be like straw in fire. What should they find incredible, since they believed no longer in a rational universe? What should they regard as too obscene, since they held that all morality was a mere subjective by-product of the physical and economic situations of men? The time was ripe. From the point of view which is accepted in Hell, the whole history of our Earth had led up to this moment. There was now at last a real chance for fallen Man to shake off that limitation of his powers which mercy had imposed upon him as a protection from the full results of his fall. If this succeeded, Hell would be at last incarnate. Bad men, while still in the body, still crawling on this little globe, would enter that state which, heretofore, they had entered only after death, would have the diuturnity and power of evil spirits. Nature, all over the globe of Tellus, would become their slave; and of that dominion no end, before the end of time itself, could be certainly foreseen.

10

The Conquered City

Up till now, whatever his days had been like, Mark had usually slept well; this night sleep failed him. He had not written to Jane; he had spent the day keeping out of sight and doing nothing in particular. The wakeful night moved all his fears onto a new level. He was, of course, a materialist in theory; and (also in theory) he was past the age at which one can have night fears. But now, as the wind rattled his window hour after hour, he felt those old terrors again: the old exquisite thrill, as of cold fingers delicately travelling down his back. Materialism is in fact no protection. Those who seek it in that hope (they are not a negligible class) will be disappointed. The thing you fear is impossible. Well and good. Can you therefore cease to fear it? Not here and now. And what then? If you must see ghosts, it is better not to disbelieve in them.

He was called earlier than usual, and with his tea came a note. The Deputy Director sent his compliments and must ask Mr. Studdock to call on him *instantly* about a most urgent and distressing matter. Mark dressed and obeyed.

In Wither's room he found Wither and Miss Hardcastle. To Mark's surprise and (momentarily) to his relief, Wither showed no recollection of their last meeting. Indeed, his manner was genial, even deferential, though extremely grave.

"Good morning, good morning, Mr. Studdock," he said. "It is with the greatest regret that I—er—in short, I would not have kept you from your breakfast unless I had felt that in your own interests you should be placed in full possession of the facts at the earliest possible moment. You will, of course, regard all that I am about to say as strictly confidential. The matter is a distressing or at least an embarrassing one. I feel sure that as the conversation proceeds (pray be seated, Mr. Studdock) you will realise in your present situation how very wise we have been in securing from the outset a police force—to give it that rather unfortunate name—of our own."

Mark licked his lips and sat down.

"My reluctance to raise the question," continued Wither, "would however be very much more serious if I did not feel able to assure you— in *advance,* you understand—of the complete confidence which we all feel in you and which I very much hoped" (here for the first time he looked Mark in the eyes) "you were beginning to reciprocate. We regard ourselves here as being so many brothers and—er sisters: so that whatever passes between us in this room can be regarded as confidential in the fullest possible sense of the word, and I take it we shall all feel entitled to discuss the subject I am about to mention in the most human and informal manner possible."

Miss Hardcastle's voice, suddenly breaking in, had an effect not wholly unlike that of a pistol shot.

"You have lost your wallet, Studdock," she said.

"My—my wallet?" said Mark.

"Yes. Wallet. Pocketbook. Thing you keep notes and letters in."

"Yes. I have. Have you found it?"

"Does it contain three pounds ten, counterfoil of postal order for five shillings, letters from a woman signing herself Myrtle, from the Bursar of Bracton, from G. Hernshaw, F. A. Browne, M. Belcher, and a bill for a dress suit from Simonds and Son, 32a Market Street, Edgestow?"

"Well, more or less so."

"There it is," said Miss Hardcastle pointing to the table. "No, you don't!" she added as Mark made a step towards it.

"What on earth is all this about?" said Mark. His tone was that which I think almost any man would have used in the circumstances but which policemen are apt to describe as "blustering."

"None of that," said Miss Hardcastle. "This wallet was found in the grass beside the road about five yards away from Hingest's body."

"My God!" said Studdock. "You don't mean . . . the thing's absurd."

"There's no use appealing to *me*," said Miss Hardcastle. "I'm not a solicitor, nor a jury, nor a judge. I'm only a policewoman. I'm telling you the facts."

"Do I understand that I'm suspected of murdering Hingest?"

"I don't really think," said the Deputy Director, "that you need have the slightest apprehension that there is, at this stage, any radical difference between your colleagues and yourself as to the light in which this very painful matter should be regarded. The question is really a constitutional one—"

"Constitutional?" said Mark angrily. "If I understand her, Miss Hardcastle is accusing me of murder."

Wither's eyes looked at him as if from an infinite distance.

"Oh," said he, "I don't really think that does justice to Miss Hardcastle's position. That element in the Institute which she represents would be strictly *ultra vires* in doing anything of the kind within the N.I.C.E.—supposing, but purely of course for purposes of argument, that they wished, or should wish at a later stage, to do so—while in relation to the outside authorities their function, however we define it, would be quite inconsistent with any action of the sort; at least, in the sense in which I understand you to be using the words."

"But it's the outside authorities with whom I'm concerned, I suppose," said Mark. His mouth had become dry and he had difficulty in making himself audible. "As far as I can understand, Miss Hardcastle means I'm going to be arrested."

"On the contrary," said Wither. "This is precisely one of those cases in which you see the enormous value of possessing our own executive. Here is a matter which might, I fear, cause you very considerable inconvenience if the ordinary police had discovered the wallet or if we were in the position of an ordinary citizen who felt it his duty—as we should ourselves feel it our duty if we ever came to be in that very different situation—to hand over the wallet to them. I do not know if Miss Hardcastle has made it perfectly clear to you that it was her officers, and they only, who have made this—er—embarrassing discovery."

"What on earth do you mean?" said Mark. "If Miss Hardcastle does not think there's a *prima facie* case against me, why am I being arraigned in this way at all? And if she does, how can she avoid informing the authorities?"

"My dear friend," said Wither in an antediluvian tone, "there is not the slightest desire on the part of the Committee to insist on defining, in cases of this sort, the powers of action of our own police, much less (what is here in question) their powers of inaction. I do not think anyone had suggested that Miss Hardcastle should be *obliged*—in any sense that limited her own initiative—to communicate to outside authorities, who by their very organisation must be supposed to be less adapted for dealing with such imponderable and quasi-technical inquiries as will often arise, any facts acquired by her and her staff in the course of their internal functioning within the N.I.C.E."

"Do I understand," said Mark, "that Miss Hardcastle thinks she has facts justifying my arrest for the murder of Mr. Hingest, but is kindly offering to suppress them?"

"You got it now, Studdock," said the Fairy. A moment later for the first time in Mark's experience, she actually lit her cheroot, blew a cloud of smoke, and smiled, or at least drew back her lips so that the teeth became visible.

"But that's not what I want," said Mark. This was not quite true. The idea of having the thing hushed up in any way and on almost any terms when it first presented itself a few seconds ago had come like air to one suffocating. But something like citizenship was still alive in him and he proceeded, almost without noticing this emotion, to follow a different line. "I don't want that," he said, speaking rather too loud. "I'm an innocent man. I think I'd better go to the police—the *real* police, I mean—at once."

"If you *want* to be tried for your life," said the Fairy, "that's another matter."

"I want to be vindicated," said Mark. "The charge would fall to pieces at once. There was no conceivable motive. And I have an *alibi*. Everyone knows I slept here last night."

"Really?" said the Fairy.

"What do you mean?" said Mark.

"There's always a *motive,* you know," said she. "For anyone murdering anyone. The police are only human. When the machinery's started they naturally want a conviction."

Mark assured himself he was not frightened. If only Wither didn't keep all his windows shut and then have a roaring fire!

"There's a letter you wrote," said the Fairy.

"What letter?"

"A letter to a Mr. Pelham, of your own College, dated six weeks ago, in which you say, 'I wish Bill the Blizzard could be moved to a better world.'"

Like a sharp physical pain the memory of that scribbled note came back to Mark. It was the sort of silly jocularity one used in the Progressive Element—the kind of thing that might be said a dozen times a day in Bracton about an opponent or even about a bore.

"How does that letter come to be in your hands?" said Mark.

"I think, Mr. Studdock," said the Deputy Director, "it would be very improper to suggest that Miss Hardcastle should give any kind of exposition—in detail, I mean—of the actual working of the Institutional Police. In saying this, I do not mean for one moment to deny that the fullest possible confidence between all the members of the N.I.C.E. is one of the most valuable characteristics it can have, and, indeed, a *sine qua non* of that really concrete and organic life which we expect it to develop. But there are necessarily certain spheres—not sharply defined, of course, but inevitably revealing themselves in response to the environment and obedience to the indwelling *ethos* or dialectic of the whole—in which a confidence that involved the verbal interchange of facts would—er—would defeat its own end."

"You don't suppose," said Mark, "that anyone could take that letter to be meant seriously?"

"Ever tried to make a policeman understand anything?" said the Fairy. "I mean what you call a *real* policeman."

Mark said nothing.

"And I don't think the *alibi* is specially good," said the Fairy. "You were seen talking to Bill at dinner. You were seen going out of the front door with him when he left. You were not seen coming back. Nothing is known of your movements till breakfast time next morning. If you had gone with him by car to the scene of the murder you would have had ample time to walk back and go to bed by about two fifteen. Frosty night, you know. No reason why your shoes should have been specially muddy or anything of that sort."

"If I might pick up a point made by Miss Hardcastle," said Wither, "this is a very good illustration of the immense importance of the Institutional Police. There are so many fine shades involved which it would be unreasonable to expect the ordinary authorities to understand but which, so long as they remain, so to speak, in our own family circle (I look upon the N.I.C.E., Mr. Studdock, as one great family) need develop no tendency to lead to any miscarriage of justice."

Owing to some mental confusion, which had before now assailed him in dentists' operating rooms and in the studies of Headmasters, Mark began almost to identify the situation which seemed to be imprisoning him with his literal imprisonment by the four walls of that hot room. If only he could once get out of it, on any terms, out into the free air and sunlight, away over the countryside, away from the recurrent creak of the Deputy Director's collar and the red stains on the end of Miss Hardcastle's cheroot and the picture of the King which hung above the fireplace!

"You really advise me, Sir," he said, "not to go to the police?"

"To the police?" said Wither as if this idea were completely new. "I don't think, Mr. Studdock, that any one had quite contemplated your taking any irrevocable action of that sort. It might even be argued that by such an action you would be guilty—unintentionally guilty, I hasten to add—of some degree of disloyalty to your colleagues and specially to Miss Hardcastle. You would, of course be placing yourself outside our protection . . ."

"That's the point, Studdock," said the Fairy. "Once you are in the hands of the police you are in the hands of the police."

The moment of Mark's decision had passed by him without his noticing it.

"Well," he said, "what do you propose to do?"

"Me?" said the Fairy. "Sit tight. It's lucky for you that it was we and not some outsider who found the wallet."

"Not only fortunate for—er—Mr. Studdock," added Wither gently, "but for the whole N.I.C.E. We could not have been indifferent . . ."

"There's only one snag," said the Fairy, "and that is that we haven't got your letter to Pelham. Only a copy. But with any luck, nothing will come of that."

"Then there's nothing to be done at present?" said Mark.

"No," said Wither. "No. No immediate action of any official character. It is, of course, very advisable that you should act, as I am sure you will, with the greatest prudence and—er—er—caution for the next few months. As long as you are with us, Scotland Yard would, I feel, see the inconvenience of trying to act unless they had a very clear case indeed. It is no doubt probable that some—er—some trial of strength between the ordinary executive and our own organisation will take place within the next six months; but I think it very unlikely they would choose to make this a test case."

Wither's attitude was paternal.

"But do you mean they suspect me already?" said Mark.

"We'll hope not," said the Fairy. "Of course, they want a prisoner—that's only natural. But they'd a damn sight rather have one who doesn't involve them in searching the premises of the N.I.C.E."

"But look here, damn it!" said Mark. "Aren't you hoping to catch the thief in a day or two? Aren't you going to do *anything?*"

"The thief?" said Wither. "There has been no suggestion so far that the body was rifled."

"I mean the thief who stole my wallet."

"Oh—ah—your wallet," said the other very gently stroking his refined, handsome face. "I see. I understand, do I, that you are advancing a charge of theft against some person or persons unknown—"

"But good God!" shouted Mark. "Were you not assuming that someone stole it? Do you think I was there myself? Do *you* both think I am a murderer?"

"Please!" said the Deputy Director, "please, Mr. Studdock, you really must not shout. Quite apart from the indiscretion of it, I must remind you that you are in the presence of a lady. As far as I can remember, nothing has been said on our side about murder, and no charge of any sort has been made. My only anxiety is to make perfectly clear what we are all doing. There are, of course, certain lines of conduct and a certain mode of procedure which it would be theoretically possible for you to adopt and which would make it very difficult for us to continue the discussion. I am sure Miss Hardcastle agrees with me."

"It's all one to me," said the Fairy. "Why Studdock should start bellowing at us because we are trying to keep him out of the dock, I don't know. But that's for him to decide. I've got a busy day and don't want to hang about here all morning."

"Really," said Mark, "I should have thought it was excusable to . . ."

"Pray compose yourself, Mr. Studdock," said Wither. "As I said before, we look upon ourselves as one family and nothing like a formal apology is required. We all understand one another and all dislike—er—scenes. I might perhaps be allowed to mention, in the friendliest possible manner, that any instability of temperament would be viewed by the Committee as—well, as not very favourable to the confirmation of your appointment. We are all speaking, of course, in the strictest confidence."

Mark was far past bothering about the job for its own sake; but he realised that the threat of dismissal was now a threat of hanging.

"I'm sorry if I was rude," he said at last. "What do you advise me to do?"

"Don't put your nose outside Belbury, Studdock," said the Fairy.

"I do not think Miss Hardcastle could have given you better advice," said Wither. "And now that Mrs. Studdock is going to join you here this temporary captivity—I am using that word, you will understand, in a metaphorical sense—will not be a serious hardship. You must look upon this as your *home*, Mr. Studdock."

"Oh . . . that reminds me, Sir," said Mark. "I'm not really quite sure about having my wife here. As a matter of fact, she's not in very good health—"

"But surely, in that case, you must be all the more anxious to have her here?"

"I don't believe it would suit her, Sir."

The D.D.'s eyes wandered and his voice became lower.

"I had almost forgotten, Mr. Studdock," he said, "to congratulate you on your introduction to our Head. It marks an important transition in your career. We all now feel that you are really one of us in a deeper sense. I am sure nothing is further from your intention than to repel the friendly—the almost fatherly—concern he feels about you. He is very anxious to welcome Mrs. Studdock among us at the earliest opportunity."

"Why?" said Mark suddenly.

Wither looked at Mark with an indescribable smile.

"My dear boy," he said. "Unity, you know. The family circle. She'd—she'd be company for Miss Hardcastle!" Before Mark had recovered from this staggeringly new conception, Wither rose and shuffled towards the door. He paused with one hand on the handle and laid the other on Mark's shoulder.

"You must be hungry for your breakfast," he said. "Don't let me delay you. Behave with the greatest caution. And—and—" here his face suddenly changed. The widely opened mouth looked all at once like the mouth of some enraged animal: what had been the senile vagueness of the eyes became an absence of all specifically human expression. "And bring the girl. Do you understand? Get your wife," he added. "The Head . . . he's not patient."

2

As Mark closed the door behind him he immediately thought "Now! They're both in there together. Safe for a minute at least." Without even waiting to get his hat, he walked briskly to the front door and down the drive. Nothing but physical impossibility would stop him from going to Edgestow and warning Jane. After that he had no plans. Even the vague idea of escaping to America which, in a simpler age, comforted so many a fugitive, was denied him. He had already read in the papers the warm approval of the N.I.C.E. and all its works which came from the United States and from Russia. Some poor tool just like himself had written them. Its claws were embedded in every country: on the liner, if he should ever succeed in sailing; on the tender, if he should ever make some foreign port; its ministers would be waiting for him.

Now he was past the road; he was in the belt of trees. Scarcely a minute had passed since he had left the D.D.'s office and no one had overtaken him. But yesterday's adventure was happening over again. A tall, stooped, shuffling, creaking figure, humming a tune, barred his way. Mark had never fought. Ancestral impulses lodged in his body—that body which was in so many ways wiser than his mind—directed the blow which he aimed at the head of his senile obstructor. But there was no impact. The shape had suddenly vanished.

Those who know best were never fully agreed as to the explanation of this episode. It may have been that Mark, both then and on the previous day, being overwrought, saw a hallucination of Wither where Wither was not. It may be that the continual appearance of Wither which at almost all hours haunted so many rooms and corridors of Belbury was (in one well verified sense of the word) a ghost—one of those sensory impressions which a strong personality in its last decay can imprint, most commonly after death but sometimes before it, on the very structure of a building, and which are removed not by exorcism but by architectural alterations. Or it may, after all, be that souls who have lost the intellectual good do indeed receive in return, and for a short period, the vain privilege of thus reproducing themselves in many places as wraiths. At any rate the thing, whatever it was, vanished.

The path ran diagonally across a field in grass, now powdered with frost, and the sky was hazy blue. Then came a stile; after that the path ran for three fields along the edge of a spinney. Then a little to the left, past the back parts of a farm, then along a ride through a wood. After that the spire of Courthampton was in sight; Mark's feet had now got warm and he was beginning to feel hungry. Then he went across a road, through a herd of cattle that put down their heads and snorted at him, across a stream by a foot bridge, and so into the frozen ruts of the lane that led him into Courthampton.

The first thing he saw as he came into the village street was a farm cart. A woman and three children sat beside the man who was driving it and in the cart were piled chests of drawers, bedsteads, mattresses, boxes, and a canary in a cage. Immediately after it came a man and woman and child on foot wheeling a perambulator; it also was piled with small household property. After that came a family pushing a handcart, and then a heavily loaded trap, and then an old car, blowing its horn incessantly but unable to get out its place in the procession. A steady stream of such traffic was passing through the village. Mark had never seen war: if he had he would have recognized at once the signs of flight. In all those plodding horses and men and in all those loaded vehicles he would have read clearly the message, "Enemy behind."

The traffic was so continuous that it took him a long time to get to the crossroads by the pub where he could find a glazed and framed table of busses. There would not be one to Edgestow till twelve fifteen. He hung about, understanding nothing of what he saw, but wondering; Courthampton was normally a very quiet village. By a happy, and not uncommon illusion he felt less endangered now that Belbury was out of sight, and thought surprisingly little about his future. He thought sometimes about Jane, and sometimes about bacon and eggs, and fried fish, and dark, fragrant streams of coffee pouring into large cups. At eleven thirty the pub opened. He went in and ordered a pint and some bread and cheese.

The bar was at first empty. During the next half hour men dropped in one by one till about four were present. They did not at first talk about the unhappy procession which continued all this time to pass the windows. For some time indeed they did not talk at all. Then a very little man with a face like an old potato observed to no one in particular, "I seen old Rumbold the other night." No one replied for five minutes and then a very young man in leggings said, "I reckon he's sorry he ever tried it." In this way conversation about Rumbold trickled on for some time. It was only when the subject of Rumbold was thoroughly exhausted that the talk, very indirectly and by gradual stages, began to throw some light on the stream of refugees.

"Still coming out," said one man.

"Ah," said another.

"Can't be many left there by now."

"Don't know where they'll all get in, I'm sure."

Little by little the whole thing came out. These were the refugees from Edgestow. Some had been turned out of their houses, some scared by the riots and still more by the restoration of order. Something like a terror appeared to have been established in the town. "They tell me there were two hundred arrests yesterday," said the landlord. "Ah," said the young man. "They're hard cases, those N.I.C.E. police, every one of them. They put the wind up my old Dad proper, I tell 'ee." He ended with a laugh. "'Taint the police so much as the workmen by what I hear," said another. "They never ought to have brought those Welsh and Irish." But that was about as far as the criticism went. What struck Mark deeply was the almost complete absence of indignation among the speakers, or even of any distinct sympathy with the refugees. Everyone present knew of at least one outrage in Edgestow; but all agreed that these refugees must be greatly exaggerating. "It says in this morning's paper that things are pretty well settling down," said the landlord. "That's right," agreed the others. "There'll always be some who get awkward," said the potato-faced man. "What's the good of getting awkward?" asked another, "it's got to go on. You can't stop it." "That's what I say," said the Landlord. Fragments of articles which Mark himself had written drifted to and fro. Apparently he and his kind had done their work well; Miss Hardcastle had rated too high the resistance of the working classes to propaganda.

When the time came he had no difficulty in getting onto the bus: it was indeed empty for all the traffic was going in the opposite direction. It put him down at the top of Market Street and he set out at once to walk up to the flat. The whole town wore a new expression. One house out of three was empty. About half the shops had their windows boarded up. As he gained height and came into the region of large villas with gardens, he noticed that many of these had been requisitioned and bore white placards with the N.I.C.E. symbol—a muscular male nude grasping a thunderbolt. At every corner, and often in between, lounged or sauntered the N.I.C.E. police, helmeted, swinging their clubs, with revolvers in holsters on their black shiny belts. Their round, white faces with open mouths slowly revolving as they chewed gum remained long in his memory. There were also notices everywhere which he did not stop to read: they were headed *Emergency Regulations* and bore the signature, Feverstone.

Would Jane be in? He felt he could not bear it if Jane should not be in. He was fingering his latchkey in his pocket long before he reached the house. The front door was locked. This meant that the Hutchinsons who occupied the ground floor were away. He opened it and went in. It seemed cold and damp on the staircase: cold and damp and dark on the landing. "Ja-ane," he shouted as he unlocked the door of the flat; but he had already lost hope. As soon as he was inside the door he knew the place was uninhabited. A pile of unopened letters lay on the inside door mat. There was no sound, not a tick of a clock. Everything was in order: Jane must have left some morning immediately after "doing" all the rooms. The tea cloths hanging in the kitchen were bone dry: they clearly had not been used for at least twenty four hours. The bread in the cupboard was stale. There was a jug half full of milk, but the milk had thickened and would not pour. He continued stumping from room to room long after he was quite certain of the truth, staring at the staleness and pathos which pervades deserted homes. But obviously it was no good hanging about here. A splutter of unreasonable anger arose. Why the hell hadn't Jane told him she was going away? Or had someone taken her away? Perhaps there was a note for him. He took a pile of letters off the mantlepiece, but they were only letters he had put there himself to be answered. Then on the table he noticed an envelope addressed to Mrs. Dimble at her own house over beyond the Wynd. So that damned woman had been here! Those Dimbles had always, he felt, disliked him. They'd probably asked Jane to stay with them. Been interfering somehow, no doubt. He must go down to Northumberland and see Dimble.

The idea of being annoyed with the Dimbles occurred to Mark almost as an inspiration. To bluster a little as an injured husband in search of his wife would be a pleasant change for the attitudes he had recently been compelled to adopt. On the way down town he stopped to have a drink. As he came to the Bristol and saw the N.I.C.E. placard on it, he had almost said, "Oh, damn," and turned away, before he suddenly remembered that he was himself a high official in the N.I.C.E. and by no means a member of that general Public whom the Bristol now excluded. They asked him who he was at the door and became obsequious when he told them. There was a pleasant fire burning. After the gruelling day he had had, he felt justified in ordering a large whisky, and after it he had a second. It completed the change in his mental weather which had begun at the moment when he first conceived the idea of having a grievance against the Dimbles. The whole state of Edgestow had something to do with it. There was an element in him to which all these exhibitions of power suggested chiefly how much nicer and how much more appropriate it was, all said and done, to be part of the N.I.C.E. than to be an outsider. Even now . . . had he been taking all this *démarche* about a murder trial too seriously? Of course, that was the way Wither managed things: he liked to have something hanging over everyone. It was only a way to keep him at Belbury and to make him send for Jane. And when one came to think of it, why not? She couldn't go on indefinitely living alone. And the wife of a man who meant to have a career and live at the centre of things would have to learn to be a woman of the world. Anyway, the first thing was to see that fellow Dimble.

He left the Bristol feeling, as he would have said, a different man. Indeed he was a different man. From now onwards till the moment of final decision should meet him, the different men in him appeared with startling rapidity and each seemed very complete while it lasted. Thus, skidding violently from one side to the other, his youth approached the moment at which he would begin to be a person.

3

"Come in," said Dimble in his rooms at Northumberland. He had just finished with his last pupil for the day and was intending to start for St. Anne's in a few minutes. "Oh, it's you, Studdock," he added as the door opened. "Come in." He tried to speak naturally but he was surprised at the visit and shocked by what he saw. Studdock's face appeared to him to have changed since they last met; it had grown fatter and paler and there was a new vulgarity in the expression.

"I've come to ask about Jane," said Mark. "Do you know where she is?"

"I can't give you her address, I'm afraid," said Dimble.

"Do you mean you don't know it?"

"I can't give it," said Dimble.

According to Mark's programme this was the point at which he should have begun to take a strong line. But he did not feel the same now that he was in the room. Dimble had always treated him with scrupulous politeness and Mark had always felt that Dimble disliked him. This had not made him dislike Dimble. It had only made him uneasily talkative in Dimble's presence and anxious to please. Vindictiveness was by no means one of Mark's vices. For Mark liked to be liked. A snub sent him away dreaming of not revenge but of brilliant jokes or achievements which would one day conquer the good will of the man who had snubbed him. If he were ever cruel it would be downwards, to inferiors and outsiders who solicited his regard, not upwards to those who rejected it. There was a good deal of the spaniel in him.

"What do you mean?" he asked. "I don't understand."

"If you have any regard for your wife's safety you will not ask me to tell you where she has gone," said Dimble.

"Safety?"

"Safety," repeated Dimble with great sternness.

"Safety from what?"

"Don't you know what has happened?"

"What's happened?"

"On the night of the big riot the Institutional Police attempted to arrest her. She escaped, but not before they had tortured her."

"Tortured her? What do you mean?"

"Burned her with cigars."

"That's what I've come about," said Mark. "Jane—I'm afraid she is on the verge of a nervous breakdown. That didn't really happen, you know."

"The doctor who dressed the burns thinks otherwise."

"Great Scot!" said Mark. "So they really did? But, look here. . ."

Under the quiet stare of Dimble he found it difficult to speak.

"Why have I not been told of this outrage?" he shouted.

"By your colleagues?" asked Dimble drily. "It is an odd question to ask me. You ought to understand the workings of the N.I.C.E. better than I do."

"Why didn't *you* tell me? Why has nothing been done about it? Have you been to the police?"

"The Institutional Police?"

"No, the ordinary police."

"Do you really not know that there are no ordinary police left in Edgestow?"

"I suppose there are some magistrates."

"There is the Emergency Commissioner, Lord Feverstone. You seem to misunderstand. This is a conquered and occupied city."

"Then why, in Heaven's name, didn't you get on to me?"

"*You?*" said Dimble.

For one moment, the first for many years, Mark saw himself exactly as a man like Dimble saw him. It almost took his breath away.

"Look here," he said. "You don't . . . it's too fantastic! You don't imagine I knew about it. You don't really believe I send policemen about to man-handle my own wife!" He had begun on the note of indignation, but ended by trying to insinuate a little jocularity. If only Dimble would give even the ghost of a smile: anything to move the conversation onto a different level.

But Dimble said nothing and his face did not relax. He had not, in fact, been perfectly sure that Mark might not have sunk even to this, but out of charity he did not wish to say so.

"I know you've always disliked me," said Mark. "But I didn't know it was quite as bad as that." And again Dimble was silent, but for a reason Mark could not guess. The truth was that his shaft had gone home. Dimble's conscience had for years accused him of a lack of charity towards Studdock and he had struggled to amend it: he was struggling now.

"Well," said Studdock in a dry voice, after the silence had lasted for several seconds, "there doesn't seem to be much more to say. I insist on being told where Jane is."

"Do you *want* her to be taken to Belbury?"

Mark winced. It was as if the other had read the very thought he had had in the Bristol half an hour ago.

"I don't see, Dimble," he said, "why I should be cross-questioned in this way. Where is my wife?"

"I have no permission to tell you. She is not in my house nor under my protection. She is well and happy and safe. If you still have the slightest regard for her happiness you will make no attempt to get into touch with her."

"Am I sort of leper or criminal that I can't even be trusted to know her address?"

"Excuse me. You are a member of the N.I.C.E. who have already insulted, tortured, and arrested her. Since her escape she has been left alone only because your colleagues do not know where she is."

"And if it really was the N.I.C.E. police, do you suppose I'm not going to have a very full explanation out of them? Damn it, what do you take me for?"

"I can only hope that you have no power in the N.I.C.E. at all. If you have no power, then you cannot protect her. If you have, then you are identified with its policy. In neither case will I help you to discover where Jane is."

"This is fantastic," said Mark. "Even if I do happen to hold a job in the N.I.C.E. for the moment, you know *me.*"

"I do *not* know you," said Dimble. "I have no conception of your aims or motives."

He seemed to Mark to be looking at him, not with anger or contempt, but with that degree of loathing which produces in those who feel it a kind of embarrassment—as if he were an obscenity which decent people are forced, for very shame, to pretend that they have not noticed. In this Mark was quite mistaken. In reality his presence was acting on Dimble as a summons to rigid self-control. Dimble was simply trying very hard not to hate, not to despise, above all not to enjoy hating and despising, and he had no idea of the fixed severity which this effort gave to his face. The whole of the rest of the conversation went on under this misunderstanding.

"There has been some ridiculous mistake," said Mark. "I tell you I'll look into it thoroughly. I'll make a row. I suppose some newly enrolled policeman got drunk or something. Well, he'll be broken. I—"

"It was the chief of your police, Miss Hardcastle herself, who did it."

"Very well. I'll break *her* then. Did you suppose I was going to take it lying down? But there must be some mistake. It can't . . ."

"Do you know Miss Hardcastle well?" asked Dimble. Mark was silenced. And he thought (quite wrongly) that Dimble was reading his mind to the bottom and seeing there his certainty that Miss Hardcastle had done this very thing and that he had no more power of calling her to account than of stopping the revolution of the Earth.

Suddenly the immobility of Dimble's face changed, and he spoke in a new voice. "Have *you* the means to bring her to book?" he said. "Are you already as near the centre of Belbury as that? If so, then you have consented to the murder of Hingest, the murder of Compton. If so, it was by your orders that Mary Prescott was raped and battered to death in the sheds behind the station. It is with your approval that criminals—honest criminals whose hands you are unfit to touch—are being taken from the jails to which British judges sent them on the conviction of British juries and packed off to Belbury to undergo for an indefinite period, out of reach of the law, whatever tortures and assaults on personal identity you call Remedial Treatment. It is you who have driven two thousand families from their homes to die of exposure in every ditch from here to Birmingham or Worcester. It is you who can tell us why Place and Rowley and Cunningham (at eighty years of age) have been arrested, and where they are. And if you are as deeply in it as that, not only will I not deliver Jane into your hands, but I would not deliver my dog."

"Really—really," said Mark. "This is absurd. I know one or two high-handed things have been done. You always get some of the wrong sort in a police force—specially at first. But—I mean to say—what have I ever done that you should make me responsible for every action that any N.I.C.E. official has taken—or is said to have taken in the gutter press?"

"Gutter press!" thundered Dimble, who seemed to Mark to be even physically larger than he was a few minutes before. "What nonsense is this? Do you suppose I don't know that you have control of every paper in the country except one? And that one has not appeared this morning. Its printers have gone on strike. The poor dupes say they will not print articles attacking the people's Institute. Where the lies in all other papers come from you know better than I."

It may seem strange to say that Mark, having long lived in a world without charity, had nevertheless very seldom met real anger. Malice in plenty he had encountered, but it all operated by snubs and sneers and stabbing in the back. The forehead and eyes and voice of this elderly man had an effect on him which was stifling and unnerving. At Belbury one used the words, "whining" and "yapping," to describe any opposition which the actions of Belbury aroused in the outer world. And Mark had never had enough imagination to realise what the "whining" would really be like if you met it face to face.

"I tell you I knew nothing about *it*," he shouted. "Damn it, I'm the injured party. The way you talk, anyone would think it was *your* wife who'd been ill-treated."

"So it might have been. So it may be. It may be any man or woman in England. It was a woman and a citizen. What does it matter whose wife it was?"

"But I tell you I'll raise hell about it. I'll break the infernal bitch who did it, if it means breaking the whole N.I.C.E."

Dimble said nothing. Mark knew that Dimble knew that he was talking nonsense. Yet Mark could not stop. If he did not bluster, he would not know what to say.

"Sooner than put up with this," he shouted, "I'll leave the N.I.C.E."

"Do you mean that?" asked Dimble with a sharp glance. And to Mark, whose ideas were now all one fluid confusion of wounded vanity and jostling fears and shames, this glance once more appeared accusing and intolerable. In reality, it had been a glance of awakened hope: for charity hopes all things. But there was caution in it; and between hope and caution Dimble found himself once more reduced to silence.

"I see you don't trust me," said Mark, instinctively summoning to his face the manly and injured expression which had often served him well in headmasters' studies.

Dimble was a truthful man. "No," he said after a longish pause. "I don't quite."

Mark shrugged his shoulders and turned away.

"Studdock," said Dimble. "This is not a time for foolery, or compliments. It may be that both of us are within a few minutes of death. You have probably been shadowed into the college. And I, at any rate, don't propose to die with polite insincerities in my mouth. I don't trust you. Why should I? You are (at least in some degree) the accomplice of the worst men in the world. Your very coming to me this afternoon may be only a trap."

"Don't you know me better than *that?*" said Mark.

"Stop talking nonsense!" said Dimble. "Stop posturing and acting, if only for a minute. Who are you to talk like that? They have corrupted better men than you or me before now. Straik was a good man once. Filostrato was at least a great genius. Even Alcasan—yes, yes, I know who your Head is—was at least a plain murderer: something better than they have now made of him. Who are you to be exempt?"

Mark gasped. The discovery of how much Dimble knew had suddenly inverted his whole picture of the situation. No logic was left in him.

"Nevertheless," continued Dimble, "knowing all this—knowing that you may be only the bait in the trap, I will take a risk. I will risk things compared with which both our lives are a triviality. If you seriously wish to leave the N.I.C.E., I will help you."

One moment it was like the gates of Paradise opening—then, at once, caution and the incurable wish to temporise rushed back. The chink had closed again.

"I—I'd need to think that over," he mumbled.

"There is no time," said Dimble. "And there is really nothing to think about. I am offering you a way back into the human family. But you must come at once."

"It's a question affecting my whole future career."

"Your career!" said Dimble. "It's a question of damnation or—a last chance. But you must come at once."

"I don't think I understand," said Mark. "You keep on suggesting some kind of danger. What is it? And what powers have you to protect me—or Jane—if I do bolt?"

"You must risk that," said Dimble. "I can offer you no security. Don't you understand? There is no security for anyone now. The battle has started. I'm offering you a place on the right side. I don't know which will win."

"As a matter of fact," said Mark, "I *had* been thinking of leaving. But I must think it over. You put things in rather an odd way."

"There is no time," said Dimble.

"Supposing I look you up again tomorrow?"

"Do you know that you'll be able?"

"Or in an hour? Come, that's only sensible. Will you be here in an hour's time?"

"What can an hour do for you? You are only waiting in the hope that your mind will be less clear."

"But will you be here?"

"If you insist. But no good can come of it."

"I want to think. I want to think," said Mark, and left the room without waiting for a reply.

Mark had said he wanted to think: in reality he wanted alcohol and tobacco. He had thoughts in plenty—more than he desired. One thought prompted him to cling to Dimble as a lost child clings to a grown-up. Another whispered to him, "Madness. Don't *break* with the N.I.C.E. They'll be after you. How can Dimble save you! You'll be killed." A third implored him not, even now, to write off as a total loss his hard won position in the Inner Ring at Belbury: there must, must be some middle course. A fourth recoiled from the idea of ever seeing Dimble again: the memory of every tone Dimble had used caused horrible discomfort. And he wanted Jane, and he wanted to punish Jane for being a friend of Dimble's, and he wanted never to see Wither again, and he wanted to creep back and patch things up with Wither somehow. He wanted to be perfectly safe and yet also very nonchalant and daring—to be admired for manly honesty among the Dimbles and yet also for realism and knowingness at Belbury—to have two more large whiskies and also to think everything out very clearly and collectedly. And it was beginning to rain and his head had begun to ache again. Damn the whole thing. Damn, damn! Why had he such a rotten heredity? Why had his education been so ineffective? Why was the system of society so irrational? Why was his luck so bad?

He began walking rapidly.

It was raining quite hard as he reached the College lodge. Some sort of van seemed to be standing in the street outside, and there were three or four uniformed men in capes. He remembered afterwards how the wet oilskin shone in the lamplight. A torch was flashed in his face.

"Excuse me, Sir," said one of the men. "I must ask for your name."

"Studdock," said Mark.

"Mark Gainsby Studdock," said the man, "it is my duty to arrest you for the murder of William Hingest."

4

Dr. Dimble drove out to St. Anne's dissatisfied with himself, haunted with the suspicion that if he had been wiser, or more perfectly in charity with this very miserable young man, he might have done something for him. "Did I give way to my temper? Was I self-righteous? Did I tell him as much as I dared?" he thought. Then came the deeper self-distrust that was habitual with him. "Did you fail to make things clear because you really wanted not to? Just wanted to hurt and humiliate? To enjoy your own self-righteousness? Is there a whole Belbury inside you too?" The sadness that came over him had novelty in it. "And thus," he quoted from Brother Lawrence, "thus I shall always do, whenever You leave me to myself."

Once clear of the town, he drove slowly—almost sauntering on wheels. The sky was red to westward and the first stars were out. Far down below him in a valley he saw the lights already lit in Cure Hardy.

"Thank Heaven it at any rate is far enough from Edgestow to be safe," he thought. The sudden whiteness of a white owl flying low fluttered across the woody twilight on his left. It gave him a delicious feeling of approaching night. He was very pleasantly tired; he looked forward to an agreeable evening and an early bed.

"Here he is! Here's Dr. Dimble," shouted Ivy Maggs as he drove up to the front door of the Manor.

"Don't put the car away, Dimble," said Denniston.

"Oh, Cecil!" said his wife; and he saw fear in her face. The whole household seemed to have been waiting for him.

A few moments later, blinking in the lighted kitchen, he saw that this was not to be a normal evening. The Director himself was there, seated by the fire, with the jackdaw on his shoulder and Mr. Bultitude at his feet. There were signs that everyone else had had an early supper and Dimble found himself almost at once seated at the end of the table and being rather excitedly urged to eat and drink by his wife and Mrs. Maggs.

"Don't stop to ask questions, dear," said Mrs. Dimble. "Go on eating while they tell you. Make a good meal."

"You have to go out again," said Ivy Maggs.

"Yes," said the Director. "We're going into action at last. I'm sorry to send you out the moment you come in; but the battle has started."

"I have already repeatedly urged," said MacPhee, "the absurdity of sending out an older man like yourself, that's done a day's work forbye, when here am I, a great strapping fellow sitting doing nothing."

"It's no good, MacPhee," said the Director, "you can't go. For one thing you don't know the language. And for another—it's time for frankness—you have never put yourself under the protection of Maleldil."

"I am perfectly ready," said MacPhee, "in and for this emergency, to allow the existence of these eldils of yours and of a being called Maleldil whom they regard as their king. And I—"

"You can't go," said the Director. "I will not send you. It would be like sending a three-year-old child to fight a tank. Put the other map on the table where Dimble can see it while he goes on with his meal. And now, silence. This is the situation, Dimble. What was under Bragdon was a living Merlin. Yes, asleep, if you like to call it sleep. And nothing has yet happened to show that the enemy have found him. Got that? No, don't talk, go on eating. Last night Jane Studdock had the most important dream she's had yet. You remember that in an earlier dream she saw (or so I thought) the very place where he lay under Bragdon. But—and this is the important thing—it's not reached by a shaft and a stair. She dreamed of going through a long tunnel with a very gradual ascent. Ah, you begin to see the point. You're right. Jane thinks she can recognise the entrance to that tunnel: under a heap of stones at the end of a copse with—what was it, Jane?"

"A white gate, Sir. An ordinary five-barred gate with a cross-piece. But the cross-piece was broken off about a foot from the top. I'd know it again."

"You see, Dimble? There's a very good chance that this tunnel comes up *outside* the area held by the N.I.C.E."

"You mean," said Dimble, "that we can now get *under* Bragdon without going *into* Bragdon."

"Exactly. But that's not all."

Dimble, steadily munching, looked at him.

"Apparently," said the Director, "we are almost too late. He was waked already."

Dimble stopped eating.

"Jane found the place empty," said Ransom.

"You mean the enemy have already found him?"

"No. Not quite as bad as that. The place had not been broken into. He seems to have waked of his own accord."

"My God!" said Dimble.

"Try to eat, darling," said his wife.

"But what does it mean?" he asked, covering her hand with his.

"I think it means that the whole thing has been planned and timed long, long ago," said the Director. "That he went out of Time, into the parachronic state, for the very purpose of returning at this moment."

"A sort of human time-bomb," observed MacPhee, "which is why—"

"You can't go, MacPhee," said the Director.

"Is he out?" asked Dimble.

"He probably is by now," said the Director. "Tell him what it was like, Jane."

"It was the same place," said Jane. "A dark place, all stone, like a cellar. I recognised it at once. And the slab of stone was there, but no one lying on it; and this time it wasn't quite cold. Then I dreamed about this tunnel . . . gradually sloping up from the souterrain. And there was a man in the tunnel. Of course, I couldn't see him: it was pitch dark. But a great big man. Breathing heavily. At first I thought it was an animal. It got colder as we went up the tunnel. There was air—a little air—from outside. It seemed to end in a pile of loose stones. He was pulling them about just before the dream changed. Then I was outside, in the rain. That was when I saw the white gate."

"It looks, you see," said Ransom, "as if they had not yet—or not then—established contact with him. That is our only chance now. To meet this creature before they do."

"You will all have observed that Bragdon is very nearly water-logged," put in MacPhee. "Where exactly you'll find a dry cavity in which a body could be preserved all these centuries is a question worth asking. That is, if any of you are still concerned with evidence."

"That's the point," said the Director. "The chamber must be under the high ground—the gravelly ridge on the south of the wood where it slopes up to the Eaton Road. Near where Storey used to live. That's where you'll have to look first for Jane's white gate. I suspect it opens on the Eaton Road. Or else that other road—look at the map—the yellow one that runs up into the Y of Cure Hardy."

"We can be there in half an hour," said Dimble, his hand still on his wife's hand. To everyone in that room, the sickening excitement of the last minutes before battle had come nearer.

"I suppose it must be tonight?" said Mrs. Dimble, rather shame-facedly.

"I am afraid it must, Margaret," said the Director. "Every minute counts. We have practically lost the war if the enemy once make contact with him. Their whole plan probably turns on it."

"Of course. I see. I'm sorry," said Mrs. Dimble.

"And what is our procedure, Sir?" said Dimble, pushing his plate away from him and beginning to fill his pipe.

"The first question is whether he's *out*," said the Director. "It doesn't seem likely that the entrance to the tunnel has been hidden all these centuries by nothing but a heap of loose stones. And if it has, they wouldn't be very loose by now. He may take hours getting out."

"You'll need at least two strong men with picks—" began MacPhee.

"It's no good, MacPhee," said the Director. "I'm not letting you go. If the mouth of the tunnel is still sealed, you must just wait there. But he may have powers we don't know. If he's out, you must look for tracks. Thank God it's a muddy night. You must just hunt him."

"If Jane is going, Sir," said Camilla, "couldn't I go too? I've had more experience of this sort of thing than—"

"Jane has to go because she is the guide," said Ransom. "I am afraid you must stay at home. We in this house are all that is left of Logres. You carry its future in your body. As I was saying, Dimble, you must hunt. I do not think he can get far. The country will, of course, be quite unrecognisable to him, even by daylight."

"And . . . if we do find him, Sir?"

"That is why it must be you, Dimble. Only you know the Great Tongue. If there was eldilic power behind the tradition he represented he may understand it. Even if he does not understand it he will, I think, recognise it. That will teach him he is dealing with Masters. There is a chance that he will think *you* are the Belbury people—his friends. In that case you will bring him here at once."

"And if not?"

The Director spoke sternly.

"Then you must show your hand. That is the moment when the danger comes. We do not know what the powers of the old Atlantean circle were: some kind of hypnotism probably covered most of it. Don't be afraid; but don't let him try any tricks. Keep your hand on your revolver. You too Denniston."

"I'm a good hand with a revolver myself," said MacPhee. "And why, in the name of all commonsense—"

"You can't go, MacPhee," said the Director. "He'd put *you* to sleep in ten seconds. The others are heavily protected as you are not. You understand, Dimble? Your revolver in your hand, a prayer on your lips, your mind fixed on Maleldil. Then, if he stands, conjure him."

"What shall I say in the Great Tongue?"

"Say that you come in the name of God and all angels and in the power of the planets from one who sits today in the seat of the Pendragon and command him to come with you. Say it now."

And Dimble, who had been sitting with his face drawn, and rather white, between the white faces of the two women, and his eyes on the table, raised his head, and great syllables of words that sounded like castles came out of his mouth. Jane felt her heart leap and quiver at them. Everything else in the room seemed to have been intensely quiet; even the bird, and the bear, and the cat, were still, staring at the speaker. The voice did not sound like Dimble's own: it was as if the words spoke themselves through him from some strong place at a distance—or as if they were not words at all but present operations of God, the planets, and the Pendragon. For this was the language spoken before the Fall and beyond the Moon and the meanings were not given to the syllables by chance, or skill, or long tradition, but truly inherent in them as the shape of the great Sun is inherent in the little waterdrop. This was Language herself, as she first sprang at Maleldil's bidding out of the molten quicksilver of the star called Mercury on Earth, but Viritrilbia in Deep Heaven.

"Thank you," said the Director in English; and once again the warm domesticity of the kitchen flowed back upon them. "And if he comes with you, all is well. If he does not—why then, Dimble, you must rely on your Christianity. Do not try any tricks. Say your prayers and keep your will fixed in the will of Maleldil. I don't know what he will do. But stand firm. You can't lose your soul, whatever happens; at least, not by any action of his."

"Yes," said Dimble. "I understand."

There was a longish pause. Then the Director spoke again.

"Don't be cast down, Margaret," he said. "If they kill Cecil, we shall none of us be let live many hours after him. It will be a shorter separation than you could have hoped for in the course of Nature. And now, gentlemen," he said, "you would like a little time, to say your prayers, and to say goodbye to your wives. It is eight now, as near as makes no matter. Suppose you all re-assemble here at ten past eight, ready to start?"

"Very good," answered several voices. Jane found herself left alone in the kitchen with Mrs. Maggs and the animals and MacPhee and the Director.

"*You* are all right, child?" said Ransom.

"I think so, Sir," said Jane. Her actual state of mind was one she could not analyse. Her expectation was strung up to the height; something that would have been terror but for the joy, and joy but for the terror, possessed her—an all-absorbing tension of excitement and obedience. Everything else in her life seemed small and commonplace compared with this moment.

"Do you place yourself in the obedience," said the Director, "in obedience to Maleldil?"

"Sir," said Jane, "I know nothing of Maleldil. But I place myself in obedience to you."

"It is enough for the present," said the Director. "This is the courtesy of Deep Heaven: that when you mean well, He always takes you to have meant better than you knew. It will not be enough for always. He is very jealous. He will have you for no one but Himself in the end. But for tonight, it is enough."

"This is the craziest business ever I heard of," said MacPhee.

I I

Battle Begun

I

"I can't see a thing," said Jane.

"This rain is spoiling the whole plan," said Dimble from the back seat. "Is this still Eaton Road, Arthur?"

"I think . . . yes, there's the toll-house," said Denniston who was driving.

"But what's the use?" said Jane. "I can't see, even with the window down. We might have passed it any number of times. The only thing is to get out and walk."

"I think she's right, Sir," said Denniston.

"I say!" said Jane suddenly. "Look! Look! What's that? Stop."

"I can't see a white gate," said Denniston.

"Oh, it's not that," said Jane. "Look over there."

"I can't see anything," said Dimble.

"Do you mean that light?" said Denniston.

"Yes, of course; that's the fire."

"What fire?"

"It's the light," she said, "the fire in the hollow of the little wood. I'd forgotten all about it. Yes, I know: I never told Grace, or the Director. I'd forgotten that part of the dream till this moment. That was how it ended. It was the most important part really. That was where I found *him*—Merlin, you know. Sitting by a fire in a little wood. After I came out of the place underground. Oh, come quickly!"

"What do you think, Arthur?" said Dimble.

"I think we must go wherever Jane leads," answered Denniston.

"Oh, do hurry," said Jane. "There's a gate here. Quick! It's only one field away."

All three of them crossed the road and opened the gate and went into the field. Dimble said nothing. He was inwardly reeling under the shock and shame of the immense and sickening fear which had surged up inside him. He had, perhaps, a clearer idea than the others of what sort of things might happen when they reached the place.

Jane, as guide, went first, and Denniston beside her, giving her his arm and showing an occasional gleam of his torch on the rough ground. Dimble brought up the rear. No one was inclined to speak.

The change from the road to the field was as if one had passed from a waking into a phantasmal world. Everything became darker, wetter, more incalculable. Each small descent felt as if you might be coming to the edge of a precipice. They were following a track beside a hedge; wet and prickly tentacles seemed to snatch at them as they went. Whenever Denniston used his torch, the things that appeared within the circle of its light—tufts of grass, ruts filled with water, draggled yellow leaves clinging to the wet blackness of many-angled twigs, and once the two greenish-yellow fires in the eyes of some small animal—had the air of being more commonplace than they ought to have been; as if, for that moment's exposure, they had assumed a disguise which they would shuffle off again the moment they were left alone. They looked curiously small, too; when the light vanished the cold, noisy darkness seemed a huge thing.

The fear which Dimble had felt from the first began to trickle into the minds of the others as they proceeded—like water coming into a ship from a slow leak. They realised that they had not really believed in Merlin till now. They had thought they were believing the Director in the kitchen; but they had been mistaken. The shock was still to take. Out here with only the changing red light ahead and the black all round, one really began to accept as fact this tryst with something dead and yet not dead, something dug up, exhumed, from that dark pit of history which lies between the ancient Romans and the beginning of the English. "The Dark Ages," thought Dimble; how lightly one had read and written those words. But now they were going to step right into that Darkness. It was an age, not a man, that awaited them in the horrible little dingle.

And suddenly all that Britain which had been so long familiar to him as a scholar rose up like a solid thing. He could see it all. Little dwindling cities where the light of Rome still rested—little Christian sites, Camalodunum, Kaerleon, Glastonbury—a church, a villa or two, a huddle of houses, an earthwork. And then, beginning scarcely a stone's throw beyond the gates, the wet, tangled endless woods, silted with the accumulated decay of autumns that had been dropping leaves since before Britain was an island; wolves slinking, beavers building, wide shallow marshes, dim horns and drummings, eyes in the thickets, eyes of men not only Pre-Roman but Pre-British, ancient creatures, unhappy and dispossessed, who became the elves and ogres and wood-wooses of the later tradition. But worse than the forests, the clearings. Little strongholds with unheard-of kings. Little colleges and covines of Druids. Houses whose mortar had been ritually mixed with babies' blood. They had tried to do that to Merlin. And now all that age, horribly dislocated, wrenched out of its place in the time series and forced to come back and go through all its motions yet again with doubled monstrosity, was flowing towards them and would, in a few minutes, receive them into itself.

Then came a check. They had walked right into a hedge. They wasted a minute, with the aid of the torch, disentangling Jane's hair. They had come to the end of a field. The light of the fire, which kept on growing stronger and weaker in fitful alternations, was hardly visible from here. There was nothing for it but to set to work and find a gap or a gate. They went a long way out of their course before they found one. It was a gate that would not open: and as they came down on the far side, after climbing it, they went ankle deep into water. For a few minutes, plodding slightly up-hill, they were out of sight of the fire, and when it re-appeared it was well away on their left and much further off than anyone supposed.

Hitherto Jane had scarcely attempted to think of what might lie before them. As they went on, the real meaning of that scene in the kitchen began to dawn on her. He had sent the men to bid goodbye to their wives. He had blessed them all. It was likely, then, that this—this stumbling walk on a wet night across a ploughed field—meant death. Death—the thing one had always heard of (like love), the thing the poets had written about. So this was how it was going to be. But that was not the main point. Jane was trying to see death in the new light of all she had heard since she left Edgestow. She had long ceased to feel any resentment at the Director's tendency, as it were, to dispose of her—to give her, at one time or in one sense, to Mark, and in another to Maleldil—never, in any sense, to keep her for himself. She accepted that. And of Mark she did not think much, because to think of him increasingly aroused feelings of pity and guilt. But Maleldil. Up till now she had not thought of Maleldil either. She did not doubt that the eldils existed; nor did she doubt the existence of this stronger and more obscure being whom they obeyed . . . whom the Director obeyed, and through him the whole household, even MacPhee. If it had ever occurred to her to question whether all these things might be the reality behind what she had been taught at school as "religion," she had put the thought aside. The distance between these alarming and operative realities and the memory, say, of fat Mrs. Dimble saying her prayers, was too wide. The things belonged, for her, to different worlds. On the one hand, terror of dreams, rapture of obedience, the tingling light and sound from under the Director's door, and the great struggle against an imminent danger; on the other, the smell of pews, horrible lithographs of the Saviour (apparently seven feet high, with the face of a consumptive girl), the embarrassment of confirmation classes, the nervous affability of clergymen. But this time, if it was really to be death, the thought would not be put aside. Because, really, it now appeared that almost anything might be true. The world had already turned out to be so very unlike what she had expected. The old ring-fence had been smashed completely. One might be in for anything. Maleldil might be, quite simply and crudely, God. There might be a life after death: a Heaven: a Hell. The thought glowed in her mind for a second like a spark that has fallen on shavings, and then a second later, like those shavings, her whole mind was in a blaze—or with just enough left outside the blaze to utter some kind of protest. "But . . . but this is unbearable. I ought to have been told." It did not, at that moment, occur to her even to doubt that if such things existed they would be totally and unchangeably adverse to her.

"Look out, Jane," said Denniston. "That's a tree."

"I—I think it's a cow," said Jane.

"No. It's a tree. Look. There's another."

"Hush," said Dimble. "This is Jane's little wood. We are very close now."

The ground rose in front of them for about twenty yards and there made an edge against the firelight. They could see the wood quite clearly now, and also each other's faces, white and blinking.

"I will go first," said Dimble.

"I envy you your nerve," said Jane.

"Hush," said Dimble again.

They walked slowly and quietly up to the edge and stopped. Below them a big fire of wood was burning at the bottom of a little dingle. There were bushes all about, whose changing shadows, as the flames rose and fell, made it difficult to see clearly. Beyond the fire there seemed to be some rude kind of tent made out of sacking, and Denniston thought he saw an upturned cart. In the foreground, between them and the fire, there was certainly a kettle.

"Is there anyone here?" whispered Dimble to Denniston.

"I don't know. Wait a few seconds."

"Look!" said Jane suddenly. "There! When the flame blew aside."

"What?" said Dimble.

"Didn't you see him?"

"I saw nothing."

"I thought I saw a man," said Denniston.

"I saw an ordinary tramp," said Dimble. "I mean a man in modern clothes."

"What did he look like?"

"I don't know."

"We must go down," said Dimble.

"*Can* one get down?" said Denniston.

"Not this side," said Dimble. "It looks as if a sort of path came into it over there to the right. We must go along the edge till we find the way down."

They had all been talking in low voices and the crackling of the fire was now the loudest sound, for the rain seemed to be stopping. Cautiously, like troops who fear the eye of the enemy, they began to skirt the lip of the hollow, stealing from tree to tree.

"Stop!" whispered Jane suddenly.

"What is it?"

"There's something moving."

"Where?"

"In there. Quite close."

"I heard nothing."

"There's nothing now."

"Let's go on."

"Do you still think there's something, Jane?"

"It's quiet now. There *was* something."

They made a few paces more.

"St!" said Denniston. "Jane's right. There is something."

"Shall I speak?" said Dimble.

"Wait a moment," said Denniston. "It's just there. Look!—damn it, it's only an old donkey!"

"That's what I said," said Dimble. "The man's a gypsy: a tinker or something. This is his donkey. Still, we must go down."

They proceeded. In a few moments they found themselves descending a rutted grassy path which wound about till the whole hollow opened before them; and now the fire was no longer between them and the tent. "There he is," said Jane.

"Can you see him?" said Dimble. "I haven't got your eyes."

"I can see him all right," said Denniston. "It *is* a tramp. Can't you see him, Dimble? An old man with a ragged beard in what looks like the remains of a British Warm and a pair of black trousers. Don't you see his left foot, stuck out, and the toe a bit up in the air?"

"That?" said Dimble. "I thought was a log. But you've better eyes than I have. Did you really see a man, Arthur?"

"Well, I thought I did, Sir. But I'm not certain now. I think my eyes are getting tired. He's sitting very still. If it *is* a man, he's asleep."

"Or dead," said Jane with a sudden shudder.

"Well," said Dimble, "we must go down."

And in less than a minute all three walked down into the dingle and past the fire. And there was the tent, and a few miserable attempts at bedding inside it, and a tin plate, and some matches on the ground, and the dottle of a pipe, but they could see no man.

2

"What I can't understand, Wither," said Fairy Hardcastle, "is why you don't let me try my hand on the young pup. All these ideas of yours are so half-hearted—keeping him on his toes about the murder, arresting him, leaving him all night in the cells to think it over. Why do you keep messing about with things that may work or may not?—when twenty minutes of my treatment would turn his mind inside out. I know the type."

Miss Hardcastle was talking, at about ten o'clock that same wet night, to the Deputy Director in his study. There was a third person present: Professor Frost.

"I assure you, Miss Hardcastle," said Wither, fixing his eyes not on her but on Frost's forehead, "you need not doubt that your views on this, or any other matter, will always receive the fullest consideration. But if I may say so, this is one of those cases where—ah—any grave degree of coercive examination might defeat its own end."

"Why?" said the Fairy sulkily.

"You must excuse me," said Wither, "for reminding you—not, of course, that I assume you are neglecting the point, but simply on methodological grounds—it is so important to make everything *clear*—that we need the woman—I mean, that it would be of the greatest value to welcome Mrs. Studdock among us—chiefly on account of the remarkable psychical faculty she is said to possess. In using the word *Psychical,* I am not, you understand, committing myself to any particular theory."

"You mean these dreams?"

"It is very doubtful," said Wither, "what effect it might have on her if she were brought here under compulsion and then found her husband—ah—in the markedly, though no doubt temporarily, abnormal condition which we should have to anticipate as a result of your scientific methods of examination. One would run the risk of a profound emotional disturbance on her part. The faculty itself might disappear, at least for a long time."

"We have not yet had Major Hardcastle's report," said Professor Frost quietly.

"No good," said the Fairy. "He was shadowed into Northumberland. Only three possible people left the College after him—Lancaster, Lyly, and Dimble. I put them in that order of probability. Lancaster is a Christian, and a very influential man. He's in the Lower House of Convocation. He had a lot to do with the Repton Conference. He's mixed up with several big clerical families. And he's written a lot of books. He has a real stake in their side. Lyly is rather the same type, but less of an organiser. As you will remember, he did a great deal of harm on that reactionary commission about Education last year. Both these are dangerous men. They are the sort of people who get things done—natural leaders of the other party. Dimble is quite a different type. Except that he's a Christian, there isn't really much against him. He's purely academic. I shouldn't think his name is much known, except to other scholars in his own subject. Not the kind that would make a public man. Impractical . . . he'd be too full of scruples to be much use to them. The others know a thing or two, Lancaster particularly. In fact, he's a man we could find room for on our own side if he held the right views."

"You should tell Major Hardcastle that we have access to most of these facts already," said Professor Frost.

"Perhaps," said Wither, "in view of the late hour—we don't wish to overtax your energies, Miss Hardcastle—we might go on to the more strictly narrative parts of your report."

"Well," said the Fairy, "I had to follow all three. With the resources I had at the moment. You'll realise young Studdock was seen setting off for Edgestow only by good luck. It was a bomb-shell. Half my people were already busy on the hospital affair. I just had to lay my hands on anyone I could get. I posted a sentry and had six others out of sight of the College; in plain clothes, of course. As soon as Lancaster came out I told off the three best to keep him in sight. I've had a wire from them half an hour ago from London where Lancaster went off by train. We may be onto something there. Lyly gave the devil of a lot of trouble. He appeared to be calling on about fifteen different people in Edgestow. We've got them all noted—I sent the next two of my lads to deal with him. Dimble came out last. I would have sent my last man off to follow him, but a call came through at that moment from Captain O'Hara, who wanted another car. So I decided to let Dimble go for tonight and sent my man up with the one he had. Dimble can be got any time. He comes into College pretty regularly every day; and he's really a nonentity."

"I do not quite understand," said Frost, "why you had no one inside the college to see what staircase Studdock went to."

"Because of your damned Emergency Commissioner," said the Fairy. "We're not allowed into colleges now, if you please. I said at the time that Feverstone was the wrong man. He's trying to play on both sides. He's for us against the town, but when it comes to us against the University he's unreliable. Mark my words, Wither, you'll have trouble with him yet."

Frost looked at the Deputy Director.

"I am far from denying," said Wither, "though without at all closing my mind to other possible explanations, that some of Lord Feverstone's measures may have been injudicious. It would be inexpressibly painful to me to suppose that—"

"Need we keep Major Hardcastle?" said Frost.

"Bless my soul!" said Wither. "How very right of you! I had almost forgotten, my dear lady, how tired you must be, and how very valuable your time is. We must try to save you for that particular kind of work in which you have shown yourself indispensable. You must not allow us to impose on your good nature. There is a lot of duller and more routine work which it is only reasonable that you should be spared." He got up and held the door open for her.

"You don't think," said she, "that I ought to let the boys have just a *little* go at Studdock? I mean, it seems so absurd to have all this trouble about getting an address."

And suddenly, as Wither stood with his hand on the door-handle, courtly, patient, and smiling, the whole expression faded out of his face. The pale lips, open wide enough to show his gums, the white curly head, the pouchy eyes, ceased to make up any single expression. Miss Hardcastle had the feeling that a mere mask of skin and flesh was staring at her. A moment later and she was gone.

"I wonder," said Wither as he came back to his chair, "whether we are attaching too much importance to this Studdock woman."

"We are acting on an order dated the 1st of October," said Frost.

"Oh . . . I wasn't questioning it," said Wither with a gesture of deprecation.

"Allow me to remind you of the facts," said Frost. "The authorities had access to the woman's mind for only a very short time. They inspected one dream only—a most important dream, which revealed, though with some irrelevancies, an essential element in our programme. That warned us that if the woman fell into the hands of any ill-affected persons who knew how to exploit her faculty, she would constitute a grave danger."

"Oh, to be sure, to be sure. I never intended to deny—"

"That was the first point," said Frost, interrupting him. "The second is that her mind became opaque to our authorities almost immediately afterwards. In the present state of our science we know only one cause for such occultations. They occur when the mind in question has placed itself, by some voluntary choice of its own, however vague, under the control of some hostile organism. The occultation, therefore, while cutting off our access to the dreams, also tells us that she has, in some mode or other, come under enemy influence. This is in itself a grave danger. But it also means that to find her would probably mean discovering the enemy's headquarters. Miss Hardcastle is probably right in maintaining that torture would soon induce Studdock to give up his wife's address. But as you pointed out, a round up at their headquarters, an arrest, and the discovery of her husband here in the condition in which the torture would leave him, would produce psychological conditions in the woman which might destroy her faculty. We should thus frustrate one of the purposes for which we want to get her. That is the first objection. The second is that an attack on enemy headquarters is very risky. They almost certainly have protection of a kind we are not prepared to cope with. And finally the man may not *know* his wife's address. In that case . . ."

"Oh," said Wither, "there is nothing I should more deeply deplore. Scientific examination (I cannot allow the word *Torture* in this context) in cases where the patient doesn't know the answer is always a fatal mistake. As men of humanity we should neither of us . . . and then, if you go on, the patient naturally does not recover . . . and if you stop, even an experienced operator is haunted by the fear that perhaps he *did* know after all. It is in every way unsatisfactory."

"There is, in fact, no way of implementing our instructions except by inducing Studdock to bring his wife here himself."

"Or else," said Wither, a little more dreamily than usual, "if it were possible, by inducing in him a much more radical allegiance to our side than he has yet shown. I am speaking, my dear friend, of a real change of heart."

Frost slightly opened and extended his mouth, which was a very long one, so as to show his white teeth.

"That," he said, "is a subdivision of the plan I was mentioning. I was saying that he must be induced to send for the woman himself. That, of course, can be done in two ways. Either by supplying him with some motive on the instinctive level, such as fear of us or desire for her; or else by conditioning him to identify himself so completely with the Cause that he will understand the real motive for securing her person and act on it."

"Exactly . . . exactly," said Wither. "Your expressions, as always, are a little different from those I would choose myself, but . . ."

"Where is Studdock at present?" said Frost.

"In one of the cells here—on the other side."

"Under the impression he has been arrested by the ordinary police?"

"That I cannot answer for. I presume he would be. It does not, perhaps, make much difference."

"And how are you proposing to act?"

"We had proposed to leave him to himself for several hours—to allow the psychological results of the arrest to mature. I have ventured . . . of course, with every regard for humanity . . . to reckon on the value of some slight physical discomforts—he will not have dined, you understand. They have instructions to empty his pockets. One would not wish the young man to relieve any nervous tension that may have arisen by smoking. One wishes the mind to be thrown entirely on its own resources."

"Of course. And what next?"

"Well, I suppose some sort of examination. That is a point on which I should welcome your advice. I mean, as to whether, I, personally, should appear in the first instance. I am inclined to think that the appearance of examination by the ordinary police should be maintained a little longer. Then at a later stage will come the discovery that he is still in our hands. He will probably misunderstand this discovery at first—for several minutes. It would be well to let him realise only gradually that this by no means frees him from the—er—embarrassments arising out of Hingest's death. I take it that some fuller realisation of his inevitable solidarity with the Institute would then follow . . ."

"And then you mean to ask him again for his wife?"

"I shouldn't do it at all like that," said Wither. "If I might venture to say so, it is one of the disadvantages of that extreme simplicity and accuracy with which you habitually speak (much as we all admire it) that it leaves no room for fine shades. One had rather hoped for a spontaneous outburst of confidence on the part of the young man himself. Anything like a direct demand—"

"The weakness of the plan," said Frost, "is that you are relying wholly on fear."

"Fear," repeated Wither as if he had not heard the word before. "I do not quite follow the connection of thought. I can hardly suppose you are following the opposite suggestion, once made, if I remember rightly, by Miss Hardcastle."

"What was that?"

"Why," said Wither, "if I understand her aright, she thought of taking scientific measures to render the society of his wife more desirable in the young man's eyes. Some of the chemical resources . . ."

"You mean an aphrodisiac?"

Wither sighed gently and said nothing.

"That is nonsense," said Frost. "It isn't to his wife that a man turns under the influence of aphrodisiacs. But as I was saying, I think it is a mistake to rely wholly on fear. I have observed, over a number of years, that its results are incalculable: especially when the fear is complicated. The patient may get too frightened to move, even in the desired direction. If we have to despair of getting the woman here with her husband's good will, we must use torture and take the consequences. But there are other alternatives. There is desire."

"I am not sure that I am following you. You have rejected the idea of any medical or chemical approach."

"I was thinking of stronger desires."

Neither at this stage of the conversation nor at any other did the Deputy Director look much at the face of Frost; his eyes, as usual, wandered over the whole room or fixed themselves on distant objects. Sometimes they were shut. But either Frost or Wither—it was difficult to say which—had been gradually moving his chair, so that by this time the two men sat with their knees almost touching.

"I had my conversation with Filostrato," said Frost in his low, clear voice. "I used expressions which must have made my meaning clear if he had any notion of the truth. His senior assistant, Wilkins, was present too. The fact is that neither is really interested. What interests them is the fact that they have succeeded—as they think—in keeping the Head alive and getting it to talk. What it says does not really interest them. As to any question about *what* is really speaking, they have no curiosity. I went very far. I raised questions about its mode of consciousness—its sources of information. There was no response."

"You are suggesting, if I understand you," said Wither, "a movement towards this Mr. Studdock along *those* lines. If I remember rightly, you rejected fear on the ground that its effects could not really be predicted with the accuracy one might wish. But—ah—would the method now envisaged be any *more* reliable? I need hardly say that I fully realise a certain disappointment which serious-minded people must feel with such colleagues as Filostrato and his subordinate Mr. Wilkins."

"That is the point," said Frost. "One must guard against the error of supposing that the political and economic dominance of England by the

N.I.C.E. is more than a subordinate object: it is individuals that we are really concerned with. A hard unchangeable core of individuals really devoted to the same cause as ourselves—that is what we need and what, indeed, we are under orders to supply. We have not succeeded so far in bringing many people in—really *in*."

"There is still no news from Bragdon Wood?"

"No."

"And you believe that Studdock might really be a suitable person? . . ."

"You must not forget," said Frost, "that his value does not rest solely on his wife's clairvoyance. The couple are eugenically interesting. And secondly, I think he can offer no resistance. The hours of fear in the cell, and then an appeal to desires that under-cut the fear, will have an almost certain effect on a character of that sort."

"Of course," said Wither, "nothing is so much to be desired as the greatest possible unity. You will not suspect me of under-rating that aspect of our orders. Any fresh individual brought into that unity would be a source of the most intense satisfaction to—ah—all concerned. I desire the closest possible bond. I would welcome an interpenetration of personalities so close, so irrevocable, that it almost transcends individuality. You need not doubt that I would open my arms to receive—to absorb—to assimilate this young man."

They were now sitting so close together that their faces almost touched, as if they had been lovers about to kiss. Frost's *pince-nez* caught the light so that they made his eyes invisible: only his mouth, smiling but not relaxed in the smile, revealed his expression. Wither's mouth was open, the lower lip hanging down, his eyes wet, his whole body hunched and collapsed in his chair as if the strength had gone out of it. A stranger would have thought he had been drinking. Then his shoulders twitched and gradually he began to laugh. And Frost did not laugh, but his smile grew moment by moment brighter and also colder, and he stretched out his hand and patted his colleague on the shoulder. Suddenly in that silent room there was a crash. *Who's Who* had fallen off the table, swept onto the floor as, with sudden swift convulsive movement, the two old men lurched forward towards each other and sat swaying to and fro, locked in an embrace from which each seemed to be struggling to escape. And as they swayed and scrabbled with hand and nail, there arose, shrill and faint at first, but then louder and louder, a cackling noise that seemed in the end rather an animal than a senile parody of laughter.

3

When Mark was bundled out of the police wagon into the dark and rain and hurried indoors between two constables and left at length alone in a little lighted room, he had no idea that he was at Belbury. Nor would he have cared greatly if he had known, for the moment he was arrested he had despaired of his life. He was going to be hanged.

He had never till now been at close quarters with death. Now, glancing down at his hand (because his hands were cold and he had been automatically rubbing them), it came to him as a totally new idea that this very hand, with its five nails and the yellow tobacco-stain on the inside of the second finger, would one day be the hand of a corpse, and later the hand of a skeleton. He did not exactly feel horror, though on the physical level he was aware of a choking sensation; what made his brain reel was the preposterousness of the idea. This was something incredible, yet at the same time quite certain.

There came a sudden uprush of grisly details about execution, supplied long since by Miss Hardcastle. But that was a dose too strong for the consciousness to accept. It hovered before his imagination for a fraction of a second, agonising him to a kind of mental scream, and then sank away in a blur. Mere death returned as the object of attention. The question of immortality came before him. He was not in the least interested. What had an after life to do with it? Happiness in some other and disembodied world (he never thought of unhappiness) was totally irrelevant to a man who was going to be killed. The killing was the important thing. On any view, this body—this limp, shaking, desperately vivid thing, so intimately his own—was going to be returned into a *dead* body. If there were such things as souls, this cared nothing about them. The choking, smothering sensation gave the body's view of the matter with an intensity which excluded all else.

Because he felt that he was choking, he looked round the cell for any sign of ventilation. There was, in fact, some sort of grating above the door. That ventilator and the door itself were the only objects to detain the eye. All else was white floor, white ceiling, white wall, without a chair or table or book or peg, and with one hard white light in the centre of the ceiling.

Something in the look of the place now suggested to him for the first time the idea that he might be at Belbury and not in an ordinary police station. But the flash of hope aroused by this idea was so brief as to be instantaneous. What difference did it make whether Wither and Miss Hardcastle and the rest had decided to get rid of him by handing him over to the ordinary police or by making away with him in private—as they had doubtless done with Hingest? The meaning of all the ups and down he had experienced at Belbury now appeared to him perfectly plain. They were all his enemies, playing upon his hopes and fears to reduce him to complete servility, certain to kill him if he broke away, and certain to kill him in the long run when he had served the purpose for which they wanted him. It appeared to him astonishing that he could ever have thought otherwise. How could he have supposed that any real conciliation of these people could be achieved by anything he did?

What a fool—a blasted, babyish, gullible fool—he had been! He sat down on the floor, for his legs felt weak, as if he had walked twenty-five miles. Why had he come to Belbury in the first instance? Ought not his very first interview with the Deputy Director to have warned him, as clearly as if the truth were shouted through a megaphone or printed on a poster in letters six feet high, that here was the world of plot within plot, crossing and double-crossing, of lies and graft and stabbing in the back, of murder and a contemptuous guffaw for the fool who lost the game? Feverstone's guffaw, that day he had called him an "incurable romantic," came back to his mind. Feverstone . . . that was how he had come to believe in Wither: on Feverstone's recommendation. Apparently his folly went further back. How on earth had he come to trust Feverstone—a man with a mouth like a shark, with his flash manners, a man who never looked you in the face? Jane, or Dimble, would have seen through him at once. He had "crook" written all over him. He was fit only to deceive puppets like Curry and Busby. But then, at the time when he first met Feverstone, he had not thought Curry and Busby puppets. With extraordinary clarity, but with renewed astonishment, he remembered how he had felt about the Progressive Element at Bracton when he was first admitted to its confidence; he remembered, even more incredulously, how he had felt as a very junior Fellow while he was outside it— how he had looked almost with awe at the heads of Curry and Busby bent close together in Common Room, hearing occasional fragments of their whispered conversation, pretending himself the while to be absorbed in a periodical but longing—oh, so intensely longing—for one of them to cross the room and speak to him. And then, after months and months, it had happened. He had a picture of himself, the odious little outsider who wanted to be an insider, the infantile gull, drinking in the husky and unimportant confidences, as if he were being admitted to the government of the planet. Was there *no* beginning to his folly? Had he been utter fool all through from the very day of his birth? Even as a schoolboy, when he had ruined his work and half broken his heart trying to get into the society called Grip, and lost his only real friend in doing so? Even as a child, fighting Myrtle because she *would* go and talk secrets with Pamela next door?

He himself did not understand why all this, which was now so clear, had never previously crossed his mind. He was unaware that such thoughts had often knocked for entrance, but had always been excluded for the very good reason that if they were once entertained it involved ripping up the whole web of his life, cancelling almost every decision his will had ever made, and really beginning over again as though he were an infant. The indistinct mass of problems which would have to be faced if he admitted such thoughts, the innumerable "somethings" about which "something" would have to be done, had deterred him from ever raising these questions. What had now taken the blinkers off was the fact that nothing *could* be done. They were going to hang him. His story was at an end. There was no harm in ripping up the web now for he was not going to use it any more; there was no bill to be paid (in the shape of arduous decision and reconstruction) for truth. It was a result of the approach of death which the Deputy Director and Professor Frost had possibly not foreseen.

There were no moral considerations at this moment in Mark's mind. He looked back on his life not with shame, but with a kind of disgust at its dreariness. He saw himself as a little boy in short trousers, hidden in the shrubbery beside the paling, to overhear Myrtle's conversation with Pamela, and trying to ignore the fact that it was not at all interesting when overheard. He saw himself making believe that he enjoyed those Sunday afternoons with the athletic heroes of Grip while all the time (as he now saw) he was almost homesick for one of the old walks with Pearson—Pearson whom he had taken such pains to leave behind. He saw himself in his teens laboriously reading rubbishy grown-up novels and drinking beer when he really enjoyed John Buchan and stone ginger. The hours that he had spent learning the very slang of each new circle that attracted him, the perpetual assumption of interest in things he found dull and of knowledge he did not possess, the almost heroic sacrifice of nearly every person and thing he actually enjoyed, the miserable attempt to pretend that one *could* enjoy Grip, or the Progressive Element, or the N.I.C.E.—all this came over him with a kind of heart-break. When had he ever done what he wanted? Mixed with the people whom he liked? Or even eaten and drunk what took his fancy? The concentrated insipidity of it all filled him with self-pity.

In his normal condition, explanations that laid on impersonal forces outside himself the responsibility for all this life of dust and broken bottles would have occurred at once to his mind and been at once accepted. It would have been "the system" or "an inferiority complex" due to his parents, or the peculiarities of the age. None of these things occurred to him now. His "scientific" outlook had never been a real philosophy believed with blood and heart. It had lived only in his brain, and was a part of that public self which was now falling off him. He was aware, without even having to think of it, that it was he himself—nothing else in the whole universe—that had chosen the dust and broken bottles, the heap of old tin cans, the dry and choking places.

An unexpected idea came into his head. This—this death of his—would be lucky for Jane. Myrtle long ago, Pearson at school, Denniston while they were undergraduates, and lastly Jane had been the four biggest invasions of his life by something from beyond the dry and choking places. Myrtle he had conquered by becoming the clever brother who won scholarships and mixed with important people. They were really twins, but after a short period in childhood during which she had appeared as an elder sister, she had become more like a younger sister and had remained so ever since. He had wholly drawn her into his orbit: it was her large wondering eyes and naïf answers to his accounts of the circle he was now moving in which had provided at each stage most of the real pleasure of his career. But for the same reason she had ceased to mediate life from beyond the dry places. The flower, once safely planted among the tin cans, had turned into a tin can itself. Pearson and Denniston he had thrown away. And he now knew, for the first time, what he had secretly meant to do with Jane. If all had succeeded, if he had become the sort of man he hoped to be, she was to have been the great hostess—the secret hostess in the sense that only the very esoteric few would know who that striking-looking woman was and why it mattered so enormously to secure her good will. Well . . . it was lucky for Jane. She seemed to him, as he now thought of her, to have in herself deep wells and knee-deep meadows of happiness, rivers of freshness, enchanted gardens of leisure, which he could not enter but could have spoiled. She was one of those other people—like Pearson, like Denniston, like the Dimbles—who could enjoy things for their own sake. She was not like him. It was well that she should be rid of him.

At that moment came the sound of a key turning in the lock of the cell-door. Instantly all these thoughts vanished; mere physical terror of death, drying the throat, rushed back upon him. He scrambled to his feet and stood with his back against the furthest wall, staring as hard as if he could escape hanging by keeping whoever entered steadily in sight.

It was not a policeman who came in. It was a man in a grey suit whose *pince-nez* as he glanced towards Mark and towards the light become opaque windows concealing his eyes. Mark knew him at once and knew that he was at Belbury. It was not this that made him open his own eyes even wider and almost forget his terror in his astonishment. It was the change in the man's appearance—or rather the change in the eyes with which Mark saw him. In one sense everything about Professor Frost was as it had always been—the pointed beard, the extreme whiteness of forehead, the regularity of features, and the bright Arctic smile. But what Mark could not understand was how he had ever managed to overlook something about the man so obvious that any child would have shrunk away from him and any dog would have backed into the corner with raised hackles and bared teeth. Death itself did not seem more frightening than the fact that only six hours ago he would in some measure have trusted this man, welcomed his confidence, and even made believe that his society was not disagreeable.

12

Wet and Windy Night

I

"Well," said Dimble. "There's no one here."

"He was here a moment ago," said Denniston.

"You're sure you *did* see someone?" said Dimble.

"I thought I saw someone," said Denniston. "I'm not positive."

"If there was anyone he must still be quite close," said Dimble.

"What about giving him a call?" suggested Denniston.

"Hush! Listen!" said Jane. They were all silent for a few moments.

"That's only the old donkey," said Dimble presently, "moving about at the top."

There was another silence.

"He seems to have been pretty extravagant with his matches," said Denniston, presently, glancing at the trodden earth in the firelight. "One would expect a tramp—"

"On the other hand," said Dimble, "one would not expect Merlin to have brought a box of matches with him from the Fifth Century."

"But what are we to *do*?" said Jane.

"One hardly likes to think what MacPhee will say if we return with no more success than this. He will at once point out a plan we ought to have followed," said Denniston with a smile.

"Now that the rain's over," said Dimble, "we'd better get back to the car and start looking for your white gate. What are you looking at, Denniston?"

"I'm looking at this mud," said Denniston who had moved a few paces away from the fire and in the direction of the path by which they had descended into the dingle. He had been stooping and using his torch. Now he suddenly straightened himself. "Look!" he said, "there have been several people here. No, don't walk on it and mess up all the tracks. Look. Can't you see, Sir?"

"Aren't they our own footprints?" said Dimble.

"Some of them are pointing the wrong way. Look at that—and that."

"Might they be the tramp himself?" said Dimble. "If it was a tramp."

"He couldn't have walked up that path without our seeing him," said Jane.

"Unless he did it before we arrived," said Denniston.

"But we all saw him," said Jane.

"Come," said Dimble. "Let's follow them up to the top. I don't suppose we shall be able to follow them far. If not, we must get back to the road and go on looking for the gate."

As they reached the lip of the hollow, mud changed into grass under foot and the footprints disappeared. They walked twice round the dingle and found nothing; then they set out to return to the road. It had turned into a fine night: Orion dominated the whole sky.

2

The Deputy Director hardly ever slept. When it became absolutely necessary for him to do so, he took a drug, but the necessity was rare, for the mode of consciousness he experienced at most hours of day or night had long ceased to be exactly like what other men call waking. He had learned to withdraw most of his consciousness from the task of living, to conduct business, even, with only a quarter of his mind. Colours, tastes, smells, and tactual sensations no doubt bombarded his physical senses in the normal manner: they did not now reach his ego. The manner and outward attitude to men which he had adopted half a century ago were now an organisation which functioned almost independently like a gramophone and to which he could hand over his whole routine of interviews and committees. While the brain and lips carried on this work, and built up day by day for those around him the vague and formidable personality which they knew so well, his inmost self was free to pursue its own life. That detachment of the spirit, not only from the senses, but even from the reason, which has been the goal of some mystics, was now his.

Hence he was still, in a sense, awake—that is, he was certainly not sleeping—an hour after Frost had left him to visit Mark in his cell. Anyone who had looked into the study during that hour would have seen him sitting motionless at his table, with bowed head and folded hands. But his eyes were not shut. The face had no expression; the real man was far away suffering, enjoying, or inflicting whatever such souls do suffer, enjoy or inflict when the cord that binds them to the natural order is stretched out to its utmost but not yet snapped. When the telephone rang at his elbow he took up the receiver without a start.

"Speaking," he said.

"This is Stone, Sir," came a voice. "We have found the chamber."

"Yes."

"It was empty, Sir."

"Empty?"

"Yes, Sir."

"Are you sure, my dear Mr. Stone, that you have found the right place? It is possible . . ."

"Oh yes, Sir. It is a little kind of crypt. Stonework and some Roman brick. And a kind of slab in the middle, like an altar or a bed."

"And am I to understand there was no one there? No sign of occupation?"

"Well, Sir, it seemed to us to have been recently disturbed."

"Pray be as explicit as possible, Mr. Stone."

"Well, Sir, there was an exit—I mean a tunnel, leading out of it to the South. We went up this tunnel at once. It comes out about eight hundred yards away, outside the area of the wood."

"Comes out? Do you mean there is an arch—a gate—a tunnel-mouth?"

"Well, that's just the point. We got out to the open air all right. But obviously something had been smashed-up there quite recently. It looked as if it had been done by explosives. As if the end of the tunnel had been walled up and had some depth of earth on top of it, and as if someone had recently blasted his way out. There was no end of a mess."

"Continue, Mr. Stone. What did you do next?"

"I used the order you had given me, Sir, to collect all the police available and have sent off search parties for the man you described."

"I see. And how did *you* describe him to them?"

"Just as you did, Sir: an old man with either a very long beard or a beard very roughly trimmed, probably in a mantle, but certainly in some kind of unusual clothes. It occurred to me at the last moment to add that he might have no clothes at all."

"Why did you add that, Mr. Stone?"

"Well, Sir, I didn't know how long he'd been there, and it isn't my business. I'd heard things about clothes preserved in a place like that and all falling to pieces as soon as the air was admitted. I hope you won't imagine for a moment that I'm trying to find out anything you don't choose to tell me. But I just thought it would be as well to . . . "

"You were quite right, Mr. Stone," said Wither, "in thinking that anything remotely resembling inquisitiveness on your part might have the most disastrous consequences. I mean, for yourself, for, of course, it is your interests I have chiefly had in view in my choice of methods. I assure you that you can rely on my support in the very—er—delicate position you have—no doubt unintentionally—chosen to occupy."

"Thank you very much, Sir. I am so glad you think I was right in saying he might be naked."

"Oh, as to *that,*" said the Director, "there are a great many considerations which cannot be raised at the moment. And what did you instruct your search parties to do on finding any such—er—person?"

"Well, that was another difficulty, Sir. I sent my own assistant, Father Doyle, with one party, because he knows Latin. And I gave Inspector Wrench the ring you gave me and put him in charge of the second. The best I could do for the third party was to see that it contained someone who knew Welsh."

"You did not think of accompanying a party yourself?"

"No, Sir. You'd told me to ring up without fail the moment we found anything. And I didn't want to delay the search parties until I'd got you."

"I see. Well, no doubt your action (speaking quite without prejudice) could be interpreted along those lines. You made it quite clear that this—ah—Personage—when found, was to be treated with the greatest deference and—if you won't misunderstand me—caution?"

"Oh yes, Sir."

"Well, Mr. Stone, I am, on the whole, and with certain inevitable reservations, moderately satisfied with your conduct of this affair. I believe that I may be able to present it in a favourable light to those of my colleagues whose good will you have, unfortunately, not been able to retain. If you can bring it to a successful conclusion you would very much strengthen your position. If not . . . it is inexpressibly painful to me that there should be these tensions and mutual recriminations among us. But you quite understand me, my dear boy. If only I could persuade—say Miss Hardcastle and Mr. Studdock—to share my appreciation of your very real qualities, you would need to have no apprehensions about your career or—ah—your security."

"But what do you want me to *do*, Sir?"

"My dear young friend, the golden rule is very simple. There are only two errors which would be fatal to one placed in the peculiar situation which certain parts of your previous conduct have unfortunately created for you. On the one hand, anything like a lack of initiative or enterprise would be disastrous. On the other, the slightest approach to unauthorised action—anything which suggested that you were assuming a liberty of decision which, in all the circumstances, is not really yours— might have consequences from which even I could not protect you. But as long as you keep quite clear of these two extremes, there is no reason (speaking unofficially) why you should not be perfectly safe."

Then, without waiting for Mr. Stone to reply, he hung up the receiver and rang his bell.

3

"Oughtn't we to be nearly at the gate we climbed over?" said Dimble.

It was a good deal lighter now that the rain had stopped, but the wind had risen and was roaring about them so that only shouted remarks could be heard. The branches of the hedge beside which they were tramping swayed and dipped and rose again so that they looked as if they were lashing the bright stars.

"It's a good deal longer than I remembered," said Denniston.

"But not so muddy," said Jane.

"You're right," said Denniston, suddenly stopping. "It's all stony. It wasn't like this at all on the way up. We're in the wrong field."

"I *think*," said Dimble mildly, "we must be right. We turned half left along this hedge as soon as we came out of the trees, and I'm sure I remember—"

"But did we come out of the copse on the right side?" said Denniston.

"If we once start changing course," said Dimble, "we shall go round and round in circles all night. Let's keep straight on. We're bound to come to the road in the end."

"Hullo!" said Jane sharply. "What's this?"

All listened. Because of the wind, the unidentified rhythmic noise which they were straining to hear seemed quite distant at one moment, and then, next moment, with shouts of "Look out!"—"Go away, you great brute!"—"Get back!"—and the like, all were shrinking back into the hedge as the *plosh-plosh* of a horse cantering on soft ground passed close beside them. A cold gobbet of mud flung up from its hoofs struck Denniston in the face.

"Oh look! Look!" cried Jane. "Stop him. Quick!"

"Stop him?" said Denniston who was trying to clean his face. "What on earth for? The less I see of that great clodhopping quadruped, the better—"

"Oh, shout out to him, Dr. Dimble," said Jane in an agony of impatience. "Come on. Run! Didn't you see?"

"See what?" panted Dimble as the whole party, under the influence of Jane's urgency, began running in the direction of the retreating horse.

"There's a man on his back," gasped Jane. She was tired and out of breath and had lost a shoe.

"A man?" said Denniston; and then: "by God, Sir, Jane's right. Look, look there! Against the sky . . . to your left."

"We can't overtake him," said Dimble.

"Hi! Stop! Come back! Friends—*amis*—*amici*," bawled Denniston.

Dimble was not able to shout for the moment. He was an old man, who had been tired before they set out, and now his heart and lungs were doing things to him of which his doctor had told him the meaning some years ago. He was not frightened, but he could not shout with a great voice (least of all in the Old Solar language) until he had breathed. And while he stood trying to fill his lungs all the others suddenly cried "Look" yet again; for high among the stars, looking unnaturally large and many legged, the shape of the horse appeared as it leaped a hedge some twenty yards away, and on its back, with some streaming garment blown far out behind him in the wind, the great figure of a man. It seemed to Jane that he was looking back over his shoulder as though he mocked. Then came a splash and thud as the horse alighted on the far side; and then nothing but wind and starlight again.

4

"You are in danger," said Frost when he had finished locking the door of Mark's cell, "but you are also within reach of a great opportunity."

"I gather," said Mark, "I am at the Institute after all and not in a police station."

"Yes. That makes no difference to the danger. The Institute will soon have official powers of liquidation. It has anticipated them. Hingest and Carstairs have both been liquidated. Such actions are demanded of us."

"If you are going to kill me," said Mark, "why all this farce of a murder charge?"

"Before going on," said Frost, "I must ask you to be strictly objective. Resentment and fear are both chemical phenomena. Our reactions to one another are chemical phenomena. Social relations are chemical relations. You must observe these feelings in yourself in an objective manner. Do not let them distract your attention from the facts."

"I see," said Mark. He was acting while he said it—trying to sound at once faintly hopeful and slightly sullen, ready to be worked upon. But within, his new insight into Belbury kept him resolved not to believe one word the other said, not to accept (though he might feign acceptance) any offer he made. He felt that he must at all costs hold onto the knowledge that these men were unalterable enemies; for already he felt the old tug towards yielding, towards semi-credulity, inside him.

"The murder charge against you and the alterations in your treatment have been part of a planned programme with a well defined end in view," said Frost. "It is a discipline through which everyone is passed before admission to the Circle."

Again Mark felt a spasm of retrospective terror. Only a few days ago he would have swallowed any hook with that bait on it; and nothing but the imminence of death could have made the hook so obvious and the bait so insipid as it now was. At least, so comparatively insipid. For even now . . .

"I don't quite see the purpose of it," he said aloud.

"It is, again, to promote objectivity. A circle bound together by subjective feelings of mutual confidence and liking would be useless. Those, as I have said, are chemical phenomena. They could all in principle be produced by injections. You have been made to pass through a number of conflicting feelings about the Deputy Director and others in order that your future association with us may not be based on feelings at all. In so far as there must be social relations between members of the circle it is, perhaps, better that they should be feelings of dislike. There is less risk of their being confused with the real *nexus*."

"My future association?" said Studdock, acting a tremulous eagerness. But it was perilously easy for him to act it. The reality might reawake at any moment.

"Yes," said Frost. "You have been selected as a possible candidate for admission. If you do not gain admission, or if you reject it, it will be necessary to destroy you. I am not, of course, attempting to work on your fears. They only confuse the issue. The process would be quite painless, and your present reactions to it are inevitable physical events."

Mark considered this thoughtfully.

"It—it seems rather a formidable decision," said Mark.

"That is merely a proposition about the state of your own body at the moment. If you please, I will go on to give you the necessary information. I must begin by telling you that neither the Deputy Director, nor I, are responsible for shaping the policy of the Institute."

"The Head?" said Mark.

"No. Filostrato and Wilkins are quite deceived about the Head. They have, indeed, carried out a remarkable experiment by preserving it from decay. But Alcasan's mind is not the mind we are in contact with when the Head speaks."

"Do you mean Alcasan is really . . . *dead?*" asked Mark. His surprise at Frost's last statement needed no acting.

"In the present state of our knowledge," said Frost, "there is no answer to that question. Probably it has no meaning. But the cortex and vocal organs in Alcasan's head are used by a different mind. And now, please, attend very carefully. You have probably not heard of macrobes."

"Microbes?" said Mark in bewilderment. "But of course—"

"I did not say *microbes,* I said *macrobes.* The formation of the word explains itself. Below the level of animal life, we have long known that there are microscopic organisms. Their actual results on human life, in respect of health and disease, have of course made up a large part of history: the secret cause was not known till we invented the microscope."

"Go on," said Mark. Ravenous curiosity was moving like a sort of groundswell beneath his conscious determination to stand on guard.

"I have now to inform you that there are similar organisms *above* the level of animal life. When I say, 'above,' I am not speaking biologically. The structure of the *macrobe,* so far as we know it, is of extreme simplicity. When I say that it is above the animal level, I mean that it is more permanent, disposes of more energy, and has greater intelligence."

"More intelligent than the highest anthropoids?" said Mark. "It must be pretty nearly human, then."

"You have misunderstood me. When I say it transcended the animals, I was, of course, including the most efficient animal, Man. The *macrobe* is more intelligent than Man."

Frowningly, Mark studied this theory.

"But how is it in that case that we have had no communication with them?"

"It is not certain that we have not. But in primitive times it was spasmodic, and was opposed by numerous prejudices. Moreover, the intellectual development of man had not reached the level at which intercourse with our species could offer any attractions to a *macrobe.* But though there has been little intercourse, there has been profound influence. Their effect on human history has been far greater than that of the microbes, though, of course, equally unrecognized. In the light of what we now know, all history will have to be rewritten. The real causes of all the principal events are quite unknown to historians; that, indeed, is why history has not yet succeeded in becoming a science."

"I think I'll sit down, if you don't mind," said Mark resuming his seat on the floor. Frost remained, throughout the whole conversation, standing perfectly still with his arms hanging down straight at his sides. But for the periodic upward tilt of his head and flash of his teeth at the end of a sentence, he used no gestures.

"The vocal organs and brain taken from Alcasan," he continued, "have become the conductors of a regular intercourse between the Macrobes and our own species. I do not say that we have discovered this technique; the discovery was theirs, not ours. The circle to which you may be admitted is the organ of that co-operation between the two species which has already created a new situation for humanity. The change, you will see, is far greater than that which turned the sub-man into the man. It is more comparable to the first appearance of organic life."

"These organisms, then," said Mark, "are friendly to humanity?"

"If you reflect for a moment," said Frost, "you will see that your question has no meaning except on the level of the crudest popular thought. Friendship is a chemical phenomenon; so is hatred. Both of them presuppose organisms of our own type. The first step towards intercourse with the macrobes is the realisation that one must go outside the whole world of our subjective emotions. It is only as you begin to do so, that you discover how much of what you mistook for your thought was merely a by-product of your blood and nervous tissues."

"Oh, of course. I didn't quite mean, 'friendly,' in that sense. I really meant, were their aims compatible with our own?"

"What do you mean by our own aims?"

"Well—I suppose—the scientific reconstruction of the human race in the direction of increased efficiency—the elimination of war and poverty and other forms of waste—a fuller exploitation of Nature—the preservation and extension of our species, in fact."

"I do not think this pseudo-scientific language really modifies the essentially subjective and instinctive basis of the ethics you are describing. I will return to the matter at a later stage. For the moment, I would merely remark that your view of war and your reference to the preservation of the species suggest a profound misconception. They are mere generalisations from affectional feelings."

"Surely," said Mark, "one requires a pretty large population for the full exploitation of Nature, if for nothing else? And surely war is disgenic and reduces efficiency? Even if population needs thinning, is not war the worst possible method of thinning it?"

"That idea is a survival from conditions which are rapidly being altered. A few centuries ago, war did not operate in the way you describe. A large agricultural population was essential; and war destroyed types which were then still useful. But every advance in industry and agriculture reduces the number of work-people who are required. A large, unintelligent population is now becoming a dead-weight. The real importance of scientific war is that scientists have to be reserved. It was not the great technocrats of Koenigsberg or Moscow who supplied the casualties in the siege of Stalingrad: it was superstitious Bavarian peasants and low-grade Russian agricultural workers. The effect of modern war is to eliminate retrogressive types, while sparing the technocracy and increasing its hold upon public affairs. In the new age, what has hitherto been merely the intellectual nucleus of the race is to become, by gradual stages, the race itself. You are to conceive the species as an animal which has discovered how to simplify nutrition and locomotion to such a point that the old complex organs and the large body which contained them are no longer necessary. That large body is therefore to disappear. Only a tenth part of it will now be needed to support the brain. The individual is to become all head. The human race is to become all Technocracy."

"I see," said Mark. "I had thought rather vaguely—that the intelligent nucleus would be extended by education."

"That is pure chimera. The great majority of the human race can be educated only in the sense of being given knowledge: they cannot be trained into the total objectivity of mind which is now necessary. They will always remain animals, looking at the world through the haze of their subjective reactions. Even if they could, the day for a large population has passed. It has served its function by acting as a kind of cocoon for Technocratic and Objective Man. Now, the Macrobes, and the selected humans who can co-operate with them, have no further use for it."

"The two last wars, then, were not disasters on your view?"

"On the contrary, they were simply the beginning of the programme—the first two of the sixteen major wars which are scheduled to take place in this century. I am aware of the emotional (that is, the chemical) reactions which a statement like this produces in you, and you are wasting your time in trying to conceal them from me. I do not expect you to control them. That is not the path to objectivity. I deliberately raise them in order that you may become accustomed to regard them in a purely scientific light and distinguish them as sharply as possible from the *facts*."

Mark sat with his eyes fixed on the floor. He had felt, in fact, very little emotion at Frost's programme for the human race; indeed, he almost discovered at that moment how little he had ever really cared for those remote futures and universal benefits whereon his co-operation with the Institute had at first been theoretically based. Certainly, at the present moment there was no room in his mind for such considerations. He was fully occupied with the conflict between his resolution not to trust these men, never again to be lured by any bait into a real co-operation, and the terrible strength—like a tide sucking at the shingle as it goes out—of an opposite emotion. For here, here surely at last (so his desire whispered to him) was the true inner circle of all, the circle whose centre was outside the human race—the ultimate secret, the supreme power, the last initiation. The fact that it was almost completely horrible did not in the least diminish its attraction. Nothing that lacked the tang of horror would have been quite strong enough to satisfy the delirious excitement which now set his temples hammering. It came into his mind that Frost knew all about this excitement, and also about the opposite determination, and reckoned securely on the excitement as something which was certain to carry the day in his victim's mind.

A rattling and knocking which had been obscurely audible for some time now became so loud that Frost turned to the door. "Go away," he said, raising his voice. "What is the meaning of this impertinence?" The indistinct noise of someone shouting on the other side of the door was heard, and the knocking went on. Frost's smile widened as he turned and opened it. Instantly a piece of paper was put into his hand. As he read it, he started violently. Without glancing at Mark, he left the cell. Mark heard the door locked again behind him.

5

"What friends those two are!" said Ivy Maggs. She was referring to Pinch the cat and Mr. Bultitude the bear. The latter was sitting up with his back against the warm wall by the kitchen fire. His cheeks were so fat and his eyes so small that he looked as if he were smiling. The cat after walking to and fro with erected tail and rubbing herself against his belly had finally curled up and gone to sleep between his legs. The jackdaw, still on the Director's shoulder, had long since put its head beneath its wing.

Mrs. Dimble, who sat further back in the kitchen, darning as if for dear life, pursed her lips a little as Ivy Maggs spoke. She could not go to bed. She wished they would all keep quiet. Her anxiety had reached that pitch at which almost every event, however small, threatens to become an irritation. But then, if anyone had been watching her expression, they would have seen the little grimace rapidly smoothed out again. Her will had many years of practice behind it.

"When we use the word, Friends, of those two creatures," said MacPhee, "I doubt we are being merely anthropomorphic. It is difficult to avoid the illusion that they have personalities in the human sense. But there's no evidence for it."

"What's she go making up to him for, then?" asked Ivy.

"Well," said MacPhee, "maybe there'd be a desire for warmth—she's away in out of the draught there. And there'd be a sense of security from being near something familiar. And likely enough some obscure transferred sexual impulses."

"Really, Mr. MacPhee," said Ivy with great indignation, "it's a shame for you to say those things about two dumb animals. I'm sure I never did see Pinch—or Mr. Bultitude either, the poor thing—"

"I said *transferred*," interrupted MacPhee drily. "And anyway, they like the mutual friction of their fur as a means of rectifying irritations set up by parasites. Now, you'll observe—"

"If you mean they have fleas," said Ivy, "you know as well as anyone that they have no such thing." She had reason on her side, for it was MacPhee himself who put on overalls once a month and solemnly lathered Mr. Bultitude from rump to snout in the wash-house and poured buckets of tepid water over him, and finally dried him—a day's work in which he allowed no one to assist him.

"What do you think, Sir?" said Ivy, looking at the Director.

"Me?" said Ransom. "I think MacPhee is introducing into animal life a distinction that doesn't exist there, and then trying to determine on which side of that distinction the feelings of Pinch and Bultitude fall. You've got to become human before the physical cravings are distinguishable from affections—just as you have to become spiritual before affections are distinguishable from charity. What is going on in the cat and the bear isn't one or other of these two things: it is a single undifferentiated thing in which you can find the germ of what we call friendship and of what we call physical need. But it isn't either at that level. It is one of Barfield's 'ancient unities.' "

"I never denied they liked being together," said MacPhee.

"Well, that's what I said," retorted Mrs. Maggs.

"The question is worth raising, Mr. Director," said MacPhee, "because I submit that it points to an essential falsity in the whole system of this place."

Grace Ironwood who had been sitting with her eyes half-closed suddenly opened them wide and fixed them on the Ulsterman, and Mrs. Dimble leaned her head towards Camilla and said in a whisper, "I do wish Mr. MacPhee could be persuaded to go to bed. It's perfectly unbearable at a time like this."

"How do you mean, MacPhee?" asked the Director.

"I mean that there is a half-hearted attempt to adopt an attitude towards irrational creatures which cannot be consistently maintained. And I'll do the justice to say that you've never tried. The bear is kept in the house and given apples and golden syrup till it's near bursting—"

"Well, I like that!" said Mrs. Maggs. "Who is it that's always giving him apples? That's what I'd like to know."

"The bear, as I was observing," said MacPhee, "is kept in the house and pampered. The pigs are kept in a stye and killed for bacon. I would be interested to know the philosophical *rationale* of the distinction."

Ivy Maggs looked in bewilderment from the smiling face of the Director to the unsmiling face of MacPhee.

"I think it's just silly," she said. "Who ever heard of trying to make bacon out of a bear?"

MacPhee made a little stamp of impatience and said something which was drowned first by Ransom's laughter, and then by a great clap of wind which shook the window as if it would blow it in.

"What a dreadful night for them!" said Mrs. Dimble.

"I love it," said Camilla. "I'd love to be out in it. Out on a high hill. Oh, I do wish you'd let me go with them, Sir."

"You *like* it?" said Ivy. "Oh I don't! Listen to it round the corner of the house. It'd make me feel kind of creepy if I were alone. Or even if you was upstairs, Sir. I always think it's on nights like this that they— you know—come to you."

"They don't take any notice of weather one way or the other, Ivy," said Ransom.

"Do you know," said Ivy in a low voice, "that's a thing I don't quite understand. They're so eerie, these ones that come to visit you. I wouldn't go near that part of the house if I thought there was anything there, not if you paid me a hundred pounds. But I don't feel like that about God. But He ought to be worse, if you see what I mean."

"He was, once," said the Director. "You are quite right about the Powers. Angels in general are not good company for men in general, even when they are good angels and good men. It's all in St. Paul. But as for Maleldil Himself, all that has changed: it was changed by what happened at Bethlehem."

"It's getting ever so near Christmas now," said Ivy addressing the company in general.

"We shall have Mr. Maggs with us before then," said Ransom.

"In a day or two, Sir," said Ivy.

"Was that only the wind?" said Grace Ironwood.

"It sounded to me like a horse," said Mrs. Dimble.

"Here," said MacPhee jumping up. "Get out of the way, Mr. Bultitude, till I get my gum boots. It'll be those two horses of Broad's again, tramping all over my celery trenches. If only you'd let me go to the police in the first instance. Why the man can't keep them shut up—" He was bundling himself into his mackintosh as he spoke and the rest of the speech was inaudible.

"My crutch please, Camilla," said Ransom. "Come back, MacPhee. We will go to the door together, you and I. Ladies, stay where you are."

There was a look on his face which some of those present had not seen before. The four women sat as if they had been turned to stone, with their eyes wide and staring. A moment later Ransom and MacPhee stood alone in the scullery. The back door was so shaking on its hinges with the wind that they did not know whether someone were knocking at it or not.

"Now," said Ransom, "open it. And stand back behind it yourself."

For a second MacPhee worked with the bolts. Then, whether he meant to disobey or not (a point which must remain doubtful), the storm flung the door against the wall and he was momentarily pinned behind it. Ransom, standing motionless, leaning forward on his crutch, saw in the light from the scullery, outlined against the blackness, a huge horse, all in a lather of sweat and foam, its yellow teeth laid bare, its nostrils wide and red, its ears flattened against its skull, and its eyes flaming. It had been ridden so close up to the door that its front hoofs rested on the doorstep. It had neither saddle, stirrup nor bridle; but at that very moment a man leapt off its back. He seemed both very tall and very fat, almost a giant. His reddish-grey hair and beard were blown all about his face so that it was hardly visible; and it was only after he had taken a step forward that Ransom noticed his clothes—the ragged, ill-fitting khaki coat, baggy trousers, and boots that had lost the toes.

6

In a great room at Belbury, where the fire blazed and wine and silver sparkled on side-tables and a great bed occupied the centre of the floor, the Deputy Director watched in profound silence while four young men with reverential or medical heedfulness carried in a burden on a stretcher. As they removed the blankets and transferred the occupant of the stretcher to the bed, Wither's mouth opened wider. His interest became so intense that for the moment the chaos of his face appeared ordered and he looked like an ordinary man. What he saw was a naked human body, alive, but apparently unconscious. He ordered the attendants to place hot water bottles at its feet and raise the head with pillows: when they had done so and withdrawn, he drew a chair to the foot of the bed and sat down to study the face of the sleeper. The head was very large, though perhaps it looked larger than it was because of the unkempt grey beard and the long and tangled grey hair. The face was weather-beaten in the extreme and the neck, where visible, already lean and scraggy with age. The eyes were shut and the lips wore a very slight smile. The total effect was ambiguous. Wither gazed at it for a long time and sometimes moved his head to see how it looked from a different angle—almost as if he searched for some trait he could not find and were disappointed. For nearly a quarter of an hour he sat thus; then the door opened and Professor Frost came softly into the room.

He walked to the bedside, bent down and looked closely into the stranger's face. Then he walked round to the far side of the bed and did the same.

"Is he asleep?" whispered Wither.

"I think not. It is more like some kind of a trance. What kind, I don't know."

"You have no doubts, I trust?"

"Where did they find him?"

"In a dingle about quarter of a mile from the entrance to the souterrain. They had the track of bare feet almost all the way."

"The souterrain itself was empty?"

"Yes. I had a report on that from Stone shortly after you left me."

"You will make provisions about Stone?"

"Yes. But what do you think?"—he pointed with his eyes to the bed.

"I think it is he," said Frost. "The place is right. The nudity is hard to account for on any other hypothesis. The skull is the kind I expected."

"But the face."

"Yes. There are certain traits which are a little disquieting."

"I could have sworn," said Wither, "that I knew the look of a Master—even the look of one who could be made into a Master. You understand me . . . one sees at once that Straik or Studdock might do; that Miss Hardcastle, with all her excellent qualities, would not."

"Yes. Perhaps we must be prepared for great crudities in . . . *him*. Who knows what the technique of the Atlantean Circle was really like?"

"Certainly, one must not be—ah—narrow-minded. One can suppose that the Masters of that age were not quite so sharply divided from the common people as we are. All sorts of emotional and even instinctive, elements were perhaps still tolerated in the Great Atlantean which we have had to discard."

"One not only *may* suppose it, one *must*. We should not forget that the whole plan consists in the reunion of different kinds of the art."

"Exactly. Perhaps one's association with the Powers—their different time scale and all that—tends to make one forget how enormous the gap in time is by our human standards."

"What we have here," said Frost pointing to the sleeper, "is not, you see, something from the Fifth Century. It is the last vestige, surviving into the Fifth Century, of something much more remote. Something that comes down from long before the Great Disaster, even from before primitive Druidism; something that takes us back to Numinor, to preglacial periods."

"The whole experiment is perhaps more hazardous than we realised."

"I have had occasion before," said Frost, "to express the wish that you would not keep on introducing these emotional pseudo-statements into our scientific discussions."

"My dear friend," said Wither without looking at him, "I am quite aware that the subject you mention has been discussed between you and the Powers themselves. Quite aware. And I don't doubt that you are equally well aware of certain discussions they have held with me about aspects of your own methods which are open to criticism. Nothing would be more futile—I might say more dangerous—than any attempt to introduce between ourselves those modes of oblique discipline which we properly apply to our inferiors. It is in your own interest that I venture to touch on this point."

Instead of replying, Frost signalled to his companion. Both men became silent, their gaze fixed on the bed: for the Sleeper had opened his eyes.

The opening of the eyes flooded the whole face with meaning, but it was a meaning they could not interpret. The Sleeper seemed to be looking at them, but they were not quite sure that he saw them. As the seconds passed, Wither's main impression of the face was its caution. But there was nothing intense or uneasy about it. It was a habitual, unemphatic defensiveness which seemed to have behind it years of hard experience, quietly—perhaps even humorously—endured.

Wither rose to his feet, and cleared his throat.

"*Magister Merline*," he said, "*Sapientissime Britonum, secreti secretorum possessor, incredibili quodam gaudio afficimur quod te in domum nostram accipere nobis—ah—contingit. Scito nos etiam haud imperitos esse magnae artis—et—ut ita dicam . . .*"[1]

But his voice died away. It was too obvious that the Sleeper was taking no notice of what he said. It was impossible that a learned man of the Fifth Century should not know Latin. Was there, then, some error in his own pronunciation? But he felt by no means sure that this man could not understand him. The total lack of curiosity, or even interest, in his face, suggested rather that he was not listening.

Frost took a decanter from the table and poured out a glass of red wine. He then returned to the bedside, bowed deeply, and handed it to the stranger. The latter looked at it with an expression that might (or might not) be interpreted as one of cunning; then he suddenly sat up in bed, revealing a huge hairy chest and lean, muscular arms. His eyes turned to the table and he pointed. Frost went back to it and touched a different decanter. The stranger shook his head and pointed again.

"I think," said Wither, "that our very distinguished guest is trying to indicate the jug. I don't quite know what was provided. Perhaps—"

"It contains beer," said Frost.

"Well, it is hardly appropriate—still, perhaps—we know so little of the customs of that age . . ."

While he was still speaking Frost had filled a pewter mug with beer and offered it to their guest. For the first time a gleam of interest came into that cryptic face. The man snatched the mug eagerly, pushed back his disorderly moustache from his lips, and began to drink. Back and back went the grey head; up and up went the bottom of the tankard; the moving muscles of the lean throat made the act of drinking visible. At last the man, having completely inverted the tankard, set it down, wiped his wet lips with the back of his hand, and heaved a long sigh—the first

---

[1] Master Merlin, wisest of the Britons, possessor of the secrets, it is with inexpressible pleasure that we embrace the opportunity of—ah—welcoming you in our house. You will understand that we also are not unskilled in the Great Art, and, if I may say so . . .

sound he had uttered since his arrival. Then he turned his attention once more to the table.

For about twenty minutes the two old men fed him—Wither with tremulous and courtly deference, Frost with the deft, noiseless movements of a trained servant. All sorts of delicacies had been provided, but the stranger devoted his attention entirely to cold beef, chicken, pickles, bread, cheese and butter. The butter he ate neat, off the end of a knife. He was apparently unacquainted with forks, and took the chicken bones in both hands to gnaw them, placing them under the pillow when he had done. His eating was noisy and animal. When he had eaten, he signalled for a second pint of beer, drank it at two long draughts, wiped his mouth on the sheet and his nose on his hand, and seemed to be composing himself for further slumber.

"Ah—er—domine," said Wither with deprecating urgency, "nihil magis mihi displiceret quam ut tibi ullo modo—ah—molestior essem. Attamen, venia tua . . ."[1]

But the man was taking no notice at all. They could not tell whether his eyes were shut or whether he was still looking at them under half-closed lids; but clearly he was not intending to converse. Frost and Wither exchanged enquiring glances.

"There is no approach to this room, is there?" said Frost, "except through the next one."

"No," said Wither.

"Let us go out there and discuss the situation. We can leave the door ajar. We shall be able to hear if he stirs."

7

When Mark found himself left suddenly alone by Frost, his first sensation was an unexpected lightness of heart. It was not that he had any release from fears about the future. Rather, in the very midst of those fears, a strange sense of liberation had sprung up. The relief of no longer trying to win these men's confidence, the shuffling off of miserable hopes, was almost exhilarating. The straight fight, after the long series of diplomatic failures, was tonic. He might lose the straight fight. But at least it was now

---

[1] Ah—er—Sir—nothing would be further from my wish than to be in any way troublesome to you. At the same time, with your pardon . . .

his side against theirs. And he could talk of "his side" now. Already he was with Jane and with all she symbolised. Indeed, it was he who was in the front line: Jane was almost a non-combatant. . . .

The approval of one's own conscience is a very heady draught: and specially for those who are not accustomed to it. Within two minutes Mark passed from that first involuntary sense of liberation to a conscious attitude of courage, and thence into unrestrained heroics. The picture of himself as hero and martyr, as Jack the Giant-Killer still coolly playing his hand even in the giant's kitchen, rose up before him, promising that it could blot out forever those other, and unendurable pictures of himself which had haunted him for the last few hours. It wasn't everyone, after all, who could have resisted an invitation like Frost's. An invitation that beckoned you right across the frontiers of human life . . . into something that people had been trying to find since the beginning of the world . . . a touch on that infinitely secret cord which was the real nerve of all history. How it would have attracted him once!

Would have attracted him once . . . Suddenly, like a thing that leaped to him across infinite distances with the speed of light, desire (salt, black, ravenous, unanswerable desire) took him by the throat. The merest hint will convey to those who have felt it the quality of the emotion which now shook him, like a dog shaking a rat; for others, no description perhaps will avail. Many writers speak of it in terms of lust: a description admirably illuminating from within, totally misleading from without. It has nothing to do with the body. But it is in two respects like lust as lust shows itself to be in the deepest and darkest vault of its labyrinthine house. For like lust, it disenchants the whole universe. Everything else that Mark had ever felt—love, ambition, hunger, lust itself—appeared to have been mere milk and water, toys for children, not worth one throb of the nerves. The infinite attraction of this dark thing sucked all other passions into itself: the rest of the world appeared blenched, etiolated, insipid, a world of white marriages and white masses, dishes without salt, gambling for counters. He could not now think of Jane except in terms of appetite: and appetite here made no appeal. That serpent, faced with the true dragon, became a fangless worm. But it was like lust in another respect also. It is idle to point out to the perverted man the horror of his perversion: while the fierce fit is on, that horror is the very spice of his craving. It is ugliness itself that becomes, in the end, the goal of his lechery; beauty has long since grown too weak a stimulant. And so it was here. These creatures of which Frost had spoken—and he did not doubt now that they were locally present with him in the cell—breathed death on the human race and on all joy. Not despite this but because of this, the terrible gravitation sucked and tugged and fascinated him towards them. Never before had he known the fruitful strength of the movement opposite to Nature which now had him in its grip; the impulse to reverse all reluctances and to draw every circle anti-clockwise. The meaning of certain pictures, of Frost's talk about "objectivity," of the things done by witches in old times, became clear to him. The image of Wither's face rose to his memory; and this time he did not merely loathe it. He noted, with shuddering satisfaction, the signs it bore of a shared experience between them. Wither also knew. Wither understood . . .

At the same moment, it came back to him that he would probably be killed. As soon as the thought of that, he became once more aware of the cell—the little hard white empty place with the glaring light, in which he found himself sitting on the floor. He blinked his eyes. He could not remember that it had been visible for the last few minutes. Where had he been? His mind was clear now at any rate. This idea of something in common between him and Wither was all nonsense. Of course they meant to kill him in the end unless he could rescue himself by his own wits. What had he been thinking and feeling while he forgot that?

Gradually he realized that he had sustained some sort of attack, and that he had put up no resistance at all; and with that realisation a quite new kind of dread entered his mind. Though he was theoretically a materialist, he had all his life believed quite inconsistently, and even carelessly, in the freedom of his own will. He had seldom made a moral resolution, and when he had resolved some hours ago to trust the Belbury crew no further, he had taken it for granted that he would be able to do what he resolved. He knew, to be sure, that he might "change his mind"; but till he did so, of course he would carry out his plan. It had never occurred to him that his mind could thus be changed for him, all in an instant of time, changed beyond recognition. If that sort of thing could happen . . . It was unfair. Here was a man trying (for the first time in his life) to do what was obviously the right thing—the thing that Jane and the Dimbles and Aunt Gilly would have approved of. You might have expected that when a man behaved in that way the universe would back him up. For the relics of such semi-savage versions of Theism as Mark had picked up in the course of his life were stronger in him than he knew, and he felt, though he would not have put it into words, that it was "up to" the universe to reward his good resolutions. Yet, the very first moment you tried to be good, the universe let you down. It revealed gaps you had never dreamed of. It invented new laws for the express purpose of letting you down. That was what you got for your pains.

The cynics, then, were right. But at this thought, he stopped sharply. Some flavor that came with it had given him pause. Was this the other mood beginning again? Oh not that, at any price. He clenched his hands. No, no, no. He could not stand this much longer. He wanted Jane; he wanted Mrs. Dimble; he wanted Denniston. He wanted somebody or something. "Oh don't, don't let me go back into it," he said; and then louder, "don't, don't." All that could in any sense be called himself went into that cry; and the dreadful consciousness of having played his last card began to turn slowly into a sort of peace. There was nothing more to be done. Unconsciously he allowed his muscles to relax. His young body was very tired by this time and even the hard floor was grateful to it. The cell also seemed to be somehow emptied and purged, as if it too were tired after the conflicts it had witnessed—emptied like a sky after rain, tired like a child after weeping. A dim consciousness that the night must be nearly ended stole over him, and he fell asleep.

13

They Have Pulled Down
Deep Heaven on Their Heads

I

"Stand! Stand where you are and tell me your name and business," said Ransom.

The ragged figure on the threshold tilted its head a little sideways like one who cannot quite hear. At the same moment the wind from the opened door had its way with the house. The inner door, between the scullery and the kitchen, clapped to with a loud bang, isolating the three men from the women, and a large tin basin fell clattering into the sink. The stranger took a pace further into the room.

"*Sta,*" said Ransom in a loud voice. "*In nomine Patris et Filii et Spiritus Sancti, dic mihi qui sis et quam ob causam veneris.*"[1]

The Stranger raised his hand and flung back the dripping hair from his forehead. The light fell full on his face, from which Ransom had the impression of an immense quietness. Every muscle of this man's body seemed as relaxed as if he were asleep, and he stood absolutely still. Each drop of rain from the khaki coat struck the tiled floor exactly where the drop before it had fallen.

His eyes rested on Ransom for a second or two with no particular

---

[1] Stand. In the name of the Father and the Son and the Holy Ghost, tell me who you are and why you come.

interest. Then he turned his head to his left, to where the door was flung back almost against the wall. MacPhee was concealed behind it.

"Come out," said the Stranger in Latin. The words were spoken almost in a whisper, but so deep that even in that wind-shaken room they made a kind of vibration. But what surprised Ransom much more was the fact that MacPhee immediately obeyed. He did not look at Ransom but at the Stranger. Then, unexpectedly, he gave an enormous yawn. The Stranger looked him up and down and then turned to the Director.

"Fellow," he said in Latin, "tell the Lord of this House that I am come." As he spoke, the wind from behind him was whipping the coat about his legs and blowing his hair over his forehead; but his great mass stood as if it had been planted like a tree and he seemed in no hurry. And the voice, too, was such as one might imagine to be the voice of a tree, large and slow and patient, drawn up through roots and clay and gravel from the depths of the Earth.

"I am the Master here," said Ransom, in the same language.

"To be sure!" answered the Stranger. "And yonder whipper-snapper *(mastigia)* is without doubt your Bishop." He did not exactly smile, but a look of disquieting amusement came into his keen eyes. Suddenly he poked his head forward so as to bring his face much nearer to the Director's.

"Tell your Master that I am come," he repeated in the same voice as before.

Ransom looked at him without the flicker of an eyelid.

"Do you really wish," he said at last, "that I call upon my Masters?"

"A daw that lives in a hermit's cell has learned before now to chatter book-Latin," said the other. "Let us hear your calling, mannikin" *(homuncio)*.

"I must use another language for it," said Ransom.

"A daw could have Greek also in its bill."

"It is not Greek."

"Let us hear your Hebrew, then."

"It is not Hebrew."

"Nay," answered the other with something like a chuckle, a chuckle deep hidden in his enormous chest and betrayed only by a slight movement of his shoulders, "if you come to the gabble of barbarians, it will go hard but I shall out-chatter you. Here is excellent sport."

"It may happen to seem to you the speech of barbarians," said Ransom, "for it is long since it has been heard. Not even in Numinor was it heard in the streets."

The Stranger gave no start and his face remained as quiet as before, if it did not become quieter. But he spoke with a new interest.

"Your Masters let you play with dangerous toys," he said. "Tell me, slave, what is Numinor?"

"The true West," said Ransom.

"Well," said the other. Then, after a pause, he added, "You have little courtesy to guests in this house. It is a cold wind on my back, and I have been long in bed. You see, I have already crossed the threshold."

"I value that at a straw," said Ransom. "Shut the door, MacPhee," he added in English. But there was no response; and looking round for the first time, he saw that MacPhee had sat down in the one chair which the scullery contained and was fast asleep.

"What is the meaning of this foolery?" said Ransom looking sharply at the Stranger.

"If you are indeed the Master of this house, you have no need to be told. If not, why should I give account of myself to such as you? Do not fear; your horse-boy will be none the worse."

"This shall be seen to shortly," said Ransom. "In the meantime, I do not fear your entering the house. I have more cause to fear your escaping. Shut the door if you will, for you see my foot is hurt."

The Stranger without ever taking his eyes off Ransom swept back his left hand behind him, found the door handle, and slammed the door to. MacPhee never stirred. "Now," he said, "what of these Masters of yours?"

"My Masters are the Oyéresu."

"Where did you hear that name?" asked the Stranger. "Or, if you are truly of the College, why do they dress you like a slave?"

"Your own garments," said Ransom, "are not those of a druid."

"That stroke was well put by," answered the other. "Since you have knowledge, answer me three questions, if you dare."

"I will answer them, if I can. But as for daring, we shall see."

The Stranger mused for a few seconds; then, speaking in a slightly sing-song voice, as though he repeated an old lesson, he asked, in two Latin hexameters, the following question:

"Who is called Sulva? What road does she walk? Why is the womb barren on one side? Where are the cold marriages?"

Ransom replied, "Sulva is she whom mortals call the Moon. She walks in the lowest sphere. The rim of the world that was wasted goes through her. Half of her orb is turned towards us and shares our curse.

Her other half looks to Deep Heaven; happy would he be who could cross that frontier and see the fields on her further side. On this side, the womb is barren and the marriages cold. There dwell an accursed people, full of pride and lust. There when a young man takes a maiden in marriage, they do not lie together, but each lies with a cunningly fashioned image of the other, made to move and to be warm by devilish arts, for real flesh will not please them, they are so dainty *(delicati)* in their dreams of lust. Their real children they fabricate by vile arts in a secret place."

"You have answered well," said the Stranger. "I thought there were but three men in the world that knew this question. But my second may be harder. Where is the ring of Arthur the King? What Lord has such a treasure in his house?"

"The ring of the King," said Ransom, "is on Arthur's finger where he sits in the House of Kings in the cup-shaped land of Abhalljin, beyond the seas of Lur in Perelandra. For Arthur did not die; but Our Lord took him, to be in the body till the end of time and the shattering of Sulva, with Enoch and Elias and Moses and Melchisedec the King. Melchisedec is he in whose hall the steep-stoned ring sparkles on the forefinger of the Pendragon."

"Well answered," said the Stranger. "In my college it was thought that only two men in the world knew this. But as for my third question, no man knew the answer but myself. Who shall be Pendragon in the time when Saturn descends from his sphere? In what world did he learn war?"

"In the sphere of Venus I learned war," said Ransom. "In this age Lurga shall descend. I am the Pendragon."

When he had said this, he took a step backwards for the big man had begun to move and there was a new look in his eyes. Any who had seen them as they stood thus face to face would have thought that it might come to fighting at any moment. But the Stranger had not moved with hostile purpose. Slowly, ponderously, yet not awkwardly, as though a mountain sank like a wave, he sank on one knee; and still his face was almost on a level with the Director's.

2

"This throws a quite unexpected burden on our resources," said Wither to Frost, where they both sat in the outer room with the door ajar. "I must confess I had not anticipated any serious difficulty about language."

"We must get a Celtic scholar at once," said Frost. "We are regrettably weak on the philological side. I do not at the moment know who has discovered most about ancient British. Ransom would be the man to advise us if he were available. I suppose nothing has been heard of him by your department?"

"I need hardly point out," said Wither, "that Dr. Ransom's philological attainments are by no means the only ground on which we are anxious to find him. If the least trace had been discovered, you may rest assured that you would have long since had the—ah—gratification of seeing him here in person."

"Of course. He may not be in the Earth at all."

"I met him once," said Wither, half-closing his eyes. "He was a most brilliant man in his way. A man whose penetrations and intuitions might have been of infinite value, if he had not embraced the cause of reaction. It is a saddening reflection . . ."

"Of course," said Frost, interrupting him. "Straik knows modern Welsh. His mother was a Welsh woman."

"It would certainly be much more satisfactory," said Wither, "if we could, so to speak, keep the whole matter in the family. There would be something very disagreeable to me—and I am sure you would feel the same way yourself—about introducing a Celtic expert from outside."

"The expert would, of course, be provided for as soon as we could dispense with his services," replied Frost. "It is the waste of time that is the trouble. What progress have you made with Straik?"

"Oh, really excellent," said the Deputy Director. "Indeed I am almost a little disappointed. I mean, my pupil is advancing so rapidly that it may be necessary to abandon an idea which, I confess, rather attracts me. I had been thinking while you were out of the room that it would be specially fitting and—ah—proper and gratifying if your pupil and mine could be initiated together. We should both, I am sure, have felt . . . But, of course, if Straik is ready some time before Studdock, I should not feel myself entitled to stand in his way. You will understand, my dear fellow, that I am not trying to make this anything like a test case as to the comparative efficacy of our very different methods."

"It would be impossible for you to do so," said Frost, "since I have interviewed Studdock only once, and that one interview has had all the success that could be expected. I mentioned Straik only to find out whether he were already so far committed that he might properly be introduced to our guest."

"Oh . . . as to being *committed*," said Wither, "in some sense . . . ignoring certain fine shades for the moment, while fully recognizing their ultimate importance . . . I should not hesitate . . . we should be perfectly justified."

"I was thinking," said Frost, "that there must be someone on duty here. He may wake at any moment. Our pupils—Straik and Studdock—could take it in turns. There is no reason why they should not be useful even before their full initiation. They would, of course, be under orders to ring us up the moment anything happened."

"You think Mr.—ah—Studdock is far enough on?"

"It doesn't matter," said Frost. "What harm can he do? He can't get *out*. And, in the meantime, we only want someone to watch. It would be a useful test."

3

MacPhee who had just been refuting both Ransom and Alcasan's head by a two-edged argument which seemed unanswerable in the dream but which he never afterwards remembered, found himself violently waked by someone shaking his shoulder. He suddenly perceived that he was cold and his left foot was numb. Then he saw Denniston's face looking into his own. The scullery seemed full of people—Denniston and Dimble and Jane. They appeared extremely bedraggled, torn and muddy and wet.

"Are you all right?" Denniston was saying. "I've been trying to wake you for several minutes."

"All right?" said MacPhee swallowing once or twice and licking his lips. "Aye. I'm all right." Then he sat upright. "There's been a—a man here," he said.

"What sort of a man?" asked Dimble.

"Well," said MacPhee. "As to that . . . it's not just so easy . . . I fell asleep talking to him, to tell you the truth. I can't just bring to mind what we were saying."

The others exchanged glances. Though MacPhee was fond of a little hot toddy on winter nights, he was a sober man: they had never seen him like this before. Next moment he jumped to his feet.

"Lord save us!" he exclaimed. "He had the Director here. Quick! We must search the house and the garden. It was some kind of impostor or spy. I know now what's wrong with me. I've been hypnotised. There was a horse too. I mind the horse."

This last detail had an immediate effect on his hearers. Denniston flung open the kitchen door and the whole party surged in after him. For a second they saw indistinct forms in the deep red light of a large fire which had not been attended to for some hours; then, as Denniston found the switch and turned on the light, all drew a deep breath. The four women sat fast asleep. The jackdaw slept, perched on the back of an empty chair. Mr. Bultitude, stretched out on his side across the hearth, slept also; his tiny, child-like snore, so disproportionate to his bulk, was audible in the momentary silence. Mrs. Dimble, bunched in what seemed an uncomfortable position, was sleeping with her head on the table, a half-darned sock still clasped on her knees. Dimble looked at her with that uncurable pity which men feel for any sleeper, but specially for a wife. Camilla, who had been in the rocking chair, was curled up in an attitude which was full of grace, like that of an animal accustomed to sleep anywhere. Mrs. Maggs slept with her kind, commonplace mouth wide open; and Grace Ironwood, bolt upright as if she were awake, but with her head sagging a little to one side, seemed to submit with austere patience to the humiliation of unconsciousness.

"They're all right," said MacPhee from behind. "It's just the same as he did to me. We've no time to wake them. Get on."

They passed from the kitchen into the flagged passage. To all of them except MacPhee the silence of the house seemed intense after their buffeting in the wind and rain. The lights as they switched them on successively revealed empty rooms and empty passages which wore the abandoned look of indoor midnight—fires dead in the grates, an evening paper on a sofa, a clock that had stopped. But no one had really expected to find much else on the ground floor. "Now for upstairs," said Dimble.

"The lights are on upstairs," said Jane as they all came to the foot of the staircase.

"We turned them on ourselves from the passage," said Dimble.

"I don't think we did," said Denniston.

"Excuse me," said Dimble to MacPhee, "I think perhaps I'd better go first."

Up to the first landing they were in darkness; on the second and last the light from the first floor fell. At each landing the stair made a right-angled turn, so that till you reached the second you could not see the lobby on the floor above. Jane and Denniston, who were last, saw MacPhee and Dimble stopped dead on the second landing; their faces in profile lit up, the backs of their heads in darkness. The Ulsterman's mouth was shut like a trap, his expression hostile and afraid. Dimble was open-mouthed. Then, forcing her tired limbs to run, Jane got up beside them and saw what they saw.

Looking down on them from the balustrade were two men, one clothed in sweepy garments of red and the other in blue. It was the Director who wore blue, and for one instant a thought that was pure nightmare crossed Jane's mind. The two robed figures looked to be two of the same sort . . . and what, after all, did she know of this Director who had conjured her into his house and made her dream dreams and taught her the fear of Hell that very night? And there they were, the pair of them, talking their secrets and doing whatever such people would do, when they had emptied the house or laid its inhabitants to sleep. The man who had been dug up out of the earth and the man who had been in outer space . . . and the one had told them that the other was an enemy, and now, the moment they met, here were the two of them, run together like two drops of quicksilver. All this time she had hardly looked at the Stranger. The Director seemed to have laid aside his crutch, and Jane had hardly seen him standing so straight and still before. The light so fell on his beard that it became a kind of halo; and on top of his head also she caught the glint of gold. Suddenly, while she thought of these things, she found that her eyes were looking straight into the eyes of the Stranger. Next moment she had noticed his size. The man was monstrous. And the two men were allies. And the Stranger was speaking and pointing at her as he spoke.

She did not understand the words; but Dimble did, and heard Merlin saying in what seemed to him a rather strange kind of Latin:

"Sir, you have in your house the falsest lady of any at this time alive."

And Dimble heard the Director answer him in the same language:

"Sir, you are mistaken. She is doubtless like all of us a sinner; but the woman is chaste."

"Sir," said Merlin, "know well that she has done in Logres a thing of which no less sorrow shall come than came of the stroke that Balinus struck. For, Sir, it was the purpose of God that she and her lord should between them have begotten a child by whom the enemies should have been put out of Logres for a thousand years."

"She is but lately married," said Ransom. "The child may yet be born."

"Sir," said Merlin, "be assured that the child will never be born, for the hour of its begetting is passed. Of their own will they are barren: I did not know till now that the usages of Sulva were so common among you. For a hundred generations in two lines the begetting of this child was prepared; and unless God should rip up the work of time, such seed, and such an hour, in such a land, shall never be again."

"Enough said," answered Ransom. "The woman perceives that we are speaking of her."

"It would be great charity," said Merlin, "if you gave order that her head should be cut from her shoulders; for it is a weariness to look at her."

Jane, though she had a smattering of Latin, had not understood their conversation. The accent was unfamiliar, and the old druid used a vocabulary that was far beyond her reading—the Latin of a man to whom Apuleius and Martianus Capella were the primary classics and whose elegances resembled those of the *Hisperica Famina*. But Dimble had followed it. He thrust Jane behind him and called out,

"Ransom! What in Heaven's name is the meaning of this?"

Merlin spoke again in Latin and Ransom was just turning to answer him, when Dimble interrupted,

"Answer *us*," he said. "What has happened? Why are you dressed up like that? What are you doing with that blood-thirsty old man?"

MacPhee, who had followed the Latin even less than Jane, but who had been staring at Merlin as an angry terrier stares at a Newfoundland dog which has invaded its own garden, broke into the conversation:

"Dr. Ransom," he said. "I don't know who the big man is and I'm no Latinist. But I know well that you've kept me under your eyes all this night against my own expressed will, and allowed me to be drugged and hypnotised. It gives me little pleasure, I assure you, to see yourself dressed up like something out of a pantomime and standing there hand in glove with that yogi, or shaman, or priest, or whatever he is. And you can tell him he need not look at me the way he's doing. I'm not afraid of him. And as for my own life and limb—if you, Dr. Ransom, have changed sides after all that's come and gone, I don't know that I've much more use for either. But though I may be killed, I'm not going to be made a fool of. We're waiting for an explanation."

The Director looked down on them in silence for a few seconds.

"Has it really come to this?" he said. "Does not one of you trust me?"

"I do, Sir," said Jane suddenly.

"These appeals to the passions and emotions," said MacPhee, "are nothing to the purpose. I could cry as well as anyone this moment if I gave my mind to it."

"Well," said the Director after a pause, "there is some excuse for you all for we have all been mistaken. So has the enemy. This man is Merlinus Ambrosius. They thought that if he came back he would be on their side. I find he is on ours. You, Dimble, ought to realise that this was always a possibility."

"That is true," said Dimble. "I suppose it was—well, the look of the thing—you and he standing there together: like *that*. And his appalling bloodthirstiness."

"I have been startled by it myself," said Ransom. "But after all we had no right to expect that his penal code would be that of the Nineteenth Century. I find it difficult, too, to make him understand that I am not an absolute monarch."

"Is—is he a Christian?" asked Dimble.

"Yes," said Ransom. "As for my clothes, I have for once put on the dress of my office to do him honour, and because I was ashamed. He mistook MacPhee and me for scullions or stable-boys. In his days, you see, men did not, except for necessity, go about in shapeless sacks of cloth, and drab was not a favourite colour."

At this point Merlin spoke again. Dimble and the Director who alone could follow his speech heard him say, "Who are these people? If they are your slaves, why do they do you no reverence? If they are enemies, why do we not destroy them?"

"They are my friends," began Ransom in Latin, but MacPhee interrupted,

"Do I understand, Dr. Ransom," he said, "that you are asking us to accept this person as a member of our organisation?"

"I am afraid," said the Director, "I cannot put it that way. He *is* a member of the organisation. And I must command you all to accept him."

"And secondly," continued MacPhee, "I must ask what enquiries have been made into his credentials."

"I am fully satisfied," answered the Director. "I am as sure of his good faith as of yours."

"But the grounds of your confidence?" persisted MacPhee. "Are we not to hear them?"

"It would be hard," said the Director, "to explain to you my reasons for trusting Merlinus Ambrosius; but no harder than to explain to him why, despite many appearances which might be misunderstood, I trust you." There was just the ghost of a smile about his mouth as he said this. Then Merlin spoke to him again in Latin and he replied. After that Merlin addressed Dimble.

"The Pendragon tells me," he said in his unmoved voice, "that you accuse me for a fierce and cruel man. It is a charge I never heard before. A third part of my substance I gave to widows and poor men. I never sought the death of any but felons and heathen Saxons. As for the woman, she may live for me. I am not Master in this house. But would it be such a great matter if her head were struck off? Do not queens and ladies who would disdain her as their tire-woman go to the fire for less? Even that gallows bird *(cruciarius)* beside you—I mean you, fellow, though you speak nothing but your own barbarous tongue; you with the face like sour milk and the voice like a saw in a hard log and the legs like a crane's—even that cutpurse *(sector zonarius),* though I would have him to the gatehouse, yet the rope should be used on his back not his throat."

MacPhee who realised, though without understanding the words, that he was the subject of some unfavourable comment, stood listening with that expression of entirely suspended judgment which is commoner in Northern Ireland and the Scotch lowlands than in England.

"Mr. Director," he said when Merlin had finished, "I would be very greatly obliged if—"

"Come," said the Director suddenly, "we have none of us slept tonight. Arthur, will you come and light a fire for our guest in the big room at the North end of this passage? And would someone wake the women? Ask them to bring him up refreshments. A bottle of Burgundy and whatever you have cold. And then, all to bed. We need not stir early in the morning. All is going to be very well."

4

"We're going to have difficulties with that new colleague of ours," said Dimble. He was alone with his wife in their room at St. Anne's late on the following day.

"Yes," he repeated after a pause. "What you'd call a strong colleague."

"You look very tired, Cecil," said Mrs. Dimble.

"Well, it's been rather a gruelling conference," said he. "He's—he's a tiring man. Oh, I know we've all been fools. I mean, we've all been imagining that because he came back in the Twentieth Century he'd be a Twentieth Century man. Time is more important than we thought, that's all."

"I felt that at lunch, you know," said his wife. "It was so silly not to have realised that he wouldn't know about forks. But what surprised me even more (after the first shock) was how—well, how *elegant* he was without them. I mean you could see it wasn't a case of having no manners but of having different ones."

"Oh, the old boy's a gentleman in his own way—anyone can see that. But . . . well, I don't know. I suppose it's all right."

"What happened at the meeting?"

"Well, you see, everything had to be explained on both sides. We'd the dickens of a job to make him understand that Ransom isn't the king of this country or trying to become king. And then we had to break it to him that we weren't the British at all, but the English—what he'd call Saxons. It took him some time to get over that."

"I see."

"And then MacPhee had to choose that moment for embarking on an interminable explanation of the relations between Scotland and Ireland and England. All of which, of course, had to be translated. It was all nonsense too. Like a good many people, MacPhee imagines he's a Celt when, apart from his name, there's nothing Celtic about him any more than about Mr. Bultitude. By the way Merlinus Ambrosius made a prophesy about Mr. Bultitude."

"Oh? What was that?"

"He said that before Christmas this bear would do the best deed that any bear had done in Britain except some other bear that none of us had ever heard of. He keeps on saying things like that. They just pop out when we're talking about something else, and in a rather different voice. As if he couldn't help it. He doesn't seem to know any *more* than the bit he tells you at the moment, if you see what I mean. As if something like a camera shutter opened at the back of his mind and closed again immediately and just one little item came through. It has rather a disagreeable effect."

"He and MacPhee didn't quarrel again, I hope."

"Not exactly. I'm afraid Merlinus Ambrosius wasn't taking MacPhee very seriously. From the fact that MacPhee is always being obstructive and rather rude and yet never gets sat on, I think Merlinus has concluded that he is the Director's fool. He seems to have got over his dislike for him. But I don't think MacPhee is going to like Merlinus."

"Did you get down to actual business?" asked Mrs. Dimble.

"Well, in a way," said Dimble, wrinkling his forehead. "We were all at cross-purposes, you see. The business about Ivy's husband being in prison came up, and Merlinus wanted to know why we hadn't rescued him. He seemed to imagine us just riding off and taking the County Jail by storm. That's the sort of thing one was up against all the time."

"Cecil," said Mrs. Dimble suddenly. "Is he going to be any use?"

"He's going to be able to *do* things, if that's what you mean. In that sense there's more danger of his being too much use than too little."

"What sort of things?" asked his wife.

"The universe is so very complicated," said Dr. Dimble.

"So you have said rather often before, dear," replied Mrs. Dimble.

"Have I?" he said with a smile. "How often, I wonder? As often as you've told the story of the pony and trap at Dawlish?"

"Cecil! I haven't told it for years."

"My dear, I heard you telling it to Camilla the night before last."

"Oh, *Camilla*. That was quite different. She'd never heard it before."

"I don't know that we can be certain even about that . . . the universe being so complicated and all." For a few minutes there was silence between them.

"But about Merlin?" asked Mrs. Dimble presently.

"Have you ever noticed," said Dimble, "that the universe, and every little bit of the universe, is always hardening and narrowing and coming to a point?"

His wife waited as those wait who know by long experience the mental processes of the person who is talking to them.

"I mean this," said Dimble in answer to the question she had not asked. "If you dip into any college, or school, or parish, or family—anything you like—at a given point in its history you always find that there was a time before that point when there was more elbow room and contrasts weren't quite so sharp; and that there's going to be a time after that point when there is even less room for indecision and choices are even more momentous. Good is always getting better and bad is always getting worse: the possibilities of even apparent neutrality are always diminishing. The whole thing is sorting itself out all the time, coming to a point, getting sharper and harder. Like in the poem about Heaven and Hell eating into merry Middle Earth from opposite sides . . . how does it go? Something about 'eat every day' . . . 'till all is *somethinged away.*' It can't be *eaten,* that wouldn't scan. My memory has failed dreadfully these last few years. Do you know the bit, Margery?"

"What you were saying reminded me more of the bit in the Bible about the winnowing fan. Separating the wheat and the chaff. Or like Browning's line: " 'Life's business being just the terrible choice.' "

"Exactly! Perhaps the whole time-process means just that and nothing else. But it's not only in questions of moral choice. Everything is getting more itself and more different from everything else all the time. Evolution means species getting less and less like one another. Minds get more and more spiritual, matter more and more material. Even in literature, poetry and prose draw further and further apart."

Mrs. Dimble with the ease born of long practice averted the danger, ever present in her house, of a merely literary turn being given to the conversation.

"Yes," she said. "Spirit and matter, certainly. That explains why people like the Studdocks find it so difficult to be happily married."

"The Studdocks?" said Dimble, looking at her rather vaguely. The domestic problems of that young couple had occupied his mind a good deal less than they had occupied his wife's. "Oh, I see. Yes. I daresay that has something to do with it. But about Merlin. What it comes to, as far as I can make out, is this. There were still possibilities for a man of that age which there aren't for a man of ours. The Earth itself was more like an animal in those days. And mental processes were much more like physical actions. And there were—well, Neutrals, knocking about."

"Neutrals?"

"I don't mean, of course, that anything can be a *real* neutral. A conscious being is either obeying God or disobeying Him. But there might be things neutral in relation to us."

"You mean eldils—angels?"

"Well, the word *angel* rather begs the question. Even the Oyéresu aren't exactly angels in the same sense as our guardian angels are. Technically they are Intelligences. The point is that while it may be true at the end of the world to describe every eldil either as an angel or a devil, and may even be true now, it was much less true in Merlin's time. There used to be things on this Earth pursuing their own business, so to speak. They weren't ministering spirits sent to help fallen humanity; but neither were they enemies preying upon us. Even in St. Paul one gets glimpses of a population that won't exactly fit into our two columns of angels and devils. And if you go back further . . . all the gods, elves, dwarfs, water-people, *fate, longaevi*. You and I know too much to think they are just illusions."

"You think there are things like that?"

"I think there were. I think there was room for them then, but the universe has come more to a point. Not all rational things perhaps. Some would be mere wills inherent in matter, hardly conscious. More like animals. Others—but I don't really know. At any rate, that is the sort of situation in which one got a man like Merlin."

"It all sounds rather horrible to me."

"It was *rather* horrible. I mean even in Merlin's time (he came at the extreme tail end of it) though you could still use that sort of life in the universe innocently, you couldn't do it safely. The things weren't bad in themselves, but they were already bad for us. They sort of withered the man who dealt with them. Not on purpose. They couldn't help doing it. Merlinus is withered. He's quite pious and humble and all that, but something has been taken out of him. That quietness of his is just a little deadly, like the quiet of a gutted building. It's the result of having laid his mind open to something that broadens the environment just a bit too much. Like polygamy. It wasn't wrong for Abraham, but one can't help feeling that even he lost something by it."

"Cecil," said Mrs. Dimble. "Do you feel quite comfortable about the Director's using a man like this? I mean, doesn't it look a little bit like fighting Belbury with its own weapons?"

"No. I *had* thought of that. Merlin is the reverse of Belbury. He's at the opposite extreme. He is the last vestige of an old order in which matter and spirit were, from our modern point of view, confused. For him every operation on Nature is a kind of personal contact, like coaxing a child or stroking one's horse. After him came the modern man to whom

Nature is something dead—a machine to be worked, and taken to bits if it won't work the way he pleases. Finally, come the Belbury people, who take over that view from the modern man unaltered and simply want to increase their power by tacking onto it the aid of spirits—extra-natural, anti-natural spirits. Of course they hoped to have it both ways. They thought the old *magia* of Merlin which worked in with the spiritual qualities of Nature, loving and reverencing them and knowing them from within, could be combined with the new *goeteia*—the brutal surgery from without. No. In a sense Merlin represents what we've got to get back to in some different way. Do you know that he is forbidden by the rules of his order to use any edged tool on any growing thing?"

"Good gracious!" said Mrs. Dimble. "There's six o'clock. I'd promised Ivy to be in the kitchen at quarter to. There's no need for *you* to move, Cecil."

"Do you know," said Dimble, "I think you are a wonderful woman."

"Why?"

"How many women who had had their own house for thirty years would be able to fit into this menagerie as you do?"

"That's nothing," said Mrs. Dimble. "Ivy had her own house too, you know. And it's much worse for her. After all, I haven't got my husband in jail."

"You jolly soon will have," said Dimble, "if half the plans of Merlinus Ambrosius are put into action."

5

Merlin and the Director were meanwhile talking in the Blue Room. The Director had put aside his robe and circlet and lay on his sofa. The druid sat in a chair facing him, his legs uncrossed, his pale large hands motionless on his knees, looking to modern eyes like an old conventional carving of a king. He was still robed and beneath the robe, as Ransom knew, had surprisingly little clothing, for the warmth of the house was to him excessive and he found trousers uncomfortable. His loud demands for oil after his bath had involved some hurried shopping in the village which had finally produced, by Denniston's exertions, a tin of Brilliantine. Merlinus had used it freely so that his hair and beard glistened and the sweet sticky smell filled the room. That was why Mr. Bultitude had pawed so insistently at the door that he was finally admitted and now sat as near the magician as he could possibly get, his nostrils twitching. He had never smelled such an interesting man before.

"Sir," said Merlin in answer to the question which the Director had just asked him. "I give you great thanks. I cannot indeed understand the way you live and your house is strange to me. You give me a bath such as the Emperor himself might envy, but no one attends me to it; a bed softer than sleep itself, but when I rise from it I find I must put on my own clothes with my own hands as if I were a peasant. I lie in a room with windows of pure crystal so that you can see the sky as clearly when they are shut as when they are open, and there is not wind enough within the room to blow out an unguarded taper; but I lie in it alone with no more honour than a prisoner in a dungeon. Your people eat dry and tasteless flesh but it is off plates as smooth as ivory and as round as the sun. In all the house there are warmth and softness and silence that might put a man in mind of paradise terrestrial; but no hangings, no beautified pavements, no musicians, no perfumes, no high seats, not a gleam of gold, not a hawk, not a hound. You seem to me to live neither like a rich man nor a poor one: neither like a lord nor a hermit. Sir, I tell you these things because you have asked me. They are of no importance. Now that none hears us save the last of the seven bears of Logres, it is time that we should open counsels to each other."

He glanced at the Director's face as he spoke and then, as if startled by what he saw there, leaned sharply forward.

"Does your wound pain you?" he asked.

Ransom shook his head. "No," he said, "it is not the wound. We have terrible things to talk of."

The big man stirred uneasily.

"Sir," said Merlinus in a deeper and softer voice, "I could take all the anguish from your heel as though I were wiping it out with a sponge. Give me but seven days to go in and out and up and down and to and fro, to renew old acquaintance. These fields and I, this wood and I, have much to say to one another."

As he said this, he was leaning forward so that his face and the bear's were almost side by side, and it almost looked as if those two might have been engaged in some kind of furry and grunted conversation. The druid's face had a strangely animal appearance: not sensual nor fierce but full of the patient, unarguing sagacity of a beast. Ransom's, meanwhile, was full of torment.

"You might find the country much changed," he said, forcing a smile.

"No," said Merlin. "I do not reckon to find it much changed." The distance between the two men was increasing every moment. Merlin was like something that ought not to be indoors. Bathed and anointed though he was, a sense of mould, gravel, wet leaves, weedy water, hung about him.

"Not *changed*," he repeated in an almost inaudible voice. And in that deepening inner silence of which his face bore witness, one might have believed that he listened continually to a murmur of evasive sounds: rustling of mice and stoats, thumping progression of frogs, the small shock of falling hazel nuts, creaking of branches, runnels trickling, the very growing of grass. The bear had closed its eyes. The whole room was growing heavy with a sort of floating anaesthesia.

"Through me," said Merlin, "you can suck up from the Earth oblivion of all pains."

"Silence," said the Director sharply. He had been sinking down into the cushions of his sofa with his head drooping a little towards his chest. Now he suddenly sat bolt upright. The magician started and straightened himself likewise. The air of the room was cleared. Even the bear opened its eyes again.

"No," said the Director. "God's glory, do you think you were dug out of the earth to give me a plaster for my heel? We have drugs that could cheat the pain as well as your earth-magic or better, if it were not my business to bear it to the end. I will hear no more of that. Do you understand?"

"I hear and obey," said the magician. "But I meant no harm. If not to heal your own wound, yet for the healing of Logres, you will need my commerce with field and water. It must be that I should go in and out, and to and fro, renewing old acquaintance. It will not be changed, you know. Not what you would call *changed*."

Again that sweet heaviness, like the smell of hawthorn, seemed to be flowing back over the Blue Room.

"No," said the Director in a still louder voice, "that cannot be done any longer. The soul has gone out of the wood and water. Oh, I daresay you could awake them; a little. But it would not be enough. A storm, or even a river-flood would be of little avail against our present enemy. Your weapon would break in your hands. For the Hideous Strength confronts us and it is as in the days when Nimrod built a tower to reach heaven."

"Hidden it may be," said Merlinus. "But not *changed*. Leave me to work, Lord. I will wake it. I will set a sword in every blade of grass to wound them and the very clods of earth shall be venom to their feet. I will—"

"No," said the Director. "I forbid you to speak of it. If it were possible, it would be unlawful. Whatever of spirit may still linger in the earth has withdrawn fifteen hundred years further away from us since your time. You shall not speak a word to it. You shall not lift your little finger to call it up. I command you. It is in this age utterly unlawful." Hitherto, he had been speaking sternly and coldly. Now he leaned forward and said in a different voice, "It never was *very* lawful, even in your day. Remember, when we first knew that you would be awaked, we thought you would be on the side of the enemy. And because Our Lord does all things for each, one of the purposes of your reawakening was that your own soul should be saved."

Merlin sank back into his chair like a man unstrung. The bear licked his hand where it hung, pale and relaxed, over the arm of the chair.

"Sir," said Merlin presently, "if I am not to work for you in that fashion, then you have taken into your house a silly bulk of flesh. For I am no longer much of a man of war. If it comes to point and edge I avail little."

"Not that way either," said Ransom, hesitating like a man who is reluctant to come to the point. "No power that is merely earthly," he continued at last, "will serve against the Hideous Strength."

"Then let us all to prayers," said Merlinus. "But there also . . . I was not reckoned of much account . . . they called me a devil's son, some of them. It was a lie. But I do not know why I have been brought back."

"Certainly, let us stick to our prayers," said Ransom. "Now and always. But that was not what I meant. There are celestial powers: created powers, not in this Earth, but in the Heavens."

Merlinus looked at him in silence.

"You know well what I am speaking of," said Ransom. "Did not I tell you when we first met that the Oyéresu were my Masters?"

"Of course," said Merlin. "And that was how I knew you were of the College. Is it not our pass-word all over the Earth?"

"A pass-word?" exclaimed Ransom with a look of surprise. "I did not know that?"

"But . . . but," said Merlinus, "if you knew not the pass-word, how did you come to say it?"

"I said it because it was true."

The magician licked his lips which had become very pale.

"True as the plainest things are true," repeated Ransom. "True as it is true that you sit here with my bear beside you."

Merlin spread out his hands. "You are my father and mother," he said. His eyes, steadily fixed on Ransom, were large as those of an awe-struck child, but for the rest he looked a smaller man than Ransom had first taken him to be.

"Suffer me to speak," he said at last, "or slay me if you will, for I am in the hollow of your hand. I had heard of it in my own days—that some had spoken with the gods. Blaise my Master knew a few words of that speech. Yet these were, after all, powers of Earth. For—I need not teach you, you know more than I—it is not the very Oyéresu, the true powers of Heaven, whom the greatest of our craft meet, but only their earthly wraiths, their shadows. Only the earth-Venus, the earth-Mercurius; not Perelandra herself, not Viritrilbia himself. It is only . . ."

"I am not speaking of the wraiths," said Ransom. "I have stood before Mars himself in the sphere of Mars and before Venus herself in the sphere of Venus. It is their strength, and the strength of some greater than they, which will destroy our enemies."

"But, Lord," said Merlin, "how can this be? Is it not against the Seventh Law?"

"What law is that?" asked Ransom.

"Has not our Fair Lord made it a law for Himself that He will not send down the Powers to mend or mar in this Earth until the end of all things? Or is this the end that is even now coming to pass?"

"It may be the beginning of the end," said Ransom. "But I know nothing of that. Maleldil may have made it a law not to send down the Powers. But if men by enginry and natural philosophy learn to fly into the Heavens, and come, in the flesh, among the heavenly powers and trouble them, He has not forbidden the Powers to react. For all this is within the natural order. A wicked man did learn so to do. He came flying, by a subtle engine, to where Mars dwells in Heaven and to where Venus dwells, and took me with him as a captive. And there I spoke with the true Oyéresu face to face. You understand me?"

Merlin inclined his head.

"And so the wicked man had brought about, even as Judas brought about, the thing he least intended. For now there was one man in the world—even myself—who was known to the Oyéresu and spoke their tongue, neither by God's miracle nor by magic from Numinor, but naturally, as when two men meet in a road. Our enemies had taken away from themselves the protection of the Seventh Law. They had broken by natural philosophy the barrier which God of His own power would not break. Even so they sought you as a friend and raised up for themselves a scourge. And that is why Powers of Heaven have come down to this house, and in this chamber where we are now discoursing Malacandra and Perelandra have spoken to me."

Merlin's face became a little paler. The bear nosed at his hand, unnoticed.

"I have become a bridge," said Ransom.

"Sir," said Merlin, "what will come of this? If they put forth their power, they will unmake all Middle Earth."

"Their naked power, yes," said Ransom. "That is why they will work only through a man."

The magician drew one large hand across his forehead.

"Through a man whose mind is opened to be so invaded," said Ransom, "one who by his own will once opened it. I take Our Fair Lord to witness that if it were my task, I would not refuse it. But he will not suffer a mind that still has its virginity to be so violated. And through a black magician's mind their purity neither can nor will operate. One who has dabbled . . . in the days when dabbling had not begun to be evil, or was only just beginning . . . and also a Christian man and a penitent. A tool (I must speak plainly) good enough to be so used and not too good. In all these Western parts of the world there was only one man who had lived in those days and could still be recalled. You—"

He stopped, shocked at what was happening. The huge man had risen from his chair, and stood towering over him. From his horribly opened mouth there came a yell that seemed to Ransom utterly bestial, though it was in fact only the yell of primitive Celtic lamentation. It was horrifying to see that withered and bearded face all blubbered with undisguised tears like a child's. All the Roman surface in Merlinus had been scraped off. He had become a shameless, archaic monstrosity babbling out entreaties in a mixture of what sounded like Welsh and what sounded like Spanish.

"Silence," shouted Ransom. "Sit down. You put us both to shame."

As suddenly as it had begun the frenzy ended. Merlin resumed his chair. To a modern it seemed strange that, having recovered his self-control, he did not show the slightest embarrassment at his temporary loss of it. The whole character of the two-sided society in which this man must have lived became clearer to Ransom than pages of history could have made it.

"Do not think," said Ransom, "that for me either it is child's play to meet those who will come down for you empowering."

"Sir," faltered Merlin, "you have been in Heaven. I am but a man. I am not the son of one of the Airish Men. That was a lying story. How can I? . . . You are not as I. You have looked upon their faces before."

"Not on all of them," said Ransom. "Greater spirits than Malacandra and Perelandra will descend this time. We are in God's hands. It may unmake us both. There is no promise that either you or I will save our lives or our reason. I do not know how we can dare to look upon their faces; but I know we cannot dare to look upon God's if we refuse this enterprise."

Suddenly the magician smote his hand upon his knee.

"*Mehercule!*" he cried. "Are we not going too fast? If you are the Pendragon, I am the High Council of Logres and I will counsel you. If the Powers must tear me in pieces to break our enemies, God's will be done. But is it yet come to that? This Saxon king of yours who sits at Windsor, now. Is there no help in him?"

"He has no power in this matter."

"Then is he not weak enough to be overthrown?"

"I have no wish to overthrow him. He is the king. He was crowned and anointed by the Archbishop. In the order of Logres I may be Pendragon, but in the order of Britain I am the King's man."

"Is it then his great men—the counts and legates and bishops—who do the evil and he does not know of it?"

"It is—though they are not exactly the sort of great men you have in mind."

"And are we not big enough to meet them in plain battle?"

"We are four men, some women, and a bear."

"I saw the time when Logres was only myself and one man and two boys, and one of those was a churl. Yet we conquered."

"It could not be done now. They have an engine called the Press whereby the people are deceived. We should die without even being heard of."

"But what of the true clerks? Is there no help in them? It cannot be that *all* your priests and bishops are corrupted."

"The Faith itself is torn in pieces since your day and speaks with a divided voice. Even if it were made whole, the Christians are but a tenth part of the people. There is no help there."

"Then let us seek help from over sea. Is there no Christian prince in Neustria or Ireland or Benwick who would come in and cleanse Britain if he were called?"

"There is no Christian prince left. These other countries are even as Britain, or else sunk deeper still in the disease."

"Then we must go higher. We must go to him whose office it is to put down tyrants and give life to dying kingdoms. We must call on the Emperor."

"There is no Emperor."

"No Emperor . . ." began Merlin, and then his voice died away. He sat still for some minutes wrestling with a world which he had never envisaged. Presently he said, "A thought comes into my mind and I do not know whether it is good or evil. But because I am the High Council of Logres I will not hide it from you. This is a cold age in which I have awaked. If all this West part of the world is apostate, might it not be lawful, in our great need, to look farther . . . beyond Christendom? Should we not find some even among the heathen who are not wholly corrupt? There were tales in my day of some such: men who knew not the articles of our most holy Faith, but who worshipped God as they could and acknowledged the Law of Nature. Sir, I believe it would be lawful to seek help even there. Beyond Byzantium. It was rumoured also that there was knowledge in those lands—an Eastern circle and wisdom that came West from Numinor. I know not where—Babylon, Arabia, or Cathay. You said your ships had sailed all round the earth, above and beneath."

Ransom shook his head. "You do not understand," he said. "The poison was brewed in these West lands but it has spat itself everywhere by now. However far you went you would find the machines, the crowded cities, the empty thrones, the false writings, the barren beds: men maddened with false promises and soured with true miseries, worshipping the iron works of their own hands, cut off from Earth their mother and from the Father in Heaven. You might go East so far that East became West and you returned to Britain across the great Ocean, but even so you would not have come out anywhere into the light. The shadow of one dark wing is over all Tellus."

"Is it then the end?" asked Merlin.

"And this," said Ransom, ignoring the question, "is why we have no way left at all save the one I told you. The Hideous Strength holds all this Earth in its fist to squeeze as it wishes. But for their one mistake, there would be no hope left. If of their own evil will they had not broken the frontier and let in the celestial Powers, this would be their moment of victory. Their own strength has betrayed them. They have gone to the gods who would not have come to them, and pulled down Deep Heaven on their heads. Therefore, they will die. For though you search every cranny to escape, now that you see all crannies closed, you will not disobey me."

And then, very slowly, there crept back into Merlin's white face, first closing his dismayed mouth and finally gleaming in his eyes, that almost animal expression, earthy and healthy and with a glint of half-humorous cunning.

"Well," he said, "if the Earths are stopped, the fox faces the hounds. But had I known who you were at our first meeting, I think I would have put the sleep on you as I did on your Fool."

"I am a very light sleeper since I have travelled in the Heavens," said Ransom.

14

"Real Life Is Meeting"

I

Since the day and night of the outer world made no difference in Mark's cell, he did not know whether it was minutes or hours later that he found himself once more awake, once more confronting Frost, and still fasting. The Professor came to ask if he had thought over their recent conversation. Mark, who judged that some decent show of reluctances would make his final surrender more convincing, replied that only one thing was still troubling him. He did not quite understand what he in particular or humanity in general stood to gain by co-operation with the Macrobes. He saw clearly that the motives on which most men act, and which they dignify by the names of patriotism or duty to humanity, were mere products of the animal organism, varying according to the behaviour pattern of different communities. But he did not yet see what was to be substituted for these irrational motives. On what ground henceforward were actions to be justified or condemned?

"If one insists on putting the question in those terms," said Frost, "I think Waddington has given the best answer. Existence is its own justification. The tendency to developmental change which we call Evolution is justified by the fact that it is a general characteristic of biological entities. The present establishment of contact between the highest biological entities and the Macrobes is justified by the fact that it is occurring, and it ought to be increased because an increase is taking place."

"You think, then," said Mark, "that there would be no sense in asking whether the general tendency of the universe might be in the direction we should call Bad?"

"There could be no sense at all," said Frost. "The judgment you are trying to make turns out on inspection to be simply an expression of emotion. Huxley himself, could only express it by using emotive terms such as "gladiatorial" or "ruthless." I am referring to the famous Romanes lecture. When the so-called struggle for existence is seen simply as an actuarial theorem, we have, in Waddington's words, "a concept as unemotional as a definite integral" and the emotion disappears. With it disappears that preposterous idea of an external standard of value which the emotion produced."

"And the actual tendency of events," said Mark, "would still be self-justified and in that sense 'good' when it was working for the extinction of all organic life, as it presently will?"

"Of course," replicd Frost, "if you insist on formulating the problem in those terms. In reality the question is meaningless. It presupposes a means-and-end pattern of thought which descends from Aristotle, who in his turn was merely hypostatising elements in the experience of an iron-age agricultural community. Motives are not the causes of action but its by-products. You are merely wasting your time by considering them. When you have attained real objectivity you will recognize, not *some* motives, but *all* motives as merely animal, subjective epiphenomena. You will then have no motives and you will find that you do not need them. Their place will be supplied by something else which you will presently understand better than you do now. So far from being impoverished your action will become much more efficient."

"I see," said Mark. The philosophy which Frost was expounding was by no means unfamiliar to him. He recognised it at once as the logical conclusion of thoughts which he had always hitherto accepted and which at this moment he found himself irrevocably rejecting. The knowledge that his own assumptions led to Frost's position combined with what he saw in Frost's face and what he had experienced in this very cell, effected a complete conversion. All the philosophers and evangelists in the world might not have done the job so neatly.

"And that," continued Frost, "is why a systematic training in objectivity must be given to you. Its purpose is to eliminate from your mind one by one the things you have hitherto regarded as grounds for action. It is like killing a nerve. That whole system of instinctive preferences, whatever ethical, æsthetic, or logical disguise they wear, is to be simply destroyed."

"I get the idea," said Mark though with an inward reservation that his present instinctive desire to batter the Professor's face into a jelly would take a good deal of destroying.

After that, Frost took Mark from the cell and gave him a meal in some neighbouring room. It also was lit by artificial light and had no window. The Professor stood perfectly still and watched him while he ate. Mark did not know what the food was and did not much like it, but he was far too hungry by now to refuse it if refusal had been possible. When the meal was over Frost led him to the ante-room of the Head and once more he was stripped and re-clothed in surgeon's overalls and a mask. Then he was brought in, into the presence of the gaping and dribbling Head. To his surprise, Frost took not the slightest notice of it. He led him across the room to a narrower little door with a pointed arch, in the far wall. Here he paused and said, "Go in. You will speak to no one of what you find here. I will return presently." Then he opened the door and Mark went in.

The room, at first sight, was an anticlimax. It appeared to be an empty committee room with a long table, eight or nine chairs, some pictures, and (oddly enough) a large step-ladder in one corner. Here also there were no windows; it was lit by an electric light which produced, better than Mark had ever seen it produced before, the illusion of daylight—of a cold, grey place out of doors. This, combined with the absence of a fireplace, made it seem chilly though the temperature was not in fact very low.

A man of trained sensibility would have seen at once that the room was ill-proportioned, not grotesquely so, but sufficiently to produce dislike. It was too high and too narrow. Mark felt the effect without analysing the cause and the effect grew on him as time passed. Sitting staring about him he next noticed the door—and thought at first that he was the victim of some optical illusion. It took him quite a long time to prove to himself that he was not. The point of the arch was not in the centre: the whole thing was lop-sided. Once again, the error was not gross. The thing was near enough to the true to deceive you for a moment and to go on teasing the mind even after the deception had been unmasked. Involuntarily one kept shifting the head to find positions from which it would look right after all. He turned round and sat with his back to it . . . one mustn't let it become an obsession.

Then he noticed the spots on the ceiling. They were not mere specks of dirt or discolouration. They were deliberately painted on: little round black spots placed at irregular intervals on the pale mustard-coloured surface. There were not a great many of them: perhaps thirty . . . or was it a hundred? He determined that he would not fall into the trap of try-ing to count them. They would be hard to count, they were so irregularly placed. Or weren't they? Now that his eyes were growing used to them (and one couldn't help noticing that there were five in that little group to the right), their arrangement seemed to hover on the verge of regularity. They suggested some kind of pattern. Their peculiar ugliness consisted in the very fact that they kept on suggesting it and then frustrating the expectation thus aroused. Suddenly he realised that this was another trap. He fixed his eyes on the table.

There were spots on the table too: white ones. Shiny white spots, not quite round. And arranged, apparently, to correspond to the spots on the ceiling. Or were they? No, of course not . . . ah, now he had it! The pat-tern (if you could call it a pattern) on the table was an exact reversal of that on the ceiling. But with certain exceptions. He found he was glanc-ing rapidly from one to the other, trying to puzzle it out. For the third time he checked himself. He got up and began to walk about. He had a look at the pictures.

Some of them belonged to a school of art with which he was already familiar. There was a portrait of a young woman who held her mouth wide open to reveal the fact that the inside of it was thickly overgrown with hair. It was very skilfully painted in the photographic manner so that you could almost feel that hair; indeed you could not avoid feeling it however hard you tried. There was a giant mantis playing a fiddle while being eaten by another mantis, and a man with corkscrews instead of arms bathing in a flat, sadly coloured sea beneath a summer sunset. But most of the pictures were not of this kind. At first, most of them seemed rather ordinary, though Mark was a little surprised at the predominance of scriptural themes. It was only at the second or third glance that one discovered certain unaccountable details—something odd about the positions of the figures' feet or the arrangement of their fingers or the grouping. And who was the person standing between the Christ and the Lazarus? And why were there so many beetles under the table in the Last Supper? What was the curious trick of lighting that made each picture look like something seen in delirium? When once these questions had been raised the apparent ordinariness of the pictures became their supreme menace—like the ominous surface innocence at the beginning of certain dreams. Every fold of drapery, every piece of architecture, had a meaning one could not grasp but which withered the mind. Compared with these the other, surrealistic, pictures were mere foolery. Long ago Mark had read somewhere of "things of that extreme evil which seem innocent to the unintitiate," and had wondered what sort of things they might be. Now he felt he knew.

He turned his back on the pictures and sat down. He understood the whole business now. Frost was not trying to make him insane; at least not in the sense Mark had hitherto given to the word "insanity." Frost had meant what he said. To sit in the room was the first step towards what Frost called objectivity—the process whereby all specifically human reactions were killed in a man so that he might become fit for the fastidious society of the Macrobes. Higher degrees in the asceticism of anti-Nature would doubtless follow: the eating of abominable food, the dabbling in dirt and blood, the ritual performances of calculated obscenities. They were, in a sense, playing quite fair with him—offering him the very same initiation through which they themselves had passed and which had divided them from humanity, distending and dissipating Wither into a shapeless ruin while it condensed and sharpened Frost into the hard, bright, little needle that he now was.

But after an hour or so this long, high coffin of a room began to produce on Mark an effect which his instructor had probably not anticipated. There was no return of the attack which he had suffered last night in the cell. Whether because he had already survived that attack, or because the imminence of death had drawn the tooth of his lifelong desire for the esoteric, or because he had (in a fashion) called very urgently for help, the built and painted perversity of this room had the effect of making him aware, as he had never been aware before, of this room's opposite. As the desert first teaches men to love water, or as absence first reveals affection, there rose up against this background of the sour and the crooked some kind of vision of the sweet and the straight. Something else—something he vaguely called the "Normal"— apparently existed. He had never thought about it before. But there it was—solid, massive, with a shape of its own, almost like something you could touch, or eat, or fall in love with. It was all mixed up with Jane and fried eggs and soap and sunlight and the rooks cawing at Cure Hardy and the thought that, somewhere outside, daylight was going on at that moment. He was not thinking in moral terms at all; or else (what is much the same thing) he was having his first deeply moral experience. He was choosing a side: the Normal. "All that," as he called it, was what he chose. If the scientific point of view led away from "all that," then be damned to the scientific point of view! The vehemence of his choice almost took his breath away; he had not had such a sensation before. For the moment he hardly cared if Frost and Wither killed him.

I do not know how long this mood would have lasted; but while it was still at its height Frost returned. He led Mark to a bedroom where a fire blazed and an old man lay in bed. The light gleaming on glasses and silver and the soft luxury of the room so raised Mark's spirits that he found it difficult to listen while Frost told him that he must remain here on duty till relieved and must ring up the Deputy Director if the patient spoke or stirred. He himself was to say nothing; indeed, it would be useless if he did for the patient did not understand English.

Frost retired. Mark glanced round the room. He was reckless now. He saw no possibility of leaving Belbury alive unless he allowed himself to be made into a dehumanised servant of the Macrobes. Meanwhile, do or die for it, he was going to have a meal. There were all sorts of delights on that table. Perhaps a smoke first, with his feet on the fender.

"Damn!" he said as he put his hand into his pocket and found it empty. At the same moment he noticed that the man in the bed had opened his eyes and was looking at him. "I'm sorry," said Mark, "I didn't mean—" and then stopped.

The man sat up in bed and jerked his head towards the door.

"Ah?" he said enquiringly.

"I beg your pardon," said Mark.

"Ah?" said the man again. And then, "Foreigners, eh?"

"You *do* speak English, then?" said Mark.

"Ah," said the man. After a pause of several seconds he said, "Guv'ner." Mark looked at him. "Guv'ner," repeated the patient with great energy, "you ha'nt got such a thing as a bit of baccy about you? Ah?"

2

"I think that's all we can do for the present," said Mother Dimble. "We'll do the flowers this afternoon." She was speaking to Jane and both were in what was called the Lodge—a little stone house beside the garden door at which Jane had been first admitted to the Manor. Mrs. Dimble and Jane had been preparing it for the Maggs family. For Mr. Magg's sentence expired today and Ivy had gone off by train on the previous afternoon to spend the night with an aunt in the town where he was imprisoned and to meet him at the prison gate.

When Mrs. Dimble had told her husband how she would be engaged that morning he had said, "Well, it can't take you very long just lighting a fire and making a bed." I share Dr. Dimble's sex and his limitation. I have no idea what the two women found to do in the Lodge for all the hours they spent there. Even Jane had hardly anticipated it. In Mrs. Dimble's hands the task of airing the little house and making the bed for Ivy Maggs and her jail-bird husband became something between a game and a ritual. It woke in Jane vague memories of helping at Christmas or Easter decorations in church when she had been a small child. But it also suggested to her literary memory all sorts of things out of Sixteenth-Century epithalamiums—age-old superstitions, jokes, and sentimentalities about bridal beds and marriage bowers, with omens at the threshold and fairies upon the hearth. It was an atmosphere extraordinarily alien to that in which she had grown up. A few weeks ago she would have disliked it. Was there not something absurd about that stiff, twinkling archaic world—the mixture of prudery and sensuality, the stylised ardours of the groom and the conventional bashfulness of the bride, the religious sanction, the permitted salacities of Fescennine song, and the suggestion that everyone except the principals might be expected to be rather tipsy? How had the human race ever come to imprison in such a ceremony the most unceremonious thing in the world? But she was no longer sure of her reaction. What she was sure of was the dividing line that included Mother Dimble in that world and left her outside. Mother Dimble, for all her Nineteenth-Century propriety, or perhaps because of it, struck her this afternoon as being herself an archaic person. At every moment she seemed to join hands with some solemn yet roguish company of busy old women who had been tucking young lovers into beds since the world began with an incongruous mixture of nods and winks and blessings and tears—quite impossible old women in ruffs or wimples who would be making Shakespearean jokes about codpieces and cuckoldry at one moment and kneeling devoutly at altars the next. It was very odd; for, of course, as far as their conversation was concerned the difference between them was reversed. Jane, in a literary argument, could have talked about codpieces with great *sang froid*, while Mother Dimble was an Edwardian lady who would simply have ignored such a subject out of existence if any modernized booby had been so unfortunate as to raise it in her presence. Perhaps the weather had some bearing on Jane's curious sensations. The frost had ended and it was one of those days of almost piercingly sweet mildness which sometimes occur in the very beginning of winter.

Ivy had discussed her own story with Jane only the day before. Mr. Maggs had stolen some money from the laundry that he worked for. He had done this before he met Ivy and at a time when he had got into bad company. Since he and Ivy had started going out together he had gone "as straight, as straight"; but the little crime had been unearthed and come out of the past to catch him, and he had been arrested about six weeks after their marriage. Jane had said very little during the telling of the story. Ivy had not seemed conscious of the purely social stigma attaching to petty theft and a term of imprisonment, so that Jane would have had no opportunity to practice, even if she had wished, that almost technical "kindness" which some people reserve for the sorrows of the poor. On the other hand, she was given no chance to be revolutionary or speculative—to suggest that theft was no more criminal than all wealth was criminal. Ivy seemed to take traditional morality for granted. She had been "ever so upset" about it. It seemed to matter a great deal in one way, and not to matter at all in another. It had never occurred to her that it should alter her relations with her husband—as though theft, like ill health, were one of the normal risks one took in getting married.

"I always say, you can't expect to know everything about a boy till you're married, not really," she had said.

"I suppose not," said Jane.

"Of course, it's the same for them," added Ivy. "My old Dad used often to say he'd never have married Mum, not if he'd known how she snored. And she said herself, 'No, Dad, that you wouldn't!'"

"That's rather different, I suppose," said Jane.

"Well, what I say is, if it wasn't one thing it'd be something else.

That's how I look at it. And it isn't as if they hadn't a lot to put up with too. Because they've sort of got to get married if they're the right sort, poor things, but, whatever we say, Jane, a woman takes a lot of living with. I don't mean what you'd call a bad woman. I remember one day—it was before you came—Mother Dimble was saying something to the Doctor; and there he was sitting reading something, you know the way he does, with his fingers under some of the pages and a pencil in his hand—not the way you or I'd read—and he just said, 'Yes dear,' and we both of us knew he hadn't been listening. And I said, 'There you are, Mother Dimble,' said I, 'that's how they treat us once they're married. They don't even listen to what we say,' I said. And do you know what she said? 'Ivy Maggs,' said she, 'did it ever come into your mind to ask whether anyone *could* listen to all we say?' Those were her very words. Of course I wasn't going to give in to it, not before him, so I said, 'Yes, they could.' But it was a fair knock-out. You know often I've been talking to my husband for a long time and he's looked up and asked me what I've been saying and, do you know? I haven't been able to remember myself!"

"Oh, that's different," said Jane. "It's when people drift apart—take up quite different opinions—join different sides . . ."

"You must be ever so anxious about Mr. Studdock," replied Ivy. "I'd never be able to sleep a wink if I were in your shoes. But the Director'll bring it all right in the end. You see if he don't."

Mrs. Dimble went back to the house presently to fetch some little nicety which would put the finishing-touch to the bedroom in the Lodge. Jane, feeling a little tired, knelt on the window seat and put her elbows on the sill and her chin in her hands. The sun was almost hot. The thought of going back to Mark if Mark were ever rescued from Belbury was one which her mind had long accepted; it was not horrifying to her, but flat and insipid. It was not the less so because at this moment she fully forgave him for his conjugal crime of sometimes apparently preferring her person to her conversation and sometimes his own thoughts to both. Why should anyone be particularly interested in what she said? This new humility would even have been pleasant to her if it had been directed to anyone more exciting than Mark. She must, of course, be very different with him when they met again. But it was that "again" which so took the savour out of the good resolution—like going back to a sum one had already got wrong and working it out afresh on the same scrawled page of the exercise book. "If they met again . . ." she felt guilty at her lack of anxiety. Almost the same moment she found that she was a little anxious. For hitherto she had always somehow assumed that Mark would come back. The possibility of his death now presented itself. She had no direct emotions about herself living afterwards; she just saw the image of Mark dead, that face dead, in the middle of a pillow, that whole body rigid, those hands and arms (for good and ill so different from all other hands and arms) stretched out straight and useless like a doll's. She felt very cold. Yet the sun was hotter than ever—almost impossibly hot for the time of year. It was very still too, so still that she could hear the movements of a small bird which was hopping along the path outside the window. This path led to the door in the garden wall by which she had first entered. The bird hopped on to the threshold of that door, and onto someone's foot. For now Jane saw that someone was sitting on a little seat just inside the door. This person was only a few yards away, and she must have been sitting very quiet for Jane not to have noticed her.

A flame coloured robe, in which her hands were hidden, covered this person from the feet to where it rose behind her neck in a kind of high ruff-like collar, but in front it was so low or open that it exposed her large breasts. Her skin was darkish and Southern and glowing, almost the colour of honey. Some such dress Jane had seen worn by a Minoan priestess on a vase from old Cnossus. The head, poised motionless on the muscular pillar of her neck, stared straight at Jane. It was a red-cheeked, wet-lipped face, with black eyes—almost the eyes of a cow—and an enigmatic expression. It was not by ordinary standards at all like the face of Mother Dimble; but Jane recognised it at once. It was, to speak like the musicians, the full statement of that theme which had elusively haunted Mother Dimble's face for the last few hours. It was Mother Dimble's face with something left out, and the omission shocked Jane. "It is brutal," she thought, for its energy crushed her; but then she half changed her mind and thought, "It is I who am weak, trumpery." "It is mocking me," she thought, but then once more changed her mind and thought, "It is ignoring me. It doesn't see me"; for though there was an almost ogre-ish glee in the face, Jane did not seem to be invited to share the joke. She tried to look aside from the face—succeeded—and saw for the first time that there were other creatures present—four or five of them—no, more—a whole crowd of ridiculous little men: fat dwarfs in red caps with tassels on them, chubby, gnome-like little men, quite insufferably familiar, frivolous, and irrepressible. For there was no doubt that they, at any rate, were mocking her. They were pointing at her, nodding, mimicking, standing on their heads, turning somersaults. Jane was not yet frightened, partly because the extreme warmth of the air at this open window made her feel drowsy. It was really quite ridiculous for the time of year. Her main feeling was one of indignation. A suspicion which had crossed her mind once or twice before now returned to her with irresistible force—the suspicion that the real universe might be simply silly. It was closely mixed up with the memories of that grown-up laughter—loud, careless, masculine laughter on the lips of bachelor uncles—which had often infuriated her in childhood, and from which the intense seriousness of her school debating society had offered such a grateful escape.

But a moment later she was very frightened indeed. The giantess rose. They were all coming at her. With a great glow and a noise like fire the flame-robed woman and the malapert dwarfs had all come into the house. They were in the room with her. The strange woman had a torch in her hand. It burned with terrible, blinding brightness, crackling, and sent up a cloud of dense black smoke, and filled the bedroom with a sticky, resinous smell. "If they're not careful," thought Jane, "they'll set the house on fire." But she had hardly time to think of that for her whole attention was fixed by the outrageous behaviour of the little men. They began making hay of the room. In a few seconds the bed was a mere chaos, the sheets on the floor, the blankets snatched up and used by the dwarfs for tossing the fattest of their company, the pillows hurtling through the air, feathers flying everywhere. "Look out! Look out, can't you?" shouted Jane, for the giantess was beginning to touch various parts of the room with her torch. She touched a vase on the mantelpiece. Instantly there rose from it a streak of colour which Jane took for fire. She was just moving to try to put it out when she saw that the same thing had happened to a picture on the wall. And then it happened faster and faster all round her. The very top-knots of the dwarfs were now on fire. But just as the terror of this became unbearable, Jane noticed that what was curling up from everything the torch had touched was not flame after all, but vegetation. Ivy and honeysuckle was growing up the legs of the bed, red roses were sprouting from the caps of the little men, and from every direction huge lilies rose to her knees and waist, shooting out their yellow tongues at her. The smells, the heat, the crowding, and the strangeness made her feel faint. It never occurred to her to think she was dreaming. People mistake dreams for visions: no one ever mistook a vision for a dream . . .

"Jane! Jane!" said the voice of Mrs. Dimble suddenly. "What on earth is the matter?"

Jane sat up. The room was empty, but the bed had all been pulled to pieces. She had apparently been lying on the floor. She felt cold and very tired.

"What *has* happened?" repeated Mrs. Dimble.

"I don't know," said Jane.

"Are you ill, child?" asked Mother Dimble.

"I must see the Director at once," said Jane. "It's all right. Don't bother. I can get up by myself . . . really. But I'd like to see the Director at once."

3

Mr. Bultitude's mind was as furry and as unhuman in shape as his body. He did not remember, as a man in his situation would have remembered, the provincial zoo from which he had escaped during a fire, not his first snarling and terrified arrival at the Manor, not the slow stages whereby he had learned to love and trust its inhabitants. He did not know that he loved and trusted them now. He did not know that they were people, nor that he was a bear. Indeed, he did not know that he existed at all: everything that is represented by the words *I* and *Me* and *Thou* was absent from his mind. When Mrs. Maggs gave him a tin of golden syrup, as she did every Sunday morning, he did not recognise either a giver or a recipient. Goodness occurred and he tasted it. And that was all. Hence his loves might, if you wished, be all described as cupboard loves: food and warmth, hands that caressed, voices that reassured, were their objects. But if by a cupboard love you meant something cold or calculating you would be quite misunderstanding the real quality of the beast's sensations. He was no more like a human egoist than he was like a human altruist. There was no prose in his life. The appetencies which a human mind might disdain as cupboard loves were for him quivering and ecstatic aspirations which absorbed his whole being, infinite yearnings, stabbed with the threat of tragedy and shot through with the colours of Paradise. One of our race, if plunged back for a moment in the warm, trembling, iridescent pool of that pre-Adamite consciousness, would have emerged believing that he had grasped the absolute: for the states below reason and the states above it have, by their common contrast to the life we know, a certain superficial resemblance. Sometimes there returns to us from infancy the memory of a nameless delight or terror, unattached to any delightful or dreadful thing, a potent adjective floating in a nounless void, a pure quality. At such moments we have experience of the shallows of that pool. But fathoms deeper than any memory can take us, right down in the central warmth and dimness, the bear lived all its life.

Today an unusual thing had happened to him—he had got out into the garden without being muzzled. He was always muzzled out of doors, not because there was any fear of his becoming dangerous but because of his partiality for fruit and for the sweeter kinds of vegetables. "'Tisn't that he's not tame," as Ivy Maggs had explained to Jane Studdock, "but that he isn't honest. He wouldn't leave us a thing if we let him have the run of his teeth." But today the precaution had been forgotten and the bear had passed a very agreeable morning investigating the turnips. Now—in the early afternoon—he had approached the garden wall. There was a chestnut tree within the wall which the bear could easily climb, and from its branches he could drop down on the far side. He was standing looking up at this tree. Mrs. Maggs would have described his state of mind by saying, "He knows perfectly well he's not allowed out of the garden." That was not how it appeared to Mr. Bultitude. He had no morals; but the Director had given him certain inhibitions. A mysterious reluctance arose, a clouding of the emotional weather, when the wall was too close; but mixed with this there was an opposite impulse to get beyond that wall. He did not, of course, know why, and was incapable even of raising the question. If the pressure behind this impulse could be translated into human terms at all, it would appear as something more like a mythology than a thought. One met bees in the garden, but never found a bee-hive. The bees all went away, over the wall. And to follow bees was the obvious thing to do. I think there was a sense in the bear's mind—one could hardly call it a picture—of endless green lands beyond the wall, and hives innumerable, and bees the size of sparrows, and waiting there, or else walking, trickling, oozing to meet one, something or someone stickier, sweeter, more golden than honey itself.

Today, this unrest was upon him in an unusual degree. He was missing Ivy Maggs. He did not know that there was any such person and he did not remember her as we know remembering, but there was an unspecified lack in his experience. She and the Director were, in their different ways, the two main factors in his existence. He felt, in his own fashion, the supremacy of the Director. Meetings with him were to the bear what mystical experiences are to men, for the Director had brought back with him from Venus some shadow of man's lost prerogative to ennoble beasts. In his presence Mr. Bultitude trembled on the very borders of personality, thought the unthinkable and did the impossible, was troubled and enraptured with gleams from beyond his own woolly world, and came away tired. But with Ivy he was perfectly at home—as a savage who believes in some remote High God is more at home with the little deities of wood and water. It was Ivy who fed him, chased him out of forbidden places, cuffed him, and talked to him all day long. It was her firm conviction that the creature "understood every word she said." If you took this literally it was untrue; but in another sense it was not so wide of the mark. For much of Ivy's conversation was the expression not of thought but of feeling and of feelings Mr. Bultitude almost shared—feelings of alacrity, snugness, and physical affection. In their own way they understood one another pretty well.

Three times Mr. Bultitude turned away from the tree and the wall, but each time he came back. Then, very cautiously and quietly, he began to climb the tree. When he got up into the fork he sat there for a long time. He saw beneath him a steep grassy bank descending to a road. The desire and the inhibition were now both very strong. He sat there for nearly half an hour. Sometimes his mind wandered from the point and once he nearly went to sleep. In the end he got down on the outside of the wall. When he found that the thing had really happened, he became so frightened that he sat still at the bottom of the grassy bank on the very edge of the road. Then he heard a noise.

A motor van came into sight. It was driven by a man in the livery of the N.I.C.E. and another man in the same livery sat beside him.

"Hullo . . . I say!" said the second man. "Pull up, Sid. What about *that?*"

"What?" said the driver.

"Haven't you got eyes in your head?" said the other.

"Gor," said Sid, pulling up. "A bloody great bear. I say—it couldn't be our own bear, could it?"

"Get on," said his mate. "She was in her cage all right this morning."

"You don't think she could have done a bunk? There'd be hell to pay for you and me . . ."

"She couldn't have got here if she *had* done a bunk. Bears don't go forty miles an hour. That ain't the point. But hadn't we better pinch this one?"

"We haven't got no orders," said Sid.

"No. And we haven't failed to get that blasted wolf either, have we?"

"Wasn't our fault. The old woman what said she'd sell wouldn't sell, as you're there to witness, young Len. We did our best. Told her that experiments at Belbury weren't what she thought. Told her the brute would have the time of its life and be made no end of a pet. Never told so many lies in one morning in my life. She'd been got at by someone."

"Course it wasn't our fault. But the boss won't take no notice of that. It's get on or get out at Belbury."

"Get out?" said Sid. "I wish to hell I knew how to."

Len spat over the side and there was a moment's silence.

"Anyway," said Sid presently, "what's the good of taking a bear back?"

"Well, isn't it better than coming back with nothing?" said Len. "And bears cost money. I know they want another one. And here it is free."

"All right," said Sid ironically, "if you're so keen on it, just hop out and ask him to step in."

"Dope," said Len.

"Not on my bit of dinner, you don't," said Sid.

"You're a bucking good mate to have," said Len, groping in a greasy parcel. "It's a good thing for you I'm not the sort of chap who'd split on you."

"You done it already," said the driver. "I know all your little games."

Len had by this time produced a thick sandwich and was dabbing it with some strong smelling liquid from a bottle. When it was thoroughly saturated, he opened the door and went a pace forward, still holding the door in one hand. He was now about six yards from the bear, which had remained perfectly still ever since it saw them. He threw the sandwich to it.

Quarter of an hour later Mr. Bultitude lay on his side, unconscious and breathing heavily. They had no difficulty in tying up his mouth and all four paws, but they had great difficulty in lifting him into the van.

"That's done something to my ticker," said Sid, pressing his hand to his left side.

"Curse your ticker," said Len, rubbing the sweat out of his eyes. "Come on."

Sid climbed back into the driving seat, sat still for a few seconds, panting and muttering "Christ" at intervals. Then he started his engine up and they drove away.

4

For some time now Mark's waking life was divided between periods by the Sleeper's bedside and periods in the room with the spotted ceiling. The training in objectivity which took place in the latter cannot be described fully. The reversal of natural inclination which Frost inculcated was not spectacular or dramatic, but the details would be unprintable and had, indeed, a kind of nursery fatuity about them which is best ignored. Often Mark felt that one good roar of coarse laughter would have blown away the whole atmosphere of the thing; but laughter was unhappily out of the question. There indeed lay the horror—to perform petty obscenities which a very silly child might have thought funny all under the unchangingly serious inspection of Frost, with a stop watch and a note book and all the ritual of scientific experiment. Some of the things he had to do were merely meaningless. In one exercise he had to mount the stepladder and touch some one spot on the ceiling, selected by Frost: just touch it with his forefinger and then come down again. But either by association with the other exercises or because it really concealed some significance, this proceeding always appeared to Mark to be the most indecent and even inhuman of all his tasks. And day by day, as the process went on, that idea of the Straight or the Normal which had occurred to him during his first visit to this room, grew stronger and more solid in his mind till it had become a kind of mountain. He had never before known what an Idea meant: he had always thought till now that they were things inside one's own head. But now, when his head was continually attacked and often completely filled with the clinging corruption of the training, this Idea towered up above him—something which obviously existed quite independently of himself and had hard rock surfaces which would not give, surfaces he could cling to.

The other thing that helped to save him was the Man in the Bed. Mark's discovery that he really could speak English had led to a curious acquaintance with him. It can hardly be said that they conversed. Both spoke but the result was hardly conversation as Mark had hitherto understood the term. The man was so very allusive and used gesture so extensively that Mark's less sophisticated modes of communication were almost useless. Thus when Mark explained that he had no tobacco, the man had slapped an imaginary tobacco pouch on his knee at least six times and struck an imaginary match about as often, each time jerking his head sideways with a look of such relish as Mark had seldom seen on a human face. Then Mark went on to explain that though "they" were not foreigners, they were extremely dangerous people and that probably the Stranger's best plan would be to preserve his silence.

"Ah," said the Stranger jerking his head again. "Ah. Eh?" And then, without exactly laying his finger on his lips, he went through an elaborate pantomime which clearly meant the same thing. And it was impossible for a long time to get him off this subject. He went back and back to the theme of secrecy. "Ah," he said, "don't get nothing out of me. I tell 'ee. Don't get nothing out of me. Eh? I tell 'ee. You and me knows. Ah?" And his look embraced Mark in such an apparently gleeful conspiracy that it warmed the heart. Believing this matter to be now sufficiently clear, Mark began, "But, as regards the future—" only to be met by another pantomime of secrecy, followed by the word "eh?" in a tone which demanded an answer.

"Yes, of course," said Mark. "We are both in considerable danger. And—"

"Ah," said the man. "Foreigners. Eh?"

"No, no," said Mark. "I told you they weren't. They seem to think *you* are, though. And that's why—"

"That's right," interrupted the man. "I know. Foreigners, I call them. I know. They get nothing out of me. You and me's all right. Ah."

"I've been trying to think out some sort of plan," said Mark.

"Ah," said the man approvingly.

"And I was wondering," began Mark when the man suddenly leaned forwards and said with extraordinary energy, "I tell 'ee."

"What?" said Mark.

"I got a plan."

"What is it?"

"Ah," said the man, winking at Mark with infinite knowingness and rubbing his belly.

"Go on. What is it?" said Mark.

"How'd it be," said the man, sitting up and applying his left thumb to his right fore-finger as if about to propound the first step in a philosophical argument, "how'd it be now if you and I made ourselves a nice bit of toasted cheese?"

"I meant a plan for escape," said Mark.

"Ah," replied the man. "My old Dad now. He never had a day's illness in his life. Eh? How's that for a bit of all right? Eh?"

"It's a remarkable record," said Mark.

"Ah. You may say so," replied the other. "On the road all his life. Never had a stomachache. Eh?" And here, as if Mark might not know that malady, he went through a long extraordinarily vivid dumb show.

"Open-air life suited him, I suppose," said Mark.

"And what did he attribute his health to?" asked the man. He pronounced the word *attribute* with great relish, laying the accent on the first syllable. "I ask everyone, what did he attribute his health to?"

Mark was about to reply when the man indicated by a gesture that the question was purely rhetorical and that he did not wish to be interrupted.

"He attributed his health," continued the speaker with great solemnity, "to eating toasted cheese. Keeps the water out of the stomach. That's what it does. Eh? Makes a lining. Stands to reason. Ah!"

In several later interviews, Mark endeavoured to discover something of the Stranger's own history, and particularly how he had been brought to Belbury. This was not easy to do, for though the tramp's conversation was very autobiographical, it was filled almost entirely with accounts of conversations in which he had made stunning repartees whose points remained wholly obscure. Even where it was less intellectual in character, the allusions were too difficult for Mark, who was quite ignorant of the life of the roads though he had once written a very authoritative article on Vagrancy. But by repeated and (as he got to know his man) more cautious, questioning, he couldn't help getting the idea that the tramp had been made to give up his clothes to a total stranger and then put to sleep. He never got the story in so many words. The tramp insisted on talking as if Mark knew it already, and any pressure for a more accurate account produced only a series of nods, winks, and highly confidential gestures. As for the identity or appearance of the person who had taken his clothes, nothing whatever could be made out. The nearest Mark ever got to it, after hours of talk and deep potations, was some such statement as "Ah. He was a one!" or "He was a kind of—eh? *You* know?" or "That was a customer, that was." These statements were made with enormous gusto as though the theft of the tramp's clothes had excited his deepest admiration.

Indeed, throughout the man's conversation this gusto was the most striking characteristic. He never passed any kind of moral judgment on the various things that had been done to him in the course of his career nor did he even try to explain them. Much that was unjust and still more that was simply unintelligible seemed to be accepted, not only without resentment, but with a certain satisfaction provided only that it was striking. Even about his present situation he showed very much less curiosity than Mark would have thought possible. It did not make sense, but then the man did not expect things to make sense. He deplored the absence of tobacco and regarded the "Foreigners" as very dangerous people; but the main thing, obviously, was to eat and drink as much as possible while the present conditions lasted. And gradually Mark fell into line. The man's breath, and indeed his body, were malodorous, and his methods of eating were gross. But the sort of continual picnic which the two shared carried Mark back into the realm of childhood which we have all enjoyed before nicety began. Each understood perhaps an eighth part of what the other said, but a kind of intimacy grew between them. Mark never noticed until years later that here, where there was no room for vanity and no more power or security than that of "children playing in a giant's kitchen," he had unawares become a member of a "circle," as secret and as strongly fenced against outsiders as any that he had dreamed of.

Every now and then their *tête-à-tête* was interrupted. Frost or Wither or both would come in introducing some stranger who addressed the tramp in an unknown language, failed completely to get any response, and was ushered out again. The tramp's habit of submission to the unintelligible, mixed with a kind of animal cunning, stood him in good stead during these interviews. Even without Mark's advice, it would never have occurred to him to undeceive his captors by replying in English. Undeceiving was an activity wholly foreign to his mind. For the rest, his expression of tranquil indifference, varied occasionally by extremely sharp looks but never by the least sign of anxiety or bewilderment, left his interrogators mystified. Wither could never find in his face the evil he was looking for; but neither could he find any of that virtue which would, for him, have been the danger signal. The tramp was a type of man he had never met. The dupe, the terrified victim, the toady, the would-be accomplice, the rival, the honest man with loathing and hatred in his eyes, were all familiar to him. But not this.

And then, one day, there came an interview that was different.

5

"It sounds rather like a mythological picture by Titian come to life," said the Director with a smile when Jane had described her experience in the lodge.

"Yes, but . . ." said Jane; and then stopped. "I see," she began again, "it was very like that. Not only the woman and the . . . the dwarfs . . . but the glow. As if the air were on fire. But I always thought I liked Titian. I suppose I wasn't really taking the pictures seriously enough. Just chattering about 'the Renaissance' the way one did."

"You didn't like it when it came out into real life?"

Jane shook her head.

"Was it real, Sir?" she asked presently. "Are there such things?"

"Yes," said the Director, "it was real enough. Oh, there are thousands of things within this square mile that I don't know about yet. And I daresay that the presence of Merlinus brings out certain things. We are not living *exactly* in the Twentieth Century as long as he's here. We overlap a bit; the focus is blurred. And you yourself . . . you are a seer. You were perhaps bound to meet her. She's what you'll get if you won't have the other."

"How do you mean, Sir?" said Jane.

"You said she was a little like Mother Dimble. So she is. But Mother Dimble with something left out. Mother Dimble is friends with all that world as Merlinus is friends with the woods and rivers. But he isn't a wood or a river himself. She has not rejected it, but she has baptised it. She is a Christian wife. And you, you know, are not. Neither are you a virgin. You have put yourself where you must meet that Old Woman and you have rejected all that has happened to her since Maleldil came to Earth. So you get her raw—not stronger than Mother Dimble would find her, but untransformed, demoniac. And you don't like it. Hasn't that been the history of your life?"

"You mean," said Jane slowly, "I've been repressing something?"

The Director laughed; just that loud, assured, bachelor laughter which had often infuriated her on other lips.

"Yes," he said. "But don't think I'm talking of Freudian repressions. He knew only half the facts. It isn't a question of inhibitions—inculcated shame—against natural desire. I'm afraid there's no niche in the world for people that won't be either Pagan or Christian. Just imagine a man who was too dainty to eat with his fingers and yet wouldn't use forks!"

His laughter rather than his words had reddened Jane's cheeks, and she was staring at him open-mouthed. Assuredly, the Director was not in the least like Mother Dimble; but an odious realisation that he was, in this matter, on Mother Dimble's side—that he also, though he did not belong to that hot-coloured, archaic world, stood somehow in good diplomatic relations with it, from which she was excluded—had struck her like a blow. Some old female dream of finding a man who "really understood" was being insulted. She took it for granted, half-unconsciously, that the Director was the most virginal of his sex; but she had not realised that this would leave his masculinity still on the other side of the stream from herself and even steeper, more emphatic, than that of common men. Some knowledge of a world beyond Nature she had already gained from living in his house, and more from fear of death that night in the dingle. But she had been conceiving this world as "spiritual" in the negative sense—as some neutral, or democratic, vacuum where differences disappeared, where sex and sense were not transcended but simply taken away. Now the suspicion dawned upon her that there might be differences and contrasts all the way up, richer, sharper, even fiercer, at every rung of the ascent. How if this invasion of her own being in marriage from which she had recoiled, often in the very teeth of instinct, were not, as she had supposed, merely a relic of animal life or patriarchal barbarism, but rather the lowest, the first, and the easiest form of some shocking contact with reality which would have to be repeated—but in ever larger and more disturbing modes—on the highest levels of all?

"Yes," said the Director. "There is no escape. If it were a virginal rejection of the male, He would allow it. Such souls can bypass the male and go on to meet something far more masculine, higher up, to which they must make a yet deeper surrender. But your trouble has been what old poets called *Daungier*. We call it Pride. You are offended by the masculine itself: the loud, irruptive, possessive thing—the gold lion, the bearded bull—which breaks through hedges and scatters the little king-dom of your primness as the dwarfs scattered the carefully made bed. The male you could have escaped, for it exists only on the biological level. But the masculine none of us can escape. What is above and beyond all things is so masculine that we are all feminine in relation to it. You had better agree with your adversary quickly."

"You mean I shall have to become a Christian?" said Jane.

"It looks like it," said the Director.

"But—I still don't see what that has to do with . . . with Mark," said Jane. This was perhaps not perfectly true. The vision of the universe which she had begun to see in the last few minutes had a curiously stormy quality about it. It was bright, darting, and overpowering. Old Testament imagery of eyes and wheels for the first time in her life took on some possibility of meaning. And mixed with this was the sense that she had been manœuvered into a false position. It ought to have been she who was saying these things to the Christians. Hers ought to have been the vivid, perilous world brought against their grey formalised one; hers the quick, vital movements and theirs the stained glass attitudes. That was the antithesis she was used to. This time, in a sudden flash of purple and crimson, she remembered what stained glass was really like. And where Mark stood in all this new world she did not know. Certainly not quite in his old place. Something which she liked to think of as the oppo-site of Mark had been taken away. Something civilised, or modern, or scholarly, or (of late) "spiritual" which did not want to possess her, which valued her for the odd collection of qualities she called "herself," something without hands that gripped and without demands upon her. But if there were no such thing? Playing for time, she asked,

"Who was that Huge Woman?"

"I'm not sure," said the Director. "But I think I can make a guess. Did you know that all the planets are represented in each?"

"No, Sir. I didn't."

"Apparently they are. There is no Oyarsa in Heaven who has not got his representative on Earth. And there is no world where you could not meet a little unfallen partner of our own black Archon, a kind of other self. That is why there was an Italian Saturn as well as a Heavenly one, and a Cretan Jove as well as an Olympian. It was these earthly wraiths of the high intelligences that men met in old times when they reported that they had seen the gods. It was with those that a man like Merlin was (at times) conversant. Nothing from beyond the Moon ever really descended. What concerns you more, there is a terrestrial as well as a celestial Venus—Perelandra's wraith as well as Perelandra."

"And you think . . . ?"

"I do: I have long known that this house is deeply under her influence. There is even copper in the soil. Also—the earth Venus will be specially active here at present. For it is tonight that her heavenly archetype will really descend."

"I had forgotten," said Jane.

"You will not forget it once it has happened. All of you had better stay together—in the kitchen, perhaps. Do not come upstairs. Tonight I will bring Merlin before my Masters, all five of them—Viritrilbia, Perelandra, Malacandra, Glund, and Lurga. He will be opened. Powers will pass into him."

"What will he *do*, Sir?"

The Director laughed. "The first step is easy. The enemies at Belbury are already looking for experts in archaic Western dialects, preferably Celtic. We shall send them an interpreter! Yes, by the splendour of Christ, we will send them one. 'Upon them He a spirit of frenzy sent To call in haste for their destroyer.' They have advertised in the papers for one! And after the first step . . . well, you know, it will be easy. In fighting those who serve devils one always has this on one's side; their Masters hate them as much as they hate us. The moment we disable the human pawns enough to make them useless to Hell, their own Masters finish the work for us. They break their tools."

There was a sudden knock on the door and Grace Ironwood entered.

"Ivy is back, Sir," she said. "I think you'd better see her. No; she's alone. She never saw her husband. The sentence is over but they haven't released him. He's been sent on to Belbury for remedial treatment. Under some new regulation. Apparently, it does not require a sentence from a court . . . but she's not very coherent. She is in great distress."

6

Jane had gone into the garden to think. She accepted what the Director had said, yet it seemed to her nonsensical. His comparison between Mark's love and God's (since apparently there was a God) struck her nascent spirituality as indecent and irreverent. "Religion" ought to mean a realm in which her haunting female fear of being treated as a thing, an object of barter and desire and possession, would be set permanently at rest and what she called her "true self" would soar upwards and expand in some freer and purer world. For still she thought that "Religion" was a kind of exhalation or a cloud of incense, something steaming up from specially gifted souls towards a receptive Heaven. Then, quite sharply, it occurred to her that the Director never talked about Religion; nor did the Dimbles nor Camilla. They talked about God. They had no picture in their minds of some mist steaming upward: rather of strong, skilful hands thrust down to make, and mend, perhaps even to destroy. Supposing one were a *thing* after all—a thing designed and invented by Someone Else and valued for qualities quite different from what one had decided to regard as one's true self? Supposing all those people who, from the bachelor uncles down to Mark and Mother Dimble, had infuriatingly found her sweet and fresh when she wanted them to find her also interesting and important, had all along been simply right and perceived the sort of thing she was? Supposing Maleldil on this subject agreed with them and not with her? For one moment she had a ridiculous and scorching vision of a world in which God Himself would never understand, never take her with full seriousness. Then, at one particular corner of the gooseberry patch, the change came.

What awaited her there was serious to the degree of sorrow and beyond. There was no form nor sound. The mould under the bushes, the moss on the path, and the little brick border, were not visibly changed. But they were changed. A boundary had been crossed. She had come into a world, or into a Person, or into the presence of a Person. Something expectant, patient, inexorable, met her with no veil or protection between. In the closeness of that contact she perceived at once that the Director's words had been entirely misleading. This demand which now pressed upon her was not, even by analogy, like any other demand. It was the origin of all right demands and contained them. In its light you could understand them; but from them you could know nothing of it. There was nothing, and never had been anything, like this. And now there was nothing except this. Yet also, everything had been like this; only by being like this had anything existed. In this height and depth and breadth the little idea of herself which she had hitherto called *me* dropped down and vanished, unfluttering, into bottomless distance, like a bird in a space without air. The name *me* was the name of a being whose existence she had never suspected, a being that did not yet fully exist but which was demanded. It was a person (not the person she had thought), yet also a thing, a made thing, made to please Another and in Him to please all others, a thing being made at this very moment, without its choice, in a shape it had never dreamed of. And the making went on amidst a kind of splendour or sorrow or both, whereof she could not tell whether it was in the moulding hands or in the kneaded lump.

Words take too long. To be aware of all this and to know that it had already gone made one single experience. It was revealed only in its departure. The largest thing that had ever happened to her had, apparently, found room for itself in a moment of time too short to be called time at all. Her hand closed on nothing but a memory. And as it closed, without an instant's pause, the voices of those who have not joy rose howling and chattering from every corner of her being.

"Take care. Draw back. Keep your head. Don't commit yourself," they said. And then more subtly, from another quarter, "You have had a religious experience. This is very interesting. Not everyone does. How much better you will now understand the Seventeenth-Century poets!" Or from a third direction, more sweetly, "Go on. Try to get it again. It will please the Director."

But her defences had been captured and these counter-attacks were unsuccessful.

15

The Descent of the Gods

The whole house at St. Anne's was empty, but for two rooms. In the kitchen, drawn a little closer than usual about the fire and with the shutters closed, sat Dimble and MacPhee and Denniston and the women. Removed from them by many a long vacancy of stair and passage, the Pendragon and Merlin were together in the Blue Room.

If anyone had gone up the stairs and on to the lobby outside the Blue Room, he would have found something other than fear that barred his way—an almost physical resistance. If he had succeeded in forcing his way forward against it, he would have come into a region of tingling sounds that were clearly not voices though they had articulation; and if the passage were quite dark he would probably have seen a faint light, not like fire or moon, under the Director's door. I do not think he could have reached the door itself unbidden. Already the whole house would have seemed to him to be tilting and plunging like a ship in a Bay of Biscay gale. He would have been horribly compelled to feel this Earth not as the bottom of the universe but as a ball spinning, and rolling onwards, both at delirious speed, and not through emptiness but through some densely inhabited and intricately structured medium. He would have known sensuously, until his outraged senses forsook him, that the visitants in that room were in it, not because they were at rest but because they glanced and wheeled through the packed reality of Heaven (which men call empty space), to keep their beams upon this spot of the moving Earth's hide.

The druid and Ransom had begun to wait for these visitors soon after sundown. Ransom was on his sofa. Merlin sat beside him, his hands clasped, his body a little bent forward. Sometimes a drop of sweat trickled coldly down his grey cheek. He had at first addressed himself to kneel but Ransom forbade him. "See thou do it not!" he had said. "Have you forgotten that they are our fellow servants?" The windows were uncurtained and all the light that there was in the room came thence: frosty red when they began their waiting, but later lit with stars.

Long before anything happened in the Blue Room the party in the kitchen had made their ten o'clock tea. It was while they sat drinking it that the change occurred. Up till now they had instinctively been talking in subdued voices, as children talk in a room where their elders are busied about some august incomprehensible matter, a funeral, or the reading of a will. Now of a sudden they all began talking loudly at once, each, not contentiously but delightedly, interrupting the others. A stranger coming into the kitchen would have thought they were drunk, not soddenly but gaily drunk: would have seen heads bent close together, eyes dancing, an excited wealth of gesture. What they said, none of the party could ever afterwards remember. Dimble maintained that they had been chiefly engaged in making puns. MacPhee denied that he had ever, even that night, made a pun, but all agreed that they had been extraordinarily witty. If not plays upon words, yet certainly plays upon thoughts, paradoxes, fancies, anecdotes, theories laughingly advanced yet (on consideration) well worth taking seriously, had flowed from them and over them with dazzling prodigality. Even Ivy forgot her great sorrow. Mother Dimble always remembered Denniston and her husband as they had stood, one on each side of the fireplace, in a gay intellectual duel, each capping the other, each rising above the other, up and up, like birds or aeroplanes in combat. If only one could have remembered what they said! For never in her life had she heard such talk—such eloquence, such melody (song could have added nothing to it), such toppling structures of double meaning, such skyrockets of metaphor and allusion.

A moment after that and they were all silent. Calm fell, as suddenly as when one goes out of the wind behind a wall. They sat staring upon one another, tired and a little self-conscious.

Upstairs this first change had a different operation. There came an instant at which both men braced themselves. Ransom gripped the side of his sofa; Merlin grasped his own knees and set his teeth. A rod of coloured light, whose colour no man can name or picture, darted between them: no more to see than that, but seeing was the least part of their experience. Quick agitation seized them: a kind of boiling and bubbling in mind and heart which shook their bodies also. It went to a rhythm of such fierce speed that they feared their sanity must be shaken into a thousand fragments. And then it seemed that this had actually happened. But it did not matter: for all the fragments—needle-pointed desires, brisk merriments, lynx-eyed thoughts—went rolling to and fro like glittering drops and reunited themselves. It was well that both men had some knowledge of poetry. The doubling, splitting, and recombining of thoughts which now went on in them would have been unendurable for one whom that art had not already instructed in the counterpoint of the mind, the mastery of doubled and trebled vision. For Ransom, whose study had been for many years in the realm of words, it was heavenly pleasure. He found himself sitting within the very heart of language, in the white-hot furnace of essential speech. All fact was broken, splashed into cataracts, caught, turned inside out, kneaded, slain, and reborn as meaning. For the lord of Meaning himself, the herald, the messenger, the slayer of Argus, was with them: the angel that spins nearest the sun. Viritrilbia, whom men call Mercury and Thoth.

Down in the kitchen drowsiness stole over them after the orgy of speaking had come to an end. Jane, having nearly fallen asleep, was startled by her book falling from her hand, and looked about her. How warm it was . . . how comfortable and familiar. She had always liked wood fires but tonight the smell of the logs seemed more than ordinarily sweet. She began to think it was sweeter than it could possibly be, that a smell of burning cedar or of incense pervaded the room. It thickened. Fragrant names hovered in her mind—nard and cassia's balmy smells and all Arabia breathing from a box; even something more subtly sweet, perhaps maddening—why not forbidden?—but she knew it was commanded. She was too drowsy to think deeply how this could be. The Dimbles were talking together but in so low a voice that others could not hear. Their faces appeared to her transfigured. She could no longer see that they were old—only mature, like ripe fields in August, serene and golden with the tranquility of fulfilled desire. On her other side, Arthur said something in Camilla's ear. There too . . . but as the warmth and sweetness of that rich air now fully mastered her brain, she could hardly bear to look on them: not through envy (that thought was far away), but because a sort of brightness flowed from them that dazzled her, as if the god and goddess in them burned through their bodies and through their clothes and shone before her in a young double-natured nakedness of rose-red spirit that overcame her. And all about them danced (as she half saw), not the gross and ridiculous dwarfs which she had seen that afternoon, but grave and ardent spirits, bright winged, their boyish shapes smooth and slender like ivory rods.

In the Blue Room also Ransom and Merlin felt about this time that the temperature had risen. The windows, they did not see how or when, had swung open; at their opening the temperature did not drop, for it was from without that the warmth came. Through the bare branches, across the ground which was once more stiffening with frost, a summer breeze was blowing into the room, but the breeze of such a summer as England never has. Laden like heavy barges that glide nearly gunwale under, laden so heavily you would have thought it could not move, laden with ponderous fragrance of night-scented flowers, sticky gums, groves that drop odours, and with cool savour of midnight fruit, it stirred the curtains, it lifted a letter that lay on the table, it lifted the hair which had a moment before been plastered on Merlin's forehead. The room was rocking. They were afloat. A soft tingling and shivering as of foam and breaking bubbles ran over their flesh. Tears ran down Ransom's cheeks. He alone knew from what seas and what islands that breeze blew. Merlin did not; but in him also the inconsolable wound with which man is born waked and ached at this touching. Low syllables of prehistoric Celtic self-pity murmured from his lips. These yearnings and fondlings were however only the fore-runners of the goddess. As the whole of her virtue seized, focussed, and held that spot of the rolling Earth in her long beam, something harder, shriller, more perilously ecstatic, came out of the centre of all the softness. Both the humans trembled—Merlin because he did not know what was coming, Ransom because he knew. And now it came. It was fiery, sharp, bright and ruthless, ready to kill, ready to die, outspeeding light: it was Charity, not as mortals imagine it, not even as it has been humanised for them since the Incarnation of the Word, but the translunary virtue, fallen upon them direct from the Third Heaven, unmitigated. They were blinded, scorched, deafened. They thought it would burn their bones. They could not bear that it should continue. They could not bear that it should cease. So Perelandra, triumphant among planets, whom men call Venus, came and was with them in the room.

Down in the kitchen MacPhee sharply drew back his chair so that it grated on the tiled floor like a pencil squeaking on a slate. "Man!" he exclaimed, "it's a shame for us to be sitting here looking at the fire. If the Director hadn't got a game leg himself, I'll bet you he'd have found some other way for us to go to work." Camilla's eyes flashed towards him. "Go on!" she said, "go on!" "What do you mean MacPhee?" said Dimble. "He means fighting," said Camilla. "They'd be too many for us, I'm afraid," said Arthur Denniston. "Maybe that!" said MacPhee. "But maybe they'll be too many for us this way too. But it would be grand to have one go at them before the end. To tell you the truth I sometimes feel I don't greatly care what happens. But I wouldn't be easy in my grave if I knew they'd won and I'd never had my hands on them. I'd like to be able to say as an old sergeant said to me in the first war, about a bit of a raid we did near Monchy. Our fellows did it all with the butt end, you know. "Sir," says he, "did ever you hear anything like the way their heads cracked." "I think that's disgusting," said Mother Dimble. "That part is, I suppose," said Camilla. "But . . . oh if one could have a charge in the old style. I don't mind anything once I'm on a horse." "I don't understand it," said Dimble. "I'm not like you, MacPhee. I'm not brave. But I was just thinking as you spoke that I don't feel afraid of being killed and hurt as I used to do. Not tonight." "We may be, I suppose," said Jane. "As long as we're all together," said Mother Dimble. "It might be . . . no, I don't mean anything heroic . . . it might be a *nice* way to die." And suddenly all their faces and voices were changed. They were laughing again, but it was a different kind of laughter. Their love for one another became intense. Each, looking on all the rest, thought, "I'm lucky to be here. I could die with these." But MacPhee was humming to himself:

King William said, Be not dismayed, for the loss of one commander.

Upstairs it was, at first, much the same. Merlin saw in memory the wintry grass of Badon Hill, the long banner of the Virgin fluttering above the heavy British-Roman cataphracts, the yellow-haired barbarians. He heard the snap of the bows, the *click-click* of steel points in wooden shields, the cheers, the howling, and the ring of struck mail. He remembered also the evening, fires twinkling along the hill, frost making the gashes smart, starlight on a pool fouled with blood, eagles crowding together in the pale sky. And Ransom, it may be, remembered his long struggle in the caves of Perelandra. But all this passed. Something tonic and lusty and cheerily cold, like a sea breeze, was coming over them. There was no fear anywhere: the blood inside them flowed as if to a marching-song. They felt themselves taking their places in the ordered rhythm of the universe, side by side with punctual seasons and patterned atoms and the obeying Seraphim. Under the immense weight of their obedience their wills stood up straight and untiring like caryatids. Eased of all fickleness and all protestings they stood: gay, light, nimble, and alert. They had outlived all anxieties; care was a word without meaning. To live meant to share in this processional pomp. Ransom knew, as a man knows when he touches iron, the clear, taut splendour of that celestial spirit which now flashed between them: vigilant Malacandra, captain of a cold orb, whom men call Mars and Mavors, and Tyr who put his hand in the wolf-mouth. Ransom greeted his guests in the tongue of Heaven. But he warned Merlin that now the time was coming when he must play the man. The three gods who had already met in the Blue Room were less unlike humanity than the two whom they still awaited. In Viritrilbia and Venus and Malacandra were represented those two of the Seven Genders which bear a certain analogy to the biological sexes and can therefore be in some measure understood by men. It would not be so with those who were now preparing to descend. These also doubtless had their genders, but we have no clue to them. These would be mightier energies: ancient eldils, steersman of giant worlds which have never from the beginning been subdued to the sweet humiliations of organic life.

"Stir the fire, Denniston, for any sake. That's a cold night," said MacPhee. "It must be cold outside," said Dimble. All thought of that: of stiff grass, hen-roosts, dark places in the middle of woods, graves. Then of the sun's dying, the Earth gripped, suffocated, in airless cold, the black sky lit only with stars. And then, not even stars: the heat-death of the universe, utter and final blackness of nonentity from which Nature knows no return. Another life? "Possibly," thought MacPhee. "I believe," thought Denniston. But the old life gone, all its times, all its hours and days, gone. Can even Omnipotence *bring back*? Where do years go, and why? Man never would understand it. The misgiving deepened. Perhaps there was nothing to be understood.

Saturn, whose name in the heavens is Lurga, stood in the Blue Room. His spirit lay upon the house, or even on the whole Earth, with a cold pressure such as might flatten the very orb of Tellus to a wafer. Matched against the lead-like burden of his antiquity the other gods themselves perhaps felt young and ephemeral. It was a mountain of centuries sloping up from the highest antiquity we can conceive, up and up like a mountain whose summit never comes into sight, not to eternity where the thought can rest, but into more and still more time, into freezing wastes and silence of unnameable numbers. It was also strong like a mountain; its age was no mere morass of time where imagination can sink in reverie, but a living, self-remembering duration which repelled lighter intelligences from its structure as granite flings back waves, itself unwithered and undecayed but able to wither any who approach it unadvised. Ransom and Merlin suffered a sensation of unendurable cold; and all that was strength in Lurga became sorrow as it entered them. Yet Lurga in that room was overmatched. Suddenly a greater spirit came—one whose influence tempered and almost transformed to his own quality the skill of leaping Mercury, the clearness of Mars, the subtler vibration of Venus, and even the numbing weight of Saturn.

In the kitchen his coming was felt. No one afterwards knew how it happened but somehow the kettle was put on, the hot toddy was brewed. Arthur—the only musician among them—was bidden to get out his fiddle. The chairs were pushed back, the floor cleared. They danced. What they danced no one could remember. It was some round dance, no modern shuffling: it involved beating the floor, clapping of hands, leaping high. And no one while it lasted thought himself or his fellows ridiculous. It may, in fact, have been some village measure, not ill-suited to the tiled kitchen: the spirit in which they danced it was not so. It seemed to each that the room was filled with kings and queens, that the wildness of their dance expressed heroic energy and its quieter movements had seized the very spirit behind all noble ceremonies.

Upstairs his mighty beam turned the Blue Room into a blaze of lights. Before the other angels a man might sink: before this he might die, but if he lived at all, he would laugh. If you had caught one breath of the air that came from him, you would have felt yourself taller than before. Though you were a cripple, your walk would have became stately: though a beggar, you would have worn your rags magnanimously. Kingship and power and festal pomp and courtesy shot from him as sparks fly from an anvil. The pealing of bells, the blowing of trumpets, the spreading out of banners, are means used on earth to make a faint symbol of his quality. It was like a long sunlit wave, creamy-crested and arched with emerald, that comes on nine feet tall, with roaring and with terror and unquenchable laughter. It was like the first beginning of music in the halls of some King so high and at some festival so solemn that a tremor akin to fear runs through young hearts when they hear it. For this was great Glund-Oyarsa, King of Kings, through whom the joy of creation principally blows across these fields of Arbol, known to men in old times as Jove and under that name, by fatal but not inexplicable misprision, confused with his Maker—so little did they dream by how many degrees the stair even of created being rises above him.

At his coming there was holiday in the Blue Room. The two mortals, momentarily caught up into the *Gloria* which those five excellent Natures perpetually sing, forgot for a time the lower and more immediate purpose of their meeting. Then they proceeded to operation. Merlin received the power into him.

He looked different next day. Partly because his beard had been shaved; but also, because he was no longer his own man. No one doubted that his final severance from the body was near. Later in the day MacPhee drove him off and dropped him in the neighborhood of Belbury.

2

Mark had fallen into a doze in the tramp's bedroom that day, when he was startled, and driven suddenly to collect himself, by the arrival of visitors. Frost came in first and held the door open. Two others followed. One was the Deputy Director; the other was a man whom Mark had not seen before.

This person was dressed in a rusty cassock and carried in his hand a wide-brimmed black hat such as priests wear in many parts of the continent. He was a very big man and the cassock perhaps made him look bigger. He was clean shaven, revealing a large face with heavy and complicated folds in it, and he walked with his head a little bowed. Mark decided that he was a simple soul, probably an obscure member of some religious order who happened to be an authority on some even more obscure language. And it was to Mark rather odious to see him standing between those two birds of prey—Wither, effusive and flattering on his right and Frost, on his left, stiff as a ramrod, waiting with scientific attention but also, as Mark could now see, with a certain cold dislike, for the result of the new experiment.

Wither talked to the stranger for some moments in a language which Mark could not follow but which he recognised as Latin. "A priest, obviously," thought Mark. "But I wonder where from? Wither knows most of the ordinary languages. Would the old chap be a Greek? Doesn't look like a Levantine. More probably a Russian." But at this point Mark's attention was diverted. The tramp, who had closed his eyes when he heard the door handle turning had suddenly opened them, seen the stranger, and then shut them tighter than before. After this his behaviour was peculiar. He began emitting a series of very exaggerated snores and turned his back to the company. The stranger took a step nearer to the bed and spoke two syllables in a low voice. For a second or two the tramp lay as he was but seemed to be afflicted with a shivering fit; then, slowly but with continuous movement, as when the bows of a ship come round in obedience to the rudder, he rolled round and lay staring up into the other's face. His mouth and his eyes were both opened very wide. From certain jerkings of his head and hands and from certain ghastly attempts to smile, Mark concluded that he was trying to say something, probably of a deprecatory and insinuating kind. What next followed took his breath away. The stranger spoke again; and then, with much facial contortion, mixed with coughs and stammers and spluttering and expectoration, there came out of the tramp's mouth, in a high unnatural voice, syllables, words, a whole sentence, in some language that was neither Latin nor English. All this time the stranger kept his eyes fixed on those of the tramp.

The stranger spoke again. This time the tramp replied at much greater length and seemed to manage the unknown language a little more easily, though his voice remained quite unlike that in which Mark had heard him talking for the last few days. At the end of his speech he sat up in bed and pointed to where Wither and Frost were standing. Then the stranger appeared to ask him a question. The tramp spoke for the third time.

At this reply the stranger started back, crossed himself several times, and exhibited every sign of terror. He turned and spoke rapidly in Latin to the other two. Something happened to their faces when he spoke. They looked like dogs who have just picked up a scent. Then, with a loud exclamation the stranger caught up his skirts and made a bolt for the door.

But the scientists were too quick for him. For a few minutes all three were wrangling there, Frost's teeth bared like an animal's, and the loose mask of Wither's face wearing, for once, a quite unambiguous expression. The old priest was being threatened. Mark found that he himself had taken a step forward. But before he could make up his mind how to act, the stranger, shaking his head and holding out his hands, had come timidly back to the bedside. It was an odd thing that the tramp who had relaxed during the struggle at the door should suddenly stiffen again and fix his eyes on this frightened old man as if he were awaiting orders.

More words in the unknown language followed. The tramp once more pointed at Wither and Frost. The stranger turned and spoke to them in Latin, apparently translating. Wither and Frost looked at one another as if each waited for his fellow to act. What followed was pure lunacy. With infinite caution, wheezing and creaking, down went the whole shaky senility of the Deputy Director, down onto its knees; and half a second later, with a jerky, metallic movement, Frost got down beside him. When he was down, he suddenly looked over his shoulder to where Mark was standing. The flash of pure hatred in his face, but hatred, as it were, crystallised so that it was no longer a passion and had no heat in it, was like touching metal in the Arctic where metal burns. "Kneel," he bleated, and instantly turned his head. Mark never could remember afterwards whether he simply forgot to obey this order or whether his real rebellion dated from that moment.

The tramp spoke again, always with his eyes fixed on those of the man in the cassock. And again the latter translated, and then stood aside. Wither and Frost began going forward on their knees till they reached the bedside. The tramp's hairy, dirty hand with its bitten nails was thrust out to them. They kissed it. Then it seemed that some further order was given them. They rose and Mark perceived that Wither was gently expostulating in Latin against this order. He kept on indicating Frost. The words *venia tua*[1] (each time emended to *venia vestra*) recurred so often that Mark could pick them out. But apparently the expostulation was unsuccessful: a few moments later Frost and Wither had both left the room.

As the door shut, the tramp collapsed like a deflated balloon. He rolled himself to and fro on the bed muttering, "Gor' blimey. Couldn't have believed it. It's a knock-out. A fair knock-out." But Mark had little

[1] "With your kind permission," or "if you will pardon me."

leisure to attend to this. He found that the stranger was addressing him and though he could not understand the words, he looked up. Instantly, he wished to look away again and found that he could not. He might have claimed with some reason that he was by now an expert in the endurance of alarming faces. But that did not alter the fact that when he looked on this he felt himself afraid. Almost before he had time to realise this he felt himself drowsy. A moment later he fell into his chair and slept.

3

"Well?" said Frost as soon as they found themselves outside the door.

"It is . . . er . . . profoundly perplexing," said the Deputy Director.

They walked down the passage conversing in low tones as they went.

"It certainly looked—I say *looked*," continued Frost, "as if the man in the bed were hypnotised and the Basque priest were in charge of the situation."

"Oh, surely, my dear friend, that would be a most disquieting hypothesis."

"Excuse me. I have made no hypothesis. I am describing how it looked."

"And how, on your hypothesis—forgive me, but that is what it is— would a Basque priest come to invent the story that our guest was Merlinus Ambrosius?"

"That is the point. If the man in the bed is *not* Merlinus then someone else, and someone quite outside our calculations, namely the priest, knows our whole plan of campaign."

"And that, my dear friend, is why the retention of both these persons and a certain extreme delicacy in our attitude to both is required— at least, until we have some further light."

"They must, of course, be detained."

"I should hardly say *detained*. It has implications . . . I do not venture to express any doubt at present as to the identity of our distinguished guest. There is no question of detention. On the contrary, the most cordial welcome, the most meticulous courtesy . . ."

"Do I understand that you had always pictured Merlinus entering the Institute as a Dictator rather than a colleague?"

"As to that," said Wither, "my conception of the personal, or even official, relations between us had always been elastic and ready for all necessary adaptations. It would be a very real grief to me if I thought you were allowing any misplaced sense of your own dignity . . . ah, in short, provided he *is* Merlinus . . . you understand me?"

"Where are you taking us at the moment?"

"To my apartments. If you remember, the request was that we should provide our guest with some clothes."

"There was no request. We were ordered."

To this the Deputy Director made no reply. When both men were in his bedroom and the door was shut, Frost said:

"I am not satisfied. You do not seem to realise the dangers of the situation. We must take into account the possibility that the man is not Merlinus. And if he is not Merlinus, then the priest knows things he ought not to know. To allow an imposter and a spy to remain at large in the Institute is out of the question. We must find out at once where that priest gets his knowledge from. And where did you get the priest from?"

"I think that is the kind of shirt which would be most suitable," said Wither laying it on the bed. "The suits are in here. The . . . ah . . . clerical personage said he had come in answer to our advertisement. I wish to do full justice to the point of view you have expressed, my dear Frost. On the other hand, to reject the real Merlinus . . . to alienate a power which is an integral factor in our plan . . . would be at least equally dangerous. It is not even certain that the priest would in any event be an enemy. He may have made independent contact with the Macrobes. He may be a potential ally."

"Did you think he looked like it? His priesthood is against him."

"All that we now want," said Wither, "is a collar and tie. Forgive me for saying that I have never been able to share your root and branch attitude to religion. I am not speaking of dogmatic Christianity in its primitive form. But within religious circles—ecclesiastical circles—types of spirituality of very real value do from time to time arise. When they do, they sometimes reveal great energy. Father Doyle, though not very talented, is one of our soundest colleagues; and Mr. Straik has in him the germs of that total allegiance (*objectivity* is, I believe, the term you prefer) which is so rare. It doesn't do to be in any way narrow."

"What do you actually propose to do?"

"We will, of course, consult the Head at once. I use that term, you understand, purely for convenience."

"But how can you? Have you forgotten that this is the night of the inaugural banquet, and that Jules is coming down? He may be here in an hour. You will be dancing attendance on him till midnight."

For a moment Wither's face remained still, the mouth wide open. He had indeed forgotten that the puppet Director, the dupe of the Institute by whom it duped the public, was coming that night. But the realisation that he had forgotten troubled him more than it would have troubled another. It was like the first cold breath of winter—the first little hint of a crack in that great secondary self or mental machine which he had built up to carry on the business of living while he, the real Wither, floated far away on the indeterminate frontiers of ghosthood.

"God bless my soul!" he said.

"You have therefore to consider at once," said Frost, "what to do with these two men this very evening. It is out of the question that they should attend the banquet. It would be madness to leave them to their own devices."

"Which reminds me that we have already left them alone—and with Studdock too—for over ten minutes. We must go back with the clothes at once."

"And without a plan?" inquired Frost, though following Wither out of the room as he said it.

"We must be guided by circumstances," said Wither.

They were greeted on their return by a babble of imploring Latin from the man in the cassock. "Let me go," he said, "I intreat you do not, for your mothers' sakes, do not do violence to a poor harmless old man. I will tell nothing—God forgive me—but I cannot stay here. This man who says he is Merlinus come back from the dead—he is a diabolist, a worker of infernal miracles. Look! Look what he did to the poor young man the moment you had left the room." He pointed to where Mark lay unconscious in his chair. "He did it with his eye, only by looking at him. The evil eye, the evil eye."

"Silence!" said Frost in the same language, "and listen. If you do what you are told, no harm will come to you. If you do not, you will be destroyed. I think that if you are troublesome you may lose your soul as well as your life, for you do not sound likely to be a martyr."

The man whimpered, covering his face with his hands. Suddenly, not as if he wished to but as if he were a machine that had been worked, Frost kicked him. "Get on," he said. "Tell him we have brought such clothes as men wear now." The man did not stagger when he was kicked.

The end of it was that the tramp was washed and dressed. When this had been done, the man in the cassock said, "He is saying that he must now be taken for a journey through all your house and shown the secrets." "Tell him," said Wither, "that it will be a very great pleasure and privilege—" But here the tramp spoke again. "He says," translated the big man, "first that he must see the Head and the beasts and the criminals who are being tormented. Secondly, that he will go with one of you alone. With you, Sir," and here he turned to Wither.

"I will allow no such arrangement," said Frost in English.

"My dear Frost," said Wither, "this is hardly the moment . . . and *one* of us must be free to meet Jules."

The tramp had spoken again. "Forgive me," said the man in the cassock, "I must follow what he says. The words are not mine. He forbids you to talk in his presence in a tongue which he cannot, even through me, understand. And he says it is an old habit of his to be obeyed. He is asking now whether you wish to have him for a friend or an enemy."

Frost took a pace nearer to the pseudo-Merlin so that his shoulder touched the rusty cassock of the real one. Wither thought that Frost had intended to say something but had grown afraid. In reality, Frost found it impossible to remember any words. Perhaps it was due to the rapid shifts from Latin to English which had been going on. He could not speak. Nothing but nonsense syllables would occur to his mind. He had long known that his continued intercourse with the beings he called Macrobes might have effects on his psychology which he could not predict. In a dim sort of way, the possibility of complete destruction was never out of his thoughts. He had schooled himself not to attend to it. Now, it seemed to be descending on him. He reminded himself that fear was only a chemical phenomenon. For the moment, clearly, he must step out of the struggle, come to himself, and make a new start later in the evening. For, of course, this could not be final. At the very worst it could only be the first hint of the end. Probably he had years of work before him. He would outlast Wither. He would kill the priest. Even Merlin, if it was Merlin, might not stand better with the Macrobes than himself. He stood aside, and the tramp, accompanied by the real Merlin and the Deputy Director, left the room.

Frost had been right in thinking that the aphasia would be only temporary. As soon as they were alone he found no difficulty in saying, as he shook Mark by the shoulder, "Get up. What do you mean by sleeping here? Come with me to the Objective Room."

4

Before proceeding to their tour of inspection Merlin demanded robes for the tramp, and Wither finally dressed him as a Doctor of Philosophy of the University of Edgestow. Thus arrayed, walking with his eyes half shut, and as delicately as if he were treading on eggs, the bewildered tinker was led upstairs and downstairs and through the zoo and into the cells. Every now and then his face underwent a kind of spasm as if he were trying to say something; but he never succeeded in producing any words except when the real Merlin asked him a question and fixed him with his eye. Of course, all this was not to the tramp what it would have been to anyone who made an educated and wealthy man's demands upon the universe. It was, no doubt, a "rum do"—the rummest do that had ever befallen him. The mere sensation of being clean all over would have made it that even apart from the crimson robe and the fact that his own mouth kept on uttering sounds he did not understand and without his own consent. But it was not by any means the first inexplicable thing that had been done to him.

Meanwhile, in the Objective Room, something like a crisis had developed between Mark and Professor Frost. As soon as they arrived there Mark saw that the table had been drawn back. On the floor lay a large crucifix, almost life size, a work of art in the Spanish tradition, ghastly and realistic. "We have half an hour to pursue our exercises," said Frost looking at his watch. Then he instructed Mark to trample on it and insult it in other ways.

Now whereas Jane had abandoned Christianity in early childhood, along with her belief in fairies and Santa Claus, Mark had never believed in it at all. At this moment, therefore, it crossed his mind for the very first time that there might conceivably be something in it. Frost who was watching him carefully knew perfectly well that this might be the result of the present experiment. He knew it for the very good reason that his own training by the Macrobes had, at one point, suggested the same odd idea to himself. But he had no choice. Whether he wished it or not this sort of thing was part of the initiation.

"But, look here," said Mark.

"What is it?" said Frost. "Pray be quick. We have only a limited time at our disposal."

"This," said Mark, pointing with an undefined reluctance to the horrible white figure on the cross. "This is all surely a pure superstition."

"Well?"

"Well, if so, what is there objective about stamping on the face? Isn't it just as subjective to spit on a thing like this as to worship it? I mean—damn it all—if it's only a bit of wood, why do anything about it?"

"That is superficial. If you had been brought up in a non-Christian society, you would not be asked to do this. Of course, it is a superstition; but it is that particular superstition which has pressed upon our society for a great many centuries. It can be experimentally shown that it still forms a dominant system in the subconscious of many individuals whose conscious thought appears to be wholly liberated. An explicit action in the reverse direction is therefore a necessary step towards complete objectivity. It is not a question for *a priori* discussion. We find it in practice that it cannot be dispensed with."

Mark himself was surprised at the emotions he was undergoing. He did not regard the image with anything at all like a religious feeling. Most emphatically it did not belong to that idea of the Straight or Normal or Wholesome which had, for the last few days, been his support against what he now knew of the innermost circle at Belbury. The horrible vigour of its realism was, indeed, in its own way as remote from that Idea as anything else in the room. That was one source of his reluctance. To insult even a carved image of such agony seemed an abominable act. But it was not the only source. With the introduction of this Christian symbol the whole situation had somehow altered. The thing was becoming incalculable. His simple antithesis of the Normal and the Diseased had obviously failed to take something into account. Why was the crucifix there? Why were more than half the poison-pictures religious? He had the sense of new parties to the conflict—potential allies and enemies which he had not suspected before. "If I take a step in any direction," he thought, "I may step over a precipice." A donkey-like determination to plant hoofs and stay still at all costs arose in his mind.

"Pray make haste," said Frost.

The quiet urgency of the voice, and the fact that he had so often obeyed it before, almost conquered him. He was on the verge of obeying, and getting the whole silly business over, when the defencelessness of the figure deterred him. The feeling was a very illogical one. Not because its hands were nailed and helpless, but because they were only made of wood and therefore even more helpless, because the thing, for all its realism, was inanimate and could not in any way hit back, he paused. The unretaliating face of a doll—one of Myrtle's dolls—which he had pulled to pieces in boyhood had affected him in the same way and the memory, even now, was tender to the touch.

"What are you waiting for, Mr. Studdock?" said Frost.

Mark was well aware of the rising danger. Obviously, if he disobeyed, his last chance of getting out of Belbury alive might be gone. Even of getting out of this room. The smothering sensation once again attacked him. He was himself, he felt, as helpless as the wooden Christ. As he thought this, he found himself looking at the crucifix in a new way—neither as a piece of wood nor a monument of superstition but as a bit of history. Christianity was nonsense, but one did not doubt that the man had lived and had been executed thus by the Belbury of those days. And that, as he suddenly saw, explained why this image, though not itself an image of the Straight or Normal, was yet in opposition to crooked Belbury. It was a picture of what happened when the Straight met the Crooked, a picture of what the Crooked did to the Straight— what it would do to him if he remained straight. It was, in a more emphatic sense than he had yet understood, a *cross*.

"Do you intend to go on with the training or not?" said Frost. His eye was on the time. He knew that those others were conducting their tour of inspection and that Jules must have very nearly reached Belbury. He knew that he might be interrupted at any moment. He had chosen this time for this stage in Mark's initiation partly in obedience to an unexplained impulse (such impulses grew more frequent with him every day), but partly because he wished, in the uncertain situation which had now arisen, to secure Mark at once. He and Wither, and possibly (by now) Straik, were the only full initiates in the N.I.C.E. On them lay the danger of making any false step in dealing with the man who claimed to be Merlin and with his mysterious interpreter. For him who took the right steps there was a chance of ousting all the others, of becoming to them what they were to the rest of the Institute and what the Institute was to the rest of England. He knew that Wither was waiting eagerly for any slip on his own part. Hence it seemed to him of the utmost importance to bring Mark as soon as possible beyond that point after which there is no return and the disciple's allegiance both to the Macrobes and to the teacher who has initiated him becomes a matter of psychological, or even physical, necessity.

"Do you not hear what I am saying?" he asked Mark again.

Mark made no reply. He was thinking, and thinking hard because he knew, that if he stopped even for a moment, mere terror of death would take the decision out of his hands. Christianity was a fable. It would be ridiculous to die for a religion one did not believe. This Man himself, on that very cross, had discovered it to be a fable, and had died complaining that the God in whom he trusted had forsaken him—had, in fact, found the universe a cheat. But this raised a question that Mark had never thought of before. Was *that* the moment at which to turn against the Man? If the universe was a cheat, was that a good reason for joining its side? Supposing the Straight was utterly powerless, always and everywhere certain to be mocked, tortured, and finally killed by the Crooked, what then? Why not go down with the ship? He began to be frightened by the very fact that his fears seemed to have momentarily vanished. They had been a safeguard . . . they had prevented him, all his life, from making mad decisions like that which he was now making as he turned to Frost and said,

"It's all bloody nonsense, and I'm damned if I do any such thing."

When he said this he had no idea what might happen next. He did not know whether Frost would ring a bell or produce a revolver or renew his demands. In fact, Frost simply went on staring at him and he stared back. Then he saw that Frost was listening, and he began to listen himself. A moment later the door opened. The room seemed suddenly to be full of people—a man in a red gown (Mark did not instantly recognise the tramp) and the huge man in the black gown, and Wither.

5

In the great drawing room at Belbury a singularly uncomfortable party was by now assembled. Horace Jules, Director of the N.I.C.E., had arrived about half an hour before. They had shown him to the Deputy Director's study, but the Deputy Director was not there. Then they had shown him to his own rooms and hoped he would take a long time settling in. He took a very short time. In five minutes he was downstairs again and on their hands, and it was still much too early for anyone to go and dress. He was now standing with his back to the fire, drinking a glass of sherry, and the principal members of the Institute were standing round him. Conversation was hanging fire.

Conversation with Mr. Jules was always difficult because he insisted on regarding himself not as a figurehead but as the real director of the Institute, and even as the source of most of its ideas. And since, in fact, any science he knew was that taught him at the University of London over fifty years ago, and any philosophy he knew had been acquired from writers like Hæckel and Joseph McCabe and Winwood Reade, it was not, in fact, possible to talk to him about most of the things the Institute was really doing. One was always engaged in inventing answers to questions which were actually meaningless and expressing enthusiasm for ideas which were out of date and had been crude even in their prime. That was why the absence of the Deputy Director in such interviews was so disastrous, for Wither alone was master of a conversational style that exactly suited Jules.

Jules was a cockney. He was a very little man, whose legs were so short that he had unkindly been compared with a duck. He had a turned up nose and a face in which some original *bonhomie* had been much interfered with by years of good living and conceit. His novels had first raised him to fame and affluence; later, as editor of the weekly called *We Want To Know,* he had become such a power in the country that his name was really necessary to the N.I.C.E.

"And as I said to the Archbishop," observed Jules, " 'you may not know, my lord,' said I, 'that modern research shows the temple at Jerusalem to have been about the size of an English village church.' "

"God!" said Feverstone to himself where he stood silent on the fringes of the group.

"Have a little more sherry, Director," said Miss Hardcastle.

"Well, I don't mind if I do," said Jules. "It's not at all bad sherry, though I think I could tell you of a place where we could get something better. And how are you getting on, Miss Hardcastle, with your reforms of our penal system?"

"Making real headway," she replied. "I think some modification of the Pellotoff method—"

"What I always say," remarked Jules, interrupting her, "is, why not treat crime like any other disease? I've no use for Punishment. What you want to do is to put the man on the right lines—give him a fresh start—give him an interest in life. It's all perfectly simple if you look at it from that point of view. I daresay you've been reading a little address on the subject I gave at Northampton."

"I agreed with you," said Miss Hardcastle.

"That's right," said Jules. "I tell you who didn't though. Old

Hingest—and by the bye, that was a queer business. You never caught the murderer, did you? But though I'm sorry for the old chap, I never did quite see eye to eye with him. Very last time I met him, one or two of us were talking about juvenile offenders, and do you know what he said? He said, 'The trouble with these courts for young criminals nowadays is that they're always binding them over when they ought to be bending them over.' Not bad, was it? Still, as Wither said—and, by the way, where *is* Wither?"

"I think he should be here any moment now," said Miss Hardcastle, "I can't imagine why he's not."

"I think," said Filostrato, "he have a breakdown with his car. He will be very desolated, Mr. Director, not to have given you the welcome."

"Oh, he needn't bother about that," said Jules, "I never was one for any formality, though I did think he'd be here when I arrived. You're looking very well, Filostrato. I'm following your work with great interest. I look upon you as one of the makers of mankind."

"*Yes, yes,*" said Filostrato, "that is the real business. Already we begin—"

"I try to help you all I can on the non-technical side," said Jules. "It's a battle I've been fighting for years. The whole question of our sex-life. What I always say is, that once you get the whole thing out into the open, you don't have any more trouble. It's all this Victorian secrecy which does the harm. Making a mystery of it. I want every boy and girl in the country—"

"God!" said Feverstone to himself.

"Forgive me," said Filostrato who, being a foreigner, had not yet despaired of trying to enlighten Jules. "But that is not precisely the point."

"Now I know what you're going to say," interrupted Jules, laying a fat forefinger on the Professor's sleeve. "And I daresay you don't read my little paper. But believe me, if you looked up the first number of last month you'd find a modest little editorial which a chap like you might overlook because it doesn't use any technical terms. But I ask you just to read it and see if it doesn't put the whole thing in a nutshell. And in a way that the man in the street can understand."

At this moment the clock struck a quarter.

"I say," asked Jules, "what time is this dinner at?" He liked banquets, and specially banquets at which he had to speak. He also disliked to be kept waiting.

"At quarter to eight," said Miss Hardcastle.

"You know," said Jules, "this fellow Wither really ought to be here. I mean to say, I'm not particular, but I don't mind telling you between you and me that I'm a bit hurt. It isn't the kind of thing a chap expects, is it?"

"I hope nothing's gone wrong with him," said Miss Hardcastle.

"You'd hardly have thought he'd have gone out anywhere, not on a day like this," said Jules.

"*Ecco,*" said Filostrato. "Someone come."

It was indeed Wither who entered the room followed by a company whom Jules had not expected to see, and Wither's face had certainly good reason to look even more chaotic than usual. He had been bustled round his own Institute as if he were a kind of footman. He had not even been allowed to have supplies of blood and air turned on for the Head when they made him take them into the Head's room. And "Merlin" (if it was Merlin) had ignored it. Worst of all, it had gradually become clear to him that this intolerable incubus and his interpreter fully intended to be present at dinner. No one could be more keenly aware than Wither of the absurdity of introducing to Jules a shabby old priest who couldn't speak English, in charge of what looked like a somnambulist chimpanzee dressed up as a Doctor of Philosophy. To tell Jules the real explanation—even if he knew which was the real explanation—was out of the question. For Jules was a simple man to whom the word "medieval" meant only "savage" and in whom the word "magic" roused memories of *The Golden Bough*. It was a minor nuisance that ever since their visit to the Objective Room he had been compelled to have both Frost and Studdock in attendance. Nor did it mend matters that as they approached Jules and all eyes were fixed upon them, the pseudo-Merlin collapsed into a chair, muttering, and closed his eyes.

"My dear Director," began Wither, a little out of breath. "This is one of the happiest moments of my life. I hope your comfort has been in every way attended to. It has been most unfortunate that I was called away at the very moment when I was expecting your arrival. A remarkable coincidence . . . another very distinguished person has joined us at the very same moment. A foreigner . . ."

"Oh," interrupted Jules in a slightly rasping voice. "Who's he?"

"Allow me," said Wither, stepping a little to one side.

"Do you mean *that?*" said Jules. The supposed Merlin sat with his arms hanging down on each side of the chair, his eyes closed, his head on one side, and a weak smile on his face. "Is he drunk? Or ill? And who is he, anyway?"

"He is, as I was observing, a foreigner," began Wither.

"Well, that doesn't make him go to sleep the moment he is introduced to me, does it?"

"Hush!" said Wither, drawing Jules a little out of the group and lowering his voice. "There are circumstances—it would be very difficult to go into it here—I have been taken by surprise and would, if you had not been here already, have consulted you at the first possible moment. Our distinguished guest has just undertaken a very long journey and has, I admit, certain eccentricities, and . . ."

"But who is he?" persisted Jules.

"His name is . . . er . . . Ambrosius. Dr. Ambrosius, you know."

"Never 'eard of him," snapped Jules. At another time he might not have made this admission, but the whole evening was turning out differently from his expectations and he was losing his temper.

"Very few of us have heard of him *yet*," said Wither. "But everyone will have heard of him soon. That is why, without in the least . . ."

"And who's *that*?" asked Jules indicating the real Merlin. "He looks as if he were enjoying himself."

"Oh, that is merely Dr. Ambrosius's interpreter."

"Interpreter? Can't he talk English?"

"Unfortunately not. He lives rather in a world of his own."

"And can't you get anyone except a priest to act for him? I don't like the look of that fellow. We don't want that sort of thing here at all. Hullo! And who are *you*?"

The last question was addressed to Straik, who had at this moment, thrust his way up to the Director. "Mr. Jules," he said fixing the latter with a prophetic eye, "I am the bearer of a message to you which you must hear. I—"

"Shut up," said Frost to Straik.

"Really, Mr. Straik, really," said Wither. Between them they shouldered him aside.

"Now look 'ere, Mr. Wither," said Jules, "I tell you straight I'm very far from satisfied. Here's *another* parson. I don't remember the name of any such person coming before me and it wouldn't have got past me if it had done, see? You and I'll have to have a very serious conversation. It seems to me you've been making appointments behind my back and turning the place into a kind of seminary. And that's a thing I won't stand. Nor will the British people."

"I know. I know," said Wither. "I understand your feelings exactly. You can rely on complete sympathy. I am eager and waiting to explain the situation to you. In the meantime, perhaps, as Dr. Ambrosius seems slightly overcome and the dressing bell has just sounded . . . oh, I beg your pardon. This *is* Dr. Ambrosius."

The tramp, to whom the real magician had recently turned, was now risen from his chair, and approaching. Jules held out his hand sulkily. The other, looking over Jules's shoulder and grinning in an inexplicable fashion, seized it and shook it, as if absent-mindedly, some ten or fifteen times. His breath, Jules noticed, was strong and his grip horny. He was not liking Dr. Ambrosius. And he disliked even more the massive form of the interpreter towering over them both.

16

Banquet at Belbury

I

It was with great pleasure that Mark found himself once more dressing for dinner and what seemed likely to be an excellent dinner. He got a seat with Filostrato on his right and a rather inconspicuous newcomer on his left. Even Filostrato seemed human and friendly compared with the two initiates, and to the newcomer his heart positively warmed. He noticed with surprise that the tramp sat at the high table between Jules and Wither, but did not often look in that direction, for the tramp, catching his eye, had imprudently raised his glass and winked at him. The strange priest stood patiently behind the tramp's chair. For the rest, nothing of importance happened until the King's health had been drunk and Jules rose to make his speech.

For the first few minutes, anyone glancing down the long tables would have seen what we always see on such occasions. There were the placid faces of elderly *bons viveurs* whom food and wine had placed in a contentment which no amount of speeches could violate. There were the patient faces of responsible but serious diners, who had long since learned how to pursue their own thoughts, while attending to the speech just enough to respond wherever a laugh or a low rumble of serious assent was obligatory. There was the usual fidgety expression on the faces of young men unappreciative of port and hungry for tobacco. There was bright over-elaborate attention on the powdered faces of women who knew their duty to society. But if you have gone on looking down the tables you would presently have seen a change. You would have seen face after face look up and turn in the direction of the speaker. You would have seen first curiosity, then fixed attention, then incredulity. Finally you would have noticed that the room was utterly silent, without a cough or a creak, that every eye was fixed on Jules, and soon every mouth opened in something between fascination and horror.

To different members of the audience the change came differently. To Frost it began at the moment when he heard Jules end a sentence with the words, "as gross an anachronism as to trust to Calvary for salvation in modern war." *Cavalry,* thought Frost almost aloud. Why couldn't the fool mind what he was saying? The blunder irritated him extremely. Perhaps—but hullo! what was this? Had his hearing gone wrong? For Jules seemed to be saying that the future density of mankind depended on the implosion of the horses of Nature. "He's drunk," thought Frost. Then, crystal clear in articulation, beyond all possibility of mistake, came, "The madrigore of verjuice must be talthibianised."

Wither was slower to notice what was happening. He had never expected the speech to have any meaning as a whole and for a long time the familiar catch-words rolled on in a manner which did not disturb the expectation of his ear. He thought, indeed, that Jules was sailing very near the wind, that a very small false step would deprive both the speaker and the audience of the power even to pretend that he was saying anything in particular. But as long as that border was not crossed, he rather admired the speech; it was in his own line. Then he thought, "Come! That's going too far. Even they must see that you can't talk about accepting the challenge of the past by throwing down the gauntlet of the future." He looked cautiously down the room. All was well. But it wouldn't be if Jules didn't sit down pretty soon. In that last sentence there were surely words he didn't know. What the deuce did he mean by *aholibate?* He looked down the room again. They were attending too much, always a bad sign. Then came the sentence, "The surrogates esemplanted in a continual of porous variations."

Mark did not at first attend to the speech at all. He had plenty of other things to think of. The appearance of this spouting popinjay at the very crisis of his own history was a mere interruption. He was too endangered and yet also, in some precarious way, too happy to bother about Jules. Once or twice some phrase caught his ear and made him want to smile. What first awoke him to the real situation was the behaviour of those who sat near him. He was aware of their increasing stillness. He noticed that everyone except himself had begun to attend. He looked up and saw their faces. And then first he really listened. "We shall not," Jules was saying, "we shall not till we can secure the erebation of all prostundiary initems." Little as he cared for Jules, a sudden shock of alarm pierced him. He looked round again. Obviously it was not he who was mad—they had all heard the gibberish. Except possibly the tramp, who looked as solemn as a judge. He had never heard a speech from one of these real toffs before and would have been disappointed if he could understand it. Nor had he ever before drunk vintage port, and though he did not much like the taste he had been working away like a man.

Wither had not forgotten for a moment that there were reporters present. That in itself did not matter much. If anything unsuitable appeared in tomorrow's paper, it would be child's play for him to say that the reporters were drunk or mad and break them. On the other hand he might let the story pass. Jules was in many respects a nuisance, and this might be as good an opportunity as any other for ending his career. But this was not the immediate question. Wither was wondering whether he should wait till Jules sat down or whether he should rise and interrupt him with a few judicious words. He did not want a scene. It would be better if Jules sat down of his own accord. At the same time, there was by now an atmosphere in that crowded room which warned Wither not to delay too long. Glancing down at the secondhand of his watch he decided to wait two minutes more. Almost as he did so he knew that he had misjudged it. An intolerable falsetto laugh rang out from the bottom of the table and would not stop. Some fool of a woman had got hysterics. Immediately Wither touched Jules on the arm, signed to him with a nod, and rose.

"Eh? Blotcher bulldoo?" muttered Jules. But Wither, laying his hand on the little man's shoulder, quietly but with all his weight, forced him down into a sitting position. Then Wither cleared his throat. He knew how to do that so that every eye in the room turned immediately to look at him. The woman stopped screaming. People who had been sitting dead still in strained positions moved and relaxed. Wither looked down the room for a second or two in silence, feeling his grip on the audience. He saw that he already had them in hand. There would be no more hysterics. Then he began to speak.

They ought to have all looked more and more comfortable as he proceeded; and there ought soon to have been murmurs of grave regret for the tragedy which they had just witnessed. That was what Wither expected. What he actually saw bewildered him. The same too attentive silence which had prevailed during Jules' speech had returned. Bright unblinking eyes and open mouths greeted him in every direction. The woman began to laugh again—or no, this time it was two women. Cosser, after one frightened glance, jumped up, overturning his chair, and bolted from the room.

The Deputy Director could not understand this, for to him his own voice seemed to be uttering the speech he had resolved to make. But the audience heard him saying, "Tidies and fugleman—I sheel foor that we all—er—most steeply rebut the defensible, though, I trust, lavatory, Aspasia which gleams to have selected our redeemed inspector this deceiving. It would—ah—be shark, very shark, from anyone's debenture . . ."

The woman who had laughed rose hastily from her chair. The man seated next to her heard her murmur in his ear, "Vood wooloo." He took in the meaningless syllables and her unnatural expression at one moment. Both for some reason infuriated him. He rose to help her to move back her chair with one of those gestures of savage politeness which often, in modern society, serve instead of blows. He wrenched the chair, in fact, out of her hand. She screamed, tripped on a ruck in the carpet and fell. The man on the other side of her saw her fall and saw the first man's expression of fury. "Bot are you blammit?" he roared, leaning towards him with a threatening movement. Four or five people in that part of the room were now up. They were shouting. At the same time there was movement elsewhere. Several of the younger men were making for the door. "Bundlemen, bundlemen," said Wither sternly in a much louder voice. He had often before, merely by raising his voice and speaking one authoritative word reduced troublesome meetings to order.

But this time he was not even heard. At least twenty people present were at that very moment attempting to do the same thing. To each of them it seemed plain that things were just at that stage when a word or so of plain sense, spoken in a new voice, would restore the whole room to sanity. One thought of a sharp word, one of a joke, one of something very quiet and telling. As a result fresh gibberish in a great variety of tones rang out from several places at once. Frost was the only one of the leaders who attempted to say nothing. Instead, he had pencilled a few

344 • C. S. L E W I S

words on a slip of paper, beckoned to a servant, and made him understand by signs that it was to be given to Miss Hardcastle.

By the time the message was put into her hands the clamour was universal. To Mark it sounded like the noise of a crowded restaurant in a foreign country. Miss Hardcastle smoothed out the paper and stooped her head to read. The message ran, *Blunt frippers intantly to pointed bdeluroid. Purgent. Cost.* She crumpled it up in her hand.

Miss Hardcastle had known before she got the message that she was three parts drunk. She had expected and intended to be so: she knew that later on in the evening she would go down to the cells and do things. There was a new prisoner there—a little fluffy girl of the kind the Fairy enjoyed—with whom she could pass an agreeable hour. The tumult of gibberish did not alarm her: she found it exciting. Apparently, Frost wanted her to take some action. She decided that she would. She rose and walked the whole length of the room to the door, locked it, put the key in her pocket, and then turned to survey the company. She noticed for the first time that neither the supposed Merlin nor the Basque priest were anywhere to be seen. Wither and Jules, both on their feet, were struggling with each other. She set out towards them.

So many people had now risen that it took her a long time to reach them. All semblance of a dinner party had disappeared: it was more like the scene at a London terminus on a bank holiday. Everyone was trying to restore order, but everyone was unintelligible, and everyone, in the effort to be understood, was talking louder and louder. She shouted several times herself. She even fought a good deal before she reached her goal.

There came an ear-splitting noise and after that, at last, a few seconds of dead silence. Mark noticed first that Jules had been killed: only secondly, that Miss Hardcastle had shot him. After that it was difficult to be sure what happened. The stampede and the shouting may have concealed a dozen reasonable plans for disarming the murderess, but it was impossible to concert them. Nothing came of them but kicking, struggling, leaping on tables and under tables, pressing on and pulling back, screams, breaking of glass. She fired again and again. It was the smell more than anything else which recalled the scene to Mark in later life: the smell of the shooting mixed with the sticky compound smell of blood and port and madeira.

Suddenly, the confusion of cries ran all together into one thin long-drawn noise of terror. Everyone had become *more* frightened. Something had darted very quickly across the floor between the two long tables and disappeared under one of them. Perhaps half the people present had not seen what it was—had only caught a gleam of black and tawny. Those who had seen it clearly could not tell the others: they could only point and scream meaningless syllables. But Mark had recognised it. It was a tiger.

For the first time that evening everybody realised how many hiding places the room contained. The tiger might be under any of the tables. It might be in any of the deep bay windows, behind the curtains. There was a screen across one corner of the room too.

It is not to be supposed that even now none of the company kept their heads. With loud appeals to the whole room or with urgent whispers to their immediate neighbours they tried to stem the panic, to arrange an orderly retreat from the room, to indicate how the brute could be lured or scared into the open and shot. But the doom of gibberish frustrated all their efforts. They could not arrest the two movements which were going on. The majority had not seen Miss Hardcastle lock the door: they were pressing towards it, to get out at all costs: they would fight, they would kill if they could, rather than not reach the door. A large minority, on the other hand, knew that the door was locked. There must be another door, the one used by the servants, the one whereby the tiger had got in. They were pressing to the opposite end of the room to find it. The whole centre of the room was occupied by the meeting of these two waves—a huge football scrum, at first noisy with frantic efforts at explanation, but soon, as the struggle thickened, almost silent except for the sound of labouring breath, kicking or trampling feet, and meaningless muttering.

Four or five of these combatants lurched heavily against a table, pulling off the cloth in their fall and with it all the fruit dishes, decanters, glasses, plates. Out of that confusion, with a howl of terror, broke the tiger. It happened so quickly that Mark hardly took it in. He saw the hideous head, the cat's snarl of the mouth, the flaming eyes. He heard a shot—the last. Then the tiger had disappeared again. Something fat and white and bloodied was down among the feet of the scrummers. Mark could not recognise it at first for the face, from where he stood, was upside down and the grimaces disguised it until it was quite dead. Then he recognized Miss Hardcastle.

Wither and Frost were no longer to be seen. There was a growling close at hand. Mark turned, thinking he had located the tiger. Then he caught out of the corner of his eye a glimpse of something smaller and greyer. He thought it was an Alsatian. If so, the dog was mad. It ran along the table, its tail between its legs, slavering. A woman, standing with her back to the table, turned, saw it, tried to scream, next moment went down as the creature leaped at her throat. It was a wolf. "Ai—ai!!" squealed Filostrato and jumped on the table. Something else had darted between his feet. Mark saw it streak across the floor and enter the scrum and wake that mass of interlocked terror into new and frantic convulsions. It was some kind of snake.

Above the chaos of sounds which now awoke—there seemed to be a new animal in the room every minute—there came at last one sound in which those still capable of understanding could take comfort. *Thud— thud—thud;* the door was being battered from the outside. It was a huge folding door, a door by which a small locomotive could almost enter, for the room was made in imitation of Versailles. Already one or two of the panels were splintering. The noise maddened those who had made that door their goal. It seemed also to madden the animals. They did not stop to eat what they killed, or not more than to take one lick of the blood. There were dead and dying bodies everywhere by now, for the scrum was by this time killing as many as the beasts. And always from all sides went up the voices trying to shout to those beyond the door. "Quick. Quick. Hurry," but shouting only nonsense. Louder and louder grew the noise at the door. As if in imitation a great gorilla leaped on the table where Jules had sat and began drumming on its chest. Then, with a roar, it jumped down into the crowd.

At last the door gave. Both wings gave. The passage, framed in the doorway, was dark. Out of the darkness there came a grey snaky something. It swayed in the air; then began methodically to break off the splintered wood on each side and make the doorway clear. Then Mark saw distinctly how it swooped down, curled itself round a man—Steele, he thought, but everyone looked different now—and lifted him bodily high off the floor. After that, monstrous, improbable, the huge shape of the elephant thrust its way into the room: its eyes enigmatic, its ears standing stiffly out like the devil's wings on each side of its head. It stood for a second with Steele writhing in the curl of its trunk and then dashed him to the floor. It trampled him. After it raised head and trunk again and brayed horribly; then plunged straight forward into the room, trumpeting and trampling—continuously trampling like a girl treading grapes, heavily and soon wetly tramping in a pash of blood and bones, of flesh, wine, fruit, and sodden tablecloth. Something more than danger darted from the sight into Mark's brain. The pride and insolent glory of the beast, the carelessness of its killings, seemed to crush his spirit even as its flat feet were crushing women and men. Here surely came the King of the world . . . then everything went black and he knew no more.

2

When Mr. Bultitude had come to his senses he had found himself in a dark place full of unfamiliar smells. This did not very greatly surprise or trouble him. He was inured to mystery. To poke his head into any spare bedroom at St. Anne's, as he sometimes managed to do, was an adventure no less remarkable than that which had now befallen him. And the smells here were, on the whole, promising. He perceived that food was in the neighbourhood and—more exciting still—a female of his own species. There were a great many other animals about too, apparently, but that was rather irrelevant than alarming. He decided to go and find both the female bear and the food; it was then he discovered that walls met him in three directions and bars in the fourth. He could not get out. This, combined with an inarticulate want for the human companionship to which he was accustomed, gradually plunged him into depression. Sorrow such as only animals know—huge seas of disconsolate emotion with not one little raft of reason to float on—drowned him fathoms deep. In his own fashion he lifted up his voice and wept.

And yet, not very far away from him, another, and human, captive was almost equally engulfed. Mr. Maggs, seated in a little white cell, chewed steadily on his great sorrow as only a simple man can chew. An educated man in his circumstances would have found misery streaked with reflection; would have been thinking how this new idea of cure instead of punishment, so humane in seeming, had in fact deprived the criminal of all rights and by taking away the *name* Punishment made the *thing* infinite. But Mr. Maggs thought all the time simply of one thing: that this was the day he had counted on all through his sentence, that he had expected by this time to be having his tea at home with Ivy (she'd have got something tasty for him the first night) and that it hadn't happened. He sat quite still. About once in every two minutes a single large tear trickled down his cheek. He wouldn't have minded so much if they'd let him have a packet of fags.

It was Merlin who brought release to both. He had left the dining room as soon as the curse of Babel was well fixed upon the enemies. No one had seen him go. Wither had once heard his voice calling loud and intolerably glad above the riot of nonsense, "*Qui Verbum Dei contempserunt, eis auferetur etiam verbum hominis.*"[1] After that he did not see him again, nor the tramp either. Merlin had gone and spoiled his house. He had liberated beasts and men. The animals that were already maimed he killed with an instantaneous motion of the powers that were in him, swift and painless as the mild shafts of Artemis. To Mr. Maggs he had handed a written message. It ran as follows: "Dearest Tom, I do hope your well and the Director here is one of the right sort and he says to come as quick as you can to the Manor at St. Anne's. And don't go through Edgestow Tom whatever you do, but come any way you can I should think someone had given you a Lift. Everything is all-right no more now. Lots of love ever your own Ivy." The other prisoners he let go where they pleased. The tramp, finding Merlin's back turned on him for a second, and having noticed that the house seemed to be empty, made his escape, first into the kitchen and thence, re-inforced with all the edibles his pockets would hold, into the wide world. I have not been able to trace him further.

The beasts, except for one donkey who disappeared about the same time as the tramp, Merlin sent to the dining room, maddened with his voice and touch. But he retained Mr. Bultitude. The latter had recognized him at once as the same man whom he had sat beside in the Blue Room: less sweet and sticky than on that occasion, but recognisably the same. Even without the brilliantine there was that in Merlin which exactly suited the bear and at their meeting it "made him all the cheer that a beast can make a man." He laid his hand on its head and whispered in its ear and its dark mind was filled with excitement as though some long forbidden and forgotten pleasure were suddenly held out to it. Down the long, empty passages of Belbury it padded behind him. Saliva dripped from its mouth and it was beginning to growl. It was thinking of warm, salt tastes, of the pleasant resistances of bone, of things to crunch and lick and worry.

[1] They that have despised the word of God, from them shall the word of man also be taken away.

3

Mark felt himself shaken; then the cold shock of water dashed in his face. With difficulty he sat up. The room was empty except for the bodies of the distorted dead. The unmoved electric light glared down on hideous confusion—food and filth, spoiled luxury and mangled men, each more hideous by reason of the other. It was the supposed Basque priest who had roused him. "*Surge, miselle* (Get up, wretched boy)," he said, helping Mark to his feet. Mark rose; he had some cuts and bruises and his head ached but he was substantially uninjured. The man held out to him wine in one of the great silver cups, but Mark turned away from it with a shudder. He looked with bewilderment on the face of the stranger and found that a letter was being put into his hand. "Your wife awaits you," it ran, "at the Manor at St. Anne's on the Hill. Come quickly by road as best you can. Do not go near Edgestow—A. Denniston." He looked again at Merlin and thought his face terrible. But Merlin met his glance with a look of unsmiling authority, laid a hand on his shoulder, and impelled him over all the tinkling and slippery havoc to the door. His fingers sent a prickly sensation through Mark's skin. He was led down to the cloakroom, made to fling on a coat and hat (neither were his own) and thence out under the stars, bitter cold and two o'clock in the morning, Sirius bitter green, a few flakes of dry snow beginning to fall. He hesitated. The stranger stood back from him for a second, then, with his open hand, struck him on the back: Mark's bones ached at the memory as long as he lived. Next moment he found himself running as he had never run since boyhood; not in fear, but because his legs would not stop. When he became master of them again he was half a mile from Belbury and looking back he saw a light in the sky.

4

Wither was not among those killed in the dining room. He naturally knew all the possible ways out of the room, and even before the coming of the tiger he had slipped away. He understood what was happening if not perfectly, yet better than anyone else. He saw that the Basque interpreter had done the whole thing. And, by that, he knew also that powers more than human had come down to destroy Belbury; only one in the saddle of whose soul rode Mercury himself could thus have unmade language. And this again told him something worse. It meant that his own dark Masters had been completely out in their calculations. They had talked of a barrier which made it impossible that powers from Deep Heaven should reach the surface of the Earth; had assured him that nothing from outside could pass the Moon's orbit. All their polity was based on the belief that Tellus was blockaded, beyond the reach of such assistance and left (as far as that went) to their mercy and his. Therefore he knew that everything was lost.

It is incredible how little this knowledge moved him. It could not, because he had long ceased to believe in knowledge itself. What had been in his far-off youth a merely aesthetic repugnance to realities that were crude or vulgar, had deepened and darkened, year after year, into a fixed refusal of everything that was in any degree other than himself. He had passed from Hegel into Hume, thence through Pragmatism, and thence through Logical Positivism, and out at last into the complete void. The indicative mood now corresponded to no thought that his mind could entertain. He had willed with his whole heart that there should be no reality and no truth, and now even the imminence of his own ruin could not wake him. The last scene of *Dr. Faustus* where the man raves and implores on the edge of Hell is, perhaps, stage fire. The last moments before damnation are not often so dramatic. Often the man knows with perfect clarity that some still possible action of his own will could yet save him. But he cannot make this knowledge real to himself. Some tiny habitual sensuality, some resentment too trivial to waste on a blue-bottle, the indulgence of some fatal lethargy, seems to him at that moment more important than the choice between total joy and total destruction. With eyes wide open, seeing that the endless terror is just about to begin and yet (for the moment) unable to feel terrified, he watches passively, not moving a finger for his own rescue, while the last links with joy and reason are severed, and drowsily sees the trap close upon his soul. So full of sleep are they at the time when they leave the right way.

Straik and Filostrato were also still alive. They met in one of the cold, lighted passages, so far away from the dining room that the noise of the carnage was but a faint murmur. Filostrato was hurt, his right arm badly mauled. They did not speak—both knew that the attempt would be useless—but walked on side by side. Filostrato was intending to get round to the garage by a back way: he thought that he might still be able to drive, in a fashion, at least as far as Sterk.

As they rounded a corner they both saw what they had often seen before but had expected never to see again—the Deputy Director, stooped, creaking, pacing, humming his tune. Filostrato did not want to go with him, but Wither, as if noticing his wounded condition, offered him an arm. Filostrato tried to decline it: nonsense syllables came from his mouth. Wither took his left arm firmly; Straik seized the other, the mauled arm. Squealing and shivering with pain, Filostrato accompanied them perforce. But worse awaited him. He was not an initiate, he knew nothing of the dark eldils. He believed that his skill had really kept Alcasan's brain alive. Hence, even in his pain, he cried out with horror when he found the other two drawing him through the ante-room of the Head and into the Head's presence without pausing for any of those antiseptic preparations which he had always imposed on his colleagues. He tried vainly to tell them that one moment of such carelessness might undo all his work. But this time it was in the room itself that his conductors began undressing. And this time they took off all their clothes.

They plucked off his too. When the right sleeve, stiff with blood, would not move, Wither got a knife from the ante-room and ripped it. In the end, the three men stood naked before the Head—gaunt, big-boned Straik; Filostrato, a wobbling mountain of fat; Wither, an obscene senility. Then the high ridge of terror from which Filostrato was never again to descend, was reached; for what he thought impossible began to happen. No one had read the dials, adjusted the pressures, or turned on the air and the artificial saliva. Yet words came out of the dry gaping mouth of the dead man's head. "Adore!" it said.

Filostrato felt his companions forcing his body forwards, then up again, then forwards and downwards a second time. He was compelled to bob up and down in rhythmic obeisance, the others meanwhile doing the same. Almost the last thing he saw on earth was the skinny folds on Wither's neck shaking like the wattles of a turkey-cock. Almost the last thing he heard was Wither beginning to chant. Then Straik joined in. Then, horribly, he found he was singing himself:

> *Ouroborindra !*
> *Ouroborindra !*
> *Ouroborindra ba-ba-hee !*

But not for long. "Another," said the voice, "give me another head." Filostrato knew at once why they were forcing him to a certain place in the wall. He had devised it all himself. In the wall that separated the Head's room from the ante-chamber there was a little shutter. When drawn back it revealed a window in the wall, and a sash to that window which could fall quickly and heavily. But the sash was a knife. The little guillotine had not been meant to be used like this. They were going to murder him uselessly, unscientifically. If he were doing it to one of them all would have been different; everything would have been prepared weeks beforehand—the temperature of both rooms exactly right, the blade sterilised, the attachments all ready to be made almost before the head was severed. He had even calculated what changes the terror of the victim would probably make in his blood pressure; the artificial blood-stream would be arranged accordingly, so as to take over its work with the least possible breach of continuity. His last thought was that he had underestimated the terror.

The two initiates, red from top to toe, gazed at each other, breathing heavily. Almost before the fat dead legs and buttocks of the Italian had ceased quivering, they were driven to begin the ritual again:

> *Ouroborindra !*
> *Ouroborindra !*
> *Ouroborindra ba-ba-hee !*

The same thought struck both of them at one moment: "It will ask for another." And Straik remembered that Wither had that knife. He wrenched himself free from the rhythm with a frightful effort: claws seemed to be tearing his chest from inside. Wither saw what he meant to do. As Straik bolted, Wither was already after him. Straik reached the ante-room, slipped in Filostrato's blood. Wither slashed repeatedly with his knife. He had not strength to cut through the neck, but he had killed the man. He stood up, pains gnawing at his old man's heart. Then he saw the Italian's head lying on the floor. It seemed to him good to pick it up and carry it into the inner room: show it to the original Head. He did so. Then he realised that something was moving in the ante-room. Could it be that they had not shut the outer door? He could not remember. They had come in forcing Filostrato along between them; it was possible . . . everything had been so abnormal. He put down his burden—carefully, almost courteously, even now—and stepped towards the door between the two rooms. Next moment he drew back. A huge bear, rising to its hind legs as he came in sight of it, had met him in the doorway—its mouth open, its eyes flaming, its fore-paws spread out as if for an embrace. Was this what Straik had become? He knew (though even now he could not attend to it) that he was on the very frontier of a world where such things could happen.

5

No one at Belbury that night had been cooler than Feverstone. He was neither an initiate like Wither nor a dupe like Filostrato. He knew about the Macrobes, but it wasn't the sort of thing he was interested in. He knew that the Belbury scheme might not work, but he knew that if it didn't he would get out in time. He had a dozen lines of retreat kept open. He had also a perfectly clear conscience and had played no tricks with his mind. He had never slandered another man except to get his job, never cheated except because he wanted money, never really disliked people unless they bored him. He saw at a very early stage that something was going wrong. One had to guess how far wrong. Was this the end of Belbury? If so, he must get back to Edgestow and work up the position he had already prepared for himself as the protector of the University against the N.I.C.E. On the other hand, if there were any chance of figuring as the man who had saved Belbury at a moment of crisis, that would be definitely the better line. He would wait as long as it was safe. And he waited a long time. He found a hatch through which hot dishes were passed from the kitchen passage into the dining room. He got through it and watched the scene. His nerves were excellent and he thought he could pull and bolt the shutter in time if any dangerous animal made for the hatch. He stood there during the whole massacre, his eyes bright, something like a smile on his face, smoking endless cigarettes and drumming with his hard fingers on the sill of the hatch. When it was all over he said to himself, "Well, I'm damned!" It had certainly been a most extraordinary show.

The beasts had all streaked away somewhere. He knew there was a chance of meeting one or two of them in the passages, but he'd have to risk that. Danger—in moderation—acted on him like a tonic. He worked his way to the back of the house and into the garage; it looked as if he must go to Edgestow at once. He could not find his car in the garage—indeed, there were far fewer cars than he had expected. Apparently several other people had had the idea of getting away while the going was good, and his own car had been stolen. He felt no resentment, and set about finding another of the same make. It took him a longish time, and when he had found one he had considerable difficulty in starting her up. The night was cold—going to snow, he thought. He scowled, for the first time that night; he hated snow. It was after two o'clock when he got going.

Just before he started he had the odd impression that someone had got into the back of the car behind him. "Who's that?" he asked sharply. He decided to get out and see. But to his surprise his body did not obey this decision: instead it drove the car out of the garage and round to the front and out into the road. The snow was definitely falling by now. He found he could not turn his head and could not stop driving. He was going ridiculously fast, too, in this damned snow. He had no choice. He'd often heard of cars being driven from the back seat, but now it seemed to be really happening. Then to his dismay he found he had left the road. The car, still at a reckless speed, was bumping and leaping along what was called Gipsy Lane or (by the educated) Wayland Street— the old Roman Road from Belbury to Edgestow, all grass and ruts. "Here! What the devil am I doing?" thought Feverstone. "Am I tight? I'll break my neck at this game if I don't look out!" But on the car went as if driven by one who regarded this track as an excellent road and the obvious route to Edgestow.

6

Frost had left the dining room a few minutes after Wither. He did not know where he was going or what he was about to do. For many years he had theoretically believed that all which appears in the mind as motive or intention is merely a by-product of what the body is doing. But for the last year or so—since he had been initiated—he had begun to taste as fact what he had long held as theory. Increasingly, his actions had been without motive. He did this and that, he said thus and thus, and did not know why. His mind was a mere spectator. He could not understand why that spectator should exist at all. He resented its existence, even while assuring himself that resentment also was merely a chemical phenomenon. The nearest thing to a human passion which still existed in him was a sort of cold fury against all who believed in the mind. There was no tolerating such an illusion. There were not, and must not be, such things as men. But never, until this evening, had he been quite so vividly aware that the body and its movements were the only reality, that the self which seemed to watch the body leaving the dining room and setting out for the chamber of the Head, was a nonentity. How infuriating that the body should have power thus to project a phantom self!

Thus the Frost whose existence Frost denied watched his body go into the ante-room, watched it pull up sharply at the sight of a naked and bloodied corpse. The chemical reaction called shock occurred. Frost stopped, turned the body over, and recognised Straik. A moment later his flashing *pince-nez* and pointed beard looked into the room of the Head itself. He hardly noticed that Wither and Filostrato lay there dead. His attention was fixed by something more serious. The bracket where the Head ought to have been was empty: the metal ring twisted, the rubber tubes tangled and broken. Then he noticed a head on the floor; stooped and examined it. It was Filostrato's. Of Alcasan's head he found no trace, unless some mess of broken bones beside Filostrato's were it.

Still not asking what he would do or why, Frost went to the garage. The whole place was silent and empty; the snow was thick on the ground by this. He came up with as many petrol tins as he could carry. He piled all the inflammables he could think of together in the Objective Room. Then he locked himself in by locking the outer door of the ante-room. Whatever it was that dictated his actions then compelled him to push the key into the speaking tube which communicated with the passage. When he had pushed it as far in as his fingers could reach, he took a pencil from his pocket and pushed with that. Presently he heard the clink of the key falling on the passage floor outside. That tiresome illusion, his consciousness, was screaming to protest; his body, even had he wished, had no power to attend to those screams. Like the clockwork figure he had chosen to be, his stiff body, now terribly cold, walked back into the Objective Room, poured out the petrol and threw a lighted match into the pile. Not till then did his controllers allow him to suspect that death itself might not after all cure the illusion of being a soul—nay, might prove the entry into a world where that illusion raged infinite and unchecked. Escape for the soul, if not for the body, was offered him. He became able to know (and simultaneously refused the knowledge) that he had been wrong from the beginning, that souls and personal responsibility existed. He half saw: he wholly hated. The physical torture of the burning was not fiercer than his hatred of that. With one supreme effort he flung himself back into his illusion. In that attitude eternity overtook him as sunrise in old tales overtakes and turns them into unchangeable stone.

17

Venus at St. Anne's

I

Daylight came with no visible sunrise as Mark was climbing to the highest ground in his journey. The white road, still virgin of human traffic, showed the footprints of here and there a bird and here and there a rabbit, for the snow-shower was just then coming to its end in a flurry of larger and slower flakes. A big lorry, looking black and warm in that landscape, overtook him. The man put out his head. "Going Birmingham way, mate?" he asked. "Roughly," said Mark. "At least I'm going to St. Anne's." "Where's that then?" said the driver. "Up on the hill behind Pennington," said Mark. "Ah," said the man, "I could take you to the corner. Save you a bit." Mark got in beside him.

It was mid-morning when the man dropped him at a corner beside a little country hotel. The snow had all lain and there was more in the sky and the day was extremely silent. Mark went into the little hotel and found a kind elderly landlady. He had a hot bath and a capital breakfast and then went to sleep in a chair before a roaring fire. He did not wake till about four. He reckoned he was only a few miles from St. Anne's, and decided to have tea before he set out. He had tea. At the landlady's suggestion he had a boiled egg with his tea. Two shelves in the little sitting room were filled with bound volumes of *The Strand*. In one of these he found a serial children's story which he had begun to read as a child but abandoned because his tenth birthday came when he was half way through it and he was ashamed to read it after that. Now, he chased it from volume to volume till he had finished it. It was good. The grown-up stories to which, after his tenth birthday, he had turned instead of it, now seemed to him, except for *Sherlock Holmes,* to be rubbish. "I suppose I must get on soon," he said to himself.

His slight reluctance to do so did not proceed from weariness—he felt, indeed, perfectly rested and better than he had felt for several weeks—but from a sort of shyness. He was going to see Jane: and Denniston: and (probably) the Dimbles as well. In fact, he was going to see Jane in what he now felt to be her proper world. But not his. For he now thought that with all his life-long eagerness to reach an inner circle he had chosen the *wrong* circle. Jane was where she belonged. He was going to be admitted only out of kindness, because Jane had been fool enough to marry him. He did not resent it, but he felt shy. He saw himself as this new circle must see him—as one more little vulgarian, just like the Steeles and the Cossers, dull, inconspicuous, frightened, calculating, cold. He wondered vaguely why he was like that. How did other people—people like Denniston or Dimble—find it so easy to saunter through the world with all their muscles relaxed and a careless eye roving the horizon, bubbling over with fancy and humour, sensitive to beauty, not continually on their guard and not needing to be? What was the secret of that fine, easy laughter which he could not by any efforts imitate? Everything about them was different. They could not even fling themselves into chairs without suggesting by the very posture of their limbs a certain lordliness, a leonine indolence. There was elbow-room in their lives, as there had never been in his. They were Hearts: he was only a Spade. Still, he must be getting on . . . Of course, Jane was a Heart. He must give her her freedom. It would be quite unjust to think that his love for her had been basely sensual. Love, Plato says, is the son of Want. Mark's body knew better than his mind had known till recently, and even his sensual desires were the true index of something which he lacked and Jane had to give. When she first crossed the dry and dusty world which his mind inhabited she had been like a spring shower; in opening himself to it he had not been mistaken. He had gone wrong only in assuming that marriage, by itself, gave him either power or title to appropriate that freshness. As he now saw, one might as well have thought one could buy a sunset by buying the field from which one had seen it.

He rang the bell and asked for his bill.

2

That same afternoon Mother Dimble and the three girls were upstairs in the big room which occupied nearly the whole top floor of one wing at the Manor, and which the Director called the Wardrobe. If you had glanced in, you would have thought for one moment that they were not in a room at all but in some kind of forest—a tropical forest glowing with bright colours. A second glance and you might have thought they were in one of those delightful upper rooms at a big shop where carpets standing on end and rich stuffs hanging from the roof make a kind of woven forest of their own. In fact, they were standing amidst a collection of robes of state—dozens of robes which hung, each separate, from its little pillar of wood.

"That would do beautifully for you, Ivy," said Mother Dimble lifting with one hand the fold of a vividly green mantle over which thin twists and spirals of gold played in a festive pattern. "Come, Ivy," she continued, "don't you like it? You're not still fretting about Tom, are you? Hasn't the Director told you he'll be here tonight or tomorrow mid-day, at the latest?"

Ivy looked at her with troubled eyes.

"'Tisn't that," she said. "Where'll the Director himself be?"

"But you can't want him to stay, Ivy," said Camilla, "not in continual pain. And his work will be done—if all goes well at Edgestow."

"He has longed to go back to Perelandra," said Mother Dimble. "He's—sort of home-sick. Always, always . . . I could see it in his eyes."

"Will that Merlin man come back here?" asked Ivy.

"I don't think so," said Jane. "I don't think either he or the Director expected him to. And then my dream last night. It looked as if he was on fire . . . I don't mean burning, you know, but light—all sorts of lights in the most curious colours shooting out of him and running up and down him. That was the last thing I saw: Merlin standing there like a kind of pillar and all those dreadful things happening all round him. And you could see in his face that he was a man used up to the last drop, if you know what I mean—that he'd fall to pieces the moment the powers let him go."

"We're not getting on with choosing our dresses for tonight."

"What is it made of?" said Camilla, fingering and then smelling the green mantle. It was a question worth asking. It was not in the least transparent yet all sorts of lights and shades dwelled in its rippling folds and it flowed through Camilla's hands like a waterfall. Ivy became interested.

"Gor!" she said. "However much a yard would it be?"

"There," said Mother Dimble as she draped it skilfully round Ivy. Then she said, "Oh!" in genuine amazement. All three stood back from Ivy staring at her with delight. The commonplace had not exactly gone from her form and face, the robe had taken it up, as a great composer takes up a folk tune and tosses it like a ball through his symphony and makes of it a marvel, yet leaves it still itself. A "pert fairy" or "dapper elf," a small though perfect sprightliness, stood before them: but still recognisably Ivy Maggs.

"Isn't that like a man!" exclaimed Mrs. Dimble. "There's not a mirror in the room."

"I don't believe we were meant to see ourselves," said Jane. "He said something about being mirrors enough to see another."

"I would just like to see what I'm like at the back," said Ivy.

"Now Camilla," said Mother Dimble. "There's no puzzle about you. This is obviously your one."

"Oh, do you think *that* one?" said Camilla.

"Yes, of course," said Jane.

"You'll look ever so nice in that," said Ivy. It was a long slender thing which looked like steel in colour though it was soft as foam to the touch. It wrapped itself close about her loins and flowed out in a glancing train at her heels. "Like a mermaid," thought Jane; and then, "like a Valkyrie."

"I'm afraid," said Mother Dimble, "you must wear a coronet with that one."

"Wouldn't that be rather . . . ?"

But Mother Dimble was already setting it on her head. That reverence (it need have nothing to do with money value) which nearly all women feel for jewelry hushed three of them for a moment. There were perhaps no such diamonds in England. The splendour was fabulous, preposterous.

"What are you all staring at?" asked Camilla who had seen but one flash as the crown was raised in Mrs. Dimble's hands and did not know that she stood "like starlight, in the spoils of provinces."

"Are they real?" said Ivy.

"Where did they come from, Mother Dimble?" asked Jane.

"Treasure of Logres, dears, treasures of Logres," said Mrs. Dimble. "Perhaps from beyond the Moon or before the flood. Now Jane."

Jane could see nothing specially appropriate in the robe which the others agreed in putting on her. Blue was, indeed, her colour but she had thought of something a little more austere and dignified. Left to her own judgment, she would have called this a little "fussy." But when she saw the others all clap their hands, she submitted. Indeed, it did not now occur to her to do otherwise and the whole matter was forgotten a moment later in the excitement of choosing a robe for Mother Dimble.

"Something quiet," she said. "I'm an old woman and I don't want to be made ridiculous."

"This wouldn't do at all," said Camilla, walking down the long row of hanging splendours, herself like a meteor as she passed against that background of purple and gold and scarlet and soft snow and elusive opal, of fur, silk, velvet, taffeta and brocade. "That's lovely," she said. "But not for you. And oh!—look at that. But it wouldn't do. I don't see anything . . ."

"Here! Oh, do come and look! Come here," cried Ivy as if she were afraid her discovery would run away unless the others attended to it quickly.

"Oh! Yes, yes indeed," said Jane.

"Certainly," said Camilla.

"Put it on, Mother Dimble," said Ivy. "You know you got to." It was of that almost tyrannous flame colour which Jane had seen in her vision down in the lodge, but differently cut, with fur about the great copper brooch that clasped the throat, with long sleeves and hangings from them. And there went with it a many-cornered cap. And they had no sooner clasped the robe than all were astonished, none more than Jane, though indeed she had had best reason to foresee the result. For now this provincial wife of a rather obscure scholar, this respectable and barren woman with grey hair and double chin, stood before her, not to be mistaken, as a kind of priestess or sybil, the servant of some prehistoric goddess of fertility—an old tribal matriarch, mother of mothers, grave, formidable, and august. A long staff, curiously carved as if a snake twined up it, was apparently part of the costume: they put it in her hand.

"Am I awful?" said Mother Dimble looking in turn at the three silent faces.

"You look lovely," said Ivy.

"It is exactly right," said Camilla.

Jane took up the old lady's hand and kissed it. "Darling," she said, "*aweful,* in the old sense, is just what you *do* look."

"What are the men going to wear?" asked Camilla suddenly.

"They can't very well go in fancy dress, can they?" said Ivy. "Not if they're cooking and bringing things in and out all the time. And I must say, if this is to be the last night and all, I do think we ought to have done the dinner anyway. Let them do as they like about the wine. And what they'll do with that goose is more than I like to think, because I don't believe that Mr. MacPhee ever roasted a bird in his life, whatever he says."

"They can't spoil the oysters anyway," said Camilla.

"That's right," said Ivy. "Nor the plum pudding, not really. Still, I'd like just to go down and take a look."

"You'd better not," said Jane with a laugh. "You know what he's like when he's in charge in the kitchen."

"I'm not afraid of *him,*" said Ivy, almost, but not quite, putting out her tongue. And in her present dress the gesture was not uncomely.

"You needn't be in the least worried about the dinner, girls," said Mother Dimble. "He will do it very well. Always provided he and my husband don't get into a philosophical argument just when they ought to be dishing up. Let's go and enjoy ourselves. How very warm it is in here."

"'s lovely," said Ivy.

At that moment the whole room shook from end to end.

"What on earth's that?" said Jane.

"If the war was still on I'd have said it was a bomb," said Ivy.

"Come and look," said Camilla who had regained her composure sooner than any of the others and was now at the window which looked west towards the valley of the Wynd. "Oh, look!" she said again. "No. It's not fire. And it's not searchlights. And it's not forked lightning. Ugh! . . . There's another shock. And there . . . Look at that. It's as bright as day there beyond the Church. What am I talking about, it's only three o'clock. It's brighter than day. And the heat!"

"It has begun," said Mother Dimble.

3

At about the same time that morning when Mark had climbed into the lorry, Feverstone, not much hurt but a good deal shaken, climbed out of the stolen car. That car had ended its course upside down in a deep ditch, and Feverstone, always ready to look on the bright side, reflected as he extricated himself that things might have been worse—it might have been his own car. The snow was deep in the ditch and he was very wet. As he stood up and looked about him he saw that he was not alone. A tall massive figure in a black cassock was before him, about five yards distant. Its back was towards him and it was already walking steadily away. "Hi!" shouted Feverstone. The other turned and looked at him in silence for a second or two; then it resumed its walk. Feverstone felt at once that this was not the sort of man he would get on with—in fact, he had never liked the look of anyone less. Nor could he, in his broken and soaking pumps, follow the four-mile-an-hour stride of those booted feet. He did not attempt it. The black figure came to a gate, there stopped and made a whinnying noise. He was apparently talking to a horse across the gate. Next moment (Feverstone did not quite see how it happened) the man was over the gate and on the horse's back and off at a canter across a wide field that rose milk white to the sky-line.

Feverstone had no idea where he was, but clearly the first thing to do was to reach a road. It took him much longer than he expected. It was not freezing now and deep puddles lay hidden beneath the snow in many places. At the bottom of the first hill he came to such a morass that he was driven to abandon the track of the Roman road and try striking across the fields. The decision was fatal. It kept him for two hours looking for gaps in hedges, and trying to reach things that looked like roads from a distance but turned out to be nothing of the sort when one reached them. He had always hated the country and always hated weather and he was not at any time fond of walking.

Near twelve o'clock he found a road with no signposts that led him an hour later into a main road. Here, thank heavens, there was a fair amount of traffic, both cars and pedestrians, all going one way. The first three cars took no notice of his signals. The fourth stopped. "Quick. In you get," said the driver. "Going to Edgestow?" asked Feverstone, his hand on the door. "Good Lord, no!" said the other. "*There's*

Edgestow!" (and he pointed behind him)—"if you want to go *there*." The man seemed surprised and considerably excited.

In the end there was nothing for it but walking. Every vehicle was going away from Edgestow, none going towards it. Feverstone was a little surprised. He knew all about the exodus (indeed, it had been part of his plan to clear the city as far as possible) but he had supposed it would be over by now. But all that afternoon as he splashed and slipped through the churned snow the fugitives were still passing him. We have (naturally) hardly any first-hand evidence for what happened in Edgestow that afternoon and evening. But we have plenty of stories as to how so many people came to leave it at the last moment. They filled the papers for weeks and lingered in private talks for months, and in the end became a joke. "No, I *don't* want to hear how you got out of Edgestow," came to be a catch-phrase. But behind all the exaggerations there remains the undoubted truth that a quite astonishing number of citizens left the town just in time. One had had a message from a dying father; another had decided quite suddenly, and he couldn't just say why, to go and take a little holiday; another went because the pipes in his house had been burst by the frost and he thought he might as well go away till they were put right. Not a few had gone because of some trivial event which seemed to them an omen—a dream, a broken looking-glass, tea-leaves in a cup. Omens of a more ancient kind had also revived during this crisis. One had heard his donkey, another her cat, say "as clear as clear": "*Go away.*" And hundreds were still leaving for the old reason—because their houses had been taken from them, their livelihood destroyed, and their liberties threatened by the Institutional Police.

It was at about four o'clock that Feverstone found himself flung on his face. That was the first shock. They continued, increasing in frequency, during the hours that followed—horrible shudderings, and soon heavings, of the earth, and a growing murmur of wide-spread subterranean noise. The temperature began to rise. Snow was disappearing in every direction and at times he was knee deep in water. Haze from the melting snow filled the air. When he reached the brow of the last steep descent into Edgestow he could see nothing of the city: only fog through which extraordinary coruscations of light came up to him. Another shock sent him sprawling. He now decided not to go down: he would turn and follow the traffic—work over to the railway and try to get to London. The picture of a steaming bath at his club, of himself at the fender of the smoking room telling this whole story, rose in his mind. It would be something to have survived both Belbury and Bracton. He had survived a good many things in his day and believed in his luck.

He was already a few paces down the hill when he made this decision, and he turned at once. But instead of going up he found he was still descending. As if he were in shale on a mountain slope, instead of on a metalled road, the ground slipped away backwards where he trod on it. When he arrested his descent he was thirty yards lower. He began again. This time he was flung off his feet, rolled head over heels, stones, earth, grass, and water pouring over him and round him in riotous confusion. It was as when a great wave overtakes you while you are bathing, but this time it was an earth wave. He got to his feet once again; set his face to the hill. Behind, the valley seemed to have turned into Hell. The pit of fog had been ignited and burned with blinding violet flame, water was roaring somewhere, buildings crashing, mobs shouting. The hill in front of him was in ruins—no trace of road, hedge, or field, only a cataract of loose raw earth. It was also far steeper than it had been. His mouth and hair and nostrils were full of earth. The slope was growing steeper as he looked at it. The ridge heaved up and up. Then the whole wave of earth rose, arched, trembled, and with all its weight and noise poured down on him.

4

"Why Logres, Sir?" said Camilla.

Dinner was over at St. Anne's and they sat at their wine in a circle about the dining-room fire. As Mrs. Dimble had prophesied, the men had cooked it very well; only after their serving was over and the board cleared had they put on their festal garments. Now all sat at their ease and all diversely splendid: Ransom crowned, at the right of the hearth; Grace Ironwood, in black and silver, opposite him. It was so warm that they had let the fire burn low, and in the candlelight the court dresses seemed to glow of themselves.

"Tell them, Dimble," said Ransom. "I will not talk much from now on."

"Are you tired, Sir?" said Grace. "Is the pain bad?"

"No, Grace," he replied. "It isn't that. But now that it's so very nearly time for me to go, all this begins to feel like a dream. A happy dream, you understand: all of it, even the pain. I want to taste every drop. I feel as though it would be dissolved if I talked much."

"I suppose you *got* to go, Sir?" said Ivy.

"My dear," said he, "what else is there to do? I have not grown a day or an hour older since I came back from Perelandra. There is no natural death to look forward to. The wound will only be healed in the world where it was got."

"All this has the disadvantage of being clean contrary to the observed laws of Nature," observed MacPhee. The Director smiled without speaking, as a man who refuses to be drawn.

"It is not contrary to the laws of Nature," said a voice from the corner where Grace Ironwood sat, almost invisible in the shadows. "You are quite right. The laws of the universe are never broken. Your mistake is to think that the little regularities we have observed on one planet for a few hundred years are the real unbreakable laws; whereas they are only the remote results which the true laws bring about more often than not; as a kind of accident."

"Shakespeare never breaks the real laws of poetry," put in Dimble. "But by following them he breaks every now and then the little regularities which critics mistake for the real laws. Then the little critics call it a 'licence.' But there's nothing licentious about it to Shakespeare."

"And that," said Denniston, "is why nothing in Nature is *quite* regular. There are always exceptions. A good average uniformity, but not complete."

"Not many exceptions to the law of death have come my way," observed MacPhee.

"And *how*," said Grace with much emphasis, "how should *you* expect to be there on more than one such occasion? Were you a friend of Arthur's or Barbarossa's? Did you know Enoch or Elijah?"

"Do you mean," said Jane, "that the Director . . . the Pendragon . . . is going where they went?"

"He will be with Arthur, certainly," said Dimble. "I can't answer for the rest. There are people who have never died. We do not yet know why. We know a little more than we did about the How. There are many places in the universe—I mean, this same physical universe in which our planet moves—where an organism can last practically forever. Where Arthur is, we know."

"Where?" said Camilla.

"In the Third Heaven, in Perelandra. In Aphallin, the distant island which the descendants of Tor and Tinidril will not find for a hundred centuries. Perhaps alone?" . . . he hesitated and looked at Ransom who shook his head.

"And that is where Logres comes in, is it?" said Camilla. "Because he will be with Arthur?"

Dimble was silent for a few minutes arranging and rearranging the fruit-knife and fruit-fork on his plate.

"It all began," he said, "when we discovered that the Arthurian story is mostly true history. There was a moment in the Sixth Century when something that is always trying to break through into this country nearly succeeded. Logres was our name for it—it will do as well as another. And then . . . gradually we began to see all English history in a new way. We discovered the haunting."

"What haunting?" asked Camilla.

"How something we may call Britain is always haunted by something we may call Logres. Haven't you noticed that we are two countries? After every Arthur, a Mordred; behind every Milton, a Cromwell: a nation of poets, a nation of shopkeepers: the home of Sidney—and of Cecil Rhodes. Is it any wonder they call us hypocrites? But what they mistake for hypocrisy is really the struggle between Logres and Britain."

He paused and took a sip of wine before proceeding.

"It was long afterwards," he said, "after the Director had returned from the Third Heaven, that we were told a little more. This haunting turned out to be not only from the other side of the invisible wall. Ransom was summoned to the bedside of an old man then dying in Cumberland. His name would mean nothing to you if I told it. That man was the Pendragon, the successor of Arthur and Uther and Cassibelaun. Then we learned the truth. There has been a secret Logres in the very heart of Britain all these years: an unbroken succession of Pendragons. That old man was the seventy-eighth from Arthur: our Director received from him the office and the blessings; tomorrow we shall know, or tonight, who is to be the eightieth. Some of the Pendragons are well known to history, though not under that name. Others you have never heard of. But in every age they and the little Logres which gathered round them have been the fingers which gave the tiny shove or the almost imperceptible pull, to prod England out of the drunken sleep or to draw her back from the final outrage into which Britain tempted her."

368 • C. S. LEWIS

"This new history of yours," said MacPhee, "is a wee bit lacking in documents."

"It has plenty," said Dimble with a smile. "But you do not know the language they're written in. When the history of these last few months comes to be written in *your* language, and printed, and taught in schools, there will be no mention in it of you and me, nor of Merlin and the Pendragon and the Planets. And yet in these months Britain rebelled most dangerously against Logres and was defeated only just in time."

"Aye," said MacPhee, "and it could be right good history without mentioning you and me or most of those present. I'd be greatly obliged if any one would tell me what we *have* done—always apart from feeding the pigs and raising some very decent vegetables."

"You have done what was required of you," said the Director. "You have obeyed and waited. It will often happen like that. As one of the modern authors has told us, the altar must often be built in one place in order that the fire from heaven may descend somewhere else. But don't jump to conclusions. You may have plenty of work to do before a month is passed. Britain has lost a battle, but she will rise again."

"So that, meanwhile, is England," said Mother Dimble. "Just this swaying to and fro between Logres and Britain?"

"Yes," said her husband. "Don't you feel it? The very quality of England. If we've got an ass's head, it is by walking in a fairy wood. We've heard something better than we can do, but can't quite forget it . . . can't you see it in everything English—a kind of awkward grace, a humble, humorous incompleteness? How right Sam Weller was when he called Mr. Pickwick an angel in gaiters! Everything here is either better or worse than—"

"Dimble!" said Ransom. Dimble, whose tone had become a little impassioned, stopped and looked towards him. He hesitated and (as Jane thought) almost blushed before he began again.

"You're right, Sir," he said with a smile. "I was forgetting what you have warned me always to remember. This haunting is no peculiarity of ours. Every people has its own haunter. There's no special privilege for England—no nonsense about a chosen nation. We speak about Logres because it is *our* haunting, the one we know about."

"But this," said MacPhee, "seems a very round-about way of saying that there's good and bad men everywhere."

"It's not a way of saying that at all," answered Dimble. "You see, MacPhee, if one is thinking simply of goodness in the abstract, one soon reaches the fatal idea of something standardised—some common kind of life to which all nations ought to progress. Of course, there are universal rules to which all goodness must conform. But that's only the grammar of virtue. It's not there that the sap is. He doesn't make two blades of grass the same: how much less two saints, two nations, two angels. The whole work of healing Tellus depends on nursing that little spark, on incarnating that ghost, which is still alive in every real people, and different in each. When Logres really dominates Britain, when the goddess Reason, the divine clearness, is really enthroned in France, when the order of Heaven is really followed in China—why, then it will be spring. But meantime, our concern is with Logres. We've got Britain down but who knows how long we can hold her down? Edgestow will not recover from what is happening to her tonight. But there will be other Edgestows."

"I wanted to ask about Edgestow," said Mother Dimble. "Aren't Merlin and the eldils a trifle . . . well, *wholesale*. Did *all* Edgestow deserve to be wiped out?"

"Who are you lamenting?" said MacPhee. "The jobbing town council that'd have sold their own wives and daughters to bring the N.I.C.E. to Edgestow?"

"Well, I don't know much about them," said she. "But in the University. Even Bracton itself. We all knew it was a horrible College, of course. But did they really mean any great harm with all their fussy little intrigues? Wasn't it more *silly* than anything else?"

"Och aye," said MacPhee. "They were only playing themselves. Kittens letting on to be tigers. But there was a real tiger about and their play ended by letting her in. They've no call to complain if when the hunter's after her he lets them have a bit of a lead in their guts too. It'll learn them not to keep bad company."

"Well, then, the Fellows of other colleges. What about Northumberland and Duke's?"

"I know," said Denniston. "One's sorry for a man like Churchwood. I knew him well; he was an old dear. All his lectures were devoted to proving the impossibility of ethics, though in private life he'd walked ten miles rather than leave a penny debt unpaid. But all the same . . . was there a single doctrine practised at Belbury which hadn't been preached by some lecturer at Edgestow? Oh, of course, they never thought any one would *act* on their theories! No one was more astonished than they when what they'd been talking of for years suddenly took on reality. But it was their own child coming back to them: grown up and unrecognisable, but their own."

"I'm afraid it's all true, my dear," said Dimble. "*Trahison des clercs.* None of us is quite innocent."

"That's nonsense, Cecil," said Mrs. Dimble.

"You are all forgetting," said Grace, "that nearly everyone except the very good (who were ripe for fair dismissal) and the very bad, had already left Edgestow. But I agree with Arthur. Those who have forgotten Logres sink into Britain. Those who call for Nonsense will find that it comes."

At that moment she was interrupted. A clawing and whining noise at the door had become audible.

"Open the door, Arthur," said Ransom. A moment later the whole party rose to its feet with cries of welcome, for the new arrival was Mr. Bultitude.

"Oh, I never *did*," said Ivy. "The pore thing! And all over snow too. I'll just take him down to the kitchen and get him something to eat. Wherever have you been, you bad thing? Eh? Just look at the state you're in."

5

For the third time in ten minutes the train gave a violent lurch and came to a standstill. This time the shock put all the lights out.

"This is really getting a bit too bad," said a voice in the darkness. The four other passengers in the first-class compartment recognised it as belonging to the well-bred, bulky man in the brown suit; the well-informed man who at earlier stages of the journey had told everyone else where they ought to change and why one now reached Sterk without going through Stratford and who it was that really controlled the line.

"It's serious for me," said the same voice. "I ought to be in Edgestow by now." He got up, opened the window, and stared out into the darkness. Presently, one of the other passengers complained of the cold. He shut the window and sat down.

"We've already been here for ten minutes," he said presently.

"Excuse me. Twelve," said another passenger.

Still the train did not move. The noise of two men quarreling in a neighbouring compartment became audible.

Then silence followed again.

Suddenly a shock flung them all together in the darkness. It was as if the train, going at full speed, had been unskilfully pulled up.

"What the devil's that?" said one.

"Open the doors."

"Has there been a collision?"

"It's all right," said the well-informed man in a loud, calm voice. "Putting on another engine. And doing it very badly. It's all these new engine drivers they've got in lately."

"Hullo!" said someone. "We're moving."

Slow and grunting, the train began to go.

"It takes its time getting up speed," said someone.

"Oh, you'll find it'll start making up for lost time in a minute," said the well-informed man.

"I wish they'd put the lights on again," said a woman's voice.

"We're *not* getting up speed," said another.

"We're losing it. Damn it! Are we stopping again?"

"No. We're still moving—oh!!"—once more a violent shock hit them. It was worse than the last one. For nearly a minute everything seemed to be rocking and rattling.

"This is outrageous," exclaimed the well-informed man, once more opening the window. This time he was more fortunate. A dark figure waving a lantern was walking past beneath him.

"Hi! Porter! Guard!" he bellowed.

"It's all right, ladies and gentlemen, it's all right, keep your seats," shouted the dark figure, marching past and ignoring him.

"There's no good letting all that cold air in, Sir," said the passenger next to the window.

"There's some sort of light ahead," said the well-informed man.

"Signal against us?" asked another.

"No. Not a bit like that. The whole sky's lit up. Like a fire, or like searchlights."

"I don't care what it's like," said the chilly man. "If only—oh!"

Another shock. And then, far away in the darkness, vague disastrous noise. The train began to move again, still slowly, as if it were groping its way.

"I'll make a row about this," said the well-informed man. "It's a scandal."

About half an hour later the lighted platform of Sterk slowly loomed alongside.

"Station Announcer calling," said a voice. "Please keep your seats for an important announcement. Slight earthquake shock and floods have rendered the line to Edgestow impassable. No details available. Passengers for Edgestow are advised . . ."

The well-informed man, who was Curry, got out. Such a man always knows all the officials on a railway and in a few minutes he was standing by the fire in the ticket collector's office getting a further and private report of the disaster.

"Well, we don't exactly know yet, Mr. Curry," said the man. "There's been nothing coming through for about an hour. It's very bad, you know. They're putting the best face on it they can. There's never been an earthquake like it in England from what I can hear. And there's the floods too. No, Sir, I'm afraid you'll find nothing of Bracton College. All that part of the town went almost at once. It began there, I understand. I don't know what the casualties'll be. I'm glad I got my old Dad out last week."

Curry always in later years regarded this as one of the turning points of his life. He had not up till then been a religious man. But the word that now instantly came into his mind was "Providential." You couldn't really look at it any other way. He'd been within an ace of taking the earlier train; and if he had . . . why he'd have been a dead man by now. It made one think. The whole College wiped out! It would have to be rebuilt. There'd be a complete (or almost complete) new set of Fellows, a new Warden. It was Providential again that some responsible person should have been spared to deal with such a tremendous crisis. There couldn't be an ordinary election, of course. The College Visitor (who was the Lord Chancellor) would probably have to appoint a new Warden and then, in collaboration with him, a nucleus of new Fellows. The more he thought of it the more fully Curry realised that the whole shaping of the future College rested with the sole survivor. It was almost like being a second founder. Providential—providential. He saw already in imagination the portrait of that second founder in the new-built Hall, his statue in the new-built quadrangle, the long, long chapter consecrated to him in the College History. All this time, without the least hypocrisy, habit and instinct had given his shoulders just such a droop, his eyes such a solemn sternness, his brow such a noble gravity, as a man of good feeling might be expected to exhibit on hearing such news. The ticket-collector was greatly edified. "You could see he felt it bad," as he said afterwards. "But he could take it. He's a fine old chap."

"When is the next train to London?" asked Curry. "I must be in town first thing tomorrow morning."

6

Ivy Maggs, it will be remembered, had left the dining room for the purpose of attending to Mr. Bultitude's comfort. It therefore surprised everyone when she returned in less than a minute with a wild expression on her face.

"Oh, come quick, someone. Come quick!" she gasped.

"There's a bear in the kitchen."

"A bear, Ivy?" said the Director. "But, of course—"

"Oh, I don't mean Mr. Bultitude, Sir. There's a strange bear; another one."

"Indeed!"

"And it's eaten up all what was left of the goose and half the ham and all the junket and now it's lying along the table eating everything as it goes along and wriggling from one dish to another and a breaking all the crockery. Oh, do come quick! There'll be nothing left."

"And what line is Mr. Bultitude taking about all this, Ivy?" asked Ransom.

"Well, that's what I want someone to come and see. He's carrying on something dreadful, Sir. I never seen anything like it. First of all he just stood lifting up his legs in a funny way as if he thought he could dance, which we all know he can't. But now he's got up on the dresser on his hind legs and there he's kind of bobbing up and down, making the awfullest noise—squeaking like—and he's put one foot into the plum pudding already and he's got his head all mixed up in the string of onions and I can't do *nothing* with him, really I can't."

"This is very odd behaviour for Mr. Bultitude. You don't think, my dear, that the stranger might be a *she* bear?"

"Oh, don't say that, Sir!" exclaimed Ivy with extreme dismay.

"I think that's the truth, Ivy. I strongly suspect that this is the future Mrs. Bultitude."

"It'll be the present Mrs. Bultitude if we sit here talking about it much longer," said MacPhee, rising to his feet.

"Oh, dear, what *shall* we do?" said Ivy.

"I am sure Mr. Bultitude is quite equal to the situation," replied the

Director. "At present, the lady is refreshing herself. *Sine Cerere et Baccho*, Dimble. We can trust them to manage their own affairs."

"No doubt, no doubt," said MacPhee. "But not in our kitchen."

"Ivy, my dear," said Ransom. "You must be very firm. Go into the kitchen and tell the strange bear I want to see her. You wouldn't be afraid, would you?"

"Afraid? Not me. I'll show her who's the Director here. Not that it isn't only natural for her."

"What's the matter with that jackdaw?" said Dr. Dimble.

"I think it's trying to get out," said Denniston. "Shall I open the window?"

"It's warm enough to have the window open anyway," said the Director. And as the window was opened Baron Korvo hopped out and there was a scuffle and a chattering just outside.

"Another love affair," said Mrs. Dimble. "It sounds as if Jack had found a Jill . . . What a delicious night!" she added. For as the curtain swelled and lifted over the open window all the freshness of a midsummer night seemed to be blowing into the room. At that moment, a little further off, came a sound of whinneying.

"Hullo!" said Denniston, "the old mare is excited too."

"Sh! Listen!" said Jane.

"That's a different horse," said Denniston.

"It's a stallion," said Camilla.

"This," said MacPhee with great emphasis, "is becoming indecent."

"On the contrary," said Ransom, "decent, in the old sense, *decens*, fitting, is just what it is. Venus herself is over St. Anne's."

"She comes more near the Earth than she was wont," quoted Dimble, "to make men mad."

"She is nearer than any astronomer knows," said Ransom. "The work at Edgestow is done, the other gods have withdrawn. She waits still and when she returns to her sphere I will ride with her."

Suddenly, in the semi-darkness Mrs. Dimble's voice cried sharply, "Look out! Look out! Cecil! I'm sorry. I can't stand bats. They'll get in my hair!" *Cheep cheep* went the voices of the two bats as they flickered to and fro above the candles. Because of their shadows they seemed to be four bats instead of two.

"You'd better go, Margaret," said the Director. "You and Cecil had better both go. I shall be gone very soon now. There is no need of long goodbyes."

"I really think I *must* go," said Mother Dimble. "I can't stand bats."

"Comfort Margaret, Cecil," said Ransom. "No. Do not stay. I'm not dying. Seeing people off is always folly. It's neither good mirth nor good sorrow."

"You mean us to go, Sir?" said Dimble.

"Go, my dear friends. *Urendi Maleldil.*"

He laid his hands on their heads; Cecil gave his arm to his wife and they went.

"Here she is, Sir," said Ivy Maggs re-entering the room a moment later, flushed and radiant. A bear waddled at her side, its muzzle white with junket and its cheeks sticky with gooseberry jam. "And—oh, Sir" she added.

"What is it, Ivy?" said the Director.

"Please, Sir, it's poor Tom. It's my husband. And if you don't mind—"

"You've given him something to eat and drink, I hope?"

"Well, yes, I have. There wouldn't have been nothing if those bears had been there much longer."

"What has Tom got, Ivy?"

"I gave him the cold pie and the pickles (he always was a great one for pickles) and the end of the cheese and a bottle of stout, and I've put the kettle on so as we can make ourselves—so as he can make himself a nice cup of tea. And he's enjoying it ever so, Sir, and he said would you mind him not coming up to say how d'you do because he never was much of a one for company, if you take my meaning."

All this time the strange bear had been standing perfectly still with its eyes fixed on the Director. Now he laid his hand on its flat head. "*Urendi Maleldil,*" he said. "You are a good bear. Go to your mate—but here he is," for at that moment the door which was already a little ajar was pushed further open to admit the inquiring and slightly anxious face of Mr. Bultitude. "Take her, Bultitude. But not in the house. Jane, open the other window, the French window. It is like a night in July." The window swung open and the two bears went blundering out into the warmth and the wetness. Everyone noticed how light it had become.

"Are those birds all daft that they're singing at quarter to twelve?" asked MacPhee.

"No," said Ransom. "They are sane. Now, Ivy, you want to go and talk to Tom. Mother Dimble has put you both in the little room half way up the stairs, not in the lodge after all."

"Oh, Sir," said Ivy and stopped. The Director leaned forward and laid his hand on her head. "Of course, you want to go," he said. "Why, he's hardly had time to see you in your new dress yet. Have you no kisses to give him?" he said and kissed her. "Then give him mine, which are not mine but by derivation. Don't cry. You are a good woman. Go and heal this man. *Urendi Maleldil*—we shall meet again."

"What's all yon squealing and squeaking?" said MacPhee. "I hope it's not the pigs got loose. For I tell you there's already as much carrying on about this house and garden as I can stand."

"I think it's hedgehogs," said Grace Ironwood.

"That last sound was somewhere in the house," said Jane.

"Listen!" said the Director, and for a short time all were still. Then his face relaxed into a smile. "It's my friends behind the wainscot," he said. "There are revels there too—

So geht es in Snützepützhaüsel
Da singen und tanzen die Maüsel!

"I suppose," said MacPhee drily, producing his snuff-box from under the ash-coloured and slightly monastic-looking robe in which, contrary to his judgment, the others had seen fit to clothe him, "I suppose we may think ourselves lucky that no giraffes, hippopotami, elephants, or the like have seen fit to—God almighty, what's that?" For as he spoke a long grey flexible tube came in between the swaying curtains and, passing over MacPhee's shoulder, helped itself to a bunch of bananas.

"In the name of Hell where's all them beasts coming from?" he said.

"They are the liberated prisoners from Belbury," said the Director. "She comes more near the Earth than she was wont to—to make Earth sane. Perelandra is all about us and Man is no longer isolated. We are now as we ought to be—between the angels who are our elder brothers and the beasts who are our jesters, servants and playfellows."

Whatever MacPhee was attempting to say in reply was drowned by an earsplitting noise from beyond the window.

"Elephants! Two of them," said Jane weakly. "Oh, the celery! And the rose beds!"

"By your leave, Mr. Director," said MacPhee sternly. "I'll just draw these curtains. You seem to forget there are ladies present."

"No," said Grace Ironwood in a voice as strong as his. "There will be nothing unfit for anyone to see. Draw them wider. How light it is! Brighter than moonlight: almost brighter than day. A great dome of light stands over the whole garden. Look! The elephants are dancing. How high they lift their feet. And they go round and round. And oh, look!— how they lift their trunks. And how ceremonial they are. It is like a minuet of giants. They are not like the other animals. They are a sort of good dæmons."

"They are moving away," said Camilla.

"They will be as private as human lovers," said the Director. "They are not common beasts."

"I think," said MacPhee, "I'll away down to my office and cast some accounts. I'd feel easier in my mind if I were inside and the door locked before any crocodiles or kangaroos start courting in the middle of all my files. There'd better be one man about the place keep his head this night for the rest of you are clean daft. Good night, ladies."

"Goodbye, MacPhee," said Ransom.

"No, no," said MacPhee, standing well back, but extending his hand. "You'll speak none of your blessings over me. If ever I take to religion, it won't be your kind. My uncle was Moderator of the General Assembly. But there's my hand. What you and I have seen together . . . but no matter for that. And I'll say this, Dr. Ransom, that with all your faults (and there's no man alive knows them better than myself), you are the best man, taking you by and large, that ever I knew or heard of. You are . . . you and I . . . but there are the ladies crying. I don't rightly know what I was going to say. I'm away this minute. Why would a man want to lengthen it? God bless you, Dr. Ransom. Ladies, I'll wish you a good night."

"Open all the windows," said Ransom. "The vessel in which I must ride is now almost within the air of this World."

"It is growing brighter every minute," said Denniston.

"Can we be with you to the very end?" said Jane.

"Child," said the Director, "you should not stay till then."

"Why, Sir?"

"You are waited for."

"Me, Sir?"

"Yes. Your husband is waiting for you in the Lodge. It was your own marriage chamber that you prepared. Should you not go to him?"

"Must I go *now*?"

"If you leave the decision with me, it is now that I would send you."

"Then I will go, Sir. But—but—am I a bear or a hedgehog?"

"More. But not less. Go in obedience and you will find love. You will have no more dreams. Have children instead. *Urendi Maleldil.*"

7

Long before he reached St. Anne's, Mark had come to realise that either he himself or else the world about him, was in a very strange condition. The journey took him longer than he expected, but that was perhaps fully accounted for by one or two mistakes that he made. Much harder to explain was the horror of light to the west, over Edgestow, and the throbbings and bouncings of the Earth. Then came a sudden warmth and the torrents of melted snow rolling down the hillside. Everything became a mist; and then, as the lights in the west vanished, this mist grew softly luminous in a different place—above him, as though the light rested on St. Anne's. And all the time he had the curious impression that things of very diverse shapes and sizes were slipping past him in the haze—animals, he thought. Perhaps it was all a dream; or perhaps it was the end of the world; or perhaps he was dead. But in spite of all perplexities, he was conscious of extreme well-being. His mind was ill at ease, but as for his body—health and youth and pleasure and longing seemed to be blowing towards him from the cloudy light upon the hill. He never doubted that he must keep on.

His mind was not at ease. He knew that he was going to meet Jane, and something was beginning to happen to him which ought to have happened to him far earlier. That same laboratory outlook upon love which had forestalled in Jane the humility of a wife, had equally forestalled in him, during what passed for courtship, the humility of a lover. Or if there had ever arisen in him at some wiser moment the sense of "Beauty too rich for use, for earth too dear," he had put it away from him. False theories, at once prosaic and fanciful, had made it seem to him a mood frousty, unrealistic, and outmoded. Now, belated, after all favours had been conceded, the unexpected misgiving was coming over him. He tried to shake it off. They were married, weren't they? And they were sensible, modern people? What could be more natural, more ordinary?

But then, certain moments of unforgettable failure in their short married life rose in his imagination. He had thought often enough of what he called Jane's "moods." This time at last he thought of his own clumsy importunity. And the thought would not go away. Inch by inch, all the lout and clown and clod-hopper in him was revealed to his own reluctant inspection; the coarse, male boor with horny hands and hobnailed shoes and beefsteak jaw, not rushing in—for that can be carried off—but blundering, sauntering, stumping in where great lovers, knights and poets, would have feared to tread. An image of Jane's skin, so smooth, so white (or so he now imagined it) that a child's kiss might make a mark on it, floated before him. How had he dared? Her driven snow, her music, her sacrosanctity, the very style of all her movements . . . how had he dared? And dared too with no sense of daring, nonchalantly, in careless stupidity! The very thoughts that crossed her face from moment to moment, all of them beyond his reach, made (had he but had the wit to see it) a hedge about her which such as he should never have had the temerity to pass. Yes, yes—of course, it was she who had allowed him to pass it: perhaps in luckless, misunderstanding pity. And he had taken blackguardly advantage of that noble error in her judgment; had behaved as if here native to that fenced garden and even its natural possessor.

All this, which should have been uneasy joy, was torment to him, for it came too late. He was discovering the hedge after he had plucked the rose, and not only plucked it but torn it all to pieces and crumpled it with hot, thumb-like, greedy fingers. How had he dared? And who that understood could forgive him? He knew now what he must look like in the eyes of her friends and equals. Seeing that picture, he grew hot to the forehead, alone there in the mist.

The word *Lady* had made no part of his vocabulary save as a pure form or else in mockery. He had laughed too soon.

Well, he would release her. She would be glad to be rid of him. Rightly glad. It would now almost have shocked him to believe otherwise. Ladies in some noble and spacious room, discoursing in cool ladyhood together, either with exquisite gravity or with silver laughter—how should they *not* be glad when the intruder had gone?—the loud-voiced or tongue-tied creature, all boots and hands, whose true place was in the stable. What should he do in such a room—where his very admiration could only be insult, his best attempts to be either grave or gay could only reveal unbridgeable misunderstanding? What he had called her coldness seemed now to be her patience. Whereof the memory scalded. For he loved her now. But it was all spoiled: too late to mend matters.

Suddenly the diffused light brightened and flushed. He looked up and perceived a great lady standing by a doorway in a wall. It was not Jane, not like Jane. It was larger, almost gigantic. It was not human, though it was like a woman divinely tall, part naked, part wrapped in a flame-coloured robe. Light came from it. The face was enigmatic, ruthless he thought, inhumanly beautiful. It was opening the door for him. He did not dare disobey ("Surely," he thought, "I must have died"), and he went in: found himself in some place of sweet smells and bright fires, with food and wine and a rich bed.

8

And Jane went out of the big house with the Director's kiss upon her lips and his words in her ears, into the liquid light and supernatural warmth of the garden and across the wet lawn (birds were everywhere) and past the see-saw and the greenhouse and the piggeries, going down all the time, down to the lodge, descending the ladder of humility. First she thought of the Director, then she thought of Maleldil. Then she thought of her obedience and the setting of each foot before the other became a kind of sacrificial ceremony. And she thought of children, and of pain and death. And now she was half way to the lodge, and thought of Mark and of all his sufferings. When she came to the lodge she was surprised to see it all dark and the door shut. As she stood at the door with one hand on the latch, a new thought came to her. How if Mark did not want her—not tonight, nor in that way, nor any time, nor in any way? How if Mark were not there after all? A great gap—of relief or of disappointment, no one could say—was made in her mind by this thought. Still she did not move the latch. Then she noticed that the window, the bedroom window, was open. Clothes were piled on a chair inside the room so carelessly that they lay over the sill: the sleeve of a shirt—Mark's shirt—even hung over down the outside wall. And in all this damp too. How exactly like Mark! Obviously it was high time she went in.